I0783599

Stone Raven Press Books
by Larissa N. N. Davila

Shorn

Cael's Shadow

Avelune

Praise for The Sky Seekers

"Larissa N. N. Davila paints a compelling portrait of a world and an individual teetering on the edge of chaos. . . . The epic clashes presented in *Avelune* are as much psychological as they are physical. . . . Jhared's journey is a compelling search for discovery and redemption that leads readers on another breathtaking flight of fantasy."

—*Midwest Book Review*

"Davila's moral intelligence and complicated world-building never waver. In *Avelune*, Volume III of The Sky Seekers, unexpected allies and enemies reveal themselves. Sparks fly in tense confrontation scenes. Pieces of the puzzle fall into place with satisfying snaps as both protagonists journey to new places and gain self-knowledge."

—Sarah Kozloff, author of The Nine Realms

"Fans in the mood for a well-written and exciting epic high fantasy can do no better than Larissa N. N. Davila's *Cael's Shadow*."

—Nancy Pearl, the "Nation's Librarian" and author of the Book Lust series

"Thoroughly engrossing on many different levels. . . . As Davila unwinds another series of escalating personal and political challenges affecting the survival of individuals and societies in this world, fantasy readers who look for swift action tempered by an attention to strong characterization and a solid sense of place and purpose will find *Cael's Shadow* hard to put down."

—D. Donavan, senior reviewer *Midwest Book Review*

"*Shorn* is a striking debut, filled with skilled world-building, complex psychological tension, and a fine sense of nuance too seldom seen in fantasy. I was engrossed in the unfolding tale, and I look forward to the continuing journey!"
—Jacqueline Carey, *New York Times* bestselling author of Kushiel's Legacy series

"Davila's debut novel, the first of a planned four-book series, creates a fascinating world of rival clans and sacred rituals . . . and belongs in most fantasy collections."
—*Library Journal*

"A grand-scale fantasy. . . . Fantasy fans will be impressed by Davila's deep characterization of the two main players; the focus on their internal development . . . makes them emotionally relatable and endearing. . . . Scenes come alive on the page through detailed descriptions, and multiple layers of political and social intrigue . . . add remarkable depth."
—*Kirkus Reviews*

"Larissa N. N. Davila has created a compelling story with an original and complex hero torn between duty and desire, loyalty and freedom. She shows us a deep and fascinating culture, a believable world, struggling with issues of faith and power in ways that reflect our own fears and dreams. More please!"
—Ari Berk, author of The Undertaken trilogy

"Larissa N. N. Davila has created a fascinating world, peopled it with vivid characters, and woven an epic tale of adventure and political intrigue with thoughtful themes of duty versus desire, bigotry versus acceptance, and the truth of history that hides behind the self-serving accounts written by the victors. She has also invented one of the more convincing religions I've seen in fantasy recently—no mere window-dressing of gods and altars and a priest or two, but a fully rounded, psychologically convincing faith. An intelligent and captivating novel by a new writer of promise."
—Victoria Strauss, author of *The Burning Land*

AVELUNE

BOOK III OF THE SKY SEEKERS

AVELUNE

BOOK III OF THE SKY SEEKERS

LARISSA N. N. DAVILA

STONE RAVEN
— PRESS —

Sante Fe, New Mexico

Acknowledgments

Writing can be lonely work, but I am lucky to have many people who keep me going when the creative process stumbles. Love to my sister, Alysia, for always making me laugh when times are tough, and to my mom, Marie, for her cookies and early morning conversations. Thanks to all the Lady Bosses (you know who you are) for their warmth and wisdom. Gratitude to the team at Stone Raven Press—especially to my dear friend and marvelous editor Kristen McDermott—and to the folks at The Writer's Ally, Ally Machate, Julie Haase, Amy Handy, and Isaac Peterson for creating a beautiful book from my necessary tale.

TO ALL THOSE STILL SEARCHING
FOR THEIR STOLEN WINGS

Principal Characters

Jhared Denaban, a young Shorn man

Mahla Denaban, his mother (deceased)

Boar and Shrill, Jhared's internal Teachers

Mayavana, Avelonian smuggler and mountain guide

Zinderdali Imiro, Sahisten smuggler

THE UNBOUND SHORN KIN

Alende, waylayer, leader of the Kin

Shira, Pathwalker

Rona and Trevazio, brothers

Kilzaro, second to Alende

Rani (Aranila), peacemaker of the group

Creaben, sometime partner to Kilzaro

Silvien, sometime partner to Alende

Lusian, rival of Alende

IN VELANTAR

Branlen Trianor, Jhared's foster brother

Ziabela Marcalo, Shorn scribe accused of treason

Jholan, Shorn boy imprisoned for theft

KEY MEMBERS OF THE COUNCIL OF CLANS

Adan Rumar, High Chieftain of Avelos

Tumal the Just, heroic former high chieftain (deceased)

Elder Tierzen Trianor, Minister of the Teaching, Jhared's foster father and one of his Teachers

Elder Toren Abrigado, Minister of the Treasury, Leader of Tumal's Legacy

REMNANTS OF JHARED'S PATROL

RIANA'S SERVANTS

Lady Nemiah Gabriana, High Priestess of Avelos

Leita, Bearer of Cael's Blade

Lady Amalia, traitorous former high priestess (deceased)

Kaliska, Temple Healer, Mistress of Guardians, Keeper of the Shadow Guards

Bena, Mistress of Maps

Captain Rom, Nemiah's Arionad

Commander Evorales, Arionad

Rien, Arionad

SONANS

Vjeran, captain of the Mila Jul

Mursa Vin Suamey, chief of the northern border guard

Luvas, young border guard

General Hrvan, great Se'yo of the Southern Quarter, Prime Advisor to the Simata'yo

Falucha, merchant, supplier for the Bird Walkers

Vyla, housekeeper to General Hrvan, one of the half-souled *hofja*

Nemaye, mother of Rathael & Ilaye

Rathael & Ilaye, siblings

Kest & Moravel, siblings

Katian, Kest's lover

Drijan, Sonan Storyteller

Hzelka, healer

AVELONIAN FOREST GUARD

Enrian Nadel, General of the Southern Towers

Lieutenant Matio Sevar, Jhared's commanding officer

Lenaro, patrol commander

Anzo Nevia, patrolman

Grion, patrolman

Esran, patrolman

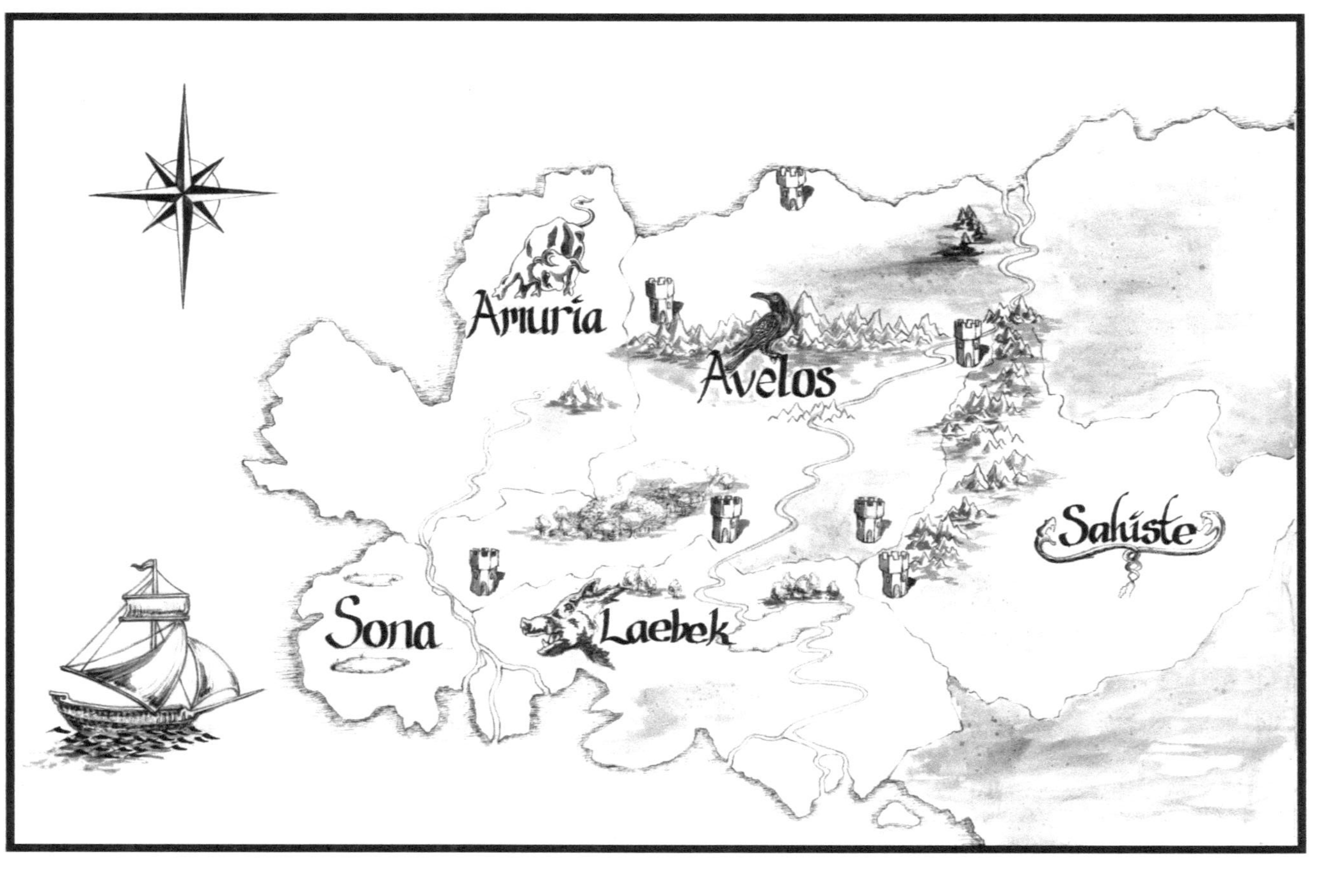

Amuria
Avelos
Salúste
Sona
Laebek

1.

Our Scars are the Same

Jhared didn't waste energy cursing the way Riana twisted his Path; he had drawn this danger on himself. Black pines and bared oaks poked accusing fingers that caught at his cloak and scraped his mare's silver coat. A bruised sun stippled the forest deadfall with shadows as he reined in and dismounted. He couldn't stop moving, not yet, but he could at least spell Seravina. He murmured gentle encouragements to her as they continued southwest, his own steps long since grown ponderous. Days of hard running with little food and almost no rest had leeched even his mare's Chosen-bred stamina. The men pursuing Jhared rode fresh horses and knew these woods as he did not. They would be on him by sunset.

Desire had led him to this, and his own lack of discipline. He had told himself that riding into a town was necessary. The provisions Lady Nemiah had given him were nearly gone; he needed grain for Seravina and a bow to hunt his own food. But what he really longed for was to walk among his people one last time. He had loved Avelos, had sworn an oath to die defending her. Now he was flailing at the border where love became hatred. He had needed to look upon the people of Avelos through unveiled eyes. He had been foolish to hope he would find anything but grief.

The town of Corbene was a stopping point for the caravans carting loads of timber and furs from the forests of Clans Nadaren and Ontera to the city. It was large enough to support the tradesmen Jhared needed. At his first stop at the bowyers' workshops, a silver-bearded craftsman had been pleased by his knowledge and his skill with the bow. The money the high priestess had given him served well enough to suppress awkward questions. Times were such that good coin could not be refused, even if it came from a solitary Shorn soldier riding a horse worth more than he could earn in two years. The bow he purchased was well made. The curve of laminated wood promised a strong, clean flight for the small quiver of arrows he negotiated into the deal. He shouldn't have pressed his good luck; he should have ridden out immediately. Instead, he wandered through town for a time, watching other men go about the normal tasks of their days, watching women with their children, and a father with his son, before pausing at a smithy's sign to see if he might afford a serviceable sword. The smith's assistant, a deep-chested man with a broken nose and a torn ear, had eyed him at first with suspicion, and then seeing Seravina, with greed.

Realizing his mistake, Jhared turned away without a blade and left Corbene quickly, moving off the road as soon as he was out of sight of the gate. At midday, he caught the faint sound of hooves behind him. Later, he heard a horse's squeal and a man's curse, abruptly silenced. When he couldn't lose the pursuit by pushing Seravina faster and confusing the trail, he rode a wide circle, hoping to come up on them, to determine who they were and what threat they offered. Although he found the tracks of six mounted men, he couldn't manage to gain sight of them. They were skilled woodsmen and knew their terrain. When he discovered the point on the trail where they had figured out his maneuver and circled back around him, he knew that running was futile.

Their tenacity made him suspect it wasn't only the mare they wanted. He hadn't expected a council courier to reach Corbene with news of his escape so soon, not if Lady Nemiah had delayed the elders from acting against him. Possibly her plea had gone unanswered. The temple possessed few allies, and who would be willing to stand for a Shorn man whose crimes carried a sentence of death? With an ache that scored his spirit, Jhared recalled the anguished look Elder Trianor had given him that last night during the council interrogation. The elders might already have announced a bounty for his capture.

His anger warred with his fear, and with a sorrow he acknowledged but wouldn't permit himself to feel, too vulnerable an emotion for a man on the run. Tierzen Trianor had called him son, had saved him time and again from the self-destructive urges of the Shorn, had nurtured his love and trust.

With that love, Elder Trianor had bound him to a history of lies.

Seravina bumped her silver head against Jhared's shoulder and lipped his arm. He pushed her nose aside. "Very well, madam. Let's ride on. I'll not let anyone drag me back."

He swung into the saddle once more and guided the mare west along a narrow stream. She moved out willingly, though no longer eagerly. The sun sank another finger's width as Jhared searched for a defensible position to face his hunters. The landscape remained stubbornly flat. He had left the hills and rock formations of the Parnas Mountains behind and hadn't yet reached the kettles and valleys of Clan Nadaren's lands. He was considering whether to settle on the shallow rise of the stream's bank, when the forest began to thin. Ahead, the shadows lightened and through the trees Jhared caught the dusty tan stripes of a cultivated field. He pressed Seravina forward until the trees gave way entirely and he found himself at the edge of an abandoned farm.

By the look of it, some clan family had tried to carve a steading out of the dense forest and make their way with livestock and grain rather than timber or trapping. It might have been a family's pride once, a place where the wilds were held at bay and order was imposed, but it was a shambles now. The hay had gone to seed. The grain had been crushed and trampled. Beyond the fields lay the ruins of a house, a barn, and several smaller outbuildings.

Jhared patted Seravina's withers. "What about some rest and a meal before we face the blades, eh, madam?"

The mare pinned her ears and danced a nervous jig in response. As Jhared turned his head, gleaming blue limned the edges of his vision and the world swung. Too late, he realized he'd been careless. He clapped his heels to Sera's sides, driving her away from the forest's edge and himself away from temptation. *Avoid the borders, the bridges, the thresholds,* Leita had warned. *At such places of transition, the Paths are always churning.* The Bearer of Cael's Blade had given him one of her sky-consuming gazes when she said it. She would never look at him so again.

He cantered out from the shadows onto the farmlands. Seravina didn't let him slow until they crossed the fields. When the world had steadied, he wheeled her about to look more closely at the wreckage. Where the farmhouse once stood lay a pile of broken timbers, nothing upright but a row of studs that poked toward the sky like the ribs of a stripped carcass. Along a worn walkway between the house and the barn, what had once been a flowerbed was crushed beneath a portion of the house's roof. The barn had fared better: three exterior walls, the loft, and several stalls remained intact, with random bits of tack still hanging from pegs, including a small saddle fit for a pony. The barn door and part of one wall had been torn away and flung toward the forest.

Jhared looked down at his fists clenched on the reins and tried not to think of the family who had lived here or of the children who had been torn. The killing winds had done this work. Little consolation existed in the knowledge that this destruction was too far west to be something he had caused.

The sun dripped gold toward the horizon. He forced himself to move again. This place would do well enough for a hide. Anyone approaching must come across the cleared acres, revealing themselves. He led Seravina into the shelter of the remaining barn walls, freed her from saddle and bridle, and settled her in one of the stalls with water and a ration of grain. He didn't tie her. The blood of Riana's Chosen, Captain Mavias, ran in her veins and made her a fierce combatant when threatened. On the other side of the stall, Jhared lit a small fire and searched through the bags that Lady Nemiah had given him. The Lady had been thoughtful in her preparations before she set him free. In Seravina's saddlebags he had found grain, dried apples, sausage and flatbread, a small pot, a coil of rope, a good hunting knife, and enough coin to buy the weapons she couldn't provide. In the smaller bag, he found more than merely what he needed to survive: a flask of brandy, a letter from Leita with the names of priestesses with whom it was safe to leave word, and the lyrics of a song written by a hand he knew. Upon consideration, he stuck the knife into his belt and took the coil of rope. Then he swung the small bag and his bow over his shoulder and climbed up to the loft to wait.

Stars blinked gradually into the purpling sky. Leathery wings whipped the air as bats flew in and out of the loft. Jhared inhaled the fading scent of horses and the metallic edge of approaching frost. Full dark descended before the deliberate hoof-beats of closely reined mounts clopped softly out of the fields, stopping somewhere between the house and the barn. Jhared braced himself with a swallow of brandy and nocked an arrow to the string. Energy hummed through his muscles. He didn't want this confrontation. Too much blood already stained his hands, but he owned too many truths now to stand before the elders ever again.

Silent moments slipped by. Jhared held his stance. Finally, one man appeared at the doorway, a tall figure, a near match to Jhared in build. Cautiously, gracefully, the man approached the fire with nothing but a short blade at his waist. His bright hair glinted gold. Then, unerring, although Jhared would have sworn he made no noise, the man looked up to Jhared's hide, staring with a green-eyed gaze full of irony.

"I do not die by your arrow, Jhared Denaban. Not on this Path."

Jhared met that feline stare, blood pounding in his ears. "Alende. You're alive!"

The waylayer tilted his head. Firelight caught his fey smile. "Riana keeps her hand over me. I've told you."

The bow relaxed in Jhared's grip. He jumped from the loft, stumbling a little as the half-healed wound in his left thigh protested. "I thought the Verael might have reached you. Then, when Seravina appeared in Murita, I imagined perhaps the winds . . ." He stopped. A smile curved his lips. "It's good to see you, Alende." With surprise, he realized how deeply he meant it.

"Good? To see me?" The waylayer's eyes went round. "Oh, my darling, what have they done with you?"

What had they done? Jhared was grateful for the waylayer's sardonic tone that allowed him to keep the question at a distance. He gestured with the bow. "Four or five others rode up with you. Who's still out there?"

"Ah, ever the keen scout." The waylayer gave an arch grin. "But as ever, the answer depends on the Path to which you're referring. On some Paths, I've brought with me a host of the untamed men who follow my story and despise the bound Shorn. On other Paths, I've come with fresh horses and a message for you from a beautiful woman. On one Path, I've bought forgiveness for myself by selling you to the Council of Clans." The waylayer looked up, his grin broadening.

Jhared made a face. He could not deny the bond his mother's memory wrought between him and the waylayer, but sometimes he would not regret it if the man fell onto someone else's Path. "I would offer you the hospitality of my fire, Alende, but not before you anchor yourself and answer me as you would have answered Mahla. Who have you brought with you? On this Path."

The older Shorn man scratched absently at the scars on his neck, and his expression sobered. Jhared knew it was Mahla's name and not any loyalty to himself that did it. "Five men from Sona," the man answered. "Travel companions, I suppose you could call them."

"Smugglers, you mean. Where are they now?"

"I sent them back to take care of the bodies of the men who were following you."

Jhared cursed softly. "Alende, what have you done?"

"Only what needed to be done. The brigands meant to slay you and steal Madam Silver. I owed you your life." Alende walked over to Seravina. The mare lowered her head to let him rub her cheek.

"You should not have killed them."

"Do you really believe so, my darling?" Alende turned, eyeing him curiously.

Jhared scrubbed a hand over his face. He had leaped across boundaries a Shorn man was never meant to cross, traveled among the infinite Paths, and called death upon those he had loved. He didn't know who that made him now, but some things he must hold dear. "Yes. I do."

"Interesting." Alende stepped around Jhared, studying him. "There are parts of you I didn't see before, aren't there?"

"Yes." Jhared didn't look aside from the waylayer.

"Tell me of them."

"Perhaps. But not now. Are you hungry?"

Alende's bitter, beautiful laughter rang into the night, a sound that hinted of the forbidden. "There is never a moment I do not hunger."

Jhared shivered, wishing he didn't understand just what that meant. He pulled a piece of flatbread from his bag and tossed it across the distance that separated them. "I meant for food."

"I know what you meant." Alende caught the bread. "Food is not the only sustenance a man must consume to survive. I think you've discovered that truth since I saw you last."

As though in confirmation, Jhared's hungers rose to taunt him: desire for Mayavana's embrace, for the touch of the sacred skies, and for the kiss of forbidden blue flames. He doused them with the recollection of the consequences of those desires: the killing winds, and the men he knew lying dead, the flesh stripped from their bones.

"Sit down," he ordered. "I have a flask of Melandrien. It's excellent."

Alende laughed again. "Oh my dear, you're clinging so very hard to your old Paths, but I can smell the wilds on you. You're not the same tamed man you were. Pass me the brandy and take some for yourself. I suspect you'll need it before you'll be able to tell me your stories."

Beside the fire, Jhared shared out the last of the sausage and the dried fruit. He did drink, more than he should have. He had been too many days alone with his losses. The stories poured from him as smoothly as the Melandrien down his throat. As the stars turned their silent spirals, he told Alende most of what had happened since they parted. He wasn't so drunk that he missed how attentive the waylayer remained, and he wasn't so far gone as to tell all. He held back Mayavana's story and Lady Amalia's. The former, he told himself, was for Maya's protection; the latter was for his own. He wasn't yet ready to speak of the meaninglessness of his sacrifice and the sacrifice of every Shorn child. Alende had already taken the final step into madness. Jhared suspected the journey for himself was not so long.

The last thing he withheld was for the sake of Avelos: he said nothing of his knowledge of the killing winds. Fear ran cold through him at the thought of Alende's unbound followers learning the winds' secret. If Jhared were correct, the unbound Shorn themselves were the secret, and he with them. If they discovered it, they would ravish the land with their hatred.

Jhared hurried through his tale and fell silent. Alende shifted from where he leaned against the wall, studying him through half-lidded eyes. "So many twists in this story, eh? The north's betrayal was clear on any Path. But the Bearer . . . what will that mean for the weaving, I wonder? And the High Priestess of Avelos who cut your chains? Fascinating! I've never seen her story. It says something different about Lady Nemiah. Very different. I wonder where it turns us."

Jhared wondered as well. *You may be needed,* Lady Nemiah had told him, but he was wandering free now and far from her Path. He shook his head. "What happened to you after the Verael attacked?"

"Ah, what happened, what happened?" Alende raked a hand across his throat. "You're a cruel one with your questions. Now I suppose you'll want me to tell my tale in order, whether or not I know it that way."

"If you please." Jhared smiled a little at the waylayer's grumbling. He suspected that forcing Alende to organize his experiences helped the man to distinguish his own Path from the tangled confusion of all the others he traveled. By Alende's admission, Mahla Denaban had required the same.

"Very well, Mahla's son. The start of the story is always the easiest. Shall we see what it offers us? I recall waking in a tree after a dream of being carried there by a hawk. Madam Silver remained with me. In the meadow lay the battered carcass of a Verael. I remember . . . the smell of a pyre. He was someone I knew, I think. No, no, no. That isn't the right tale." Alende rose to his feet, his gaze darting about the barn as though seeking an answer.

"It was one of my patrolmates," Jhared volunteered. "Jase."

"Ah, yes. The Clan Nadaren man. I remember his story. A sad one. A cheerful heart, a useless death."

It never occurred to Jhared that Alende might have known Jase, but the men had been of an age, after all. They might even have been recruits to the Forest Guard at the same time, before Alende had failed the Becoming. Jhared said nothing.

"The patrol was gone, and you and the Bearer with them," Alende went on, "but Madam Silver and I didn't follow. The doors had opened, and I . . . I wandered for a time. There were dark Paths to travel." He turned, as though to pace, but brought himself up short with one hand on the barn wall. Effort twisted his features.

"What happened next is . . . difficult. Two armies came through the pass, but one marched north and one marched south. I'm not certain if they belong to this story. Do they?" The waylayer glanced up in confusion. The tension that strung through every line of his body seemed the only thing holding him together.

"On this Path, an army marched south," Jhared said gently. "The northerners coming to confront the high chieftain."

"Right, right." Alende let out a relieved breath. "I might have let them go, but I caught sight of your lieutenant. Sevar. He'd been ill-treated and was clearly kept against his will. I expected you and the Bearer to be held as well. I expected it might be the end of our song. The northerners can't abide Shorn soldiers and they fear more than respect the power of Cael's Blade."

Jhared thought of Leita and nodded mutely.

"I followed them all the way to Parnas Pass," Alende continued. "As the story goes, however, you were not among them."

"No. By then I was separated from them." Jhared stopped, uncomfortable pressing his lies any further.

"Mm, indeed." Alende narrowed his eyes with a look that, for a moment, held no hint of madness. "You said you traveled toward Velantar with the news of northern betrayals. You also told me how this tale ends. Your escape from the northerners' camp, the battle, and the killing winds coming so swiftly."

Jhared turned from the waylayer's gaze, which suddenly seemed too knowing. "Is that where your Sonans rejoined you? In Parnas Pass?"

"Is it? No. Earlier, I think. Good boys and useful on the trail. You should meet them. They're not the swamp rats Avelos has told you they are." Alende took another swallow of brandy, then focused his gaze on Jhared. "I want you to come with me."

Jhared looked up. "With you where?"

"To winter with my band in the south."

"With the unbound?"

"The unchained."

Jhared frowned. "You shouldn't speak of them to me. I'm a soldier, still. Some things I should not hear."

"Wrong, Mahla's son. You are no longer a Forest Guard or an elder's fosterling. And you promised me a season of your life."

Jhared straightened so abruptly his head bumped against the post behind him. "What?"

"Isn't it so like a Shorn man to forget his promises?" Alende *tsked* between his teeth. "Outside of Brenia you promised me a season of your life if I told you where to find your patrolmates."

"You tricked me into believing they had fled."

"Perhaps. But you offered the promise freely."

Jhared went still. What else had he to do with his life? Since Lady Nemiah set him free, he had been following a dream of Mayavana toward Sona, but in fact he had abandoned the Avelun with no reason for her to expect or even to wish him with her. Everything he was meant to be had been stripped from him at birth, painted anew with Shorn Law, and now had been stripped a second time by the truth. Where did he expect to find a place?

"Why do you want me to come with you?"

"Oh, my darling, why must you always ask such tangled questions? On what Path does a man move for only one reason? Perhaps I would like you to know what Mahla began when she saved my life. Perhaps I believe it would ease you to understand what a Shorn man's life can be in the wilds. Perhaps I want to know what you can offer to my people."

"And what of the destruction of the weaving? The quest for the Bearer? The end of our song?"

The waylayer inclined his head. "The Bearer has slipped out of reach, but you and I have found one another. There's balance in that, don't you think? She is Cael's Lady and you . . . I think perhaps Cael touches you in ways I've not yet untangled. Perhaps in ways that you've not untangled. If I follow you, I think I will find what is needed before the end."

Jhared stared into the fire. Touched by Cael indeed. The Bearer herself had called him Cael's Beloved. Perhaps all that remained to him was to join those who had never been bound at all. "I'll think on it."

"Good." The waylayer gave him a sly smile and Jhared knew whatever the man told him it was not everything he meant.

The high moon watch had come and gone. Jhared climbed to his feet to stretch and felt the land bobble beneath him, a token of the Lady's brandy. He had indulged more than he meant to. If he tried to sleep now, he would pay for it come morning.

"I'm going for a walk," he muttered.

Alende chuckled and gave him a mock salute. As Jhared wandered out of the barn, Seravina snorted and kicked a hoof against the stall door. He paused in the barnyard and surveyed the darkness. Starlight veiled the farm's destruction, turning broken timbers and crushed hope into soft shadows. He wondered if Alende's Sonans were out there keeping watch. Why did Sonan smugglers involve themselves in the matters of the unbound? Alende had claimed they sought ancient Avelonian texts, and Mayavana had told him such texts sold for high prices in their undeveloped land. Maya hoped to find the means to reach the skies in those ancient volumes. What did the Sonans want?

The cold air felt good on Jhared's fevered skin. He closed his eyes, then quickly opened them as the brandy set him spinning. The night was deep and clear, a good night for hunting. A good night to catch the breeze beneath strong wings and soar through the sacred skies. Jhared tilted his head and stared upward, yearning to fall into the boundless depths of the star-dusted darkness. He thought of Mayavana stretching her wings at the edge of a cliff. He thought of her quick smile and sharp wit, her competent hands and gentle voice. He indulged in emotions he hadn't let himself recall since his capture and felt the heat swirl up from his center into his limbs. Abruptly, he realized he was falling; a jarring thud shook him loose from his thoughts. Sprawled on his back, he laughed aloud, throwing his arms open to the splendid night, inviting the darkness to consume him.

Without warning, he was falling again, into the embrace of blue flames.

The fall ended swiftly. He could almost believe he had steered himself there, for the place he landed was a familiar refuge. On this other Path, a breeze as mild as summer rustled the reeds along the lake and sunset turned the water to amber. He ran along the shore toward the odd cottage on its rows of stilts. Sand and pebbles crunched under his steps and waves lapped at his boots. Maya was there, sitting on the old grey pier, her shift pulled up to her knees and her long legs dangling toward the water. Jhared halted at the base of the pier, breathless, not from his run but from the startling beauty of her. One wing wrapped around her body, revealing the way her feathers shifted through every shade of night, from frosty twilight at the wing's leading edge to blackest midnight at the tips of her primary feathers. As she bent to her preening, a wave of her dark hair fell across her cheek.

She stopped and glanced up before his boot even touched the pier. "Jhared."

His heart drummed against his ribs. How long had he known what it was to be acknowledged by that steady, sage gaze? Even before he had found her on his own Path, he had met her here. He wanted to gather her into his arms, to breathe in the wild tang of her, but he didn't move, hearing no condemnation in her tone but also no welcome. "Ah, Mayavana, I didn't mean to leave you. Not like that."

She stood, both wings furling neatly against her back. "I know. I found the place where you fought the guard in the pass. Don't regret it. You are a soldier of Avelos. You did what you must."

He winced. "I feared for you. With fighting men swarming the mountains and the winds come again, I was so afraid."

A smile quirked one side of her mouth, breaking through her neutral mask; then she was running, her bare feet slapping the wood. Jhared staggered a surprised step backward as she tumbled into him, smelling of berries and feathers and fresh water.

"Gods of seas and skies, soldier, among all the infinite Paths, you found me here. Don't waste this treasure explaining things that were clear the moment I saw you."

She kissed him, flooding him with need. She knew him, even his horrible strength, and was not repulsed. How had he imagined he could ever turn his back on her? With one arm around her waist, he drew her closer.

And nearly knocked her flat as pain bolted through him and he crashed to his knees.

Maya stumbled backward. "What's happening? Are you attacked?"

Jhared hunched over the sand, gasping. Flames seared through his vision, slashing apart the pier, the lake. "The waylayer," he choked. "He must mean to cut me free."

"Oh gods, Jhared, this is wrong. Ugly and wrong!" Maya's voice twisted in anguish. "I feel the doors ripped open and the web tearing. You must return to your Path before they wrench your spirit from your body!"

For a heartbeat, her gaze found his, and he saw the sorrow in her as she pushed him away. Unbalanced, he dropped into the blue flames and scrambled through agony to grasp a sense of himself, to find his own place in the weaving. *Soldier. Brother. Singer. Lover.* He made a litany of the names that he claimed as his own and tracked his way to the moment where he belonged. When his fall came to a rough halt, he opened his eyes to see the waylayer bending over him.

Hurt and loss and unfulfilled longing lent Jhared the strength to haul himself upright. He swung hard and his fist connected solidly with flesh. Alende staggered and went down.

The only sound in the barnyard was Seravina's urgent whinnying. Then came the waylayer's beautiful, dangerous laughter.

"Right! I was right! I *knew* the Bearer claimed you for a reason. You are touched, a true caelevano!" The waylayer sat up, dabbing at his chin with the back of his hand. "All this time. All this time you sat before me. How very delicious. What else have you hidden from me, Pathwalker?"

The rush of deadly cold through Jhared's veins spared him the need to answer. He hit the ground again like a bag of sand, his muscles twitching and twisting. His teeth clenched as his life's heat poured out of him. No longer laughing, the waylayer dropped down beside him. Distantly, Jhared was aware of an arm wrapped around his shoulders and hands bracing his head before he was forced to focus on breathing.

An age passed until he finally won free of the ice and discovered himself sprawled across the waylayer's lap, his body clammy and limp as a speared fish.

"Mahla's son," Alende murmured, brushing damp strands of hair from Jhared's brow. "You don't belong among the bound any longer. Please say you'll come with me."

"I cannot," Jhared croaked, collecting himself and drawing away from Alende into an aching heap.

"What is it you cannot do? Walk among those who refuse to wear the chains?" The waylayer's tone turned caustic. "Do you not see that you are anathema too?"

Jhared no longer understood how words such as "anathema" applied to the unbound. The crimes for which they had to answer were not the ones he had been told. "It's not that, Alende."

"Then what? Has the Bearer ordered you to some task for her own purpose? Because I must warn you—"

"No." Jhared closed his eyes. He had seen Mayavana, and she had met him with warmth. He must at least learn where the road would lead if he went after her. He tried to think of a safe way to share what that meant with the waylayer. "Alende, I have seen a Path where joy still exists. I hope to . . . I think I might . . ."

"You hope to chase it? Like poor deceived Lusian chasing starlight over the mountains? Oh, my darling, the Paths are ever shifting. Whatever moment of joy you saw was already lost to you in the instant you welcomed me to your fire or the moment I dragged you free of the weaving or any other of a thousand moments before or since. Madness lies in chasing such visions." Alende lifted his chin, revealing the complex network of scars across his throat. "You know I speak the truth."

Jhared touched one hand to his own throat and felt the wound Alende had inflicted parallel to the scar the Bearer had given him. Maya had never needed a blade to bring him back from a journey. He wanted what she knew. He would not follow Alende into madness. "I'm sorry. I cannot go with you."

"Is that the only answer you have for me?"

"Yes. For now."

Jhared expected the waylayer to show his anger, but Alende only smiled sadly. "Then I must wait until your Path turns again, mustn't I? Come back to the fire, my darling. I have something to ease your aches."

By the time Jhared had limped back into the barn, Alende had set a pot of water over the fire and was crumbling dried leaves into a cup. When the water was steaming, he poured it over the leaves. "Here. Let it steep a few minutes before you drink. It's something my Sonans brought to me. It will help to anchor you."

Jhared took the cup, watching the unfamiliar leaves swirl and settle before he sipped. "That's awful," he said, choking back a swallow. "I'd rather have the brandy."

Alende shrugged and waved a hand. "I'm not one to deny a man his means of escape, my darling. You've seen what the liquor does for me."

Jhared stopped with his arm halfway to the flask. He *had* seen. The brandy didn't close the Gate or cool the blue flames; it only made the waylayer weak and pathetic. Jhared hunkered down and tried another sip of the tea. It wasn't so disgusting, just a little fusty. The heat felt good in his stomach.

Alende watched him drink. "How long have you known the Gate?" the waylayer asked, standing at the fire.

It was hard to remember how long ago Jhared had first seen the tongues of blue licking at the edges of his awareness, but it wasn't until the Bearer discovered him that the flames had been given a name. "Since Brenia," he answered.

"Hmm, Brenia." Alende scowled and stared at the ground, as though trying to recall something.

"That was just before you and your Sonans found me in the forest."

Recollection flashed in the waylayer's eyes. "I know, I know," he grumbled. "I remember that part of the story."

Jhared nodded noncommittally and forced down another swallow of tea.

"The Bearer taught you," Alende said. It was not a question.

"She tried. I have no skill. That's why . . ." Jhared made a gesture indicating his fall in the barnyard.

The waylayer uttered a little laugh. "I imagine it will give you no pleasure to know we're the same in that."

"You imagine correctly." Jhared finished the tea and set aside the cup, starting to feel just how weary he was. "Did someone teach you?"

"No. But I saw what the Bearer tried to teach the false caelevano in Shorn Circle. It never worked for them because they had no true sense for the Paths. It never worked for me because . . ." The waylayer shrugged again. "Who knows. The Shorn were not meant to touch the weaving."

Jhared's vision was clouding with exhaustion. He straightened and wiped a hand across his eyes. This conversation was important. Maya's knowledge and his own nightmarish experiences led him to believe the killing winds sprang somehow from those Shorn survivors who had access to the Paths, the Shorn who had not been properly bound. Alende led a band of the unbound; he might know something that could shed light on the winds' source. "Are all those who follow you sensitive to the Paths?" Jhared asked.

There was that quick, keen gleam in the waylayer's gaze again. "You could come with me to find out," he said slyly.

Jhared pressed his lips together. They tingled. He touched a finger to his bottom lip.

"Never mind, my darling. You're worn out. I'll not argue it further." The waylayer waved a blurry hand. "Very few of my people know the Paths. And the weaving leaves its mark on us."

Very few? How did that fit? Jhared had felt the killing winds at his core; they rose from his own Paths. He was nearly sure of it. For a man to possess their power, didn't he also need to sense the weaving and know the blue flames? If so, did that mean the unbound had nothing to do with the killing winds? Or that only a few of them did? Had any of them realized what destruction they held? Surely not, or they might have flattened all of Avelos by now. Jhared shook his head to clear it, an effort like dragging an anvil through water.

"Truly, the weaving does leave its mark," Alende murmured.

"No. Not the weaving," Jhared managed. "Something's . . . wrong." Belatedly, he realized he was slumping backward. With a remote thud, his back met the barn wall. Alarm rang through him, but his body refused his command to straighten.

Numbness slid its dead hands over him. Through a blur of black spots, he watched Alende stalk toward him. Jhared's fingers scrabbled to draw his knife, but he couldn't make them form a fist.

"Ah, my darling, I did hope the story would not twist this way. I do not wish to spill the blood of Mahla's son on any Path."

Jhared strained against the invisible ties enwrapping his limbs. His heart labored against the poison in his veins. With all his fading strength, he dragged one foot beneath him and then the other. Slowly, he pushed himself upright along the wall.

Alende laid a hand on his shoulder and shoved him back down. "Don't. You'll only injure yourself when you fall."

"You *swore* . . . on Mahla's name!"

"I swore not to harm the Bearer," Alende replied coldly. "And you're in no position to name me oath breaker."

As Jhared's body slowed and failed, his thoughts raced. What was it the waylayer wanted? What did he have to give the man?

What else have you hidden from me, Pathwalker?

Jhared choked on air that was too heavy. What had Alende guessed? The waylayer had been in Parnas Pass when the killing winds struck. He had seen the northerners attack the high chieftain's men. What else had he seen?

Alende crouched in front of him, a hostile smudge of gold and green. "Which way will you lead me, my darling? Toward peace or anguish?"

Around Jhared, the world was shutting down. He couldn't see more than a few inches in front of his face, couldn't lift a hand, couldn't form a word. He would have welcomed the blue flames with their power to set him free, but he had been truly chained. The waylayer disappeared from his field of vision. Jhared heard a whistle, then the sound of horses. Men entered the barn. The Sonans. They smelled of rosemary and mint. They murmured in their muddy tongue.

Rough hands grasped Jhared and dragged him into the night. He fought, but someone merely slapped his fist away and took a better grip on his arm. He heard harsh laughter as they deposited him in the barnyard. The stars no longer lit his darkness.

As they hoisted him into the air and slung his body over a horse, he seethed with helpless fury and cursed his need to trust.

2.

CAEL'S CHILDREN

"Cael knows you have failed your family, your people, and your land. Cael knows and bears witness. Come to me.

"Cael sees you are the slayer of order and the beloved of chaos. Cael offers you rest. Surrender to me."

The demon's voice echoed hollow and otherworldly, the essence of condemnation. Jhared heard water tripping over stone. He might have been floating in a black ocean, left with nothing but his leaden thoughts. He tried to see, as though eyes might still have meaning in this darkness. Cael's great raven head glared down at him, a blur of fear and death. Its vicious beak gripped a fragile human skull. In one pale hand, the demon wielded a long, grey feather; the other hand clutched Cael's Blade.

"You of the Shorn have earned your torments by tormenting others. Cael will count out your punishments by the beating of your heart."

Was this death, then? Had he come to the Hidden Paths? Jhared remembered a man who had gone to the edge of death and returned: General Nadel had faced the killing winds and the demon and had survived them both. In a dark cave, Jhared had found the general clinging to life. The grey feather curse had marked his trial, but the general had not surrendered.

"You, the spawn of betrayal, heir to the tainted blood of Lady Amalia, it is right that you should despair. Give yourself to me."

"No!"

To speak the single word left Jhared dizzy with effort, but he drew defiance around him like a shield. A choice existed here, as it had existed for General Nadel, a choice to yield or endure. He had known Lady Amalia in the hour of her death. She had given him her trust and the words to mark it. Even lying helpless, at Cael's mercy, he would honor her name, she whom Avelos had so wrongly dishonored. "No," he said again.

New sounds rose around him: footsteps, cloth rustling, another voice not otherworldly at all but young and filled with very human urgency. Cael's chanting broke off with an angry squawk.

"He said something! I heard it! Shira, move away. He's like to be a beast when he comes to."

"This soldier belongs to Cael!" the demon insisted. "You must lay no hand on him."

"According to Alende, he belongs to us," a third voice answered, more ill-tempered than urgent but with the same crisp city accent as the young voice. "Give me the rope, Trev. I'll not have him running to betray us to his own kind."

"Only Cael determines what torments a body deserves!" The demon's voice spiraled higher. "You will lay no hand on this soldier. You will lay no hand!"

"Here's the rope," the young voice offered. "Rona, maybe we ought to leave him be. Shira says no."

Through the ground, Jhared felt the faint vibration of someone stepping closer, then a yelp. "Damn it, girl! You nearly cut me with that thing. Move away, will you? We only mean to keep him from bolting."

"He will not be bound! He will not be bound! You will not bind the power of chaos!"

The demon wailed with a sound of rising panic. Jhared strained to move. His vision was nothing but a smear of motion. He closed his eyes and tried to orient himself by sound alone. Behind him, someone came running.

"Rona, Trevazio, get rid of that rope. Now!" Alende's voice pierced the turmoil, commanding and clearer than Jhared had ever heard it. "Easy, Shira. Easy, love. You know you're safe here, always."

"We only wanted to be sure the soldier didn't run," the young voice gasped. "Truly, Alende. We didn't mean to upset her."

"He wouldn't be able to run if you had simply done what I told you and kept watch. Now get out of my sight and Shira's, Trevazio. Unless you'd like me to use the rope on you and Rona both."

"No! No body will be bound!" the demon whimpered.

"Ah love, of course not. Only Cael can say who is bound, eh?"

"You've brought a wasp into our nest, Alende," the deeper voice, the one called Rona, replied sulkily.

"We've all been the wasp, Rona. It's a chance we take each time we bring a new one among us. You and Trev included."

"It's not the same. Not with this one. This one's a Forest Guard and long tamed."

"Don't speak of things you don't understand, Rona. I've seen the boy on this Path and others—and I've seen you. Leave me now. Give me the space to calm her."

As two sets of footsteps turned away, Jhared heard the demon murmuring sadly: "Some torments we deserve. Some torments we deserve. Some torments—"

"Hush, Shira. Do not say so. There is no torment you deserve." Alende's voice had gone quiet.

"It's too late to pay the debt," mourned the demon. "They should never have tried to bind what belongs to the sacred skies. In the binding, they have wrought destruction."

"It's not too late, love. I've not let Rona use the rope. Look here, see? Chaos cannot be bound. Not in this story. The boy is free and safe and listening to us even now. Aren't you, Mahla's son?"

Jhared opened his eyes and stared in bewilderment. The slender figure of Cael, garbed all in midnight, crouched over him, wringing its hands beneath its cruel beak while Alende gently stroked its back. At the demon's feet lay the grey feather and Cael's Blade.

From over the demon's shoulder, Alende smiled. "You'll not be feeling yourself yet, Denaban, but don't fear. By this evening, I expect your sight will have cleared and your limbs will have returned to you. We'll speak then."

Jhared glared, trying to make his tongue form the scathing words he wanted to whip at Alende. His attempt turned into a muffled cry as the demon lifted both pale hands and tugged off its avian head. From beneath the mask, a fall of golden hair slipped over narrow shoulders and a woman appeared.

She darted forward and pressed her face close to his. Her fine features came into focus above him, looking disturbingly like Alende's. Her green eyes glinted.

"It is right that you've come to us," she whispered. "The beloved of Cael will find a place among the shadows."

"Let's leave him be for now, Shira."

"No." She turned an accusing glare upon Alende. "I smell blood on him."

"Not my doing, love. You know it's not. Avelos had him for too long. Now that he's with us, he will have the chance to rest and heal. Come now. Kilzaro will keep him safe."

"No," the demon said again. Sitting back on her haunches, she picked up Cael's Blade from the dirt. "I will watch him."

Jhared couldn't see the waylayer's expression, but he heard Alende utter a long, thoughtful sigh. "I see. I suppose I should have recognized what it would mean to you to find him like this. Are you certain, Shira? He has served among the soldiers."

"Oh yes. He knows about the danger of bonds. I can see it." The woman waved the Blade uncomfortably close to Jhared's eyes. "When he is well, we will speak on the importance of chaos and the inevitability of conflict."

"Very good then, love. If you're certain, I will leave him in your care."

The guileless smile that lit the woman's face was impossible to reconcile with the demon's haughty condemnation. "Yes, you will!"

This time, Jhared did see Alende's expression. The waylayer hunkered close, his eyes dark with warning. "Harm her in any fashion, my darling, and it will not matter that you bear Mahla's blood or carry this story's secrets. You will suffer. Remember, I have traveled far and seen methods of destroying a man this Path has never imagined." He brushed a callused hand across Jhared's brow, then stood with a smile for the woman. "Guard him well."

Jhared's awareness slipped away before his captors had finished speaking. In his dreams, demons transformed into golden women and grey-winged Avelune offered him their feathers.

When he awoke again, the light had changed to pale orange. Above him, the branches of a willow tree swayed gently, and beyond them, tufts of pink-tinged clouds drifted in an evening sky. He blinked to be sure of it. A root was digging a notch into his shoulder and the cold seeped into him from the ground. But he welcomed the minor discomforts as the most marvelous of sensations, realizing that he was in possession of his body once again.

Atop a blanket not far from him, the woman lay curled like a cat, one arm tucked over her eyes, her bright hair tumbled about her head. He shifted slowly so as not to disturb her, but she sprang up with a predator's vigilance. Before he could move, she had pressed the curved Blade against his throat.

"There are no torments I deserve!" she declared.

Jhared inclined his head a little to see her better and the knife scraped against his skin. Shira glared. Her anger was palpable, but it was anxiety that filled her eyes when they flashed over him.

"I am sorry, Lady," he breathed, motionless. "I didn't mean to startle you."

"Take care," she warned. "Cael decides who lives and dies."

Without turning, he slid his gaze to the place where the demon's mask lay on the ground, then back to her. "Do you speak for Cael?"

"I speak for all that has been defiled." Her chin jutted upward, as though daring Jhared to challenge her.

With her knife at his vein, he had no mind for a challenge. Instead, he used the moment to study her. She was a treasure of gold and emerald and pearl, with the same feral grace as Alende. Although she and Alende shared the bright coloring so rare among the Shorn, they did not share the same features after all. Her face and hands were narrow and delicate. Looking at her brought to mind a young doe, wild nettles, fall leaves. Alende, by contrast, was all swift streams, bright serpents, and hunting cats. In the soft light, Jhared saw one more thing the woman shared with the waylayer: the pattern of scars across her throat.

"You travel the Paths," he observed.

"I've strolled among the shining threads. I've known the stories and the blood." She twisted the Blade under Jhared's chin, forcing him to expose his throat to her. "You have as well, it seems. When they brought you in, I felt the doors swing wide. And perhaps something more?" She cocked her head, birdlike, considering him.

"Is that why I'm here?"

Her laughter brushed the air, a sound as fragile as snowdrops. "For shame! That's Alende's story. Do you think I will tell you what he has not?"

Jhared had hoped so. For now, though, it was relief enough that she moved the knife away from his throat. As she returned it to its sheath, he realized that although the curved blade mimicked Cael's, the grip was only roughly polished wood and the steel was a dull grey, with no sense of power in it.

"I'm going to move now, Lady," he warned. "I promise not to go anywhere."

She watched him warily, but didn't try to stop him as he sat up. He stretched, newly appreciating the sensation of his muscles lengthening and contracting. He felt stiff and bruised and desperately hungry. His head ached, although it might have been from the brandy as easily as the poison. He seemed well enough otherwise. With one eye on Shira, he assessed his surroundings. The gnarled willow beside him rose, with a concealing curtain of other trees, from the bank of a river that had long ago receded to a narrow stream. The place where he had slept abutted an earthen wall about waist high that once would have been the river's edge. Not far along the bank, a big, bearded man tended a kettle over a fire, and behind the man, a picket of horses stirred for their evening feed. Jhared was glad to catch the silver flash of Seravina's coat among them. Few other signs of occupation disturbed the setting. It might have been any hunters' camp.

"Is this Alende's band of unchained?" he asked, turning back to the woman. He had expected something more dire.

"We are not Alende's," she said, "not creatures to be possessed. We're the untamed Kin, who choose freely to follow his story. The group here is but one part of us who follow. The head, some would allow. The rest are scattered at different tasks."

"Tasks, Lady?"

She laughed again and gave him a look that told him he was foolish for trying. "You speak so prettily. You're city born, aren't you?"

He smiled a little at the way she turned the topic. He let her. "Yes. I'm from Velantar."

"They say you're a Forest Guard, but I don't see a soldier's heart in you."

He grimaced. "Because I've deserted Avelos?"

"Because you're willing to learn about a thing, rather than beating it to fit the shape of your own beliefs."

Jhared's face heated. The ability to question was no more than Elder Trianor had taught him, and one of the reasons he was here now, exiled and no longer certain of any belief. "Where are you from?" he asked, needing to change the topic himself. Her clear speech might have marked her as a daughter of Clan Manitar, but he thought he heard a hint of Clan Valador's soft slur.

"I come from the darkest heart of hopelessness," she murmured.

"Your failed Becoming?" Jhared asked.

She tensed and lowered her gaze.

"You're a Pathwalker. Is that why you failed?"

Without warning, her hand flew. She smacked Jhared across the cheek, hard enough to make his eyes water. "Some torments are deserved!" she cried. "Would you know them for yourself?"

"No. No, I'm sorry. It was a thoughtless question."

She balanced on her toes, her fists clenched near her heart, her eyes wide. Where her sleeves had slid up her arms, Jhared spied two sets of ragged scars that raked the insides of her wrists. In whatever town or village she had tried the Becoming, the temple had cut her and thrown her out into the wilds to die.

"I'm sorry," he said again. "Forgive me."

"It's too late for forgiveness! They bound what should never have been bound and cut apart what should have been whole. Now all must pay the price."

She lifted the demon's mask and fitted it over her head. As the avian shape concealed her features, her stance changed, growing imperious and menacing. Jhared regretted the transformation. Madness touched her, but not in the same form it touched Alende. When she looked at him, Jhared could see that she knew him and knew which Path she trod. Instead, fear and fury overwhelmed her. The two emotions vied for dominance in her tone and in her teetering expressions. He wondered where her true self had fled and if she ever allowed anyone to see it.

They were interrupted by the man at the kettle. Jhared saw him glance over before setting aside his ladle and heading up the bank. He was strongly built and dark-bearded, with the look of a wild northerner about him. His features were unlovely and blunt, as though someone hadn't quite finished molding his image in clay. A heavy limp marred his gait, but he called out cheerfully before he reached them.

"Halloo, Shira! Alende said ya were back. What's the state'a things, my girl?"

The demon swung around to face the newcomer. "Cael knows your intentions, Kilzaro. It is well for you we judge them benign."

"Ay, I'm ever thankful for it," the man said, rubbing the heel of his palm against his left thigh as he stopped beside Jhared. "What's your report'a the road?"

"Cael spied a teamster with a lumber cart stealing coins from his partner's purse, a farmer and his son hauling sheep toward Corbene for slaughter, and a young mother carrying a sick child."

"Ah, indeed," the man murmured. "No clanguard? No soldiers?"

"None today." The demon's voice echoed through the human skull.

"There's a bit of a gift, at least, with Lus and Silvi still wanted back."

"Lusian," the demon grumbled. "Cael sees discord in that one. He need never come back at all. You should also be aware, Kilzaro, that Cael is displeased with Rona. Should he continue this way, his punishments will number like the pebbles along this bank."

"Not much of a surprise there," the man muttered. "I'll talk to him again." He gave Jhared a glance. "What'a this boy?"

Shira turned her head and Jhared found himself once more under the severe regard of the raven's eye. "He prefers to ask questions than to answer them. And he thinks he has the right to look beneath others' veils. But we believe him only misguided, not malevolent."

Kilzaro's glance grew thoughtful, and Jhared realized the man was seriously weighing the demon's words. "Could be worse. Alende will shape him up well enough. Dinner's soon. Will ya join us tonight?"

The avian beak tipped back and forth. "Not with our two spirits still away. Cael watches for those who wander in the dark. For now, I put the boy in your care."

"Of course. I'll see he stays put." The big man gave the slender figure an awkward bow. "Take care with yourself, my girl."

The demon turned its head toward Jhared, and he saw the woman's eyes judging him from behind Cael's features before she glided up the bank toward the trees. As she drew away, the cruel raven's beak and the human skull made a strange silhouette in the lengthening light.

"Alende said ya'd wake hungry." Kilzaro reached through Jhared's thoughts. "Join us at the kettle if ya wish. The others will gather by nightfall."

"Where's Alende?" Jhared demanded.

"Careful now. Keep some respect in your tone when ya say his name."

"Respect for a man who uses poison before a fire of hospitality?"

"That," the man said with a shrug of his wide shoulders, "was for your own good."

Jhared gave the other an incredulous glare. "How so?"

"Ya'll fare better among your own kind than in the wilds alone."

Among your own kind. A short time ago, Jhared would never have let anyone compare him to the unbound, but he had changed and so had his understanding of what these people were. If he were honest, he knew Alende had likely saved his life on the road.

Kilzaro was looking at him with a bemused smile. Jhared realized the man expected some response. "Shira told me you each chose freely to be a part of this band, but you'll stop me if I choose to leave, won't you?"

"Yes," Kilzaro replied.

"Why? What do I mean to you?"

"What ya mean ta me doesn't much matter, but Alende has asked me ta see that ya stay, and I follow his story." Kilzaro's blunt features softened into an expression of pity. "Look, boy, Riana don't bother with her castoffs out here, so don't look for the kind'a order ya knew in the Forest Guard. If you're hungry, come eat. After that, Alende might answer your questions. Maybe ya'll be heard tomorrow. Or maybe the next day. Ya'll find patience is a trait worth fostering in this group."

Jhared closed his eyes and saw Mayavana's wry smile, her steady regard, and the gleam of her wings. She was out there. He must only untangle himself from these unbound and find her. But he did know the value of patience. He settled his features into a more neutral expression for Kilzaro. "If you think I've not been drilled in waiting, you've never been part of a garrison."

The northerner limped toward the fire. "Come on then."

Jhared followed. One whiff of the soup steaming in the big kettle reminded him he was a long way past famished. Kilzaro caught his expression and laughed.

"Just a bit now for the food," the man said. "Ya have freedom'a the camp. Your packs and tack are on the stone with our things." He pointed down the bank to a small collection of bags and bedrolls. "Alende figures he'll keep hold'a that pretty bow'a yours for a time. 'Til we see how ya settle in."

"And if I run?"

The big man nodded as though the question were expected. "Alende says you're a soldier and a quick scout, so ya might manage ta slip by our watch, but ya won't pass the Sonans. They can track a fish through the sea, and they're deadly with them staves. When they tow ya back, I'd wager you'll not be in as good a shape as when ya left."

Jhared kept quiet. If it came to it, he would take his chances.

"No use stewing over it." Kilzaro snorted. "Ya know your way around horses, eh? Go see ta their fodder until the others arrive."

Jhared set about it, glad to have something to do. As he approached the picket, Seravina stretched her head toward him and greeted him with an irritated swish of her elegant tail. He smiled at her petulance and rubbed her neck. Among the pile of gear, he found his bags intact, as Kilzaro had indicated. He ran his fingers over the folded pages in his smaller bag, wondering if Alende had looked inside and read the letter from Leita. A conversation awaited in that. Jhared stifled a rill of frustration. Patience, he reminded himself.

As he distributed fodder to the motley herd, Jhared observed Kilzaro limping about the fire. The northerner had a steadiness and an unassuming confidence about him. They were not traits Jhared associated with the unbound, but then Alende was the only unbound man he had known.

"Kilzaro," Jhared murmured. "Cael's Chosen commander who feeds upon the misfortunes of others and devours the spirits of the dead. That's an interesting—" He stopped, belatedly recognizing the pattern: Kilzaro, Shira, Trevazio, Rona, even Alende. Each one was the name of a Chosen spirit or an ancient hero. "Ahh, I see."

The older man paused over the kettle with two hands full of wild greens. "What do ya think ya see, boy?"

"The names you bear were chosen after your failed Becomings, weren't they? After you began your new life."

"Close enough," Kilzaro growled, dropping the leaves into the soup. "Don't ever let me hear ya say it so effortlessly again. Each of us died in the wilds before we earned our names. We lost our friends, our families, and our homes."

"I understand," Jhared said.

Kilzaro eyed him for a long moment, then relented with a gruff nod. "Ay, perhaps ya do. Somewhat."

"You haven't yet told the soldier why the name of the spirit-eater fits you, Zaro!"

At first glance, Jhared took the Shorn man leaping into the riverbed for a boy. He was about the height of old Anzo, but what was only somewhat short for a whole man was right for a Shorn youth of twelve or thirteen winters, and stocky Anzo made up for his height with girth, while this man was slender as a birch. Jogging heavily behind the small one was another who matched Kilzaro in size. As the slender man landed lightly and sprang up like a hare, the larger one clambered down the bank and hauled up beside the fire. A pair of speckled trout hung from his callused fist.

"Aw, Rani, don't frighten the soldier with the list of Kilzaro's strange appetites," the large man panted.

"Frighten? It's that list what makes him interesting." The small man gave Kilzaro a wink.

"Creaben, Rani, don't either'a ya settle down if those fish aren't cleaned," Kilzaro warned.

The small man grinned, his dark eyes sparkling, as he poked his face over the soup pot. "Cleaned and ready for the coals," he said. "I saw Rona on the way in. What's flown up his nose?"

"You need ask?" The bearlike Creaben jerked his head in Jhared's direction.

"Naw. That's not the heart'a it," Kilzaro said. "Rona's still trying to get his feet under him. Remember what it's like on the new road."

The slight man's gaze brightened. "He's keen for the territory."

"No keener than the rest of us," Creaben muttered.

Kilzaro glanced sidelong at Jhared, scowling. "Rona can't see so far ahead yet. And that business don't need discussing right now."

"If I can't see ahead, it's because there's nothing left on the Path worth seeing," a grim voice interrupted.

Jhared hadn't spied the other's face before, but he recognized the precise speech of the upper circles of Velantar. It came from a rangy young man near his own age, with straight black hair and aristocratic features that any elder's daughter and some sons might have named handsome. Rona, the others had called him, the name of the northern hero who had sacrificed his life to save the son of his rival. Trailing him like a sheepdog was a boy with a worried gaze and a fistful of feathers. Trevazio? Jhared frowned. He was a child in truth, younger than Branlen. Years away from trying the Becoming.

"Don't, Rona," the boy murmured. "It will be well."

"Ay, you'll find your way. Listen to Trev." Kilzaro turned to smile at the child. "Eh, boy, that's a nice sample of feathers you have to add to your collection. Is that a nightshiver's flight feather I see?"

Trev still had an eye on Rona, but he held up the hand gripping the feathers. "I think so. I found it near the water. I've a blooddaw and a jay, too!"

"My *way*?" Rona spat. "As an aimless exile?"

Creaben looked up, a hint of threat folded in his heavy features. "Careful there. We're all on the same road."

Rona kicked at the end of a log sticking out of the fire, sending sparks flying. "Indeed. A road to nowhere. In the company of oath breakers."

Trevazio's expression went wide with dismay. Rani shook his head in warning.

With unexpected speed, Kilzaro swung around on his bad leg and pushed a bowl into Rona's hands. "Enough. If ya want ta stay out'a trouble, boy, ya'd do well ta use your mouth for eating and not for talking. None'a us want Trev and ya ta be out on your own. Not with winter coming."

Rona paled at the threat and all the protest in his expression died. Silent, he accepted the soup. As he picked a place at the fire, he threw an accusing glare at Jhared. The others seemed eager not to speak of it further. They brought their own cups or bowls to the fire, passing them around to be filled. Someone tugged Jhared's arm. The slight man, Rani, offered him a mug.

"You look like you've been on half rations for a while, soldier. Go ahead. Fill it up. Kilzaro's cooking's decent enough."

"Thank you," Jhared said, taking the mug.

"No debt, eh? It's not often we have a new face among us, and I already know more than I want to about these fellows."

"I don't imagine you'll find anything interesting about who I am."

"Jhared Denaban of the Forest Guard Fourth? Oh, I suspect you've some stories worth hearing." The little man grinned, white teeth flashing. "As you heard already, I'm Rani."

Jhared ignored the man's angling for information. "Rani?" he echoed.

The man's grin widened. "That's *Aranila* to those I dislike."

Aranila was the spirit of one of Cael's Chosen, trapped now in the form of Aranael, the spider that hunted in hordes. Jhared had once seen an Aranael horde take down a bull moose, smothering with a hundred thousand soft abdomens and stinging with venomous fangs. By the end, so many spiders swarmed the carcass that Jhared could only tell it was a moose by the one antler poking up from among the feasting bodies. "I'm glad not to fall among that group," he said.

"Not yet," the other man replied cheerfully.

Rani pointed out a place to sit, and Jhared followed. The circle remained quiet for a time as six Shorn men worked to sate their hunger. Jhared drank down the soup, thick with beans, shreds of tender meat, and various wild leaves. Without complaint, Kilzaro filled his mug a second time, and when the fish had finished searing near the coals, offered him a generous portion. Rani chuckled as Jhared swallowed his last morsel of trout.

"It has been a while since you fed well. Been running hard, eh?"

Jhared nodded noncommittally. He'd been running from the moment Lady Nemiah set him loose—from the moment he had lost his place in Avelos and every future meant for him. It seemed unreal. He felt nothing but a dull, unyielding weight in his chest. "How far are we from Corbene?" he asked. "We must be nearing Clan Nadaren's lands."

"It's three days south and west to Nadrona. That is, if there's no clanguard to avoid and no rain to make the forests mud."

Good news there at least. Alende had carried Jhared in the direction he wanted to go. In truth, Maya might not be so far away. She was traveling on foot and had no reason to push as hard as he had been. He thought of her moving through the night, with her staff in one hand and her wings furled under her cloak. He wondered if she had crossed this same riverbed on her way.

"Not a good idea to think about it."

Jhared blinked at the man beside him. "What?"

"You had that look meant you was thinking of home. We all have it for the first while. Poor Rona still has it."

"Oh. No, not home." Jhared pressed a hand to his chest. Home had been a place of bonds: love and shame, duty and debts. Mayavana was something other.

"Well, wherever you were, better to think forward than back. You're with the Kin now."

"I was brought here against my will," Jhared said, frustrated by just how matter-of-factly the others seemed to take his abduction. "You don't fear I'll seek to betray you?"

Rani's friendly gaze narrowed. "Alende wouldn't have brought you to us if that were likely. And anyway, the Sonans have seen you now. If you flee, they'll deal with you."

It was Jhared's second warning of the evening. He berated himself for his lack of caution. That Alende placed value on his life was the only reason these men had for accepting him, and the waylayer's regard was unpredictable at best. He would do well not to go rousing enmity. "I'm sorry," he sighed. "You're right, you know. There's no looking back for me. The only thing waiting at home is execution."

The man nodded. "I figured it was some such thing. Deserter, eh?"

Jhared bristled at the ugly word, but it was the simplest label for what Avelos saw in him. "Near enough."

So Alende hadn't shared his history with the others, or at least not with all the others; Kilzaro seemed to play a part in leading the band. Jhared wondered if he knew more. A jug had been going around the fire with a fierce drink that tasted faintly of plums and felt like ice going down the throat. *Slu*, Rani called it, a gift from the Sonans. When it came to Jhared, he was loath to let it go.

With only a bit of encouragement, Rani was far more forthcoming than Shira had been and chatted candidly, though somewhat tangentially, in response to Jhared's questions. It seemed that numerous small bands of the unchained Kin roamed across Avelos, coming together each winter near the Sonan border. Through the rest of the year, Alende drifted from band to band in an attempt to maintain the ties among them, but Rani said, with a tone of pride and genuine fondness, that it was this group the waylayer first brought together and this group he considered family. Rani had less to say about the bound Kin, like Ziabela and Enaro, who had passed the Becoming and paid their debts with service, but still allied with Alende. Jhared gathered that the Kin had multiple established routes of communication with the bound, though Rani offered no details about just how such routes were managed. Jhared thought of Leita's birds.

Across the fire next to Rona, Trevazio laid out rows of feathers, organizing them by size and color. Every once in a while, the boy would lift one up and smile at it. Sometimes he would show it to Rona, who nodded perfunctorily. Closer to Jhared, Creaben had taken out a knife and was carving on a small piece of wood as he and Kilzaro spoke quietly in a mix of Velos and the muddy Sonan tongue. Jhared glanced up at the sky, brilliant with stars, and let his thoughts creep beyond the firelight. By now, the high chieftain's company would have limped its way home from Parnas Pass. Rumar would be trying to hold the council together, while deciding whether to maintain the force at the Sahisten border or draw off men to march on the traitorous northerners. The decision would matter; it would change the shape of Avelos. People Jhared knew would live or die because of that decision. His thoughts darted toward those he had left behind. Anzo. Leita. Tierzen. Branlen. So many had already died in Parnas Pass, some by the hand of the traitors, but not all. The killing winds had torn apart— No. Jhared yanked his thoughts away. Not there. Not a safe direction.

"Well now, is this the band of Alende's Kin I've taken unawares?"

Rani and Creaben shot to their feet, Jhared with them, his gaze arrowing in the direction of the voice. At the edge of the riverbed stood a woman, tall and strongly built, with steel at her waist and a bow over her shoulder.

"Silvien!" Trevazio cried happily.

"Aw, it is her," Creaben said, looking abashed.

In the dusky light, Jhared could just make out the woman's expression: her eyes shone as shrewdly as a magpie's and her features cut sharp lines against the night. Her short, curly hair appeared to be the only soft thing about her. "For shame, Kilzaro! Letting me slip all the way up to camp."

Kilzaro was still climbing to his feet. "We didn't do any such thing, ya fox. Our watch is there behind ya. I'd bet my good leg on it."

"Cael is not surprised by chaos!" the demon agreed as Shira's slender figure stepped out of the trees wearing the skull mask. Beside her stood Alende.

"How'd you know?" the newcomer asked, her eyes sparking.

Kilzaro smiled. "Ya would'a asked of Alende first if ya hadn't already seen him."

The woman laughed, a round, pleasant sound at odds with her sharp angles, and jumped across the bank into the riverbed. "Ah, well. You have me there," she said, offering Kilzaro a hearty embrace. The others hurried over to welcome her with hugs and slaps on the shoulders. Jhared stood aside.

"Let the girl come up for air!" Kilzaro finally roared, parting the others.

Grinning, Silvien emerged from the welcome, shrugged a laden bag from her back, and offered it to Alende.

"Success?" Kilzaro asked.

"Yes and no," the woman answered. "A few old volumes in there should please our friends. But Corbene is finished. Not enough of value left in town to risk another run."

Alende opened the pack, nodding as he ran his hands over the spines of several books. "We knew it was almost ended. This won't be enough for Mursa Vin, but it's something."

"What of Lusian's find?"

"He's not back yet," Kilzaro replied.

Silvien's eyes turned to catlike slits. "He should'a been. You think he's finally run off?"

"A better thing if he has," Kilzaro muttered.

The woman shook her head. "It won't be good for any of us if he—"

Alende stopped her with a hand on her arm. The expression he gave her held both reprimand and reassurance. "Don't turn toward trouble, Silvi. In this story, Lusian will bring what we need. Come to the fire."

Kilzaro took the bag of books as Alende led Silvien to the warmth. Jhared frowned. They were plundering ancient writings from Avelos to give to the Sonans in exchange for aid. He had seen Alende at it before. It cut him to watch them blithely stripping Avelos of her treasures.

"You must be famished, Silvien," a voice said shyly. "Take some supper?" From where he had hung back by the kettle, Rona held out a bowl of soup like an offering to the goddess.

"Thanks, Rona. I could stand a meal or three." The woman waded through her well-wishers, took the bowl in one hand, and ruffled Rona's hair absently with the other. "Rani, go get your flute! Crea, warm your throat. I've been too long with the discordant noises of town in my ears. I hunger for the music of my Kin!"

As the night deepened, the mood grew merrier. The jug of *slu* continued around, adding sparkle to the music and wildness to the laughter. It could almost have been a gathering of Jhared's patrolmates after a successful skirmish. Rani played reels and spins and the ballads of Clan Delsio on a brightly tuned flute. He was skilled, though not as inspired as Zia. For the ballads, Creaben sang in an unsteady but willing baritone, with Kilzaro sometimes adding a surprisingly tender harmony. Still wearing Cael's mask, Shira sat cross-legged between the sentinel-like figures of Alende and Silvien. The demon's avian beak bobbed in time to the music. Even Rona's expression lifted from its angry gloom as he hung close to Silvien and listened to her stories. Jhared discovered himself smiling a little at the unlooked for sense of camaraderie that pervaded the circle. He was taken off guard when Rona's voice rang across the fire.

"I choose the soldier for a song!"

The unbound young man was grinning evilly, his face flushed with drink. Jhared straightened from where he'd been speaking with Rani.

"Let the soldier sing for his supper!" Trevazio echoed.

Rani wiped a speck of dust from his flute with a finger and shook his head. "You're a troublemaker from start to finish, Rona. He's a guest. Leave him be."

"I don't see a harm in letting a stranger pay his way," Silvien said, reclining against a log, long-legged and sleek as a mountain cat.

Rona puffed his chest at the woman's support. "It's a song I've requested, not a duel. Alende says the soldier knows the meaning of our story. That he's heard the tales of the Storytellers. Well, let him prove it. Let him sing one of the old songs."

"Why not?" Creaben asked.

Kilzaro shifted. "Well, now—"

"I'll sing."

The others swiveled their heads to look at him. Jhared thought he caught a gleam of amusement in Alende's eye, but it might have only been the *slu* the waylayer had been steadily consuming.

"Good. Excellent. What will it be?" Rani asked, brandishing his flute with nervous cheer.

It was only a song Rona demanded, but Jhared had worked among fighting men long enough to know a challenge for what it was. This would be only the first of the tests. They wanted to know if he shared enough with them to become a part of their group rather than a threat to it.

"I will sing," he said again, "but not one of the old songs. You can judge for yourselves whether it says something of our story." He cleared his throat and reached for the jug. Someone put it into his hand. He took a swallow of the icy *slu*, closing his eyes to shut out Rona's smirk and the mixed curiosity and wariness of the others. It had been a lifetime since he'd sung for an audience. He had been but a child and had only ever sung before his mother's friends, musicians all. He remembered it now only in dreams. Tonight, though, he knew exactly what song he must sing. "Alende's Flight."

He had never put the words to the music for anyone but himself. The piece was challenging, stretching across a span of octaves as the mood of the tale slid from the heights of determination to the hollows of despair. He took the time necessary to gather himself, breathing evenly and drawing on the quiet at the core of him.

He opened his throat on the first notes with his eyes still closed. The verse was well within his range and came out full and rich. There was joy at the start: the tale of a Shorn youth who found peace in his music and happiness in running beneath the sacred skies, a youth who conquered his restlessness with the dream of finding a place among his people. The mood of the piece changed gradually, and with it Jhared changed registers, flawlessly the first time, then faltering a little and steadying again. When called by Avelos to prove his worth, the youth had offered his blood and service, but met only with rejection. For his failure, his people had called him a traitor and drove him into the wilds to die.

It was *loss* that Jhared had in common with these Kin, and his intention in selecting the song was to answer their test. He hadn't expected the music to abrade his own wounds, though he should have. "Alende's Flight" was the story of a man's Path unraveled, of shattered beliefs and lost purpose. The lyrics had been set down by Ziabela and given to him by Lady Nemiah, but they were his mother's words. Mahla Denaban had written it for the boy Alende, whom she had loved. Tonight, for Jhared, the story meant something even more personal.

His voice quavered as the song approached its ambiguous close. It had been too long since he had pushed his range so far, not with such emotion in a piece, not with an audience who understood the song. At the end, the tension in the story was left unresolved. For some, Alende's survival could be taken as a triumph, but for others there could be no consolation for the loss of all he had known and loved. The chance for reparation had slipped away.

Silence greeted Jhared as he released the last note. Some of the Kin gifted him with their unshielded expressions: Rani offered a nod of acknowledgment, tears tracing twin trails down his face. Creaben let out a long, shuddering sigh and brushed a hand over his eyes. Others looked angry and guarded: Silvien stabbed at the ground with her knife; Shira sat motionless, Cael's expression unaltered; Rona stared at Jhared with blatant loathing, his body clenched as though gripping something he wasn't willing to reveal.

It was Alende who split the stillness, scrambling to his feet, his breathing loud and harsh. "That's one way the story goes," he muttered. In a flash, his knife was in his hand, the steel reflecting the orange flames. He staggered drunkenly, then wrenched himself away from the others and strode off alone. From the horse line, came a long, ringing whinny. Seravina.

Jhared didn't need the mare's warning to know what Alende was battling. A drum pounded against his chest and the whole forest seemed to tremble in answer. "Alende, wait!" He came to his feet, following the waylayer out of the circle and down the dead riverbed. He hadn't yet reached the trees when a broad shadow stepped into his way.

"Not you," Kilzaro said. "He's hunted enough without you chasing after him."

"I know what hunts him, Kilzaro."

The big man didn't budge, but glared at Jhared in the darkness. "We all know. He sees the ways and must pay their toll. But you're the one who sang his song and laid him bare."

Jhared hadn't considered how the song would tear at Alende, but some part of him had no doubt known it. It was, perhaps, a response to poison and helplessness.

"Let him go."

The soft voice belonged to Shira. Jhared turned in surprise. She had pulled off the demon's mask. It dangled from one hand as she faced them with her own gaze. "The boy knows what it is to fall. He's walked the tangled web himself and still knows which Path is his own. Let him go, Zaro."

Kilzaro hesitated, then reluctantly moved aside. "You'd best have a care with him, soldier. It's Shira I trust, not you."

Jhared hurried into the woods. He found Alende under a lightning-struck pine tree, twisting a knife against his throat behind his jaw. His gaze held desperation and need as he fought to hold the Gate at bay. Blood trickled down his neck. Jhared thought of Lady Nemiah and how the Paths had depleted her. Though his anger remained, he couldn't wall himself away from Alende's pain.

The waylayer didn't look up at his approach. "You did a lovely job with Mahla's song, my darling. Have you come now to push the blade deeper?"

Jhared knelt. Slowly, he reached out and wrapped his fingers around Alende's knife hand. The man stiffened.

"No, Alende, not deeper. There are other ways to keep from falling."

"Mm, I've seen how well they work for you," the waylayer growled.

"They do work. Sometimes. It's not only pain that can hold you in the moment."

The waylayer's gaze clouded. "That's . . . familiar. Mahla said something like that once. Perhaps even on this Path."

"She didn't like to see you use the knife?"

Alende shook his head.

"Then in her memory, turn your senses to the night and remind yourself who you are in it. It will anchor you."

The waylayer blinked at Jhared, then closed his eyes with a sigh.

"No. Open your eyes. Engage *every* sense in this moment."

Jhared was taking a risk. He had seen Alende at the edge of the Gate, aggressive and volatile, but he could not abandon the man to this suffering, not with Mahla's song lingering in his head. The Old Man had once helped him to find his own place in the web; he could at least offer Alende that much. He tightened his grip on the waylayer's hand and tried to draw the knife away.

Alende's green eyes flashed open. His arm tensed. "No. No, don't. *Please.*"

It was a command and a plea. Alende's eyes gleamed with hunger for the blue flames and the terror of being consumed by them. Jhared knew those conflicting needs. With effort, he confronted them, keeping the pressure on the blade insistent and his breathing steady. This was only another test—to learn whether he would surrender his borders and tumble through the Gate with Alende or hold firm and pull the man back to the safety of his own Path.

"You will not bleed out your desire, Alende. Not tonight."

For a moment, he thought the waylayer would strike him, but instead the man's expression shifted, yielded. Finally, with a look that might have been resignation or relief, he allowed Jhared to take the knife.

"Very well. Watch me fall," Alende said, his voice vague and defeated. "Before the flames, we have no more volition than a feather in a breeze."

"That's not so," Jhared replied, setting aside the blade. "It takes force to knock us from our own Paths. You must only remember yourself to keep you where you are."

The waylayer chuckled softly. "Very little of me remains on this Path, I think."

Jhared tried to consider a way to help the man. When he thought on it, he realized he knew hardly anything about Alende, and everything he did know was tied to the past, to Mahla. Then it occurred to him who would know more: "Something of who you are is held safe by those who follow you. Tell me how they came to you. Who you are to them."

Alende hesitated, looking lost. From his time with the Old Man, Jhared thought it important that the waylayer find his own way, but he tried prompting: "Kilzaro knows you and holds you dear."

"Does he?" The waylayer's brow furrowed. "I suppose he's seen enough of me in all these years. He was the first I found."

"When?" Jhared asked.

"So many lives . . . years ago . . ." Alende licked his lips, then seemed to put effort into concentrating. "I think . . . it wasn't so long after my own failure. Mahla wished me to stay close to the city, but she knew the danger. And she had her own son to worry for. I fled as far from my lost life as I could. Northward. Stopped only when I came to the shores of the Tregata Sea. The Path led me to Kilzaro's village in Clan Lasla on the morning of his Becoming. I found him on the shore. They had run a stake through his leg to pin him to the ground until the tide would end him."

Jhared hissed a breath. "What are you to Kilzaro—on this Path?"

"A friend. A guide, perhaps. Sometimes." Alende laughed drunkenly. "A map read upside down would serve him better."

"Stop that. Claim what you are." Jhared recalled the prodding, powerful voice of the Old Man. "What of the others?"

"After I freed Kilzaro, my searching became deliberate. Every spring, I—all of us now—hunt the wilds for those who have been thrown away. It's how we've grown."

"A hunter, then?"

"Yes," Alende agreed, leaning back against the tree. "More often than not we are too late or the Arionade on watch are too vigilant, but sometimes . . . sometimes we can save them."

"Rona's the most recent member of your group, isn't he?"

"Indeed. He's a familiar part of this story. He came from Velantar this past spring. Same as you. Poor boy has no mind for lists and dates. He couldn't keep the histories straight. When he failed, his brother ran into the wilds to find him."

"Trevazio," Jhared murmured.

Alende nodded. "That's right. No more than ten winters that boy. But he gave up his own chance to try the Becoming in order to save Rona. I may be freedom to them, but I'm also the face of their sorrow."

A pang slashed through Jhared. He had known the kind of devotion that would lead a boy to give up his life for his brother. He had known and lost it. "What else?"

"Silvi, bless Silvi for her strength. She managed to staunch her wounds and stagger halfway across the Parnas Mountains before she found us herself."

"You mean something very particular to her. I saw it."

Alende's gaze sparkled, his expression nearly lucid. "We have been both gift and curse to one another. Mentor and student; student and mentor. There is no single name that can tell the story of what I am with that woman, and no other name I will share with you."

"You need only know it yourself." Jhared hid a hopeful smile. "And Shira?"

Without warning, pain crumbled the waylayer's features. It was a different pain from before, not self-destructive but filled with regret and anger. A low moan escaped his lips, the sound of heartache. Jhared feared all their work had shredded, but Alende reached out and grasped his shoulder, as though to physically anchor himself. Panting through clenched jaws, the waylayer lifted his head. His eyes were clear.

"Ah, Shira, Shira. I saw her on a thousand twisted Paths. She's the only one I ever knew before I found her. With dying eyes, she met me on every journey. I had no clue if she were my future, my past, or some present that had nothing at all to do with me, but I began to hunt for her. I found her in the wilds outside a small village of Clan Valador. I don't recall the name on this Path . . . Olar . . . Obile . . . Oblent . . ."

"Obled?"

"Yes. Obled. Curse the name and its people."

"They have been cursed," Jhared answered. Death had come to them in the form of the killing winds. "Are you saying you used your journeys to find Shira on the day she failed?"

Alende pushed himself upright, his expression haggard. "No. If I had managed to find her that first day, she would still be intact."

"Alende, she survives because of you. You are salvation to her."

"She survives because her will is steel and stone!" Alende replied. "She had already committed a crime before her Becoming, you see. She loved a boy. The eldest son of her Teacher. Perhaps that's why she failed. Perhaps the judges knew. But after the priestesses cut her and the Arionade left her to die, the boy found her. He carried her to an abandoned hunters' shelter and treated her injuries. He begged her to flee with him. But she refused to let him throw away the life she would have given anything to regain. She refused him."

Alende's knife was in his fist again, but the ferocity in his eyes suggested no risk remained that he meant to use it on himself.

Jhared's expression darkened. "And he hurt her for her refusal?"

"No, not as you're thinking. Someone in the town discovered she lived. A mob of them came for her. The boy reached her in time. He held them off and gave her the chance to escape. She ran, though not so far that she couldn't see it when they stoned him to death. Have you ever witnessed a stoning, soldier?"

Jhared shook his head, sickened.

"It's a slow, ugly way to die. Shira watched while they shattered his bones and crushed his skull. After, someone pinned a robin's wings to his broken back."

Ah goddess. The fear and fury that consumed Shira made a horrible kind of sense now. She had watched while they killed the boy she loved, the boy who had saved her. Was it any wonder she masked herself in Cael's rage? *No one who stands beside you is safe.*

The waylayer nodded as though hearing Jhared's thoughts. "We are the bane of Avelos. When I found her in the wilds, she was out of her senses with shame and grief. For a long while, I thought her final links to this Path would snap."

Alende's gaze was lucid and his stance straight. He appeared more stable than he'd been all night. Jhared didn't think it was the recollection of the horrifying past that steadied him, but his focus on the needs of another.

"Look," Jhared said quietly. "You've kept yourself here."

The waylayer closed his eyes, then opened them again, with an expression of amazement absent of irony. "The blue flames have gone to ember."

Jhared smiled, one hand pressed against his chest.

Alende glanced at the knife. He touched the crisscross of scars on his throat. "That is . . . astonishing. The Bearer didn't teach you how to do that."

"No. She didn't."

"You figured it out for yourself?"

Jhared didn't reply.

"Another secret?"

"Is that why you brought me here? To pry out my secrets?"

"Yes. In part. I told you I need your help to reach the Bearer."

With a sigh, Jhared pushed the man's knife aside. "The Bearer is not your foe, Alende. She fears the unraveling of the web as you do."

The waylayer rose and began to pace. He moved once around the tree, looking intensely present on his own Path. "If you don't know where the cliff lies, the fear of falling in the dark is not enough to prevent it. Even if she does not desire chaos, the Bearer may still be its cause. I've seen it! Please. Tell me how Cael has touched you. I need to understand!"

Jhared pressed the heels of his hands against his eyelids until lights flashed in his vision. "I cannot."

"I could force it from you, you know." Alende said the words as if they startled him, but his features settled into something like resolve.

"You won't."

"Do not think that because Mahla—"

Jhared held up a hand to stop him. "I just heard you tell Shira's story. You won't force me because you know such violence is unbalanced and you despise it. You believe that the lack of balance has something to do with the unraveling. I think the Bearer believes the same."

True Chaos. He heard the heretics' words in Leita's voice.

Alende remained quiet.

"How long do you imagine you can hold me here?" Jhared asked.

"You could make a place with us. Take a new name for your new life. *Ularian* would suit you. On another Path, you might have served as Riana's Chosen archer, don't you think?"

"How long, Alende?"

The waylayer shrugged bonelessly. "You promised me a season, but time means very little to one who wanders forward and back among all the seasons of the intricate web."

"I see." Jhared swallowed his frustration and stood, suddenly in no mood to deal further with the waylayer. "Good night."

As he began to walk away, the waylayer called out. "Wait, my darling. I'd best return with you or you're likely to face blades when you reach the riverbed."

Jhared nodded and paused for the other man to join him. They walked toward camp without speaking, deadfall crunching under their boots. When they neared the stream, every set of eyes turned toward them at once. The intensity of those joined stares formed a wall. Jhared knew what those stares meant; he had seen them all his life.

"I don't belong here," he muttered.

Unexpectedly, a hand alighted on his shoulder, a moment of warmth for all to witness. Jhared startled at Alende's touch. The waylayer squeezed his shoulder and gave him a sideways smile.

"Ah, my darling, open your eyes to your own Path. You don't belong anywhere else."

3.

Uncommon Visions

Jhared jerked upright, arrowing his gaze across the camp. Milky starlight revealed the sleeping forms of the others sprawled close to the fire. The arguing voices he thought he had heard had only been the wind tugging through the last of the leaves or part of a twisted dream. At least, he hoped that was so. His Teachers hadn't spoken to him since Shrill attacked him on the far side of the Gate. He had answered her attack with violence, and he didn't care to consider just how Shrill and Boar would punish him when they returned.

Thinking on his Teachers left him well and truly wakeful. He stood, stretching out the kinks in his back carved by the pebbled ground. The scent of pine and earth hung on the chilly air. Silently, he crossed the riverbed to the stream and followed it away from camp until the dark and the trees closed around him. There he stripped off his clothes and stepped into the water, his skin prickling in the cold. As he scrubbed away days of travel grime with a handful of pine needles, his fingers walked the trail of his scars: the parallel lines on his throat where Leita and Alende had cut him free of Riana's web; the curved stroke across his ribs made by a Legacy sword; the inverted *V*'s in the muscle of his upper arm, like spread wings, that represented his oath to Avelos; and the twin weals down his back that marked what he was supposed to be.

Ah goddess, what he was supposed to be.

Tawny and gold flashed in the sunlight as his wings unfurled. Muscles stretched and feathers caught the wind. His body rose on a current of air.

"No. Oh no."

Vertigo whipped the forest into a blur. From a distance, he knew he had tumbled into the stream as the Gate called him toward its blue flames.

Full-bellied clouds tugged shadows across summer-kissed valleys. The lands of Avelos unrolled beneath him. He knew a sense of connection to the sacred skies and every creature in them, a sense of well-being and rightness.

Lady help him, he yearned for that Path with a force that left him breathless. If he chose it, he could let go and lose himself beyond the Gate—lose himself in a life that might have been—but that sense of well-being and connection was only an illusion. He had been taught to reach for the truth.

Gold soared against flawless blue. He passed over the land and saw the pattern of the paths below, not just the roads of men but Riana's ways as well.

Jhared gritted his teeth. If he could help Alende to evade the Gate, he could help himself. "That is not my place," he breathed. He drove his fingers into the streambed, forcing himself to focus on the cold water, the scent of pine, and the sound of birdsong. He closed his heart to temptation and grasped at the moments of joy he had known in this life: Branlen's devotion, Mayavana's friendship, Lady Nemiah's trust.

The whoosh of wings against the air grew fainter. The patterns below him began to fade. Reflexively, he grasped for the wondrous moment once more:

Soaring. All the world laid out below him like a map—

"No! I have no claim to the sacred skies. I am *Shorn*."

The truth of that name reverberated through him. Deep within his center, something powerful shifted and clashed. The impact cut off his sense of wings and sky like a dam dropped abruptly across a river or a door slammed shut on a conversation.

Wet and naked, he hunkered in the stream, his fists full of sand and stones. As a breeze brushed his body, he felt each hair on his arms rise and each droplet of water roll across his flanks. Light painted lavender on the eastern horizon. As the forest stirred under morning's touch, he heard the music of it. He was present on his own Path in a way he hadn't been in weeks.

"How very strange," a voice mused. "No gift from Cael, that."

With a curse and a splash, Jhared lunged across the water. He snatched up his cloak and swirled it around him to conceal his scars. Sitting on a branch overhanging the stream, Shira watched him with Cael's features.

"I didn't expect the demon to follow a man to his bath," Jhared muttered.

"So you don't enjoy others peering at you as much as you enjoy peering under others' veils?" Beneath the mask, the woman grinned. "You just turned away the flames. You closed the Gate without going through. That's a thing worth remarking."

Jhared hesitated. Was it a closed Gate that explained the uncommon quiet in his mind and the clarity returned to the world? "How can you tell?"

The demon swung her legs on the branch like a child on a swing. "How could I not? The Paths that have been atremble since Alende brought you to us have stilled. Your own chaos is no longer shaking the web."

"My chaos? What does that mean?"

"You know well enough," she replied. "Don't think you can shirk responsibility by claiming ignorance. I felt your turmoil tangling the Paths long before I first saw you. We're each to blame for the torments we cause."

He frowned up at her. "Shira, I *am* ignorant. I want to learn. What can Cael tell me about keeping the Gate closed?"

"Nothing." She gave a haughty shrug. "What use has the Demon of Disorder for closed doors?"

"But you've found a way to close them, haven't you?"

The woman shushed him and cocked her avian head. After a moment, she straightened. "Time to go, Jhared Denaban. Our watchers have come for a visit. Go back to camp and stop trying to peer around other's veils. Or you may find that someone will rip all yours away."

Jhared heard horses. Men's voices rose in greeting. "Alende's Sonans? Have they—Shira?"

He looked up. The unbound woman was climbing higher into the tree. Her boots scraped against the rough bark. "Go on. Alende will be looking for you." Jhared thought he caught a smirk behind the mask. "Although you might consider dressing first."

He did, swiftly and without glancing again at the slender figure disappearing overhead. A bustling scene greeted him in camp. The Kin were cheerfully hailing five Sonan warriors. Kilzaro was speaking in Sonan to a young man who had offered over a string of fish and was helping to set the kettle on the fire. Creaben and Rani assisted with tethering the horses while Rona hefted a bag of grain, scowling over his shoulder at a grey-eyed man who seemed to be trying to flirt with Silvien in a combination of his own language and halting Velos.

The warriors were a short, tightly muscled folk, garbed in dun, with pale eyes in lean faces, and straight hair the grey-brown color of oak bark. Each man wore a knife and kept a staff strapped to his saddle. Their horses appeared cast from the same mold as Seravina, only smaller, with the strong, slender legs, arched necks, and dished faces of Clan Everen coursers. At some point, the Sonans had gained access to Clan Everen bloodlines. Jhared wondered if the Kin had helped them to it.

The Sonan leader swung down from his mount, wafting the scent of rosemary and mint into the air as he greeted Alende with a gruff embrace. Many seasons creased his austere features. Silver shot through his thick hair, but like his men, he was strong and fit. Jhared recognized the leader from outside Brenia, where Alende had turned over books stolen from Lady Esania's library. That time, Jhared had experienced the speed with which a Sonan warrior could wield a staff.

As though sensing Jhared's gaze upon him, the leader looked over and smiled, a curl of lips over yellowed teeth. Alende turned and gestured for Jhared to join them.

"Good morning, my darling," the waylayer said merrily. "I'm glad for you to finally know Mursa Vin Suamey, *cir'yo* in the Sonan border guard and a generous provider to the Kin. Mursa Vin, Jhared Denaban is a fascinating story. It might do you well to know more of it."

The warrior looked Jhared up and down in dubious appraisal. "If you tell me so, *se'yo*, it must be true, eh? You are gifted to see things my eyes cannot."

Alende laughed. He seemed coherent this morning and genuinely pleased to see the Sonans. "Gifted or cursed, we can debate, my friend, but in this story it's the truth nonetheless. Talk with one another. Negotiations can wait until you and your men have shared our food and fire."

"Ah. Perhaps you think that a full belly will dull my bargaining edge, eh, *se'yo*?"

Though the words seemed pointed, the Sonan was grinning. Alende grinned back and tapped the center of his forehead with three fingers. "I would never make such a foolish mistake, *cir'yo*. Ancient poets have declaimed the skill of the Sonans in negotiation. And I know you too well." To Jhared he gave a wink as he went off humming "Lusian's Light." Jhared watched the waylayer use some excuse to draw Silvien away from the flirtatious young Sonan, then turned awkwardly to face Mursa Vin.

"You look better than the last time I saw you, Forest Guard," the warrior observed. "Standing on your feet this time."

"I'm no longer a Forest Guard," Jhared replied.

"No?" The man chuckled. "Then why do you glare at me like a bear guarding her cubs? I think you don't like that we've crossed your borders uninvited."

Jhared opened his mouth, closed it. Sona wasn't an enemy of Avelos, but for certain it was no ally. A small, swampy land pressed between Laebek and Amuria and freed of Amurian occupation barely fifty years before, Sona had neither military strength nor significant trade to offer. The Council of Clans had never considered it worth the effort to maintain active relations with the Sonan sovereign, but that didn't make Jhared feel easier. "Why are you here, Mursa Vin?"

"Aha. No laughter for you in this, I see. Very well, Forest Guard. I will answer you, but first I ask the same. Why are you here?"

"I was dragged here. With your help, if you recall."

The warrior shook his head. "That's not my meaning. Why does the *se'yo* risk his life for you? Why is he so keen to have you here?"

"*Sayo.* You mean Alende?"

"Yes. *Se'yo.* In Velos, it is 'river captain' or 'river pilot.' A man worthy of respect. Like Alende. You?" The warrior shrugged dismissively. "I know your kind, but not you."

"I don't know why Alende wants me here. I didn't choose it for myself."

Mursa Vin appeared to consider that, his manner patient and self-possessed. He spoke Velos more fluently than many clansmen and made observations worthy of a scout. Jhared was impressed and disturbed by that.

"I have warned the *se'yo* that you will mean blood for him, but he ignores me. Some of his madness, maybe."

"Maybe." Jhared offered the Sonan a meaningful look. "Perhaps it would be better for everyone if I were to leave."

"Perhaps, yes. But I have told the *se'yo* I will help to keep you here, so I will see that you stay. Understand?"

"I understand well enough," Jhared answered. "Alende has bought your loyalty."

"No!" Mursa Vin slammed one fist against his palm. "I do so because he is *se'yo*. That is not a thing you can earn with pay." The Sonan narrowed his eyes. "I think you cannot understand. Everything in Avelos is about debt. About what you owe or don't. No place remains for honor."

Jhared sucked a sharp breath. "If you find no honor in Avelos, why are you here stealing our histories?"

The Sonan raised a brow, his pale eyes glittering like water in the sunlight. "You want to know in truth?"

"Yes."

"Our *Simata'yo* is building a great archive. He is bringing the stories and knowledge of many places to Sona."

"The truth? You're smuggling out the ancient treasures of Avelos for a library?"

In the man's gaze, Jhared caught a flash of pride. He had never thought of Sonans as proud. When he thought of them at all, it was as a slippery, unctuous people, smelling of fish. Something hard and resentful in the warrior's manner told Jhared he knew that.

"Why do you have such surprise?" Mursa Vin replied. "The people of Avelos live in the center of everyone." The warrior made a circular gesture indicating Avelos surrounded by the border nations. "But you talk to no one. We will take your histories and stories. We will take the stories of Laebek, Amuria, Sahiste. Then you all will come to us. You will beg to see what we have. To learn."

The idea of such an archive—of a world's worth of knowledge compiled in one place—fascinated Jhared, but his words twisted on the other man's arrogance. "You should read some of the work you've smuggled, Mursa Vin. Anarava will warn you of the dangers of seeking glory through corrupt means."

Mursa Vin froze. Slowly, a thin, dangerous smile etched his face. Jhared tensed, prepared for whatever the man might start.

A long, high-pitched whinny knocked the moment in another direction. Jhared glanced away to see one of the other Sonans tying his gelding too near to Seravina, who was trumpeting her ire and threatening to tear free of her tether. As Jhared strode over to steady her, the Sonan warrior swatted her soft muzzle. She snapped at the man, who jumped backward, glaring at Jhared and hissing something in his own tongue that did not need translating.

"Her grandsire was a Mavaye stallion," Jhared replied stonily. "The blood of Riana's Chosen, Captain Mavias, runs in her veins. Do not expect her to suffer strangers readily."

"No stranger here but you," the Sonan replied, his eyes flashing.

Jhared's fingers clenched on Seravina's lead. The mare stomped and swiveled in his grasp, her hooves grinding the dirt.

"Wait, wait! All is well!" Rani appeared, inserting his small frame between Jhared and the young Sonan. "Luvas was taken by surprise is all. We're friends here. No one means to tread on that friendship. *No one.*" The slender Shorn man gave Jhared a meaningful glare.

"As you say," Jhared muttered. He tethered Seravina farther from the other mounts, though he would have preferred to take her out for a run. He was acting rashly and knew it. The Sonans could offer no true threat to Avelos and were crucial to the survival of Alende's people. It was petty of him to risk that relationship over things that had no meaning among the unbound.

At Alende's invitation, Mursa Vin and his men remained in camp for the day, waiting for the return of one of the Kin called Lusian, who Rani said would bring another supply of books. Jhared witnessed the bag of volumes from Corbene given into the foreigners' hands. In exchange, the Sonans offered a number of provisions and promised their continued services as outriders and watchmen. The promise was given by a stern-faced Mursa Vin and cheered by both sides. Jhared couldn't deny that the interactions he witnessed seemed to include mutual respect, but it left him feeling further adrift. For the first time, he truly believed the words he had said to Mursa Vin: he was no longer a Forest Guard. He could no longer even say with surety who his enemies were.

After breakfast, Mursa Vin, Alende, and Kilzaro came together and headed away from camp, deep in conversation. Curious and bored, Jhared considered following, but Rani caught his arm.

"Oh, no. That's not for you, soldier."

Jhared watched Alende bend close to Mursa Vin as they disappeared into the trees. "Why not?"

"Because you just came near to taking off Luvas's head, and that storm is still in your eyes. It's no secret what they're discussing. They don't need complications like you added to the conversation."

Jhared pulled free of Rani's grasp, somewhat chastened. "What conversation would that be?"

"Alende's negotiating the price for our protection this winter and whether the unchained will shelter in Avelos or Sona."

"Sona? Is it safe for you there?"

"Safer than here. If we provide enough gifts for his library, the *Simata'yo* says we can take sanctuary in his lands. There's wilds enough near the border for us to hunt and find shelter without dealing with the Sonan clans."

Jhared tried to reconcile the fact that the unbound Kin, who didn't even exist in the minds of the Avelonian people, had been acknowledged by a foreign head of state—even if it was only the Sonan sovereign. "Why not simply go, then?" he asked. "Why would you stay?"

Rani's features twisted. "Because Avelos belongs to us! We deserve a piece for ourselves, and hiding in the swamplands won't win it. A man who gets in the habit of retreating from his dreams forgets what they mean to him."

"Taking a piece of Avelos for the Kin is a dangerous dream," Jhared replied.

The unbound man glanced over his shoulder. Caution seemed to hold his tongue for a heartbeat before he surrendered to his nature. "What new danger should we fear? We've already lost our lives. And in the wilds, we must every minute fear crossing the path of a clanguard patrol or some woodsmen's hunting party."

"Rani, when you talk about claiming some of Avelos for yourself, you're not talking about facing ragged clanguard or drunken hunters. You're declaring war." Jhared's heart thudded. "How do you ever imagine you might win?"

The little man gave him a wild, hopeful grin. "With the killing winds."

Even familiar with that answer as he was, Jhared struggled to restrain his revulsion. To exchange the knives of the Shearing for the knives of the killing winds was no solution. As he considered his response, he felt himself observed. A few yards away, Cael's avian features appeared from behind a tree. His eyes met Shira's for a moment before she pulled out of sight. He looked at Rani. "You would wash a new land in the blood of our own countrymen?"

"Not my countrymen, soldier."

It was the same argument Jhared had confronted in Ziabela, and he doubted he would find the unbound Kin any more receptive to his challenges. He rubbed a hand across his eyes.

"Is it you?" Rani asked, his voice dropping lower. "Is that why Alende brought you among us? You've found the secret in your travels?"

Jhared gave a startled laugh. "Because a Shorn deserter would be privy to such secrets?"

"Shira named you Cael's Beloved when they brought you in. She knows something of the demon's ways. Maybe Cael has gifted you somehow."

"Rani, if I knew anything of the killing winds, do you think Avelos would have let me go?"

The little Shorn man looked up at him, deflated. His thin shoulders slumped. "That's what I said to Crea. Still, you can't help hoping, eh? This endless wandering wears sometimes. I think . . . I think it would be pleasant to have a home."

Jhared bowed his head. It had been easier to face Ziabela's self-righteous anger. "I'm sorry," he murmured.

As swiftly as he could, he extricated himself from the conversation. That left him with little to do. He made himself useful completing tasks in camp, but had no good excuse to decline when Rani drew him into a game of dice with the foreigners. He felt absurdly out of place as the Kin and the Sonans bantered easily and joked as though they were old comrades. In the afternoon, Creaben went out to hunt with the young Sonan, Luvas; two others rode out on a short patrol. Shira remained mostly invisible, though Jhared caught her surreptitiously watching the camp twice more during the afternoon. When he asked Silvien why Shira was uncomfortable with the Sonans, the woman gave him a withering look. "Maybe it's not the Sonans she can't tolerate."

With the additional company around the fire that night, dinner quickly grew into a raucous affair. If Mursa Vin was a shrewd, steady commander, his men seemed inclined to more varied temperaments. Grey-eyed Luvas hovered attentively near Silvien, who appeared amused by his flirting, while Rona, across from them, did not. Two of the other warriors argued good-naturedly in their own tongue with Kilzaro. The last Sonan, a laughing man with one brown eye and one blue, named himself a singer. Jhared, who had resolved to make up for his earlier rudeness, feigned enthusiasm when the others begged to hear the Sonan's melodies. By the end of the first cycle, however, Jhared found himself nodding in genuine admiration. The singer owned a powerful voice with an impressive range. The anthems he offered crashed against the night, and his impassioned ballads threatened to set the forest aflame. Jhared couldn't call the songs lovely, for they rang out raw and unmodulated compared to any Avelonian melody, but they were intriguing. He remained at the fire as the nature of the Sonan spirit took shape in song. The generations of defeat and occupation that shaped the Sonan way of life were no more than unsung harmonies implied by the themes of determination and fortitude. The pledge voiced repeatedly in the singer's bold baritone was the pledge of a people not merely to endure but to flourish. In each song, Jhared recognized another piece of the connection between the Sonans and the Kin.

The fire was a red-gold glow by the time the warriors took their leave. As Mursa Vin's men mounted their horses, the *cir'yo* embraced Alende and addressed him soberly in Sonan.

"I understand, my friend," Alende replied in Velos. "When Lusian returns, I hope we'll have sufficient gifts that you won't need to face such a decision."

Mursa Vin swung into the saddle and saluted Alende with a flick of his fingers against the center of his brow. "We watch for you in the darkness, *se'yo.*"

At their leader's signal, the warriors rode out, with only the sounds of their horses' hooves to mark their passing.

"Do they always keep to their own camp?" Jhared asked Alende when the sound of the riders had faded and the other Kin had dispersed to their blankets.

"Not always," the waylayer replied. "But it keeps us both easier to conceal. Swifter to move." Alende yawned and swayed a little, not entirely sober. "Did you see clear to the truth of them, my darling?"

"I saw they respect you and seem to have a fondness for the Kin."

"But?"

"They're full of resentment. They have no love for Avelos, no matter that they seem excessively comfortable here."

The waylayer snorted.

"What would you have of me, Alende? Your truth comes from a different vantage than mine."

"Fair enough," the waylayer sighed. "Perhaps I'll ask you again some other time. Still, you heard the heart of their music, didn't you?"

"Yes. I did. It was . . . unyielding."

"They're an unyielding folk." Alende crouched beside the embers. "Sona's been either ignored or occupied by its neighbors on every path. Yet the Sonans I've met don't bemoan their past. They're resolute. Proud. It's in their music. We could take a lesson."

Jhared looked up at the stars, thinking of music and of pasts. "Did Mahla approve of your alliance with them?"

The waylayer shook his head, sadness in the gesture. "She never knew. Mursa Vin only came to us a few years ago. She never had the chance to hear Sonan music. I'm sorry for that. I think she would have appreciated it."

"I think so too." Jhared smiled in spite of himself, and Alende smiled in return. At that moment, his mother's memory seemed a gentler bond between them.

"Go to sleep, my darling," Alende said softly. "Enjoy the memory of music while you can."

A different kind of music stirred Jhared sometime later.

Mayavana reached for him in the silky evening light and kissed his throat. "Ah, Jhared, do not turn from me. You only fear your body because they taught you to fear it. Because they do. Let me teach you the meaning of joy."

Jhared pulled her closer. Desire ran like sunlight through his veins and reflected in Maya's bright gaze. It grew as they entwined themselves, until he could no longer hold anything back from her. She was compassion and courage and unbridled longing. His need roared through him, loosing the cache of Shorn energy that ever waited for release.

Desire in a Shorn man is death.

"Have a care!" Maya gasped. "The doors are slamming open!"

Fear shot through him. He had reached for what he craved and touched the forbidden. The doors of the infinite Paths flew wide, freeing what had too long been caged. From afar, he heard Maya cry his name, but the storm had risen around him. It keened and wailed, a sound of devastation and fury.

The killing winds drove their knives through Maya, leaving long fingers of blood streaming across her skin. Jhared threw himself around her, trying to shield her, but it wasn't enough. Not nearly enough. She was flayed by the power his desire had released. Jhared begged for aid from Riana, from Cael, from whatever being might listen, but none took mercy. The winds wreaked their violence. Mayavana's blood-slicked body slipped from his grasp.

Jhared sobbed a breath, wrenching himself from sleep. He opened his eyes to escape the horror and found another nightmare waiting.

Cael glowered down at him, a grey feather and the curved blade inches from his face.

With a startled hiss, he jerked against the ground, but there was nowhere to go; the skull hovered just above him. "Shira! What are you doing?"

It was the echoing demon's voice that answered. "If you call to Cael in the darkness, he will come."

"Lady, have mercy," Jhared breathed.

"The Lady of Order has no mercy for our kind. Did she not turn her back while they bound what belongs to the sacred skies? Did she not cause this despair?"

Jhared blinked up at the empty eye-sockets of the human skull. Riana had thrown Shira into the wilds and abandoned her and the boy who loved her. "I understand."

The avian head twitched. "Do not presume, soldier. We shall see how much you understand. Come with me."

Jhared considered the straight-backed figure with its condemning features, the curved blade in one hand and the grey feather in the other. Whatever purpose Shira's demon had for him, he would rather confront it than return to his nightmare. Without argument, he tugged on his boots and buckled his belt. He reached for his knife, but the demon made a harsh, disapproving sound.

"Only Cael determines a body's torments. Leave the blade."

Jhared dropped it atop his bedroll.

"Good. Come."

With one slender arm, the demon gestured for him to walk ahead. It was a strange and uncomfortable thing to move through the trees with the figure of Cael at his back. Almost, Jhared could have imagined that he still dreamed. The raven head cast a long, sharp shadow in the moonlight. It was another crystalline night, cold and still. He breathed deeply, hoping the chill would clear his head.

"Did Alende send you to me?" he asked, glancing over his shoulder.

"No!" The demon's head lifted sharply. "Cael will not be used by others."

The depth of her indignation was enough to cause him to believe her. Alende would not force her to some task unwilling. "Then why do you keep following me?"

"Hush," she ordered. "You've not earned the right to peer beneath my veils."

She gestured him onward. They traveled south, until the forested land began to dip, gently at first, then with increasing steepness, until Jhared had to lean into the hill to keep from sliding on the loose scree. When he glanced up, he could see that the slope curved away to either side of them, forming a wide kettle. They moved across the slope, descending in a gradual spiral. It was slow going, but the demon moved like someone long acquainted with the night. Jhared was glad for a task to keep his attention off the sky. He crouched closer to the ground and stepped around a patch of exposed stone, worn smooth and slippery. Eventually, the land began to level. In the distance, he caught the gleam of moonlight on water.

The demon prodded him the rest of the way down the incline. At the bottom, the trees gave way to stony shoreline. Reeds rustled at the water's edge. Moonlight turned the peaks of the little waves to milk and lit the planks of a decaying pier. Jhared stopped abruptly. It took several heartbeats to convince himself this couldn't be Mayavana's lake. That place was in Sona.

He knelt on the shore and plunged his hands into the water. It was fresh and icy. He swallowed a handful.

"What does the night mean to you, soldier?"

The demon hovered behind him. Water trickled from Jhared's fingers as he stood, taking in the pristine starlight, the gleaming lake, and the ancient forest. Above the kettle, an owl glided on silent wings. The night was Cael's realm, but he had long found comfort in it. "I'm a soldier, Lady. A scout. At times, night is a refuge, other times a danger. Tonight?" He let out a breath and smiled. "It is a thing of beauty."

"Good. Yes, that's good." As the raptor's head nodded in approval, her hand shot toward him, flashing steel. With a curse, Jhared flung up an arm and twisted sideways. The blade missed his heart but cut a stinging line across the back of his hand.

He took a quick step backward and dropped into a fighting crouch. She chuckled, the sound echoing disturbingly through the avian and human skulls.

"Every moment of joy and beauty comes with pain to balance it. You needn't fear, soldier. That was only a reminder."

"I would think this Path provides reminders enough," he growled, watching to see if she meant to strike again.

Behind the mask, her expression changed. "Do not mock! We are the cause of all pain. *We* are the evil, and for that, Cael determines our torments. Do you understand?"

Images came to him, fierce and unbidden: the killing winds whipping through Parnas Pass, his comrades slashed and bloody, Mayavana dead in his dreams.

Shira's love had been stoned to death for defending her.

He bowed his head. "Yes. I do."

"You do," she agreed. She didn't sheathe the knife, but moved away from him toward the water where she stared out at the lake. In her left hand, she twirled the grey feather absently. The tableau had a thread of uncomfortable familiarity about it.

"Cael has watched you wander, soldier. Did you know?"

"I've been told Cael's shadow follows me."

"Not that." She waved a hand as though to brush aside the obvious. "I mean that I've watched you travel the roads of men. I've heard you sing while Cael's Bearer rode at your side. I've watched you bargain with my waylayer. I've seen you riding in the rain to escape your grief."

Jhared shifted self-consciously, feeling the packed sand compress beneath his boots. "You watched me? You mean you traveled with Alende? Chasing after my patrol?"

"Not exactly. Cael roams alone. But at times I follow Alende. The guardian of the Kin sometimes needs guarding. When his journeys sap his strength, Cael keeps his heart from faltering."

The avian head tilted, and Jhared saw Shira's eyes anxious behind the demon's features. Her words were beginning to seem, not a sign of madness, but only a language he didn't fully comprehend.

"This tonight. Bringing me here. Is it about protecting Alende?"

"Yes." She went quiet, peering intently at the feather and blade in her hands. "Cael sees a fear in you that I might put to rest. I would do so to keep your fear from turning to aggression."

"Shira, I have no wish to harm Alende. Or any of his band."

"In your life, Jhared Denaban, how often have you ever received that which you wished?"

He opened his mouth. She held up a hand, the one with the feather in it, to silence him. Something about the demon presenting the grey feather made his heart race with a memory of dread. He didn't understand it. He had come to see grace and beauty in the gift of Mayavana's grey wings. And Shira offered him no real threat. The tangled thought made the shoreline rock gently.

"Of all the ways we may be bound, the bond of love is the most dangerous," she murmured, as though answering a question he had asked. "Chains forged from love can never be truly broken, but only twisted into sadness or fear or hatred. Have you learned that?"

Jhared had learned it. He had once named love as the reason for everything he had sacrificed. Love for Tierzen Trianor and his family had been the tie that kept him from the cliff edge. He hadn't yet allowed himself to consider what would become of that love now, or whether it had ever existed at all. To Shira's question, he only nodded.

"Alende has forged such a bond to you, and I to him," she continued, her voice beginning to sound more her own and less the demon's. "Those bonds draw me to act tonight, despite what it may mean."

"What does it mean?" Jhared asked, feeling not bound at all but very much adrift.

"It means that Avelos has torn what belonged to the sacred skies and Cael has crafted torments from those wounds. None of the others believe me when I tell them, but I have cause to know." She let out a low moan and sank to the ground, her hands clutching at the avian skull. "Darkness forgive me, I have earned my torments!"

Jhared's heart turned over in the face of her anguish. He took a tentative step toward her. "Shira, please don't. There are no torments you deserve. You need not tell me this thing."

She shook her head hard, the mask sliding on her shoulders. "Don't you see? The bonds of love demand that I speak. I will not be his death again. I will not!" She picked herself up and held out pleading hands.

"Soldier, tell me you understand. Creaben, Lusian, Rani, and the others yearn for a land for our kind. They would fight for it. But to Alende that land is no longer of significance. What import a spot on a map when the weaving itself is unraveling? When every spirit on every Path will be undone? Hear me, Jhared Denaban, you need not fear that Alende seeks the killing winds. He has witnessed too much horror on the other side of the blue flames to consider them as a weapon for the Kin."

Jhared stood motionless. "Why do you tell me this?"

Through the mask she met his gaze. "Because you do not wish to share your secret, and I would not have you driven to violence against Alende to guard it."

It did not occur to him to lie to her. The despair in her eyes said she knew. He stepped toward her, a reflexive gesture to offer comfort, perhaps to seek it, but as he moved, the landscape changed. The Gate flared before him with searing blue light. Instinctively, he flung himself back into his own moment, grasping tightly to the place where he belonged. In the last two days, he had managed to anchor Alende, to find Maya, and to close the Gate. He held fast now, unwilling to be ripped into the Nowhere. As he clung to his own Path and the image of the forest at night, the Gate threatened to drag him into the glorious weaving, through doors and into lives best left unknown. His thoughts strained under the pull of the opposing forces, like a worn bowstring.

Without warning, the bowstring snapped. His awareness fractured. A part of him leaped toward the blue flames while the rest of him clung to his rightful place. Every sensation doubled into maddening impossibilities. Sand crunched beneath his knees as his steps thudded against stone. Clean night air purged his lungs while the scent of blood and death filled them. The vast sky stretched overhead as he hunkered in the confined shadows of a cave. Cael stood beside a starlit lake while Cael crouched before a wounded soldier.

On his knees by the lake, Jhared gasped as General Nadel leaned against the cave wall, a grey feather in his fist and his big frame shredded by the killing winds. The demon stared down at the general, its cruel beak nearly touching the soldier's chest. Tears filled the very mortal eyes behind the demon's mask.

"I know this Path," Jhared breathed, *"but it does not belong to me."*

As he watched, Cael lifted one small hand and placed it gently over the general's heart.

"Avelos should never have bound what was meant to soar freely in the sacred skies," the demon murmured. Shira's voice. Shira's hand. *"In the binding, we have been*

broken. Now Cael will use the pieces to tear us all. Take that torment with you on your next Path."

With a growl, General Nadel grabbed up his dagger and struck at the figure, but he had been too badly wounded, and Cael was already disappearing beyond the cave's threshold.

The light in the cave had shifted across the stone by the time Jhared saw himself enter and heard General Nadel whisper: *"Demon."* He crouched at the general's side, and the man caught him unbalanced and off guard, shoving the dagger under his chin.

"Demon!" the general cried again. *"I am not yet finished with this path."*

Months and miles away from that cave in southern Avelos, Jhared jerked his head up, forcing himself to see Shira before him, Shira as she was on this Path, amidst the forest and the open water. He pulled himself back from that night in Lamirna, when he had searched for the victims of the first killing winds attack and found General Nadel. The Gate fought him, but he shoved at it with the names he had claimed for himself: *Jhared Denaban. Shorn Traveler. Son of a Storyteller. Unbound.*

Inside him, something twisted and clashed. Pain came with it this time, a dislocated joint being snapped back into place: tension, then a sharp ache, then sudden relief. General Nadel vanished. The blue flames winked out. Jhared sagged to the sand.

His eyes reported only Cael on the ground not far from him, but he knew what he had witnessed. In early summer, he had lived that moment. General Nadel had been near death, clutching the grey feather and cursing at the demon, the demon who had never truly come from Cael's realm, but only from the warped need of an unbound woman.

"Ah, Shira. It was you, wasn't it? You started the storm that first time in the south. You know the source of the killing winds too."

She huddled on the shore, her knees pulled to her chest and her arms wrapped around her head. "Quiet! Only Cael determines the torments of others," she moaned.

"Forgive me, I cannot be quiet. We must speak of this. Does Alende know?"

The woman shook her head without looking at him.

"Do any others carry this terror? Do they know what they hold?"

"Choke on your questions!" she cried. "Avelos should not have bound what belongs to the sacred skies. Only devastation comes of it. We are that devastation!"

How much could a spirit endure and still move forward on her Path? Jhared heard the shame and endless grief in Shira's voice. He understood it.

"Easy," he murmured, putting some distance between them. "Shira, be easy. We hold one another's secrets now. Perhaps we might help—"

"Don't! I told you not to look beneath my veils. I told you to leave the knife behind. You should have listened!"

She leaped to her feet, her midnight cloak unfurling as she fled up the slope.

"Shira, please stay. We *must* speak."

She didn't look back as she disappeared into the darkness. Jhared restrained himself from running after her. No matter his need, he would not cause her more fear.

He waited by the lake, forcing himself to maintain a mask of calm, hoping she would return. When the false dawn began to smear the sky, he realized he must go back to camp. He wouldn't give her away. He couldn't. Though Alende might not seek the killing winds, Jhared had seen Rani's longing and heard the bitterness in Rona. Some of the others might not scruple to take what they so desired.

He crept up the kettle and jogged slowly toward the riverbed, enwrapped in his thoughts. Shira owned the secret of the killing winds. Her vulnerability had transformed into uncontrollable strength. What had she sensed from him that had given him away? He thought of the small southern villages where he had spent most of the summer helping to clean up the wreckage. He thought of the destruction in Velantar and Obled. Shira had come from Obled. The eldest son of her Teacher, the man she loved, had been murdered there. Jhared recalled the two children, Tomen and Natiani, the only survivors of their family when the killing winds struck. Their father had been a Teacher. Cold settled at Jhared's center. He wouldn't have noticed the bird at all, if it hadn't nearly tripped him.

It was an owl. Its white and sable wings had been shorn from its body, and the creature had been laid on a nest of pine needles and dried leaves. Beside it, someone had opened and arranged the wings with care. The bloody feathers had been smoothed and the hooked beak wiped clean.

Jhared went to one knee, remembering a shorn raven outside of Obled whose death throes had nearly knocked him through the Gate, and a lark in the rain at Aven Fork, where he and Alende had taken shelter. He had believed those mutilations to be a villager's talismans against the cursed, but now? He forced himself to look at the owl. The severed muscles in his back twitched. This death was no warning for the Shorn. It was a symbol of the agony of someone who both loathed and loved what she had slain.

"Shira?"

No one answered.

Jhared found he couldn't leave the owl disregarded on the ground. *Cousins*, Maya had called the birds. He had fallen through the Gate enough times to know the truth of the name. He looked around until he found a tree with suitable branches, then he tucked the creature with its torn wings into one edge of his cloak and climbed. Twenty or so feet in the air, one outstretched arm of the tree formed a V with the trunk. Jhared nestled the owl there. Let Cael's carrion eaters take nourishment if they would; at least it wouldn't be trod upon or stolen by the wolves.

The sky had gone to pale gold by the time he dropped back to the ground. He pressed a hand over his breast where he had once felt the shaft of his own arrow claim the life of a hawk. Behind him, the underbrush rustled. He spun, hoping to find Shira, but Rona stared at him instead.

"Lady of Order," the young man breathed. "What are you doing?"

"Leaving an offering," Jhared replied.

"For the demon?" Disgust was clear in Rona's city-bred inflection. "Do you seek darkness as the rest of them do?"

Jhared closed his eyes and let out a breath. "You don't know me, Rona. Don't throw your anger this way. Not now."

"Oh, I know you. I know Trianor's Folly."

Jhared uttered one hoarse laugh, taken off guard by the irony of that name reaching him here. "The men who first chose that epithet were playing a game of power in the council. They wanted to discredit the high chieftain's ally. What is it *you* want, Rona?"

"I want you to know I see who you are, even if the others don't. In Shorn Circle, we all knew you. An elder's pet."

It was a longstanding taunt that had never been true, yet it ached like an old scar. "That life is gone," Jhared said heavily. "You needn't fear me. I have no wish to betray you or any of Alende's people."

"Fear you?" Rona spat. "Should I fear the dung on my shoe? I want to know what you're doing here. You care nothing for your own kind. You spurned Shorn Circle and claimed an elder's family for your own. You would have stepped on a bleeding Shorn man in the street to mount your horse. We all knew that."

Jhared stared, dumbstruck. After his mother's death, no one had been willing to claim him, not one friend or family member, not one person among all Shorn Circle. He had clung to his foster family gratefully and believed their care for him sincere. "Rona, if you think that the gossip of fools is equivalent to the truth it's no wonder you failed the Becoming."

The boy's eyes flashed with hatred. "Don't speak to me of failure. You were supposed to fail. Only your Elder Trianor made certain you did not!"

"Never!" Jhared no longer curbed the energy hurtling through him. "Never once did Elder Trianor show favor. Do you know who my judges were? Clans Amerre and Lasla. Do you call that favor, Rona? The leader of the Legacy and a northerner who hates the city-born almost as much as the Shorn? Think on it! If the Minister of the Teaching had favored his own pupil, the council would have stripped him of his position."

"Humble the high chieftain's dearest friend?" Rona gave a caustic snort. "Oh, certainly. Do you even know what happened to the initiates whose Becomings followed yours? Tell me you know what the elders did to us."

Jhared was trembling now, anger running through him like a fault line ready to crack open. "I don't know."

"Well, I do," Rona said. "Mine was the first Becoming after yours. And the councilors were out for blood."

"You're saying *I'm* the reason you failed?"

"They wouldn't have pressed so hard otherwise! I knew the Laws and all the debts. I even knew the history of the high chieftains and their elders. But they pressed and pressed for dates. What matter the day the forty-third council passed the ninety-ninth Law? The council needed to prove the Shorn disloyal. They couldn't do it with you. So they did it with me."

It might have been true or not. Jhared couldn't know, didn't want to know. "Rona, look at me. There's nothing for you to envy. I've lost what family I had and every purpose in my life. I'm an outcast just as surely as you."

"That's just it!" Rona cried brokenly. "What are you *doing here*? You *passed* the Becoming! You had a place in Avelos and the favor of an elder. How could you throw it away?"

Outrage contorted the young man's features. With a snarl, he rushed headlong to attack.

Whatever type of service Rona had trained for before failing the Becoming, it had not been soldiering. His assault was unplanned and clumsy. He owned no great speed or strength to compensate, only his anger and despair. Jhared could have evaded him, could have kept him at bay until the man exhausted himself, but Jhared needed to taste blood. He let Rona inside his guard and took a blow that clicked his jaws together with a burst of cleansing pain. Then he swung hard. His fist struck the man's abdomen, sending Rona reeling backward.

Only a sudden weight on his arm stopped him from striking again. Cael's features glared at him as Shira grappled for his fist. "Stop, soldier! Stop! What was chained has broken free. Your need grows into the storms of war! Please, come away! Please!"

Jhared let her pull him back from Rona, who was doubled up in the dirt gasping for breath.

"What's happened? Was that Shira? Who's on watch?"

The voices came from the direction of camp. Rani and Silvien were the first to appear, blades in hand, then Creaben. Trevazio, following Alende, yelped at the sight of Rona on the ground. He pushed past the others and dropped beside his brother, worry raw in his young voice.

"Evare . . . Rona! Brother, are you all right?"

Jhared looked away.

"What happened?" Kilzaro demanded, limping up last, his plain face red with effort.

"Looks like Rona's mouth finally got him in trouble," Rani said with a hint of satisfaction.

Creaben shook his head. "Let's be careful, eh? Rona's one'a us. He's taken a name and given his word. The soldier hasn't."

"Let them speak for themselves," Alende growled. "Rona first."

Still grey and breathless, the young man clambered to his feet, leaning on his brother for support. "I know what he is. And I told him so," Rona gasped. "He . . . attacked me for it."

"And what do you think you know about what he is, Rona?" Alende's tone was tired.

"He's the son of an elder! Trianor's Folly they call him. We all knew of him in the city. A pampered pet. Given a chance, he'll betray us to the council!"

Jhared's gaze moved over the others, uncertain what he would see. Creaben and Rani showed varying degrees of surprise. Silvien showed nothing. Kilzaro rolled his eyes. The northerner, at least, had already known.

"A man with a death mark on his name is hardly likely to run to the council to whisper our secrets," the waylayer said. "Rona, you'll live longer if you think more. Trianor's Folly, what do you have to say for yourself?"

Jhared grimaced. Calling Rona on the lie would win him nothing, and the truth was that he needn't have hit the man. "I let him bait me. I shouldn't have."

Kilzaro looked disgusted. "What do ya want ta do with them, Alende?"

The waylayer's expression was pinched. "We are not going to do this. Not in this story. We've been torn enough. Rona and Jhared, you've had your brawl. It's finished. We break camp at sundown. If Lusian still hasn't returned, Rona and I will ride back toward the city to find him. Kilzaro, take the others and continue . . . continue south. If we've not reached you by the time you make it to Sona . . . If we've not reached you . . ."

Alende trailed off, a scowl creasing his brow. His gaze searched the air for the thread of the story he'd lost. The pause grew awkward. Someone coughed.

"We'll catch up with the other bands and wait for you at the border," Silvien finished matter-of-factly.

"Yes, yes. Wait at the border." Alende closed his eyes and exhaled.

"Ya heard it," Kilzaro said to the group, clapping his hands. "Tonight we move!"

"Where's Shira?" Silvien asked.

Jhared darted a look among the trees. The slender figure of Cael was nowhere in sight.

"She couldn't bear the violence."

Alende answered Silvien, but Jhared knew the words were for him.

"She'll be all right," Kilzaro said. "She's like ya more than a little, my friend. She heals best on her own."

Alende didn't respond but only stared toward the depths of the forest as the others went about following his orders.

Jhared waited. Kilzaro gave him a warning look, but he waved the northerner away and took a step closer to the waylayer. "Alende, I am sorry. I didn't intend to—"

"I don't need to know. You and Rona share too much in common. This was bound to happen. Next time . . ." Alende frowned and licked his lips. "Next time . . ."

"I won't let him bait me."

"That's right. You won't. You could kill the fool faster than he could draw a blade, and Rona's too impulsive to consider that."

Jhared winced.

"And Denaban."

"Yes."

"If I must leave tonight, I want you to watch over Trevazio. He'll try to follow his brother, and I can't risk him trailing us. Do you understand? I'm making you responsible for his safety."

"Alende, please don't. If the boy didn't hate me before, he does now."

The waylayer gave a distant smile. "I've seen you with the elder's son. Branlen, isn't it? I've seen you lay down your life for him on more than one Path. Most of the others no longer understand that kind of bond, but you cling hard to what you loved. I trust you to take care with a child."

Jhared lifted his head. To Branlen, he had never been cursed, had never been Trianor's Folly. Trevazio showed the same blind love for Rona. He thought of Shira's words about the dangers of the bonds of love. "Very well. I'll do my best."

"Good. I'll see to it Kilzaro gives you back your bow. You're a bodyguard again. You may need it." Alende nodded, his gaze somewhere between his Path and the infinite. "And Jhared."

"Yes?"

"I thank you."

The waylayer's genuine tone caused Jhared to look over in surprise. "No debt. Not for this thing."

4.

MURDER AND THEFT

Dusky violet skies stretched over the forest, and Lusian hadn't yet returned. Jhared could see that Kilzaro and Silvien worried over Alende's tremulous grip on his Path as he prepared to ride off to find their missing Kin, but they limited their opposition to unhappy glances. They weren't alone in their discontent. Misery drew Trevazio's features as he watched his brother and Alende trot away. When Kilzaro ordered the others to mount up and set off in the opposite direction, the boy complied with the mien of a condemned man.

Kilzaro led them off the roads and across the wildest terrain, heading south and west. Avoiding villages required a circuitous trek, but Jhared rejoiced in the freedom of traveling again. The others seemed glad of it as well. They shared stories and posed riddles as they rode, weaving a pattern that felt comfortable and familiar, but that didn't include Jhared. It surprised him how much their coolness rankled. He had never expected they would accept him, but he regretted that his fight with Rona and the revelation of his upbringing seemed to have fueled their aversion.

He occupied himself by keeping a close watch on Trevazio. Within the first hours of their journey, the boy had already given away his intentions: ever so gradually reining in his gelding until he slid to the rear of the group. When Jhared flashed him a warning look, the boy evaded his gaze, showing sudden interest in a buckle on his saddle pack. It reminded Jhared of Branlen trying to evade notice as he planned some prank, but Branlen had never needed the type of resolve that sent a boy into the wilds alone and carved a man's worries into his young face. Jhared was loath to crush Trevazio's determination, so he allowed the boy room to consider the situation for himself. He hoped Trevazio would realize the impossibility of his plan, although Jhared knew it was unlikely to stop him.

Their route carried them slowly toward the forests of Clan Nadaren. Near the heart of night, they reached a wide tributary of the Jhanaza River, where they paused to rest the horses. Fog as dense as lamb's wool cloaked the stars and made it difficult to see one another. As Jhared began to dismount near the riverbank, Seravina spooked and nearly took off from under him. He hopped backward, one hand still clutching the reins, and brought her up short. With ears pinned, she snaked her head around and snapped at him. Before them, the river ran silently, draped by the mist.

"Hope you don't mind getting a little wet," Rani said, a grey ghost farther along the bank. "This lady's like to kiss you."

Jhared eyed the wide river and the steep bank as he stroked Sera's sweat-spotted neck. She sensed the Paths churning around this borderland, even if he didn't. "That's quite a swim for the horses."

"It's not so bad as it looks," Kilzaro answered. "Bit rough going in, but they can walk it most'a the way. All but the middle. Your long-legged demon shouldn't have any trouble."

As the others remounted, Jhared remained close to Trevazio, who was tightening his girth and checking his packs. Water splashed as the horses began to enter the murky river. Rani's mount stumbled going in. Jhared hissed as horse and rider went under to the chin before recovering. Given a choice, he wouldn't have chosen this place to cross. Not in the dark and the fog with the river near its crest.

Mindful of Seravina's warning, he turned his attention inward and reached cautiously toward his center. No flames greeted him. In fact, he still felt as secure in himself as he had two mornings ago. Shira had told him then that he had closed the Gate. For whatever it might be worth, he clung to that belief. He glanced over his shoulder. "Ready, Trev?"

The boy shrugged and climbed back into the saddle. "Don't call me Trev."

They entered the river together. Jhared knew from watching the others that the bank dropped off sharply. Still, when Seravina stepped forward and sank to her shoulders, he sucked a breath as cold water filled his boots.

Sera wanted none of it. She whinnied in alarm, crow-hopping to escape the current thrusting against her body. Jhared kept his seat as she twisted one way and then the other, but his calming murmurs didn't reach her. With a sudden gathering of muscle, she reared, kicking her hooves over the river, as though it were a predator. For an agonizing moment, she held her balance. Then the current shoved her over.

She crashed downward, pluming river spray into the air. A wall of water slammed against Jhared as they went under. He fought to stay with his mare, clutching her neck and wrapping his legs around her barrel. Beneath him, she flailed, futilely seeking solid ground. He knew her panic and wondered if they would find air before it was too late. Water blinded him, burned his nose, and squeezed his lungs. From somewhere near the opposite bank, the others cried out. Jhared heard a name, distorted below the surface. Then somehow Seravina organized her legs and the flailing became swimming. They popped to the surface. Jhared coughed grateful breaths.

Across the water, the others were pointing and calling out, but not to him. Upriver, he registered another great splash and turned in time to see Trevazio's stocky bay leaping onto the bank and streaking back the way they had come.

Jhared cursed. He was the closest. None of the others could reach Trevazio before the boy disappeared. And he had given Alende his word.

"I'll get him!"

"Soldier? Ya certain?" Kilzaro's tone stuttered through the fog, full of doubt.

Of course they doubted him. He wasn't one of them. Abruptly, that knowledge stung. "Go on. I'll bring him back!"

"See you do. We'll meet you by dawn. Caves west'a the river. Ya hear?"

"I hear. We'll be there."

By the time Jhared turned Sera and they had lurched back up the steep incline, Trevazio was out of sight, sprinting through the trees. Sera struggled to find her stride, still blowing from her fright in the river. They pounded through the forest at a speed that could spell disaster, but the boy had committed to his flight. Jhared galloped after him, one mile then another, cursing at the confounding fog, until he realized he no longer heard Trevazio's gelding.

He drew to a halt. In the mist-shrouded darkness, he had no chance of finding tracks. He inclined his head, picking out the sounds of the night: Seravina's deep breaths; night creatures conversing in soft chitters; and from some distance, the muffled crunch of hooves on deadfall.

He nudged Sera back into motion, a slower pace this time. They followed the periodic crackle of a twig, a horse's low wicker, and the thud of an unshod hoof on stone, but sounds bounced unpredictably in the fog, making their source difficult to decipher. Then the rain started, with a fine, steady hiss just loud enough to mask the rest.

At the bottom of a sheer ridge, far from the river, Jhared stopped again. The boy had evaded him. He debated going back to the others for help, but by the time he went and returned, Trevazio would have gained that much more of a lead. It was wild, dangerous territory. He wouldn't leave the child riding deeper toward trouble.

A grey dawn came and went, and Jhared continued to search. He rode back and forth along the flank of the ridge, hunting for an opening where Trevazio might have scrambled through. In the rain, he could hardly see past Seravina's ears. The slick, uneven stone threatened to break legs. Jhared could too easily imagine Trevazio's gelding floundering and the boy somersaulting down the rocky hillside. He pushed on.

It was Sera who finally revealed the boy. As they approached a twisted tree jutting out from the edge of the ridge, she snorted and flicked her ears forward with interest rather than alarm. Jhared urged her closer. By the glistening of water on stone, he could make out a gap in the slab of rock. As he drew up to explore, Seravina lifted her head and let out a whinny of greeting. From within the gap, came an enthusiastic equine reply. Jhared wiped at the dampness that clung to his face and grinned in relief.

"It's time to come back, Trevazio."

A string of obscenities echoed from the gap.

Jhared waited without comment, allowing the boy time with his disappointment.

"How did you find me?" Trevazio grumbled, not emerging.

"With some difficulty," Jhared admitted. "You chose well."

"I'm not going back. I'll hurt you if you try to make me. I'll . . . I'll kill you!" The words burned with the boy's rage.

"You have a right to be angry," Jhared replied calmly. "Are you coming out on your own or are you going to force me to drag you out?"

Silence stretched for a span of heartbeats. Then Trevazio's ululating cry stabbed the air in answer. His gelding leaped out of the gap, scrambled for footing, and leaped again. Jhared wheeled Seravina to avoid a collision, but as the boy sped past, Jhared flung himself at the fleeing horse and grabbed one side of the wet reins. The force jerked him half out of the saddle. For several harrowing steps, the horses cantered together, shoulder bumping shoulder on the slippery stones. Jhared clung to the reins of Trevazio's mount with one hand and kneed Seravina into a circle, giving the gelding no choice but to turn as well. With his guidance, Seravina plunged into a tighter turn and a tighter one, until finally both mounts could do nothing but come to a snorting, huffing stop.

Trevazio glowered from under a mat of rain-plastered dark hair. Water ran down his face and dripped from his cloak.

Jhared rubbed ruefully at his right shoulder before he leaned forward and lifted the reins over the gelding's head. "Come on. The others will have long settled into camp. You can put on dry clothes. Kilzaro will feed you and give you something hot to drink."

The boy didn't respond. Jhared led them down the hill, with Sera picking her footing carefully. The fog remained thick. When Jhared glanced back, he could barely see Trevazio's furious expression.

"Why are you bringing me back?"

Jhared rolled his shoulder once more. "Because I want to see you safe."

"You have no right to choose my path. I need to be with Rona!"

"Does this mean you're going to make me tie you to keep you from running again?"

"Shira won't let you tie me," the boy said, more smugly than was good for Jhared's patience.

"Perhaps. But Shira's not yet returned to camp."

Trevazio made a dispirited sound. "You could tell them you couldn't find me," he pleaded. "Or . . . or we could both run. Alende dragged you in. You don't even want to be with the Kin!"

"I won't, Trevazio. I promised Alende to watch over you."

"Oh, a promise. As if that matters to a deserter." The boy's voice twisted unkindly. "How many promises did you break to end up with the unbound?"

Seravina's back hoof kicked a stone down the ridge. "I've lost count."

"You know none of them like you," the boy went on. "Creaben says a soldier is useless. Silvien says you're a gold coin to pay off the clanguard when they must. They don't trust you."

Jhared whipped around, causing Trevazio to look up, wide-eyed. "Well, they do trust you! And you're betraying them with your selfishness. What do you think will happen when you stumble into Nadaren hunters or a Forest Guard patrol from the Barlona garrison? What will you say when soldiers ask why a city-bred Shorn boy is so far from his Teachers?"

Trevazio's bold gaze lowered, but defiance remained in his tone. "Stop talking to me. You can't understand."

Jhared sighed and drew back. "Don't tell me what I can't understand. You at least will have the chance to see your brother again."

Trevazio's brow knotted before he looked away.

The rain never ceased, not as they worked their way down the ridge and not as they entered the forest and crossed the river. It wasn't a hard rain, but neither of them had been truly dry since the first attempt at the river the night before, and the cold and effort had taken their toll. Trevazio's mount was stumbling with exhaustion and near lame from the rocky footing. The boy was shivering hard enough to make his teeth chatter. Jhared stared up at the blanket of black clouds pressing over them. Darkness would catch them again soon. By now, the others would think he had run, abandoning the boy, but there was nothing for it. If they kept going, they were just as likely to miss the camp in the dark. He sat back; Seravina stopped.

Trevazio's head snapped up and he looked around in confusion. "What happened? Are we back?"

"We're making camp. Come down off that poor beast. We'll get you warm and figure out something for you to eat."

The boy did as he was bid, moving stiffly to care for his gelding. Once Jhared had a fire crackling, he managed a steaming broth with the wild onions and greens he had forged, and shared the lump of cheese and chunk of dry bread he had in his bag.

They ate in silence. Trevazio hunched in an unhappy ball near the fire. Jhared finished the small meal and checked the horses, then sat with his back against a tree, prepared for a long night.

"Is he younger or older than you? Your brother?"

Jhared glanced up. "Younger. Branlen's near to your age."

"Is he Shorn?"

"No."

"Oh." Trevazio's tone was contemptuous. He tossed a twig into the flames. The wet wood sizzled and spit. "Then you don't really know each other. You didn't grow up together. They wouldn't have let you."

Jhared thought of all the years that Branlen had been a part of his life: tagging after him to the stables, to the garrison, and to the woods; asking for stories about the Forest Guard; absorbing everything Jhared could teach him about tracking. The boy's mother hadn't liked it, but Madam Trianor had never been able to stop him. Elder Trianor had seemed to think it a good thing for his son to learn about Shorn Law. Or perhaps Branlen had merely been another bond calculated to hold Jhared fast. "We did grow up together. We were close."

Trevazio's mouth opened. Then his look grew thoughtful. He set his chin on his fists. "You kept your little brother safe? When you were in Velantar. You took care of him?"

"I tried. Trevazio, what is it you're really asking? Do you need to know that others can care as much for their family as Rona cares for you? Do you need to see that others have failed those they love as well?"

"You don't understand."

"You could explain," Jhared said. "We've an entire night for it."

The boy didn't answer, but returned to his sullen silence with his arms wrapped around his knees. After a time, he lay down on his side and pulled his hood over his head. Eventually, he began to snore, the deep, flat sound of exhaustion.

Jhared thought of Branlen. He wondered what Elder Trianor had told the boy about the debacle in Parnas Pass. He wondered if Bran knew that his foster brother was no longer bound and what he would say if they ever saw one another again.

Dawn hadn't yet found the forest when Jhared awoke to the sound of a horse's nicker. He was rising to his feet even before coming fully awake. With a lunge, he intercepted Trevazio's gelding as the boy was still trying to swing into the saddle.

They stood that way: Jhared blocking the boy's path and Trevazio staring in furious silence.

"Trevazio, enough of this. Please! What would Rona do if you died searching for him?"

"No! You listen to *me*!" the boy cried. "Don't you see? *Rona's* the one who's like to die! He can't stay out of trouble. Look what happened at his Becoming. And don't think I can't guess who started the fight between you two. He needs me with him!"

The boy stood angry and taut, ready to fight or flee. The agony in his expression tore at Jhared's heart. In the boy's pained words, Jhared recognized something he hadn't before.

"Ah, Trevazio. You were right. I didn't understand." Jhared rubbed a hand over his face. "I think Alende spoke truly."

"About what?"

"He said your brother and I share too much in common."

Trevazio frowned. "Does that mean you'll let me go?"

"No. It means I understand something I think you do not."

"What could you know? You don't even—"

Jhared held up a palm against the boy's dissent. "Why do you think Alende took Rona with him?"

"To keep him from picking another fight with you."

"That's not it. Alende took Rona to give him the chance to find his own way. He failed the Becoming and lost not only his own hope for a life but yours as well. He needs to feel he's strong enough to carve a place for himself. And to protect you."

"I don't need protecting!"

The words echoed in the air. Jhared said nothing. Trevazio glanced down.

"I see Rona has given you cause to fear for him," Jhared said gently, "but he isn't traveling by himself. Alende has known these forests for nearly as many years as you've been alive."

"Alende's reckless!"

"Yes. But not with the lives of his Kin."

Eventually, Trevazio nodded.

"Perhaps it's good for you to have some time with the others as well," Jhared added. "Let them see you as your own person."

A mistake. The boy bristled and drew back. "No! Rona's *all* I have. I don't care if the others know me or not."

Jhared sighed. "Does that mean I'm going to have to swing you over my shoulder and carry you back?"

"It means I'm loyal to my brother."

"Very well. Then prove it by being safe and healthy when he returns."

The boy seemed to consider that. When he looked up at Jhared, some of the fight had left his gaze. "All right. I think . . . I'm ready to go back now."

He helped Jhared to break camp, but remained quiet and thoughtful. Jhared didn't push the fragile truce between them.

"You know," the boy murmured as they mounted and started through the forest, "It's not right what Silvien and Creaben said about you. Even if you're not Kin. Our scars are still the same."

Jhared caught a breath. But his gratitude was given to Trevazio's back as the boy kicked his mount into a trot.

When they finally caught up with the others, it caused something of a furor. Creaben, it seemed, had riled the others with stories of how Jhared had fled, leaving Trevazio lost. Silvien had wanted to ride out after them, but Rani argued they should wait and give Jhared time to prove himself. The result was an intense and noisy greeting. The others only quieted to hear Trevazio's story of hiding among the rocks and how Jhared had found him in the fog. As the boy finished, they all looked at Jhared.

He shrugged out from under their scrutiny. "I said I would keep him safe."

Kilzaro's face had gone dusky with anger. The gaze he turned upon Trevazio could have stripped bark off a tree. "Trevazio, hear me now. Ya can't—"

"I know, I know," the boy said swiftly, standing straight against Kilzaro's fierce regard. "I've given my word not to go after Rona again."

"Good. See ya keep it. Survival is an uncertain thing for us. Unchained we might be, but we depend on each other. A risk to you is a risk to us all."

That evening they ate well, snug in a cave beneath a low hill. Silvien told stories of the ancient Avelune, thrilling Trevazio with a tale of his namesake, Riana's Chosen scout *Trevaye*, and his Avelun companion, a mighty red-winged Traveler named Tormelay. Jhared listened, a part of him hungry for tales of his ancestors, another part of him unable to stop thinking about what Trevazio had said: how Silvien had assessed his worth. Was that why Alende had poisoned him and dragged him back to the Kin? To use as surety? To buy them safety? He didn't realize someone had asked him a question until Rani poked him in the ribs.

"What?" he snapped.

The others blinked at him as if he had fractured the mood. Silvien chuckled as she took up the flask of *slu*. "Well, we needn't fear the soldier means to worm his way into our hearts with his charm, eh?"

"Why would you ever expect such a thing?" Jhared replied. "Did you hope for a shinier coin to give over to the council, Silvien?"

The woman looked neither chagrined nor apologetic. "Kilzaro said it tonight: our survival is uncertain. We must consider the gifts that come to hand. It was my obligation to make the suggestion to Alende."

The others were silent. Jhared didn't move. "And?"

"Alende said it's not an option. And that's the end of it."

"So quick as that?" Jhared demanded.

"So quick as that." Silvien stood and stretched, long and lithe as a mountain cat, and as dangerous.

She came at him, and Jhared shifted into a balanced position, prepared to spring. She saw it and smiled before leaning forward to offer him the flask.

"You did well with the boy, soldier. I don't mind saying it. You can't expect us not to be wary, but trust is a thing that must go both ways, eh?"

The landscape changed as they entered the holdings of Clan Nadaren. The forests grew older and graver. Sentinel trees it would take six men to circle formed a canopy against the sky, permitting light to pass only in narrow blades. Centuries of deadfall formed a thick carpet that hushed all sounds and camouflaged loops of vine that reached for horses' legs. Ravines cut deep and straight into the ground, often unseen until a man was swaying at the very rim. Jhared felt they had entered a wild place that had no reason to welcome them. It was easy to conjure images of unclaimed spirits, such as the Bloodless, drifting among the dappled shadows. He thought he understood a little better the superstitious men of Clan Nadaren, who wore their prayers tattooed across their faces to keep misfortune at bay, yet celebrated each moment with joyful irreverence.

The band traveled three days closer to the Sonan border. After Trevazio's return, Kilzaro began to assign Jhared more of the regular tasks of the camp, even occasionally those that took him off alone. His skill with a bow was appreciated when he returned from a hunt with fresh meat. When he had the opportunity, Jhared searched for evidence that Shira might be following on her spotted mare, but he found nothing. Rani caught him at it one afternoon and shook his head. "I used to worry for her, too. But she'll be back. She follows her own Path."

By the fourth night, they were bumping the shoulder of civilization near the clan seat of Nadrona. Kilzaro called the band to a halt on the stream side of a hill.

"Bit early to camp, isn't it?" Silvien asked.

"Settle in," Kilzaro replied, dismounting awkwardly. "We're staying put for a while."

Creaben frowned. "It's not what he told us to do."

"It's what we're doing just the same," Kilzaro said.

Silvien tapped her knife. "You think he's had trouble?"

"No. But I'd rather not go hunting up the other bands until he's with us. No need ta set the others ta wondering."

Days passed. Trevazio marked their passing on a strip of leather around his wrist, but Jhared saw that everyone was keeping just as careful track. Each morning, Silvien rode from camp—to keep an eye out for unwelcome visitors, she said—but she always rode north and east, the direction from which Alende would return. Rani flitted about like a sparrow in spring, working at unnecessary tasks and chattering until Creaben barked at him to be still. Kilzaro's characteristic calm spiraled down into brooding.

Jhared was finishing the evening chores, washing up at the stream, when he heard horses approaching. This close to Nadrona it could be anyone: a tradesman who had lost his way, a group of trappers searching for new game trails, a Nadaren clanguard patrol. He dumped the water from the kettle he'd been scrubbing and, gripping it like a weapon, hastened back. Trevazio's hoot of joy rang out before he arrived.

Alende and Rona were still ahorse in the center of camp. Jhared saw Trevazio charge toward his brother. With an unabashed show of emotion, Rona threw himself from the saddle and gathered the boy into a hug.

"Now there's a welcome to covet!" a voice laughed.

A stranger swung down from the back of a lanky black stallion. Lusian, Jhared presumed. About eight winters Jhared's senior, he had a Shorn man's height and a fighting man's bearing, but his face was pink-cheeked and fresh as a girl's. As he handed his reins to Rani, Jhared saw he was missing the last three fingers of his left hand.

"What took you so long?" Silvien demanded of the newcomer.

"When one dares what I have, my warrior beauty, it's necessary to go to ground for a time. You'll have to wait for the story." With his maimed hand, the man caught Silvien behind the neck and planted a kiss on her mouth. "That is, unless you're willing to give me the kind of welcome I deserve."

In answer, Silvien cuffed him on the side of the head, staggering the man several steps. As he regained his balance, he gave her a bared-teeth grin.

"We found Lusian already on the way back from Velantar," Rona said, ruffling Trev's hair. "It just took a little longer for us to get there than we thought it would."

Alende cast a sharp glance in the brothers' direction. "Rona, water the horses, would you? In this story, they prefer your attention to mine."

Rona smiled, a thing Jhared hadn't seen before. "I will. And an extra measure of grain for them all tonight. They've earned it."

From Rona's joy and Trevazio's relief, it was easy now to see that Rona had been the one dependent upon his little brother, not the reverse. But something had changed. Rona carried himself a little straighter and stepped more lightly. Whatever he had encountered on his trip, perhaps he'd come closer to finding his place. Jhared envied him a little. He turned away to help Kilzaro and Rani unload the laden bags from the horses.

"Five bags. And brimming all," Kilzaro observed. "This should settle our debts through the winter and beyond."

"Oh, it will," Lusian said. "No one else has matched this find, I promise you."

Lusian and Rani strapped the bags to a tree branch to keep them from the damp ground. They swung there—pilfered fragments of the country's history—like carcasses hung for gutting.

"All looks well here," Alende said, surveying the group. His gaze was bruised and weary. A line of fresh blood crossed his throat.

"Better now," Kilzaro said. "Poor Trev nearly . . ." The big man trailed off, looking at the waylayer more closely. "What is it?"

Alende shook his head. "Later."

Kilzaro nodded, hustling the others toward the remnants of the fire. "Crea, stir up the embers. Jhared, draw fresh water. We've a reason to celebrate."

Lusian made himself comfortable among the others, drinking his share from the flask and laughing at old jests in which Jhared couldn't take part. Still, a guarded air hung over the group that not even the Sonans had evoked. Silvien sat near Alende, her features stiff and observant. Kilzaro and Creaben hunkered beside one another like twin guard dogs. Rani's laughter was stretched thin. Only Trevazio seemed oblivious, delighted to have Rona back and excited to repeat his own adventures to a new audience. It took some time before anyone commented directly about the treasures Lusian had brought them.

"So, five bags," Kilzaro said at last. "Did you strike the council library?"

The shift in attention caused Lusian's face to light in a way that suggested he'd been waiting for this moment since he arrived. "No. Not the council."

"Private libraries," Silvien guessed. "Elders' homes."

"I helped myself to the elders' collections a time or two. But that's not where I found the greatest part of the treasure. Can you dare to guess once more?"

Silence fell around the circle.

Lusian grinned extravagantly. "The home of the Great Lady herself. The high temple!"

"The high temple?" Trevazio's gaze touched his brother's. "Riana will punish you!"

"Well now, she's already punished me, eh?" Lusian waggled the thumb and remaining finger of his left hand. "It's my turn now."

"You'll have to change your name to Verilen the Trickster," Rani said, chuckling faintly.

Silvien's expression remained unimpressed. "What books did you take?"

"Books? Not anything so mundane, my warrior queen! Not from the temple. Look here!" Lusian leaped up and grabbed one of the bags where it hung. With his good hand, he rooted around and pulled out a handful of slender scrolls. "Ask Alende. He'll tell you their value." He fumbled with one of the scrolls until he could unroll it and waved it before them. "I promise you the Sonans have never seen the like!"

"It looks like a lot of scribbling. What is it?" Furrows carved Creaben's brows.

Honey-sweet warmth lapped over Jhared's shoulders like sunlight over open meadows, like a warm breeze over mountain peaks. Graceful lines marked the vellum Lusian held. It looked like a drawing of a slender tree with many branches, or a cluster of graceful vines with tendrils that wound in every direction, reaching for connections with others. Neatly printed notes lay at each point where the tendrils divided.

"It's a map," Jhared said. Oh goddess, such a map. From the high temple.

The others stared at him.

"A map of what?" Rani asked, reaching out to touch the vellum.

"The priestesses' sacred journeys along Riana's Paths."

Rani whistled softly and drew his hand back.

Silvien's gaze was keen. "Do you know how to read it?"

"I do not." Jhared had never even seen one, but Leita had told him about them and about the four Principles of the Paths they represented. Lady Nemiah had told him how they had been stolen.

"Will the Sonans know how to read them?" Rani asked.

"They wanted ancient writings," Lusian replied with a shrug. "If they don't know how to read them, it'll give them something to do figuring it out."

"How'd you get into the high temple?" Trevazio's gaze held wary admiration. Lusian made the most of it.

"Getting in is no problem, boy. The question is how to get out! It took a good bit of cleverness, I don't mind telling you."

Poison. Lady Nemiah had said that her Arionade were poisoned, and every map of every sacred journey since the Exile had been stolen. The loss had devastated her. Jhared had seen it when she told the story. The taproot of her strength had been crushed.

"How many of Riana's servants died of your cleverness, Lusian?"

The unbound man swung around, eyeing Jhared directly for the first time. "Don't know. Fewer than Shorn who are killed each spring, no doubt."

Jhared didn't flinch. This was beyond stripping the country's histories; this was sacrilege and death. What Lusian had stolen was the heart of a sacred mystery. If he concentrated, Jhared could still sense the warmth against his shoulders, the goddess's touch. A glance at the others told him they felt none of it. "This is wrong. It doesn't serve us to live up to our legacy of conspiracy and deceit."

Lusian's lip curled up in a smile. "Ah, but that's what I am. Tainted blood runs in my veins. Temple says I'm cursed. Nothing to be done for it."

"A hound acts according to its nature, eh?" Rani suggested.

"It's not," Jhared growled. "It's not in your blood. You've only found yourself a way to justify murder for your own gain."

Lusian reached into his pocket and pulled out a sealed clay vial the width of two fingers. The smile never left his face as he tossed it into the air and caught it again. "I need find no gain to justify your death, soldier."

Across the fire, Alende jerked upright, his green eyes sparking. "Too far, Lusian! Jhared Denaban is my guest. A threat against him is a threat against me. Is that what you intend?"

Lusian's smile faded, but as he shuttered his gaze under long lashes, Jhared caught a flash of anger. "Of course not, Alende."

"I thought not," the waylayer replied. "Jhared, leave us. The Kin have a need to speak."

Jhared stood, the flames hot on his face. "In Mahla's name, Alende, don't surrender those maps. They hold the most meaningful records of our history."

Alende only lifted a hand and gestured at the darkness.

As Jhared strode away from the group, the arguments exploded behind him. Lusian's voice and then Alende's rose over the others'. Jhared marched into the trees until he could no longer hear them. He stamped around the perimeter of the camp, trying to siphon off his anger. The memory of Lady Nemiah's devastated expression burned in his mind. *Every map of every sacred journey since the Exile is gone,* she had said. It meant the loss of more truths. While the tales that were passed down by the Storytellers couldn't help but warp over years of telling, the map of a sacred journey was as clean as an observer of events could make it. What would Avelos lose if a century and more of maps went to Sona?

The waning moon had lifted in the east by the time he heard Alende's fluid step behind him. When the waylayer wasn't drunk, he moved like a dancer. Jhared halted, and Alende paused at his shoulder. They stood in silence, side by side, listening to the dark forest.

"Do you think there's anything of use to me in those maps?" the waylayer asked eventually.

Jhared didn't turn. "Of use? No. If they held some clue about the web's unraveling, the Bearer wouldn't have been looking for Pathwalkers. And if they held an answer to the killing winds, Lady Nemiah wouldn't have sent the Bearer north."

Alende sighed deeply. "Then I'm afraid I have no choice but to give them to Mursa Vin. They will buy us a place to winter and the protection we need."

"Then you buy protection and sell a part of who you are."

"Who we *are*? Oh, my darling, what's to be done with you? *Sulosan, surma sen.* Our scars are the same, brother. Why must you fight us so?" The waylayer's tone offered only sadness.

Jhared spun to face him. "Our scars are not the same! No matter that I am exiled and unbound, I will not brag of theft and murder."

Alende remained composed, his expression bemused. "It truly troubles you, the loss of those Arionade?"

"They were Riana's servants and innocent!"

"No. Not innocent."

"Very well. Would you condemn every man who serves Riana for spilling our blood? Just as Avelos has condemned every one of us for the crimes claimed of our ancestors?"

"It is a kind of balance," Alende observed.

Jhared thought of Lady Amalia and the false accusations that had led to her execution, to the Exile War, and to the destruction of the Avelune. He thought of the poisoned Arionade. "No, Alende. They were unjust deaths, then and now. One evil cannot balance another."

"As you will," the waylayer said tiredly. "It is, at the least, a way to survive. Fewer of us will die if we earn the Sonans' aid."

Jhared leaned his head in his hands.

"Oh, my darling, you see you do not belong among the bound, yet you have not let them go. You cannot move forward until you mourn them, I know. But, brother, I only hope you find your way to it . . . soon."

Against his will, the strain in the waylayer's voice made Jhared look up. "Why?"

"I don't think I can wait through the winter. The end looms too close, and the Bearer is too far. It may be time to take up the hunt again and seek the end of our song."

"Leita has been tortured and blinded," Jhared bit out. "Will you poison her too?"

The waylayer's expression grew brittle. "I . . . don't know. I don't know any more whether her existence dooms us or perhaps will save us all. Two nights ago, I felt something out there." Alende waved a hand at the darkness.

"Something?"

"A tangle in Riana's weaving. A massive knot of Paths. Warped, writhing, wrapping itself around me." The waylayer shuddered.

"It seems the knife served you well enough to escape it," Jhared replied, gesturing at Alende's throat.

"No. You misunderstand. This thing wasn't behind the Gate. Rona saw it too."

"I didn't take Rona for a Pathwalker."

"He's not. The boy has less sensitivity to the Paths than a bale of hay. He didn't feel its call or know what it meant, but he saw how it distorted the land. It was only the size of one of your precious maps, hovering over a fork in the trail, but by the demon, I wouldn't have escaped its pull without Rona's help. It nearly turned me inside out."

"Just like brandy will turn you inside out?"

"Be still and listen!" Alende barked. "There are few enough things that I'm certain exist on our Path. This is one. Rona tossed two stones at it. Good, fist-sized chunks of granite. The first stone never came out. The second exploded into pieces. One stone into a hundred pebbles in a heartbeat. As if the Paths had yanked it in different directions until it shattered. I've a new nightmare now: the image of what would have happened had either of us stumbled into it."

For a change, the waylayer wasn't drunk or raving; he was scared. Jhared wasn't certain what to do with that. His understanding of the man had grown since he'd come among the unbound. Alende was more than caelevano; he led the Kin, loved them, struggled to do what he thought best for them. Jhared respected him for it, admired him even. He might have had more sympathy now if he weren't thinking of the murdered Arionade. "You've known such a thing before, haven't you?"

"No. Well, perhaps. Yes, I suppose so. No one has ever been with me to see it, and I've always believed the thing to be a product of my own confusion." Alende groaned. "Nothing I've seen has been as monstrous as this."

"Maybe it *is* of your own making. Maybe you tangle the Paths when you tumble. Is that possible?"

"I don't know. How could I know?" Alende pounded his fist against a tree trunk. "All I see are broken threads. I cannot see the pattern!"

The camp was still, Alende and the others long asleep, when Jhared awoke to find Shira sitting cross-legged at his side. Her hands lay empty in her lap, and her eyes studied him from behind Cael's features.

They watched one another in silence. Below the mask, Jhared could see the faint silver gleam of scars along her throat. On this Path, she was cursed and damaged. On another Path, she would have been a priestess.

"I'm glad you're back," he said softly, sitting up. "Where were you?"

The human skull stared, hollow-eyed, from within the raven's beak. "We needed to follow Alende. We do not trust Lusian, and Rona is but a boy."

"Perhaps a little less of a boy now?"

She shrugged.

Jhared desperately wanted to talk with her about the winds, but her uneasy expression said she would only flee. He tried another direction. "Shira, is Lusian a danger to Alende?"

Surprise registered behind the mask. "You ask for Alende and not for yourself?"

"I figured that answer was obvious."

She nodded sadly. "He is not yet a danger. Lusian likes an audience. If he means to act, he'll wait until the unchained Kin have come together. Then he'll try to break Alende into bits."

Jhared grimaced. "He wants to lead the Kin?"

"Lead? He doesn't understand what that means. He has been twisted by his bonds. Now, he can only hold himself together by tearing others apart."

"Can Silvien and Kilzaro prevent him from causing harm?"

"Cael will prevent him. If it becomes necessary." The dark strength in her voice, utterly at odds with her fragile frame, made Jhared think of birds, shorn and bloody, in the forest. He had little doubt that Shira would be willing to stop Lusian if she felt she must.

The skull pushed closer to his face. "Have you studied the Lady's maps yet, soldier?"

"That's an odd question." He looked at her sideways. "I haven't. I'm not sure if I want to. If Alende is going to—"

"Look at them. They are rare."

He raised a brow. "You've seen such maps?"

"I do not need to see them to know what they are. Cael and Riana do not often come together in peace."

He shook his head gently. "Shira, the Pathwalkers' maps belong to Riana. Cael has no part in them."

Her laughter was as deep as the night sky. Just for a moment, it reminded him of the Bearer. "Soldier, how would we ever travel the infinite ways without Cael? Have you never stopped to wonder what order is to be found in leaving one's proper Path and tumbling about the web?"

He hadn't. Not truly, though it seemed the contradiction had lurked at the edge of his awareness since he met Leita. "If you understand how rare they are, then you know what we lose by giving them to the Sonans."

"I do," she murmured.

"But you won't encourage Alende to keep them?"

"Avelos is already cut to the heart and dying, Jhared Denaban. This small injury does not signify."

Jhared pressed his fingers against his thighs to keep from clenching his fists. "I don't believe that's true. Wounds can be healed. And we have an obligation to ease suffering when we can." As he said it, Jhared realized he meant it. It was easier to glimpse the pale remnants of his hope beside her darkness.

"Avelos has bound what belonged to the sacred skies," she replied. "The Lady watched as her Chosen were torn and flung from the cliffs. She caused our suffering. We have no obligation to her."

"If the only thing left to us is grief, Shira, then why should I bother to read the maps?"

She took off Cael's mask and looked at him with her own conflicted gaze. "Because to understand ourselves, we must know what it is we mourn."

After dawn, Jhared made no attempt to hide his intention from the others. He marched toward the tree that held the bags and began to take one down. Lusian and Alende were not in sight. Shira was sitting in a tree at the edge of camp nibbling on a strip of dried meat. None of the others tried to stop him, although he could feel them staring. He ignored them and sat beside the great trunk with the first bag open beside him.

Dozens of scrolls poked from the bag in small spirals. Jhared wiped his hands on his shirt, keenly aware of the mystery before him. He found himself breathing faster as he dared to touch the sacred. He drew out one of the larger scrolls and unrolled it, placing small stones at the corners to hold it.

It was beautiful, fragile, flawed. He traced his finger along slender trails of dark ink. The map took the form of a young grape vine, with one primary shoot at the center of the page and half-a-dozen smaller shoots curling tentatively in different directions. In five rows near the top right corner, in neat small script it read:

Lady Pahlina's Journey, Dwngs Eve 4753.

Plc. Hunt at Shivrey Hill.

Tme. Rule of Matio the Giving.

Per. Priestess, unkwn.

Par. Near past, estbld; one knwn repetition.

At the bottom of the page, in even tighter text was what must have been the Mapmaker's signature: *Lady Bna Shefra, By the Lght of R.*

Jhared tilted his head to read the notes printed beside some of the tendrils. Along the primary shoot, he read: *Running the hounds after a grey buck, Eldr. Friam thrown from his stallion.* The smaller shoots told the story of a hunt and the death of a city elder in some detail. One of the shoots lined the words, *See repetition at Lady Pa, Wedding of Eldr Friam's dghter.*

Leita's teaching returned to him as he read. The four Principles were the key, she had said. Together they allowed a Pathwalker to understand where a Path belonged in the web. Place and Time were the first Principles, and easy enough to understand. Jhared looked at the map again: *Plc. Hunt at Shivrey Hill; Tme. Rule of Matio.* Those shards of information set the hunt in the foothills just outside of Velantar at least seventy years ago, when Lord Matio ruled as high chieftain. Perspective, Leita had explained, had to do with which doors a Traveler opened onto a Path. One door might lead to the perspective of a person who lived that story, while another door only allowed the Pathwalker to view the story from a distance, like standing on a height above a battle. The importance of varying perspectives made sense to a scout. Parallel, however, was more difficult. Leita had said that Parallel revealed the particular thread of the web from which a Path originated, but Jhared had trouble imagining how to distinguish one line of history from another in a web that was infinite. Carefully, he rolled up the map of the hunt and drew out another.

He couldn't have said how many hours he spent reading, sliding into the perspectives of the priestesses who had slid into the perspectives of others. The intimacy disarmed him, left him vulnerable, but he was compelled to reach for one map after another. At some distance, he knew the Kin went about their day. He knew they still watched him, but their regard was irrelevant. The maps were pieces in Riana's puzzle. He wanted one that could give him a clearer understanding of where Avelos belonged, of where he belonged. He pulled a slender scroll from among several that appeared more recent than the others, with vellum that was lighter and not yet crackling with age. At the top, written in a thin-veined script, it read:

Lady Nmh's Journey, 4823.

Plc. High Temple in Velntr, Sahiste.

Tme. Varied, Unkwn.

Pers. Lady Nmh and Unkwn.

Par. Not estbld.

A breeze brushed Jhared's cheek, carrying the scent of dusty archives and new wool. The soft murmur of doves filled his ears. He sucked a breath as Riana enwrapped him. It was one of Lady Nemiah's journeys. He read it, then reread it.

When a shadow fell across the page, he nearly expected to find Lady Nemiah standing before him, with her summer-bright hair and goddess-lit green eyes. The sight of Alende frowning down jammed him roughly back into the present.

"What are you doing, Mahla's son?"

"Exploring." Jhared leaped to his feet and had to catch Alende's arm for balance as the immensity of the mysteries rushed over him. "Look at this! Lady Nemiah watched while a Sahisten priest sealed the alliance between Sahiste and Laebek with the bite of vipers. Alende, this journey came from a Path I know. Lady Nemiah has walked through Shorn lives. There are more. So many more journeys exist here. About Arionade and elders. About a farmer laboring in his field and the birth of temple hounds. *True* threads. Not the lies we hold now. These are a part of the pattern."

"Slow down, my darling." Alende grasped Jhared's shoulders, his expression wavering from amusement to irritation to concern. "You'll throw yourself into the Nowhere if you keep this up."

Reluctantly, Jhared closed his eyes and drew a breath. His heart was galloping in his chest. Riana's honeyed warmth pooled across his shoulders. "Alende, please," he said, forcing himself to shape each word with care. "If Lady Nemiah is to have any part in what's to come, she needs a foundation from which to draw strength. These maps represent the power of generations of priestesses. She needs them."

"Why would we want the temple to play any part in our future?"

Jhared turned. He hadn't heard Rona approaching. The city man stood stiffly, his features pale with anger.

"Because she has seen the truth of us," Jhared replied.

Rona scowled. "Lady Nemiah is a cold, imperious bitch with no heart to care whether the initiates of the Becoming live or die."

Jhared glanced down at the precious map in his hand, reminding himself of all that Rona had suffered. "I understand what you saw at your Becoming, Rona. The face Lady Nemiah wears before the council is not all of her. You don't—"

"And her *healer*," the man spat the word, "was so eager to spill blood that she sent away the priestess who was meant to cut me so she could do it herself!"

"The temple healer? Madam Kaliska?" Jhared shook his head. "She is a friend to the Kin. Ask Alende. No doubt she saved your life as much as Trev did. She knew how to give you time. Rona, be careful how your veils shape you or you'll know nothing but hatred."

Jhared turned back to the waylayer. "Alende, please reconsider. Riana's gifts *must* remain in Avelos."

Alende's gaze wandered from Jhared to Rona and then to someplace past Jhared's shoulder. Jhared glanced behind him and saw Lusian observing them.

"Let it be," Alende replied softly. "Lady Nemiah walks the web. She'll have more journeys to map soon. Do not let *your* veils keep you thinking like a chained man." Without meeting Jhared's gaze, the waylayer strode away. The finality of his words echoed in the heaviness of his steps.

Lusian smiled and gave Jhared a mocking salute. Jhared stared back. He had erred in pressing Alende in front of the other man. Alende couldn't back down before Lusian, and the rest of the Kin would never go against Alende's word.

As if they knew the direction of Jhared's thoughts, the others avoided him for the rest of the day. Even Kilzaro decided abruptly that he would fish with Creaben and Rani rather than keep to his usual tasks about camp. Jhared knew it was just as well he stayed clear of them. A thought had entered his head, a thought that followed him about as he watered the horses and reset their picket line, a thought that refused to be discarded, although the others would have trussed him up and poisoned him again if they knew it. When he lay down to sleep that night, the thought only came clearer. If he returned the maps to the temple, the unbound Kin might suffer for it—Alende, Shira, Kilzaro, Trev. People he had begun to care about, people who might eventually call him one of their own. Yet if Lady Nemiah owned the strength for it, she might find a way to stand for the Shorn—all the Shorn, not just the few who lived outside the Laws. If she succeeded, he might one day return home; he might belong again rather than merely wander at the borders of others' lives. If he aided Lady Nemiah now, one day all of them might return.

Jhared told himself it was the greater goal that caused him to rise and bid farewell in his heart to the sleeping forms around him. The fact that Lusian stood watch when he decided to act might have been chance, or the Path's way of letting him know he was stepping exactly as he should.

He rose silently, pulled on his boots and his cloak. His heart ached as he looked down at Trevazio, sleeping with one arm flung above his head, fingers clenched around a feather that Creaben had carved for him. Shira was curled like a cat atop her bedroll. Alende lay passed out from *slu* and exhaustion.

Lady, let this be the right thing for them all.

Jhared turned away and moved unhurriedly toward the tree. Lusian sat against the trunk, a pipe gripped between his teeth.

"What do you want?" the man drawled.

"I want to look at the maps."

"My, you have been enthralled, haven't you?"

"You could learn from them, Lusian. You believe your own Path is the only relevant part of the weaving. That makes your world dangerously narrow."

Lusian clenched his pipe and flashed his snarl of a grin. "You know, soldier, it's never been so easy to steal from the elders as it was on this trip."

"Oh?" Jhared began untying the first bag. Only three bags held maps. The rest contained histories, rare books but not unique.

"Indeed. It happens that while I was there, the elders all left the city to attend some council gathering in Parnas Pass. Can you believe my luck? Easy enough to slip into a house when the protector is away." Lusian glanced sidelong at Jhared. "Of course, some elders' wives aren't opposed to a pretty face in the house at any time.

You know Sarena Trianor, don't you, Trianor's Folly? Pretty little thing. Soft in all the right places."

'Jhared schooled his features, setting the first bag down and working on the second. In the Forest Guard, he had met one or two men like Lusian, those who cloaked their need for cruelty in smiles and jests; those who knew where best to strike to cause others to bleed. "Lusian, you're wasting your energy by aiming your arrows at me. I no longer have any connection to Elders' Circle."

The man gave an elegant shrug. "I can't help it. I am Shorn, after all. Treacherous. Malicious."

A grim smile stretched Jhared's face. He tossed the second bag down, and pulled at the third. It came free with a soft snap. Lusian skittered to his feet.

"Stop that. What are you up to?"

With a swift step, Jhared closed on the man. "You believe the maps have no importance to you," Jhared whispered. "But that's only because you refuse to look beyond your own Path. The maps document the sacred journeys. I will tell you of a journey now. The Avelune had no part in any betrayal. Lady Amalia was falsely accused after her Arionad tried to protect her from Tumal's threats. We are Shorn for naught but Tumal's fear. You are no throwback to a treacherous people. You have no excuse for your foul core."

Jhared continued to advance. Lusian stumbled backward, past the edge of camp, his hard gaze going wide. "You've no way to know such a thing!"

"I saw it." Jhared pushed the unbound man farther away from the sleeping figures, anger and sadness pounding through him. "I saw Lady Amalia on her death walk. Caught her in my arms when Tumal's men beat her."

"If that's so, why didn't Alende speak of it? Or any of the others?"

"They don't know. No one knows besides Lady Nemiah, myself, and you. It's a thing that changes the world. It's a thing that can drive a person mad. Keep your stolen books and let the Sonans be satisfied. Avelos must not lose more of the truth. I'm returning the maps to where they belong."

A swift jab to the throat with the edge of his hand dropped Lusian to the ground. With the straps that had held the bags, Jhared gagged the man and bound him hand and foot; then left him where he wasn't likely to wake the others with his moaning.

A strange calm settled over Jhared as he returned to camp to scoop up the bags and untie Seravina. He led her away, praying she didn't call out to the other mounts and certain she would not. She was the granddaughter of a Mavaye stallion, Riana's Chosen, and he was acting for Riana's temple.

He left the Kin behind, gripping the sacred mysteries in three worn sacks.

5.

SANCTUARY

Near the western border of Avarel Forest, Clan Nadaren supported a temple. Jhared recalled his patrolmate Jase speaking of it. "The priestesses in Avarel Forest are wilder than those in the city, but they still know just how to place their needles." Saying it, Jase had tapped his tattooed cheek and offered a wicked grin. Avarel wasn't among the temples Leita and Lady Nemiah had named as safe for a Shorn man, but the forest temple wouldn't require Jhared to negotiate his way through a town, and it wouldn't be too far. A day's ride, if he were lucky, maybe two. He wanted the Pathwalkers' maps out of his hands as swiftly as possible and back with those meant to hold them.

He kept Seravina moving through the darkness. Although she stepped out eagerly, the miles crept along. The terrain was treacherous, carved into gullies and ravines, requiring vigilance and an agonizing pace. Dawn arrived too soon, bringing with it a steady rain that transformed the leaf-strewn hillsides into hazardous slides. Jhared gritted his teeth as he navigated the mare around another steep ridge, losing time. The Kin knew where he was bound. He had told Lusian clearly enough. His only hope was to stay ahead of them.

When he encountered the river flowing south in its deep, sheer bed, Jhared swore aloud. It was the Jhanaza. No other river in Avarel Forest matched it. An excellent waterway for shipping Nadaren timber, the Jhanaza was no good for a man on horseback who needed to cross. If he had been where he expected to be, he shouldn't have encountered the river at all. He'd made an error in the night and had thought himself already far enough south that the Jhanaza was curling along the Amurian border, much farther west. Here it stopped his flight dead. The bridge lay a day's ride in the wrong direction, north toward Nadrona town. As he stared out at the grey water, Seravina huffed and pranced, sharing his frustration. There was nothing better to be done; they would have to ride south along the river until it turned west, and they could continue toward the forest's edge.

He rode on, only pausing from time to time to spell Seravina. By late afternoon, the rain stopped and the sun pierced the clouds. It wasn't enough to dry his sodden clothes or Seravina's silver coat, but the rays falling on his face told him how far the river had shifted. They were moving southwest now, and still turning. He kept Seravina trotting over the slender trail at the river's edge. On the left, the forest remained thick. Jhared rode easily, tired but relieved that he had spied no sign of the Kin behind him. He might have had the rain to thank for that, or perhaps Alende, unpredictable and ambivalent, had decided to let him go.

Night crept in. Stars dusted the blue cap of the sky. Jhared slowed Seravina, wary of the narrow trail and precipitous drop. He was considering whether it would be wise to pause for the night rather than risk the difficult trail in the dark, when he heard the rustling in the brush ahead. It was Sera who warned him that no forest hunter hid in the brush. She flicked her ears with interest and let out a long call. Another horse answered, a familiar whinny. Jhared put his heels to the mare's sides and she lunged into a gallop.

A figure rose out of the brush. "It's him! It is him. Rona, he's coming!" Trev's shout went shrill with excitement.

Jhared hissed. Not far ahead, a downed tree barred the path. It was one of the ancient grandmothers of the forest, with a massive trunk and heavy branches reaching eight feet toward the sky. It made an ideal place for an ambush, a place Jhared would have chosen himself had he been tracking raiders. He thought quickly: The rest of the Kin would be waiting for him, likely deeper in among the trees. Alende would have set them up to net him when he veered off the trail, away from the fallen tree and away from the river, in the only direction left to him.

The only direction left if he hadn't been riding a descendent of the Chosen. He leaned close to Seravina's neck and prepared for the jump. The fallen oak loomed above him, its branches scratching at the night. Rona ran out in front of it, waving his arms and screaming in triumph. Another horse would refuse the jump, must refuse it. Jhared put his trust in Seravina and told her so. She swerved around Rona. The trunk rushed up; her head came down. Jhared felt her hindquarters slide deep beneath her and propel her upward. Together they stretched higher and higher. For an instant, Jhared feared they would be impaled upon the branches. His blood roared in his ears. With all his spirit, he yearned for the skies. Then the mare was clear, her body rotating, her forelegs stretching. She touched earth, recovered, and galloped onward.

Jhared smiled mirthlessly, reveling as the damp air slapped his skin. After a little way, he drew rein, listening for pursuit. Sera fought him, throwing her head sideways and dragging on the bit. He thought it only her desire to run free, until he heard the pounding hooves behind him and knew they were coming.

Seravina didn't need encouragement. Jhared loosed the reins and she dashed once more through the darkness, flowing like molten silver and pouring like moonlight around trees and over obstacles. Her bright mane lashed Jhared's face. The granddaughter of Riana's Chosen rejoiced in racing along her own Path. Behind him on his left flank, another mount crashed through the undergrowth. Rona cried out dire threats. Jhared didn't hear the others, but they were out there. They knew this forest. They had known how far south to travel to cut him off. It was only a matter of time before they closed on him. If he found no way to escape, the Kin would come, and with them Alende. Jhared dreaded that confrontation more than he feared the council.

Seravina ran the tortuous trail between water and forest. The river roared in the ravine at Jhared's right. He needed to end this, to make a response the Kin wouldn't expect. He glanced sideways, trying to assess the span of the ravine. Twelve feet, thirteen maybe, with a sharply rising slope on the opposite side. Given better options, it wasn't a jump he would choose to make in the dark with uncertain footing, but right now it seemed that Sera could fly if he asked it of her.

He pushed her harder, leaving Rona behind; then took her wide, away from the edge. A risky maneuver to wheel back among the trees. They managed it, and pounded straight toward the drop-off, with Jhared judging the strides as they approached. Seravina leaped without hesitation, as cleanly as the tree. Jhared sucked a breath as once more they stretched weightlessly into the air.

Her front hooves contacted the opposite bank. Then her hindquarters. Then she shrieked. Her pain and terror shredded the night, a sound that held too much suffering for one animal on one Path. She tried to halt: her forelegs stiffened and she went sliding, skidding on stone. Her head whipped upward, as though to avoid a barrier. Her haunches collapsed beneath her. Jhared kicked free of the stirrups and threw himself out of the saddle, hoping they had landed far enough from the edge to avoid falling into the chasm. Seravina went down thrashing. Jhared struck the dirt, rolled, and scrambled to get clear.

Not six feet in front of them, the distortion writhed over the ground, a tangle of impossible shadows in the darkness, repulsive and wrong in ways he had no time to understand. That wrongness smashed through his chest. He was glass shattered against stone, stone crushed under steel. His self scattered across uncountable moments. So many Paths tangled here, spilling through doors where they didn't belong, pushing across times when they shouldn't have been.

And they would kill him. Already, each Path plucked up the pieces of him, like vultures plucking flesh. He knew he must move before he lost awareness entirely. On hands and knees, he scrambled away from the ravine and up the rocky slope. Innumerable Paths called him back. He tried to breathe, but how did one draw air when his head was on one Path and his chest on another? He crested the incline, lost his balance, and tumbled down the opposite side.

At the bottom, he lay stunned, watching the stars and trying to remember how to inhale; wondering if he sat up what parts of himself he would discover missing; wondering if Seravina had fallen or fled.

On the other side of the ravine, someone crashed through the underbrush. In that part of Jhared's mind still aware enough to consider consequences, an alarm blared.

"Stop." It came out a whisper. He pulled in a deeper breath and forced it from his lungs, "Rona, stop! Stop! Don't cross! Don't—"

He was too far away and Rona was focused on the chase. Jhared heard the leap, then two animals screaming, a horse and a man. Then silence.

Trevazio's voice came from farther away, still on the opposite ledge.

"Evared! Evared, what happened? Are you . . . Evared!"

"Trev, stay back," Jhared gasped, clambering to his feet. "Please, stay back!"

"I'm coming after you, traitor!"

Trevazio and his gelding were farther down the ravine. A narrower gap there, but they barely made the jump. The gelding's hooves scrabbled at the edge before the beast heaved itself onto level ground. Trevazio wheeled around, searching for his brother.

"On your life, Trev, don't move!" Jhared cried. He flung himself back toward the deadly knot of Paths. Up the hill, then down, in a barely controlled slide. He staggered into Trevazio's way just as the boy approached the tangle. The gelding pulled up hard. Trevazio's gaze went past Jhared to the wreckage of horse and man behind him.

"You've killed him!"

The boy leaped from the saddle. Jhared grabbed for him and missed. Trevazio ran.

The horse was dead, its neck in an untenable twist. A few feet away, Rona sprawled directly across the tangle. At first, Jhared thought his own disorientation shaped what he saw. Then he recognized it for the truth. On either side of the distortion, Rona's body appeared intact, but where the shadows coiled, where his torso should have been dark and solid, there was a wavering fog. The lines of him shifted back and forth, as though seen through water or through the heated air of a summer day. The tangle was splitting him apart.

Trevazio hurled himself at his brother, screaming his name. Not his new, chosen name, but the one his family had given him, the one he had lost. Jhared barely managed to hook his fingers in the collar of Trevazio's shirt and drag him backward, wrapping his arms around the boy's chest.

"You can't touch him, Trev! You can't!"

The boy kicked and bit, wild to get free. "Traitor! You've killed him!"

"Trev, stop! I'll get him out. But I'm not going to let you go until you promise not to run at that thing. Promise me!"

It took time for the words to penetrate the boy's panic. He gulped for breath and slowly stopped his flailing. "I promise. I promise. Just please help him!"

Cautiously, Jhared released the boy and pushed him toward the hill. Then he turned to face the half-Rona, swallowing back sickness. He moved slowly, aware how easy it would be to trip into the tangle himself. This close to it he felt like a beam of light split by a prism or a stream of sand poured through a sieve. As he hunkered beside the fallen Shorn man, Jhared fought to hold all the streams together.

Mahla's son. Soldier. Unbound. Brother.

Music maker. Oath breaker . . .

He leaned over Rona. The air before him hummed like a swarm of bees. He clenched his teeth and reached for Rona's right arm where it lay free of the tangle.

Traveler.

Traitor.

The man's skin was cold as a corpse. Jhared grabbed Rona's other arm. With a groan, he threw all his strength into tugging backward.

The Paths clung to their prize. Jhared leaned into the pull, digging into the dirt with his boots. Soon he was panting, aware that his self was slipping, fraying, falling toward Riana's Gate. His arms trembled with the effort. He tightened his grip around Rona's cold wrists and murmured an incoherent prayer.

Rona's body broke loose suddenly, sending Jhared backpedaling. He held on and kept dragging until even Rona's feet were clear of the shadows.

He stared down at the body. The man was intact from boots to head, but so cold. "What's wrong with him?" Trevazio cried. "What happened?"

"Get wood," Jhared ordered. "We need a fire. We need to warm him. Have a care where you step. There could be more of these tangles."

The boy nodded his understanding and hurried off. Jhared stood, swaying, before trying to drag Rona farther from the danger. He made it only a short distance before he dropped to his knees, dizzy and out of breath. His vision fragmented until the trees all danced around him and he saw a row of wavering Ronas on the ground. He had to close his eyes and grasp up the pieces of himself once more before he could creep back to the unconscious man's side.

"You aren't going to die here," he said, yanking off his muddy cloak and draping it around Rona's icy form. "We won't do this to Trev, you and I."

Rona made no response. Under the cloak, his chest rose and fell shallowly. Jhared began to chafe the man's hands between his own, trying to ignore it whenever one of the vultures flew out of the tangle and tore away another part of himself.

Trev returned without success. After so much rain, damp branches and sodden tinder were his only harvest. Jhared struggled with the fire, his fingers clumsy on the striker. He swore over it as nothing took the spark. Finally, he had to give up. He drew back his cloak from Rona's body.

"Lie close," he ordered Trev. "It's the best way to warm him. And it will let him know you're here."

Obediently, Trev scooted down beside his brother, pressing against him and stretching one arm over his chest. Jhared tucked the cloak around them both.

"The others are coming. They'll hurt you when they find us," Trevazio said.

"Probably." Jhared didn't bother opening his eyes. Everything at which he looked insisted upon splitting into pieces. He kept his hands moving over Rona's, trying to rub warmth back into them, trying to pray life back into him.

None of his prayers were answered. Rona never woke. His body fought to suck enough air to feed his spirit. And then he stopped fighting.

Trevazio's howl rang out like the cry of a broken animal. He clambered to his knees, shaking his brother's body and crying his name.

Jhared reached for the boy, staggering when the ground wasn't where it should have been.

Trevazio yanked away. "Don't touch me! Run! Run if you can, traitor! You did this thing."

"Don't, Trev," Jhared murmured. "I'll stay here with you. Until the others—"

"No! You made me trust you. You pretended you understood what it meant to love a brother. Then you went back to *them*! I saved Evared from the Becoming, but I couldn't save him from you!"

The boy picked up something from the ground and hurled it. A stone, it must have been. Jhared felt the impact, dull and distant. Another one went up into the boy's hand and whipped through the darkness. Violent flowers of light bloomed in Jhared's head.

"What's wrong with you?" Trevazio cried. "I want you to go. I want you to run!"

"Trev . . . I'm sorry."

"There is no sorry big enough for this. They will kill you. Go!"

Another rock struck Jhared. Numbly, he turned.

"Never seek the Kin again, traitor! You belong nowhere! Nowhere!"

"Goodbye . . . Bran. I didn't mean to leave you alone. I didn't mean it."

Jhared knew only that his legs moved up the hill, away from the boy and death, away from the ones he had betrayed, away from the grotesque wound in the web. He staggered through the trees without seeing his way or having any awareness of time. If he looked behind him, he was sure he would find little pieces of himself scattered like breadcrumbs. The image made him laugh, and then stop when the desolate sound echoed back at him from a thousand Paths. Sometimes he imagined that he heard an irritated whicker or felt the bump-bump of a heavy head against his arm, but Seravina could be nothing more than a wish that existed only on some other Path. He moved until he couldn't move any more. When the earth invited him down, soft and welcoming, he accepted.

Maya's singing reached him first, a cheerful melody in Sonan, then the sound of water splashing. He shivered as it bathed his fevered skin.

"Jhared, you're back!" Her voice was startled, breathless. More splashing. "Wait. Wait a moment."

She stepped out of the lake, her ombré wings drawn back like a swan's, her wet body glistening under the morning sun. He saw myriad versions of her, as though he peered through a faceted gem. Through those facets, she picked up her cloak from the pebbly shore and wrapped it around herself.

"What are you doing? You shouldn't have returned so soon. You're traveling too often."

He tried to explain about the maps, about the tangle and Rona, but his voice echoed back to him from a thousand different sources. They overlapped one another, escalating until they smeared into nothing but noise.

Maya clapped her hands over her ears. "I can't understand you. There are too many of you. What's happened?"

She turned in a slow circle. The water lapped at her bare feet. A breeze caressed her hair and kissed her throat. Jhared wanted to be that breeze.

"I see you, parts of you, again and again. It's as though you've pulled open the doors of a hundred Paths and left a portion of yourself on each of them. Jhared, stop this! You must return to your own place."

"How?" He barely breathed the single word, but it clamored back at him over and over.

"Ah, gods of seas and skies! I can't help you from here." She stopped and closed her eyes. Jhared felt her reaching for composure or perhaps he was the one who reached. "It will be all right," she said more softly. "Do you remember where you belong?"

He opened his mouth, then closed it and merely nodded.

"And you remember how to claim who you are?"

He nodded again, bleakly.

"You must track your way back as you have before. Not just from one Path, but from all of them—" Maya cut herself short. Her tone changed abruptly, as if she had recognized something in his expression. "What's happened? Why don't you wish to return?"

He had no way to tell her what he had done and why he didn't have the will to face his own Path, but she saw it or perhaps she felt it, just as he felt her dismay.

"Come to me," she ordered. "Not through the Gate. On your own road. Return to your place and find me. Cross the Sonan border where it touches both Avelos and Amuria. Follow the Jhanaza River and put the Amurian hills at your back. You know the house near the lake. Please, Jhared. Find me."

It was a purpose, something that could focus him. Maya breathed out slowly, a long stream of calm. It helped Jhared to collect his strength.

"You are a gift," he said softly. But the words reverberated into meaninglessness as he stepped from Maya's Path and tumbled into the Nowhere.

6.
DARK PLACES

"You dared *refuse* them?"

Bena's ancient voice scalded the air. She cracked her walking stick across the leg of the table. It resounded against the stone walls.

"Of course," Nemiah replied, wiping at the blue blur in the corners of her eyes as if she could brush it away.

"You have finished us this time, Lady. That you have."

Beside Bena, Kaliska's keen grey eyes were as clear and calm as ever, but worry lines folded the skin above her nose. "Mistress Bena, I believe what the Lady is saying is that she has delayed her response to the council so that the Higher Circle can determine how best to answer the elders' demand."

"Bah!" The vehemence of the Mistress of Maps flew in a fine spittle across the table. "There's no need for discussion. Only one thing can be done and you know it as well as I do. The girl must go back to them."

Nemiah rested her hands on the smooth tabletop, composed despite the argument howling before her. She hadn't intended to confront this challenge now; others needed her. The Mapmaker and healer had converged upon her as she returned from the morning devotions. It had been a futile hope that she could cut short their protests by dealing with them together here in the small dining room off the main hall. The two women, who rarely took the same side on any issue, were united by one thing: their fear of the consequences of Parnas Pass. They had seen the shattered regiment of Forest Guard soldiers escorting Nemiah and High Chieftain Rumar back into the city. They knew she had defied the council. And they had seen Leita. Now both women stared at her, waiting: Bena with a decade of disgust in her expression; Kaliska with an air of reserved judgment and a pressing need to know.

"Mistress Bena is correct in one thing, Madam Kaliska. This discussion is unnecessary. Ziabela Marcalo will remain under Riana's protection. I have sent my formal refusal to Lord Rumar."

"You've made it a matter of record?" Bena nearly choked on her fury. "First, you lose us every sacred map in the temple—five generations of Mapmaking! Then you meddle with a Shorn deserter. Now this? Protecting a treasonous scribe? Elder Abrigado has dreamed of such a day. He will send the city garrison against us with swords and battering clubs to take the girl. And goddess help whichever of us gets in his way. Blood will be spilled, mark my words. It will be Lord Tumal in the temple all over again!"

"Bena, you are becoming unbalanced," Nemiah said. "I suggest you sit back down and drink your tea. You haven't thought it though."

"There's more? Once the water is over your head, Lady, you're going to drown. It doesn't matter how much deeper it grows."

"Then perhaps you should learn to swim." Nemiah refilled the old woman's teacup and set down the earthenware pot with a thump. "Toren Abrigado is not going to raid the temple. He needs to condemn more than one Shorn scribe to save his bid for Rumar's seat. He needs me. There will be a tribunal."

The Mistress of Maps dropped her walking stick so abruptly it was nearly comical. Her creased features arranged themselves into a problematic mix of feigned regret and genuine hope. "You think the council will dare it? To bring the Lady before them?"

Nemiah laughed. Now that she had stated it aloud, nervous anticipation cantered through her. "Half the elders are clamoring for it, and Abrigado has the impetus to make the others act. He cannot leave me intact for fear I will lend credibility to Jhared Denaban's accusations against him. Neither does he want to further agitate the western clans by attacking the temple directly. Not while he still hopes to gather support to topple Rumar. Once he has me, he will leave you alone. I will see to it."

"And to your successor?" Bena said slyly.

"Bena, enough!" Kaliska cried. "Standing before the tribunal need not be a death sentence."

Nemiah smiled grimly. "The Mistress of Maps is only being practical, Kaliska. Of course I will guide the Circle in the selection of my successor before I go to the tribunal. To do otherwise would be irresponsible. And no, Bena, I will not recall Carian."

The Mapmaker was nearly grinning, her thin lips drawn back over yellowed teeth. Beside her, the silver-haired, straight-backed Kaliska, healer and spy mistress and superb observer of others, made no comment. She would recognize that Nemiah was holding something back.

A sliver of regret pricked Nemiah. Kaliska more than most people needed to know the truth. As the healer responsible for seeing each Avelun babe brought to the temple to be Shorn, Kaliska needed to know that Lady Amalia was innocent of all Avelos accused her and that the Shearing was not a tool of salvation Riana offered to High Chieftain Tumal but a terrible blasphemy. Only dread made Nemiah bide her time: dread of the harm that would be done if the truth flew out carelessly. Nemiah had already tried to carry Amalia's story to where it must be heard, but her words had remained unspoken. Bloodshed would follow the truth, bloodshed as had not been known even during the Exile War. On a battered night, sitting alone with Adan Rumar, she had seen that Path, had nearly been undone by it. Avelos need take only one small step to cause the people, in their growing fear, to burn out the Shorn and exterminate them entirely from this Path.

"You've made a brave decision, Lady, keeping the girl."

Nemiah yanked herself away from the images of death. Kaliska's tone had shifted from neutrality to something more probing. Her nature and her duties would drive her to seek what she didn't yet know. Only a heavy pounding on the hall door postponed the woman's next question.

Before Nemiah could utter leave to enter, a sinewy, fair-headed Arionad crashed into the room. Not one of her own men, he was one of those Lady Ansa had sent after the high temple's Arionade had been attacked. An impulsive man, Rien, and tending toward arrogance. Nemiah didn't like him.

"He's here! They've sent him!" the young man blurted, barreling up to the table.

Kaliska stopped him with an expression of ice. "Arionad Rien, you are in the presence of the Lady. Conduct yourself properly."

The man hissed a breath between his teeth, but made an attempt to pull himself together. "Lady Nemiah, Elder Tierzen Trianor has come to the sanctuary. He says he must speak with you."

"They've come for you!" Bena said gleefully.

Kaliska stood, nearly knocking over her chair. "Not yet!"

"How many men are with him, Arionad Rien?" Nemiah's tone remained quiet but her heart thundered beneath her breast.

"None, Lady."

"I mean City Guard. Not elders."

"The elder is alone, Lady. I invited him to wait in your receiving room, but he refused. He asks for you to join him in the outer courtyard."

"Alone?" Bena wheezed. "Why? What does he want?"

"Perhaps he has come for a blessing," Kaliska replied, sardonic.

The elder hadn't come seeking the goddess's peace, Nemiah knew. Jhared Denaban had been Tierzen Trianor's fosterling. The charges that threatened her shadowed the elder as well. There was only one reason he would risk being seen at the temple.

"Very well. I will speak with him. Arionad, come with me."

The healer blocked her way. "Lady, I should join you. We should greet the elder together, Temple to Council."

"This isn't council business," Nemiah said, moving around Kaliska's tall figure. "I will deal with it myself. There are things I owe this man."

"Lady, there are other things we must discuss—"

"Kaliska." Nemiah added a warning to her tone.

"Lady Nemiah, the Guardians have named three Avelune babes of age to be brought to the Shearing."

Nemiah's breath locked in her throat. It took all her will to keep walking toward the door. "Well, prepare the acolytes for the ritual. It is four days before the new moon. I imagine I will have returned before then."

She led the Arionad toward the outer courtyard, pausing at her tower long enough to retrieve her winter cloak and exchange her delicate slippers for her boots. As she laced the leathers, her thoughts darted away from Kaliska's final words, slipping instead over that first terrible night after the killing winds had shredded Parnas Pass and the northerners had shredded the Forest Guard. That night Amalia's story and Leita's torture had pushed her in a direction she had never before walked. She had taken steps toward a man she had never before dared to trust. Part of the consequences of her daring waited for her now in the courtyard. What she hadn't yet determined was whether she had stepped too far on that night or not far enough.

She stood, adjusting her cloak. She wished she could bring Capalino with her—Elder Trianor had reason to like the hound—but Capa had been too long cooped inside the walls and she had sent him to the Mistress of Kennels for several days of hunting in the valley.

In the outer courtyard, the cold morning drizzle strung silver beads over the bare bones of the bushes and trees. Tierzen Trianor stood alone, his long hands braced against his thighs, his earnest face lifted toward the sky. Silver glistened across his cheeks.

"Elder Trianor."

He turned toward her with a weary urgency, like a man who had long been a stranger to sleep. No pleasure registered in his blue-grey eyes at seeing her. "Lady Nemiah. Thank you for coming out. We must hurry, I think. Before the City Guard has too much time with him."

Nemiah halted, the world slipping sideways from where she had expected it. "Time with whom? Hurry where?"

"Ah, forgive me. I've only just received word myself and I am not . . ." The elder rubbed a hand across his face. "The City Guard has captured the man responsible for the theft of rare books in the city. I'm on my way to Aelend Prison. Will you come?"

The thief responsible for stealing rare books: the one the heretics claimed was responsible for stealing Riana's maps and for poisoning her Arionade, the one who sought to unravel the world.

"Of course I'll come. But why are you here? Why did the City Guard not send a message?"

"Perhaps they will. Though if Elder Abrigado gets to him, I doubt it. The thief is Shorn. A young man. They only sent for me as Minister of the Teaching. I thought of you."

She turned to Rien. "Fetch Commander Evorales. We are going to Aelend."

"Yes, Lady. Should I tell Captain Rom?"

Rom would be in his quarters, by now wondering why she had not come to him. The thief with his poison had stolen not only Riana's sacred maps, but Rom's strength and health, and nearly his life. He could not help her in this, and she had nothing but torment for him. "Leave the captain to his morning duties."

Rien bowed his head and hurried off, revealing nothing of what he knew of his injured captain's duties. For that, he rose a notch in Nemiah's estimation.

She wrapped her arms about herself beneath her fur-lined cloak. In the mountains, the drizzle would be turning to snow, and the air shivered with the promise of that cold. The elder waited in silence beside her, all his friendly vigor frozen into something painfully detached.

"The thief. Where did they catch him?" she asked.

"At the home of the Secretary of Records. An apt target, as it happens. His family library contains several volumes considered the last of their kind."

"Our thief is well-informed then."

"No doubt. The Shorn in this city receive a thorough education."

Nemiah winced at the self-recrimination in the elder's tone. The allegations of treason against his fosterling and Jhared Denaban's subsequent escape had destroyed Tierzen's influence in the council and with the high chieftain. That he still held his position as Minister of the Teaching Nemiah suspected was a testament to the disorder in the council more than any will to keep him in power. She had come to understand the elder well enough to realize that this Shorn thief struck yet another blow against his hopes for the Teaching. He had meant for the Teaching to save Avelos from the Shorn and to save the Shorn from themselves. Tierzen couldn't know that all his hopes were based on lies. He knew only that she had made it possible for his condemned fosterling to flee.

"Elder Trianor, I did not expect you to greet me again with anything but questions and antipathy."

"Lady Nemiah, if it were possible for you to answer my questions you would have done so already. As for antipathy . . ." He shrugged loosely. "If your intent were malicious, you could have caused me equal damage without incriminating yourself. Therefore, I must assume that some other motive—pity perhaps—drove you to act as you did. Ultimately, however, the choices of the deserter derived from the flaws in my Teaching and in his character. I do not hold you culpable."

The man's precise, unemotional analysis disturbed her far more than his rage would have done. *The deserter.* A young man he had raised as his son. Again, she felt Amalia's truth pressing for release.

"What pity I have is for us all," she replied.

The elder's gaze on hers remained devastatingly direct and considering. It was the same unforgiving intensity his fosterling possessed. Nemiah wondered if he knew.

Whatever the man might have said next was cut short by the appearance of Commander Evorales. Understanding they were to descend from Travitar Hill and cross the clan circles to Aelend Prison, the commander offered to prepare the Lady's litter, or failing that, to call for her mount and a full escort. Nemiah refused both. For the elder's sake, she wished to draw as little notice as possible. None were likely to molest them with two armed Arionade as guardians, and the man responsible for attacking the temple had apparently been caught. Evorales capitulated with a strained expression. Nemiah nodded to Elder Trianor and they set out on foot.

Aelend Prison was an ancient gargoyle of stone and wood that sprawled against the city wall. Some believed the oldest sections of the structure had been built in the time of Alende Isan to serve as a garrison. The unreachable guard posts near the top of the two round towers lent some weight to such a belief. It still provided garrison and offices for the City Guard, but since well before the Exile, Aelend's primary purpose was to confine the men and women deemed dangerous to Avelos. Thick, thorny vines caged the dull grey stone, and a row of arrow loops squinted through the drizzle. As they were meant to do, the scourging columns came into view from as far away as the streets of the clan circles: five columns in the outer yard, arranged in a half-circle. Rain ran in red droplets from the rusting iron chains bolted near the crown of each column and left bloody stains on the ground. The stones of Aelend had witnessed centuries of suffering. Tumal had favored the prison as a place to punish and store away those who opposed him. From the prison gate, those named traitors began their march to the steps of the wall to be—

Nemiah stumbled, struck by a nightmare realization: she had been here. Aelend would have been Amalia's last, terrible home. The sensation of a dark cell closed around Nemiah, and with it, the despair of the generous Avelun who had become her friend. Nemiah would never forget the battered woman chained to the floor, the long night when she had offered her own inadequate song as comfort, or the moment when she understood that Amalia had never shaped a plot against Lord Tumal.

"Lady, are you well?" Evorales had moved to her shoulder. Concern echoed in his tone.

She breathed slowly. Cold sweat trickled between her breasts. "Perfectly, Commander."

Elder Trianor did not look at her or at the row of scourging columns. "It sickens me as well," he declared, marching resolutely toward the gate.

The captain of the prison guard, a block-shaped man with a shining pate, recognized the elder and let them in without fuss, leading them past a small guardroom, where a handful of men ate and diced, past a number of offices, then down a set of slippery stairs and into the heart of the prison. The air grew dank and heavy with the odor of decaying wood and abused bodies. Black, moldy walls gave way to a series of barred doors. With a shudder, Nemiah wondered about the men and women who lay behind each door. Who other than a Shorn thief who poisoned the innocent servants of Riana deserved such treatment? She thought of Amalia, who hadn't deserved it at all, and shuddered again. The guard stopped halfway down a corridor and fumbled with the bar before drawing open a door. Nemiah stood, cold and ill, at the threshold.

No sound came from within the cell. The guard lifted his lamp, throwing a film of light over a floor of damp stone, a low pallet of hay, and a prisoner curled on the hay like an injured animal.

Nemiah rounded on the guard. "What have you done? This is no corrupt Shorn man. He's no more than a helpless child!"

"He may be young, but helpless he is not." The guard rubbed his jaw. "And he was thieving. That's certain. Caught him crawling out'a window with the books."

"Where are his Teachers?" Elder Trianor demanded, ashen in the wan light.

"Don't know. He wouldn't say. That's why we sent for you. Don't make me out as some monster what takes pleasure in beating children. I only did what I had to."

"Let us in," Elder Trianor said, his voice hard and flat.

The guard stood aside. Nemiah followed the elder, who gestured the lamp closer. As the light dropped on the boy, he scrambled upright. He was ten winters, maybe eleven, but no child's roundness remained in his long, gaunt frame. A mat of black hair fell over his hunted gaze. Bruises and scrapes discolored his cheeks. His clothes might have been made from sturdy, colorful fabric of the type the mountain folk wove, but were now limp and grey with dirt. His wrists stuck out from the frayed sleeves.

"What's your name, boy?"

The wary green eyes took in the elder and then Nemiah. "Who are ya?"

"Elder Tierzen Trianor. I am the Minister of the Teaching. This is the Lady of Avelos."

"Are ya here ta take me ta the wall?"

"No, boy. We're not here to punish you. We're here to learn what happened. You're from the northern mountains, aren't you? Is that Clan Hilera I hear in your words?"

The boy shot a nervous glance at the guard, then back to the elder. The prefect of Clan Hilera had not joined the rest of the northern five in the uprising at Parnas Pass, but neither had the clan yet denounced its neighbors for their treason. Nemiah wondered how much a Shorn child understood of his people's precarious position.

"Yes," the boy said bravely. "Hilera."

"You're a long way from your clan. Tell me your name. Why were you stealing books?"

"Elder, slow down. Look at him. The boy is swaying with hunger." Nemiah turned to the guard. "What have you and your comrades for lunch?"

"Oats and a bit of lamb, Lady. But I don't—"

"You can spare a plate for the child. And some fresh water for him to clean up."

The guard puffed himself like a porcupine, ready to protest, but after a moment he deflated. "Very well, Lady. Right away."

Nemiah and Tierzen waited while the boy first washed his grimy hands and face with a care that suggested a civilized upbringing, then fell upon the bowl of hot porridge with a ferocity that suggested too long living with deprivation. He bolted his food, one arm wrapped around the bowl possessively. Only after scarfing every drop did he look up.

"What happened, child?" Nemiah asked gently. "Won't you tell me how you came to be so far from home?"

Perhaps it was because hers was the first kind voice the boy had heard in Aelend or perhaps the strain of keeping silent finally snapped his caution. He began to blurt out his story. His name was Jholan. He had traveled to Velantar for the fall gathering with his family and many of his clan. When the killing winds struck the city on Dawnings' Day, his mother, father, and younger sister had all been slain. For weeks, he had searched for his Teachers, but presumed them dead as well. Knowing no one and having no coin, he had no way to travel home. Instead, he had become one of the multitudes of displaced children, scrambling about the wreckage in the poorest parts of the city, hiding, thieving, and clinging to the ragged remainder of his life.

The boy ended his story with his arms crossed over his thin chest. Although bravado stiffened his words, his expression was all over bewilderment, like a friendly puppy kicked by a stranger.

"Who hired you to steal the books?" Elder Trianor asked.

"Didn't say anything 'bout someone hiring me," the boy protested. "Books are treasures. My Teachers always told me so. I thought someone might buy 'em."

"You thought so, eh?" Elder Trianor sighed and rubbed a hand over his eyes. "Jholan, your Teachers were right: books are treasures. And what did they tell you about the lies of a Shorn boy?"

The child swallowed and stared past the elder without speaking.

"Jholan, you know what you owe to Avelos," Elder Trianor said soberly. "You know what you owe your family. What would they say if they saw you now? You've committed a great wrong. There is a need for reparation."

The boy remained drawn up straight, but his face screwed tight, as though to force back tears. Nemiah's heart broke.

"Elder, that's not right. Please, stop this!"

A dagger glance from the man silenced her. In that glance, his own heartbreak was exposed. His fosterling had been meant for this prison.

"For the memory of your family, Jholan, tell me why you stole the books."

It was too much. With a small cry of defeat, the boy sank into himself, knees to chest, head bowed. "A man wanted them. He had silver. He told me and some'a the other boys he would pay if we stole the oldest books from Elders' Circle. He told us the houses we should try."

"Who was this man?"

"Don't know." A flash of defiance, then a groan of surrender. "Said he worked for the king'a Sona. Said he was a royal agent. I'm no fool. I know the swamp rats don't have a king. He looked and spoke like a clansman, sure enough, but I didn't care about that. He had real silver."

"Do you know where he can be found?" the elder asked.

A hard, quick head shake. Fear in the gesture. The elder opened his mouth as though to prod again, but Nemiah restrained him with a hand on his shoulder.

"He threatened to harm you, didn't he?" she said to the boy. "If you reveal him."

A small nod.

Nemiah pressed her lips together. "What can we do for him, Elder?"

Elder Trianor bowed his head, as if in some internal debate, before speaking again. "Jholan, if you tell us all you know of this man, I will see you are sent back safely to your people in Clan Hilera."

A long pause, then the boy held up his hand. "He told us ta call him Lusian, like the hero in the stars. I don't think that was his name. He just liked ta be called hero. He could fight. And he had only two fingers on his left hand."

"Was he Shorn?" The elder's tone was implacable.

"Yes . . . no . . . I can't say. He looked like one'a us, but he didn't talk like any bound man I know."

Nemiah met the Shorn boy's gaze. "Did the man ever speak of the temple or encourage you to steal from Riana?"

"Oh yes," Jholan said, wide-eyed. "He spoke evil words against our Lady. Called her things not right ta say about any lady. He boasted he would sneak right inta the temple and take what he wanted. Said he'd take a girl or two as well, if he fancied it." The boy scowled. "He liked ta boast. He liked us all ta follow him and tell him fine things about himself. He was more dags than wool, my mama would say . . . would'a said." Jholan's scowl deepened and he dropped into a sad silence.

"I'm sorry, child," Nemiah said quietly, her thoughts raging. "I'm so sorry we failed to help you before it came to this."

It didn't take long to draw out the rest of what Jholan knew about the clansman who was turning children into thieves. For what purpose, the boy truly didn't seem to know. It was clear enough the child himself hadn't anything to do with the theft at the temple. Nemiah thought of the woman who had claimed she knew about such things. According to the heretic Yarla, the theft of books had nothing to do with the passive people of little Sona. It had to do with madness and True Chaos.

When the boy had no more to share, Elder Trianor informed the captain of the guard that they would be taking the Shorn prisoner with them. The guard showed no surprise, but appeared suddenly as though he wished himself someplace else.

"Of course, Elder Trianor. If you would just pass me the order from Chief Karwen for the boy's release, he can go with you."

Elder Trianor did not move or display an ounce of uncertainty. "The order does not come from your prison chief. It comes from the Minister of the Teaching. Every Shorn child before the age of his Becoming is in my charge. The authority to take custody of the boy rests with me."

Jholan stood stiff and straight beside the elder. The captain shifted his square frame. "Not in this case, I'm afraid. I'm sorry, Elder Trianor. I'm not to allow you to take the boy."

Nemiah had witnessed Elder Trianor angry before. He did not bluster or growl. Everything about him grew still and sharp. "Who gave that order, captain?"

"Elder, I have no argument with you. You know it. I always—"

"*Who?*"

The captain straightened. Whatever his ambivalence about balking an elder of the council, he was doing his job and knew it. "Minister Rud. Take it up with him, if you like."

Gilior Rud was the council elder for Clan Makri, the Minister of Prisons, and a stalwart ally of Toren Abrigado. Nemiah grew lightheaded with her own anger.

"I see," Tierzen said calmly. "The minister told you to send for me. Then he warned you I would want to take the boy."

"Elder, it's time for you and the Lady to be on your way," the captain responded woodenly. "This Shorn creature is a thief and will stay safely detained until he's sentenced."

Nemiah stepped toward the guard. "Captain, the Lady of Avelos—"

"Has no say here!" the man cried. "I made allowance for you, Lady, because you came with the elder, but we'll not let another of our prisoners disappear into the temple. No! Nor escape into the wilds either. Come along, now. Both of you. Don't make me call my men."

There was a soft, stifled whimper. Jholan. He hadn't moved from the elder's side.

Something raw flashed in Elder Trianor's expression when he looked down at the Shorn boy, but he wiped it away with one pass of his hand. "It all goes toward reparation, child. Just think on that. I'll return for you."

Jholan's chin rose and he turned his back. "That's what my papa said before he sent me inta the city and died in the killing winds."

There was nothing for it. Nemiah laid a blessing on the boy. Then she unclasped her cloak and pulled it from her shoulders. Elder Trianor stopped her before she could give it to the child, his own cloak of thick, warm wool already in his hands. He draped it around Jholan. Nemiah nodded. She had no choice then but to let the captain of the guard, with his sword and the threat of his nearby garrison, herd her out of the cell. Before she stepped free of Aelend Prison, she halted once more. The ring on her little finger was cunningly wrought of silver, with a precise spiral twisted around a skystone of cerulean. It had been a gift from Rom's niece, a piece of her own crafting. Nemiah dropped it into the captain's palm.

"I expect the boy to receive regular meals and clean water. I expect he will have no new bruises when next I see him. He may not have family left in Velantar, but the High Temple of Avelos is watching over him now."

The delicate ring vanished in the captain's thick fingers. "Of course, Lady."

Then Evorales and Rien were behind her and Nemiah was once more passing the bloody scourging columns. She clenched her fists.

"That was Abrigado taunting us," Elder Trianor observed as they reached the bottom of Travitar Hill. The rain had stopped but the muddy water coursing down the narrow lanes sprayed out from the wheels of passing carts.

Nemiah kept walking, disregarding the water. "He means to use it against us? Our attempt to claim the boy?"

"I imagine so. I've done you no favors today, Lady."

She looked at the elder, but saw no rancor in his gaze. He hadn't planned this encounter by way of retribution.

"Lady, you do know Abrigado hopes to accuse you of crimes against the council?"

"I assumed he would try," she answered. "Will you be considered complicit?"

"Perhaps. I still have some protections. There are certain things Abrigado won't yet dare. The temple does not have that shield." The elder paused. "You will have to surrender the Shorn scribe, Lady."

Nemiah stiffened, ready to protest, but she forced herself to remain steady. "You believe Abrigado cannot be convinced to let her go?"

"He will not."

"Because of what she knows?"

"Yes," Tierzen replied. "And because of who she is."

Nemiah hesitated. "Do you mean that the crimes of a wellborn Shorn woman will cause more outcry than if she had merely been another lost body from Shorn Circle?"

The elder looked mildly surprised. "You recognized her roots. I thought you might. I believe, however, you haven't realized who her family is." He ground out a breath. "I suppose, after all, it was my meddling that brought us to this point. You wouldn't have invoked the Law of Advocacy and taken her otherwise."

Elder Trianor lifted his eyes to the golden dome of the temple and the elegant tower of Elders' Hall where they rose side by side above the mud and the noise and the noxious city smells.

Nemiah stopped beside him. Somewhere along the street, the rhythmic clanging from a smithy beat the air. A horse uttered a long, high whinny.

"Why, Elder? Why did you see to it I would stand for Ziabela? Why have you exhausted your political influence fighting for the Shorn?"

"Because I believe the well-being of our country is tied to the well-being of those citizens who are the most vulnerable, the most damaged. I've always believed we must help the Shorn to find a place, else the threads that weave Avelos together will fray and split." He stared over her shoulder at Elders' Hall. "In that, I have failed spectacularly. My efforts have caused precisely what I most feared."

Nemiah gazed at him, hearing another voice generations away, Amalia's voice: *"The Avelune are Riana's mortal webweavers, yet still a part of the pattern itself. Can you understand, then, what it means to tear us? Imagine what happens to a pattern on the loom if you slash apart the warp."*

It startled her how close to the truth the elder had tread, but with a Teaching based on lies, of course he could only fail. It was a sad irony: she had witnessed his honesty and compassion. As the Minister of the Teaching, Tierzen Trianor could influence the life of every Shorn child. Had he been given a better map, he might have helped to lead Avelos toward a safer position among the border nations.

He needed to know Amalia's truth. And she could not give it to him. Not yet. She had seen the consequences of speaking too soon.

"We have all failed the Shorn, Elder Trianor."

He looked at her with a level of perceptiveness she had known in only two other men, but she did not fear he would guess at the truth. None of them would ever guess it.

"There are a thousand ways for a man to fail, Lady. Has the goddess given you insight into all of them?"

"Only the one that matters." She turned and started again to walk. How long could she wait? If she was to be tried for treason, she might not have so very much time. She shivered and put her focus back on the moment. "I'll not turn Ziabela over to the council. You know what they would do with her."

"Yes. I also know that you cannot make your own reparation by trying to save her."

Nemiah quickened her pace, putting distance between herself and the temptation of speaking further. She couldn't speak of Amalia, couldn't speak of the blood she herself had spilled on the altar. Not yet. Her gaze sorted through the crowd, as if there were an escape to be found among the laborers and the clerks, the farmers and the merchants, the artisans and the apprentices. She spied a soldier across the street in front of the stall of a bone carver, a grizzled clansman in Forest Guard green. His broad, sturdy figure was bent over a selection of dice. She didn't recognize him until he lifted his head to speak with his companion, a handsome, black-haired man, and she spied the soldier's pleasant face still mottled with bruises. As she stepped across the street to greet him, she heard Elder Trianor moving up beside her. Evorales made a sound of objection, quickly extinguished.

"Patrolman Nevia, isn't it?"

The soldier turned, the stiffness that hints of injury tainting his movements. When his eyes fell upon her, his easy expression hardened. He removed his hand from the shoulder of his companion.

"Lady Nemiah. Minister Trianor. How unexpected. This is my comrade Temen."

The soldier's dark-eyed companion made a spiral to Riana and a small bow to the elder. The soldier did not.

"I am relieved to see that you're recovering, Patrolman."

"Good of you to say, Lady. I imagine I'll take a lashing or two more before the end." He didn't smile. His features remained even and unengaged.

"Patrolman Nevia, the temple owes you for what you did for the Bearer of Cael's Blade. *I* owe you."

"The temple owes me nothing, Lady. The Bearer sacrificed herself trying to aid us. All I did was lead her out of the fighting. I was not the one who set her free."

"Nevertheless, she has spoken well of you."

Nevia managed a nod. "Then she's generous as well as courageous. Please take her my good wishes."

"I will," Nemiah promised. "I hope your patrolmates are also recovering."

The clansman's gaze chilled another degree. "Some of them, Lady. But that's the fate of a soldier, isn't it? To fall to a blade?"

Nemiah sighed inwardly. "I see. I'm sorry. I will light candles and pray that the guides find those who have gone to the Hidden Paths."

"I'm sure your prayers will mean something to those we have lost."

The soldier rocked forward like a man about to speak again, but his companion set a hand on his back and he sank once more onto his heels. "Forgive me for taking up your time on this cold street, Lady Nemiah. Minister Trianor. I won't delay you any longer." With a perfunctory bob of his head, the clansman turned to leave.

Nemiah didn't blame the man for his manner. He was battling grief. She had seen it in other soldiers, in a general. She called out as he began to walk away. "Patrolman, I understand your anger. You have been battered, and your comrades have fallen to traitors. The northerners should have been your allies. I know it seems that all reason has fallen to chaos."

The soldier halted like a horse drawn up too sharply. Temen pressed him onward, speaking in a quick, dire whisper, but the patrolman shook him off and stalked two steps back toward Nemiah.

"Chaos, Lady, is something a soldier learns to live with. Most days. Other days, even a man as simple as myself does sometimes wonder on the reason for things. Just for an instance, I wonder what your reasons might'a been for what you did in Murita. I was there, you remember, when you convinced the boy to come out with you. It must'a been a very good reason that caused you to ruin a youth so close to becoming a fine man. I'm a great fool for being free with my thoughts this way, but I've years enough behind me to see what must be said. You wrecked something that might'a been solid and good. Not whole. Not perfect. But strong and big-spirited and kind. You should know that. I hope your reasons were worth the cost."

Nemiah opened her mouth, but no sound came out. Elder Trianor cleared his throat.

The clansman's accusing gaze swung up to meet the elder's. "And you didn't leave him any choice. Jhared Denaban ran across most of Avelos alone to warn you of treachery; he saved our patrol and the Bearer. And you let the council cut him up for it. You left him no other way out." The soldier made a sound of disgust. "Now. So long as you don't mean to have me arrested right here, I'll go. If you change your minds, I'll be in the garrison awaiting orders to march north or south. Seems we're determined to destroy ourselves, but no one can decide whether to do it from the outside in or the inside out. Good day to you both."

Nemiah watched him stride away, her vision blurring. "There was some honesty."

Elder Trianor looked grim. "When your tool is a sword rather than subtlety, it's easy to have that kind of honesty."

"No, Elder. Nothing about that was easy." Nemiah turned and looked up. "Do you intend to see him punished?"

"To what purpose? To salve my dignity? No."

"Some would call his words seditious. To defend a soldier accused of crimes against the council."

The elder offered Nemiah his troubled blue-grey gaze. "You and I know it's more complicated than that, don't we, Lady?"

She wanted to answer that what she had done in Murita had been necessary. That it was a small step to return Avelos to the right Path, but she was no longer certain it was so: Jhared Denaban was gone and could not return without facing death; an orphaned Shorn child shivered in a dank prison; and three more babes had already been named for the knife.

"Indeed. More complicated." With a sigh, Nemiah turned away from the elder and continued walking.

7.

FRIENDS AND HERETICS

Nemiah parted from Elder Trianor bearing his promises to share what he learned about the man Lusian. Then she marched straight to Kaliska to order her Shadow Guards to begin investigating. She had just set her hand on the door to Kaliska's rooms beside the infirmary, when a high, urgent voice accosted her.

"Lady Nemiah! Thank the spheres I've found you. The Bearer of Cael's Blade has been asking for you all morning."

Merisel scampered up the hall, her butter-colored plaits fluttering back from her round face. Nemiah halted, guilt and worry filling her.

"What's happened? Is she . . .?"

"It's all right, Lady. No storms yet." The young girl reached Nemiah's side and wove a hasty spiral. "The Lady Bearer told me not to return until I found you and to find you before we all return. She says you have something to tell her."

"Do you mean she has something to tell me?"

"No, Lady."

"I see." Nemiah sighed. "Thank you, child."

Leita's apartments perched at the top of the tower opposite Nemiah's own, at the end of a stairway that curled upward in a narrow, slippery spiral. Since her return, the Bearer had refused the offer to move her quarters down to the east corridor, just as she had refused the aid of a dedicated acolyte or the company of one of the temple's hounds.

"Cael's Bearer was never meant to walk a straight Path," Leita had said, turning her back on the novice selected to help her. "I will not take a guide, Nemiah. I am meant to be the guide."

Nemiah hadn't argued. So much had been stolen from her friend; she would not also steal her dignity. Leita must have sensed something of her thoughts—might have sensed pity—for the expression on her scarred features had darkened.

"Once I would have been given a skull-topped staff and a raven to assist me. The one I can have made. Will you find me the other?"

Nemiah had pressed her lips together. Whatever she answered would hurt both of them, and Leita's balance was precarious. Her moods, always quick-changing, since her capture could flash from deep brooding to wild fury. The destruction that often accompanied her fury Leita had ruefully named her storms. Nemiah strived to shield her friend from the things most likely to unbalance her: Leita had not yet returned to the sanctuary or the Higher Circle. When she left her rooms at all, it was only to sit in the inner courtyard, her face turned up toward the stars that she would never see again. They did not speak of what Leita had suffered at the hands of Commander Ciam. And neither of them had dared to broach the issue of Leita's association with Yarla, of heresy and misplaced alliances. Those questions festered still.

Now, Nemiah wiped her palms against the soft wool of her gown, gathered herself, and began to climb the tower stairs.

Dewy strains of an ancient melody reached her on the landing, arresting her steps. The pearl and silver sounds of the flute strung themselves in idyllic strands. Stories hid within the old music, stories that Tumal's purges had never been able to extinguish. Some comfort could be found in that knowledge, even now. A low voice murmured and the music halted abruptly. Footsteps approached the door, and before Nemiah knocked, the door opened.

A fierce green gaze, glittering and imperious, pinned her. Nemiah recognized the spirit of a warrior glaring down at her. Then Ziabela's forbidding features relaxed. Quickly, she stepped aside to allow Nemiah into the room.

"Lady, she will be glad you've come."

"Thank you, Ziabela. What has she—?"

The Shorn woman shook her head quickly, a warning.

"You may torment Ziabela with all the expected questions," called the low voice from further in the apartments. "Or you may light a candle and come to receive the truth from the oracle herself."

Nemiah sent her best attempt at a reassuring smile toward Zia and stepped into the receiving room.

The Bearer kept her chambers simple and orderly. Even in this room where she greeted her guests, nothing sat on a shelf or took up space on the mantel unless it had a purpose. In the furniture, the blankets, and the shutters, the colors were all shades of earth and night. The only splash of sunlit color hung on the wall, a series of intricate tapestries designed from the stories of the creation and woven by Leita herself before she had become the Bearer. With a pang, Nemiah saw that one of the tapestries had been viciously slashed in a wide arc from one side to the other, leaving bright threads dangling. She looked about for the knife that could do such damage and spied Cael's Blade discarded on a side table. She had presented the sacred weapon to the Bearer at her return to the high temple. She had thought it might help Leita to find her place again. It had not. So far as she knew, the Blade had only been lifted to destroy the tapestry.

Leita sat in the deep casement of a window, dressed in a loose gown of midnight wool. Her black hair, hacked short by her captors, had been evenly trimmed and brushed smooth to the nape of her neck. The best of the day's dreary light folded over her cheek and into her lap, where her long fingers lay quiet on the pages of a book. Nemiah swallowed. Today, no sash of blue silk hid the bruised, sunken lids forever closed over empty sockets. The bones of Leita's face strained her fine skin, and although she retained her harsh, dry wit, at times her head would turn toward nothing and she would go quiet, as though disappearing somewhere inside herself or onto some distant Path. Nemiah had learned to stifle her outward response to the sight of this new Leita, but her heart ached with it.

As she crossed the room to the Bearer, an army of scents assailed her: the pungent smell of pine from little pots on the desk to her left and on a table near the hearth; the sweet, crisp scent of mint from a candle burning by a doorway; and the moist, mossy smell of herbs from a bowl on the top of the wardrobe. The powerful scents all competed with one another. Nemiah longed for fresh air.

She coughed softly before bending to touch her cheek to Leita's.

"You needn't be so solicitous," the Bearer said, lifting her face unerringly toward Nemiah. "I know where you are. Your clothes smell like incense and wood smoke and a little of . . . mold. Where did he take you?"

Nemiah straightened. "So Kaliska's been here?"

"Yes. She came a short while ago to tend her favorite flower. She said the Minister of the Teaching had whisked you off. Did he come to convince you to give up Ziabela or was he looking for answers about more personal matters?"

Ziabela had busied herself preparing tea at the hearth, but Nemiah saw the woman flinch at the Bearer's bald question.

"What he wanted had nothing to do with Ziabela. He had something other to show me."

Leita drew back a little. "Oh? Tell me."

"Later."

"Shall we send Zia away so that we might talk?"

"No. She is safest here. I don't want her to leave these apartments unless it is with a detail of Arionade. Zia, do you understand me?"

"I do, Lady." The scribe's tone bundled the same energy as ever, but she too had changed since Parnas Pass. She had grown shy and awkward with Nemiah and had swiftly offered herself as servant to Leita when the Bearer seemed willing to accept her. The subtle defiance that once colored Zia's every response had gone. In its place was an uncharacteristic sense of uncertainty, or perhaps it was better named surprise, as if her own choices had startled her. She had stayed with Nemiah when she might have fled and been free.

"Safest?" Leita snapped. "You mean because even Abrigado's City Guards wouldn't dishonor themselves by harming the poor blind priestess and her serving woman?"

Anger and self-scorn often heralded the start of one of the Bearer's storms. Nemiah pushed her hands along the folds of her gown, willing tranquility into her tone. "I mean that if they come for me, you will be the authority in the high temple and will be able to offer her the greatest protection. What book is that on your lap? I don't recognize the hand."

"I've been told it is a history of the temples in the lands of Clan Aglar by Drus. But I suppose Zia could have been humoring me."

"You're still searching for Sabela's temple? For the killing winds?"

"That is why you sent me north, is it not?"

You sent me north. An accusation there that had not yet been fully voiced. "Zia is reading to you, then. From these books?"

"No, I can sense the flow of the dry ink on the page. Of course Zia reads to me! You aren't really saying I should worry over what mysteries she gleans after you've allowed her so far into our circle, Nemiah. Stop evading the things that must be spoken! I have lost my sight, not my mind. Do not treat me like an addled child!"

"I am treating you like a person recovering from a grave assault."

Because I do not want to treat you like a Bearer who has committed heresy.

"I am as recovered as I will ever be." Leita shoved the book from her lap. It thudded to the floor. "Some darkness will not abate."

"Very well," Nemiah said, still quiet. "Then let us talk about your return to the Higher Circle. You could start by rejoining the devotions. And perhaps . . . perhaps it is time you consider taking an Arionad."

Leita gave a humorless laugh. "If I am unable to serve Riana as one type of Bearer you will have me serve as another? I think not. Even were there an Arionad willing to take on Cael's Blade, it is not my role on this Path to bear daughters for you to fill the sanctuary."

"That was not my intention! Leita, the days ahead are uncertain ones for the temple. For all of Avelos. It would be good for you to have a capable guard at your side. We have already suffered one attack."

The Bearer smiled slowly, a pale shadow of the expression that had once consumed everyone around her. Genuine power had existed in Leita's gaze. That was why the northerners had burned it away.

"Ziabela," she called, "you have drawn out the preparation of that tea quite long enough. Would you please pour for us and then take yourself to my study?"

The Shorn woman did as she was asked, evading Nemiah's glance before closing the door between them. The Bearer nodded at the sound of the door latch catching. "Stop this absurd talk of Arionade, Nemiah. You don't mean it."

Despite herself, Nemiah bristled. "I am protecting you."

"It is too late for protection."

Painful that, and true. "Leita, I will not do this now. I am the Lady of Avelos. Some things I cannot know without taking action."

"I need you to ask me. Ask me the question, Nemiah."

"Leita! Anything else. Choose anything else to speak of!"

When the Bearer stood, her head lifted like a hound sniffing the air. When she stepped away from the casement, she moved slowly but with confidence. Only then did Nemiah recognize the purpose of the various scents arranged about the room. The pine and candles and herbs created a map of sorts. With scent, Leita had transformed the imperceptible back into the perceptible. She stopped beside Nemiah's chair.

"Ciam's men were creative in their torments."

"Oh, Leita—"

"Four clanguards were assigned as my keepers. At first, they only used me to control Lieutenant Sevar and the patrol, threatening, taunting, occasionally beating me to prove they would carry out their threats. Sevar tried to shield me, tried to shield all of us. The clanguard liked that. They used violence against me to provoke him. One morning, I thought they would kill him outright. Aglar's men had already murdered Forest Guard at the fortress, after all. So when the opportunity came to break free, I called upon the goddess's power and opened the doors to their terror. It almost worked. Those clansmen I could reach were lost, weeping with uncontrollable fear. They hated me for it. But there were too many. Ciam had anticipated our attempt to escape and had men on watch nearby. They killed Twitch and Carn that day. And then . . . then they . . ."

The Bearer slammed her hand down on the little side table and swept it across the surface. Cael's Blade flew into the air, narrowly missed Nemiah, and clattered against the stone hearth. Embers colored the steel a bloody red. Nemiah looked at the Blade and back at the Bearer and shivered with a new, terrible understanding: they had used Cael's own weapon to blind her.

"After that," Leita whispered, "I became a challenge for them. They bet to see which of them would unravel me. They came at any hour, usually when I had just drifted into sleep. So I learned not to sleep. Sometimes they would drug what food they gave me. Just enough to leave me helpless, not enough to steal awareness. So I learned not to eat.

"Do you understand? They could not forgive me for exposing their fears. It would have been easy to push them into killing me. To make Cael's Escape my own."

With a keening heart, Nemiah stretched out her hand to her friend. The Bearer recoiled at the light touch.

"I'm sorry," Nemiah murmured, drawing back.

Leita braced herself, as though fighting off memories she could not flee. "I did not choose escape then because I believed that I still had a critical task to complete.

Now that I am home and useless, I recognize my blind arrogance—" She gave one caustic laugh. "I wonder whether that task is truly mine . . . or if I care that it is. Nemiah, I need you to ask me about the things you have tried so hard to avoid."

"Leita, you are asking me to give you a reason to live by breaking you."

"I am already broken. I am asking you to help me gather the pieces and move forward."

Silence fell. Nemiah stared at her hands in her lap, glad in that moment Leita could not see her expression. "Very well. Tell me how long you have been working to destroy Riana."

The taut lines of Leita's body eased. She nodded as she sank into the chair beside Nemiah, her arms outstretched to check the way. "I understand you see it so. And I understand why. But it is not Riana's destruction we seek. It is the restoration of the Unbroken One. The one who came before the goddess. The one from whom all existence sprang."

"The temple does not acknowledge an Unbroken One. It does not exist in any of our Teachings or on any of our maps."

"There are maps? Then the archive hasn't been emptied? Nothing lost?"

"Clever," Nemiah said dryly. "And unnecessary. I know our journeys are easily lost and our teachings swayed. Leita, be certain I understand how swiftly our knowledge is corrupted. Yet—"

"Yet to give up the beliefs you've been taught since childhood is to give up who you are?"

"No! I am not the Lady of Avelos merely because I can recite the doctrines. I have been touched by Riana. She has given me her gifts. I could not turn my back on her any more than I could turn my back on you. I cannot comprehend how you have done it. Tell me why."

Why have you betrayed me?

The rain tapped and clicked against the window as it turned to sleet. The receiving room was warm and close. Nemiah hoped the Bearer might save them both by deciding not to answer.

"The first time I felt the web unraveling I was just six winters," Leita finally started. "It was at the chapterhouse in the Parnas Mountains where I'd been sent to be tested as a Pathwalker. I'd been given a break from all the questions, from the prodding and the potions, and had raced into the forest with one of the new puppies. Cliva. A sweet, brindled thing. We played without any thought of danger, as only children can. Whatever we collided with I never saw, but I felt it. At first it was like a thicket of spider webs. Sticky and binding. Then a tearing pain and a fog of confusion. My spirit ripped and flung across . . . centuries. I don't remember how I broke free, but I awoke in the darkness with the Mistress of Novices, a pack of Arionade, and two of the temple's best tracking hounds crouched over me. Two days had passed. Cliva was dead."

Nemiah sat back in her chair, appalled. "You were untrained. The tests had opened you too far and pushed you into a journey. You should never have been left unsupervised at such a time."

"That's what the Mistress said. Then she looked at the poor contorted body of little Cliva and said that after I had fallen, the pup must have grown hungry and eaten something poisonous in the forest."

"Why did you not believe that it was just as she said?"

"Oh, Nemiah. I was a child. Of course I tried to accept it. But I knew something was wrong. I was already weaving." She waved her hands in the approximate direction of the damaged tapestries. "I could sense when the warp and weft were in harmony and when they were not. What I felt in the forest was something so terribly misshapen that nothing could exist within it. It killed Cliva. It nearly killed me."

"Did you try to explain that?"

"I tried for a time to make the Mistress of Novices understand, but even young children can perceive when others are uncomfortable around them. As the only Pathwalker among the young ones, I was already strange. My insistence on this wrong thing in the weaving made me frightening. Some of the acolytes began to whisper that perhaps I had poisoned Cliva. They were scared of me, and I had not yet learned how to turn their fear into power. So I stopped speaking about it."

The Bearer went quiet, still facing the fire as though she could see the dancing flames. The silence extended. A log popped and settled.

"Leita?"

"I did not experience the unraveling again—that I remember—in my childhood. The next time was something over ten years ago. Just before we lost Lady Pahlina and you were appointed Lady. It was a failed Becoming. After the initiate's failure, the Arionade and I took him to the heart of the valley, where the river touches the forest. I had finished the prayers. His blood was still on my knife. This time I recognized the sensation of the Paths shifting. This time I didn't just feel the binding webs and the pain, I saw a preternatural mist writhing above the ground, obscuring and revealing the body of the maimed boy before me. Again, I felt that horrible wrongness. A kind of agony that overwhelms every other sensation. I had no idea what it meant, but more than anything, I yearned to throw myself into that mass of Paths and put them all back into their proper places. It took all my will and the blade at my throat to force myself to run away. The Arionade found me wandering so close to the Gate they had to leave off their vigil over the failed initiate and carry me back to the city."

"What did Pahlina say of it?"

"That I had seen Cael's influence. That of course a failed Becoming would be marked by a change in the Paths, and of course the wrongness of it would hurt. She said the fact that I could perceive the demon's hand so clearly proved I was meant to be the Bearer. To guide others away from it."

"But you didn't accept Pahlina's explanation. Despite the fact that she was Lady of Avelos and a strong Pathwalker in her own right."

The Bearer twisted to face Nemiah, her sunken eyelids twitching. "Nothing about that wound had to do with Cael. I only suspected it then. Now I have borne his Blade for long enough to know I am right."

"In what way?"

"In a way you will not be able to hear if I tell you," the Bearer said crisply.

"Do you mean to say there is wisdom in the creature we have so long cursed? Beauty even?"

Leita's head jerked upward.

Nemiah smiled faintly. She could not remember a time when anything she said had surprised the Bearer. "No, it wasn't your queen bee Yarla who helped me see beauty in Cael's work."

Leita tilted her head. "Was it my Shorn Pathwalker?"

Leita hadn't fought Nemiah's decision to help Jhared Denaban escape, but her continuing possessiveness of the man was another thing that made Nemiah uneasy. "In part. Why are you so certain this disorder in the Paths is not a manifestation of Cael's strength?"

"Because what I witnessed was the horror of annihilation. It was not the wisdom of change or the beauty of the unexpected. It was a mass of threads slipping loose from the web, unraveling the whole of the world. It was not merely disorder. It was a sign of—"

"True Chaos?"

Another start of surprise. "I think so. Yes. Where on this Path did you learn of True Chaos?"

Nemiah stood and picked up the volume Leita had pushed to the floor. "Not on this Path, precisely. It was in the description of a sacred journey. In an ancient book of map notes buried deep in the archive. Before the theft."

"Ah, I had forgotten about that one." Leita's expression was ironic. "I did hope you might find it sooner."

"You knew of it? This treasure from the past. And you never shared it?"

"I tried. There have been many things I've tried to share with you, Nemiah."

Nemiah pressed her lips on a quick retort. For too long she had foolishly equated openness to new knowledge with a deviation from her principles. "The book was a gift from your heretics?"

"A small one. Yes."

"How did you find them? Leita, how many followers does Yarla have?"

"You might say we found each other. I was seeking an understanding of the wounds in the weaving. They needed my skill on the Paths. They gave to me the Unbroken One."

"And their followers? Who else in the temple acknowledges the idea of the Unbroken?"

Leita didn't respond. Instead, she felt around on the chair beside her until her hands landed on the small lap loom with the grey and red pattern in it. She drew the loom close and began to untangle the dangling tails of yarn.

Nemiah squeezed her eyes shut and opened them again. The things she needed most to know Leita was not readily going to give her. How far was she willing to press? Unfazed, the Bearer continued to organize the threads in the loom's pattern. Nemiah wondered how she did so without error.

"What will you do with me?" Leita asked mildly. "It is within your right to have me exiled and my name scarred in the book of the Higher Circle."

"Do you really wish me to speak it aloud when you know what I must say? You have already paid a debt and more for the sake of the temple. I will not also scar your name. You must only disavow the heretics. You must tell me what you know of their intentions."

The Bearer gave one dry chuckle. "I believe what I miss most about being able to see is the ability to read your face. You cannot make me deny what I know or spill secrets that are not mine. That much of myself, at least, I will keep."

Nemiah rubbed at her eyes. "Leita, we need not be at cross-purposes. Please. Do you understand? I know the web is unraveling. I accept that what you saw was a sign of it. Just as the killing winds are a sign of it."

We are the mortal webweavers. Amalia had told her as much about the Avelune.

"Then the Unbroken One," Leita gasped, "do you believe—"

"No!" The word fell harsh and heavy into the space between them. Leita jumped. "No," Nemiah said more gently. "Do not mistake me. We are the cause of our own impending destruction. I do not adhere in any way to your heresy."

Everything in Nemiah's line of sight stretched into a long blur, like paint smeared across a wall, like every alternative to this single moment overlaid on each other. In this instant, she might walk out of the room, berate Leita for her obstinance, capitulate to the heretics, stand her ground. Other, darker alternatives existed as well. On some Paths, this moment led to bloodshed. Nemiah looked away in horror. "Why did you force us to this now, Leita? My friend, I warned you."

The Bearer slumped backward, putting her scarred face into shadow. For a moment they were both silent.

"It is a strange thing, torture," Leita began again quietly. "The men who perpetrate it don't look like monsters. They appear like any other men: they laugh and cry, as other men do. They talk about their family and their sweethearts. They sing to their horses. When you have been hurt by such as those, screaming until there is no breath left in you, how do you encounter any person again without recognizing the monster in them? How do you stop yourself from turning away in terror and disgust? How do you consider the weaving worth saving?

"Only a portion remains of the person I was, Nemiah. That is all I have left. Will you force me to surrender it?"

Unshed tears burned in Nemiah's eyes, tears of sadness and helplessness and anger. "Does it not matter that I love you? That every day of your absence I have missed the wise disorder you brought to my life?"

"Perhaps one day it will matter. Now, it is not enough."

"Leita, please understand. I cannot afford to wage another battle in the temple. All my advisors must speak with one voice if we are to survive the things that are coming. I need you with me. With Riana. Please."

The Bearer turned her head away. One hand came up slowly and pressed hard against her brow. "Forgive me. It is difficult sometimes to think through the headaches. Would you please call Ziabela to me before you leave?"

Nemiah sat unmoving, then with a silent sigh, she stood. "Leita, may I—"

"Later, my lady. I am sure we will speak of this again. When you have decided what to do with me."

Nemiah gazed down on her Bearer with no meaningful comfort to offer. Frustration overwhelmed her. She marched to the study to call Ziabela and scowled when the Shorn woman belatedly grabbed up a book to pretend that she had been reading.

"Ziabela, every delicate conversation you overhear is one more weapon Abrigado will possess to use against us if the City Guard forcibly takes you. Have you thought on that?"

"Yes, my lady."

Nemiah recoiled. "Yes?"

The scribe gave Nemiah a fierce, hard look. "I will honor your trust, Lady. If they take me, they will learn nothing."

And if they hurt you as the Bearer has been hurt? Will you honor our trust then? Nemiah swallowed down the words. "Please see to the Bearer."

"Of course." Ziabela rose, towering over Nemiah. "Cool cloths and quiet music sometimes ease the headaches."

Nemiah left the chamber, her own sight blurred nearly to uselessness by the Paths sprouting into existence all about her.

Leita offered no acknowledgment of her leaving.

8.

KNIVES AND CHAINS

In the darkness of that first, battered night after the killing winds struck Parnas Pass, with injured soldiers and exhausted elders sleeping in the rooms all about her, with Leita returned to her as a fractured shadow, Nemiah had gone to Adan Rumar, High Chieftain of Avelos, to tear away the veils that had bound Avelos for more than a century. She had been prepared to do whatever was required to prove to Rumar that Amalia's story was the goddess's truth. She had scrubbed the dirt and blood from her body, brushed her bright hair into long waves, and donned her green gown. The high chieftain had been alone, as she knew he would be; the grey hours he kept for himself. Papers had littered the table in his room, letters waiting to be sealed and sent by swift couriers to the clan leaders, to the Sahisten border, and to the north.

He had not attempted to hide his grief from her. It had sharpened the hard edges of him and lit sparks in his pale eyes. He nodded her into the room, then poured them both wine and gestured her to a chair. Bruises and wind-torn gashes interrupted the strong plains of his face. She knew he would have stayed in the thick of the killing storm, shredded by the crystal-sharp knives, until his men and his council had made their way to safety. Clues to his weariness could be seen in his overtight grip on the cup and the angle of his body against the arm of his chair.

"I've had the last report," he said, his voice flat. "Aglar and Lasla are both dead. A handful of their men managed to escape. They've fled north."

Nemiah nodded. It was what her Arionade had told her. "Will you pursue them?"

"No," he replied shortly. "I've no soldiers left to do it. It will be days before General Nadel can respond to the message I've sent. The best I can do just now is to remind Clan Hilera about the consequences of providing shelter to traitors." He lifted his cup to his lips, swallowed, and slammed the cup back onto the desk. "What we do with the few traitors who fled isn't the pressing issue, of course."

"I know," Nemiah said quietly. "You must decide whether to pull forces from the Sahisten border."

"Yes, I must decide. Do I risk opening us to attack by Sahiste? If Javahari learns that the border defenses are weakened, he's likely to seize the opportunity to push through. Do I risk it? Or do I leave Aglar Tower in traitors' hands? Leave more loyal men to die? Watch as Avelos breaks apart?"

Rumar sagged in his seat, and for a moment Nemiah saw how dazed he was. "I did not believe even Ondal Aglar could go so far, Lady. Not treason. Not this. But for fifty Shorn soldiers and the killing winds, we are dead tonight."

Nemiah looked at the wine in her cup, deep red like old blood. The blood that stained Riana's altar. The blood crusted on Leita's face. There were things she had come here to say. "I have thought on that too."

Rumar lifted his head. "Your Lady Bearer, is she . . . recovering?"

It was a small thing but a meaningful one that on this night the high chieftain would ask after Leita. "She is alive and safe. For tonight that is all I can hope for."

"I did not believe Aglar could go so far," Rumar repeated, rubbing his thumb and forefinger over his eyes. "You know you should not have come, Lady Nemiah. You should be distancing yourself from me. While Abrigado makes kindling of my position, he will happily snap the remnants of your power as well."

"None of your people know I've come."

"Oh?" Rumar's head turned a fraction. He hadn't expected that.

Nemiah felt the Path swinging, knew the moment was approaching. "Adan, is Clan Aglar's brutality truly unexpected? This is not the first time we have betrayed and tortured our own."

He shifted to look at her directly. "There may be generations of conflict among the clans, Nemiah, but this—"

"I don't mean clan conflict. For a century and a half, we have named a portion of our own people cursed, blamed them for our ills, tortured them, and cut them apart. In naming the Shorn wrong and wicked—something different from ourselves—did we make it easier for Clan Aglar to do the same to us?"

Rumar's expression was open at first, considering. She saw her words reach him before he suddenly shook himself, as if flinging off cold water. His look grew wary. "Lady, what is it you hoped to find here?"

Nemiah took a swallow of the bitter wine. She could offer the one answer to his question, but this night demanded complete honesty. If she were to have any hope of reaching him, he needed to see the whole of her. She had come for herself as much as for Avelos. "I seek to remove veils and to share a burden, Adan."

"It has been near a decade since anyone believed sharing a burden with me might be a comfort."

"Tonight is not a night in which we will find comfort," she replied, "but perhaps we can offer Avelos our joint strength to face what is to come."

He hesitated, pushing one hand through his autumn-colored hair. "Perhaps. Yes. I think we must at least try."

"I would be grateful for that." She straightened in her chair, feeling the ache of her own bruises. Lady Amalia's story filled her. Once she spoke, nothing would be the same. The blood of babes had been shed upon the altar.

The ground heaved. From some distance, Nemiah felt her cup slip, heard it shatter. Around her, the Path split and split again: a shining blue vine shooting out new tendrils; a flock of doves dividing in the air; a span of ice fracturing in every direction. She swayed at the edge of her own moment, watching it unfurl: Adan Rumar overwhelmed by the truth of Amalia's innocence and compelled to share it; his words reaching scheming hearts, arousing anger and fear across the country; a good leader struck down in violence and a new high chieftain spouting lies; mobs roaming the streets, hunting those they blamed for their misfortunes; men and women screaming; children broken; scarred flesh burning.

"No! Oh no." Nemiah staggered back into her own moment, shaking at the evil she had seen. Here were the consequences for speaking the truth and ripping away old veils. A cry of protest rose in her throat. She swallowed it down. It could not be spoken. They sat at a point of influence, and she was the one with the power to cause more death. The high chieftain knelt beside her. When she looked into his eyes, knowing her horror was plain to see, he didn't recoil. Instead, he laid his hand over her trembling fingers, his expression one of concern. Reluctantly, she drew away. She could share no burden after all. This direction was barred. She would have to seek another way to change the Path.

What she had done after that, setting a cursed soldier free, had destroyed her tenuous link with the man, a good man, who had just begun to trust her.

The grey in the windows had turned to black before Nemiah finally returned to her own apartments to face the piles of correspondence that awaited her. Still robed for the evening devotion, she stood over her desk, sifting randomly through letters and reports. One letter caught her eye: it bore the seal of Clan Manitar but not the seal of Avelos. It did not come from the high chieftain but from his clan. Nemiah dropped the letter back onto the desk unopened. Prefect Falina Rumar, the high chieftain's aunt, was no ally.

As she turned away, Nemiah stumbled over nothing and barked her shin against the sharp corner of a drawer. She yelped in pain, annoyed and exhausted by the way every object around her endlessly shifted and multiplied as new Paths flared into existence. She longed to crawl into her bed, shut her eyes, and cling to her own moment until sleep claimed her. Instead, she considered the list of tasks that remained undone: a stack of reports and requests from the chapter houses to be addressed;

each of the members of her Higher Circle who must be pacified; and Kaliska, who must hear the news about Jholan's master thief, about Leita, and about Ziabela. Nemiah massaged the corner of her eyes with her fingers. Those tasks could wait. There was one other thing she would not put off.

The corridor to the barracks led past the kitchens, where guards now watched at every hour, past the priestess's dining hall and the Arionade's mess, past Kaliska's infirmary and the passage to the guards' bathing rooms. The lamps in the corridor had already been turned low. Men's voices rumbled out from the common room. A hound barked once. The two guards who encountered Nemiah stopped short and each gave her a thoughtful spiral. Since Rom's return, the Arionade had grown accustomed to the Lady of Avelos walking through their section of the temple compound.

Before the barracks entrance, the statue of Lord Arion swearing his life to Riana stood sentinel. Rom's quarters sat just beyond. As Nemiah approached, she saw the door was slightly open, allowing a wedge of pale light to fall across the dim corridor. It surprised and pleased her; on most nights, Rom would have retired by now. As she reached the door, a familiar voice rose in an unfamiliar tone.

"... and there's the gentleman, dripping wet and mad as a cat in the rain. The stable boy looks him up and down and, without blinking an eye, says, 'If you please, sir, remove yourself and your mare to the paddock where you'll both have more room.'"

The answering chuckle rose from a different throat. A dear sound, that one. Rare and precious. Nemiah was smiling as she stepped into the room.

The two men sat on either side of Rom's large desk, the fire warm and crackling in the small hearth beside them. Commander Evorales, still in his whites, had slung his cloak over the back of his chair. In one hand he clutched a small cup, filled from the decanter on the desk. It was the blackberry wine Rom's family sent from the mountains. Rom did not have a cup in hand, nor was he dressed for duty. The open collar of his shirt revealed the stark line of his throat. His neat beard could not conceal the hollows of his cheeks or the waxen tone of his skin.

Facing the door, Rom spied her first. His black eyes caught and held her. Commander Evorales, seeing his captain's sudden change in demeanor, turned and scrambled to his feet. Rom did not stand, but his spiral was precise and not only for Riana.

"Captain Rom, Commander Evorales."

"Lady Nemiah, forgive me. I didn't intend you should find me so disordered." The blunt-featured commander set his cup on the desk with a look of chagrin.

"It is well, Evorales. Even Lord Arion enjoyed wine and the companionship of his comrades." Nemiah had not heard Rom laugh since before poison had nearly ended his life. The commander had earned her debt.

The man offered another prompt spiral. "Captain?"

"Yes, Evorales. You are dismissed. In the morning see to moving the men. Make certain Fial knows he's to include them in drills. All of them."

"Of course, sir. We'll make them sweat, eh?"

"You will." Rom returned the other man's salute; and then his attention was for Nemiah.

"Moving the men?" she asked, as Evorales closed the door behind him.

"The unattached men among our displaced folk in the guest quarters. Some of them have started causing trouble among the families. It's not all their fault. They're heartsick and angry and dangerously bored. I've chosen to move them into the barracks and start them drilling with us before any harm comes of it."

"After which, they'll have no energy to cause trouble."

"Exactly," Rom replied. "And perhaps some of them will find a new direction. We'll not be able to shelter them forever."

Her Arionad gazed up at her from where he sat, his long legs stretched beneath his desk, his forearms braced on top. "My lady, it is good to see you tonight."

She smiled faintly. "I'm sorry it's so late."

"No debt, my lady. Not ever."

She set her palms flat on her side of the desk to remain steady. "It's well past dinner. What would you like tonight? Do you care for a game of gems?"

"No more games, Nemiah. Please. All these weeks I have not been an Arionad to you. I cannot be yet, but I should very much like it if tonight we might start back in that direction."

Nemiah gazed at the tall, gaunt figure of her captain. Illness had eaten the flesh from him until he was no more than leather and bone. She hadn't dared to hope that he would ever return to her side. She still wasn't certain whether he would regain the strength to allow it, but she would never reveal a moment of doubt to this man who had never once doubted her.

"I would also welcome that step, Captain."

There was a pause as Rom slowly straightened, pushed his chair out from the desk, and stood. Although his features remained studiously neutral, his breathing sped. Nemiah restrained the urge to offer her arm, knowing it was the surest way to cut him.

He led her into the chamber off the receiving room. It was sparsely furnished with a soldier's bed, a chest, and a table with two chairs. Only a brazier warmed the room. Rom's sword and captain's cloak hung on hooks by the door. On the shelves above the bed lay a book on the breeding and training of hounds and one on the history of the Arionade. Many unusual objects filled the shelves. Nemiah's favorites included a scrap of vellum painted brightly in a child's hand, a statue of a dog with a lolling tongue carved from bone, and a lump of copper formed roughly in the shape of a bumblebee. Each had been a gift from one of Rom's nieces. When Nemiah looked at the room, she saw it as the space of a man who kept his life uncluttered, but not empty of love or beauty.

Beside her, Rom was still standing, waiting for her. She took a seat in one of the chairs. He shut the door to the outer room and lowered himself into the other chair.

"I can see the weight you are carrying tonight, my lady. Perhaps we might imagine ourselves somewhere earlier on this Path and you could share your worries, as once you would have."

"I would not burden you before you are ready for it, Rom."

He gave her a rueful glance. "That weight, at least, I can still bear."

She couldn't deny the cool rush of relief she felt at being able to speak without guarding herself. She told her Arionad of her fears for Leita and her dilemma about how to guide her Bearer. She spoke of the conflicts with her advisors in the Higher Circle and her doubt that she might ever bring them together. And finally, knowing it would strike Rom hardest and knowing she must tell him anyway, she shared what she had seen at Aelend and what she had learned of the thief called Lusian.

Her Arionad, who had listened intently without interruption, scowled at Jholan's story.

"This Lusian is the one who poisoned us?"

"It is possible. The boy's story fits."

Rom went quiet.

"Do you remember him? Did you see him in the temple? A man with two fingers on his left hand?"

"I'm afraid I remember little of that day, my lady, or many of the days following it. I was just considering whether the thief might have some connection to the Clan Amerre man our Shadow Guards caught buying ancient books from the northerners earlier this fall."

"The clanguard? Ranz?" Nemiah drew one knee up to her chest and hugged her arms around it. The sale of rare volumes from the north to the south was a mystery Kaliska's spies had not yet unwoven. "I can't imagine it. Jholan said this Lusian claimed to have something to do with Sona. What would Clan Amerre have to do with Sona?"

"What would anyone have to do with Sona? Lusian lied to protect his true purpose."

"I suppose if that is so, then our thief and our clanguard may have nothing to do with one another, yet still have a common connection. Perhaps someone else is paying for rare volumes. Lusian and Clan Amerre may be naught but suppliers."

Rom made a sound of agreement. "The question remains, why is someone in search of our ancient history?"

"Yarla says it is to push this Path toward True Chaos."

Instantly, Nemiah regretted naming the heretic. Yarla and her followers had tended Rom when he walked the edge between the Paths of the living and the Hidden Paths of the dead. They had kept him alive when four other Arionade had died. She could not blame him for developing a connection to the heretics, but after her conversation with Leita that morning, she was in no mood to hear them praised.

At her abrupt silence, Rom leaned forward. His eyes did not waver from hers.

"She saved my life, Nemiah. I did not sell my heart or my beliefs in exchange for it."

Nemiah glanced aside. "You read me too well. Even when my thoughts are unworthy. Of course you didn't. I could never think otherwise."

"To be fair, her people did not ask it of me. They are not as fanatical as the Arionites or Cael's followers. They know the material from which they work is flawed. They interpret what they can and strive toward what they believe is our best hope."

"Yet somewhere along the way they lost the truth," Nemiah said.

"Yes. Yes, I fear that's so."

Nemiah swallowed back further comment. "I will speak with Kaliska about the possible associations between our book thief and book buyer. Perhaps it will help her to decipher their purpose."

Rom nodded. Belatedly, Nemiah saw how his shoulders had stiffened and how one hand made a fist against his thigh. A current of remorse found her. Rom would never voice his pain.

"The night is slipping by, Captain. I should leave you."

As she stood, her Arionad reached out and caught her by the wrist. "You needn't leave."

Despite his pain, or because of it, power still existed in his grip. Nemiah caught her breath.

Rom's characteristic scowl turned self-mocking. "My lady, from that look on your face, you give me credit for speedier healing than I can boast. Still, perhaps I could offer you a moment of peace and a sleep in which the Gate does not hound you."

Of course he had observed the signs that the Paths were spinning around her. The Bearer had taught him what to look for. She couldn't regret his knowing. The intensity of Rom's devotion was what bound Nemiah to her own moment.

"I would be glad to stay," she said, feeling the depth of her exhaustion in every limb. She longed for stillness, for a moment in which she saw only her own Path and not the blur of infinite possibilities.

He stood and, bending carefully over her, kissed her brow. "On another night, my lady, I will ask you once more for Riana's blessing. That night is somewhat further along our Path."

He wrapped his arms around her, and she relaxed against him, allowing him to bear her up. She stood enveloped in his devotion, her eyes closed, until abruptly, something tipped. Their embrace suddenly felt awkward, unbalanced. Nemiah straightened, understanding the change. It was her place now to protect him. Rom had already made his sacrifice. Amalia and the Arionad Ambri had given Nemiah a better knowledge of what the Lady of Avelos and Lord Arion were meant to be to one another.

Rom frowned at her as she stepped away. "Lady?"

She took his hand and led him to the bed, pressing him back until he sat. When he tried to draw her down beside him, she knelt at his feet and began to remove his boots.

"No," she said before he could protest. "There is balance in this."

"Lady, my oath—"

"*Our* oaths entwine our Paths. We must share one another's burdens. Your place is at my side, not behind me."

Nemiah stopped. She knew what she said was a truth retrieved from before the Exile, but something about her words to Rom did not fit the weaving.

"Not on this Path," he said, echoing her thoughts. "Do not imagine I have given you my devotion blindly all these years, Nemiah. I wear the face of the champion. I am not the consort or the guide. Not truly. I thought once that place might be meant for Enrian Nadel." He turned his gaze from her. "Perhaps not. But it has never been meant for me."

She hushed him with a finger to his lips, then unlaced her gown and let it slide from her shoulders. With only her thin shift outlining her body, she lay down beside him.

They spoke in quiet voices, no longer about their fears for the future or moments that did not fit or the things he desired that she could not give him. They spoke of family and hounds and the training of young men for the Arionade. Rom did not ask about the things he must still wonder—about a freed Shorn soldier and a treasonous Shorn scribe and all of the events of Parnas Pass. Someday soon he would ask and she would tell him, but not tonight.

Nemiah floated to sleep, aware of Rom's deep, even breathing and the weight of his head against her shoulder.

The Shearing took place at midday in the inner circle on the first day of the new moon. Rom was not present. No Arionade took part in this ritual.

Merisel set the warm, breathing bundle that was the first babe into Nemiah's arms. His head lolled gently against her breasts. His unfocused gaze moved vaguely across her face. The karianta berries had done their work.

Sun streamed from the oculus across the altar, lighting the dark stains on the stone from years of rituals. Nemiah's father had been a healer. Long before she became the Lady of Avelos, she had come to understand that an infected limb must sometimes be sacrificed to spare the patient. That was what she told herself every time she stood before the altar with the blade in her hand.

Kaliska stood beside her, sober and silent, ready to stitch the wound. To try to put back together what should never be cut apart. Nemiah laid the babe on the altar on his stomach as the members of the Higher Circle began the prayers. Their somber voices echoed up into the dome. Nemiah recalled from a memory not hers that it should have been joyous song echoing here. It should have been the moment when young wings spread and caught the breeze on their own for the first time. She parted the blanket, and the child's wings slid loosely down each side of his back. Small, blunt feathers: pale grey speckled with cinnamon. So soft. Tender muscle and cartilage bound them to his back.

Outside, something heavy battered the door of the inner circle. A voice barked an order and others answered. Steel rang against stone.

Cold sweat slicked Nemiah's body. Her vision fogged and cleared and fogged again. If she wasn't quick with the knife, the babe would bleed to death. It happened sometimes.

The noises in the corridor grew louder.

Tears ran unbidden down Nemiah's cheeks. No place existed in the world for an Avelun. If she sent the babe away uncut, it would be the obligation of any citizen who found him to kill him.

"Why are you waiting?" someone hissed, a voice she knew, a friend she had thought lost.

"Oh, Lady, if I speak the truth, I condemn them all!"

"Your silence has already condemned them."

The door of the inner circle burst open. Men in City Guard uniforms charged into the chamber, swords unsheathed. Merisel let out a squeak of fear.

The leader strode into the circle of priestesses, his boots punishing the flagstones. His cold gaze assessed the women. "Where is the Lady of Avelos?"

Merisel, small and brave and full of young confidence, leaped forward. "Leave this holy place! You will not touch our sacred Lady!"

The guard grinned. "Will I not?"

"Merisel, no!" Nemiah's warning went unheeded. The girl took another step toward the guard and his fist flew. Nemiah saw only the blur of it, then Merisel flying backward. Her body struck the stone altar and slithered to the floor.

Nemiah let out a cry and tried to go to the girl, but the commander turned on her.

"Give us the babe. You were meant to make him Shorn. Relinquish the babe and we will let your people live."

"I will not," Nemiah said, standing straight before the man's anger. "There will be no more blood spilled upon this altar!"

"Oh but there will be, dove. A sacrifice will be required."

The man's blade flashed in the candlelight. When he lunged toward her, Nemiah knew an instant of disbelief. The steel touched her, entered her. Her body screamed of heat, then cold, then shattering pain.

She staggered. This could not be her Path. She wasn't meant to die so futilely. If they killed her they would take the child. This could not be right; a sacrifice must have meaning. Anger rose up through her pain.

"Lady Nemiah!"

This could not be her Path. A sacrifice must have meaning.

"My lady, wake! There's danger!"

Nemiah opened her eyes. A man loomed above her. She yanked back her hand to strike him and he caught it. The candle on the table illuminated his profile. She gasped.

"It's me, Nemiah. Get up. Dress quickly. Something's happening in the sanctuary. I've sent Evorales with a detail to check it."

Nemiah sat up, blinking away her nightmare, panic still rushing through her veins. "What's happening? What time is it?"

"Just past hunters' hour." Rom tossed Nemiah her gown. In the faint light, she saw he had donned his white coat. He grabbed his sword belt from its hook. In the hall, the growl of men's voices and the quick thud of boots began to grow. She shuddered.

"Rom?"

"I don't know, Nemiah. It may be your thief returned or some new assault from the ones Yarla warned us about. I'm going out. Bar the door. I'll leave a detail with you."

"No, Rom. I can't stay here. I have to find—"

Before she could finish her protest, he had gone, moving with stiff determination and slamming the door shut behind him.

She yanked her gown over her head and pushed her feet into her slippers. It wasn't the thief. She was sure of it. The man who liked to be called Lusian had used poison and bragged about being sly. This invader wanted her to know he was coming. In the dead of night, while Riana slept, this one meant her to know his power and to feel fear. This was Toren Abrigado's doing.

Rom had left Rien and Avjay at the door. As she hurried out, they came to attention, looking stern and protective. With one sharp order, she cut off their attempts to stop her. Rien hesitated, his expression a little wild—invaders in the night were not something he had faced serving Lady Ansa—before falling in behind her.

The temple's stone walls kept their secrets. As she strode along the corridor, she couldn't yet hear anything from the sanctuary, only the sound of Arionade moving away from the barracks. If it were the City Guard pushing their way into the temple, however, the peace would not last much longer. She had only a few minutes to do the three things that most mattered.

At Kaliska's door, her pounding brought the healer out still tucking her shift into her breeches, her satchel slung over her shoulder. "Who needs care—Lady?"

"They've come, Kaliska. They're in the sanctuary."

The healer took a half-step backward. "The council?"

"I think so. Listen to me now. You must get Ziabela out of the temple. You must hide her in the city, or outside the walls if you can manage it."

"Nemiah, you are the one we must hide! Abrigado cannot get you in his power."

"No, Kaliska. If they take Zia, she will die. You know it. But City Guard ordered by the council will not dare to harm me. And I still have several ways that I might keep them from doing damage to the temple."

The healer blanched. "You intend to go with them."

"I told you I would. Can you do this?" Nemiah searched the older woman's even features.

Kaliska answered her gaze with unapologetic openness. Nemiah saw something she had never guessed at. If she had time to reflect, she imagined it wouldn't have been a surprise, but no time remained for reflection.

"I can. I will, Lady."

"Good. Take Avjay. And, Kaliska, if I am gone when you return, there is one other thing you must do."

The healer gave a nod. "Tell me."

"The three babes named for the Shearing this moon: they are too small."

"What?"

"They are all of them below the weight required by ritual law. They cannot be brought to the temple. Do you understand?"

"I understand and rejoice, Lady."

"Not yet, Kaliska. It is nothing more than a delay. We have no cause to rejoice. Just go, and have a care." She gave the woman a shove.

Kaliska and Avjay started toward the Bearer's tower. When they had turned the corner out of site, Nemiah smiled up at Rien. The bright-haired man, hand on sword, was drawn for battle.

"Lord Arionad, your duty now lies with the women and young ones of the high temple. Get to the east corridor and make certain everyone has barred themselves within the priestess's quarters. You will stay with them until this is over. I command you in Riana's name."

Rien's eyes widened, his objections rising. Then, without a word, he drew a breath, lowered his shoulders, and gave a small nod, as if to himself. Perhaps he was ordered after all, this Arionad. "In Riana's name, Lady. I will keep them safe. May the goddess smooth your way."

"And yours, Rien."

Nemiah watched him go. Then she closed her eyes, centered herself with a prayer, and ran for the sanctuary.

Only when she reached the main corridor did the sounds of the conflict echo along the carved walls: barked challenges and answering threats coming from the first circle, the holy place where every devotion rose to Riana. It was the only part of the sanctuary with direct access to the streets. Nemiah did not hear steel. *Please, Riana, not steel against your servants.* The corridor was deserted. She crept through the door that led behind the altar.

They didn't notice her, small and silent behind the large stone. Rom and his men formed a barrier preventing the invaders from breaking into the rest of the temple. A slim barrier. The captain must have split his numbers to secure the other accesses into the compound. Twice as many attackers surrounded him, hard men, alert and ready. City Guards. The Arionade had apparently caught them in the midst of their vandalism. The devotion candles had been crushed and the glass lamps shattered. Oil spread in long, glossy pools across the floor and dripped down the white walls. Near the outer doors, two Arionade lay unmoving. They would have been the night watch on the stairs facing Elders' Circle. Nemiah couldn't see who they were.

Small ears of flame quivered over one of the oil pools and sparkled across broken glass. Nemiah caught the sheen of summer blues and brilliant greens and jerked her gaze upward. High above the arched entry, Riana's eye, that glorious colored glass window created centuries ago with techniques long forgotten, remained only as a jagged hole, open to the night.

Fury beat like wings in Nemiah's chest. It was an adequate substitute for courage, she decided as she strode out from behind the altar.

"Why have Riana's servants been savaged? Why has Riana's high temple been profaned by those who are meant to keep order?"

To a man, the line of Arionade turned, pride and shock interwoven on their features. Nemiah didn't look at Rom. She knew the expression his face would hold. The leader of the City Guard appeared pleased.

"Lady Nemiah Gabriana, the Council of Clans demands that you relinquish the Shorn scribe called Ziabela Marcalo so that she may answer for crimes against the council."

He was an unremarkable-looking man of middle years with the sandy hair and hazel gaze that placed his origins anywhere among the central clans. His grip on his short sword was competent, and his tone in the face of Nemiah's sudden appearance spoke of unruffled confidence.

Nemiah pulled herself straighter. "What is your name, Officer? You have violated the sacred and will pay the debt for it."

"I am Commander Pedrin and I've done what I was ordered. The council said to get your attention. If I have it now, I'm to tell you to give up the scribe or my men will be forced to search the rest of the temple in a like manner."

Nemiah said a quick prayer and straightened her stance. "Ziabela Marcalo is no longer with us."

A faint smile curled the man's thin lips. "Dead, eh? A shame that. I suppose the council will have to be content with her body then."

"Riana accepts our spirits through the flames, Commander. We have no trace of her. Seek her spirit on the Paths, if you must."

"I think we must seek her in the women's quarters. If she is gone, perhaps there are other bodies we might find."

Some of the City Guards chuckled—low, threatening sounds.

Nemiah stepped through the line of her Arionade, each one of them tense and vigilant. Rom's desire to snatch her back behind their shield of swords was a near tangible force.

The threat of violence thrummed through the room. In a moment, the conflict would flare. *"Tumal in the temple all over again,"* Bena had said. The old Mapmaker had been right.

Nemiah knew what must be done. She met the commander's gaze, searching him for what she needed. It was not simply cruelty that moved the man, she thought. It was pleasure in doing his duty and unalloyed joy at the power he had been given, power that a man in his position could rarely wield. In such a man, it would be all too easy to call together his experiences of resentment or hostility. She needed another motivation. She hoped that deep within him something else existed.

"Commander, it is the duty of the City Guard to protect those who are vulnerable. Where is your pride in serving as our guardian?"

As she said the words, she held his gaze and called upon Riana's strength. At her invitation, the doors of his Paths burst open, pouring out his every experience of pride in his work, his confidence in his own strength, and his sense of duty to protect those less able than himself.

His own moments flooded him and his arrogant expression dissolved, turning first into one of uncertainty and then into one of beaming pride. "We are here to protect you and all of Avelos from the threat of traitors, Lady. Do not try to stop us. We have no wish to harm Riana's servants."

The commander's men murmured uneasily. Pedrin's head twitched toward the Arionade. From the corner of her eye, Nemiah saw one of Rom's men touch his sword. The commander frowned. Nemiah would have kicked the Arionad if she could have reached him. Whatever Pedrin's feelings about his duty to protect, he could not reconcile Nemiah and the temple as vulnerable while her Arionade postured behind her.

She stepped farther from the altar and from her own men. "Commander, forgive me. I cannot give to you a person who is no longer in my custody. However, I will offer you a thing that is within my ability. Something that will please the council."

The City Guard blinked consideringly. "What is that, Lady?"

The men behind her shifted. Nemiah did not dare to pull her gaze from Commander Pedrin. This sacrifice would have meaning.

"If you promise to leave without laying a hand on Riana's servants, I will put myself in your care. I will go with you to stand before the elders."

"Nemiah, no!"

The two words rang out with her Arionad's anguish. Commander Pedrin's head snapped up, breaking Nemiah's hold. Doors all over his Paths slammed shut. His expression altered as his experiences of gentle strength and single-minded protectiveness grew distant. Hostility flashed back into his gaze.

"What was that? What did you do to me?"

"I only reminded you of who you are, Commander Pedrin. You have promised to keep order in the city and to protect those unable to protect themselves. I will go with you to allow you to fulfill both parts of your promise."

Rom was at her side before she saw him move. Determination carved his colorless features. He had once threatened the life of a priestess for her sake; she had no doubts about what he would do to this arrogant guard.

"Rom, stand down!" she hissed.

He did not look at her. "If the Lady of Avelos orders it, Commander, my men will stand aside and let you depart. I cannot, however. My oath is different. If you wish to take the Lady, you must take me as well."

Nemiah closed her eyes.

Oh, Rom.

The commander gave a shrug. "Why not? Plenty of room in Aelend. Give me your weapon."

Rom sent the City Guardsman a scornful stare as he unbuckled his sword belt. Then, slowly and deliberately, he passed his sanctified blade to Commander Evorales. The other Arionad accepted it in grave silence.

Commander Pedrin shrugged again. He gestured to two of his guards. "Take him."

Rom had barely started to turn—his gaze was still on Evorales—when the first guard struck. Nemiah shouted a warning, but too late. The grip of the man's knife caught Rom across the head with an audible thud. The second guard caught him as he went down.

"He had surrendered!" Nemiah cried. "He was unarmed!"

A growl rose from the rest of the Arionade. Commander Evorales moved forward with Rom's sword in his hand. Paths multiplied around Nemiah, blurring the world. So much blood would be spilled. Her Arionade were outnumbered. Her priestesses had little means to defend themselves. She spun to face her own guardians.

"Hold, Arionade! I command you to hold! You are the wardens of the high temple and must remain to keep Riana's order! I have an agreement with this commander. He will honor it!"

Commander Pedrin assessed the Arionade nervously, perhaps realizing at last that flaunting his power could have consequences for his own men. "That's right, Lady. Come along. My people will see to your captain. We are done here."

"Evorales, go to the Bearer," Nemiah ordered. "Tell her what's happened. Tell her to send to our allies in the council."

It was the only thing she had time to say before a phalanx of City Guards surrounded her and began to hustle her out. Their boots crushed fragments of colored glass as they marched. Riana's eye, a work of beauty that had survived centuries of weather and war and the killing winds, would never again offer anyone joy or peace.

The streets were black and eerily quiet. A chill mist hovered over the city. Nemiah tried to catch sight of Rom. Two of the City Guards were half carrying, half dragging him. She couldn't tell if he was conscious.

They thrust her into Aelend, through the dank, dark corridors, and into the heart of the prison. She thought she was not so far from where Jholan was held, but she had lost track of the halls that belonged to her moment amidst the ones appearing and fading around her. One of the guards opened a cell door to reveal nothing but impenetrable blackness. The odor of decay crept out to choke her. Nemiah had been here before, not just that morning, but with Amalia. She already knew the chains and the pain and darkness that had smothered Amalia's bright spirit. As the guard shoved Nemiah toward the threshold, panic clutched her. Instinctively she resisted, grasping at the door frame and bracing herself.

"Wait. Wait!" she gasped.

Behind her, Rom tore free of his captors and kicked the guard who was pushing Nemiah. The others shouted. He had surprised them, but they swarmed around him. They struggled briefly before once again subduing him, his arms wrenched behind his back.

Nemiah's fear turned to savage anger. "Stop! Leave him be!"

Commander Pedrin made a noise of irritation. "Put them both in there. It won't change anything in the end. When the council calls for her, she'll go to the elders alone."

Nemiah stumbled into the cell and they shoved Rom in after her. The door slammed shut and the bar grated against wood as it was dropped into place. In the absolute dark, she could see nothing.

She stood motionless, fighting off vertigo. Rom's breathing, quick and loud, gave away his shifting location.

"What are you doing?"

"Figuring out what else is in here with us," her Arionad answered. There was a catch in the rhythm of his steps, then a soft rustling and an uncharacteristic curse. "A straw pallet in the corner left of the door. Don't sit on it." Nemiah heard more footsteps, then a knocking and the sound of metal clinking against metal. "A locked door on the west wall. A set of shackles bolted to the floor in the corner."

Nemiah shivered. They had chained Amalia so that she could not use her wings. "We won't be held here long. Abrigado means to demonstrate his authority, but we have some friends still."

"Friends who will dare to speak for us?" Rom's disembodied voice this time came from the opposite side of the cell.

Nemiah heard the words he did not say: *Who will dare to speak for us after the Lady of Avelos has been called before the council?*

"Even if Clan Ontera and Clan Everen are unwilling, Clan Nadaren will not abandon us. Once Leita sends word, Elder Nadro will respond." Nemiah wrapped her arms tightly about herself. "You should not have followed me, Rom."

"It is exactly what I should have done." His whisper came from just above her. She jumped. "Evorales has grown into his command in the past months. He will care for the temple. My oath is to you, my lady. I will climb out of the Hidden Paths of the Dead before I allow harm to come to you."

His hand touched her shoulder, then slid around her back, drawing her to him. When she laid her head against his chest, his heart thumped hard in her ear. She had known that defying the council would have consequences, yet somehow she had never imagined herself here, in Amalia's place. She thought of Amalia and of Ambri, who had tried to protect his Lady and instead had been used to start a war and a century of horror. She said a silent prayer for Rom and for the Path that was unrolling beneath them.

9.

AELEND

Stone walls had long meant safety, stability, and order to Nemiah. Even as a child, she had appreciated the enclosed spaces, small and dark, that others feared. Walls provided protection from the uncertainties of the immense world. They kept her from losing herself among the infinite Paths or sliding into the Nowhere.

Never had they been used as a means to unravel her.

In the absolute darkness of their cell, time could no longer be measured by the turning of Riana's spheres, but only by the appearance of the guards—who twice a day brought a cup of stale water and a measure of rancid oats—and by the demands of her body for food and sleep and relief. Three men came each time: two of them to corner Rom with their heavy batons, while the third laid down their meager meal.

The first time the guards appeared, Nemiah attempted to gauge their commitment to Riana. She greeted them as the Lady of Avelos should greet her people and spoke a blessing over them. One of the men barked at her to keep quiet; another mumbled something ugly under his breath; but the youngest of the three, who was carrying the lamp, ducked his head and made a surreptitious spiral. She smiled at him and asked his name.

Without warning, the guard who had yelled at her swung his baton. It cracked against Rom's back. Her Arionad staggered to his knees.

"Do not speak to my men again," the guard snarled. "You will speak only to me and only if I ask something of you. Understand?"

Nemiah nodded, helpless outrage filling her. Her gaze on Rom's begged for forgiveness. The young guard did not appear again, and Nemiah did not dare to speak.

Although harsh and dangerous, at least order ruled the morning guards. The evening guards sparked true terror in Nemiah; they had no order and followed no rule. From the moment they entered the cell, she felt their eyes on her, and mockery tainted their every word. If she remained quiet, they claimed she was uncooperative and struck Rom. If she answered their questions, they declared her answers insufficient and struck him twice. Nothing of duty existed in their actions: the men merely enjoyed tormenting others. One night the largest of them offered her a spiral that ended close to his body in a very different kind of gesture. For a mercy, Rom did not see that gesture. Her Arionad watched each of the three with black fire in his eyes. If any of the men crossed a boundary with her, he would stop them. And then, she had not a doubt, they would kill him.

Hours passed, then days. Nemiah feared for her priestesses and for Ziabela. She consoled herself by believing that if Kaliska or Zia had been caught, the council would have made her aware of it—at the very least, Abrigado would have come to gloat. She knew Leita would do her utmost to motivate their allies to speak on her behalf. Elder Nadro, who had so long been a devoted follower, would surely come to reassure himself she was well—unless Rom were right and even Nadro did not dare to associate with her follies.

When the walls closed in and hopelessness stalked her, sharing her thoughts with Rom helped to keep her mind ordered. They sat against the cold stone, their hands entwined, and he helped her to corral her fears and consider her resources. He did that for her, pulling hope, thin and fragile, back into the imagined possibilities. In exchange, in the moments when Rom grew quiet, Nemiah offered him the escape he needed, telling the sacred stories of Riana and Lord Arion, speaking of the meaning of the Paths, or just talking of his family in the mountains. Guessing at the hours as best she could, she completed what she might of each devotion and lifted her Arionad's name before Riana.

Neither of them slept much. The damp chill and the creatures that skittered across the floor kept Nemiah from anything deeper than an uneasy drowse. She and Rom took turns keeping the rats at bay while the other rested.

On what might have been the fifth night, Nemiah awoke to a sound she thought was someone clicking stones together.

"Rom?"

The sound stopped abruptly. "Here, my lady."

She rose and shuffled her way toward where he stood. Before she even touched him, she felt the heat pouring off his body and the deep shudders he was struggling to restrain. She choked back a cry.

"Rom, you didn't say!"

"There is nothing useful to be said. I am sorry to have awakened you."

"Sit," she ordered.

He didn't protest. When he was down, leaning against the stone, she ran her fingers lightly across his face, feeling the skin stretched tight and dry over his cheekbones. The poison that had stolen his strength left him vulnerable to the unrelenting cold and the repeated battering. His eyes were closed. His pulse beat too rapidly against her fingertips.

"I have not released you from your oath," she whispered. "You do not have permission to go, Captain Rom."

"I have no intention of going anywhere except out of this accursed prison with you, my lady."

She squeezed his hand. "Rom, your nearly good humor worries me most of all."

He offered an irascible grunt.

"Sleep now," she murmured. "I will watch for you."

"Not yet." He leaned forward, touching his fevered brow to her cool one. "Nemiah, I would have awakened you deliberately in another moment. You were crying out a name in your sleep."

"What? I—"

"Amalia." He said the name softly, with a reverence Nemiah did not expect.

"I'm sorry. I didn't realize."

"It's not the first time. She fills your dreams, doesn't she? The traitorous Lady. It has something to do with the reasons you took in the Shorn scribe and freed the soldier."

Nemiah sucked in a slow breath. "Yes."

"Are you questioning the place of the Avelune on our Path?"

He knew her. Too well. "Rom, there are things you must understand. I—"

"No, don't," he said quickly. "That you haven't spoken already means there is a reason you should not. I will say this now only because the future is uncertain, only because if I err, then I will make reparation for it here in Aelend. Lady, the debt of Amalia's people has been paid. It is time and past time to question what was passed down from a council that has hated us as deeply as it hates the Shorn."

Nemiah stared at him through the darkness.

"Will you punish me for disordered thinking, Lady? Will Riana?"

"No, not I, Rom. We are in a time when the meaning of order is difficult to see." She hadn't known he guarded such thoughts. He had supported her without question when she claimed Ziabela from the City Guard, but she had seen nothing in that other than his unfailing loyalty. He had offered no judgment when she freed Jhared Denaban, but he had been so ill she hadn't guessed he had truly considered it. Something came clear then in a way it rarely had before: Rom had not surrendered his own beliefs when he devoted his life to her. His abiding sense of justice had turned him toward the Shorn, and he had seen readily what it had taken Amalia's death to make Nemiah understand.

"Captain, there is more you must know."

Footsteps echoed in the hall. Nemiah startled as the bar scraped against their door. She had thought it somewhere in the depth of night, but if the morning guards had come already then hours had escaped her. She moved away from Rom to give the guards no excuse to beat him again. The door creaked open and a lamp thrust into the room, blinding her.

"Someone's come to see you."

An unfamiliar voice, not the morning guard and not Commander Pedrin.

She tried to peer around the light to see out the door. "What time is it?"

"Too late for visitors. Unless they pay well, of course."

"Who's come?"

"Someone who thought you'd be more comfortable above ground. Are you coming or should I tell him you're content here?"

Rom took a step toward the door. A second guard shoved out his baton. "Not you."

Nemiah shook her head at her Arionad. "Elder Nadro, Rom. It must be. It will be all right."

"It will be all right only when you're free of this place and safe in the temple," he growled.

She stretched up on tiptoe to lay a blessing on his brow. "By Riana's ways, Lord Arionad."

"By her ways," he murmured, making his spiral. Then he bent and kissed her.

The guards escorted her through the corridor, up the stairs, and along the main hall. As she caught the scent of clean air from unglazed windows, she grew increasingly aware of her creased, limp garments and the smell of her unwashed self. From a guard room just ahead came the sounds of men laughing and throwing dice. Her escort stopped and opened a door. A cushion of warmth enveloped Nemiah. It was an office, brightly lit, with a desk in one corner, a shelf holding half a dozen large volumes—records of the prison perhaps—and a table and chairs. On the table sat a decanter of wine and a plate of bread and cheese.

One man occupied the room, sitting with a glass of wine before him, as comfortable as if he sat in Elders' Hall. He looked up with a smile, smooth and charming. Nemiah's guard shoved her across the threshold. The door shut. Nemiah stood in silence staring at the person who had despised her since the moment she had become the Chosen Lady of Avelos.

"Lady Nemiah."

"Elder Abrigado."

"It seems I've taken you by surprise. You were expecting someone else, I imagine."

Nemiah didn't respond. He had come to taunt her.

Oh, Ziabela, forgive me for failing you.

Abrigado brushed a hand across his fine blue coat. "Won't you sit down? Can I pour you some wine?"

"Has a date been set for the tribunal?"

"Oh my. So blunt. Just five days in prison and already you've reverted to your village manners."

Nemiah pressed her lips together. Abrigado chuckled.

"Of course I know you, Nemiah Rustania. You have endangered Avelos. Did you not think I would want to understand why? The third child of a healer and a weaver. Raised in a village too small even to earn a name in the records. Two elder sisters who married tradesmen, and a brother who died young. The only thing I have never been able to uncover is who it was that passed a hint of the curse to you. Do you know which of your ancestors gave you your green eyes and your penchant for treachery?"

Nemiah stood very still. Nothing he said of her had been overly difficult to learn. There were city records linking Lady Nemiah Gabriana to the name Rustania. He was simply trying to unbalance her. She drew a slow breath and reminded herself she needn't let him.

"Luckily, I've never had to worry about being mistaken for Shorn." She waved a hand back and forth over her head. "My lack of stature, you see. Now, do you have a point to make or have you disturbed my sleep merely to tell me my own history?"

The elder frowned and shifted slightly in his chair. "Very well. We will get to business. Where is Ziabela Marcalo?"

Relief, deep and potent, flooded through her. Nemiah pulled it close. "You needn't have come to me for that. Your City Guards told you where she is."

"Are you going to insist upon that story?"

Nemiah remained silent.

"I've a man who says he saw Ziabela with us at Parnas Pass. Dressed as a priestess."

Breathe, Nemiah reminded herself. Think only of the moment. "I told you she was lost to us."

"Lost, Lady? Do you mean to say dead or run off? Perhaps she fled with Trianor's fosterling. Perhaps you sent them off together."

The elegant elder sat back, considering his wine without drinking. After a moment, he returned the glass to the table. Abruptly, his smooth manner dropped away and his blue gaze clouded. "I truly don't understand. Two Shorn traitors set free to face no consequences for their crimes. Is it some kind of retribution, Lady? Do you hate Avelos so much that you take pleasure in empowering her enemies?"

For the first time Nemiah heard Abrigado's overcontrolled tone slip. "Elder Abrigado, we've made mistakes about who we name our enemies."

"Yes, I have made mistakes." He rubbed a hand over his eyes and let out a sigh. For a moment, Nemiah was shocked to see a different man, one with remorse in him. "It was my mistake years ago to allow Tierzen Trianor to become Minister of the Teaching. A scholar so obsessed with testing his strange theories about insight and rehabilitation that he cannot see the truth of the world. There's more danger in his failed Shorn experiments than there would be if he truly loved the Shorn. It was another mistake to allow Ziabela Marcalo to use her position as my scribe. My authority allowed her to cause death at Panetar. *My* mistake. Now all of Avelos may pay for it. Tell me where she is."

Nemiah remained silent a moment, trying to decipher the man—a man who played a complex game and knew so well how to press others in the directions he wanted. "Elder, why are you here? You don't need Ziabela Marcalo to grab the Seal of State from Rumar. Is it that you fear Ziabela would have spoken of your collaboration with Prefect Aglar? Would she have supported every word Jhared Denaban spoke about you during his interrogation? Was that another mistake?"

Abrigado sighed again and shook his head. "Lady, we are speaking of your mistakes now. You are going to stand before a tribunal of elders to answer for crimes against the council. Your only allies have turned from you in an attempt to salvage their own positions. The people in this city are angry and afraid. Any remnant of devotion they may have held for the goddess will drown in their fury when they hear all you have done. You must speak or you will die at traitors' wall."

He paused. Nemiah watched him with a semblance of calm. He had moved quickly from questions to threats, but threats were meaningless unless he had something else to offer. "You already know you will not have Ziabela Marcalo," she said. "You don't care where the scribe is. What is it you wish to bargain for, Elder?"

A beat of silence. Abrigado blinked. "Nicely done, Lady. You've learned to think beyond the walls of the temple, it seems. Yes, I have an offer to make. That is, the noble Council of Clans has an offer."

She didn't move. "Which is?"

"Make reparation for your errors. Travel to Sahiste as an envoy. Meet with King Javahari and Prince Ashani to stop this impending war and all your debts will be paid."

Nemiah hesitated, surprised not because of what was offered but because of who offered it. Abrigado had something to gain from a war with Sahiste; General Nadel had shown her that. A war that started with Adan Rumar as high chieftain would end with Toren Abrigado in that seat, which meant there was only one thing Abrigado truly desired of her.

"All debts will be paid because I will be dead at the hands of Sahiste. You want a reason for Avelos to retaliate. You want a way to start this war."

"What I want, Lady Nemiah, is a way to rescue our country from those who have done nothing but break it apart!"

He was telling her to leave the temple, to leave Avelos and face retribution in Sahiste. Once before she had offered to go to Sahiste to balance what she had believed to be Amalia's crimes. If she went now, would it offer her an opportunity to turn the Path? If she could not speak Amalia's truth in Avelos, might she offer it to Sahiste? Agreeing to go meant leaving Leita alone. It would mean leaving everything she loved. Yet in the eyes of the council, she had committed treason.

On every Path she would die, now or later. Where might her steps make the most difference before that time came?

"Abrigado, you steaming piece of dung."

The composed and caustic voice came from behind Nemiah. She spun to see a woman in the doorway, a woman straight and tall as a pine tree. Pearls gleamed in her ears. Her ginger hair, marbled with silver, swept softly across her brow. As she glared at the elder, her eyes flashed with an energy Nemiah recognized. She had seen it in this woman's nephew.

For a moment Abrigado looked nearly as dismayed as Nemiah felt, but his smile swiftly reasserted itself. "Prefect Rumar, if I had known you would join us, I would have brought more wine."

"This is not as we agreed," the prefect snapped.

"I did not realize we had agreed I could not speak to a prisoner in the custody of the council."

"Don't play at innocence, Abrigado. It's an ill-fitting suit. I will take her now."

"And if I demand my rights as the appointed chief of the tribunal that will judge her?"

Chief of the tribunal? Abrigado had saved that nugget of information. Nemiah felt dizzy.

The woman scoffed. "Demand your rights, if you will. If you care to endanger Clan Amerre's relationship with the watermen's guild. Perhaps your clan has no goods to move upriver, so it is no matter to you." The woman crooked a finger at Nemiah as though gesturing to a lapdog. "Come, Lady."

The Paths rippled wildly around Nemiah: a point of influence rising. "To where? What is this?"

"This is where I remove you from this wretched hole and this miserable man and take you somewhere you can have a bath."

"And my Arionad?"

"Not just now."

Nemiah stood firm. "I won't leave without him."

"Yes, yes, I understand loyalty, Lady. Captain Rom will be back in the high temple before you are. Are you coming? Or would you prefer to continue your banter with the Minister of the Treasury?"

Elder Abrigado tilted his head appealingly. His gaze on her was toxic.

"I'm coming," Nemiah replied.

"Safe travels, Lady." Abrigado raised his wine glass to her with a smile somewhat more strained now. "May justice be done."

"May it indeed," Nemiah said.

The prefect swept out of the little office and down the corridor at a long-legged pace that forced Nemiah to hurry to keep up. Some direct words and a number of coins changed hands between the prefect and the captain of the guard. Then Nemiah stepped out of the heavy doors and into the cold air.

The heart of night beat softly over Velantar. The moon shed silver across the prison yard and into the street. Nemiah had never been so relieved to be outside, beyond the reach of walls. Paths curved and twisted and slipped in every direction. She swayed.

"Are you going to faint?" Prefect Rumar loomed over her, a derisive twist in her lip.

"No," Nemiah replied, locking the Gate as best she could.

"Good. Then follow me."

She led Nemiah to an enclosed carriage drawn by two horses, grey in the darkness. The driver, a young woman in Manitar livery, saluted the prefect and opened the door. Falina Rumar helped Nemiah inside. When she tapped on the roof, the carriage lurched into motion.

Nemiah leaned back against the fine leather seat. "Where are we going?"

"Someplace Abrigado and his friends cannot gain access to you."

"Why?"

The prefect stared. "You don't read your correspondence, do you, Lady?"

"Forgive me," Nemiah said coolly. "I seem to have been occupied of late."

"Then the only *why* I can tell you is that my reckless nephew insists on risking the future of his clan yet again. This time for the sake of a powerless priestess."

Nemiah knew an unexpected spark of ire. "Adan Rumar would only risk his clan for the sake of his country."

The prefect gave a dubious snort, but her gaze grew measuring.

The steady clop of the horses' hooves and the gentle rocking of the carriage were soporific. Nemiah fought off sleep by trying to anticipate their direction. In a short time, they were riding through Alende Gate out of the city and into the valley. When they crossed the river and started along the far bank toward the great country houses of the elders, she knew where they were heading.

"Your own estate? Abrigado will guess it."

"It doesn't matter what he guesses. No one will reach you here unless we allow it."

Nemiah shivered. *We* meant the power of all Clan Manitar. In other words, Manitar now held the key to her prison.

She studied the woman seated across from her. Falina Rumar remained the only woman to serve as prefect of one of the fifteen first-clans. Nemiah had always been told that Clan Manitar bowed to a woman's leadership merely to benefit from her connections to the high chieftains: her brother first and then her nephew, but the prefect had always seemed to be a phenomenon of strength and energy in her own right. She had single-handedly tamed the watermen's guild and won their hearts. She had kept trade flowing through her clan, even when the killing winds were devastating crops and flocks and trade routes. In some ways, Nemiah thought Falina Rumar was very like her nephew: blunt, impatient, and innovative. Nemiah had never found a way to gain her trust.

The horses turned up a tree-lined road, trotting in and out of the shadows cast by the moon. A word from the driver and they slowed and stopped before the manor house.

Falina Rumar bounded out of the carriage before it had fully come to rest. "This is the end of my part," she said, dropping her disapproving glare upon Nemiah once more. "You've made a mess of things, Lady of Avelos. I would appreciate it if you would try not to spread your prison stench over my family's seat during your stay."

She strode away, up the great stone steps. A young man grasping a writing tablet hastened to join her. They vanished into the manor.

Nemiah climbed out of the carriage, her head spinning. Servants in Manitar's green and silver livery hurried from the house, and she found herself in the hands of two large, capable women, who fussed over her in the way her mother had fussed over her when as a girl she came home grimy from a day of working in the kennels. She let the women lead her into the ancient manor, let them take her to the bathing room and strip away her ruined garments. The beautiful marble tub could have held four people. As she stepped into it, Nemiah had never been more grateful for hot water. One of the women helped to scrub the dirt from Nemiah's long hair and rinse it clean. When Nemiah finally rose from the water, they cocooned her in a soft robe that was far too long for her. They rubbed ointment onto the swollen insect bites that marked her limbs and neck and slid slippers of fine lambswool over her feet. Finally, they combed her hair and drew it, still damp, into a long braid.

She was shown to a suite of rooms off a gallery on the second floor and told that these would be hers while she remained a guest of the prefect. As she stepped into the receiving room, the door clicked shut behind her. The chamber was lovely, with thick rugs over the smooth wood floors, comfortable chairs near the fireplace, and a sideboard with silver trays of food and drink. Beyond the next doorway lay the bedroom. She could see the wide bed laden with blankets and fat pillows.

She had asked the maids for ink and paper to be brought to her. Waiting for her instead was the High Chieftain of Avelos. Nemiah stopped dead when she saw him. He sat in one of the receiving room chairs, his back to her as though he hadn't heard her come in. He was dressed no more finely than one of his guards, in a simple green tunic over grey breeches and black boots. Tension drew the broad span of his shoulders as he sat uncharacteristically still. She had begun to appreciate the value of this man, had once seen something stranger and deeper for them along a possible Path. For a short time, she thought he had also found reasons to trust her. She had shattered that trust when she freed a Shorn soldier accused of treason. She hadn't spoken to the high chieftain since that day.

She forced herself to face him. Only then did she see the sword.

It lay across his lap, bright and cruel. As she approached, his fingers tightened around the grip, but he did not look up. She struggled to draw a steady breath.

"Lord Rumar."

"This sword will not shatter when it kills," he said mildly. "It is a finely crafted blade more likely to flex than snap. In all of Avelos, we could not match the quality of the steel."

"Amurian smiths know their craft," she said, still composed. "Have you received a gift?"

"Of a sort." He lifted his gaze. His grey eyes gleamed as bright and hard as the blade. "This sword was found near the body of Prefect Aglar in Parnas Pass. More than a dozen others like it were found with his men and among the debris."

Another betrayal. One with dire implications. One that Rumar would feel deeply. "Have the northern five bought support from Duke Branald?"

"I have been waiting for certain messages to confirm it. If it is true, then Aglar has given Amuria an excuse to march into the north. Branald wants more than a trade deal for his weapons. He wouldn't have dismissed my overtures last spring otherwise. He wants the furs and the minerals in the Sandien Mountains. He wants the silver mines. And he wants Avelos to finally bend the knee before the Amurian bull."

"This means you have no choice but to pull forces from the Sahisten border to reinforce the north."

"I've already sent word to General Nadel," he replied. "Whether or not we have the men to put down the traitors and regain Aglar Tower, we must guard the passes in the Sandien Mountains and place a stronger guard in the west."

Nemiah sank into a chair, hearing the words of the patrolman in the market: *"We're determined to destroy ourselves, but no one can decide whether to do it from the outside in or the inside out."*

"I am sorry, Lord Rumar."

She hadn't meant to say it, but it was the truth. She was sorry for the ways he had been betrayed and regretted the way she had betrayed him. The most important sentiments often escaped that way, in an unguarded moment. A type of disorder, some of Riana's priestesses would say, to speak so artlessly. Nemiah once was such a priestess, demanding deliberation in all things. She wasn't any longer. Truth, in whatever form it reached the world, was the proper order.

Rumar's expression shifted toward her then away. He ran a callused hand through his hair, darker and more intense than his aunt's fading ginger. "I would not have allowed the council to execute the boy," he said finally. "You might have trusted me."

His own vulnerability in that admission startled her. She hadn't meant to open him. It was dangerous. Her own balance, precarious just now, was somehow tied to his.

"If you had intervened on his behalf, it would have finished you," she sighed. "The council would not have tolerated such favoritism. You know it."

"Perhaps. But you did not free Jhared Denaban to save me from accusations of favoritism."

She poured herself a glass of wine. Adan Rumar was scathingly intelligent and sometimes damagingly impatient. He was a good man shadowed by chaos. Not long ago, she had feared him.

"Shall we discuss the tribunal?" she suggested. "Elder Abrigado has made an offer that—"

"You came to me that night in Parnas Pass to warn me, didn't you? There was something you wanted to say but didn't."

She pressed her hands against her robe to still their sudden trembling. "That is true."

"If you had found a way to speak, perhaps we would be working together now. Instead, you have forced me into a position I never wished to take."

"I regret that, Lord Rumar."

A powerful man, broad and well-built, he could move with a soldier's swiftness. He exploded out of his seat, sending the Amurian sword tumbling to the floor.

"Nemiah, leave off! You have seen me alone and low in the depths of night. I have picked you up bruised and battered from the street. I thought we had declared a truce. I thought we had found a way to move forward."

Nemiah's heart thudded painfully. He was opening himself too far, offering a gift she could not return. She needed to bring him back, before they both took steps they could not retrace.

"We did move forward, Adan. I aided the escape of two Shorn captives and you locked me in Aelend Prison."

The speed with which her words took effect stole her breath. Regret shone clear in his craggy face, then anger, then all emotion left his features.

Nemiah looked down, aching with her own regret, fighting the urge to say something to remove the sting. There was no space in this night for gentleness, however; only truth. She needed to remember that.

"Clearly spoken," the high chieftain said. "You have laid out the issue so simply. Then let us speak simply of the offer that was made to you."

She nodded once. "An envoy to Sahiste. Tell me, was it Abrigado's idea or yours?"

"It was your idea. I've only let Abrigado believe he conceived it. He posed it to the council as a necessary attempt to pacify Sahiste, but he fears you, I think."

"He fears that Ziabela Marcalo has told me his secrets."

An auburn brow lifted. "Did she?"

"One. She told me that Abrigado fears the consequences if the two of us unite our strength."

Rumar looked thoughtful.

"Why did you take me out of prison, Adan?"

"Because we cannot survive both a civil war and a war in the south. The bitter irony, of course, is that we have a quicker road to solving the conflict with Sahiste than with our own people."

"By sending one disgraced priestess to the Sahisten court?"

"You will not go alone. Elder Trianor will accompany you."

That halted her a moment. She let out a sharp laugh. "Oh, I see. Very neat. Are there any other allies you must dispose of? Send them along. We will make a merry party."

Rumar ran his fingers through his hair again, standing it on end. "I cannot blame you for perceiving it that way."

"Is there another interpretation? When I have nothing left to offer them but the opportunity to take their retribution? When Tierzen Trianor has become an emblem of your failure?"

Something flickered in the grey gaze that might have been pain. "Lady Nemiah, I do not mean to send you or Elder Trianor as a sacrifice. Steps will be taken."

"Steps?"

"I will give you something else to offer them."

Nemiah sat back. She wasn't always clever in diplomacy, but she had a talent for understanding men's needs and wishes. One night, this man had allowed her to see what he wished for Avelos. The realization stole her breath. "Bright goddess. You're going to give them what they want. You're sending me to negotiate the terms to open our borders."

"Yes."

"You have of course made this decision with the council's approval?"

Rumar entrusted her with a dry smile that was answer enough. Nemiah rubbed her forefingers over her closed eyelids.

"It is what Sahiste wants and it is something Avelos needs," the high chieftain said.

She dropped her hands into her lap and looked up at him. "And if I offer it and they accept, will you still be in the high chieftain's seat to fulfill the terms when I return?"

He did not evade her gaze. "I will."

"Boldly spoken for a man facing a summons to the Trial of Integrity." She could not seem to stop baiting him. She was angry and frustrated and scared, and Rumar's certainty goaded her. It always had.

"It is only a trial," he said calmly. "I still have the chance to respond to the accusations before the second vote."

"Do enough of the elders among the remaining thirteen support you?"

"Not yet, but they will."

"I see. And how many votes will you win by sending the Lady of Avelos into Sahiste to pay for the crimes of the past and her own treachery?"

This time the pain in his expression could not be mistaken. "It is a feint, Nemiah. Think on it. Abrigado thinks he wins something this way. If he believes I am so weak as to give in to him, he will be less guarded. I need him cocky and overconfident. I need him to make a mistake. I cannot yet prove his connections with the northern traitors, but I must. It is one of the reasons I agreed to make this offer to you."

"And the other?"

Rumar stood, retrieved the Amurian sword from the floor, and laid it on the table. His gaze remained on the blade as he spoke. "If you stand before the tribunal with Abrigado as its chief, only one outcome is possible. I will not see you sentenced for treason, Lady. I will not let Abrigado turn me into Tumal."

Nemiah closed her eyes and opened them again. This night needed to be about truths, and if she were truthful with herself, only one direction made sense for her to move.

"Very well. I will rid you of the problem of my presence by going to Sahiste. I will take your offer to the court. I will do everything in my ability to pull us away from war. In exchange, some things must happen."

Rumar looked oddly ambivalent, as if he hadn't really expected her to agree—or hoped perhaps she wouldn't. "What things?"

"Captain Rom is free to remain in the temple. He will not travel with me."

"I suspect, Lady, that is a decision to be made by you and your captain. But, no, he has not been charged with a crime. Following you to Aelend was his own choice. He is not required to leave the city. What else?"

"Palace guards will stand at the doors of the high temple in my absence."

He had done that for her once, after her Arionade had been poisoned. Now she needed guards loyal to the high chieftain to keep the temple safe, not from theft, but from the violence of the council.

Rumar was sober. "I will see to it."

"And you will vouch for the well-being of the priestesses and displaced families there."

"They will be safe, Nemiah."

"One thing else," she said, "there is a Shorn boy imprisoned in Aelend, a child from Clan Hilera. Jholan is his name. His family died when the killing winds struck the city. He must be returned to his people."

"I have been made aware of that case. It is a regrettable one. I am sorry. For this request, nothing can be done."

"Abrigado will destroy him."

"You have already touched upon it, Nemiah. I cannot intervene on behalf of Shorn lawbreakers. Not now. He will stay in Aelend and face his sentence."

"He is a child!"

"He is old enough to know that what he was doing was wrong."

"What he was doing was trying to survive!" Her voice came out fierce and keen. Amalia had died to salve the country's fears. The blood of babes had been spilled upon Riana's altar. She had spilled it, knife in hand.

Nemiah wrapped her fingers around the arms of her chair and met the high chieftain's gaze. "Put me back into Aelend then, Lord Rumar. I will serve his sentence. He is a boy not yet past his Becoming. A guardian can take his crime upon herself, and he has no other person in Velantar to claim that role."

"Nemiah, don't be absurd. You cannot sacrifice yourself so uselessly. You are needed!"

She remained silent, unwavering, though she heard the depths of meaning in his words and wondered at it.

Rumar was standing once more, glowering over her. "You are needed," he said again, his tone altered.

It was not a night for gentleness, only truths. There was a story she needed to tell—for Jholan, for all of them—but could not yet. She desperately wished she could see the step that was required before she could share Amalia's tale without turning the Path toward a massacre. She wondered if there were a way for Rumar to see it for himself. If only she might carry him through the Gate and show him all the things she could not say. A foolish wish. She had never heard of a Pathwalker doing any such thing. Yet Adan Rumar had just offered her an opportunity, a frightening opportunity that would change the Path. Was this the step she needed?

She tilted her head upward. "What is it you hope, Adan?"

"I would not have you fail," he breathed.

"I am no diplomat."

"That is not what I mean." He waved away her words. "Nemiah, something between us is . . . necessary for Avelos. I did not seek it. I do not understand it. But I can no longer deny that it exists."

You are the body of Avelos as I am the spirit. Let us heal the discord between us and end the suffering in our land.

Nemiah had said those words on another Path. In that moment, she had known the importance of the union between them. It never occurred to her that he might feel it too.

Truths tonight, only truths. "What have you seen, Adan?"

"I have dreamed of hunting a bird with golden wings and green eyes. She comes to me, although I carry a bow to slay her. She alights, briefly, beside me and I am compelled to reach for her. In her talons she carries something long lost. Something treasured. As I reach for it, she soars away. Even as she touches the sky, I know she will fall to another hunter. And I know an opportunity has slipped from me that will never come again. There is a terrible sadness in that knowledge."

Dreams were reflections of the Paths colored by one's own hopes and fears and insights. They did not offer the same clear vision a sacred journey might, but they could sometimes reveal patterns a person was unwilling or unable to recognize in the light of day.

Nemiah found her breathing escaping her control. Not long ago she had despised this man, feared him, fought him to hold onto the last shreds of the temple's influence. Her understanding of him then had been deeply flawed.

"What do you think it means, this dream?"

"Don't," he growled. "I know something of you, Nemiah. I know you see the meaning in it. Probably clearer than I do."

Truths. Only truths. "I do see some things. I … don't know what to do with them."

"You told me once you believed it was your place to be my guide."

"And you rejected that possibility."

"I did and I do. I will not be led. Not by Clan Manitar, not by the council, and not by the temple."

He had been bred especially to serve the needs of his own clan—Manitar had held the high chieftain's seat since long before Lord Rumar—but he had always been his own, and he had loved Avelos. He was still standing over her. Lamplight caught in the deep red-gold of his hair and made cliffs of his features. Nemiah smelled bitter boldblood on him and wood smoke and rain.

"Something vital exists here, Nemiah. I have no patience for things unexplainable. I am no poet, but I feel a sense of *completeness* when that golden bird is beside me."

You are the body of Avelos as I am the spirit. . . .

He looked down at his hands—large, callused, ink-stained—then back up at her. "I am sorry, Lady. There are not words for some levels of regret. Can there be any meaning in an apology offered for acts committed over so many years?"

"There can be. If it is offered with true intent."

He nodded. She could see him struggling and was not inclined to make it easier for him.

"I am uncertain just what I am asking of you. I don't know what role the goddess should have here. I know only that the completeness I sense is important for Avelos."

"For Avelos, Lord Rumar?"

"And for … that is, I do not wish to know such a depth of loss again. I wish for you to trust me. I don't know how we reach that place. I only know we haven't yet."

Blood pounded in her ears and tingled through her fingertips. He had invoked the goddess. He had asked for forgiveness. It was within her power to offer such a thing in Riana's name.

Once before she had felt the harmony that might come from this step and had denied it, still afraid of her own failings, but that fear no longer drove her. The High Chieftain of Avelos had asked for forgiveness. Would the goddess acknowledge it? She closed her eyes and sought within the deepest parts of her for Riana's strength, bright and hot and hopeful.

Summer sunlight poured through her, spirit and flesh, immolating doubt. She winced at the force of it, wondering how she did not burn to ash and float away. When she stood, Rumar gasped, but held his ground, his grey eyes dark. She read in them respect, not awe; fascination, not fear; and a profound, inescapable need.

"Riana offers her blessing for some, Adan Rumar, High Chieftain of Avelos. For those who seek her peace or strength or forgiveness. For those who are worthy. Are you asking this of her? Of me?"

"I am not devout," he said stiffly. "I will not yield to her."

"Riana knows what you are. And we must yield to each other if there is to be trust." She lifted her hand to his brow and drew a languorous spiral with one finger. He caught a shallow breath.

This time he did step away.

"Nemiah, stop. This is not what I intended. Here on my family's land you are hardly less a prisoner than in Aelend. You cannot offer such things freely."

She smiled, confident in the glow of the goddess's strength. "You have no ability to coerce me in this, Adan Rumar. What I offer is a gift from Riana. It can only be given by her grace."

On another Path she had drawn him to her and he had given himself before the goddess. On this Path she raised his fingers to her lips and brushed a blessing across his hands, hands that had shaped Avelos for nearly a decade, might yet shape the future. He quivered like a tightly reined horse.

"Do you understand?" he said thickly. "I have been alone these ten years since Aviya's death. I have not played the games with eligible daughters that Clan Manitar has wished me to play. The women in my bed have known me only as a duty, or an opportunity. There have been fewer of them than you might guess. All have been well paid."

This was not a night for gentleness.

Nemiah spoke the first prayer then, opening herself to the goddess and to the man before her. Riana's heat flowed through her core. Healing was to be found here.

His eyes held hers, making himself vulnerable. Only one other man had so readily held her cursed green gaze.

Without letting go of his hands, she stepped backward slowly, through the doorway and toward the bed.

"It is a mistake for me to send you to Sahiste," he said, allowing her to draw him forward. "There is another hunter. There is loss."

"I am the one who must go," she answered. "Reparation must be made. The truth must be told."

"Ah, Lady, I have admired your courage. You must know that."

She guided his hands beneath the soft robe to her body, knew a moment of fear after all as he clutched her. She did not quail: Riana had led her here. Order existed in it. She and Adan Rumar were meant to rule Avelos side by side.

His whole body tensed with urgency, but his hands only stroked the bell of her hips, lightly, shyly. She had not expected shyness. The warmth that flashed through her was just as unexpected, and not all of the goddess's making.

She uttered the second prayer—naming him before Riana, offering herself as a tool of consecration. Some aspects of the ritual could not be exact here: she had no water from the holy springs beneath the temple, but she touched her fingers to her eyes, to the tears there, and reached out with both hands to purify him: touching his eyelids, his lips, his throat. His grey eyes and dark copper stubble were so different from the dark eyes and black beard of the man who was devoted and dear to her, from the fair eyes of the man she had loved. Yet Adan Rumar was the one meant to lead Avelos beside her.

As she completed the prayer, she leaned back against the bed, letting her robe fall open. Rumar gasped. The Paths swung around her, rushing toward the point of influence to which she had drawn them. The point through which balance might be found. Heat radiated from her, the heat of Riana's strength and of her own desire.

"Ah, Goddess," he whispered, a man who did not pray.

"You are the body of Avelos, Adan Rumar, as I am the spirit. Let us heal the discord between us and end the suffering in our land."

She pulled him down to her, turning the Path of her own will. The mystery came upon her, consuming her, until no more space existed for restraint within either of them. In that flame, Nemiah saw that the love they shared for their land forged a link stronger than any bond between two people, and that after tonight, there might be hope, but there would almost certainly be loss.

10.

FOREIGN WAYS

When Jhared opened his eyes, he didn't recognize the branches drooping above him or the rock-strewn hill below him. He blinked at the sky, trying to remember where he lay and why. Then he heard a long, low whicker and recalled the terrible steps that had carried him there. Seravina lowered her head to snuffle his face. He climbed to his feet, using the mare to steady himself.

Relief filled him to see her safe, but she had saved him twice over and it had cost her. Beneath the mud that plastered her silver coat, patches of raw skin marked where the stone had scraped her when she had fallen. The saddle had twisted sideways, grating her flanks. When she stepped close to bump his shoulder, she favored her left foreleg.

Gently, he unbuckled the girth and pulled away the saddle and bags. When he ran his hands down her leg, he found it warm and swollen below the knee. She snorted and drew the leg away from him. There would be no more mad flights through the forest.

He did what he could to care for her, scraping away the worst of the mud and bathing her cuts with clean water. He hunted until he found some boneroot for her pain, but he would have given a lot for a store of medicinals like the one Maya kept. He had fled the Kin without even a sack of grain, and Alende would be after him soon.

"I'm afraid we've a ways to go before they'll let us be," he murmured to the mare, wrapping cloth soaked in boiled boneroot around her foreleg. "But we'll find some peace when we reach Sona. Food and rest and safety."

There would be peace. Maya was waiting.

He clung to those notions as they set out. It took all his energy and focus just to move in the right direction. He felt like a child's puzzle tossed about and shoved back together the wrong way. Throughout the long day, he led Seravina south, toward Sona. They camped at dusk near the bank of a river. The next morning was the same, and the next, until the days and nights merged into an undifferentiated blur. They walked, snatched short spans of fitful sleep, and set off again. It was slow going, for the mare must graze to survive and the only food Jhared ate he had hunted or foraged.

At first, every alarm that was sounded by the forest creatures caused him to leap to alert, expecting the Kin to converge upon him. When several days passed and they did not, he wondered if he had successfully thrown them off his trail. They had no reason to guess he was heading for Sona. Alende might even believe he had run back toward Velantar and the Bearer. The thought made Jhared hesitate. What if Alende had given him up entirely and gone to hunt for Leita? What if? He scowled and pushed on through the undergrowth. Leita was protected by Arionade behind city walls. He could do no more for her. His duty to Avelos had ended.

Alende told him he didn't belong among the bound, and so he did not, no more than he belonged among the Kin.

You belong nowhere!

Gradually, he and Seravina put miles between them and the tangled Paths, but the world around Jhared remained unstable. Once more the blue flames singed his thoughts. Once more, Seravina pinned her ears and gave him wild-eyed glares when they approached some transition: the edge of a valley, a river crossing, twilight. When he reached inward, seeking to close the Gate as Shira had assured him he had, nothing happened. Whatever strength or skill he had gained since Parnas Pass seemed to have deserted him, or perhaps had been ripped away by the tangle. It left him always a little dizzy and never fully certain that when he took a step forward he would land in the place he expected to.

Nothing could be done for it but to march on. He had long ago left behind the lands that were familiar to him. The nature of the country continued to change as he approached Sona. Rivers and streams ran full and fast, hurrying toward the sea. The trees shifted from broad, straight sentinels that kept their distance from one another to lush, gnarled gossipmongers dripping with vines. Even the air changed, growing heavier and wetter. Jhared knew he must be very near the border when he caught the faint tang of the marshes on the wind. Seravina caught it too, flaring her nostrils and shaking her head at the foreign scent.

Two days later, they crossed the river that marked the border. No Forest Guard patrol watched the southwestern edge of Avelos. Sona was no threat and Amurian raiders crossed the Jhanaza River farther north. Still, as he urged Seravina into the dark, still water, Jhared realized this would be the first time he had left Avelos of his own volition. Although no tower or barrier marked the crossing, when Sera scrambled up on the far back, dancing nervously, he knew they had entered Sona. Within him, the last bond snapped.

"Aha! Found you, my aberration!"

Something pounced, fast and heavy. Jhared stumbled against Seravina, barely catching his balance, before he realized the intrusion was within him.

"Where have you hidden all this time, boy? We thought they had killed you!"

It was Shrill, her presence as sharp as talons in his flesh. For what he had done to her beyond the Gate, he had expected punishment long ago. He braced himself.

"They did not kill me. Is that why you have returned?"

A disturbing chuckle rumbled in his head. *"Of course not! We mean you no harm. We're your guardians. Your Teachers!"*

"I have left behind Shorn Law and all of Avelos," he replied. *"There is nothing more you can teach me."*

"Is there not?" Her voice turned sly.

He thought quickly. He sensed her waiting, and knew he should be wary. *"You told me you didn't know how to control the killing winds."*

"No. Not the winds, boy."

"You know about traveling the web?"

"We do," she answered.

"But I am abomination. You warned me I must not travel. Why would you teach me now?"

Shrill sighed. *"How do you keep a child from burning down his house if you do not teach him how to hold the lamp? Your dark priestess failed to teach you properly, so clearly we must."*

Jhared didn't dare to be hopeful. *"You will help me to close the Gate? To keep it closed?"*

"We will. If you promise to obey us in three things."

He let out a growl. *"Yet another price to pay? Perhaps I have obeyed you long enough."*

A flicker of fear licked from her. Just a flicker before she turned sly again. *"Then you have no wish to reach your feathered woman in one piece?"*

Jhared gritted his teeth. *"What things?"*

"You will not hide from us again. You will answer any questions we put to you. And when you reach your woman, you will do what you must to learn how she provokes the killing winds."

"Mayavana has nothing to do with the winds."

"She must. We saw the consequences when you loosed her desire."

But they hadn't seen him in Parnas Pass and they hadn't seen him with Shira or they would know Mayavana hadn't touched the killing winds. He pushed down the realization as soon as it arose. *"Why do you seek knowledge of the killing winds?"*

Shrill's presence hardened. *"Do we not exist to keep Avelos safe? How else might we help to end the destruction?"*

The answer was an evasion. He sensed it in the pitch of her voice and in the way her presence closed against him. He wondered what she could be hiding from him, then swiftly shackled his questions to prevent her from sensing them. *"I will do what you request. But only if you also promise no retribution for what happened beyond the Gate. No nightmares."*

The thin smile that curved around his thoughts made him shudder. *"Retribution? How can you say so? We are Teachers, concerned with reparation, not retribution. Surely, even now you would rejoice to play a role in stopping the killing winds. Surely, you still bear that much love for Avelos. Go to your feathered woman. Let her heal you. We will be there with you."*

She went silent abruptly, ripping through his memories as she did. Jhared caught his breath. Her invasion left him feeling soiled and torn. He would have dived into the river if he could have scrubbed away the feel of her inside him.

The remainder of the day he could not keep his attention on the trail. He needed to think through what Shrill had told him, but he knew it unwise to draw her notice and reveal his doubts. That evening, he camped early at the edge of a marsh, where black cranes and long-legged gravewalkers kept watch from the reeds. Although it required wading into the muck up to his knees, he managed to catch enough frogs to make a marsh-flavored meal. They went down easier with the last of the Melandrien brandy that Lady Nemiah had given him. With his head spinning in a way he hoped might mask his thoughts, he lay by his small fire and carefully considered his Teachers.

They hadn't always loathed him, at least he didn't think so. They had helped him to survive the death of his mother and the rigors of Shorn Law. They had been a touchstone connecting him to Avelos, an enlightened presence who understood him and the complexities of his loss. When he followed the Laws, they rewarded him. When he strayed from their instruction, they were wrathful.

But he had strayed so far that they believed he had deliberately hidden from them, and now he only wished it were true. If he could close himself to them, he would have less cause to fear Shrill's probing. How could he hide from a presence so integrally a part of him? He tried to remember how he had flung her into the Nowhere. He had witnessed Lady Amalia's death and carried Lady Nemiah toward her proper Path. Shrill had been furious with him for revealing himself as a Pathwalker to the Lady of Avelos. When Shrill attacked him in the Nowhere, he had somehow gripped the essence of her and thrown her from his awareness. For a short time then he had been free. How had she found him again? And where was Boar?

He wished he had been forward enough to ask Shira or perhaps Rani of their experiences with the Teachers. He had never dared to speak of them with any of the bound Shorn. It was an intimate topic, and he had come among Shorn companions too late. With a sigh, he put away all thoughts of his Teachers, folding and tucking them deep in hopes he might keep them inviolate. He closed his eyes, listening to the *chirrups* rising from the water and appreciating the warmth of the brandy in his blood. As he began to drift, the words of "Alende's Flight" came to him. He sang it softly, accompanied by the gentle keening of a marsh bird.

By the time he found Maya's lake, Jhared had tramped back and forth across the northwest corner of Sona, avoiding villages and searching every waterway. The moon had waxed and waned. He and Sera were thoroughly coated in mud and smelled of rotting vegetation. When he finally spied the cottage, he feared at first that wishful thinking had carried him through the Gate to Mayavana's Path. Only the mare, quiet and attentive beside him, convinced him it had not. The setting was as he had known it on his journeys: a breeze blew little silver-capped waves across the water and carried a mineral scent to the sand and pebbled shore. Long reeds swayed at the lake's edge. Past the reeds thrust a rotting pier and a single rowboat that drifted to the end of its mooring. Beyond the pier and a small, wild garden, the cottage squatted above the damp ground, braced on rows of stilt-like posts. Wide shutters framed large windows. A ladder leaned against the house to reach the door.

Jhared scanned the shore, expecting to see Maya—she had always been a part of this landscape—but the shoreline offered only a flock of excited gulls wheeling above the water. He strode toward the cottage, smiling absurdly. When he reached the shade beneath the house, he tethered Seravina to one of the posts and looked toward the top of the ladder. The door stood partially open. Jhared imagined Maya stepping from the water, wet and glistening, running into the cottage still breathless from her swim. He imagined climbing the ladder and catching a glimpse of glossy feathers, the curve of her waist, the short sweep of her dark hair. He shook away imagination and set to climbing. As he won the top, he flung the door open wide.

A collection of impressions assailed him: colorful rugs, pale wood, a smoldering hearth, a furnished loft. All of those impressions dropped to the back of his awareness when he saw the man bent over the table on the far side of the room. His back was to the door and he was focused intently upon some task at the table. He was clad in nothing but breeches, belted and rolled up to the knee. His red-gold hair hung in a braid across his smooth, muscled shoulders. He was Sahisten.

At the sound of Jhared's entrance, the man swung around, a knife in his hand, gore on his fingers. Around his wrists, he wore entwined snakes. Jhared had seen those snakes twice before: once as tattoos inked around the wrists of a Sahisten spy, and once as live vipers writhing around the arms of a Sahisten priest. On this man, they gleamed silver with hostile eyes of jet. Yet it wasn't only the snakes that caused Jhared's blood to spark. As the Sahisten assessed him, his austere features contorting into a grin, a scarf swung against his bare chest, a scarf Jhared knew—soft wool dyed the brilliant colors of a starling's wing and worked with a pattern of interlocking feathers. When he had last seen it, it had been stained with Maya's blood.

Jhared stood at the threshold. Beneath him, the Paths split and split again. Shorn energy flew to his limbs, setting his muscles humming.

"What have you done with her? What have you done, viper?"

The Sahisten's eyes widened as Jhared tossed aside his bags and strode across the room, grabbing up one of the chairs and swinging hard.

The knife clattered to the floor as Jhared struck. Speedily, the Sahisten caught the chair in his other hand and yanked it in the direction of Jhared's swing. Jhared stumbled past him, carried by the force of his blow and the Sahisten's strength. He struck the wall with one shoulder and rebounded, expecting a blade in the back. But when he spun to face his foe again, the knife still lay on the floor. Jhared gauged the distance, gauged his chances of reaching it before the Sahisten. Too far. Instead of betting on it, Jhared discarded the chair and dove for the knife in a feint. When the Sahisten leaped after him, he shifted his dive and caught the man hard in the stomach with his shoulder. The Sahisten gave a grunt as Jhared rammed him against the wall. Quick as flame, a fist crashed down on the back of Jhared's head. Red bees swarmed in his vision and he met the floor on hands and knees. Out of the haze, he saw a booted foot shoot toward him. He grabbed it and jerked backward. His foe went down with a hard thud. Jhared scrambled to pin the man and dug a knee into his middle, leaving him gasping. The knife lay within reach now. He stretched for it.

"Don't! Don't touch the blade! Move away from him or I'll take off your head! Move away—

"Jhared?"

Behind him, the tone of hot fury dropped into astonishment. But Jhared had already risen and spun toward his new opponent, his fist cocked for a blow. His heart broke open when he caught sight of a sage gaze and wings that spanned the shades of grey from frost to midnight. He had no time to avoid the staff already hissing toward him. It bashed against his temple and sent him reeling into the table. He slid to the floor, scrambling to hang onto awareness.

"Maya . . . !" He started a warning, but his mouth couldn't quite shape the sounds he needed.

She didn't look at him. To his horror, she tossed her staff aside and crouched beside the fallen Sahisten, who was slowly sitting up. Gently, she touched the man's bare shoulder and murmured something in the feathery words of Sahine. The man replied in the same language, then glanced at Jhared and gave him an arch appraisal before saying something further to the Avelun.

Maya smiled in response, an uncharacteristically shy curve of her lips that Jhared had rarely seen. His spirit bled as she stood and turned to him with a very different expression, one that was too complex for him to unravel but surely meant he had lost something he had begun to cherish.

"Oh, Jhared," she sighed. "I'm sorry. I never imagined it could be you. This man is a friend. His name is Zinderdali Imiro."

11.

Snakes of the South

The Sahisten rose and took a step toward Jhared, who came swiftly to his feet. He thought he saw amusement in the man's expression and drew himself straighter, his anger smoldering.

At that, the Sahisten halted and said something to Mayavana that sounded like a question. His silky voice tumbled the syllables of his language like water over polished stones. Maya shook her head and replied in the same language, though more slowly. The man nodded.

"Zin, this is Jhared Denaban. Patrolman of the Forest Guard Fourth."

The Sahisten bore the aquiline nose, wide cheek bones, and high brow that gave him the hawkish look Jhared had seen in others of his kind, but the man's eyes belied that severity. They were pale lavender, long-lashed, and too pretty for his fierce features. They studied Jhared with an astuteness that suggested Zinderdali Imiro already knew some things about him.

"Let Lumati find no reason to mourn our meeting," the man said in accented Velos. "Let us find meaning in the crossing of our roads."

It was an odd greeting, odder still for the courteous manner in which the Sahisten delivered it. Jhared shifted his weight, painfully aware that he was the intruder here. Yet if Maya hadn't been standing beside him, nervously biting the edge of her lip, he couldn't have found it in him to be civil. "Forgive me," he told the man. "I didn't realize you were here for . . ." He shrugged and pointed toward the Sahisten's neck. "That scarf. It's Maya's."

"Ah, the scarf." The Sahisten brightened. "We don't believe we have ever been attacked for wool before, although Yavi would not leave us be until we made one for her." He frowned at Mayavana. "Where is yours? Not lost, we hope."

"No, no." She looked chagrined as she glanced at Jhared. "I'm afraid the blood wouldn't come out of it, after all."

"Blood?" The Sahisten narrowed his eyes.

Mayavana said something in Sahine and turned her wrist, setting her bangle of silver and copper god charms to jingling. Along the inside of her forearm ran a raw, red scar that Jhared knew.

The man's expression darkened at the sight of it. "Ah, yes. A gift of the Avelonian clanguard. Barbaric butchers. May wolves and crows feast on their flesh."

"They are," Jhared answered.

The Sahisten glanced up. His expression did not reveal the hatred Jhared expected, but the frank appreciation one hunter might show for another. "Very good, Patrolman. That is right and just."

Jhared didn't respond. The deaths had been necessary. Nothing about that ambush had been right.

"Enough talk of blood." The Sahisten's expression softened. "A Forest Guard must have things to say not for the ears of a stranger, yes? We will take ourselves down to the garden. The fish is in need of some fennel."

"Thank you, Zin," Maya murmured.

With a smile, the Sahisten leaned forward and pressed his lips to her brow before disappearing out the door. Jhared heard only the faintest creak of the ladder as he climbed down barefooted.

In the quiet, Maya looked down at her boots, then up at Jhared. "I'm sorry about the staff," she said finally. "Are you all right?"

"Fine," Jhared replied, touching the blossoming bruise on the side of his head. "I'm the one to blame. I attacked someone protected by the hospitality of the house."

"I just never imagined it could be you," Maya breathed. "How in all the Paths did you find me?"

Not *I'm glad* you found me, but *how*. Jhared felt as though the world had twisted. "Maya, you told me how."

The Avelun frowned, a knot of puzzlement folding between her brows.

"When I came to you behind the Gate," Jhared prodded.

She shook her head.

"I saw you swimming in the lake," he went on a little desperately. "You knew I had traveled too much. You told me to come to you. You knew . . ." He trailed off. The look she was giving him made his chest hurt.

"It wasn't me, Jhared. At least, it wasn't me on this Path. The last time I saw you, the killing winds were howling over Parnas Pass and you were sleeping in a cave after taking viremur."

A stone dropped into his middle. *Parallel*, he heard Leita say. Here was an example of the importance of knowing the Parallel of the Path you were traveling. The Mayavana he had spoken with beyond the Gate, the one who had forgiven him for leaving her and embraced him on the pier, had known the same things about their history as he did. He had supposed that meant she was his Maya. The Parallel must have been very close to his own. But not close enough.

"Do you understand?" Maya's tone was gentle, but she fanned one wing the way she did when worried or annoyed. "You went back to your people. I never expected to see you again."

"I understand," he said flatly. "Should I leave?"

She pierced him with her sage gaze, then glanced toward the ladder where the Sahisten had vanished. "Do you have it in you to stay?"

Jhared grimaced, thinking of the silver snakes on the Sahisten's wrists and the dead Sahisten spies in Avelos. "Who is he? He's more than just a smuggler."

"Zin trades in jewels. Primarily between Amuria and Sahiste. He passes through Avelos because it's a faster route." She glanced aside. "Jhared, I know what Sahiste represents to you. If you can't—"

"No, Maya. Even I don't know what Sahiste represents anymore. The things I've seen. The things that have changed . . ." He shook his head. The change was so immense; he didn't know if he had the right to burden her with it.

"Stay and rest," she said. "You look done in."

Abruptly, he realized what a pathetic figure he made, bruised and ragged and smelling of the swamps. "Very well," he muttered, and then, because that sounded ungrateful, "Thank you."

Her wings furled against her back. She nodded, biting again at the edge of her lip.

Words existed that he had said once before, words of concern and warmth he believed she had heard but that had gone instead to a different Maya. If he said them again, perhaps they could ease the bow-string tension between them. He discovered, however, that everything he wanted to say refused to leave his throat. All the gentle words remained wedged there, like a crust of stale bread.

Somewhere outside, the Sahisten began to hum a cheerful melody.

"I know this wasn't the road you imagined for yourself, Jhared, wandering alone beyond the borders of your homeland. I do know that. I hope you'll tell me how you've come here."

"If you'd like," he murmured. "Later, I think." His eyes went to the bags he had thrown aside when he'd charged into the house. Maya's gaze followed his.

"You stole something, didn't you? Is that why you had to run?"

"Yes. And no." He pinched the bridge of his nose between his fingers. "I didn't mean to steal them. The truth is I'm not sure what I'm going to do with them."

"What are they?"

She braced one hand on her hip. He knew that smooth curve, the feel of her competent, callused fingers, the scent of her. He pushed the memories away. "Let that wait until I share the whole story."

She nodded, but her gaze remained troubled. "If you'd like a safe place for them, take them up to the loft. There's a chest. They won't be disturbed."

"Thank you. Again, I'm indebted."

It was the wrong thing to say. He recalled that as soon as he said it.

She drew a breath, but instead of the sharp reply he expected, her voice went small. "I had hoped you might remember. There are no debts between friends."

"Every relationship is based on debts, Mayavana." He exhaled hard and shook his head. "Someone is always counting what is owed."

"In your world, perhaps." She lifted her hand, as though she meant to touch him. Her fingers trembled between them, perhaps waiting for him to take a step toward her. He remained in place, trapped by his disappointed hopes and by the melody of the Sahisten man outside. Eventually she lowered her hand and turned away.

To put up Seravina, Maya sent him to the far side of the house from the lake, where a generous paddock held a small shed, a herd of goats, and a leggy blue roan. Seravina tossed her head haughtily at the others. Jhared stood outside the fence with her, the reins gripped in one hand, trying to come to a decision. He could ride away now—ride away and pretend as though he had never found the cottage—but where would he go? What place anywhere would welcome him?

"You admire our Rashina, we see."

Jhared turned. He truly was tired. He hadn't heard the Sahisten approach. "Rashina?"

The man gestured at the roan mare. She had an elegantly carved head set high on an arched neck. Delicate white spots were scattered across her shoulders and rump. "She is a rare cross. Bearing the blood of both Sahisten and Avelonian lines."

"Maya didn't tell me you smuggled horses as well."

The Sahisten smiled. "Oh, no. Why should we risk trying to smuggle something strong willed that doesn't even fit in our pockets? Gems are compliant no matter who is their master. Rashina's granddam was a gift to our family. From a Forest Guard soldier. One like you."

"A deserter?" Jhared said acidly.

"No. One of the Punished." The man stretched a hand over his shoulder to tap his own flawless back.

"Ah. Shorn."

"As you say. This soldier fell while climbing in our mountains. His comrades abandoned him to death, but the Sahisten woman who found him took pity. My grandmother. He repaid her kindness with gifts of his own. His horse was one. A long-legged mare like your beauty here." He gestured at Seravina.

"So your grandmother bred horses of a Sahisten-Avelonian cross?" Jhared said, skeptical of the story.

"Indeed. It is evidence, perhaps, that the intermingling of our peoples can happen without conflict."

"Or perhaps imminent war and a century and a half of spilled blood suggest otherwise." Jhared looked at the man—his smooth back, his lively, pale eyes, and his silver snake bracelets—and realized he had no wish to know what Zinderdali Imiro meant to Mayavana. "It's no matter. You needn't try to convince me. I'm not staying."

"What? No, you mustn't leave." The Sahisten stepped forward and caught him with a strong hand, his expression sober. "Yavi has told us about you. How you spared her from the clanguard. We think perhaps you are more like the soldier our grandmother knew than the rest of them. We would dearly like to speak with you."

Jhared broke free of the man's grip. "Did she tell you I was stationed at Ravia? That I patrolled the border?"

"You mean to say do we know it has been your duty to kill those like us?" The Sahisten put his hand over his breast. "We do know it. Would you feel more comfortable if we hated you for it?"

Jhared grimaced at the bluntness. "Probably."

"Yet if we carried our hatred with us, waiting for the day we might meet you, then we must either slay you in reprisal for what you have done or let the hatred burn through our spirit. Either way, a waste of life." The man shrugged, but when he smiled this time, it was oddly bashful. "Besides, we find fighting tedious. No beauty exists in it."

It was an unexpected thing to hear from a Sahisten. The man carried himself like a warrior, and whatever he might think of combat, he possessed ample skill. Jhared thought of the Sahistens his patrol had encountered in Avelos; neither of them had carried weapons, but they had both borne the snakes. He had thought them priests, like the snake priest he had seen in Sahiste.

"And is it more comfortable for you to hate us, Patrolman?" The tone that interrupted Jhared's thoughts was curious.

"Why does a gem smuggler care what I think or who I am?"

"Aha, so you do see." The Sahisten stroked the serpent head on one of his bangles. "We wondered. It is a reasonable question, but do not expect it to be answered yet."

"Why not?"

"Stay. Take care of your lovely mare. Take care of yourself. Then decide if you are more interested in knowing the answer than in putting an arrow through our heart. If so, ask us again."

"Us? Why do you speak of yourself as more than one person?"

"Why do you speak of yourself as only one? Do you not carry others with you? The voices of your mother, father, friends, teachers?"

Jhared made a face. "Some of them. Yes."

"Just so. Likewise, I carry the voices of my gods. They deserve no less than the honor of my acknowledgment. Go on now. By the time you've cleaned up, the fish will be ready. It would be a sad thing for you if you missed one of our meals. Some have named our cooking . . . how do you say it? Unpaired?"

"Unmatched?"

"Just so." The Sahisten offered an incongruously sweet expression in his solemn face, before padding away as silently as he had come.

As the man disappeared, Seravina whinnied and jerked against her lead. Jhared had an instant to catch at her withers before the ground rippled and the Path beneath him twisted. He laughed grimly. On the day he conversed with a Sahisten about horses and cooking, he didn't need the world to swing out from under him to tell him his life had changed direction.

"I need your help," he called to his Teachers, hanging precariously to his self. *"You promised to teach me to close the Gate."*

No one answered. He waited, drawing steady breaths and willing the dizziness to subside. Finally, despite the blue flames tickling the edges of his thoughts, he forced himself to go about his chores, placing his focus on each moment. When he had taken care of Seravina, he walked out to the shore, staring far out over the water and breathing in the scent of vegetation. He would have dived into the lake and stretched his muscles with a swim, but he had no wish to drown if the Gate should take him while he was in the deep. Instead, he stripped off his clothes and waded in to his waist. With a rough stone, he scrubbed himself and then his garments. When his skin was alive and tingling, he climbed onto the pier and spread his clothes to dry in the afternoon sunlight. He lay back on the rough wood, staring at the clouds as they spiraled slowly above him, not daring to close his eyes with the flames so close.

The sun tipped toward the horizon, trailing gold over the clouds as it sank. A gull squawked and splashed into the water. Jhared glanced back at the house, where warm yellow light poured from the open shutters. He dressed in his damp clothes and girded himself to return.

Laughter floated from the house as he climbed the ladder. Hesitantly, he opened the door. The Sahisten was at the hearth, muttering in Sahine as he fumbled with a pair of tongs to retrieve something from the coals. At the table, Maya was filling cups from a pitcher, her wings uncloaked, her eyes brilliant. It was her laughter Jhared had heard, musical and lighter than he'd ever known it. He hung back, hating to intrude.

Maya turned, her wings fluttering as she spied him. "Jhared! Come join us. Zin has created a feast. Although I'm afraid he thinks yams taste better when charred."

"Little lark, men have traveled for miles to taste our yams." With a sound of triumph, the Sahisten caught up the escaped and now somewhat blackened tuber and plunked it onto a platter with the others.

"So it's been said," Maya replied, straight-faced.

The Sahisten flashed a frivolous grin.

The scene was unreal: a Sahisten man, an Avelun woman, and an exiled Shorn soldier. In the world Jhared had known, such a party was impossible. He stood motionless, afraid anything he did or said would shatter the whimsical moment and lead back to reality.

"Are you going to come in?" Maya asked him, her smile fading. "Won't you eat with us? Or are you already regretting joining the cursed?"

"Of course not." Jhared cleared his throat and made a move toward the table. "That is . . . I'm happy to eat with you. I'd be grateful."

The Sahisten swung around from the hearth and set his platter onto the table. "Be gentle, Yavi. The soldier doesn't yet know whether he's supposed to use that knife to cut his meat or the Sahisten cooking it."

Maya settled her steady gaze on Jhared. The weight of that gaze held the power to break him open and expose all his desires. She reached one hand across her breast and touched a feather on the inside of her left wing. "Not so long ago, you took a feather and accepted the hospitality of my fire, Jhared Denaban. Do you keep that oath, still?"

He swallowed. His heart kicked against his ribs. "I do. Although every other oath lies in tatters around me, I do."

His footing shifted. He slipped and grabbed the back of a chair, cursing under his breath.

"Whoa! The Paths reach for you!" Maya clasped his shoulder, a warm support, a spot of heat that shot sparks through his blood and fed the blue flames.

He flinched. "Don't. Don't touch me."

She released him as though stung. Urgently, he clutched at her sadness, at the feel of the wood beneath his fingers, at the scents of cooking food, pulling it all toward him, the moment where he belonged.

Soldier. Brother. Traitor. Thief.

He repeated the names, a litany of himself, but this time the labels he claimed had no effect. He began to fragment as the Gate refused to close. The flames roared higher and his Path slipped further away. He would be helpless soon, a pitiful heap at the Sahisten's feet. He spotted the knife on the table, slapped it into his palm, and thrust it against his throat. Maya cried out. The Sahisten murmured something in Sahine. Jhared shoved the blade into his flesh, rejoicing at the clean pain with the power to free him. In that instant, he understood why Alende returned to the blade time and again. He cut until the burn of his own blood replaced the burn of the blue flames, until he no longer floated outside of himself, until the Gate relinquished its hold.

The moment snapped back into focus, sharp and immediate. He let the knife tumble from his fingers.

"Gods of seas and skies," Maya muttered.

"Perhaps," the Sahisten replied, pulling out a chair and pointing Jhared toward it, "but we think not."

Jhared sat, one hand pressed against his throat. "I'm sorry," he said hoarsely. "Nothing else was working."

"In our country, there are gods we rarely mention," the Sahisten said. "Shadow gods who creep through the desert caverns or stir in the black cold of ancient wells. For the power those gods offer, some people are willing to shed their own blood, as you have. Tell us what it is you have done here."

Maya began speaking in Sahine, but the Sahisten stopped her. "In Velos, lark. The soldier is already too isolated. We manage just fine."

"Jhared is a Traveler. Like me. Just not always of his own will."

"The pain anchors me. That's all." Jhared despised the looks the other two were giving him.

"Ah." The Sahisten nodded. "You think pain keeps your attention—how do you say it—in the now?"

"The present," Maya said.

"It does. When other things can't," Jhared answered.

A number of unreadable thoughts sifted across the Sahisten's face. "That seems . . . inconvenient," he said finally.

Jhared gave a sharp laugh. "It is."

From a drawer in the sideboard, Maya took a clean cloth and dipped it into the water in the pitcher on the table. She handed it to Jhared, who wiped at the blood trickling down his neck.

"*Zi*, soldier, but you are unexpected. We hope you decide to speak to us rather than to shoot us, but that decision can wait. The food is hot." The Sahisten strode back to the hearth and returned with another platter, this one filled with steaming fish dressed in lacy fronds of fennel. "You'll feel better when you eat. How could you not? As our gran often said, *'Masi vithra revundi, sheril ria jur rufil ria lur.'*"

"Food prepared lovingly brightens life's joys and lightens life's burdens," Maya translated, taking a seat across from the Sahisten.

Jhared did as he was bid, grateful not to dwell on his near fall. In truth, he hadn't eaten so well since he'd left Elder Trianor's home and Neta's cooking. The roasted fish fell apart in tender flakes flavored with fresh fennel, garlic, and onions; the yams bubbled until their sweet orange centers spilled out and turned to caramel; triangles of flat, crispy bread absorbed pads of rich goat-milk butter.

As he ate, he observed the house more closely. Compared to a home in Elders' Circle it wouldn't be called large, but it was airy and filled with the outdoors in a way the heavy stone of an elder's home could never be. The ceiling arched high to accommodate the loft. Weavings worked in natural patterns and earthy colors decorated the walls and covered the floor around furniture carved of honey-colored wood. In one corner stood an upright loom of raw grey timbers, with an unfinished pattern in red and cream. From windows opened to each direction, a mineral-scented breeze and the sound of the lake breathed into the house.

"I thought you told me this wasn't your home," Jhared said.

Maya looked around. Her eyes held a hint of wistfulness when they lit on the loom. "It isn't. It never truly was."

"But you lived here as a child?"

"Yes. Until my mother died. Others help me care for it now."

Jhared paused with a bite of yam halfway to his mouth. "Others?"

"Zin. When he comes through." She smiled at the Sahisten. "Others I've guided who have become friends." She looked sidelong at Jhared. "Shared adversity throws people together in surprising ways."

Jhared flushed. Zinderdali grinned. "We'll not forget our first trip with you, lark."

"Because I lost us in the mountains and nearly walked us into the border patrol?" Maya said with a snort.

"Because of the fearless way you faced that expedition. Those two Laebeki brutes would just as soon have seen the rest of us drown."

The Avelun's wings rustled. "It was the last time I dealt with Laebeki trappers, that's certain."

"Ah, but we did turn a fine profit on those mirror rubies from Amuria." The Sahisten chuckled. "Which reminds us, we've some lovely skystones we just acquired from the Sangren Mountains. We'll show you later. Perhaps you'll see something you like."

A sparkle entered Maya's gaze. "It's all right, Zin. Jhared knows I'm seeking the skies. Don't tease! You have some news for me?"

The Sahisten finished a bite of bread and took a drink of water. "Two things. I met an old friend in the Sangren. A man who spends his days digging for skystones in the mountains. He's seen the Wanderers."

Maya set down her spoon. "When? Did he speak with them?"

"No, no. He's not the sort of man to win the attentions of the Reverent Folk, but he's seen them more than once. Enough he thinks he might find them again." The Sahisten made a face. "If properly enticed to do so."

"Why the face, Zin? That's better news than I've had in months! Perhaps I should travel to Sahiste now rather than wait for spring."

"Oh, Restless Wing, you know our thoughts on that search."

Jhared looked from Maya to the Sahisten. "Who are the Wanderers?"

"The most ancient peoples of Sahiste," the man said, a flash of pride in his lavender eyes. "Generations ago, we were all Wanderers, but most of us have long since traded the gift of travel for the comfort of walls and property. Those who hold to the nomadic ways keep our oldest history. They keep our secrets."

"I've never heard of them."

"You mean you've never fought them," Maya said drily.

The Sahisten touched one of his snake bangles. "You will never see them at the borders or hear of them at court. The Wanderers have no more interest in the castles of kings or the armies of chieftains than do the rocks and rivers. But they have seen more of our history than any court historian could recount."

"You believe they might know something about the Avelune? About flight?" Jhared wished his need didn't ring so clearly in his voice. It helped a little that Maya's gaze was just as laden.

"No doubt they own something of that history," the Sahisten replied. "Yet speaking with them is tricky. First, you must find them. They live true to their name and travel all about the crags of our western mountains. If you manage to find them, then they must deem you worthy of their words, for they hold our history to be sacred. *If* you find them and *if* they think you worthy, you may still not learn anything you hope to learn. They do not view the world as we do. They speak from the perspective of the land. If they tell you their people spied an Avelun a short time ago, it may mean they saw him a few days ago or a few decades. Men's lives are brief. In their view, only a span such as the growth of the trees or the crumbling of a mountain can be called a 'long time.' We cannot rely upon them to keep their legends out of the now."

Maya's wings drooped. "I understand all this, Zin. But your Wanderers may have the history Avelos has destroyed. I may have no other choice but to try them."

The Sahisten placed his hand over hers, his voice curving low and sympathetic across the table. "Which is why we have carried this news to you. We look to the day when you will soar above us."

Maya glanced up at him, gratitude soft on her face.

Jhared plunked his cup down hard. "You said you had two things to tell."

"True." The Sahisten sat back, removing his hand from the Avelun's. "My friend mentioned something else of interest. Yavi, have you not said the demand for ancient writings is growing in Sona? That you have made a good trade of it?"

"Yes."

The Sahisten smiled. "We now know why."

Maya inclined her head. "Why? What is it?"

"The stone traders say Sonans have come trying to buy pieces of Sahisten history. They say the *Simata'yo* is gathering all the knowledge of the world to fill a secret archive."

"It's no secret," Jhared said. "I've heard of it. A Sonan told me of it."

Maya looked simultaneously astonished and excited. "A Sonan, Jhared?"

"They were smuggling books out of Avelos. They didn't conceal their purpose. They're very proud of this new archive."

"Where will it be?" The Avelun's wings beat powerfully once, then twice. If she could have, Jhared thought she would have lifted out of her seat. He hated to drag her back down.

"I don't know."

"South," the Sahisten said. "Near the capital. Saimbor."

"Why didn't you tell me this first, Zin? So much knowledge in one place!" Maya's eyes gleamed. "What I need might be there already. Waiting for me."

"We wish it weren't waiting in such a dangerous place, lark."

Maya looked undaunted. "Are you offering to come along?"

The Sahisten ran his fingers over his bright scarf. "You know we would like nothing more. It has been a long time since we've smelled the sea. And there are pearls to be had at good prices in Saimbor. Sadly, we have obligations we cannot set aside. When would you leave?"

"I don't know. Soon. What's to stop me?"

"You know well enough what's to stop you. It is not a journey to be taken without consideration. Even if the pearls are well priced."

Jhared opened his mouth, then closed it without speaking. She hadn't even glanced at him. He would not impose himself.

"I'll think on what you say." Maya smiled demurely, but Jhared recognized the expression in her eyes. She was already working out plans.

When the meal was finished and cleared and night had snuffed out the sun, Maya went about the house closing the shutters, while the Sahisten settled into a chair by the hearth, drawing a small woven basket to his side. The domestic ease of their routine was more than Jhared could bear. As much as he longed to hear of Maya's escape from Avelos and to tell her all that had befallen him, he was too weary to continue the pretense of composure before the Sahisten.

"I'll go," he said softly at the Avelun's shoulder as she latched the last shutter.

"Go?" She turned, her expression startled.

"To sleep. I'll find a place outside."

"Oh." She frowned, chewing her lip. "You needn't. There's plenty of room by the hearth."

The Sahisten had taken a ball of yarn and needles from the basket and was beginning to knit.

"Not quite enough," Jhared replied. Although he told himself that years of Forest Guard training made it impossible to close his eyes under the same roof as a Sahisten, that was a partial truth. Outside he wouldn't have to watch Zinderdali Imiro smile at Mayavana or lead her up to the loft.

"I see," she murmured. "In the morning, then."

"In the morning." Without glancing back to catch her expression, he left the house and skimmed down the ladder.

12.

SHARED STORIES

Jhared ran along the shore, trying to quiet his thoughts with exertion. As he ran, his boots crunching sand and stones, Trevazio's broken cry came back to him in a measured cadence: *"You belong nowhere. No. Where."* Only when exhaustion finally forced him to slow did he find himself a place to sleep with the shed at his back and the lake down the slope before him.

He felt Shrill groping at his thoughts before he even lay down.

"Is there something in particular you're searching for?" he asked.

She ignored the stiffness of his tone. *"Who is this Sahisten? What is the feathered woman doing with him?"*

"You saw him? You were awake? Why did you not respond when I called for you?"

"You forget yourself. We are not hounds to be called." She gave his memories a painful tweak. *"Why would the woman want a Sahisten? Sahiste crushed the Avelune Exiles with their hatred as surely as Avelos did. Your ancestors died by their fire and spears."*

"I know," Jhared said. *"I've read* Maren's Burn.*"*

He had done far more than that: on another Path, he had flown above the archers, trying to escape two armies. His beloved had been slain by an arrow and he had died in the fires. He didn't lift that thought forward, though. He didn't want Shrill to interfere with the memory. He needn't have worried; her anger had turned into a tirade.

"They breached the border, the snakes of the south! Slithered into lands that had once been beautiful and green. They caught the refugees fleeing from Tumal's sword and slew them all! Old men. Young girls. Babes in arms!"

"I know," Jhared repeated. *"My earliest lessons included those horrors. What do you want of me?"*

"We don't want you to be so foolish as to trust the Sahisten."

"That's what you have to say? Don't trust a Sahisten? Will you next tell me not to stick my hand in fire and not to leap from cliffs?"

Shrill's irritation smacked against his awareness like the flat of a blade, setting his senses stinging. It was only a token blow. She could have dropped him to his knees—she had proved that well enough over the years. Her restraint now suggest-ed she was afraid, genuinely afraid. In Parnas Pass, he had gripped her essence and thrown her clear of his thoughts. She didn't realize that he didn't know how he had done it or how to do it again.

"I speak only out of concern for you," she lied.

Jhared squelched his annoyance. *"There's something you did not teach me about the Exile War, isn't there?"*

Shrill hesitated. *"What do you mean?"*

"Our attack on Sahiste was unprovoked. We assassinated their ambassador only because he dared to offer aid to Lady Amalia. All the violence that came after was of our own making."

"Foolish, boy. Why would you believe such a thing?"

"Lady Nemiah told me. She saw it. I've seen parts of it myself."

Silence, sudden and cold, radiated from his Teacher. *"So, you saw it among the Paths,"* she said finally. *"You, an untrained, undisciplined Shorn man. Don't be so naïve as to interpret every journey as a part of your own. The web is infinite."*

"Do you not trust the abilities of the Lady of Avelos?" he pressed.

"Do not trouble me with absurd questions!" she cried. *"You've not yet done what I asked of you!"*

Shrill hadn't known the truth about Lady Amalia. Jhared felt it in her fury. He held tight to his surprise. *"I will do what you've asked. I haven't yet had time to talk with Maya about the killing winds."*

"You promised us."

"And you promised to help me with the Gate."

She fumed. He held himself quiet. Never in his life had he owned any power over his Teachers. The freedom of it astounded him, but he knew he must take care. *"Please. If I lose myself in the web, I have no hope of learning the secret to stopping the winds. You know I have no skill. Is there not something you might share to help me?"*

"No skill," she grumbled. *"Of course you have no skill. You are Shorn. Broken. Tainted."* She trailed off, as though distracted by her own thoughts. Jhared forced himself again to wait in silence. *"Very well,"* she said finally. *"I give you this. Listen carefully. When the blue flames come, stop gripping your own moment like a babe on his mother's teat! The harder you grip, the more easily the flames will drag you in."*

"But if I don't cling to my own Path, the Gate will swallow me into the Nowhere."

"You are thinking of it all wrong!" she snapped. *"If you grasp tightly to a rope, what happens when someone at the other end jerks it toward them? You stumble! Instead, hold to your Path gently. Let the rope slide through your fingers and you will keep your balance."*

"I see how that might be. But what of stepping back to my own place once I have traveled? How is it Mayavana can glide through the Gate without pain, when the knife and the cold are necessary for me?"

Her presence hardened. *"Talk to your feathered woman. Find out how she woke the killing winds. Ask me no more questions about how you can further defile the shining web."*

Shrill departed with one last angry slap against his thoughts. Jhared tried to settle himself, but found sleep unreachable. Instead, his thoughts circled around her words, landing eventually on her warning against Zinderdali Imiro. Jhared's instinct was to despise the man. If he tried to see around that instinct, he wasn't certain what to make of him. The Sahisten had shown kindness and ferocity. He had been self-deprecating and frivolous, but beneath the silliness, he seemed intelligent and carefully composed. If Jhared relied on his own experiences and a lifetime of lessons, he expected to see someone who was aggressive, shrewd, and treacherous. Setting those lessons aside took effort and left him very little by which to judge the stranger. Other than Mayavana.

Maya possessed a generous, open spirit that allowed her to collect an assortment of unlikely companions. Jhared couldn't guess—didn't want to guess—at the others who shared her home and heart. It would be easy to be bitter about that, if it hadn't been her openness that had allowed her to aid an injured Shorn soldier when all sense said she should have ended him.

He sighed and turned over on the hard ground. Mayavana was not deceitful or cruel, nor was she foolish or rash. She would not befriend someone with a false heart or a hateful spirit. He could acknowledge that truth, or let his old veils continue to dictate his dealings.

His thoughts kept him tossing restlessly. When dawn finally scented the darkness, he rolled to his feet and stretched the stiffness from his limbs. From the paddock, Seravina let out a warning snort.

Although he had heard no one leave the house, Jhared spied the Sahisten moving among the animals in the near-dark. Moonlight silhouetted his long frame as he stood beside his roan mare. From that perspective, Jhared recognized something familiar about the man's build and bearing. He might have been a Shorn soldier preparing for a patrol. For several moments, Jhared watched, undecided. Then he strode to the paddock.

The Sahisten tossed a saddle blanket across his mare's back. At his feet lay a saddle and two small packs. He nodded in acknowledgment as Jhared swung up and onto the top rail of the paddock fence.

"You're leaving," Jhared said, and winced at the relief so plain in his tone.

"Briefly," the man answered. "We plan to return. By tomorrow dusk, if all goes well."

Rashina danced in place, eyeing Jhared coquettishly from beneath long lashes. Behind her, Seravina paced, her silver head lifted and her ears pricked. Jhared clicked his tongue at her to distract her from mischief.

"Is it the business of stone smuggling that takes you away?" he asked the Sahisten. "Or some other thing?"

The man only smiled and turned to retrieve his saddle. As he did, Seravina sidled closer to his mare, her tail high and trouble sparkling in her gaze. Abruptly, Rashina's head snaked toward her, teeth snapping. Sera squealed and cantered to the other side of the enclosure, scattering the sleepy goats. The Sahisten chuckled and set a firm hand on his agitated mount.

"We do admire the mares," he said amiably. "Honest creatures. Reasonable, if not always tractable."

"No, not always tractable," Jhared agreed, swinging off the fence and dropping into the paddock. He closed on Seravina, who was scuffing the ground with a fore-leg, considering whether to press her challenge.

"Of course mares will test one another, lay out their conflicts with flattened ears, a bite, a kick." The Sahisten patted his roan. "But once they've determined their hierarchy, they get on with the task of caring for the herd. Not like stallions. Stallions will batter one another to death for nothing more than the favor of a mate or the claim to a patch of hill. Prideful. Unforgiving. The world is run by stallions, we fear."

Jhared glanced over his shoulder. "If you admire candor, then tell me what you are about. I know you for a spy. I wonder if perhaps you serve as a priest as well. I would know what that means."

Only a momentary hesitation betrayed surprise in the Sahisten. He slipped the bridle over Rashina's head. "A priest? Ah, no. The Favored of Lumati groan in dismay at the thought. We have no discipline for such vows. And *spy* is such an ugly word in the Velos. Deceptive as well. You think that it reveals our intentions."

"Does it not? Are you not delving for information from Avelos for the benefit of your people?"

The Sahisten tightened the saddle girth another notch. His mare stamped a hoof. "How much do you care if we are?"

Jhared gritted his teeth. "Just because I left Avelos does not mean I wish war upon her."

All flippancy slid from the Sahisten's features as he led Rashina out of the gate. "Indeed. You give us some hope, soldier."

"That's no answer," Jhared insisted.

Zinderdali Imiro turned and stepped close. He was subtly scented with something serpentine and smoky. The only time Jhared had ever stood so near to a Sahisten, he had been battling for his life. He did not step back now, but kept his gaze on the man and his hands loose at his sides.

"Is your spirit supple enough to bear what we say without breaking, Jhared Denaban of the Punished?"

"Leave off your vague warnings," Jhared growled. "Either tell me or do not."

Zinderdali Imiro smiled. "Very well. We will give you an answer when we return. We vow it. Will that satisfy you?"

"I will hold you to it," Jhared said, not capable of answering the man's smile.

"Good." The Sahisten vaulted into the saddle, moving easily with his mare as she jigged and skittered. "You have a shadow on your heart, Jhared Denaban. But this life is short, and beauty exists for you in this place. Do not brood over our words when we have gone. Rejoice in what the day offers."

He loosed the reins and his mare leaped after the edge of light on the eastern horizon. Jhared watched the pair disappear. From the distance, Rashina let out a long, high-pitched whinny. Seravina stretched her neck and bugled in answer.

Jhared shook his head. "Now she's a part of the herd, is she?"

He fed Seravina and then the goats, who insisted upon it by butting his legs and nibbling his shirt. After, with a shovel and rake he found in the shed, he cleaned up the paddock. In the process, he noticed that a nail on one of the posts had worked loose. He pounded it flat. Then he took his time examining the other posts, repairing or pulling loose nails. By the time he finished that task, the day had brightened to blue and gold. For a time, he wandered listlessly around Maya's steading. He glanced up at the house and circled wide of it, ending near the garden. The rows of kale, carrots, and yams looked near to revolt. He bent to pluck a prickly weed, and before he knew it, he was crouched in the dirt trying to impose some order.

"Jhared?"

Maya stood at the end of a row of squash. She was dressed in brown breeches that skimmed her long legs and a laced shirt of pale green. Her wings gleamed in the early sunlight, a thousand shades of frost and night.

Jhared's breath caught. "Good morning."

She tilted her head, a sardonic expression shaping her face. "You're weeding the garden?"

He shrugged. "It seemed to need it."

"Was that easier than coming back to the house where you might have to talk to me?"

Heat touched his cheeks. He stood, brushing dirt from his hands. "I suppose so."

Her nod suggested she had expected nothing else, but he thought he caught a flash of regret as well. They stared at one another in awkward silence. She looked away first.

"If you're hungry, I've food laid out," she murmured. "You needn't fear. I won't press you."

He ducked his head. "I . . . thank you. You never have."

He meant it well. She had always carefully respected the matters about which he could not speak, but this time he was certain he saw frustration in her gaze before she turned her back and started toward the house. He followed with a sigh.

The table was laid with the last of the yams from the night before, sliced and drizzled with honey, a wedge of crumbly cheese, and morsels of smoked fish. Maya moved from the hearth to the table without speaking, setting down plates and pouring tea as Jhared watched. Even early in their travels, they had worked together in a compatible rhythm. Sometimes Jhared would have said he knew her reactions as his own. It wasn't a wholly unfamiliar feeling for a scout. Tracking was an intimate business. Studying another's movements taught him the things his target feared and loved; whether he was a sound or restless sleeper; how he reacted when tired, injured, or angered. Eventually, such observations allowed Jhared to predict another's actions. With Maya, he had shared that link almost as soon as their Paths had crossed. Now he longed for its return. He sat self-consciously, feeling disconnected and lonely.

Maya folded herself into a chair and speared a slice of yam onto her plate.

"You seem to live well here," Jhared said, searching for a way to ease the silence. "The Sonans accept you?"

"Mm. That's somewhat complicated. Do you truly want to know or are you just trying to avoid the awkward quiet?"

He didn't look at her. "Please tell me."

She set down her fork and licked a drop of honey from her finger. "The village on the other side of the lake is named Vris. They tolerate me there for my mother's sake. Many among them remember how generous she was with her skills as a healer. Even if she was from Avelos."

"And beyond the village?"

One ombré wing lifted. "You must understand that this close to the border, they've heard the stories of Avelune betrayals. Tolerance such as Vris allows is the exception. Most stay well clear of me. Open hostility is rare."

Jhared frowned. "But it happens?"

"There are reasons I do not call this place home."

She spoke matter-of-factly, but Jhared felt a surge of protective anger. Maya deserved a place that was safe and hospitable. He wished he knew of such a place for her. "Will you stay here through the winter?"

"I don't know." She peered around the comfortable room. "Zin has given me an excuse to travel. Maybe I'll go to Sahiste to seek the Wanderers."

"Or to southern Sona to find the archive?"

"Perhaps."

"Your Sahisten fears you going south," Jhared said. "Do they hate you there as well?"

"Ah, no. No, the southerners don't hate me." She chuckled, a small strained sound. "Zin exaggerates the danger."

"But you wish to go whatever the danger."

"What would you risk if you might find a way to reach the skies, Jhared?"

He faced her without flinching. "Everything."

She smiled, not her wry smile or the warm, welcoming one, but a hard thing, jagged with determination. "Just so."

He had no reply to that. No way would ever exist for him to reach the skies.

Silence fell once more. Jhared sipped the strong, smoky tea.

"What happened after you left me at Parnas Pass?" Maya asked eventually. "Did you reach your people in time? I hoped for you."

He looked up. It seemed so long ago since two Shorn soldiers had dragged him away from Maya and into the high chieftain's camp. "I reached them in time."

He didn't say that his message didn't matter, that the council had discovered his crimes and decided not to believe what he told them, that Leita had been maimed and most of his comrades slain. Those words refused to come forward.

Maya bit the edge of her lip. "The winds struck the pass again after you left. Was that you?"

"Yes." His fist dropped onto the table, more heavily than he meant it. Maya jumped.

"Jhared, what's wrong? Have you forgotten how to trust me?"

He scrubbed his hands over his face, feeling the burden of too many nights of little sleep and too many days of running: from the council, the unbound, the tangle. No time to think, only to act. Keeping secrets had become reflexive. Yet reflexes played a role in a man's survival.

Are you not delving for information from Avelos for the benefit of your people?
How much do you care if we are?

"The Sahisten makes things different," he replied.

Maya winced, as though she had known that answer was coming. "He's not here now."

"But our people are a heartbeat away from war. And you . . ." *You hold him dear.*

"He's not one of those who stir conflict, Jhared. He does not seek to spill Avelonian blood." She lifted her eyes. "Will you trust me in that, at least?"

Her gaze shone a silver green, like the Parnas foothills after the first thaw or the sage growing in the rocky canyons of Sahiste. He felt the faintest tug in his chest as his spirit trembled toward hers. He sensed a thread of hope, his own and not his own. The slender connection between them twisted like spider silk. He let out a careful breath, afraid to tear it.

"Very well," he answered. "I will. Just let me have one day of nothing more than weeding gardens and tending animals. Let me have some time to consider things without needing to watch the trail behind me."

"Of course. Of course you shall have it." She smiled, softly this time, an expression he had missed.

"You did promise not to press me," he said.

"I meant it. I did!" She made a helpless gesture. "I just don't like the silence. Too much exists between us for that."

The spider-silk connection faded as she rose from the table and began to clear the plates.

Jhared could not remember a day when he had owned the freedom to do whatever he pleased, and he reveled now in choosing the most mundane of domestic chores. When he asked Mayavana what he might do to help her prepare for the winter, she had looked at him at first with bemusement, and then with the kind of artless pleasure he had only ever seen in Branlen. Throughout the morning he worked in the garden, first weeding and plucking snails off the greens, then digging up the last of the yams and the onions. After brushing the dirt from the tubers and bulbs, he filled bucket after bucket and carried them to the house, where a rope and pulley had long ago been arranged to draw bulky loads up to the door. He made trips back and forth, filling the bucket and transferring the food into barrels for winter storage.

While he worked at that task, Maya carried a basket of soiled laundry down to the shore. It was on his last trip from the garden that he heard her singing. He recognized the melody: a Sonan lullaby she had once sung for him. He halted, his chest suddenly too constricted to draw an easy breath. She was kneeling at the water. Her body rocked slightly as she scrubbed the clothing against a stone. One of the first times he had crossed her Path, she had been at the same task. It had been colder then; she had been wearing her cloak and he hadn't yet known what she was. It had been one of the most peaceful moments he had ever experienced.

She stopped. Her head came up and her gaze went directly to where he stood. Abashed to be caught staring, he waved and strode toward her, as though it were what he intended all along.

Maya slapped a shirt once more against the stone and tossed it into the basket with the other wet things. "Still a scout spying out others, Jhared Denaban?"

"Not others," he said quietly. "Not any longer. Only you."

Her lip quirked into something that wasn't quite a smile. "Oh? And what have you learned from such observation?"

He hesitated. He hadn't truly meant to say something so revealing, and now he'd made them both vulnerable. With a fabricated grin, he picked up the basket and started for the house. "A great deal about how to scrub stains from a shirt."

To his relief, she laughed and jogged to catch up with him. Her black hair rippled past her shoulders and across the curve of her wings. It had grown since he'd seen her last. "I had no notion a soldier could make himself so useful," she said. "If you've finished in the garden, how are you at working with goats?"

His turn to laugh. "I couldn't say. As it happens, soldiers aren't *that* useful."

"Well, you handle that silver queen of yours without a problem. This should be easier." She gestured to the basket in his hands. "Hang these over the line beneath the house while I grab my tools."

She returned with a small knife and a rasp and led him into the paddock. Immediately, several of the goats came crowding over, nuzzling and nibbling at Jhared's hands. A red and white nanny bleated expectantly until Maya pulled an onion from her pocket and fed it to them all in pieces. Just a few feet away, Seravina huffed and snorted and looked askance at the Avelun.

"She's frightened of me," Maya said, glancing at the mare.

"No, that's not it at all." Jhared watched, amused and surprised, as Seravina scuffed the dirt and put on airs. "She thinks you're a threat to her status."

"Ah. I see. Even your mare counts me as more beast than woman."

From her acerbic tone, Jhared recognized the scar of an old wound. It startled him. He had never considered she could believe such a thing of herself. "Maya, Seravina's grandsire was Chosen. It's Riana who's acknowledging you."

The Avelun made a skeptical face before turning toward one of the wandering goats. "I only need you to hold them and keep them from bolting."

She gestured to a grizzled black billy near the fence. Together, they separated him from the herd, then Jhared took firm hold of the animal's ridged horns and wrapped one arm over its flank.

"Good," Maya said, bending over her work. She lifted a cloven hoof and set to it with her knife.

The goat bleated in complaint and tried once to buck out of Jhared's grip, but Jhared murmured reassurances and gradually it quieted. When Maya finished trimming all four hooves, Jhared released his hold, sending the billy scrambling back among its kin. Maya pointed to a grey nanny next.

By the time they had finished with the entire herd, the sun had sailed past midday. Jhared was dusty and smelled vaguely of goat. Across the enclosure, Sera still eyed Maya dubiously, prancing and fretting her sentiments.

"A queen indeed," Maya muttered.

"She needs a stretch," Jhared replied. "I'm going to take her out."

Maya's hand stilled where she'd been scratching the poll of a grey kid. "Now?"

Jhared waded through the goats to Seravina, who seemed pleased to claim his attention. He ran a hand down her injured foreleg: no heat or swelling. In the last few days, she had moved out soundly. He patted her shoulder and vaulted onto her back, not bothering with tack. She danced an eager circle.

"Is there a reason we should not?" he asked.

For a moment, he thought Maya meant to tell him no and send him out—he anticipated Seravina's speed with a grin—but instead she took a tense step toward him. "It's the villagers. A foreign soldier is a threat. Someone might follow you back to see where you've come from and then . . ."

His grin faded. "Then I will be a danger to you."

"I'm sorry."

"No, Maya. It's for me to be sorry. For what I've brought to you." He swung down from Seravina and turned her loose.

"Come inside?" Maya suggested.

Jhared gazed over the landscape, the garden, the lake, and the wilderness beyond, not certain what he was looking for. "I think I'll swim for a while. I smell of goat."

She nodded, looking unexpectedly shy. "Later then."

He swam for several hours, enjoying the effort of crossing the lake, and the strange landscape along the shore. Stunted trees with glossy leaves twisted up from between large rocks. Brightly colored lizards hung from the tree branches and sprawled on the stone. The beasts were an impressive size, thicker than a man's forearm and as long as the distance from Jhared's wrist to his shoulder. As he swam past them, the lizards merely blinked impassively and flicked their tapered tails.

Only when a storm blew in, bringing pelting rain and wild spears of lightning, did Jhared retreat to the cottage. By then, afternoon had melted into evening, and dusk had stolen the color from the Sonan wilds. As he climbed the ladder, he heard the sound of the bar being lifted from its cradle. Maya smiled to see him, even when he came in dripping wet. She threw him his cloak from where it had been hanging on a peg. "Dry off. Then sit. You're famished."

It was an absurd thing to feel pleased simply because she could understand the scale of his appetite, because she experienced the same thing herself, but there it was nonetheless. He rubbed the cold droplets from his skin, then hung his cloak and dropped into a chair, pleasantly weary. Maya laid out for each of them a half-shell of a large squash mounded with a golden, crispy filling. When he spooned a bite of the mixture into his mouth, it melted with a tender, creamy warmth that offered both sweetness and spice. She had mashed the flesh with onions, cheese, and some type of sausage before baking the whole, tremendous concoction. He ate slowly, savoring every bite and promising himself he would hunt tomorrow to contribute to her larder.

When they had finished the meal and cleaned up, Jhared sat back in his chair, listening to the whispers of the lake against the sand. Maya had pulled out a piece of mending and was making small neat stiches in the cloth. A wisp of her black hair brushed her cheek. She reached up absently and tucked it behind her ear. Her wings, furled against her back, gleamed softly in the lamplight.

It was a simple, perfect moment. He wished he could halt the anguished flow of his thoughts to enjoy it, but sitting in this strange country with the Avelun beside him seemed less real than all the blood and death he'd faced in the past weeks. Nightmare images—Rona's body, Trevazio's grief, Leita's anguish, Amalia's chains— burned in his mind, had been burning him all day, although he had done his best to extinguish them. Tired and with no distractions now, those memories threatened to ambush him.

"Mayavana, do you know that once again you have saved my life?"

"With squash?" she asked, an arch curve on her lips.

He smiled a little, then shook his head. "Allowing me sanctuary when you've no reason to do so."

She snorted without looking up from her work. "Did you imagine I would send you away?"

"You could have."

This time she looked at him, her expression perplexed. She studied him for several long moments. "No. No, I don't think I could."

She set aside her mending and went to the sideboard. From inside the cabinet she lifted a large, earthenware jug. It thunked heavily as she set it upon the table. She poured two cups, handed one to Jhared, then retrieved her mending and drifted toward the chairs near the hearth. Jhared sniffed the contents of his cup—it had the plum-blossom scent of *slu*. With more relief than he should have felt, he took a deep swallow and quickly poured again before following Maya.

They talked for a long while about very little: the care of goats, the quality of the local fishing, the length of the Sonan growing season. Maya told Jhared that the colorful lizards by the lake were called *cissanu*, for their bright hues. They were harmless, so long as they stayed out of the garden, she said, and palatable enough if roasted with the right spices. Jhared told Maya of Seravina's breeding and her sensitivity to the Paths. The Avelun smiled at his description of the mare's haughtiness.

Jhared hoped the *slu* would make it easier to push aside the other images hounding him, but everything he said seemed to circle back to the reason he had ended here, with three bags of sacred maps and nowhere else to go. Finally, he stood, walked to the table, and filled his cup once more.

"Maya, the story you've asked for is terrible, path-twisting. Before I start, consider whether you truly want to know it."

She looked up quickly from her mending. "I do."

"No. I said *consider*!" He strode back to the middle of the room and stared down at her. "You asked for my story once before, and regretted it."

"That wasn't regret, Jhared. I was angry and sad. I don't regret learning about who I would have been. Who you are." Her green gaze turned fierce. "Do not think me afraid to hear this."

"Are you not?" he murmured. "I am afraid to speak it."

The house grew quiet. He turned away and moved to a window, unlatching the shutters to reach the cool air. When Maya replied, the iron had melted from her voice. "The Sonans say even the strongest pillar does not support the house alone. Share your story with me. Share this much of yourself. Please."

The rain had stopped, but no starlight graced the darkness. Still, her plea was a kind of grace. She had asked not only for the story, but for a part of him. He drew hope from that. With his back to her, he started to speak. The story came out in a spiral, as Alende might tell it. He formed the first loop from the events that seemed a lifetime ago: his patrol's capture by Commander Ciam, his discovery of treachery at Aglar Tower, and Lieutenant Sevar's order that he run south to warn the council. The winds that had struck the Sandien Mountains then had been of his own creation. They had pushed him into Maya's cave. She nodded with understanding, and he knew that questions she had never asked were being answered. He spun out another loop of the spiral: the day, weeks later, when he had left Maya in Parnas Pass and was captured by the Forest Guard. He held nothing back in this telling. He told her of the northern traitors, his own crimes, Commander Ciam's accusations, and Elder Trianor's sorrow.

He moved around the room restively as he relived those Paths. Again he fled his own camp to hunt for his patrolmates; again he hid in the treetops listening as the prefect of Clan Aglar ordered their deaths. His voice grew rough when he spoke of how Leita had been tortured, how the killing winds had gathered and struck in the moment Commander Ciam meant to slay him. Maya refilled his cup and he drank before describing his interrogation by the council. He spun another loop and yet another: telling her about Alende, the unbound, Mursa Vin, and stolen sacred maps. He had to pause to collect himself before he could go on to tell how he had betrayed Alende and how Rona had died.

Only at the very tail of all those loops did he finally come to the circle that encompassed them, the reason Lady Nemiah had cut him free of his bonds—Lady Amalia's story. Anger and anguish fired his words as he spoke of Lord Tumal's threats against the temple and of the Arionad who meant to protect Amalia but had caused her destruction instead. He spoke of the Exile War and Shorn Law and babes torn apart because one man loved and one man hated an Avelun woman. He spoke of Amalia's grace and the trust words she had shared with him. Jhared didn't glance at Maya again. She had asked this of him. He gave her everything without restraint.

Then, suddenly, nothing else remained to be said. He halted at the edge of the room, facing one of the autumn-colored weavings on the wall, a pattern of linked circles.

The grey haze of morning filtered through the shutters. Sometime in the night, it had started to rain again, and drops played unevenly against the roof. Over the lake, the gulls had taken up their keening.

The Avelun sat without speaking. She looked stunned. Her wings pressed flat against her body.

"Maya?" he whispered.

"Gods of seas and skies, Jhared. I didn't understand. I thought what I saw in you before was merely duty. But you truly care for them, don't you? Your elder, your patrolmates, even the dark priestess. You *love* them. I didn't believe it possible."

He stared at her, taken off guard. "They were the ones who raised me. Who taught me. Who—"

"Who broke and betrayed you." She shivered. "At least the Kin were straightforward about what they stole. Poor Rona. And the child. Trevazio? What will become of him?"

Jhared closed his eyes. "Alende will care for him. I don't know what he will become."

"Perhaps your dark priestess is right: the web is unraveling." Maya's wings lifted, then resettled.

"And Lady Amalia?" Jhared said tautly.

"Ah, yes. Sweet, brave Amalia. I have often wondered what manner of woman she was. Whether greed or stupidity or trust led her to death. Now we know."

"Now we *know*?" Jhared's eyes snapped open. "Mayavana, my people are Shorn for no reason other than Tumal's hatred! We have been stripped of our very selves. Bound into service. For naught!" He trembled with outrage too long pent.

"Oh, Jhared. Nothing has changed in that. There was never any justification for those things."

"That's not true!" He swayed on his feet, from exhaustion, from too much *slu*, from too many lies in his past. "They gave a reason for my losses. There was *balance* in it!"

"No," she said, unyielding. "What was done to you was always an evil thing. Nothing can balance it."

He opened his mouth. At the back of his throat, desperate words scrabbled to form. A part of him longed to let loose of his sanity, to splinter everything around him, to shake Mayavana free of her composure.

What was done to you was always an evil thing.

Branlen's arms thrown around him in a guileless hug. Loyal comrades at his back in the midst of battle. Summer mornings in the mountains.

Babes bleeding upon Riana's altar. Oaths demanding the sacrifice of the self. Brilliant skies forever lost.

What was done to you was always an evil thing.

If balance had ever existed, it no longer mattered. It did not exist now.

The fight drained from him all at once. He bowed his head. "I don't know which direction to step," he said hoarsely. "I have been carved by Avelos to serve one purpose. That purpose has been taken from me, but I don't know how to move beyond it."

He felt the loss like the wings torn from his back: even now, there was pain where they were meant to be.

Feathers rustled as the Avelun moved closer. "To fully enslave a person, Jhared, to prevent him even from using his own strength to free himself, he must be taught that his strength is corrupt. He must be shamed for his dreams of freedom. And he must believe that the teaching and the shaming are signs of love."

Jhared sucked a breath and stepped away from her. In his fantasy, she had understood the immensity of his losses, but in truth, she only judged him as weak for giving his loyalty to the people who had been his family, people she viewed as monsters. Movement was necessary now to keep that hurt from catching him. He turned toward the door.

"Jhared . . ."

He paused to look back at her, but whatever she saw in his expression made her shake her head and let him go.

He visited Seravina, stroking the mare's arched neck, resting his brow against her warm withers. When the skies opened wide, a torrent washed over him, and he let it. Eventually, he was forced to return to the house, wet and cold, to face the unsettled quiet that hovered between him and Mayavana. In some ways, the Avelun was a mirror, reflecting back the things he least wished to face. He'd told himself that he had broken free of Avelos, so why were her words such a knife in the gut? He didn't know the answer to that question, and then he did: If he acknowledged the evil of those who raised him, what choice did that leave but to throw away everything that had been his life?

Maya would tell him nothing of that life was worth keeping, yet it was *his*. It was everything he knew. Could a drowning man cut the last thread connecting him to shore? If everything he knew was evil, what did that leave him?

To distract himself, Jhared spent the day attending to chores he had long neglected: stitching down loose buckles on Sera's tack, oiling his saddle, cleaning his boots. Maya said nothing about his restiveness as she went about her own day. They moved around one another carefully. At some point, Maya disappeared into the loft for a nap, but Jhared did not sleep. The soldier's skill of catching rest whenever the opportunity arose had never been his. As ever, his Shorn body compensated, feeding him energy and strength from a cache that perhaps had been meant to support the demands of flight. All his life his Teachers had warned him that relying on his Shorn energy was dangerous. When he thought on it now, he realized how many times that strength had kept him alive—and had allowed him to keep others alive. The afternoon passed and evening crept forward. While he tended his bow, Maya crept down the loft ladder. The rain had stopped and night enwrapped the house. She held out three grey-black feathers to him. Her feathers. He hesitated.

"Why?"

"The grey symbolizes the in-between," she replied, laying the feathers on the table beside him. "The border between the end of one Path and the start of another."

"The Nowhere. The twilight where Riana will not tread." Jhared stared at the feathers. In Avelos, they formed a curse. He needn't see them that way now, but his thoughts went there reflexively, like a horse turning the same way back to the stable.

"For some, the border spaces are sacred," Maya said. "Places of fertility and growth. Places to make new commitments without the hindrance of old expectations. The feathers are only a symbol of the sacred, but they can be a reminder of the promise of things to come. If you let them."

He ran one finger lightly across the glossy vanes of the longest feather. They were a part of her, and she had offered them freely. "Thank you," he murmured.

She nodded and started to turn. He caught her sleeve.

"Truly, Maya. No one else knows everything I've told you."

She said nothing, but set a hand on his shoulder. He looked down and let out a long breath. Within him, something opened, like the untangling of a knotted cord. Only slowly did he register that she genuinely had heard his secrets, even if she could not accept them all. It was no small gift.

She is lovely, certainly. If you reached for her now, she might be yours.

Her fingers left his shoulder before he could decide whether the last thought was a worthy one.

"It's perfect outside," Maya said, moving away from him and retrieving her cloak from its peg. "The storm has cleared. Would you come with me to see the stars? Riana's spirals are endless."

"A reminder of my insignificance?"

She lifted one shoulder in a shrug. "There can be comfort in considering one's own troubles against that vastness."

He smiled a little; he couldn't help it. In some ways, she knew him so well. He set aside the bow and followed her.

The clouds had fled, leaving a sky of unsullied black gleaming with infinite points of silver. As Maya walked toward the lake, her palest feathers glowed under the starlight.

"Beautiful," Jhared murmured, as though he were only appreciating the landscape.

"I didn't think so as a child," Maya said ruefully. "It was a trap and a torment. A place I needed to escape."

"Because your mother didn't allow you to reveal yourself?"

Maya looked up at him. "You saw that, didn't you? You had touched my Path even then."

He nodded, remembering a woman fueled by a mother's fear chasing a younger, defiant Maya along this very shore.

The Avelun sighed. "After we escaped from Avelos, she never overcame her fear that someone would come to make me pay. She taught me to contort my shoulders to keep my wings hidden. Each day she made me practice twisting and flattening them. Gods of seas and skies that was painful." Maya stretched her wings to the trembling edge of their span. Jhared's lungs filled with the scent of clean feathers.

"Did it work?" he asked, a little roughly.

"Until I grew older. Then no amount of contorting could hide what I was. She made me bind them instead. I hated her for it. It kept me weak, and I blamed her. I thought it was her fault I couldn't fly." The Avelun looked aside, a shame in her

Jhared had never witnessed. "I was a cruel and foolish child. I didn't understand what my mother had saved me from. I didn't understand what a monstrously difficult thing it was for her to surrender everything she loved to make a life in this wet country."

"Not everything she loved," Jhared said.

Maya bit the edge of her lip, and after a moment, nodded. "Thank you for that."

"It's what I saw, Mayavana."

She nodded again.

"You don't blame her anymore?"

"No." Maya picked up a pebble and flung it into the water. It skipped across the surface and disappeared, shaping circles within circles. "I left home so I might be free of the bindings. I worked hard to strengthen my wings. Now there's nothing wrong with them. They're strong and healthy. There's only something wrong with me."

"What we've lost," Jhared said softly.

She gazed at him, her eyes glistening. "Oh, Jhared. I am sorry."

Simple words for the complex emotion in her gaze, but she didn't need to say anything else. She reached for his hand, and he closed his fingers gently around hers. In companionable silence, they continued along the shore.

A gull rose over the dark water, a grey ghost gliding. Mayavana stared at the bird with bittersweet intensity. Something in Jhared stirred to life. He knew her longing. This was the connection he had so missed. With sudden, intrusive clarity he recalled the feel of her body around his.

Soft. Strong. Welcoming.

He glanced sidelong at her. She smiled, a little shyly.

The scent of her skin. Her feathers brushed across his bare chest.

Again, Jhared felt a stirring deep within him. More memories trickled into his head unbidden.

Her lips on his throat. His fingers exploring the sweet curves of her.

"Don't fear the memories. Draw closer. Savor her warmth."

It crossed his thoughts that this was not right. Not yet. Not when he still felt the remnants of anger. Not when a Sahisten stood between them.

"Draw closer. Feel the heat rising from her body. See the seed of desire in her gaze."

He stopped to study her and was suddenly certain he did see it. When she squeezed his hand, need flooded through him.

"Awaken her longing. Remember what to do: your hands to stir the heat; your lips to spark the fire."

He kissed her, tentatively at first, and then with a flare of passion he thought must consume them both. His arms encircled her. She struggled to free herself of laces and clothing. Cloth ripped as he gripped her tightly, needing her touch too urgently to let her pull away.

"Jhared?"

His name on her lips. A gift. His tongue trailing over her breasts. His teeth in her flesh.

"Reach for her. Reach for her now!"

Her wings beat the air as her body arched against his. Her nails scored his flanks, tumbling him to the very brink of control. The first time they had fallen together, she had freed him from shame and offered him joy. He longed to return that joy to her.

"Jhared, please—"

"See, she calls for you. Feel her desire building. Her body opens to yours."

He groaned with need.

"Take her!"

"Jhared, stop! Please, stop. Do you hear me?"

Her tone reached him. The sound of alarm. It arrowed through his desire and clawed the fog from his awareness. Suddenly, he saw her on the shore looking stiff and scared, not at all impassioned. Mired deep within his memories, he sensed Shrill. Understanding and horror drove through his chest.

"Demon, what have you done?" he cried. "I will tear you apart and fling you into the Nowhere!"

Shrill darted like a rabbit among his thoughts. Her terror bolted through his awareness.

"I will shatter you!" he shouted. "For this, there is no pardon!" He lunged at her, aiming to wrap his self around her and throw her from him, as he had done once before, beyond the Paths. But his thoughts closed around nothing. She sprinted and he spun, focusing all his anger again in her direction. But how does one lay hands on a thought? On a nightmare?

Just beyond his reach, Shrill froze, her terror changing slowly to shock, and then to relief. Enraged, he threw himself at her a third time, and again he slipped against her as harmlessly as raindrops against a window. She eyed him with cold contempt. He felt her laughter. Then abruptly her presence winked out.

Heavy with dread, he forced himself to look outward. He was on his knees in the sand. From several strides away, Maya stared down at him, breathing fast. Her wings mantled above her shoulders like an angry raptor. "Gods of seas and skies!"

Jhared climbed unsteadily to his feet, his heart squeezing hard in his chest. "Ah, Mayavana. Forgive me. Please forgive me."

"Stop!" She threw out a warning hand. "Don't take another step until you tell me who you mean to tear and shatter."

Jhared halted, realizing suddenly what she had heard and how she might interpret it. His rage at Shrill had not been contained within his thoughts. "It was my Teacher. It was Shrill. She distorted my senses with memories of . . . us."

Maya remained unmoved. "Why would she do such a thing?"

"My Teachers believe you carry the secret of the killing winds. That your desire unleashes them. They want to learn from you."

"But the winds arose from *you*. Didn't they?"

"Shrill doesn't believe so. I am Shorn. Broken. I can wield no power." He sucked a breath. The winds were of no matter in this moment. It took effort to meet Mayavana's gaze. "Please tell me what I've done. I will not forgive myself for any harm I've caused you."

A troubled knot tightened between her brows. "Jhared, you did not harm me."

"But I . . ." He looked at her more closely. Her color was high, her posture vigilant, but no teeth marks marred her throat. Her shirt remained whole and demurely laced. He shook his head against what he would have called memories. "Goddess, Maya. Please tell me what happened."

"You kissed me. Sweetly, at first." Her flush deepened. "Then hungrily. But something happened to make you pull free. You seemed to lose sight of me. Of all the outside world. You were braced, as though someone were trying to drag you someplace you feared to go."

"Indeed." Jhared closed his eyes. "I heard you call to me."

"I thought you were fighting the Gate. I wanted to give you an anchor, but I wasn't willing to use the knife."

"It was your call that pulled me back to the moment. I was so afraid I had harmed you."

She inclined her head, her look serious and considering. "The time when you might have done me harm is long past, Jhared. You would not hurt me now. Do not fear it. These Teachers, as you call them, cannot make you someone you are not."

"You don't understand." He looked away from the trust in her eyes. "My Teachers have been a part of me for so long they're enwrapped within my thoughts. What they tell me to see, I see. Shrill twisted my own memories to make me believe what I sensed was the present. In that moment, I could not judge reality from veil. What I thought I saw in you . . . that desire. Goddess, forgive me, I might have—"

"Stop, Jhared. You did not."

He swallowed and nodded.

"It's a good thing," she said briskly. "I would have regretted being forced to break your arm."

It relieved him to hear the fire in her voice. He nodded again.

"It's done now," she said more gently. "Come back to the house with me."

"In a while," he mumbled. "I can't yet." She didn't realize how Shrill had set need coursing through him, how that unsated longing coursed through him still. She couldn't know how much his Teacher's manipulation terrified him. Just now, he didn't dare to be close to her.

"Very well," Maya murmured. "When you're ready. I'll leave the door unbarred."

He watched her stride away, Shrill's laughter echoing in his ears.

That echo made him shudder. In the last moment before his Teacher left him, she had seen the truth of him. Her laughter held her realization that he did not possess the strength she had feared. She would return.

The house was silent and shadowy when he finally climbed the ladder. Maya had banked the fire and retired to the loft, leaving one candle flickering on the table. Jhared marched straight for the *slu*. He drank until his body felt numb and his thoughts grew distant. It was a barrier of sorts, the only one he knew to erect. Shrill had used him in a way she had never dared before. She had altered his perceptions almost entirely. So close. He had come so close to violating a boundary he would never trespass of his own will.

Mayavana wouldn't approve of this solution, he knew. He could imagine the look in her eyes and her crisp tone as he tossed back another icy swallow of *slu*: "What are you doing, soldier?"

He was taking what steps he might to keep his will under his own control.

Even this far gone, he could appreciate the irony, but he had no better answer than to cloud his mind until his Teachers couldn't reach him. Shrill had burrowed into his memories like a wood roach into a log, gnawing his perceptions into the shape that fit her needs. How would he trust his senses after this? It occurred to him he couldn't even be sure of the few gentle moments when he and Maya had shared one another's confidences. Was it a memory or Shrill's violation? What had Maya truly shared with him?

He might have hurt her tonight. The terrible awareness of that wouldn't leave him.

He reached across the table and pulled the jug close again.

13.
SPIES

Jhared's last clear memory was of staring out at the lake watching the mist rise over the water. He didn't know exactly how he had ended in a chair by the hearth with a blanket draped over him.

A shaft of light from the window cut a bright square in the middle of the room and told him that morning was growing old. He sat up slowly, so as not to upset the precarious status of his innards. The stillness in the house said he was alone. Better that way. He didn't wish to face Maya as he pushed through the aftereffects of the *slu*.

He padded to the open shutters, rubbing at the grit in his eyes and studiously ignoring the pounding in his head. There was no sign of the Avelun at the lake or in the garden. In the paddock, Sera grazed contentedly amidst the goats. He watched the animals for a while, then turned from the window to make tea. He drank it in sips, not entirely certain how it might be received. When nothing untoward occurred, he risked enough movement to wash up at the basin near the door and tried to make himself more presentable. The only items of clothing he possessed were his travel-worn Forest Guard gear. Although he no longer had a right to wear that uniform, in the forest colors he at least felt like a scout and a tracker, parts of himself he was still willing to claim.

He spent the remainder of the morning wandering about Maya's home, trying not to think of anything that might awaken Shrill, trying not to look too deeply within himself. Inconsequential tasks occupied him—sweeping the floor, scooping ash from the hearth, carrying up fresh water from the old well between the house and the garden. Then he approached the loom.

The upright frame stretched from floor to ceiling, a rectangle of rough-hewn timbers, bound together by rope and the dozens of slender ivory threads that formed the warp. A fine red-and-cream pattern filled the first ten inches of the loom, but from the faded stripes that marked the yarn, it was evident that it hadn't been touched in many years. Dust and daily doses of sunlight had taken their toll. Beside the loom, balls of the same red and cream yarn were crisp with age. He wondered how long it had been abandoned, waiting for skilled hands to finish the pattern.

With an intense flush of regret, he thought of Leita. She had been a master weaver—of Paths and people. She had tried to weave his Path into something he could not imagine and still feared.

What was she weaving now that she could no longer see the pattern?

With the tips of his fingers, Jhared plucked at the warp, wondering, if Leita were here, what she would have him do about Shrill. The Bearer drew her power from transformation and disorder. What others had named abomination in him, she had called strength. But she had no patience for weakness or the comfort of avoidance. Even that horrible night when Jhared had found her brutalized and maimed, she had demanded that he give her a blade and had been prepared to fight. She would have nothing but contempt for his self-indulgence now.

He straightened, staring at the unfinished work before him. Leita had offered him knowledge no others would. Knowledge was what he needed now. Once, just once, he had been able to throw his Teacher from his awareness. What dark strength had allowed him to do it? Where might he learn to do it again?

His gaze was drawn toward the loft, where he had stored the sacred maps.

They hold the most meaningful records of our history.

He had said as much to Alende. The maps told the stories of Avelos, and the Shorn were a part of those stories. He rose and turned away from the loom.

The loft was Maya's private domain and he entered it self-consciously. More than in the rest of the house, here he saw something of the Avelun's straightforward, practical nature. The single floor covering was of undyed wool. Surfaces were clean and uncluttered, the furniture simple and serviceable. Amidst that order, however, three items spoke of other aspects of Mayavana's spirit: a lush blanket of cerulean wool tossed over a chair, a small owl exquisitely carved from a rose-colored stone, and a copper bowl with a collection of bright feathers. Jhared ran his fingers across the long, silky vanes—green, blue, gold, peach—wondering at the birds who had dropped them. He smiled to think of Maya retrieving and treasuring them, like a child picking shells off the beach. Beside the table lay the precisely made bed. He speedily shifted his gaze past it to the chest where she had allowed him to keep the maps.

He opened the chest's heavy lid to find the bags inside undisturbed. He piled all three bags beside him and began to unlace one. Nothing about the Teachers had caught his attention the first time he had looked through the journeys, but he hadn't read all of them and he hadn't been looking then. He upended one bag, brushing scrolls to the side, and sat down.

With no windows, the loft remained dim and the air touched with cold. Jhared pressed his back against the bed and unrolled the first map on the floor. It was a familiar one, but he reviewed the journey thoroughly, following the tight script as best he could and working to understand the four Principles. The journey followed a morning in the life of a shepherd, the uncle of the Pathwalker, if Jhared read the perspective correctly. The young man had fallen while climbing down a ravine to retrieve a lamb and had broken his shoulder. His unlikely rescuers had been a group of novices from the nearby chapterhouse riding out with their hounds to hunt.

Jhared set the map aside and picked up another. He didn't truly expect to find a journey centered on the Teachers, but they had been a key to the training of the Shorn for near a century and a half. Mightn't some Pathwalker have brushed their thoughts? Mightn't a mapmaker have commented on their purpose or their nature? He unrolled the next map and the next. The first time he had read the maps, they had entranced him. He had felt Riana's kiss and been awed by the wealth of her gift to Avelos. As he studied them closely, however, the tendrils that shaped each journey seemed thin and sparse, like vines withered by drought. Although the temple taught that within the infinite weaving every Path was interconnected, most of these stories occurred in isolation, with no tendrils binding them to others. One after another, Jhared searched each sacred map for what he needed, but with each story, he felt a growing sense of emptiness.

Below the loft, the sun was slanting against the east wall. He dropped the last map and pinched his brow between two fingers. He could speak on the preparation of fleece for dyeing, the wedding of an elder's daughter, and the rivalry between two unknown priestesses, but not on the Teachers. At his side lay the last of what he'd stolen from Alende, an old volume that had been tucked in with the maps. A brief glance when he'd first taken the book had revealed a journal of sorts, but he hadn't yet spent any time with it. He debated giving up and going downstairs to find something to eat, but instead he stifled a yawn and pulled the volume onto his lap.

It might have been something beautiful once, finely stitched and bound with good leather, but a dark crescent marked where a clasp once existed, and smoke and damp had stained many pages. Some pages had been cut free.

Gently, he turned the brittle vellum, attempting to read the faded words, and discovered something unexpected. The book hadn't been written in the old, formal Velos that most scholars called ancient; this text was in a Velos so old it was nearly a different language. Many words were unfamiliar. Sentences curved and twisted in foreign ways. Jhared ran his hands over smoke-singed pages. His first guess had been wrong: this was no journal kept by a single priestess. The script changed often, revealing it had been written by numerous people, and the headings of each entry included the four Principles. He pulled out a map, observing the careful headings there, then glanced back to the book. The book's entries dealt with specific journeys. It was a volume discussing the maps. From the archaic Velos and the condition of the book, he guessed that the maps these notes referenced were far older than the ones scattered about him.

For some time, he struggled to decipher the work. His ancient Velos was good, but this was more foreign than any history he'd ever read. Some priestesses wrote with the formal phrasing of ritual. Others wrote as though in correspondence with a friend. Some entries discussed points of theology well beyond his ken. Most entries seemed impossible to fully understand without the original maps to give him context. Frustrated, Jhared finally leaned against the bed and closed his eyes. A fascinating book, no doubt a treasure to the temple, but still nothing about the Teachers.

The bed against his shoulders was soft and carried the faint tang of autumn berries, Maya's scent. Safe enough to indulge the thoughts that came of that when she wasn't near, or so he hoped. The book slipped off his lap. Eventually, he slid down to a place where frustration didn't reach him.

He awoke gently, knowing she was there. Some part of him must have recognized her step or perhaps the way her movements stirred the air. She was sitting in the chair across the room, one knee drawn up to her chin, her wings settled gracefully around her shoulders. She wasn't looking at him, but into some vague distance, a perplexed frown canting her features. For a moment, he watched her as she sat unaware. Then her gaze came back to him, and she startled.

"You're awake! You might have said, rather than staring quiet as clouds."

"You seemed preoccupied. I didn't want to disturb you."

She snorted and peered at him closely. "Are you . . . all right?"

He sighed, wondering if this awkward inquiry would of necessity become the start of their every interaction. "I seem to be in my own place and time, with no Teachers painting over my perspective, if that's what you mean."

She nodded, as if about to add something more. Instead, she rose from the chair, her eyes on the scrolls.

He fidgeted, aware of her bed at his back. "The maps," he said. "I thought I might learn something about my Teachers from them. I didn't mean to intrude upon your space."

"And did you learn anything?"

"Not about the Teachers."

"What then?"

She crouched beside him. Her warmth radiated against his side. A row of ebony-tipped feathers brushed his arm. Abruptly, Jhared ached with the need to reach over and stroke those feathers. He didn't pause to assess whether the desire was his own or inspired by Shrill, but leaped to his feet and grabbed up the book.

"Here." He thrust it at her, a wall between them. "Look here. It's a collection of notes. All on the sacred journeys. And it's old. Very old. Much of it may have been written before the Exile."

"Truly?" She balanced the book in one hand and opened it, her eyes consuming the pages with sudden eagerness. "Does it say anything about flight?"

"Nothing. At least not that I've found so far. The translation is a challenge."

She chewed the corner of her lip. "I wonder how it survived Tumal's purges."

"Look at those smoke stains. It seems it almost didn't."

She closed the book and turned it over in her hands. "Might I keep it? I mean, just to study it more closely?"

"Of course." He smiled to see the light in her gaze.

She tightened her arms around the book. "Zin will love it. And his ancient Velos is better than mine."

Jhared's smile died. "You can't show it to the Sahisten."

"Why not?"

"Maya, how can you ask? I've not turned traitor. I won't reveal the heart of Avelos to her enemies."

"Jhared, this isn't a book of Forest Guard secrets. It's ancient history."

"That history is more tangled with the present than ever. If it weren't, Avelos and Sahiste wouldn't be on the brink of war."

"What if they are? Just what do you imagine Zin might do with a book of map notes?"

"I don't know! I don't know what he's searching for!"

Her voice dropped low, but the waver in it exposed her strain. "I told you he doesn't seek conflict. You said you trusted me."

"Well and good. A spy who has nothing to do with conflict and war." Skepticism dripped from Jhared's tone. "What of the others of his kind? If Sahiste were to learn the source of the killing winds, do you know what would happen? Every one of the unbound would be hunted down until the Sahistens caught someone they could use to destroy Avelos. They would capture Shira and—"

He broke off jaggedly, aware of the tension in his body, anger coiling into something dangerous. The control he had once trusted had become a slippery thing.

Maya laid the book down between them and took a step backward. "That's what this is about, isn't it? It's not the book. You fear I will tell Zinderdali your secrets."

Jhared forced himself to uncoil. His hands dropped loosely at his sides. "It's not only that. I shouldn't have stayed. After what Shrill did, I should have left last night. There are too many ways this can go wrong."

Maya's mouth opened. For a moment, he thought she would protest, but whatever first impulse he saw in her rose and died. She had never pressed him for what he dared not give.

"If you believe that's true," she said carefully, "I only ask that you wait until Zin returns. It's important he speak with you."

"Why is it important?"

"I don't know. Not all of it."

"Wasn't he meant to return last night?"

"The rain must have slowed him. He'll return today or perhaps this evening. Jhared, please stay until then. You know that you—"

"Owe you?" he finished.

Her gaze snapped upward. Coldness frosted her expression. "I was going to say you needn't fear that I would share your story, but have it as you will."

He turned away from her, wretched. Somehow he had just rejected his only sanctuary. He should leave now, before more damage was done, but the truth was that he did owe her.

"Very well," he answered. "Until the Sahisten returns."

Zinderdali Imiro did not appear that evening or the next day or the following night. Each evening, Maya left a lamp burning low for him. Each day she appeared more uneasy. She grew quiet at first, then distracted and short. By the third night, her glance never trailed far from the window.

It pained Jhared to see her distress, even while he hated how much the Sahisten's fate meant to her. When he longed to touch her hand and offer her comfort, he kept his distance, constrained by his fear of Shrill and the specter of the foreign man between them. By the fourth night, she did not sleep at all. He stayed with her. They spoke carefully of nothing as she paced before the hearth. Finally, Jhared came to a decision.

"Tell me where he's gone, Maya. In the morning, I'll ride out to search for him."

She turned, misery scribed across her features. "I don't know where he's gone."

"He didn't tell you?"

"Some things are unwise to share. We've grown into a habit of not asking."

"Do you think he's gone to Avelos?"

"It's possible. I don't know. He was just *in* Avelos. After you left me, I found him south of Parnas Pass. In one of our old hides. We returned to Sona together."

Another sting, that, to know the Sahisten had watched as Avelos ripped itself apart, to know Maya had traveled with him, all thoughts of a Shorn soldier gone. Jhared drew a breath. "Why?"

Many questions existed in the single word. She shook her head, refusing them all. "He can only tell you that himself."

"Would you tell me if this were about Sahisten retribution?"

"It's not!"

"All right, all right." Jhared lifted his hands against her indignation. "I'm only trying to understand."

"I know." She plucked unhappily at a feather. It came free. She made a face and rubbed her wing with the heel of her palm. "I'm sorry. It's a generous thing you've offered. I wish I could make use of it."

Evening was deepening on the fifth day when Seravina's long whinny rang up from the paddock. Jhared knew what it meant even before he heard the uneven hoof beats hurrying along the shore.

"Rashina's coming."

"Zin!" Maya dropped the onion she'd been chopping and spun toward the door.

Jhared stepped in front of her. "Wait. Something's gone awry or he wouldn't have been so long. Take your bow."

She looked as though she would argue, but nodded and did as he bid. Jhared slipped his own quiver over his shoulder and grabbed his bow before striding to the north-facing window. Rolling lowland stretched away from the lake, covered by clumps of scrubby trees that twisted over the long grass. A single road, hardly more than a serpent of worn earth, wound from the northwest toward the house. It was empty but for the familiar horse and rider moving closer. Jhared followed after Maya.

The Avelun ran to greet the Sahisten as he rode into the yard. His mare's head was drooping, but he gave Maya a smile.

"Your face is one we dreamed of seeing," he said, drawing his mount to a halt. "Forgive us, Yavi. We were delayed on the road."

"You know I must forgive you anything," Maya said, her features light with relief.

The Sahisten's expression was a gleam of white teeth in the dusky light. "In that case, we might have spent some time collecting sins."

Jhared strode up more slowly. He had been trained to observe and exploit an opponent's weaknesses. He noted the subtle way the Sahisten leaned in the saddle, the tension in his hands on the reins, and the way his smile flickered when Maya glanced away.

"Should we expect anyone else?" Jhared asked, coming up on the mare's right shoulder.

The Sahisten shot him a sharp glance. "We would never lead danger here."

Jhared looked up and hissed a breath. A crude bandage wrapped the man's right knee and thigh. His breeches were torn and stained black. "I hope that's not all yours," he muttered, gesturing at the blood.

"Why, soldier, do you take us for a thief?"

Jhared didn't smile. A bolt of the loathing he'd been trying so hard to stifle flashed through him. He knew what Sahistens were. He had seen their savagery. Did an Avelun's word really make it different? "Among other things."

The man's expression remained set, but Maya's voice trilled with sudden concern. "What is it? What's happened?"

Zinderdali slipped his feet free of the stirrups, grunted as he swung his right leg over the saddle, and landed awkwardly.

Maya made a choking sound. "Gods, Zin! And you let me tease with you? For that I could kill you myself."

"We were not teasing, silverwing. Your smile always gives us hope."

"Words and more words, while you bleed out your life in my yard? Lumati save me from the foolishness of men! Come. I'll help you with the ladder."

The Sahisten didn't follow but swung his gaze back to Rashina. Whatever other emotions the man evoked, Jhared respected him for that.

"Go on," Jhared said. "I'll take care of her."

The Sahisten hesitated, then gave a nod and handed over the reins.

Jhared worked quickly to care for the beast. She was spent, her coat sweat stiffened. She had come a long way at a hard pace, but other than several superficial scratches, she appeared uninjured. None of the blood staining her right flank was hers. When she was clean and watered and turned into the paddock, Jhared hastened back to the house. Foreboding knotted in his stomach.

At the top of the ladder, he heard the Sahisten speaking, wearily insistent.

" . . . for both of you, Yavi. It can't wait."

"It will wait," Maya replied. "Be still. This is going to hurt."

The sound of cloth ripping, then strained amusement from the Sahisten. "You know we love when you speak so."

"Hush. I know well enough what you love."

The man's tone changed, grew quiet. His words were Sahine. Maya answered tenderly in the same tongue.

Jhared pushed the door open and entered. The Sahisten had collapsed into a chair near the hearth. Mayavana knelt beside him, her red box of medicines at her knee. They both turned as Jhared approached.

"How is it?" he asked.

"We will give Lumati no reason to weep today," the Sahisten said with forced cheer.

Maya's expression was more guarded. She had torn away the bloody breeches and had managed to remove some of the bandage, exposing a portion of the wound. The surrounding flesh was tight and swollen. Jhared recognized the work of a blade, and what it meant.

"You killed the man who gave you that."

The Sahisten closed his eyes. "Yes."

"Was he a Forest Guard or just an unfortunate farmer who crossed the path of a Sahisten spy?"

Maya scowled. "Jhared, not now."

"We can still answer for ourselves, Yavi." The Sahisten spoke gently, but it was a reprimand all the same. Maya opened her mouth, then subsided. When Zinderdali looked at Jhared, his lavender gaze revealed grief. "There were three, soldier, not one. And they were not Avelonian. They were Sahisten."

Maya made a sound of surprise. Jhared took a steadying step as a series of ripples warped the ground beneath him, his Path turning. "A necessity to save your own life?"

The Sahisten lifted one hand heavily. "To save something of much more significance. That does not mean I regret it less."

Not *we* this time. This act he did not share with his gods.

"Be still now, *vi shik*." Maya bent over the leg and with competent fingers attempted to pull away another layer of the bloody cloth where it had clotted to the wound. Although the man made no sound, his body strained against the back of the chair.

Maya ceased without success, shaking her head. "Jhared, put the—"

"Water on the fire. I have it."

"Thank you. And bring the other lamps. I need better light."

"While you work, Zinderdali Imiro has a story to tell," Jhared replied, moving toward the hearth. "One he promised me before he left."

Maya whipped around, disapproval hard in her eyes.

"This is the time, Yavi," the Sahisten breathed. "We were foolish for thinking it safe to wait. We won't wait longer."

While the man began to speak, Jhared kept busy: stoking the fire and heating water; brewing a tisane from the Avelun's pain-dulling herbs; ripping clean cloth for a bandage. He avoided looking on the intimate circle formed by Maya and Zinderdali. It wasn't the care she gave the Sahisten that constricted Jhared's chest—she was a healer and would do as much for a stranger; she had done so for the Shorn soldier who had stumbled onto her Path weeks ago. It was the depth of affection he saw in her face; the soft, reassuring words she murmured in Sahine; the way the man closed his eyes and gave his body into her hands with total trust. Jhared had no right to envy that intimacy, but somehow he couldn't stop.

"Do you have it in you to believe that, soldier?"

Jhared coughed and turned around. He'd lost track of the Sahisten's question. "Believe?" he echoed.

"That the heir to the throne of Sahiste does not want war."

Jhared set a mug filled with the bitter tisane on the table beside the man. "I don't know."

Zinderdali took the mug with a deep sigh. "At significant risk to his standing at court, Prince Ashani convinced the king to propose open borders with Avelos. At risk to his life, he entered Avelos to speak with your council. You know the result of his efforts."

"The council rejected the proposal," Jhared answered.

"Not even leaving an opening for negotiation," Zinderdali said, emotion slipping through his weariness. "A door slammed shut in the face of our king. It was not well done."

"You know enough of our past to know why," Jhared replied.

"Not everything comes down to history between our peoples, soldier. That rejection arose from something more immediate. We know enough of your High Chieftain Rumar to believe he would have welcomed the opportunity King Javahari offered. He was forced to refuse it. But that part must wait—"

The man caught a sharp breath as Maya touched his leg with a cloth soaked in hot water.

"I'm sorry," she whispered.

The Sahisten licked his lips and continued a little breathlessly. "Rumar's refusal dangerously divided the *Camril Fi*, the king's circle of advisors. Some have withdrawn their support from the prince, and that has forced Javahari to distance himself from his heir. Despite it, Prince Ashani continues to work toward peace, while for others the idea of peace with Avelos is intolerable."

"And what is your part in this division?" Jhared asked.

The Sahisten clenched his jaw as Maya began to work the dirt and grime from his wound. "We are tasked with avoiding this war."

The words shoved at the bounds of plausibility. A short time ago, Jhared would have dismissed them as lies without consideration, but too many things had changed. He glanced at Maya and saw a level of surprise in her face. She hadn't known, at least not all of it.

"Are you an agent of the prince?" he asked.

The Sahisten shook his head. "You called us a spy and a priest. We call ourselves a Hand of Lumati. The Hands do not answer directly to the court but to our temple. It is our duty to strive until Lumati no longer has any reason to weep for the world."

"Then you are one of Lumati's Favored?"

"Ah, no. Not by far." The Sahisten trailed off raggedly with a gesture at Maya.

"The Favored of Lumati are his most powerful priests," she said. "If they choose to show themselves, it is only to those of royal lineage. Most often they keep to their temples in the mountains."

Zinderdali held up one silver-bound wrist. "These snakes signify that we have studied enough to be one of Lumati's lowliest servants. The Favored are his companions."

Maya paused, cursing under her breath as she picked another shred of filthy cloth from the Sahisten's wound.

Zinderdali leaned his head back and smiled wanly. "Have you decided to surrender us to the gods, lark?"

"You must keep heat on the leg as long as you can tolerate it. I can't close it yet. Too much poison within."

"We understand," Zinderdali replied. "Do not bear any blame for what happens now."

Maya rinsed the bloody cloth in the bowl of boiled water beside her, wrung it out, and set it again on the Sahisten's leg. "Do you want to tell what happened?"

"Yes . . . yes. We suspect the soldier will need to hear it before he'll truly start to listen." Zinderdali seemed to gather himself. He sipped from his mug and set it aside. "We rode into Laebek to meet another Hand who carried word from the Avelonian border, but he had been clumsy. He was followed by men loyal to the cause of vengeance. They attacked us. It was three days before we managed to lose the last of them."

"What of your companion?" Maya asked.

The Sahisten shook his head. "We were forced to flee in different directions to split our enemy's strength."

"What did you hear from him about the state of the border?" Jhared asked.

"Your Forest Guard stands ready at Ravia," the man replied. "In the past moon, however, the number of troops has shrunk. Our colleague did not know why or to where the forces have been withdrawn."

"But you know," Jhared said. "You were at Parnas Pass."

Zinderdali glanced at Maya. "We do. We know General Nadel has drawn men north to deal with traitors."

Jhared hadn't been sure the high chieftain would risk pulling men off the Sahisten front to chase after the treacherous northern five. His anger clashed with his helplessness. "What else?"

"Prince Ashani's remaining supporters are being forced down by those who protest the possibility of peace. Without his heir's strength, King Javahari will likely revert to the purpose most familiar to him."

"Retribution," Jhared muttered.

Zinderdali gave a faint response. Jhared realized the man's energy was guttering, but he pressed again: "Javahari means to take advantage of our diminished defenses, doesn't he?"

The Sahisten nodded. "He will strike first, we imagine. And soon."

Soon. Nightmares fed on that word. Soon hosts of Sahisten warriors would collide with a depleted Forest Guard demoralized by a summer of killing winds and the threat of civil war. Soon Sahistens would tear through the villages of Clan Amerre and Clan Makri, slaying villagers, Shorn first, in retribution for losses over a century old. Soon Sahistens would ride north, burning their way toward the city.

Jhared's heart pounded and his muscles buzzed. He needed to run now, to fly north to warn all those he had once loved, but something was missing from the pattern. The Sahisten heir did not want war. King Javahari had sued for peace. Jhared could feel the missing element. Zinderdali had almost said it. *We know enough of your High Chieftain Rumar to believe he would have welcomed the opportunity Javahari offered. He was forced to refuse.* Jhared licked his lips as the meaning came clear. "You believe someone has deliberately maneuvered our countries to this precipice."

Surprise brightened the Sahisten's fading gaze. "A subtle mind. Yavi said so. Do you see it? These storms of shattered glass—killing winds, you call them. They upset the balance in your council. They made your high chieftain's position precarious and forced him to reject our king's proposal to open the border. That rejection in turn weakened Javahari and estranged him from his heir. Now your ruler is in danger of being unseated and ours is backed into a corner from which he has no choice but to fight."

Jhared drew a measured breath. He saw before him a trail he didn't want to tread. "You're saying the killing winds were used to bring about this unbalance, but whoever understands how to call the killing winds owns the knowledge to destroy our lands. They have no need for subtlety."

"Unless their purpose is to watch Avelos and Sahiste savage one another. If their hatred is that immense . . ." The injured man lolled toward the edge of awareness. He shook his head hard and tried to straighten.

"Easy, *vi shik*," Maya murmured. "It's only the tea reaching you."

Jhared thought of Shira, who had first unleashed the killing storms in Avelos not far from the Sahisten border. Who but the unbound owned reasons to hate both Sahiste and Avelos with such force? If Shira lacked the guile and focus to devise such a far-reaching plot, had someone else found a way to use her? Had that been a part of the remorse and fury that drove her? Or were others involved who had discovered their own strength? What did it mean to Jhared if some among the Shorn had found a way to seek retribution? He cleared his throat and faced Zinderdali. "Do you know who it is?"

With visible effort, the Sahisten lifted his gaze. His lavender eyes were dark with drunken intensity. "Not yet. Not for certain. Do you?"

Jhared shot a glance toward Maya.

The Avelun stroked the Sahisten's brow. "Enough now, my friend. Speak later. War will not reach you here."

"Soldier, do not flee this truth just because it comes from me." The Sahisten's eyes were closing under Maya's touch. "If hatred sets the direction of your path, Lumati will have more cause to weep for the children of both our lands."

Maya covered the unconscious Sahisten with a blanket as Jhared began to pick up bits of bloody cloth. What was unsalvageable he fed to the fire. The rest he carried to the table along with the pot of blood-swirled water, which he emptied from a window. Maya washed her hands and face, then retrieved another pot of clean water from the bucket and set it over the hearth. Jhared brought out the small canister of smoky tea she preferred. She took it from him without speaking.

For a time, they moved in silence, dealing with small necessary tasks. They had been preparing dinner when Zinderdali returned. Maya pushed aside the half-chopped onion and the uncut squash and brought out instead a basket of flatbread, a jar of plum jam, and a partial round of cheese. She put them on the table as Jhared poured the tea.

"Would they believe you?" she said finally, "If you tried to warn Avelos?"

He swallowed. Even now she could arrow to the core of his thoughts. He recalled his last days as a Forest Guard: the high chieftain's look of disgust when Commander Ciam had revealed his lies, Elder Abrigado's smug confidence at the council interrogation, his foster father's final question. He had broken Laws. He had shattered his bonds. Whatever trust he had once been given had been destroyed. They meant to execute him.

"Jhared?"

"No. They wouldn't."

"I see." She broke off a piece of bread, but didn't eat it. "I saw what it meant to you when Zin spoke of the killing winds. You think it's possible. You think the unbound Shorn may have manipulated Avelos and Sahiste toward war."

"It is possible."

She sat back in her chair. One hand scratched at the leading edge of her left wing. "I see," she said again.

He stared at her, thinking of Lusian, twisted and corrupt, who had poisoned innocent men. He thought of his own betrayals.

"What is it you see? A Shorn man trained to kill? Do you also expect me to wreak violence in retribution for years of pain and hatred?"

"I didn't mean any such thing. I only thought that after all Avelos did to you—"

"That I must wish others to lose what's dear to them? For men to be burned and women raped? For children to die of hunger and disease?"

"Jhared, I only wanted—"

"That's not who I am! Just because I am done with them does not mean I wish them misery." He wrenched his gaze away from her.

"As you say, soldier."

He sucked a painful breath. He had become *soldier* again, so quickly. Well, he was a soldier, and Shorn. Skilled at little more than causing pain and death. Maya had always seen the truth in him.

"Go. Rest," he said flatly. "You haven't slept well in days. I'll stay with Zinderdali."

Silence radiated from her side of the table. Then her chair scraped the floor and she rose. Jhared heard her pause briefly beside the Sahisten before she climbed the ladder and disappeared into the loft.

14.
CUTS AND BRUISES

The rumbling started deep within him. Jhared thought of spring in the Parnas Valley when the thaw often caused avalanches in the mountains. Among his patrolmates, he had usually been the first to know it, feeling the vibration in his bones and the low, low rumble in his chest.

This time, however, the sound grew clearer rather than louder, until it was no avalanche but a deep voice. Jhared's heart sped at the sound of his Teacher speaking. He held his breath and clutched his thoughts close.

"*. . . and the boy calls us his Teachers!*" Boar growled. "*What did you think to gain by such abuse?*"

"*He's given up learning,*" Shrill spat. "*I warned you months ago this would come. We might just as soon have let him die in Velantar. He's a deserter now. The elder has turned from him. I thought—*"

"*You didn't think. You only acted, as you ever have. You've shattered what remained of the boy's trust!*"

"*You're a fool if you count him still a boy. He will no longer aid us. I had no other choice. If you still cared for your people you would have seen it too.*"

"*Quiet! No more. Do not touch him again in such a manner or you will answer to me.*"

"*You?*" Laughter sharp enough to draw blood pierced Jhared's thoughts. "*You've not the strength. You've wasted it mourning necessary losses.*"

There was a pause. Jhared felt a tremendous, effortful gathering. Then Boar's rage rose so forcefully that Jhared flinched. He sensed Shrill do the same. "*Do not speak to me of loss! You will see what strength I still own. Now go. And do not open those doors again.*"

His Teachers' presence faded from his awareness, and yet Jhared waited, holding himself still and his thoughts quiet. Only when he felt certain Boar and Shrill had not realized he was awake did he open his eyes.

Zinderdali Imiro stirred, grimacing in his sleep. Jhared rose from where he had stretched before the hearth and poked the fire back to life. Wind squeaked softly through the shutters. Night was at the cusp of the dead moon watch. He set about making tea simply to have something to do.

What did you think to gain?

Weeks had passed since he had sensed Boar. That his Teacher had returned and accused Shrill of violating a boundary raised Jhared's hope. It meant she must respond to some rein after all.

Do not open those doors again.

Doors kept each of the Paths separate on the infinite web. Leita had taught him that. His thoughts went to the sacred maps tucked in the chest upstairs, maps representing each time that a Pathwalker had passed through the Gate and opened some series of doors to reach moments not her own. The world danced about him as he realized something crucial. It felt like something he had long known but hadn't allowed himself to acknowledge: Shrill and Boar existed on some other Path. It would explain why they didn't own his every memory and why he couldn't always sense them. It would explain how they reached their Shorn pupils.

"'They are Pathwalkers opening the doors between us." To say it aloud somehow made it real. Pathwalkers as Teachers. Was it possible? Did Pathwalkers exist who were so skilled they could reach a chosen moment again and again? If so, from what distant moments did they travel? It could not be his own Parallel: Leita had told him but for herself and Lady Nemiah, with perhaps a scattered handful of others such as Alende and himself, the Pathwalkers had vanished. That was troubling. Without knowing their Path, he could not know their motivations.

"You've gone far away, soldier."

Jhared returned to the moment to find himself standing with a pot of hot water in one hand and an empty mug in the other. Zinderdali Imiro was looking up at him.

"Yes, I had." Jhared released all thoughts of his Teachers as he recognized the pain that stained the Sahisten's expression. "Forgive me. I should have been paying better attention. You need another dose of Maya's tea."

"No. No more tea. Not yet." Zinderdali shifted uncomfortably. "Though we'd give our healthy leg for a cup of *slu*."

Jhared set aside the water and poured two cups of *slu*. The Sahisten sipped his slowly. Jhared looked over the rim of his cup at the man before him, torn open and stinking of blood.

"Are you trying to decide how much of our story you believe?" the Sahisten asked.

"I believe all of it," Jhared replied. "You wouldn't lie to Mayavana."

An upward twitch of a red-gold eyebrow. "No, we wouldn't. We are glad you see that."

"I'm trying to decide why you care about stopping a war when you know Avelos is already torn from within. Sahiste almost certainly has the strength to overwhelm her."

"Overwhelm her to what purpose?" Zinderdali turned one hand, palm up. "Avelos is too large for Sahiste to hold for long. And the drawn-out struggle would kill many, through illness and starvation, if not by steel and fire. In the end, war benefits no one but the wolves. Is that not a sufficient motive to stop it?"

"I don't know you well enough to answer that for you," Jhared replied.

The faint smile that curled the Sahisten's lips was broken by a flicker of pain. Jhared retrieved the cloth Maya had used to bathe the man's wound. To the boiled water he added numbing ice root from Maya's stores and dropped in the cloth.

"I like to believe that peace is a reward I would seek no matter the circumstances," Zinderdali murmured. "My duty is to work in the world so that Lumati has no cause to weep. But you are right to wonder. I have wondered often enough myself."

Jhared offered over the compress. "Then there is more?"

A barely perceptible nod as the Sahisten pushed the hot, damp cloth over his injury. "The Avelonian soldier our grandmother rescued. The Shorn man who gave up his mare. His name was Elrian. He was our mother's father."

Jhared stared. "You have Avelune blood in your veins."

"And across Yavi's rugs, we fear. Yes."

A Forest Guard soldier and a Sahisten woman paired in affection. Jhared grappled with the idea of it. "How did your mother survive in Sahiste? How did you?"

Zinderdali laughed, a complex sound formed of amusement and frustration and perhaps a trace of sadness. "Even after all Avelos has done, you still see *Sahiste* as the monster. What abuses do you imagine were perpetrated against me? Perhaps I was cut and scarred, my spirit trampled and an oath exacted demanding that I sacrifice my unworthy self? Would that cruelty fit the repute of a heartless people and a barbarous country?"

Jhared stiffened and didn't respond.

Zinderdali sighed something in Sahine. "I am sorry. Why should you believe Sahiste is more than hostility and blood? You know only what you have been taught. Only what you have seen. We ask your pardon."

"Given," Jhared muttered. "Your irony is deserved."

Zinderdali waved one hand dismissively. "In truth, soldier, if Sahiste did not cut me, neither did she warmly claim me. I have long lived at the borders. That distance makes some things easier to see—the absurdity of continued conflict between our peoples, for an instance—but it puts other things out of reach."

"A home in your own land, perhaps?"

Zinderdali considered his cup, then tossed back the last of his *slu*. When he spoke, his voice had lost its water-smoothness. "You see clearly, Jhared Denaban. No doubt you've reason to know such things. Those who end at Yavi's door do share some experiences."

Jhared tried not to think on all the possible meanings of that. "You speak to me as though you hope I will see the war as you do."

"Not precisely. You are a Shorn soldier. You have seen more."

Jhared took the compress from the Sahisten and dipped it again into the herb-infused water. As he knelt, setting cloth to torn flesh, he caught the Sahisten's smoky scent beneath the odor of blood. The emotions roiling in his chest surprised him: they included nothing of hatred. He adjusted the hot cloth and stepped back.

"What are you asking?"

"As a soldier and an elder's son, you have insights into the workings of Avelos that our scattering of Hands could not possibly hope to win. You can reach places and people we cannot. If you returned to Avelos, you might learn things we've spent the past two seasons trying to uncover. We are asking for your knowledge and aid to help turn our people away from war."

Before Jhared could answer, the Path wrenched hard beneath him. With such a decision before him, how could it not? But he had braced himself. This time the turn did not unbalance him.

Zinderdali watched with wonder in his eyes. "Was that the touch of your goddess?"

"No," Jhared replied. "Only the step of a man trying to find his own way."

The Sahisten looked thoughtful. He set aside his cup. "If King Javahari knew what I have shared with a once-soldier of Avelos, my eyes and tongue would be cut out and burned. I would be slashed repeatedly—many fine, shallow gashes—and staked to the rocks of the Barren at the heat of the day to feast the beetles and the carrion birds."

Jhared met the man's gaze; it was open and undefended. They watched one another. After a moment, Jhared nodded. "I hadn't thought. Of course this is a danger for you too."

"Does it make a difference?" The Sahisten's tone was gently curious.

"Some."

"Will you aid us?"

What Jhared meant to say was "Yes," but a part of him to which he was still unaccustomed pressed in another direction. Avelos was done with him. He had been cut apart and then cut free. They had ripped away everything he was meant to be and bound him to an image of his kind that had been created from Tumal's jealousy and fear. Even his foster father had seen him as no more than an object on which to test his theories. A current of dark anger swirled up in him. Although the feeling was growing uncomfortably familiar, he didn't push it away. It gave him strength. He had told Maya he didn't wish to watch others suffer for what had been done to him. But how much was he willing to risk to stop their suffering? Suddenly he knew.

"I won't give myself to your cause," he answered. The words came out calm and steady. He didn't expect to feel so certain.

Zinderdali's features clouded. "You needn't speak so quickly. Think on it first."

"No. I won't give my life to it. The debt has shifted. Some things are owed to me."

Disapproval shadowed the Sahisten's expression. "Your people will die."

Jhared's anger lifted again, not wild and out of control, but contained and lethal. "They are not my people."

Zinderdali looked askance. "Is that what you believe?"

Jhared's heart beat hard against his ribs. He had never dared to say such a thing, had tried never to think such a thing, even when pressed by Alende and the un-bound. Part of him expected his Teachers to rise raging into his thoughts. At one time, they would have kept him sleepless for days, tormenting him with inescapable nightmares for far less a crime. No one came. Riana did not step from her weaving and destroy him. Carefully, he stood and turned toward the hearth. "I am finished speaking of this."

"You are uncomfortable because this decision does not match who you are," the Sahisten observed.

"It matches who I must be if I am to find a life beyond what Avelos made me." Jhared faced the man again, forcing his expression to stillness. He recognized now the little signs of Zinderdali's improbable heritage—the tall, lithe frame, the lean, muscled limbs. What would have happened if Zinderdali had been born Avelun? Might Sahiste have owned tolerance enough to allow him to survive intact?

"We have done you a disservice, Jhared Denaban. We are deeply ashamed if we have pushed you to a point where you are unwilling to give aid that might stop the death of innocents."

"You did not push me. It is a decision I have made. My own."

"We regret if you believe that is so," Zinderdali sighed.

In that moment, Jhared might have unbridled his outrage against the injured man. To prevent it, he moved toward the door, slung his bow and quiver over his shoulder, and left the house.

The following days spun around necessary tasks. Maya spent most of her hours tending Zinderdali, coaxing broth and herbals into him, bathing his injury, and changing the wrappings. The Sahisten was strong, and after several days battling fever—days Maya didn't leave his side—he began to show signs of healing. Despite everything, Jhared was glad for it. He respected the man, a thing he wouldn't have imagined possible just a few days earlier.

As Zinderdali recovered, Jhared knew it was time to leave. He had told himself that Maya needed his help. He did his best to make himself useful, caring for the animals, gathering fuel, providing fresh meat, preparing meals. Still, it did not ease the tension thrumming through the house.

In many ways, it would have been easier to say yes to Zinderdali. Working for Lumati's Hands would have given him a new purpose. It might have kept his doubts at bay. At night, Jhared thought of Branlen, his foster father, and his home. It was hard at those times not to wonder if his decision had been a wrong step. Was there any meaningful difference between spreading the poison, like Lusian, or failing to stop those who did? Jhared lay in the darkness considering, until he felt the ache of his severed muscles twitching uselessly in his back and recalled Lady Amalia in chains. Then his anger flared strong and bright, immolating his doubts. He would no longer sacrifice himself for Avelos. He owed her nothing. He would feel nothing for turning away from her.

Committed to that road, he still needed a purpose that included more than weeding Maya's garden and caring for her goats. He had told Zinderdali his life was his own. If he meant to make those words true, he could no longer evade the destructive thing within him: he needed to figure out how to control the killing winds.

Some part of him had made this decision long ago. Near the Sonan capital lay the *Simata'yo*'s archive: a library where all the written wisdom of the surrounding nations was being collected and catalogued. If the secret of the killing winds had been written, chance said it would be there.

He would go. No other choice made sense. With the ability to control the killing winds, he could face the Kin—be a help to them if they would let him, and be a help to Shira. If he were to have any hope of a life beyond his binding, he needed to control the horror within him.

"In truth, would it be so different from seeking final reparation?"

Jhared tripped, nearly dropping his bow. Boar chuckled softly in his head, a sad sound.

"Final reparation is meaningless!" Jhared growled, gathering himself on the road outside Maya's cottage. *"This I do for my kind. For myself. Do not seek to Teach me what I owe. I am beyond such things."*

"Will you allow that, with the passage of years, some teachings may change?"

"I will allow you nothing. You have taken what you wanted from me, yet I know nothing of you. What Path do you tread? Why have your returned to mine?"

Boar's sigh carried a dream-crushing sense of futility. *"Your desire to know has frequently brought you trouble, my aberration, yet we never could beat it out of you. I did not come here now to satisfy your endless seeking."*

Jhared sifted through his own thoughts, trying to sense his Teacher more thoroughly. If Boar traveled the Paths, there should be some way to *see* the man. No matter how he moved through his own memories, he could only hear the voice and sense the emotions carried with it.

"Then why did you come?" he demanded.

"Perhaps because I remember a young boy vulnerable at his mother's deathbed. Perhaps because I remember that child's kindness, his healing hands on the injured

doves, before it was battered out of him. Perhaps because all things must end and it is good to have some farewell.”

Resignation echoed in Boar's voice, like a man deep in his drink and dark with it. Jhared recalled how frightened and lonely he had been after his mother's death. He remembered his Teachers coming to him, their demanding voices speaking as one. They had flogged and bullied him out of his grief. His Teachers had never been comforting, but they had pressed him to keep going when he might have curled into himself and faded away. Now Boar sounded like the one who was fading.

"Are you giving up my Teaching?”

"Yes.” Remorse and reluctance clung to the word.

"Is this because of what Shrill did to me?”

Deep, careless laughter rose from Boar. Jhared realized with chagrin the name he had used.

"An earned name,” Boar murmured ruefully. *"I might offer some apology for her actions, but she would not. You have been her purpose for too long. Watching our work burned to ash by your failures has not been easy. Still, what she did was ill-considered.”*

"Ill-considered? She stole my senses and turned them against me! She would have hurt Maya! It was a heinous—”

"I have said we will leave off your Teaching.”

Jhared went still. Boar was undone in a way he had never before known, but that did not make him less dangerous.

His Teacher might have sensed his unease, for Boar quieted, then tried again, heavily. *"Go on your way. Find the Sonan's archive. Perhaps you will convince your sweet Avelun to come with you. You could shape a life around such a smile as hers.”*

No matter what Boar and Shrill had done to him over the years, Jhared knew they had intended to help him survive Shorn Law. Entangled in Boar's emotion as he was now, he couldn't help but feel reluctant empathy for his Teacher's regret and loss.

"I cannot thank you for what has been. But I will bear you no grudge when you've gone. I offer my gratitude to you for returning my life to me now—and for a day outside the walls of Velantar when you forced me to take another breath.”

"Eloquent,” Boar murmured. *"You always had a honeyed tongue. A bard's son. An elder's. Find your archive. Do what is needful to win some joy. It is all a man can do on the Path we tread, and we've few enough opportunities for it. Do not miss yours.”*

Boar went silent. Jhared thought his Teacher was considering something more to say. Then he realized he was alone.

He returned to the house, dizzy and drunk with the mix of Boar's regret and his own astonishment. This was a step forward on the Path. His own Path. Thinking about the implications of that forward step, he was very aware of something else changing as he strode through the door.

Maya and Zinderdali were sitting at the table, heads bent close. They abruptly drew apart at his entrance. Zinderdali gave him a sharp look. Maya glanced away.

Jhared knew without asking what was different. "You told him."

"Yes." With obvious effort, Maya drew her gaze to his. "The truth of Lady Amalia."

"Ah." Some relief there. Lady Amalia's story wasn't the one he feared to set free. He blew out a slow breath. "I suppose I should not have kept the truth of the Exile War from a man who bears the blood of both sides."

Maya relaxed a little; a downy grey feather floated free as her wings settled lower on her shoulders. She smiled at him, hesitantly.

As Jhared set his bow and quiver beside the door, he studied Zinderdali. "Does that story change something for you?"

The Sahisten's gaze shone fever bright. "How could it not? The Avelune who invited Sahiste into Avelos did so without ill intent. The murder of our ambassador was one man's doing, not a country's. Yes. That is something. It could matter."

"As soon as he's well enough to ride, Zin will return to Sahiste," Maya said.

"We have channels to reach the prince. He must know the truth." Zinderdali grimaced as he stretched his injured leg. "You could come with us. You wouldn't have to return to Avelos to be valuable. You could be of use to Prince Ashani."

"No," Jhared said, more forcefully than he meant to. "My life is my own now. I'm going south to the Sonan archive." He paused, then plowed forward. "I mean to find a way to control the killing winds."

Wariness carved Zinderdali's features. "It will be dangerous for you in the south. Memory of the occupation still scars this country. A foreign soldier will not be welcomed."

"I am no soldier. And I have no country."

"Yet claiming control of the winds is not the goal of someone who intends to remain neutral. You have denied us your help, Jhared Denaban. Do you mean to make us your enemy?"

"Zin, he doesn't!" Maya's gaze darted from Zinderdali to Jhared. "Jhared, please. It is time to speak of this. I trust Zinderdali with my life."

Jhared folded his arms over his chest, his gaze unwavering. "And with mine?"

"Please, my lark, say what you know," Zinderdali demanded. "War will tear all and mend nothing."

Mayavana nodded slowly at Jhared, but her words went to the Sahisten. "Jhared is not searching for the winds to bring about war, Zin. He has other reasons."

"Maya, stop!" Jhared stepped toward her, fury and fear thudding through his limbs.

She didn't flinch from his anger. She never had. "Very well," she replied. "I will leave it for you. I know you see the importance of it. Else you wouldn't have told us your purpose."

Zinderdali leaned forward, shaping five sharp words: "Who calls the killing winds?"

"I do!" Jhared cried. "A poorly disciplined Shorn man who has broken his bonds."

The room went silent. Outside, waves bit at the shore over and over.

Zinderdali sat back in his chair. "Surely not. You're no witch. No mage. No Wise One."

"But he is a Traveler," Maya said quietly. "More than a Traveler. And the killing winds have something to do with the Paths."

"You know for certain it's you?" The Sahisten's tone remained dubious.

"I am certain." Jhared said grimly, seeing again the deaths he had caused in Parnas Pass.

"By gods of stones and sky," Zinderdali murmured. Slowly, his doubt began to turn into a more thoughtful expression. "If the winds have something to do with the Paths, with Travelers, then why does Maya not have the capacity to call them?"

"I don't *call* them. Or control them. Not any more than I could control a rabid dog." Jhared shrugged. "They're merely a sign of how broken I am."

"But you are not the only one," Zinderdali mused.

Jhared grimaced. He had dreaded this very thing. "I can't be. The winds have traveled farther than I have."

"We see. We see." The Sahisten fidgeted in his chair as though he wished to rise and pace.

Jhared glared. "You do realize that if Avelos learns this truth, all the Shorn will be slain."

"The blood of the Shorn, of the Avelune, runs in our veins just as it runs in yours, Jhared Denaban. We serve Lumati, the Owl Who Guards His Children, the Lover Who Weeps for the World. We would not betray our kind. All we do now is to prevent bloodshed. Can you say the same?"

"I told you I want no part of war."

But killing is what Shorn men are born for.

A never-forgotten taunt. Another kind of scar. Jhared pushed it away, determined to move beyond it. "When I learn the secret of the killing winds, I will stop them."

"Go carefully," the Sahisten muttered. "We see a need for vengeance in you. Perhaps you work with others who would make Avelos pay. Is that why you have refused to aid our cause?"

"You cannot ask for my trust, Zinderdali, and at the same time reject my promises. If you cannot find the grace to see me clearly, then judge me as you will. It will not change my Path."

Jhared turned, wanting to escape before either of them could make more accusations.

"Jhared, wait!"

He glanced over his shoulder as Mayavana rose to her feet.

"I want to come with you."

Zinderdali's gaze snapped toward her. "Yavi!"

"The archive holds the wisdom of all the surrounding nations. You said it yourself. Amidst so much knowledge is my best chance of finding the key to flight."

Zinderdali shook his head. "Silverwing, there is danger for you in the south! You know it. The Bird Walkers—"

"Pose no more of a threat than I'd face anywhere, Zin." She frowned and folded her arms over her breasts. "Jhared, if you don't want my company, you will have to say it yourself."

Jhared opened his mouth. "That's not it. I just didn't expect you to offer. I didn't hope . . ." He stammered into silence.

"Perhaps you will convince your sweet Avelun to come with you," Boar had said. He had sounded remorseful, contrite. Jhared wanted to believe his Teachers truly had left him, but they had been creeping through his thoughts for half his life; a few things he believed he knew about them, and Shrill had been seeking the killing winds.

He took a step toward the Avelun and touched the grey feathers of her left wing with one hesitant hand. "It's not safe for you to be with me. Not while I have no way to control my Teachers."

Her frown turned to a scowl. "Do you seek to bind me as you have been bound? Is this what happens now that you have claimed yourself to be free?"

"Maya, that's undeserved! I only want—"

"To limit my ability to choose? To protect me? Because my own weakness does not allow me to protect myself?"

"No. That's not it at all."

She shivered as his hand drew down her wing and away. He felt the ripples of her response deep within his own body and closed his eyes. He was aware of the Sahisten man watching them.

"Jhared, you know the empty place within my spirit that must be filled by flight. You know what I am willing to risk. How can you seek to prevent me? Is this your envy showing itself at last?"

"No! Don't you see? I could not bear it if I brought you harm!"

He expected that Maya would turn away, but she stared at him, into him. "I've never let my own fear or yours curb my steps. If you cannot tolerate the thought of the dangers I may face, I can travel south on my own. But that seems foolish. We have saved one another on this Path. I think . . . I think the pattern we weave together is a brighter one."

He wondered at her courage, as he had from the first time he spoke to her in a cave in the north. Standing before her now, as the light glinted off her ebony hair and midnight-tipped wings, he felt humbled by her strength—and proud of it. Zinderdali was right: the three of them shared the blood of the Avelune. It came to him then what he might do, must do. Though he would never be whole, Maya had hope of reclaiming the sky. The only true retribution would come when she could touch the clouds. Perhaps it could be his place to help her to heal.

"Forgive me," he murmured. "You are right. I have no cause to stop you."

"Does that mean you will travel with me to explore the Sonan archive?"

He smiled a little at her reversal. "I will."

She stretched her wings wide. He inhaled and caught her wild scent.

As she drew back, smiling, Zinderdali's expression was grim. Jhared didn't ponder it. He had noticed that something he had come to expect was missing: the world remained stable beneath him. Although he had taken a leap to change his Path, he was not overwhelmed with the rippling of lost possibilities. His next step would be on solid ground.

15.

NEGOTIATIONS

"I should not be sending you to Sahiste," Adan Rumar had said again.

He had been lying beside her. Dawn edged the Parnas Valley, slipping a line of gold between the heavy window curtains and across the room, marking the transition from night to day. On any other morning, Nemiah would have been filled with the surging of the Paths as they multiplied in that moment of change, but last night she had taken hold of her own Path and turned it sharply. Now it was as though exercising her own will had steadied her. She felt still and settled, more so than she had felt in many years.

Riana had sent grace and strength to bless the High Chieftain of Avelos, and he had accepted the goddess's blessing. At least a century and a half had passed since the Lady of Avelos and the High Chieftain completed such a ritual. That marvel would mean something. Yet some moments in the night had not been a part of any ritual at all. They had been too human, beneath or perhaps beyond the notice of the goddess. There had been fear at first—in both of them, Nemiah had realized—but fear had given way to other things: her own anger, keen and fierce, for the years of conflict, for the damage done to the Paths, and for the blood of babes spilled on the altar. Rumar had borne her anger, not evading or denying it, and gradually her anger had transformed into emotions more welcoming, though no less intense. Finally, when permitted the space for it, Nemiah had discovered her own desire and Adan Rumar had revealed his capacity for wonder.

"You cannot send me, Adan. I chose this. Long before Aelend and Abrigado."

The High Chieftain of Avelos lifted himself on one elbow and gazed down at her. "But this other thing, *we* chose it?"

The uncertainty in his expression, the rarity of it, was somehow endearing. She smiled. "Riana would not have been here otherwise."

"And she was here, Nemiah. I felt her."

Nemiah reached up to cup his cheek. Rumar had sensitivity enough that he had responded to the goddess's presence within her. A joy in that.

"It was a healing step," she said, running her fingers across the copper stubble on his chin.

"Perhaps not entirely healing," he said, falling back heavily onto the blankets.

She smiled again, but something in the honesty of his gesture, in the vulnerability of the moment, as the new sun drew a lazy line of light across the two of them, made her uneasy. Neither of them could afford to be unguarded right now.

"Adan, Riana may have led us here, but this will not be good for you. The elders will be furious, especially Abrigado's people."

"Let them be furious. There are certain decisions in which the elders do not have a say."

Here was the impulsive man, the impatient one who had alienated so many. She sat up to look at him directly. "You must take care. Avelos needs a high chieftain who understands compassion and self-sacrifice. Abrigado is not that man."

"I am relieved to hear you say so after such a night."

He leaned forward and brushed his lips against Nemiah's. Heat flooded her chest. With effort, she pushed him away. "Adan, slow down. You must not lose the Trial of Integrity. No one can know what has happened between us."

The lightness left his tone and he met her gaze, his grey eyes serious. "Nemiah, I won't deny you. It was more than just a blessing offered and taken here. There was . . . is a new sense of—"

"Clarity?"

"Not just clarity. For most of my rule, every step I've taken, every step toward change has been a struggle. I have been chained by my clan, by the council, and by the past. I thought that admitting a link between you and me would be another chain, but instead I feel unfettered. As if I couldn't move freely before because I was trying to move without you. As if somehow we were bound together long before this moment. That we must move together. Do you understand?"

"Yes, I do."

"I don't intend to lose that, Nemiah."

"I am only suggesting that we wait until I return to acknowledge it before the council."

"And then?"

"There is ancient precedent for what we've done. When I return and the threat of war has eased, it will be a time for renewal. Shall we speak then of the changes we wish to bring about in Avelos?"

He leaned over her. One hand smoothed a curl of her bright hair where it lay across her shoulder. "When you return."

They had said *when* over and over, as if the anticipation of success would be enough to shape the Path. Neither of them had spoken again of how dire it was for her to succeed. Neither of them had said the word *if*.

Now the Parnas Mountains had become a silhouette of blue and purple growing ever smaller behind her. The walls of Velantar had been out of sight for two days. Her focus must turn to Sahiste and to considering how to negotiate with a people who had hated the Lady of Avelos for more than a century.

The wind gusted through the bare grey trees on either side of the road and poked under her cloak. She shivered and glanced up at the colorless sky. More rain tonight, or sooner if they were unlucky. The road was already all ruts and mud.

At her left, Rom rode in stiff silence. She had not owned the right to ask him to foreswear his oath by remaining behind. She did not have the right to spare her own heart by keeping him safe. Neither had she been able to spare Rom's heart. Although she had not spoken of what transpired between her and the high chieftain during her night in the custody of Clan Manitar, Rom had sensed the change and knew what it meant.

"You gave Riana's blessing where it was needed," he had said when she returned to the temple and found him waiting for her. "I have long known the Path was meant to twist this way." Then he had walked away from her toward the sanctuary.

They had departed just days after. She had pushed for it, knowing that if Abrigado suspected she and Rumar had united their strength, the elder would have her standing before the tribunal before she could escape. The escort around her included Rom and four of his men—Avjay, Rien, Jern, and Falerian—all she was willing to spare from the temple, as well as five City Guards. She had expected Forest Guard to accompany them, but the only soldiers left in Velantar were Shorn men and the injured few who had been captives with Leita. To travel all the way to Sahiste, the council had given her city men, most of whom she guessed had never traveled farther from Velantar than the Heartsblood River. They were an undisciplined lot who seemed even more awkward on horseback than her earthbound Arionade, falling behind, disappearing and reappearing at will.

Their captain was a coarse, terse man, who possessed only one barking tone that he used whether he was ordering his guards, saddling his horse, or addressing the Lady of Avelos. In the three days they had been on the wet road, Nemiah already had more than enough of him. He largely ignored her, treating her as a prized hound to be delivered to a breeder. His attitude toward the Arionade demonstrated nothing but contempt. She suspected he was one of Abrigado's creatures.

So far, she had kept her speculations to herself. Rom didn't need the added burden and Elder Trianor seemed indifferent. The Minister of the Teaching was no longer the curious, gregarious man he had been on their first journey together. He rode his fine horse with his hands clenched and his shoulders tight, as though restraining himself from looking back toward home. He had left a wife and a young son in Velantar. Nemiah remained acutely aware it was her fault he'd been forced to leave them. During the long, dull days, few things brought the elder out of his reflective silence, but he seemed to view it as his duty to instruct her on Sahisten politics and what little he had of the language. She accepted his instruction willingly, regretting the cold distance he maintained. Of the entire party, he had the best understanding of Sahiste and seemed the only one of the group genuinely interested in meeting the Sahisten people.

"The *Camril Fi* includes King Javahari's key advisors from the twelve most powerful families in Sahiste," he told Nemiah one afternoon. "The translation of *Camril Fi* is something like 'Strong Council' or 'Great Council.' But do not mistake, Lady, the *Fi* is not a Council of Clans. Javahari maintains his sovereign right in all matters."

"I know the *Camril Fi*." Nemiah grasped the edge of her cloak and shook off the raindrops beading on it. "What can you tell me of the families in it? Their alliances and motivations?"

"Not as much as I would like." The elder frowned and wiped the dampness off his face. "From Prince Ashani, we know that the core detractors of his bid for peace come from within the *Camril Fi*. They are proud, ancient families, with long memories of the hostilities between our countries. I suspect that reparation for losses suffered in the Exile War is still the goal for many within those families. But it is not so simple. Each family is allowed three members in the *Fi*: the elder, elder-consort, and heir. Not all families speak with one voice. Each member has a right to speak." He shook his head. "There will be nuances expressed we cannot begin to understand, coalitions we won't see. We cannot even speak their language. Isolation has not served us well in this, Lady Nemiah. In most ways, we are walking into these negotiations dangerously ignorant."

Nemiah nodded faintly. "Then we will move cautiously. To gather a clearer understanding of the terrain."

The elder glanced at her sidelong. "There is another source from which we might win support. *You* might win support."

"Oh?"

"The priests of Sahiste are highly respected. Some move through the court and wield power that even the royal family acknowledges."

Nemiah knew from Rumar that the royals of Sahiste listened to their gods in a way the Council of Clans had not done in generations. It offered a possible opening for her to win the respect of the *Camril Fi*. Yet it also offered another potential challenge.

"What welcome will the goddess receive?"

"Sahisten gods fill their forests, mountains, and deserts. And the Sahisten people seem open to acknowledging wonder in the world. I don't believe they will see Riana as a threat."

"The people may not see a threat, but I doubt their priests have any desire to share their power."

"That may be." The elder's pale eyebrows drew together. "It is perhaps a shame the Bearer of Cael's Blade did not come with us."

There was another confrontation Nemiah did not care to revisit. Refusing the Bearer's request to join the company had resulted in one of Leita's violent, raging storms, after which she had shut herself in her room and refused to speak to Nemiah. "How do you mean, Elder Trianor?"

"Raptors are symbols of strength in Sahiste. Only noblemen may own them. Not only are they trained as hunters, they are often present at important rituals."

"You believe Cael and his messengers would draw respect from the priests."

"I do. The Bearer might have used that."

"You know a curious amount about Sahisten theology, Elder. I've read no such description in the histories or in any of the documents Rumar sent with us."

"We've had scouts on the border since the Exile War, Lady. That source of knowledge does not always make it into the histories."

"Ah, of course. The boy was your informant."

The elder stiffened in the saddle. "Jhared Denaban did what he could to earn reparation. And I used what tools I possessed to keep the Seal of Avelos around Adan Rumar's neck."

Nemiah winced inwardly. A mistake to mention the elder's fosterling. "I've only ever thought you a loyal advisor to our high chieftain, Elder Trianor."

"Yet your thoughts on the matter mean little to the council, Lady."

She had no good response to that arrow. It was the closest he had come to speaking of blame. Nemiah felt the familiar rise of regret and the yearning to share Amalia's truth, but she wouldn't risk it now, not to relieve one man's grief. Sahiste was her hope. She prayed the truth would mean something to the Sahisten court. She prayed she would find a way to speak that would not turn the Path toward greater bloodshed. Elder Trianor rode beside her in silence for a time. Then, with a small tug on the rein, he slowed his mount and dropped back among the clanguard.

A fine cold mist had enveloped them through the morning and into the afternoon when she found herself riding even with Captain Kajhar. The man glanced at her once and grunted in a way that seemed meant as an acknowledgment. She had despised him instantly upon meeting him. In his City Guard colors, she could not help but see the men who had vandalized the high temple, destroying Riana's eye, beating her Arionade, and terrorizing her priestesses. Now she must rely on him to help steer them safely into and out of Sahiste. With difficulty, she pushed aside her dislike and set herself to create some order between them.

"I hope the rain ends soon or it will be even slower going tomorrow," she offered.

He grunted a second time.

She looked out between Rigojan's ears. In the distance, she could see a town wall. A relief at least for that. Unaccustomed to spending days in the saddle, her muscles were protesting the abuse, and the constant mist had begun to reach through her cloak: a hot bath and a dry bed would be welcome. "Have you visited Marenhan before this, Captain?"

"Never been to Marenhan. Not before and not now."

She turned, frowning. "What? You don't mean to stop?"

"At Marenhan? Not likely."

"Captain, it's nearly dark. And the next town is beyond reach tonight."

"That's right."

Nemiah waited for him to say more. He didn't. "Captain Kajhar, with the killing winds tearing through this part of the country and the Forest Guard at the border, the bandits own the roads. Why would we not stop while we have the benefit of walls?"

"Lady, I've worked inside walls all my life. Walls are good for one thing: they tell you who's outside and who's inside. Some folks think that makes you safe."

"You don't?"

"Walls don't tell you who the enemy is. They only keep you from getting a clear view of the terrain."

It was an echo of her words to the elder the day they had gone to Aelend. The captain glanced over his shoulder toward where one of his men was lagging. "Guardsman, keep up! You need my boot in your ass to get moving?"

The man who had dropped behind the packhorses kicked his mount into a canter to catch up.

"You might notice, Lady, we're outside the walls just now."

She looked at him: his gap-toothed sneer and thinning hair, his broken nose and pale eyes. In those eyes she glimpsed something attentive and deliberate. Perhaps the man was more subtle than she had assumed. "You believe there's danger for us in Marenhan?"

"There's danger everywhere. Else you and the elder'd be riding to Sahiste on your own."

He set heels to his mount and wheeled back to the end of their line, where his guardsman had finally returned to their little file. Nemiah wondered how long the guard had slipped out of sight. She had been too focused on the road ahead to notice. She couldn't hear their conversation, but the man looked sober and concerned. No doubt he was concerned. Captain Kajhar was like to take a piece out of his hide.

Nemiah let out a frustrated breath. Rom was watching. She caught his eye and he gave a small, tight nod. He and his men would be vigilant.

Several miles past Marenhan, Captain Kajhar led them into the forest along a road that Nemiah would never have spotted on her own. It was muddy and leaf-strewn, but rutted enough to suggest periodic use. It seemed the isolated type of road bandits would smile upon. Through the trees and the grey mist, Nemiah spied the ruins of a wall, perhaps once marking the edge of a farmer's land, but long ago left to disintegrate. Rigojan pricked her ears as somewhere farther up the hill, hooved creatures scattered. Nemiah glanced at Elder Trianor through the gloaming, but he appeared to be deep in his own thoughts. They continued around the base of the hill and along a rocky ridge. The sun would be nearing the horizon, although the iron clouds made it impossible to see. Nemiah shivered.

"Captain, where are you leading us?"

"Here."

Just ahead, two tall pillars loomed on either side of the road. Part of a wall curved away from the right pillar; it was beautiful stone, delicately carved. At one time, the wall had been well built and expensive and no doubt there had once been a gate. Kajhar led them through the pillars.

The farmyard was not so different from that of any productive household Nemiah had known in her childhood, with its stables and animal pens, brew house, dye house, and ovens. The farmhouse itself was an oddity, however. Built of ancient stone, the architect had situated its two sections such that they topped the yard in an inverted V. Each wing loomed to an unexpected height, with wooden stairs rising like an afterthought to a balcony that ran just below the roof. The entire house seemed to lack any proper doors, but large shuttered windows lined the upper levels.

Nemiah's vision rippled. She bit her cheek and drew Rigojan to a halt. Rom stopped beside her.

A man and two boys appeared from the stables. The man held an ax. Another youth poked his head out of the brew house. Kajhar signaled to his City Guard and they began to dismount. Rom kept his men in the saddle.

Nemiah searched for some sign of welcome in the approaching figures. They did not appear openly hostile, but wariness filled every face. Kajhar had implied they would know him here, but she saw no recognition. Two women stepped out from a wide window onto the balcony and glared down on the commotion in the yard. The woman closest to the rail was straight backed and small, with severely bound grey hair that gleamed with a shadow of the gold it might once have been. The rich, heavy fabric of her gown was cut in a style that half a century ago would have been fashionable sweeping across the marble floors in the palace or the large manors outside of Velantar. Nemiah was certain she had never met the woman, yet some things about her seemed familiar: the impression of abiding anger that sculpted her stiff shoulders; the sharp, clever gaze. Standing behind her with a lamp held high, the second woman looked of a similar age, but was tall and narrow and dressed practically in breeches and a vest.

"I don't believe we're being welcomed," Nemiah said quietly to the elder beside her.

He had finally glanced up and was staring at the balcony, his expression grave and tired. "No. Neither of us is welcome here."

"You know those women?"

"I know the family. Madam Sevar's late husband was an elder some years ago. Lady Nemiah, you need to be aware—"

Before he could finish the thought, the practically clad woman marched down the stairs. She had haughty, disapproving features and an air of influence. She gave a dismissive glance to Kajhar and Rom, but she raked the elder and Nemiah with an obsidian gaze.

"Elder Tierzen Trianor, Minister of the Teaching. Lady Nemiah Gabriana, Chosen of Avelos. I am Sesara, steward of this household. Madam Sevar demands to know why you have entered our gates."

"We apologize for intruding, Steward Sesara, and ask for the hospitality of a night for ourselves and our men," the elder answered.

"Why did you not stay in Marenhan?"

"The importance of our mission pushed us farther."

The woman looked unimpressed. She stared without speaking.

Nemiah began to lift her hand in a spiral of blessing, then caught the coldness in the woman's gaze and stopped. "We would be grateful for the shelter of the house. We are on our way to the southern border."

"We know where you're headed and who sent you. Adan Rumar is so very good at convincing others to sacrifice themselves for him. Is he not, Elder Trianor? I am only taken aback that he did not ensure you had adequate accommodations along the way. Something befitting your rank before you die in Sahiste."

Captain Kajhar cleared his throat and spat. "I was told by one who has reason to know it that safety could be found here for those who serve Avelos truly."

Sesara narrowed her eyes at the City Guard. "You claim to serve truly, do you, soldier?"

"No soldier." He barked a laugh. "But when it comes to serving, I do what my betters tell me. As you must also, eh steward?"

The old woman didn't respond to Kajhar, but lifted her head to the imperious woman on the balcony. Some signal must have passed between them because she turned back and gave a grudging nod.

"Come along. You'll have one night."

Nemiah climbed out of the saddle, regretting she hadn't pushed harder to stop in Marenhan.

"You needn't find beds for my men," Kajhar said. "The stable's enough for us. However, I think these fine folk will be glad of clean sheets and a fire." The captain grinned rudely at Nemiah. She ignored him as he took Rigojan's reins and the reins of the elder's gelding. The steward pointed him toward the long, low stone building on the west side of the yard.

Nemiah was glad to see the rest of the City Guard follow him out of sight. Above, Madam Sevar's expression might have cracked granite. She was staring at Elder Trianor. After a moment, she turned and disappeared into the house.

"Come along then," the steward repeated, heading toward the stairs.

They climbed to the high balcony, Rom at Nemiah's side, with his four men in a neat file behind them. Sesara held one side of the shutters back so that Nemiah and the others could step through, effectively preventing any further private interactions among the party.

Inside, Nemiah found herself standing on a narrow gallery that stretched to her left and right into the wings of the house. Before her, another stairway led down into a gathering hall, where it looked as though the household had been finishing their supper. Two bright-haired girls, neither much older than Merisel, hurriedly stacked empty platters and whisked them from the hall. A young boy built up the fire in the yawning hearth. As he worked, smoke curled lazily past Nemiah and toward an impossibly high ceiling. Faded frescos of a summer sunrise could still be seen on the ceiling, adding to the dizzying sense of openness. What appeared to be four trap doors disguised as clouds marked each corner.

Nemiah looked closely at the stairway and at the gallery on which she stood. The wood shone, still bright with clear grain, rather than with the dark, smooth patina that years of hands would have left along its surface. She glanced back at the ceiling, at the odd trap doors and the tall, shuttered windows. The farmhouse was ancient; the stairway was not.

"Come," the steward snapped.

Madam Sevar waited near the hearth. A greying, wiry-haired dog lounged at her feet, its ears pricked toward the strangers.

"Elder Trianor, Lady Nemiah. How very pleased we are to receive such favored friends of our high chieftain."

Nothing about her hinted at pleasure. Elder Trianor stepped forward. "No longer favored, Madam. But hoping still to serve Avelos. We thank you for sharing your roof with us for the night."

"Ah, Elder Trianor. I did hear something of your sordid tale. Rumar has finally thrown you over, has he? Well, it seems the Paths have turned a full circle at last. If only Elder Sevar might have lived to see it."

Nemiah glanced at Elder Trianor, wishing she knew exactly what lay between him and this woman. Sevar was a common enough name among the families of Clans Manitar and Delsio, but she didn't recall an elder of that name since she had been Chosen. That Madam Sevar knew of Elder Trianor's disgrace said the woman remained well informed. Nemiah wondered who her informants might be.

The lamps in the room cast shadows across Tierzen's features, revealing the day's grey stubble across his cheeks and a strained composure as he addressed the woman.

"Indeed, Madam, your husband's wisdom has long been missed."

The woman laughed, a sound that might once have been lovely. "Oh, Tierzen Trianor, you are no longer in Elders' Circle or Council Hall. On the farm, we leave the shit in the fields."

Tierzen's calm mien didn't change. "You know I've never been less than honest with you. The late Elder Sevar was a man of integrity. I respected him, as did many others."

"False! My husband was a coward, afraid of doing anything he thought might cause others to dislike him. No one respected him, least of all you." The old woman's silver gaze flashed. Then she seemed to catch hold of herself. Her voice softened. "But those days and those debts are long behind us, aren't they? I am very rude to neglect our other equally notable guest." With a hiss of her stiff skirts, Madam Sevar turned from the elder and eyed Nemiah.

"Lady Nemiah Gabriana, I have heard so much of you. Funny. You are so much smaller than the stories suggest."

Of all the cutting comments Nemiah could imagine, this odd remark was not included. Ironically, she found herself to be of a size with Madam Sevar. "Stories, Madam?"

"Of a woman powerful enough to defy the council and courageous enough to drive a company of armed City Guard out of the high temple. All for the sake of a traitorous Shorn scribe too weak to discipline her own ugly desires. How strange."

Beside her mistress, the steward tensed. "Madam, now that introductions have been made, shall I settle our guests?"

Madam Sevar let her gaze drift to Elder Trianor and back to Nemiah. "I see now. It seems Rumar decided to be rid of all his problems at once. How very clever of him." She glided away with a swish of fabric. "Yes, Sesara. See our guests settled. After, Lady Nemiah and I will go to the baths."

Sesara threw a sharp look at her mistress. "But the rain, Madam."

"Not more than a drizzle. The Lady has had a long ride. The hot water will do her good. Don't fear, Sesara, I will take her. My aging bones are always glad of the heat." Madam Sevar offered a frozen smile that Nemiah suspected no amount of heat would melt. "You would like a bath and a soak after your long travels, wouldn't you, Lady Nemiah?"

"I would be glad of it." Nemiah answered. What she would be most glad of would be riding away from this farm and its unpleasant occupants. Still, at least they would be dry and warm tonight, and she wouldn't shun a bath.

The steward rang a bell, bringing a lanky, pale-haired youth hurrying to her side. At her direction, the boy bobbed his head to Elder Trianor and Rom and indicated they would be staying in rooms off the east gallery. As Sesara made to lead Nemiah to the stairs, Rom remained close, his expression forbidding.

Madam Sevar laughed again. "Don't be randy, my friend Arionad. Allow your Lady time to rest. You needn't follow her to her bed or to the baths. I promise to return her to you clean and refreshed. What you do with her after, of course, is up to you."

Nemiah touched Rom's arm with a quick warning. He answered her with a scowl, but held his tongue and led his men up the stairs behind Elder Trianor.

Sesara left Nemiah in a dim, cold bed chamber. Although the room was spacious and boasted its own fireplace, the slightly dank smell and the dust on the desk and headboard suggested long disuse. Heavy shutters sealed the windows, not merely with a latch but with a length of thick chain. In this relatively quiet center of Avelos, Nemiah wondered what threats Madam Sevar meant to keep out.

Gratefully, she slid off her cloak and set down the single bag she had claimed from Rigojan's saddle. She sat on the bed, with her arms wrapped around her, and tipped her head slowly from side to side, stretching the aching muscles in her neck and shoulders. As she tilted her face toward the ceiling, she saw that frescos decorated this room as well: a wild, stormy sky swirled above her. In the corner of the ceiling, she spied another trap door with a dull brass handle that hardly interrupted the painted clouds.

She stared at the ceiling for a long, silent moment. She had never seen any such thing outside of the city. The unremarkable village of her childhood offered nothing but small farmhouses and a tradesman's cottage or two crafted without ornamentation. The vast manors of wealthy families, such as the one belonging to the high chieftain, had been thoroughly made over since the Exile War. The inheritors of this farm apparently had lacked the funds or the energy to renovate the structure. The signs it had once belonged to Avelune remained.

Nemiah looked at the tall, chained shutters and imagined them thrown open to the evening breeze, imagined some young Avelun balancing at the threshold, her wings unfurled. Deep within Nemiah, the Gate trembled. If she crossed onto the weaving, perhaps she might share the moments of the family who had once lived here. Perhaps she could learn something about the skills and duties of the Avelune on the Paths that could help her to stop the unraveling. Rom would tell her the risk of such travel was too great. He had watched helplessly when she lay senseless, trapped on the far side of the Gate. She didn't dare risk the success of their mission to Sahiste by throwing herself onto the weaving, and yet the truth was that if she did not find some way to halt the unraveling, then negotiating with the Sahistens to stop a war would be meaningless.

At a rap on the door, Nemiah snapped back to her moment. One of the serving girls Nemiah had seen in the hall stood outside with a pail and firewood.

"If you please, Lady, I will lay the fire while you are out."

"Out?"

The girl's gaze fled over Nemiah's shoulder and nervously scanned the room. "The baths. Madam Sevar is waiting for you downstairs."

"Settled" to Nemiah had a different meaning than Madam Sevar apparently gave to it, but she smiled at the girl and made to leave.

"Forgive me, Lady, but you will want your cloak."

Nemiah paused. "To cross the yard?"

As the girl set her pail by the hearth, she gave a little shudder. "The baths are not in the yard. They are in the rocks by the ridge."

Caverns and heated springs honeycombed the Parnas Mountains and the valley below. Nemiah supposed it wasn't so odd that some such sites existed farther south as well. She fingered the damp wool of her cloak unenthusiastically. "Very well. Thank you."

Madam Sevar met her at the landing at the top of the stairs. A pebbled trail marked their way from the farmyard into the woods. Another of Madam Sevar's girls walked behind them, a basket slung over one shoulder filled with towels and oils and a bottle of wine. In her hand, she held a lantern high, throwing elongated shadows of Nemiah and the older woman ahead on the trail. Frogs chirped among the trees. It was cool and damp, but the clouds had scuttled away, leaving a pure, depthless sky pricked by a sharp, bright moon.

A blast of cold struck Nemiah, as if she had opened a door on a winter day. She gasped as the ice frosted down her throat and into her lungs.

"Oh, Lady, you needn't fear," Madam Sevar said, mistaking her gasp. "Nothing dangerous treads this path. Most nights, the wolves and wild cats stay well away from the farm."

Nemiah pulled her cloak close around her. "The night doesn't trouble me. I just took a bit of a chill. That cold wind."

Madam Sevar gave a honeyed smile and said nothing.

Nemiah kept walking. "Never mind. I'm sure the hot water is what I need."

The land began to rise on their left, becoming a stone ridge that gleamed in the lantern light. In some places, the ridge stretched upward into a sheer plane that tabled far above Nemiah's head; in other places, the ridge fell into no more than a tumble of fractured rocks all settled at odd angles. Ahead, the light fell upon an ancient door that had been carved to fit between two such rocks. As Nemiah watched, the door banged open. A tall, dark-bearded man appeared. He was laughing, a lovely, full-throated laugh, and looking back the way he'd come, as if still talking to someone inside.

"No, you goose, what I said was to keep your *feathers* out of the water!"

He stepped outside, whistling a cheerful tune. He was nude but for the towel wrapped around his hips. His dark wings furled gently against his muscled back.

Nemiah froze; then forced herself to take another step. "Hello?"

The Avelun gave no sign of hearing her. She walked closer. As she crossed in front of him, the man vanished. Only she and Madam Sevar stood on the pebbled lane.

"Lady Nemiah, are you quite well?"

Nemiah squeezed her eyes shut and yanked her attention inward. The blue flames licked gently at her spirit, as they ever did. The Gate that separated her from the infinite Paths remained closed. So what had she seen? The cold of the Nowhere blew through her again. She shivered and opened her eyes. Madam Sevar looked keenly inquisitive.

"I am very well. Shall we go in?"

Warm, steamy air met her as she stepped inside. She paused, adjusting to the deeper darkness and the acrid mineral scent, but the serving girl slipped past her with the lantern and hurried around the cavern, using a curl of bark to light a half-dozen other lanterns set atop stone pedestals. The gold and ruby flames reflected back from a myriad sources—the moist walls, the still surface of the pool, the slender columns of crystal dripping from the ceiling—turning the chamber into the heart of a gem.

"How beautiful," Nemiah breathed, reluctant to disrupt the sense of the sacred with speech.

"Once I had marble tubs and glass lamps in a bathing room within my manor," Madam Sevar said derisively. "This is dirt and rock in the forest. But it's what we have."

She led Nemiah behind a wooden screen where benches lined a narrow space. Some benches held empty pitchers; others offered bowls filled with balls of soap, brushes, and clean cloths. A large barrel held rain water that ran in from a wooden pipe sloping down from the ceiling of the grotto. Madam Sevar's serving girl helped her mistress out of her gown, shift, and shoes, hanging them on pegs on the screen. Then shyly she offered help to Nemiah, who thanked her and declined. Nemiah hadn't been willing to risk the life of Merisel or any of her ladies for convenience sake; thus, the garments she wore were all easily managed.

Once she had undressed, the air did not seem nearly so warm. Following Madam Sevar's lead, Nemiah filled a pitcher with water from the barrel and poured it slowly over her shoulders. She bit the inside of her lip to keep from yelping as the icy water reached every part of her. Quickly and vigorously, she scrubbed away the road dirt with the sweet-smelling soap, then poured another pitcher of water over herself, rinsing away the last of her warmth. She had the impression the serving girl was giggling.

Madam Sevar had already padded across the rocks and stepped into the pool by the time Nemiah came out from behind the screen, exposed and naked and trying not to shiver.

The older woman stared openly, a knowing glint in her grey eyes. "You've never borne a child."

Nemiah stepped onto the stairs that led into the depths of the pool. Heat kissed her toes and lapped at her ankles. Gratefully, she stepped all the way into the water and settled on one of the stairs, the warmth snuggling up to her neck. "My Path has not yet turned that way."

Madam Sevar chuckled. The unpleasant sound echoed against the stone. "Yet? With those green eyes of yours? I suspect you have made very certain which way your Path would turn. A wise choice to avoid giving birth to the cursed."

Nemiah shivered again, wondering what had spawned such vitriol in the woman. A thwarted sense of ambition? A need for power never sated?

"Does he know?" the other woman continued. "Does your handsome Arionad know that you have kept him from giving the goddess children?"

Nemiah shoved aside a fleeting thought of Rom, pressing her palms against the edge of the stone until it hurt. "What is it you are seeking, Madam?"

"I want to learn something of who you are, Lady Nemiah. The High Priestess of Avelos who keeps Riana's order and influences the Paths. You take others' daughters and claim they are for the goddess, but I see now you are only playing a role you cannot otherwise play."

Nemiah met the old woman's grey gaze.

The light changed. In Madam Sevar's place, candles flickered. Small lights danced among the rocks and around the pool as well. A harpist pulled a sweet melody from the steamy air as lovers floated together, murmuring and caressing: a pair of grizzled warriors, both with short, barred wings; a young man with heavy golden wings and a woman with wings of ombre grey; a blue-winged woman and a smooth-backed man.

Once more, Nemiah sought inside her own spirit: the blue flames had risen, as though to feed the alternate moment, but the Gate remained closed. Those walking on the other Paths didn't seem to sense her. She had not reached out to the infinite web. Some disorder had damaged the Paths of this place: moments were bleeding on top of one another, like one dye bleeding into another on the same cloth.

"Lady Nemiah?"

Cold hissed through Nemiah again. No music now, only a low groan: the sound of hinges twisting, a door half-torn from its frame. A narrow stream of moonlight fell across the pool, no lovers now, only a still, grey form floating there. Nemiah stood, one hand pressed against her mouth. It was an Avelun man, face down, his wings splayed wide. His blood swirled on the surface of the water.

Another abrupt shift and two soldiers barreled into the chamber, drunk and armed, and roaring an old children's rhyme about stoning crows. One of them gripped a terrified Avelun girl.

The door was new and solid. A little green-eyed girl pounded on it, shrieking in terror: "I will be good. I will be good. Please, please, please let me out. I promise I'll be good!"

A young man, bright-haired, sat alone and silent among the rocks. The flute he gripped in one hand had been smashed. It would never be played again.

Nemiah dug her nails into her wrist, but the pain did nothing. She didn't know how to find her own moment: she hadn't traveled; she shouldn't be able to see these Paths. Riana's infinite ways were unraveling.

We are the mortal webweavers.

"Lady Nemiah!"

An unwelcome voice clanged in her head. Someone was shaking her. Her body was warm and weightless. "What . . . is it? What?"

"You fell asleep. As I was speaking to you."

"I'm sorry. I just . . ." Nemiah shook her head. At the edges of her vision, she caught glimpses of other moments, layered across time, like the layers of stone in the cave. "What were you saying?"

"No matter. Clearly, my company bores you." Madam Sevar turned her head away, but not before Nemiah caught a sly, satisfied expression flitting over her face.

Cold settled in Nemiah's middle. "You know something about this place. You see them too!"

Madam Sevar stepped out of the water, her withered body dripping, and smirked down at Nemiah. "What I've seen is that the cursed become ill and unbalanced when they enter this place. I've seen the earth itself rebel against their touch, driving away those who are weak and rotten. You, with your green eyes and your love of traitors, it seems the earth has sensed the rottenness in you as well."

"Foolish, ignorant woman," Nemiah gasped. "You have no idea what is happening here. These Paths are damaged!"

Nemiah forced herself to stop. Of course the old woman had no idea. She had been taught what to see when she looked at the Shorn. She had been taught how to hate. It would take much more than anger to change her.

"A mystery exists here that you cannot understand, Madam Sevar."

"We are the mortal webweavers," Amalia had told her.

"The *mystery*, Lady Nemiah, is that after sheltering traitors you are being sent to Sahiste as an ambassador rather than being made to pay on the wall. Adan Rumar would have gained new allies within the council by pushing you off like the Shorn lover you are. So why didn't he?"

Nemiah winced as other Paths began once more to encroach on the present. The doors to this place were open. That's what she sensed. Open doors allowed the Nowhere to blow through, allowed infinite moments to slip into the wrong times.

"We keep the balance," Amalia had said. *"We open the doors to the Paths and see them closed again. Can you understand, then, what it means to tear us apart?"*

Oh, Amalia. How can we ever stop the unraveling if I cannot even share your story?

"Lady Nemiah? Lady, you seem quite overcome. Shall I call for your Arionad?"

"No. Go back to your hall, Madam. There are prayers I must say here."

The woman looked as though she meant to refuse. Nemiah closed her eyes. She wouldn't call Riana's power to force Madam Sevar to comply, not with the doors already flung wide in this moment. Who knew what consequences that might have for the both of them? But she lifted her arms above her head and called to Riana to ask for strength.

There was a rustling, then a gasp from the serving girl. Nemiah let the rill of Riana's grace flow deep into her. She thought she heard the others leaving, then turned away from that moment and into herself. When she could contain no more of the goddess, Nemiah began the prayers of the evening devotion, the ones meant to heal the damage to the web from all the day's disorder. She walked around the pool to each of the lanterns, blessing the Paths before her, the ones behind, and the one on which she stood in the present. Then she drew on her own will and on the energy that Riana lent her and tried to find the open doors.

They lay before her like knife wounds in flesh: deep gashes in the web. The doors from this moment into the infinite ways had been ripped open and never closed. Row upon row of them, doors to every moment from every Perspective on every Parallel that had ever occurred in this Place. In response to Nemiah's healing prayers, a few of them shivered. She reached for them with the strength of her own spirit and the strength that Riana offered. The injury here blighted the entire weaving. It hurt—knife wounds in flesh. She wrapped herself around those wounds, wrapped them with her knowledge and her memories. She drew from the core of her being. Moments of her life tore away, shredded. Parts of herself fell through those open doors—

She dropped to the ground, breathing hard. She couldn't do it, had no idea how it might be done. Once the Avelune had made it their duty to prevent such damage, Amalia said. But the Avelune were gone and Pathwalkers had nearly disappeared from this Path. Nearly. Nemiah sat up carefully. There was the elder's fosterling. Jhared Denaban had tracked her among the infinite ways and carried her back to her own moment. Every door had opened to him. Had she been wrong to send him away? Could she find him now? Could she find others?

A scattering of unbound Shorn lived in the wilds. Denaban had reported as much to the council. She needed to find them—find him, if she could. He possessed not just strength but something she had to name instinct. Despite his lack of training and a lifetime of warnings against touching the mysteries, he had been able to find his way across the weaving. She needed someone with that kind of reach to help her to heal these scars.

But first she needed to survive her mission to Sahiste.

An Avelun woman lazed in the water. A child cried among the rocks. The stone surged and crumbled. A man kissed his beloved. Molten rock shifted. . . .

The moments continued to leak onto Nemiah's Path. She watched them tangle together: her past, her future, and that of a thousand others. A story told all out of order. Winter come in the midst of summer. Chaos.

True Chaos?

"Forgive me. I do not have the wisdom or skill to put things right here. I am sorry."

Her words echoed sadly back at her. This place had once known beauty and peace. It had been a sacred space filled with love and music. How many other moments in the weaving had unraveled like this one? What would happen here? Could the open doors and displaced Paths form the deadly tangles Leita had known? How much of the world—past, present, and future—had already been lost?

Dizzily, Nemiah pulled on her clothes. The harpist started playing again as she pushed her way out of the grotto into the night.

16.

RAPTORS

Nemiah didn't realize how much time had passed until she left the cavern and settled more firmly into her own moment. As she walked the pebbled trail toward the house, the moon peered over her shoulder from the west. The trees pressed against the trail, creating a black wall on either side, as if to prove she had no other way to step. She was still within sight of the ridge when somewhere ahead a twig snapped and the stones crunched, like something moving out of the forest. She thought of the wolves and wild cats Madam Sevar had mentioned and touched her hand to the little knife at her belt.

She wondered that Rom hadn't come looking for her. She hoped it meant he had found some rest. He had looked so tired, her Arionad, although she suspected few but her would see it. She thought of the room and soft bed awaiting her at the house, but they didn't tempt her. The shadows of the Avelune who had once thrived on this land—who had died here—hung about her. She breathed the clean night air. She had never imagined a time when the open sky might give her more comfort than the safety of stone walls or a night when Cael's darkness might offer peace.

A horse whickered and another answered, breaking her meditation. She heard a harsh whispered voice she recognized. The sounds came from beyond the stables. She walked past the low building and turned the corner, opening her view to the gate and the road. A small group of horsemen was moving out. Moonlight picked out the mountainlike profile of Captain Kajhar and touched the heads of his men. Nemiah stared, scrambling to contrive some just explanation, but she knew only one: they were leaving, abandoning her and Elder Trianor in order to avoid the dangers of Sahiste. Cowards! They would not slip away without a confrontation.

She couldn't say what warned her: a near-silent footfall on the soft dirt? The sound of an indrawn breath? She started to turn just as a hand landed on her shoulder and steel fingers pinched muscle to bone. She rammed her elbow toward the unseen assailant and collided painfully with the smooth, unyielding surface of polished leather. Armor. Fear flared up with her anger. She wrenched her shoulder, but couldn't break the man's grip. She drew a breath, and a hand clamped over her mouth before she could scream.

"Silence, girl!"

The man's voice had a Clan Delsio edge to it. Nemiah fought a moment of despair. Here was the reason Kajhar had scorned Marenhan and forced them to stop at the edge of the wilds. They weren't just being abandoned; they were being attacked. Had Kajhar planned it with Madam Sevar? Was this a moment of retribution for perceived wrongs against her family? Or had it all been orchestrated by Abrigado? Nemiah kicked and twisted in her assailant's grip.

"Stop fighting!"

The stranger fumbled his hold, just for an instant. It was enough to free Nemiah's left hand. She grabbed the little belt knife at her waist and slashed blindly over her right shoulder. The sharp steel met unprotected flesh.

His half-stifled outcry scored the night. The hard edge of his hand struck her wrist, and her knife flew into the darkness. She sucked a breath, clutching her arm to her chest. Pain threw bright spots across her vision. Before she could recover, he began to drag her backward. She stumbled with him into the stable.

A faint glow came from one of the stalls, a shuttered lamp. A horse in the crossties lifted its head. Other men were moving about, dim, faceless figures. She tried to scream.

"What have you got there, Grion?"

"Cursed little falcon flapping after Kajhar's boys. Came near to blinding me with her talons."

"Silly little thing," another voice said. "I suppose one'a the City Guards made her promises tonight, eh?"

"Don't know. Don't care. I did my job and stopped her from making a fuss."

A third figure came around the horse in the darkness. "Did you keep it quiet?"

"Lieutenant said quiet, so I was quiet!" the one called Grion snapped. "Now come get her. She'll bolt if I let her go, and I can't see a cursed thing."

Nemiah knew she had only another moment before they realized who she was. Escape must be now. Her best hope was to reach the open yard where she could be seen—where she might have a chance of alerting Rom and the Arionade. On another night such a short time ago, she had reclaimed Riana's place as the guide of Avelos. She must live to fulfill that duty, to return order to her people. Beyond any expectation, there was a man in Velantar who might grieve if she did not.

Her assailant had pinned her against his body. She swung her right heel backward as fast and hard as she could. Her foot slid up the inside of her captor's leg, along his inner thigh, and connected sharply with her goal.

He roared in pained fury, bending double and sending Nemiah tripping forward. She nearly fell under his weight, but caught her footing and fled toward the door.

In that instant, the door jerked open. A barrel-shaped shadow filled the doorway. She cried out as she tumbled headlong into the new arrival. Strong hands caught her.

"Whoa! Whoa now, girl! What cause for that kind of speed?"

This voice she knew. Firm and calm, with Clan Everen steadiness. Dread and confusion filled her. She shoved herself upright and backed away, but she had no more weapons and there were at least four men in the stable. Four Forest Guard. She panted for breath. "Patrolman Nevia, is your anger at me so terrible that you have joined this evil undertaking?"

The stocky veteran darted his gaze to her face, and in the thin light, his features shifted to dismay. He glanced at the men behind her and at the big man groaning on the floor. "By Cael's cold cock, you fools, what have you done?"

"Nothing worth griping over," one of the other soldiers said, a burly, fair-headed man. "Grion just stopped the girl from making a fuss."

"What is it, Nevia?" The fourth man slid open the shutter of a lantern on its peg, allowing more of its yellow light to trickle through. He was smaller than the one who had grabbed Nemiah, but he spoke with authority and strained patience.

Patrolman Nevia looked at Nemiah, his expression touched with chagrin. "Lady Nemiah, Chosen of Avelos, these two are Commander Lenaro and Patrolman Esran of Clan Ontera. On the ground there, that's Grion of Clan Delsio. All with the Forest Guard Fourth. Or perhaps *formerly* with the Fourth, eh?"

The one named Esran made a strangled sound. "Holy Lady, forgive us!"

"Damn you, Grion," Lenaro said in disgust.

Nemiah looked warily at the group of them. But for Anzo Nevia, she had only ever seen them at a distance, when all the world had been tumbled sideways in Parnas Pass. She knew very well who they were, however. All of them had shared the Bearer's captivity.

"What is this?" she demanded. "Why is Kajhar fleeing while you sneak in like brigands?"

The stocky veteran scratched his chin and looked at Lenaro. The other man faced Nemiah. "I'm afraid that's a story better told by someone else, Lady. Are they on their way, Anzo?"

"Yes, Commander," Nevia replied. "City Guard and our best attempts at a match for the elder and the Lady, eh?"

"Good." Lenaro didn't smile. "I hope the Lady will accept our apologies. Grion was overenthusiastic."

The patrolman Nemiah had felled was climbing to his feet. A three-inch gash above his right eye bled down the side of his face. Under the blood, he still looked a somewhat sickly grey. "Following orders is all," he grumbled.

The damage Nemiah had caused shocked her. She might have blinded the man. She had believed she was fighting for her life and had reached for her knife without hesitation. This was what came of the repeated attacks on the temple and on her own person: so much violence had led her to an unthinking animal response that allowed for no consideration of others, only an instinctive striving to survive. As if she needed more proof that fear caused the most violent kind of disorder.

"Escort the Lady to the house, where she might have her questions answered," Lenaro ordered.

Anzo Nevia stepped forward and offered his arm uncertainly. "Lady?"

She stepped past him toward Grion. The bloodied soldier looked as though he wanted to recoil, but he just glowered at her. She stretched to touch his brow and place a blessing there. "Forgive me," she said quietly. "I did not act in the name of order." The man's mouth opened in an O of surprise. Nemiah turned and strode out of the stables into the night.

Anzo caught up with her. They walked in silence until they reached the stairs to the house.

"Do you have anything to say to me before we enter, Patrolman?"

He shifted his weight from one foot to the other. "No, Lady. Nothing that's mine to say anyways."

"Very well. I will ask you only one question. Answer it truthfully or not at all. Who sent you after us?"

He looked at her as though trying to come to a decision, then gave a small sigh. "High Chieftain Rumar."

She nodded once, wondering if the patrolman could read her relief. "Thank you."

The house was quiet. At the far end of the hall, the fire shed an orange glow that illuminated the people standing or sitting on the benches there. Madam Sevar's steward Sesara stood at the head of the group, her arms crossed over her breasts and her cold stare spearing a lean, golden-haired soldier. Despite the still-healing cuts across his cheeks, Nemiah recognized him at once: Lieutenant Matio Sevar. A well-ordered man she had thought him before he had left for the north with Leita. Well-ordered but hard and closed and without a hint of reverence in him. She had disliked him. Elder Trianor, standing with unlaced shirt and no vest, looked as though he had just awoken and was still recalling his nightmare. Rom was present as well, fully dressed and armed. Why had he not come looking for her? Why was he bent solicitously over a slender figure on the bench closest to the fire? Nemiah couldn't see who the figure was. And then she could. Her relief of a moment ago evaporated.

"No. Oh, Leita, no."

"Did I not tell you she would be pleased to see me?"

Nemiah crossed the room and came to a halt before her Bearer, who was dressed for travel and still wrapped in the thick cloak of Cael's midnight. "What's happened? Has the temple been attacked? Are the young ones safe?"

"All is well, Nemiah. As well as when you left, that is. Kaliska is wrangling the rest of the Higher Circle like a goatherd. The displaced families have trampled all the roses in the outer courtyard. And the new cook's bread remains dry and hard."

"Leita, why are you here?"

"Because I was bored in Velantar." Leita tossed her head, flicking back the silk tails of the binding concealing her scars. "Is this truly a conversation you wish to have here and now?"

"There are two conversations that must be had here and now," Nemiah said, clinging to her self-composure. "The first requires that you tell me the reasons you followed me with a patrol of Forest Guard. The second," she shot the lieutenant a direct look, "requires an explanation for our abandonment by Captain Kajhar."

Both Rom and Elder Trianor darted shocked glances at her: they hadn't yet heard.

"Abandoned?" The lieutenant frowned, shifting the fine scars on his cheeks. "What did Kajhar tell you about why he was leaving? About why we've come?"

"Kajhar told us nothing," Nemiah said stonily.

The lieutenant lifted his gaze skyward. "Damned City Guard."

"What are you up to, Matio Sevar?" The steward waved a finger in the lieutenant's face. "First one group of soldiers shows up here and then another. Bringing who knows what shame and danger. If your father were alive . . . well, you owe a greeting to Madam Sevar, and then you owe her explanations!"

"Not at this hour, Sesara. When she wakes, you may send for me and I will offer what explanations I have."

"Years ago, you might have come back to us," the woman snapped. "Years ago. It's too late now. You should not be here."

"On the contrary, good steward." Leita's voice was low and quiet, but nothing of softness existed in it. "Lieutenant Sevar is a hero of Avelos. You should welcome him."

The steward turned on Leita with a sneer. "Oh, we've heard about the goings on in the north. Even exiled as we are, we've heard. If Matio Sevar is such a hero, tell me, what happened to the rest of his men? Tell me, Lady, how is it you lost your eyes?"

Leita jerked backward as if she'd been stabbed. Nemiah took a step toward the steward, but the patrolman beside her set a restraining hand on her arm.

"Graceless to turn your anger at me onto others, Sesara. I would not have come had a better choice existed. Be certain I will not remain long."

The lieutenant spoke with perfect city-bred courtesy. His lack of emotion in the face of the woman's cruelty made Nemiah's heart ache.

"Fine," Sesara snapped, unrepentant. "I will have the girls make up a place for you. I'm afraid your old room is already occupied. Will your sister's room do?"

"Don't trouble yourself. I will bed in the stable with my men."

The steward remained indignant. "That's not proper! Not for one who should'a been—"

"I believe we are some ways past concerns of propriety," the lieutenant interjected. "However, I would be in your debt if you could send some soup and bread to the stable. And we would have a bottle of the Melandrien at the fire, if it's not too dear. Thank you, Sesara. Goodnight now."

The old woman fumed, then, with a huff of disapproval, marched toward the kitchens.

"Please forgive Sesara. She believes if I had remained home I could have restored the broken influence of our family. It makes her bitter. She is wrong, of course. Did you find all that gratifying, Elder?" The lieutenant's tone remained painfully mild. He turned to the old soldier still in the room. "Nevia, you have a report?"

"Yes, sir. Captain Kajhar is clean away. Our boys are hunkered down in the stable, awaiting your orders."

"Good. Tell Lenaro to set a watch on the road. Let me know immediately if there is movement. Otherwise, you're to remain confined to the stable."

"Understood, sir." The patrolman saluted his lieutenant and left them.

One of the serving girls brought out a bottle and a platter of small, brightly glazed cups. As she began to pour the amber-colored brandy, Lieutenant Sevar waved her away and took up the pouring himself. The others sat on the benches on either side of the table. Nemiah sat across from Leita.

"Rumar intended from the start that you should have a Forest Guard escort," the lieutenant said, "but he could not send us openly. He knew Abrigado would be likely to push the council to refuse such an escort."

"On what grounds?" Nemiah said.

The lieutenant gave one humorless laugh. "That you, Lady, our dignified Elder Trianor, and I are linked by those who have been accused of treason and possibly by treasonous acts."

Tension thrummed like a plucked harp. It was true: the three of them were strangely bound—Jhared Denaban had been Sevar's soldier and Elder Trianor's fosterling—but the treasonous acts had been only Nemiah's. "That accusation is unsupportable," she said.

"Perhaps. But the council would have taken weeks to deliberate over it, and a few more of us were likely to end in Aelend at the conclusion of such deliberations." The lieutenant took one of the cups of brandy and set it near enough to the Bearer's right hand that it brushed her fingers, then passed the platter to his left. "Rumar meant my men to serve as a complement to support Kajhar. We were supposed to rendezvous in Marenhan and continue to Sahiste together."

"What happened?" the elder asked.

"Kajhar realized you're being hunted."

Nemiah caught a breath. She thought of the party's rear guard vanishing and reappearing over the past two days. She had considered it a result of poor discipline and paid it little attention. "You and Kajhar have been in contact on the road?"

The lieutenant nodded.

"Abrigado," Rom spat.

Elder Trianor considered his cup of brandy. "I don't think so, Lord Arionad. Abrigado wins nothing if we're attacked on our own soil. To meet his goal, it must clearly be a Sahisten assault. He wants a spark to ignite the war."

"He doesn't need to wait for you to cross the border," the lieutenant replied. "We've caught Sahisten spies much farther north than this. It would not be so hard for a clever man to see to it that an attack looked like aggression from Sahiste. Of course, it's not an innovative strategy—blaming your enemy for your own violence— but it has a history of success."

Rom was sharply alert. "Then you believe it is Abrigado, even as you say it might just as well be Sahistens. Why? What have you found?"

"Yesterday morning, we caught three of the men following you."

Nemiah thought the others must hear her heart pounding. It was so easy to die on this Path. *An arrow flies through the trees. A horse tumbles down a concealed ditch. A spear slashes open yielding flesh.* She dashed her bruised wrist against the table leg to force away the shifting possibilities. She would not turn toward those possibilities. She did not mean to die yet; she had truths that must be shared. She had to find a way to stop the unraveling. "Who are they?"

"Two men from Clan Amerre. The third was maybe Amerre or perhaps from Rehamra."

"Was?" the elder noted.

The lieutenant nodded. "He refused to lay down arms."

It was easy to die on this Path.

Elder Trianor scrubbed a hand over his face. "What precisely did they intend for us?"

"We can't yet speak precisely, Elder. Under some duress, Ranz and Liramerre, the two from Clan Amerre, both admitted to arranging an ambush farther south, near Makri lands. However, I suspect it was something they had agreed beforehand to reveal if captured. To protect the rest of their strategies."

Ranz? That name seemed familiar. Nemiah strained to remember. Clan Amerre men would be likely to have Legacy sympathies and would have reason to be loyal to Toren Abrigado. Ranz . . . Goddess, she was tired. They had planned to kill her even before she reached Sahiste. Her own people.

"Lady?" Rom asked softly.

She shook her head.

"Do you know anything of the others involved?" the elder asked.

"Not yet."

An ominous tone in that. Nemiah thought of a dank cell and cruel men. "Where are they now? Ranz and the other?"

"Safely held. Soon on their way back to the city."

Nemiah nodded at the wisdom of that. "Once the council hears that Clan Amerre has threatened us, Abrigado may be prevented from acting further for fear of proving his connection to the scheme."

"A possibility, Lady," the lieutenant replied. "But we cannot assume what happens in the city will reach the ears of those who are already on the road or in the wilds. We presumed they're watching for you in Marenhan, which is why I told Captain Kajhar to bring you to the farm instead. It is also the reason Kajhar has gone on with his City Guard. He'll stick to the main road south. We hope for at least a brief misdirection."

"Whoever is hunting us isn't likely to miss the fact that Lady Nemiah and I are no longer with the group," the elder said.

Nemiah thought of the riders she had seen under the moon. She thought of what Nevia had said in the stable. "Two others were sent to fill our places, weren't they?"

"Yes. If we have any fortune at all, they will confound the hunters long enough for us to lose them."

Confound the hunters. A woman Nemiah didn't know was riding into danger for her. Nemiah said a silent prayer.

Lieutenant Sevar turned to her. Abruptly, she recognized the lines of Madam Sevar redrawn in him: the even features, the bright coloring, the iron gaze. She wondered if Madam Sevar's cruelty existed in him as well.

"There is one thing more that Kajhar was meant to address with you, Lady. It would improve the quality of our decoy if we create a reason for the City Guard to be traveling without the Arionade."

"You mean send the Arionade back up the road to Velantar," Elder Trianor mused. "That could work. It wouldn't be hard for anyone to imagine a falling out between city and temple. But why not just send the Arionade with Kajhar now. If they—"

"No."

Rom's voice reverberated against the stone. His black eyes smoldered with an anger he rarely indulged. "The Arionade will not leave Riana's Ladies in the hands of the Forest Guard. Not for a week. Not for a day. We will not make that mistake a second time."

The lieutenant went very still. Beside him, Leita made a small movement with her hand beneath the table. Nemiah sighed inwardly. She understood Rom's anger, but he should have had better control just now. In the coming days, they would be forced to depend upon this hard, clever lieutenant.

Sevar kept his gaze on Nemiah. "Does Captain Rom speak with your authority, Lady?"

"Always," she replied, as she must. "It will not serve us to separate from the Arionade. But we welcome you and your men, Lieutenant."

"Very well, then. We will stay the morning to rest the horses. Be ready to depart before midday. Leave behind whatever in your packs is not essential. From tomorrow we will avoid the roads, traveling rough and at speed."

Elder Trianor frowned. "The packhorses? They carry gifts for the king and heir. We mustn't leave them."

"Gifts can be replaced, Elder."

"Lieutenant, we are trying to convince the Sahistens they will benefit more from trade with Avelos than from war. Those gifts represent some of the best our artisans have to offer. They are essential to our diplomacy."

Sevar looked as if he would argue again, but instead he blew out an exasperated breath. "If your horse can carry it, it can come. Keep in mind that to negotiate with Sahiste *you* must reach the border, Elder Trianor. Jewelry, cloth, and brandy needn't."

Tension filled the silence that fell upon the group, but nothing more could be said. Elder Trianor made a noise of assent and said his goodnights. Rom looked a question at Nemiah, who sent him to speak with the Arionade and then to his rest. As Rom departed, Nemiah marched around the table to the Bearer, who was speaking quietly to Sevar. The lieutenant's mild expression didn't flicker, but he kept his gaze lowered as the Bearer turned from him.

"Well, that was bracing," Leita said brightly, facing nearly precisely the place where Nemiah stood.

"Come with me," Nemiah replied. She guided Leita's hand to her shoulder. As the Bearer stepped with unexpected confidence across a room she had never before known, Nemiah saw that color had returned to her cheeks. The journey from Velantar did not appear to have done her any harm.

"What's wrong with your arm?"

Nemiah blinked at the Bearer's question. "What?"

"I can hear your right arm brushing against your cloak as you walk, but not your left. You must have your forearm bent close to your body. But your step doesn't suggest that you're carrying anything, so you must be favoring it. What happened?"

Nemiah straightened her arm self-consciously. "A bruise. I struck my wrist. Nothing remarkable."

"A bruise? Oh. You slipped out while Captain Kajhar was leaving, didn't you? Did you perhaps strike your wrist against a Forest Guard?"

Nemiah glanced up and saw with relief that Rom had already disappeared up the stairs. "Leita, enough."

The Bearer looked unrepentant. "You should not forget that Cael's messengers can see in the dark."

They entered the chamber Nemiah had been given for the night. The fire in the hearth had dispelled some of the dampness. She walked with Leita to the bed. The Bearer stretched a hand to the mattress, sat, then promptly slid across the blankets until her back touched the wall.

Nemiah dropped her cloak over a chair. If she had been at home, Merisel would have hurried to hang it on a peg and Zia would have given her the green shawl warmed near the fire. There would have been boldblood tea. Nemiah stood with her arms wrapped around her chest and stared at the Bearer, afraid of where the next word would lead them.

Leita had never feared to tempt chaos. "I have news of Ziabela."

Nemiah remained coiled. "Yes?"

"Kaliska reports she is out of the city. That she has friends beyond the walls with whom she will seek shelter."

"Friends?"

"Kaliska didn't say more of them. Though I suspect she could."

"Yes, I suspect so too." Nemiah had recognized something in the healer in those days after the City Guard attack. Something that one day might bode well for Avelos but just now could be very dangerous. "Did Kaliska give Zia my message?"

"She did. Zia was reluctant to go, you know. She sent a message back to you."

"What is it?"

"Let me recall. Oh, yes. She apologized for not transcribing all the lyrics of the *Cycle of Stars* before she left. She said you must not push away food when Captain Rom brings it to you. And she said . . . she said do not let men of power determine your Path just because they believe they can."

"Ah, Ziabela." Nemiah felt a strange hollowness in her chest. When she had taken the bitter, battered Shorn woman from the custody of the City Guard, she had hoped to provide her with a temporary refuge and some sense of order. She had not expected to learn from her. She had not expected to gain a friend.

Leita shed her cloak and folded the yards of soft wool in her lap. "You know I will not go back, Nemiah."

Nemiah drew a long breath and let it out slowly. "We've already had this conversation."

"We had no conversation," Leita replied. "You merely told me I could not join the delegation. You have no right to keep me from Sahiste in order to avoid your own distress."

"I do not," Nemiah agreed. "However, as Lady of Avelos, I have the right to say where your duty lies."

"Has that ever changed the course of the Bearer of Cael's Blade?"

"Leita, why do you want to die in Sahiste?"

"All Paths end, my love."

Nemiah dropped into the chair, her eyes still on the Bearer, who bore the hint of an arch smile. She had not seen so much focused will in her friend since before Leita had left Velantar to seek Sabela's temple in the north. She knew she should be glad of it, but the intensity disturbed her.

"Stop playing with disorder, Leita. What is it truly that makes the risk worthwhile to you?"

"You know what it is. I want to find the way to curb the killing winds."

"Are you so certain the answer might be found in Sahiste that you're willing to put yourself at their mercy?"

A shudder shook the Bearer's slender frame. The question cut close; Nemiah had meant for it to. If things went wrong in Sahiste, they would go badly wrong. She knew what they did to captured Shorn soldiers in the south. They would not be more forgiving to a priestess.

"Fear will not deter me," Leita said very low. "In Sahiste they have cherished their history, while we have demolished ours. If ever Sahiste has known the killing winds, if they've heard of them in stories or seen them in the deserts, they are likely to have some record."

"Leita, tell me this is not about heresy. Not about the Unbroken One."

"It is about the killing winds," the Bearer repeated. "It is about playing a role that will make a difference on this Path."

The answer wasn't entirely satisfactory, but Nemiah thought she could understand it. She leaned her head against the back of her chair.

"I may be of use to you as well," Leita continued. "Cael's messengers are valued in Sahiste. Do you know that their priests bear raptors into their rituals?"

"I do know."

Elder Trianor had said the same. Leita likely had learned it from the same source as the elder. Nemiah gathered herself; she saw few options, none of them good ones. "If I agree to your joining us, you must agree to my condition."

"Which is?"

"You must renounce the heretics."

The Bearer went silent. "I cannot renounce what I know to be true."

"Leita, you are endangering her order! I cannot have this now. Not only for the importance of the journey to Sahiste. The web is unraveling! I've seen more evidence of it tonight. If you hinder me, you are no better than that which causes it!"

A sharp, pained sound broke from the Bearer's throat. Fear entered her face in a way Nemiah had never seen, not even at the mention of captivity.

"Leita?"

The Bearer shook her head, whipping the silk tails of her binding back and forth. "It's not possible. Whatever you've seen on the Paths comes from some other Parallel. Not ours! Not ours! All I do here is to stop the unraveling!"

Nemiah watched her friend with a sudden rush of pity. "Leita, I spoke only as Riana's Lady. I've not seen the cause on any Path." She paused, staring at the Bearer. "Have you?"

"I have not!" Leita stretched a trembling hand toward the warmth of the candle on the bedside table and held it over the flame until it must have hurt. It seemed to calm her. "Nemiah, if you allow me to travel with you, I swear to have no more contact with Yarla or her followers."

Nemiah searched the Bearer's face. She never could read Leita as well as Leita could read her, but she hadn't expected so much of a concession. It had been genuine fear the Bearer expressed. "Do you swear it by Riana's ways?"

Leita hesitated, then reached under her cloak and unsheathed the knife with the black hilt and the wicked curve: Cael's weapon. Nemiah hadn't known Leita was carrying the Blade. She truly was the Bearer once again.

"I swear it by the darkness of Cael's Blade and the light of Riana's order," Leita said, drawing the knife across the fleshy part of her palm. "May chaos take me if I should be foresworn."

Nemiah stepped across the room. She touched two fingers to the blood welling up from Leita's hand and drew a spiral above her brow. "By your blood, the blood of the Bearer of Cael's Blade, Riana witnesses your oath and accepts it. May you keep your word or wander in the Nowhere forever."

The power of the binding burst between them. Leita gasped. Nemiah stumbled backward. It was the second time that night she had touched Riana's strength.

She caught herself against the hearth, panting. "You have chosen."

She sent out a silent prayer that neither of them would regret it.

A bird cried to the morning just outside the shuttered window. Nemiah awoke, shivering. Something she needed to remember hovered just out of reach. It had taunted her in her dreams. Amalia had been with her. They had walked through Sabela's temple in the Sandien Mountains looking at a library missing all its books. Books that had been sold for blood. Nemiah kept her eyes closed, as the pieces slowly returned to her. Looted libraries. Rare books. Books in the north being sold. That was it!

The Forest Guard had captured a man who had been stalking the company. A man named Ranz. She remembered the name now. Ranz had been a failed initiate of the Arionade and a clanguard for Clan Amerre, but he also had an odd connection to the traitorous northerners—as a buyer of precious books. Now he had been caught carrying out the will of Toren Abrigado.

Nemiah rolled off the bed, careful not to disturb the Bearer. Ranz could be the connection that bound Abrigado to the northerners' treason. He could be the critical link to allow Adan Rumar to prove the minister's perfidy. Nemiah lit the stub of a candle at the smoldering hearth, then dug from her bag the ink and leaves of paper that Merisel had packed for her. She wrote two letters in the near dark and sealed them, one to the high chieftain and one to Kaliska.

When she left the room, dawn was still just a promise, but already in the hall a sleepy serving boy was stirring the fire in the great hearth. Nemiah asked for Sesara and was directed to a room behind the hearth, a small office with no windows. The steward sat at her desk, hunched over what looked to be a book of accounts. When she saw Nemiah at the threshold, her jaw set.

"Good morning, Lady."

"Good morning, Steward Sesara."

"You are about early. I'm sorry the household isn't up to greet you. One of the girls will come shortly to see to your breakfast."

The old woman's gaze dropped back to her books, her reed poised, Nemiah dismissed.

Nemiah marched across the little room. "I've no need for food, thank you. I have two letters I must send to the city. As swiftly as possible."

The steward did not bother to hide her irritation. "Swift is not the word we use when sending correspondence from our little farm all the way to Velantar."

Nemiah drew herself straighter. "Do not threaten Riana's web with half-truths, Sesara. You knew the purpose of our travels before we even arrived. It took hard riding for that information to reach you faster than we did. Madam Sevar has couriers posted from here to Velantar."

The steward set down her reed and gave Nemiah a reassessing stare. "I've always heard it said the Bearer of Cael's Blade is the clever one in the high temple."

"The Bearer is cleverer than I, but today I am the one with less patience. Why do you think it wise to play games with me?"

The old woman faced Nemiah as she had the lieutenant the night before, with an undaunted sense of authority. "You will excuse me if I have no inclination to assist Riana's Lady, who has only ever caused my mistress hardship."

"Sesara, I do not know this family's story. I do not know in what way I have failed you. You might simply tell me and save us both some pain."

"For what reason? You cannot undo what has been done." The steward gave her a sour expression, which shifted slowly into something sly. "Although if you would like to pay some of what you owe, I have a question you can answer. I will see your letters sent, if you will answer me truthfully."

"If I answer, it will only ever be truthfully. I will not make a promise without knowing the cost. Ask your question and I will answer if I can."

"What has become of the girl? The traitor Ziabela Marcalo?"

A chill of warning frosted through Nemiah. She hesitated. "What concern is a Shorn woman to Madam Sevar?"

"Madam Sevar is not concerned. She has forbidden us to speak of it. Only I ask."

"Then you treat your mistress's orders with no more respect than you treat your guests?"

"Do not judge what you do not understand, Lady. I know Madam Sevar better than she knows herself. Someday she will want to learn the truth. If I don't have the answer, she will regret it, and then I will regret it."

Whatever influence Madam Sevar lost when her husband gave up his position, she clearly still kept her attention on the political terrain. Yet this was not about the politics of the moment. *Someday she will want to learn the truth.* Nemiah thought of the conflict between the Minister of the Teaching and Madam Sevar, thought of the woman's cruelty and her hatred for the Shorn, and then Nemiah thought of one thing more:

You take others' daughters. . . .

Nemiah groaned. "Oh goddess, Ziabela is Madam Sevar's daughter."

The steward came to her feet. "That Shorn traitor is no longer a part of this family in any way!"

"How is that? Because the family disowned her?"

"Only after she left of her own volition, the little demon. Elder Sevar ruined himself, his family, and the prospects of his only son by stepping down from the council in the vain hope he could bring her into line. She would have none of it. She never could govern her filthy Shorn urges."

Nemiah felt ill. She had witnessed some of the consequences of Ziabela's impulsiveness, and she had also witnessed Zia's fierce strength and loyalty. "And Marcalo?"

"The girl pulled that vulgar name from her ancestry. Someone on her father's side. One of the cursed before the Exile."

"We are linked by those who have been accused of treason," the lieutenant had said. Nemiah hadn't fully understood him then. She thought of a bright-haired young man sitting alone in the grotto, grief in his eyes, a ruined flute in his hands.

"I understand. I do now," she said quietly. "Elder Sevar gave up his position for the sake of his Shorn daughter, and shortly after, Adan Rumar favored Tierzen Trianor by allowing him to take in a Shorn son."

Sesara leaned over Nemiah. "Tell me, Lady, is she dead?"

Nemiah met the steward's gaze, aware that the moment might be a point of influence, aware of her conflicting obligations to speak the truth and to protect a friend. "Ziabela has traveled beyond a place where we might seek her."

The old woman wilted back into her chair. "Ah. The Hidden Paths, then."

Nemiah frowned and stepped closer to the steward, wondering if she had misjudged her. "Do not grieve. The Paths are infinite, for the living and the dead. Ziabela will walk Riana's web forever, as we all shall."

The old woman continued to gaze down at her books, then shook her head. "No, no. Of course. Better she died quietly. Avoided the scandal of an execution at the wall. Avoided the chance others might connect a traitorous Shorn scribe with the family. It was a favor you've done us after all."

"A favor?" Revulsion shook Nemiah. She pressed her hands against the wool of her dress to still them. "Did you know, Steward, that the City Guard tortured Ziabela before I claimed her for the temple? They beat her and made sport with her in the guise of an interrogation. Did you know that?"

The old woman looked up, eyes wide. "The Shorn deserve their punishments. She was a traitor!"

"What is a traitor, tell me? When the killing winds struck at Parnas Pass, Ziabela stayed by my side. Although I was lost on the Paths and helpless. Although she could have easily escaped to freedom. She stayed to be certain I reached safety. Tell me, is that how you define *traitor*?" Nemiah shoved the letters into the steward's hand. "See these go swiftly to Velantar."

The woman nodded mutely.

Nemiah strode out of the room before she said things that would damage Riana's order. In her heart, she repeated words of apology to Zia that the Shorn woman would never hear.

Neither Madam Sevar nor the lieutenant appeared at the table with the others when the serving girl brought out the morning meal. Near midday, Sevar marched into the hall and announced they were ready to depart. His expression remained cool and unrevealing. Nemiah tried to see something of the grieving young boy in him and couldn't. As Rom brought Rigojan to the mounting block, Madam Sevar stood at the balcony rail, staring down at them in grim disapproval. Nemiah had never been so glad to ride into the wilds.

17.

SWAMP RATS

"This was a bad idea. He doesn't like me. He'll have me off in a moment."

Jhared glanced at the Avelun and the roan gelding ambling through the mud beside Seravina and smiled. "If he didn't like you, you'd be off already. Sink into the saddle. Don't perch. You were telling me what Amuria found so valuable in this damp land that it was worth fifty years of occupation."

Maya rearranged herself on the gelding's back, then rubbed irritably at one wing. A feather floated free. "I was not meant to be a rider."

"One day soon you'll have no need. But I couldn't leave Sera behind, and we're making better time with both of us astride than we would have otherwise." Jhared gestured to the poor little road ahead of them. "You promised me a lesson in Sonan history while we traveled."

"I suppose I did." Maya tilted her head thoughtfully, letting herself be redirected. "Let's start with the invasion. Tell me what you've been taught of *Losiin Rakva*."

"I've never heard the term."

"No? *Losiin Rakva*? Vicious wave?"

Jhared shook his head.

"It's the name Sonans gave to the first incursion of Amurian soldiers into the country. Jhared, thousands died in that attack. And Avelos doesn't even acknowledge it?" Scorn flashed across her face; Jhared saw her work to quell it. "The campaign tore along the coast, overwhelming every major town. Duke Anold was young and eager to prove himself, and Sona's temperate ports and deep harbors enticed him. Amuria had a well-funded army. The Sonan farmers and fisher-folk had hoes and nets. It took barely one summer for the Amurians to batter the population into submission."

Mud eels, fish herders, swamp rats: those were the names Avelos used to describe the Sonan people. No one raised a hand to save a swamp rat. "Did none of the border nations offer aid?"

"They say Laebek sent troops west. Unfortunately, Laebek has no great navy and no particular geographical advantage. Avelos, on the other hand, might have used her long border with Amuria to drain resources away from the invasion."

"Avelos was facing the consequences of her own war near that time."

Maya turned, jerking the reins hard enough to make the gelding start. "Do you truly believe the Exile War, already more than fifty years past, was the reason Avelos did not intervene?"

Jhared leaned over to return Maya's hands to a neutral position over her mount's withers. "No. No, I don't. The council would have had no interest in aiding Sona. The borders were closed after the Exile War, and Sona had nothing tempting enough to open them."

"You should know, Jhared, that when Sonans speak of the occupation, they recall how Avelos stood aside and watched it happen. It's one reason we're traveling the smaller roads. We'll avoid confrontations as long as we can."

"If we hope to gain access to the archive in the capital, we won't be able to hide."

"I know." She shrugged one shoulder. "The capital will be different."

"Different how?"

She didn't look at him, fiddling with the reins instead. "Saimbor is a city. A place of trade. They're accustomed to strangers."

It was a partial truth. He could hear it in her tone and see it in the way she turned from him. He didn't press. They were still days from the coast. But he suspected her hesitance had something to do with Zinderdali's warning to him before they left.

He had been making final preparations, packing bags. Although Maya had convinced him to bring the ancient volume of map notes for them to study, he would leave the sacred maps behind where they would be safe. Zinderdali, still limping, had cornered him while Maya was outside.

"Soldier, we both know Yavi can care for herself, but when it comes to the search for our life's desire, the wisest of us may act rashly. Saimbor is a place where years of scarcity and violence are just now lifting. People coming out of such extremes are wont to take what they hunger for without care or consent. We trust you will not abandon her if Yavi should become entangled."

"Of course. I would never leave her in trouble."

"You left her at Parnas Pass trapped between two armies."

Jhared knew a spear of guilt. "I didn't have a choice."

"In history, 'I didn't have a choice' is the common refrain of those who chose evil."

"Zinderdali, if you care for her as much as you doubt me, it seems you would come to aid her yourself."

The Sahisten sighed. "A fair blow. We would. If our messages were not so urgent."

"Then trust me in this. The ties that forced me from Maya's side are broken. I will not leave her again."

The Sahisten's eyes brightened. "We think you have begun to see she is a rare spirit. She is also our dearest friend. We will hold you to your promise."

The three of them had left Maya's house the following day. The shutters were latched and the house locked. Two younglings from Vris, a brother and sister, had taken the goats to care for them with their own herd. With Maya's help as interpreter and the promise of two breeding nannies, Jhared had obtained the stocky gelding from the children's father several days earlier. Before Jhared and Maya set off for the south, Maya had clung to Zinderdali and kissed his cheek. She had spoken to him in Sahine. Jhared imagined she had offered to change her mind and come with him. Zinderdali had shaken his head as he mounted Rashina and turned eastward.

"Our injuries have healed well enough, silverwing. When next we meet, you will have mastered the skies." He had said it in Velos. His gaze had caught Jhared's.

That was five days ago, and they hadn't left the sight of water since then. The lake had turned at first to rivers, splayed like talons across the open land, and then to sprawling, endless wetlands. Reeds and tall grasses in every shade of green and tan stretched nearly to the horizon, where a line of short, twisted trees rose from the muck. Above, round-bellied clouds floated through depths of cerulean. Jhared glanced at Maya sitting awkwardly on the grey, her sage gaze catching his with wry good humor. He couldn't worry about the vague hazards that might lie ahead. In this moment, he had a sense of purpose and the grace of Maya's trust. With every mile, the Path he trod felt more his own. Something came to him then.

"Maya, I must learn Sonan. And Sahine as well. I don't wish to continue living with the veils Avelos gave me. I want to hear the stories these people tell of themselves."

"I'm glad," she said, with a smile that sped his pulse. "The languages will also be useful if you intend to search the archive."

"Will you teach me?"

"*Sumpra novja re hrevka, vi shef.*"

"What is that?"

"Sahine." Her lip curled upward. "It was a yes."

"It seemed somewhat more lengthy."

"It did, didn't it? I suppose you will have to wait for the rest until you've learned enough to interpret it for yourself."

He canted his head, the twist of a smile on his lips in spite of himself. "That seems an odd way to start a lesson."

"Indeed." She maintained her private expression. "Ask me something else then. Anything."

He thought on it. There were things she had said to Zinderdali. Things he wanted and didn't want to understand. "What is *vi shik*?"

She blinked. "Oh, that is an interesting case in Sahine. *Vi* is possessive. 'My' in this case. No good translation exists in Velos for *shik*. It is a name for someone very dear."

"Very dear?" he pressed unwisely.

"It's what you call someone to mark them as family when they are not related to you by blood or marriage."

"I see." Heat rose to his face as he realized how awkward the conversation was about to become and how much he had already revealed. "Perhaps let us stay with Sonan for now."

Surprise registered in her eyes and perhaps some disappointment, but Jhared suddenly had no wish to speak further of Zinderdali. "As you wish," she replied. "Why don't we start with the local flora?"

As the hours of travel passed, Jhared worked to develop a basic grasp of the Sonan language. Although it shared very little in common with Velos, once Maya began to provide the interpretations for common phrases, he began to absorb the rhythm of it. It was the language of a people for whom respect was vital. Personal titles were numerous and colorful and often based on metaphors related to water or mastery of the water. He had no need to question the reason for that. By the time he and Maya were leading the horses ankle-deep in muck, he had learned the appropriate water-related curses.

Despite Maya's warning before they had departed, he hadn't fully grasped the extent of the endless damp they would encounter. Already it threatened to chew his bowstring and leathers. Morning and night, the horses trod through wet and mud, which brought the risk of hoof rot. Adding to such dubious pleasures, each afternoon grey, gravid clouds dropped the rain they had carried inland from the coast and halted before dusk to the joy of swarms of stinging insects. Jhared spent each night waxing and oiling his bow and the horses' tack. For the animals, there was little he could do. There was no way to avoid it. The wetlands slogged and gurgled down the center of Sona like blood down a fullered sword, saturating the land from the northern border all the way to the country's toe, near the capital. He and Maya had started out from her home at a good pace, moving south through the river-streaked grasslands. Then they had turned west. The crossing to the coast was the shortest at that point, Maya had said, grimacing at the endless stretch of marsh before them. The passage would take days, if they were lucky enough not to be slowed by the rains, by the illnesses that plagued travelers, or by the predators that ruled the marshes. On the far edge of the swamps, a slender river valley awaited, where Zin had encouraged them to use one of his connections, a Sonan boatman, to travel the remainder of the way to Saimbor.

That evening, darkness caught them still searching for a tolerable place to pass the night. When they finally found a hillock dry enough to lay a fire, Jhared was all over mud and sweat. He sat with Maya before their smoky flames and ate some of the bread and dried fish they had carried. The horses made soft noises as they grazed on the coarse grass, their tails swishing and feet stomping against the siege of insects. Jhared smacked at a blood sucker on his neck and Maya handed him the jar of rosemary and mint-scented balm that the Sonans used to protect themselves from bites. After rubbing the balm into his exposed skin, he took it to the animals and smeared it around their eyes and ears and soft nostrils.

As his boots squelched through the long grass, Jhared thought of Velantar, of Elders' Circle, and of the sparkling dome of the high temple overlooking the three shining hills of the city. By this time of year, a lacy shawl of snow would enwrap the Parnas Mountains, shifting from lavender to apricot to gold as the sun rose. He understood that land, had learned the skills of a scout in the valleys and crags of the mountains. Here in the wilds of Sona, even the night sounds were foreign. The sound like a lamb lost in the marshes, Maya told him, was a type of frog. The mad old man cackling amongst the reeds was only an orange and brown water bird. A wide assortment of large and small rodents and their predators skittered over the waters during the day. At night, herds of bad-tempered creatures Maya called water boars rooted among the swamps for prey. In the marshlands, no wind whispered to the trees or played among the mountain passes; instead, water grumbled through runnels of grass and moss and mud. He wondered if such a place could ever feel like home.

Maya settled quickly to sleep, wings and blanket wrapped closely around her. Habit made Jhared sit up into the night, listening. It wasn't only Sonan's spoken language he wanted to learn; he needed to understand the language of the land as well. At first, he focused on the scents and sounds, working to distinguish and identify them, to make the foreign patterns his own, but gradually his attention lifted to the sky. The patterns of the stars, at least, were familiar and dear: Lusian chasing his children in the west; Ularian the Archer endlessly hunting Cael in the east; and Lord Arion, the brightest of them all, gleaming fiercely in the south. The glorious depths offered themselves to any who could reach them. Without his Teachers to flog him for it, Jhared allowed himself to drift into a fantasy of flight, only paying the price when the scarred muscles of his back twitched and cramped. He exhaled against the pain.

"What is it?" Maya asked drowsily.

"Nothing. Or no . . ." He rolled his shoulders, trying to unbind them along with his thoughts. "Have you ever considered that other children may have been saved from the Shearing? As your mother saved you?"

She was quiet for a time, then shifted onto her back, her wings nestled around her shoulders. "When I was small, I was so sure of it. I would stare at the sky for hours, searching for an Avelun. Every time I caught a glimpse of wings, I'd run to tell my mother. She'd tell me it was nothing but an eagle." Maya laughed ruefully. "When I discovered I was a Traveler, I tried to search for Avelune on the Paths, but I was never very good. I couldn't open the Gate reliably and didn't know where to go once I did. Eventually, I realized how unlikely it was that any others had escaped, or if they had, how unlikely it would be for me to find them. I gave up and set my focus on the one thing I could make mine."

"Your ability to fly."

She made a motion of agreement in the darkness. Firelight gilded the line of her throat and the gentle incline of her breasts.

"You will fly, Mayavana. Soon." The reality of the words struck him hard. When they found the lessons she needed in the archive, she would open her wings and embrace the sky, and he would watch her soar away.

"Perhaps it's foolish," she said, "but your faith means something. I think this time I truly will find the answer."

She shifted again on her blankets, a soft rearranging of feathers. "Jhared, I have thought about what it will mean. For you. I would understand if you didn't want to be a part of it."

As ever, she had touched his thoughts and taken them one step beyond what he had been willing to claim. "It won't be easy. I won't lie about that. But your flight will be one measure of healing against a century of pain. Nothing could make me turn from that."

The firelight picked out her tentative smile. "Thank you."

The night remained quiet, and eventually Jhared allowed himself to sleep. When he rose at the edge of dawn, Maya was already up, drawing a brush through her straight, black hair and shaking out her feathers. He stretched, trying to pretend he wasn't watching her, then walked to the bank to organize himself. The marsh water he splashed over his face smelled of decaying vegetation, but in his head was the berry tang of the Avelun. When Seravina whickered and stomped for attention, he turned to care for her and the roan, glad for the distraction. *Brenka*, the children had called the gelding. It meant plum, he knew now. He patted Brenka's neck and turned to calm Seravina.

When Jhared finished with the horses, he picked up one of the pieces of bread that Maya had left toasting near the coals, munching at it while he surveyed the morning. Although it looked to be a clear day, with only a few puffs of clouds in the west to disrupt the blue expanse, the air hung thick and heavy over the marshes. Swarms of gnats and shiny green and blue biting flies gloried in the stillness, discouraged only somewhat by the herbal balm. He spied no sign of humanity other than the rough trail. The heart of Sona was wide and wet and empty.

"We should get moving before the rains return," she said, rubbing at one wing. "Some roads are likely to grow impassible."

"Do you want to start on the ground or in the saddle?"

She shook out her feathers. "On the beast, I suppose. I'll never enjoy riding, but I can at least learn not to embarrass myself."

That morning travel quickly grew more challenging. The marsh encroached upon the trail until it was hard to judge stable ground from the deep, sucking muck. A wrong step could trap a horse, causing panic and broken legs. The danger forced Jhared from the saddle. He helped Maya down as well that they might better evaluate the footing and spare the horses. As they lurched slowly through the wetlands, sinking past their ankles with each step, they alternated time in the lead where it was necessary to beat back the tangled grasses. The need for constant vigilance meant Jhared's lessons in Sonan had to wait. Conversation was reduced to terse observations and sharp warnings. It was slow, tedious work. Jhared would gladly have traded the muck and the flies for a narrow, rocky ledge high in the Sandien Mountains or even the dry, clean desert of Sahiste. Just after midday, the skies opened with a rumble and added a dull, steady rain to the challenge. They covered little ground that day. Night was a dreary affair, with no fire and the rancid, greasy remains of a cissanu lizard Maya had caught the day before. The subsiding rain heralded the return of the insects. Jhared hummed a patient tune as he and Maya rigged a shelter that might protect their more vulnerable possessions—the grain, their bows, the volume of map notes—and give them some cover. Swamp cats yowled in the night as they marked their terrain and fought over mates. At dawn, Jhared awoke from an unsatisfying doze, soggy and cramped. The sun scrambled up, revealing another day of marsh travel.

That day and another passed before Jhared acknowledged a challenge of a different kind. Following Maya, he caught himself studying the rhythmic shift of her hips, the gentle dip and sway of her wings. He tasted her scent on the air, and abruptly became aware of the heat rising in him. He called for a rest for the horses, and after, arranged to take up the lead himself. The constraints of rough travel permitted only the barest privacy, and the consequences of inescapable proximity—the sleepy warmth of her voice in the early morning, the gentle sound of her breathing in the night, the sure movement of her competent fingers on the bow, a quick glimpse of tawny skin—fueled the memories of the single joyous encounter he had shared with her. He didn't lash himself for his response as he once would have done, but he drove down his desire with uncompromising finality. A list of reasons existed why he could not reach for her. He refused to make their journey untenable by exposing a longing that had no place on this Path.

Instead, he sought out ways to insert distance between them. When practicing his Sonan became dreary, he took up reading the book of map notes. Discussing a difficult patch in the translation, arguing points of ancient theology, considering theories about Path travel gave him innocuous and relevant topics of conversation and kept his thoughts safely engaged. He swiftly realized that he should have been studying the notes all along. He meant to find the key to controlling the killing winds, and the winds were somehow entwined with the Paths.

In the evenings, if the rain had stopped and it was dry enough for a fire, he drew the book from its waxed leather wrapping and studied the notes—blurred by age and smoke and blood—written by priestesses who had traveled the Paths more than a century before.

One step closer to success today. That we did not succeed was fully my own and none of Guide Hendren's failing. He led me to the very moment of Lady Anin's labors. I saw the bed, the birthing candles, the . . . women around her. Yet I could not open the final doors to reach her. I had spent my strength in the Nowhere and . . . failed me. I did not learn if the child lived and whether, as some Elders have recently proposed, he was the son of Clan Amerre. My thoughts and my vision blur. I will rest now. We will set off again as soon as . . . me able. The answer we seek will shape the next Council. The implications for the future of the temple are . . . V. N.

Today we said good-bye to Lady . . . Although our loss cannot be unwoven . . . her Higher Circle saw her one last time beyond the cerulean flames and each lay blessings upon her. . . . We chose the moment when her illness became critical to seek her out. Thus, she already understood her fate when we touched her from farther along her Path. Now, as she walks the Hidden Paths to which our eyes are yet veiled, she will . . . Riana's order and the gift of our love. Shamina, our Lady of Rituals, opened the final doors so that we could each touch the Chosen Lady spirit to spirit while she lay on her deathbed. I was the one who closed the doors again. It was, without doubt, the most difficult closing with which I have ever been tasked. In that moment, I closed the final doors on the woman who was my mentor and my friend. F. R.

Oh! What wonders does our Lady Riana offer to those who are willing to strive! Nine cohorts participated in the spring competitions this year. Nine of the most powerful Pathwalkers in Avelos and with them the most accurate, devoted Guides. The challenge set for us . . . unmatched in the history of the competitions . . . to find the point of influence that caused Lord Kalminen . . . and his war. Our Lady . . . and for her wonders . . .

Jhared read and gleaned what he could about how Pathwalkers had traveled across the infinite Paths in the days before the Exile. They traveled in cohorts, no less than two, it seemed, with some taking the responsibility of a guide, leading the others to their goal, and some using their strength to open and close the doors to each Place and Perspective. The Nowhere had been respected, perhaps feared, even by the trained priestesses, and the doors caused even those ladies to struggle sometimes. He found something reassuring in that. No matter how far he read, however, he learned nothing particularly useful about the mechanics of such struggles, which was what he needed most to understand: How did one seek and find a specific Path? How did one deny the blue flames when they reached for him? What must he do to keep from spinning away into the deadly Nowhere? More interesting, if less pressing than those questions, he began to wonder at the daring possibilities of travel. Could one jump to a later place on his own Path to see the consequences of a specific decision? Could someone exceptionally skilled travel to the Perspective of someone known to him as a means to communicate? Could one travel the Hidden Paths of the dead?

Among all the priestesses who logged their travels, he recognized a commonality: what they accomplished they did through deliberation and care. They chose their destinations, prepared their journeys, and opened the Gate with purpose. Although he read of mistakes that sometimes meant injury, and failure was a reality, the map notes did not detail accidental journeys or speak of Pathwalkers who slipped unintentionally through the blue flames. It inspired him to strengthen his own thready ability. He began to create drills for himself. He started very simply, as Leita once had directed him, to find the flames and back away. Maya observed his efforts with uncharacteristic disapproval thinning her lips.

It was late afternoon and warm. They had stopped early to fish and to give the horses time to graze. Frogs chirruped in the marshes. Green and grey swamp hens giggled to one another from their grassy nests. In the embers, the rewards of their fishing slowly roasted. With his other duties completed, Jhared had taken the first step to open himself to the Gate. Sitting cross-legged by the fire, his muscles shed their tension and his heart beat strong and slow. He gentled his thoughts until all went quiet within him. It was the palpable intensity of Maya's stare that forced him to abandon his meditation. He opened his eyes to find her standing before him, arms crossed over her chest, an unyielding expression in her eyes.

"You once encouraged me to try this very thing," he said into the silence.

"Once. Before I understood how completely the flames hold you. I am no guide, Jhared. I could not find you if you wandered."

"You found me before."

"I was lucky. And you were only so far as a bird on the bush beside us."

"I must learn, Maya. You know I must."

She dug her fingers into the feathers of each wing. "I do know. But it needn't be now. You haven't fallen since we set out. Why risk yourself when you might find better instruction in the archive in Saimbor?"

"Because I've known such a respite before. When the flames returned during the skirmish at Parnas Pass, they consumed me without warning. I cannot wait. While the Paths are stable beneath me, I might develop some skill. It's too late to learn to hold a sword when the battle is raging."

"And if you are set drifting? If I throw myself after you and am lost as well? Who will find us?"

The thought startled him. He'd never considered the possibility that Maya could lose her way. He lifted his eyes to hers. "If I fall, you mustn't come after me. Use the knife."

She turned away with a look of disgust. He continued as though he hadn't seen it. In this thing, he was certain. He could not afford to be made helpless time and again by the blue flames. He had the freedom now to reach for the Gate as he never would have had in Avelos. He would use it.

As ever, finding the Gate was easy. He was a scout and had already come to recognize the terrain. This time, however, he sought only to stand before the Gate without tumbling through. The blue flames burned with the purity of the stars. They sang to him of beauty, of longing. They reached out with promises of boundless journeys. Holding himself back from them took effort, like holding back at the edge of the final, urgent moment of release. This release was of the spirit, and it was a gift he would not allow himself, not until the decision could be fully his. He stood firm before the Gate, rejoicing at each instant he did not fall, then hastily quelling his triumph before it broke his concentration. As the moments gathered and restraint became painful, he kept himself in the present by counting his heartbeats, pushing himself to hold fast until the count of one hundred, then pushing himself to one hundred more, and yet one hundred more. The flames beckoned, and he refused. Only when he felt his defenses trembling and knew they would soon give way did he step back, turn from the Gate, and flee for security in the heart of his own Path.

He was aware first of the desperate heaving of his lungs, of the heat steaming off him, and of his heart, no longer steady but galloping and stumbling like a runaway horse.

Maya crouched in front of him, her eyes dark and angry, her knife gripped in her fist.

He sucked a long, fortifying breath. Then he allowed himself a smile. "You don't need it. I'm here."

She stood without comment and tossed the blade aside. Night had dropped over the marsh, but the ruddy fire, so different from the bright pure blue on which he had turned his back, lit the irritated snap of her wings.

He rose to go after her, and promptly lost his sight to a swarm of buzzing white bees. The ground came up hard beneath him.

She glanced over her shoulder. "Your little game takes its toll, doesn't it?"

He crouched, hands braced against the dirt, waiting for the dizziness to pass. "Maya, is there a reason you wish for my failure?"

"What?" The sound behind him signaled her abrupt turn. "No, Jhared. Not your failure. I've never wished for that."

"What then?"

She made a sound of unwillingness, then sighed. "Jhared . . . what if your Teachers are hunting for you on the Paths? Don't you risk drawing their attention each time you travel? Aren't you more vulnerable when you exhaust yourself?"

He shook his head. She truly didn't understand. "If Shrill seeks to possess my senses, nothing is stopping her from doing so right now. The only possible way to keep her out is to learn to stay on this side of the Gate and to close the doors to my own Path."

Maya bit the edge of her lip and frowned.

"This is one reason I told you not to come with me," he said darkly. "I did tell you."

She didn't reply, but stabbed the roasting fish with particular violence as she turned them over the coals.

As Jhared rose—slowly this time—to help with the meal, he discovered the cost of his foray: a weariness that saturated every part of him. Despite it, and despite Maya's pessimism, he felt pleased with his small success. After eating, he fell into a solid sleep that even the biting insects couldn't disrupt, regretting only the way Maya avoided his gaze for the rest of the evening.

The following day did not begin as well. The sun was still stretching up from the eastern horizon when Brenka stumbled, wrenched to his knees by a deep, muddy hole. Although the gelding didn't snap his leg and Maya managed to avoid coming off, several of the packs he carried, including the bag of grain, dropped into the water. The packs they managed to retrieve, but the grain spilled and was lost. Worse, poor Brenka stepped out of the hole badly lame. Jhared did what could be done to ease the beast and redistributed the packs between Sera, Maya, and himself, but their progress fell to a limping pace through some of the nastiest terrain they had yet crossed. The long concealing grasses and short gnarled trees made it impossible to see more than a few feet on either side of the trail. They moved through slippery mud with no likely shelter or shield. Jhared led with increased vigilance, even before Seravina plunged to a halt in the center of the trail, standing with braced feet and flattened ears. When his cautious investigation revealed nothing amiss, it took all his skill and the trust she gave him to convince the mare to move on. Experience taught Jhared to accept her warning. Although he couldn't know if the danger she sensed lay on his Path or someplace beyond the Gate, he kept his bow close to hand and pressed Maya until she took up her staff.

It did not reassure him that over the past two days they had encountered increasing evidence of the Sonans who occupied the region—sporadic tracks, the remnants of a fire, a boat moored among the reeds, and far to the south, tendrils of smoke from what must have been a village. Yet he had never glimpsed a person. He suspected they were being observed, and it kept him alert and quick. He couldn't help but consider every story he'd ever heard of the swamp dwellers, rarely seen and often deadly, who preferred poison on their arrows and on their brutal spears, hooked like the ones they used for fishing. When he asked Maya whether the local guard would seek to bar their passage, she gave him an exasperated look.

"Guard? In the wetlands you'll find only the *Rivan Vutro*, the Water People. They're a shy, peaceable folk. Too peaceable, many who survived the occupation would say."

"And the sight of foreign travelers won't stir them? It's said their poison kills faster than their aim, but I'm in no great haste to test either one."

"It's said? Do you mean drunken soldiers tell such stories by the fire? Sonans don't use poison to kill. The *Rivan Vutro* learned to survive by keeping to themselves. They don't like to leave their rivers, and you'll rarely ever see their kind in the cities. The last thing they would care to do is draw the attention of strangers. Gods of Skies and Seas, Jhared, how can you still believe what Avelos told you?"

The level of aversion in her voice took him by surprise. He stopped and turned to stare at her. "Maya, Avelos told me everything I know. It's not always clear that a thing must be questioned."

"Then you must question everything!" she snapped, rubbing crossly at her wings.

"I should think," he replied with strained calm, "the fact that I am traveling to Saimbor with an Avelun rather than helping to prevent a war against Avelos suggests I already have."

The one word—*Avelun*—came out harshly and with an implication he hadn't intended. He saw it strike her. The heat of her anger transformed into something frozen.

"Oh? And have you questioned that decision as well?"

"The decision to ignore the plight of the people I once called my own? A dozen times a day."

She shook her wings, sending feathers floating out behind her as she began to walk on. Brenka limped at her side. "Perhaps," she said to the air, "you have made the wrong choice."

Twelve years of the Teaching made tamping down his anger as instinctive as breathing, but Jhared no longer answered to his Teachers, and his frustration broke free. "If everything I thought to be true is false, then I've made a host of recent mistakes, haven't I?"

"Like traveling with an Avelun? Is that what you were trying to say last night? Telling me that I shouldn't have come with you? The Avelun is such an odd beast, after all. As fractious as your mare, though not nearly so useful. Still, in the depths of some night, in your need, perhaps you will find a use—"

He sucked an audible breath. "Maya, what are you doing? Stop!"

She shook her wings again and was silent. Beside Jhared, Seravina's hooves splashed into the mud and slurped out. They went on without speaking. Maya's straight back declared her resentment and hurt. Jhared trudged behind her, dismayed at how quickly their companionship turned caustic. But how could it not? When it came to it, Maya despised everything that had shaped him. In her eyes, he was a fool for ever devoting himself to Avelos.

The rest of the day remained tense and quiet. Maya evaded Jhared's gaze, and when by chance she did glance his way, her cheeks glowed with a hectic flush. He didn't have anything else to offer but his own aggravation. To avoid provoking another kerfuffle, he put his effort into marching through the long, wet grasses. They pushed hard, walking more than riding, eating while they walked. The sun was red and swollen in the west by the time the trail finally climbed enough to lift them to a patch of firmer ground.

"We'll stop here," Maya announced, dropping her packs under the branches of one of the short, twisted trees that scarred the landscape.

Jhared took Brenka's reins. The gelding and Seravina were both caked in mud from hoof to hock. He tethered the horses and began the significant task of scraping the mud off them, while Maya collected what fuel she could for the fire. He was still tending Brenka's strained foreleg when she returned, retrieved her bow, and slipped away through the trees. Jhared made no comment when she brought back a cissanu for the pot. They ate the tough, oily beast without speaking.

It might have been the scent of the meat that drew the predators into camp that night. At Seravina's scream, Jhared sprang awake, already reaching for his bow. Maya rolled to her feet and caught up a brand from the dying fire. The lurid glow fell over four heavily muscled bodies covered with tough, pebbled skin. Blood-drop eyes gleamed above tusked snouts, and clawed feet tore up the earth as the creatures paced at the edge of camp. Water boars, Maya had called them when Jhared first heard their ugly grunt-growling deep in the marshes. Other than their nasty temperament, they had little in common with the boars that roamed the forests of Avelos. They hunted and scavenged in the darkness. Their thick, hairless hides served them well in the water and resisted the hunters' spears, while their powerful frames were unexpectedly agile.

Jhared nocked an arrow to the bowstring and drew, his shoulders shifting to lead his target and compensate for the breeze from the south. He could have mapped the exact flight of the arrow, even before he loosed. The bowstring hummed. The stalking beast leaped and twisted in the opposite direction. The arrow flew past harmlessly and impaled the ground.

Cursing, Jhared grabbed up another shaft. Seravina kicked at an approaching beast, while Brenka whinnied in terror. Jhared loosed again. The arrow flew, piercing the boar at the shoulder. It shrieked, but kept running, with a bolt sticking from its body that should have driven through its heart. In a breath, Jhared fitted the third arrow. This shaft buried itself in the beast's eye. With a night-shattering screech, the vicious bundle of tusks and claws tumbled head over heels and lay still.

"Jhared! Guard your left!"

With a hiss, Jhared threw himself backward as another boar rushed him, a broad grizzled creature. Maya dove to his exposed side, swinging her torch. It cracked against the beast's back, but the unmovable bulk staggered her. Her wings battered the air as she fought to recover her balance. Jhared grabbed her by one arm, steadying her, as he warned back the boar with a kick under its chin. The creature paused, stymied more by the fluttering, shouting Avelun than by the futile blows. Jhared loosed another arrow, sending the attacker to its death.

Fire and noise and the discovery that its prey was not helpless drove off the third beast. The final creature was still menacing the horses, its tusked snout swinging back and forth hungrily. Seravina spun, rump outward, and landed a sharp hoof against the beast's ribcage. With a squeal, the boar stumbled sideways; then, regaining its feet, it too fled, a humped shape barreling into the night.

Jhared hastened to control the horses. Seravina had pulled free of her tether and Brenka had tangled in his lead. Behind him, Maya panted furiously. Neither of them spoke.

By the time Jhared had secured the animals and calmed them, Maya had fed the embers back into flames. The orange light exposed the taut lines of her face.

"I don't suppose they taste any better than cissanu," Jhared said, returning to deal with the carcasses.

"They don't. Although the hide is useful. Sonan hunters use it for armor." She shrugged a little shyly. "I've heard it can resist not only arrows but barbed speech and sharp words as well."

He glanced at her. "I'll consider that."

She offered another stick to the fire. Jhared drew his arrows from the dead water boars and retrieved the stray shaft from the dirt. It was Maya's quiet hiss that caused him to turn. She clutched at her right wing just below her shoulder, a handful of feathers coming free in her hand. With a scowl, she let them scatter. Where her hand had drawn away, a patch of bare skin showed raw in the red light.

Jhared straightened. "You're injured. Why didn't you tell me?"

"I'm not injured," she replied grumpily, poking another slender branch into the fire.

"Your wing—"

"It's nothing."

"Maya, tell me plainly if you have no more wish for my questions or company, but do not lie to me."

With slow deliberation, she brushed her hands against her thighs and stood. "I'm molting."

"Molting?" He stopped short. "Truly? Like a—"

"Yes!" she snapped. "Just like a bird. My winter plumage is coming in. It started before we left home."

The vulnerability under her annoyance sobered him at once. "Forgive me," he said quickly. "It never occurred to me. I never had reason to think of it." He frowned at the patch on her wing. It wasn't truly bare, he saw now; rows of tiny new pinfeathers were beginning to show. "Does it hurt?"

"Yes. No. It's not painful, exactly, but it's damned uncomfortable." She glared over her shoulder at the offending feathers, then blew out a breath. "It does make me horrible. I'm sorry."

"No debt, Maya. Is there anything I can do?"

She stretched both wings and beat the air. Feathers puffed around her. "Do you have something I can use to store these feathers? Perhaps I'll make a pillow."

Jhared couldn't help it; he laughed aloud. With relief, he saw a dry smile lift her features. She shook her head. "There's nothing to be done. It will be a week or so more until I scratch the last of the old feathers out and the new feathers poke through. The moon will wax full again before all returns to order. It's disgusting, really."

"It's not disgusting. It's astounding! Of course you must have new feathers to replace the worn ones. It will be even more important when you begin to fly."

"I know that's true," she said, plucking absently at a row of grey vanes.

"Will you change colors?"

She shrugged. "Just like other birds."

Jhared grinned; he couldn't stop. She flushed and looked aside.

The following morning, Jhared delayed their journey. The horses would benefit from the rest, he said, and Brenka was still lame. Then he set to a task of his own, dealing with the two slain water boars. Their muscled bodies were thick with an insulating layer of fat that would provide a useful tallow. In response to Maya's queries, Jhared only shook his head. It was a smelly, messy business to render the carcasses without the proper tools, but in the end he won a jar full of yellow tallow. While it settled, he gained Maya's puzzled permission to search through her box of herbs and medicinals. He chose tinctures of vel bark and poplar buds for inflammation, and brightmint to ease itching. A search around the edge of the water revealed long, willowy filly-tail, which he stripped of its outer layer and crushed for the cleansing fluids within it. All of the ingredients he carefully blended with a portion of the tallow. When it had set, the result was a greasy, pungent ointment.

"It should have more time to steep," he said, offering it to her. "And it doesn't smell so good, but it will calm the irritated skin."

She accepted it with pleased surprise. "Mother used to make an ointment for me when I molted. I didn't take the recipe when I left, and never bothered to experiment for myself. I don't know why." She rustled her wings uncomfortably. "How did you learn such a thing? I thought healing forbidden to the Shorn."

"Neta, our . . . the Trianor's household cook. She made simple remedies for the family. Whenever she needed help, she would ask me to clean herbs or stir the pot. I remember some of her recipes."

He shrugged, as though those moments hadn't been some of the happiest of his childhood. He shouldn't feel homesick. Maya was right: he had been bound to lies. He had acknowledged that, had even imagined that he'd accepted it. But Neta had been the one person in his life willing to engage him in tasks that made a child feel accepted, the one who would pat his shoulder or rub a smudge from his cheek without hesitation. It occurred to him only now that she would never really have needed his help to mix her ointments and tisanes. There had been a kitchen maid and an errand boy for such things. The cook would never have needed the aid of a Shorn child. Why had she pushed the boundaries of Shorn Law? Had she seen his interest in healing? Had it been an act of kindness or merely another kind of test? He would never know.

"I'm grateful you remembered," Maya said, renewed warmth in her words.

He smiled silently in return and walked away to wash the remains of the grease from his hands.

18.
TANGLES

Jhared began to mark the days of travel not by the repetitive cycles of sun and rain but by the changes in Maya's wings. It startled him to realize that in trying so hard not to notice the glory of her, he had also failed to notice the lack of luster in her feathers or the bare patches that marred their order. Her new feathers were small at first, each constrained by a thin sheath that she preened away nightly. As they grew, the frost-to-midnight ombré of her summer plumage gave way to a brilliant snow that started at the leading edge of her wings and sleeked to within an arm-span from the trailing edge, where bars of deepest ebony scalloped against the gleaming white.

"Light and shadow," Jhared murmured. "You were meant to be in the snowy mountain crags come winter. In the heights of Altan Mar."

Maya scoffed quietly and flipped her cloak over her wings. "Perhaps you could make a song of it."

"If I thought I could capture the truth of you, I would." He considered melodies for a moment, and key changes, then he spied the pink tinging Maya's cheeks and put his gaze back on the trail. "When we reach the river, where will we find this sailor of Zinderdali's?"

"His name is Vjeran. He docks his barge, the *Mila Jul*, at Nebov on his way downriver to Saimbor. His pennant presents two salmon entwined."

"And Zinderdali is sure of our welcome?"

"Sure enough. He says Vjeran can be prickly and he has no love for Avelos, but I've some stones from Sahiste that will smooth the way, if necessary."

Jhared frowned. "There's nothing sure about a man who can be bought."

"Perhaps. But traveling on our own would take twice as long and require us to ride through every hamlet along the valley. This way we only wait at Nebov until Vjeran returns from his upriver run."

Jhared's frown deepened. "Maya, even cloaked you can't hide for long under any deliberate scrutiny. What will the Sonans do when they see what you are?"

"We've come this far without trouble."

"We've come this far by avoiding contact with anyone other than water boars and cissanu. I wish I had a sword and a patrol of men I could trust."

"Don't, Jhared. Don't think like a soldier. Just because they're strangers does not make them enemies. If they've no favor for those with Avelonian blood, they've earned the right to it. We'll just need a dose of diplomacy." The corner of her lip curled. "The son of an elder must have some claim to such talents."

"The exiled fosterling of a disgraced elder recommends we avoid relying on his diplomatic abilities." Jhared shook his head. "I hear you, Maya. I'll try not to assume every man is a threat, if you will promise to parcel your trust with caution."

He found her nod not entirely convincing, but her enthusiasm kept him quiet. The tension in their interactions continued to wax and wane. He would do nothing now that might dull the shine in her eyes or damage the hope in her expression.

As though her eagerness influenced the land itself, gradually, the ground grew firmer and the stunted brush stretched tall, until finally Jhared found himself on a rutted road above the swamps at the borders of a lush, dense forest. A breeze from the west rushed away the stench of rotting vegetation, filling his lungs with the welcome scent of fresh water and clean growth. Elegant curtains of moss draped the branches, and high in the trees, birds of wild colors conversed in whistles and shrieks. Seravina pranced and snorted, her neck arched, as though pleased by the sound of her own hooves on solid ground at last. Stocky little Brenka tried to imitate her, throwing Maya off balance.

As Jhared leaned from the saddle to calm the gelding, he caught Maya's gaze and saw his own pleasure reflected there.

"Thank the gods of skies and seas for water that doesn't smell like rotten cabbage and a place to lay my blanket that isn't all mud," she said. "Shall we pause and enjoy it?"

He straightened. "Are you sure? The river can't be far now."

"Another day," she answered. "And I have no wish to negotiate with Vjeran while reeking of the swamp."

Jhared grinned. "Well enough. Let's find a place to make camp."

They stopped as the sun passed midday, the horses hooves muffled by springy moss, their shadows dancing under a canopy of bright leaves. The season stretched late so far south; many of the trees and bushes still bore their fruits, scenting the air with sweetness. Jhared drew Seravina to a halt in a small clearing deep in the forest. Maya set about establishing camp. Jhared hummed as he untacked and settled the horses. The river was only a day away and Saimbor perhaps six days south from there.

"Are you hoping for something other than fish or frogs for dinner?" Maya asked as he took up his bow.

He turned. In her arms, she held a small bundle of soiled clothes.

"Won't you miss the cissanu?" he replied.

She grimaced, then chuckled as she strode off. Jhared watched her move away, the curve of her wings sweeping beneath her cloak.

He walked alone through the woods, only half attending to the game trails. The birds that flitted in the branches offered a strange and splendid palette of brilliant blue and purple, green and yellow, red and orange. They chased one another in pairs, teasing in the air and across the branches. He paused, watching them play. When one of them balanced on the branch above him and tilted its peach head in his direction, he felt a faint tremble in the world. Gleaming cerulean flames flickered in his vision. Quickly, he shifted his focus, not tightening his grip on his Path, as his Teacher had warned him, but letting it spin out gradually as he turned away from the cousins and moved on. Once more, the ground beneath him settled and grew stable; his perception remained his own. He let out a breath, enjoying a cautious sense of competence.

For a time he foraged in the rich forest, selecting from among the fruits that were the most familiar. Eventually he turned from foraging and picked up the trail of a small herd of deer. The trail led to a narrow lake that stretched north and south, with a notch on the east bank in the shape of a mare's ear. As he crept toward the water, he spied his first glimpse of Sona that he could truly name beautiful: Smooth-barked trees with long, slender leaves draped the gentle curve of a bank fuzzed blue with delicate blossoms. Afternoon sunlight melted across the lake, turning the water to gold. A flock of swans drifted silently in and out of the dappled light not far from the shore.

In their midst, Maya stood bare to the elements, her wings unfurled and the water sliding over her hips. As a swan glided toward her, she lifted a hand to stroke the silky white cheek. The bird allowed it. An artless smile curved Maya's lips.

Jhared froze, his bow loose in his hand. The long days of travel side by side and the hours of suppressing his awareness of her exploded against him, blasting apart his restraint. His body responded with swift, painful assent to a question she hadn't asked.

Some subtle signal must have alerted her. Maya looked across the water directly into his eyes. No surprise or alarm registered in her precisely carved features. She made no effort to cover herself. A net of golden water droplets sparkled across the white and ebony of her new feathers, over her pale breasts, and down her supple waist. The swans continued to sail.

Jhared held her gaze, finding there the honest regard and unshielded spirit he had first encountered beyond the blue flames. As then, her openness astounded him. It aroused him to impossibly opposing desires: to protect what was so unguarded in her and to throw away his own defenses; to delve her courage in the face of his fears and to nurture her with his strength.

He allowed himself none of those impulses. Drawing on a lifetime of practice, he caught hold of his raging need and turned away. His boots crushed the fragile blue blossoms as he strode up the bank.

"Jhared, wait." Her voice floated across the water, calm and curious, but with a sadness that such an open spirit could not conceal. "Might I at least know why?"

His back was to her. He looked at his hands, callused and scarred. "Because I have been used as a tool with the potential to harm you. Because freeing my desire leads only to destruction. Because I respect the man who loves you."

A sweet treble, water falling gently into water, broke the silence. "Am I not allowed to give answer to such reasons?"

"Maya, you cannot."

"To the first," she went on, "I have already spoken. No matter the demands or the accusations of others, you are your own person. I do not fear you would ever cause me harm. I do not fear you, Jhared."

Nearly silent footfalls touched the bank. The grasses hissed. She had risen out of the water. He did not turn. "To the second," she continued languidly, "not in vain have you strengthened your skills. Although I did not think it possible, more than once now you have walked away from the blue flames. Without the flames and the Paths beyond, the killing winds do not come to you."

He drew a breath and caught the berry tang of her. She was drawing closer. The very rhythm of her approach held him fast.

"To the third, I cannot pretend I do not know what you mean, and yet—"

"Yet you set yourself before me, like Riana before Arion, knowing what it would do to me. Ah, Goddess, you must know—" He broke off. She was close enough that he could sense the chill of the water beading over her skin and the core of her heat beneath. "Mayavana, I did not think it in you to be cruel."

Her footsteps stopped. She did not try to touch him, and he did not look at her. The playful modulation in her voice ended. "Jhared, Zinderdali's affections lie in a different direction. He does love me. As I love him. I am not his beloved."

Jhared closed his eyes, controlling his breathing with effort.

"Won't you look at me and know the truth of what I've told you?"

Slowly, carefully, he turned his gaze to hers. He saw her candor, her intelligence, her kindness, and her own desire. Not as Shrill had forced him to see it, as an echo of their first joining, but as fit this moment.

"There is no more need for restraint," she said, her voice soft, unwavering. "You are free of Avelos, Jhared. I know the strength of your hunger and I welcome it."

It was enough. He took the last, fierce step to bring them together, colliding against her with a force that made her gasp. The smooth muscles of her shoulders flexed under his hands. She stumbled backward, and he thought she would go down. Instead, her wings unfurled in a sudden blur of snow and ebony. She caught her balance and took his weight, halting them both. Her arms came around his neck. Her voice near his ear was warm.

"Whoa there, *vi shef*. Did you think I would let you rush this?" She arched her hips, causing him to step back swiftly or lose himself. He laughed, a breathless, needful sound. The Gate sparkled in the distance. He turned away from it and reached for her again.

"Mayavana, I know nothing."

She smiled, slow and enticing. "Shall I show you then?"

Their first joining had been impulsive and powerful, an unexpected gift of joy. Their second was more careful, a gentle exploration of new paths. Jhared shackled his abandon with mindfulness of the flicker of blue flames and the rattling of doors. Something ugly and powerful in him could bring together his every experience of desire and create a force with the capacity to destroy. In the past days he had proved himself increasingly able to turn away from those doors, to lend them none of his own energy, but Maya had no mercy. She expressed her own need without chagrin until Jhared struggled for control. When she slipped from his grasp with a playful shriek, she fled along the bank, her bright wings tight against her back, her black hair streaming. For a handful of strides she outstripped him, but they were well matched. As he reached out to catch her, she swung around and surprised him by throwing herself once more into his arms. This time she let him draw her down to the moss.

They claimed one another with a surge of need that allowed no possibility of retreat. In that moment Jhared knew nothing but the depth of his yearning as it roared across the skies, the intensity of his joy as it shaped a new song, and the brightness of his affection as it flared hot and blue. Maya gripped his hand and her gaze held his, a gaze that saw him, knew him, and did not turn away. His fear remained, a necessary thing reminding Jhared of the damage he had caused and the danger he signified. He tried to reject those thoughts, reaching for the innermost place within his spirit, that place of openness and peace, and found something other.

"Oh goddess, no. No!"

He ripped himself from Maya's embrace, his body crying out against the interruption. With a gasp of protest, she reached for him and caught only emptiness.

"Strike me," he panted, kneeling at her side. "Hard. Now."

She sat up, her eyes wide. "What? No, Jhared. I—"

"Do it!" He grabbed a rock from the bank and shoved it into her hand. "You must!"

She didn't flinch or make any motion at all. "I won't."

The roar that had started in his head was growing into something beyond his capacity to direct or rebuff. Terror charged through him. "Don't you understand? I warned you I would bring you harm!" Cursing, he stumbled to his feet and raced toward the water, leaping in from the bank. Vigorous strokes shot him toward the center. Swans scattered in a white, trumpeting cloud. When he reached the depths,

Jhared dived. He was a strong swimmer. He had learned about currents and eddies and submerged rocks in the fast-running Heartsblood River. Warm at first, the water grew swiftly colder as he kicked himself into the darkness. Cold tightened its fists around his chest and around his laboring limbs. His lungs began to protest. Once, in Parnas Pass, the winds had come to the call of his unbridled need and had faded again when viremur carried him into oblivion. A second time, when his fury had loosed murder against his own comrades and the traitors of the north, injury had stolen his awareness and the winds had also gone. He continued kicking down through the murk.

The sunlight paled to weak, wavering ribbons. When he reached the bottom of the lake, he grasped a bundle of slimy weeds and held himself there. His heart hammered in his ears. Someone very distant seemed to be singing, a sweet, tuneless song. He forced himself to hold, forced his spirit to dwindle, leaving no part of him to drive the winds.

Only when the first dense strands of lethargy wrapped about him did he finally release the lake bottom and thrust himself back toward the light. He knew he had judged it close, perhaps too close. He had no intention of ending in the water, but neither would he once again give life to the horror of the killing winds. His lungs screamed, threatening to suck in the breath that would drown him. He swept half-circles with his arms over and over through the iron water. Far above lay a plate of rippled glass separating him from the sky. It was, perhaps, the place he belonged, this watery world, a place where his losses meant nothing, where grace did not rely on feathers and wings. He hesitated, then stopped kicking. Peace might be found here.

A shadow blocked the light as it reached toward him. Something strong and certain wrapped around his shoulders and tugged him toward the sky. He thought to fight it, but found his limbs no longer obeyed him. When his face at last broke the plane of glass, a great, involuntary gasp jolted through him. It took time before he could help Maya to help him toward the shore. He staggered up the bank and dropped onto his back, his chest heaving.

In the world of forest and sky, the air was still. The birds had started calling again.

"It worked," he gasped when he was able.

She scowled down at him. "Your attempt to drown yourself? Not quite."

"I stopped the killing winds."

"You did. I'm not sure it was worth the cost."

Jhared pushed himself up on one elbow, ready to speak of what she had refused to do. Then he saw the worry in her expression. He offered a small grin instead. "I had some need to cool off."

She bared her teeth at his flippancy. "Perhaps. But I don't care to get my feathers wet."

He collected himself and rolled, a little cautiously, to his feet. The last of the light was gilding Maya's flesh. His grin faded and he shifted his gaze to the water beside her. "It's all right. The river is a day's ride, you said. Or a night's. We might reach Nebov by morning."

She gave no retort to that but only nodded. Travel would be a distraction. It would mean they didn't have to think about the incomplete moments between them or risk sleeping beside the same fire.

"You've figured out what they are, haven't you?"

They had been riding since sundown. They kept off the road, an extra precaution that held its own danger in the dark, but made it less likely they would be forced to deal with Sonans before reaching Nebov. Sera was a silver ghost and Brenka a smaller shadow nodding beside her. Jhared felt the vastness of what he and Maya had lost.

"Please tell me what you guess," Maya murmured. "Do you understand? I need to know what part I play in it."

"It isn't you. It has nothing to do with you." The words sounded harsh. Jhared tried to wave them away. "They come in moments of failed discipline. In my fury or pain or . . ."

"Other times of heightened emotion?" she suggested.

He offered a bitter smile. "Something changes among my Paths. Doors open on my every experience of those needs and they . . . they crash together. Like a thousand mountain streams colliding suddenly into one riverbed."

"Your own experiences. So they rely upon your strength. That's why they die when you are gone."

"I think they draw on that reserve of energy our bodies harbor. The extra heat that carries you farther and longer than a normal person could manage. The winds feed on it."

She tilted her head. Starlight caught the edge of her frown.

"You must know it too," Jhared said. "A flash of fire in the blood. Strength loosed when you need it to survive. It will be valuable when you begin to fly."

"No. I don't know it. I'm not sure I've felt it."

"Oh." He trailed off. His eyes turned toward the myriad stars gleaming through the canopy.

"What is it?" Maya asked.

He scrubbed one hand across his face. "It's just that I was taught to see Shorn energy as a dirty and dangerous thing, but I had begun to imagine it must be something natural to the Avelune body. A thing we shared. If not, well . . ."

"Jhared, tell me."

He blew out a breath. "The killing winds are a sign of True Chaos. The Bearer knew that. Now we also know the Shorn are responsible for the killing winds. Amalia told Lady Nemiah that the loss of the Avelune would have consequences for Riana's web. I believe those things are related. Don't you see? The killing winds are one of the consequences Amalia spoke of. The Shorn may in fact *be* True Chaos. We may be the root of more destruction than even Avelos credited us."

Maya stretched her hand across the span between the horses and touched his shoulder. "I do not see it. Chaos is not something subject to control. And you are coming close to bridling the killing winds."

"I would have been closer if you had let me drown," he said without vigor.

"I'm sorry."

"For pulling me out of the lake?"

She snorted. "That wasn't what I meant, but keep talking and I may begin to wonder."

He chuckled softly. He was still chuckling when Seravina shied hard. She spun off the trail with a frightened squeal, backing on her haunches and trying to bolt in the opposite direction. Brenka, panicked by Sera's alarm, took off at a gallop. Jhared turned his mare tightly, struggling to keep her under control while searching the darkness for the cause of her terror. He spied nothing but a glimpse of Maya as she disappeared through the trees, dragging on Brenka's reins. The terrified gelding's arrhythmic hoof beats thudded into the distance, halting sharply as a resounding crack echoed through the forest. Maya's frightened cry entwined with the shriek of a beast in agony. Then silence descended.

Sera continued to fight an invisible threat as Jhared threw himself from her back and tore after Maya. He knew what he would find. He prayed for the Path to turn again.

A downed tree dissected Maya's trail. Propped at one end by its massive roots, it lay as high as Jhared's chin. In the darkness, running at speed, Maya would have had no chance to veer around it, and stocky little Brenka could never clear such a jump. Jhared called Maya's name and heard only the slow creak of branches in return. He hurtled over the bole, his heart slamming against his ribs.

Brenka's body was a twist of broken limbs. Maya lay farther from the tree, thrown clear of the gelding and onto the moss. Jhared knew some hope at that. Then he spied the ugly thing shifting in the starlight and felt only a cold well of dread.

He dove toward the Avelun, his mind filled with the image of Rona torn and dying. Too far yet to reach her, he collided with the miasma surrounding the tangle. Paths coiled like serpents around him, dragging him in different directions, toward different places and times. With a viselike grip on his own moment, he held himself in one piece and flung himself to Maya's side. She was sprawled like a discarded doll, her left arm and wing penetrating the tangle. She was breathing, but her features had gone slack, and under the starlight, her skin had turned the color of milk. Jhared grabbed her right wrist. No flicker of a response. Her skin was already growing cold. Rona had been as cold as death. Jhared clutched her arm more tightly, prepared to pull her free of the tangle's reach. He had been able to free Rona, but he hadn't been able to save him.

A terrible thought caused him to stop abruptly: What if dragging Rona out of the tangle was the thing that had killed him?

Jhared remained crouched over Maya, vertigo swinging him to and fro. He knew something more about the tangle now, had felt what it was to have his spirit splintered by a thousand different Paths. What if tearing Maya's body away from the tangle meant leaving her spirit behind?

Moments were passing and he had no way to answer his questions. It was hard to think. He fought to keep his breathing even, while parts of him were ripped away. If he lost consciousness, neither he nor Maya would wake to this world again. He drew his hunting blade. "Forgive me," he murmured.

The blade fit neatly in the tender place beneath her ear. He pressed the steel hard enough to dimple her flesh. She didn't flinch or moan. Jhared shouted her name, shaking her by the shoulders. Her body was growing colder as her spirit streamed away toward places she could not exist. He returned the knife to her throat. She despised the way he used the blade to anchor himself, but he saw no other choice. This time he cut a fine line along her jaw. Then a deeper one. Blood welled from the wound. Maya didn't move.

He cried out in frustration. The tangle swirled like mist through the trees as the Paths drew her spirit farther from him. He covered her with his cloak to keep her body warm a little longer. The vultures were plucking at his thoughts. He jumped as someone touched his shoulder. Glancing up, he felt a surge of hope.

"Leita, you are a guide. You can find her. You must help me to find her!"

The Bearer of Cael's Blade smiled down at him without speaking. Her midnight gaze swallowed the light, consumed him. Her midnight gaze. "Wait!" He shouted the word to try to grasp some clarity. When had the Bearer come to him? How had the others come here? Among the trees stood Alende, Shira, and Nemiah. Behind them stood a strange Avelun man. The threads of the weaving were not where they should be. All was unraveling. Swiftly, Jhared turned the blade and jabbed it against his own throat.

He knelt in the dirt beside Maya. Just the two of them, for the moment. Until his thread twisted out of place again. He realized what he must do.

"Goddess, guide me."

He lay down beside Maya and pulled the cloak over them both. Wrapping his arms around her, he closed his eyes and sought the Gate.

The flames greeted him eagerly, taking what he offered and stealing him from his own Path. He murmured the litany of names, his own and Mayavana's. He would find her, every fractured piece of her, and bring her back. For a moment the thought of such an impossible task undid him, sending him tumbling over the woven threads of blue and red until they were distant and untouchable. *"No, no!"* Desperately, he repeated his litany until he could see the snarl of Paths once more. It was a tumor within Riana's infinitely complex web, a ravaged knot of stories with a grotesque pattern. Here was the unraveling that the Bearer had so feared. It must be. A base animal drive for survival pressed Jhared to leave Maya and flee, but he stood against it. He had guided Lady Nemiah safely home. Guiding Maya would be no different. He must ignore the repulsiveness of the snarled pattern. The task simply involved more Paths and more pieces. He would retrieve Maya one Path at a time.

He tracked the Avelun first to her lake; they had met so many times in that haven. She saw him in the same moment that he saw her and ran to him. He grabbed her hand. "Maya, quickly! Tell me what's happened! From what Path have you traveled?"

She shook her head with a pretty frown. "What are you talking about, Jhared? I've been waiting here all day for you. As we planned. Kiss me, my love, and tell me what stories you've brought for me. We haven't much time."

He groaned. He had known this could happen. She wasn't his Maya, though the warmth in her tone and the delight in her expression made him wish that she were. He leaned forward and touched his lips to her cheek. "I'm so sorry. I'm not the one you're waiting for."

Without stopping to think or regret, he spun away and threw his thoughts toward the blue flames. The tangle caught him and he was flung back into the chaos. The next Maya he tracked was not his either, or the next. Panic pounded in his chest. His memories were beginning to fray. He took deep breaths and grasped for focus. His method of tracking, picturing the Avelun, imagining the shape of her wings, recalling her skill with a bow and her preference for sweet things—all her attributes and skills—was working. Repeatedly it led him to the woman called Mayavana who knew a Shorn man called Jhared. But in the infinite web an uncountable number of Mayas matched the image he had created. He needed to invoke the essence of *his* Maya in *this* moment. His Maya was more than a set of abilities. She was shaped by her connection to others, by her connection to him. In order to track the Maya who existed on his Path, he must acknowledge who she was *to him*.

He only hesitated an instant before opening himself wide and drawing forth the core of his feelings for her, emotions too rich and complex for any language he knew. As those emotions touched the web, he realized how vulnerable he had made himself. He offered up all the things that Maya meant to him and the web twisted toward him, as though hungry to swallow everything that he was. But as parts of himself become one with the Paths, he began to truly see the Paths and everything that composed them: the needs and wishes of others, the causes and consequences of actions, and the subtle connections among those living and gone. In that moment, he realized it was not possible to know a person fully or love them honestly unless he understood himself. Understanding coursed through him. He saw the answers to every question he had ever asked and those questions not yet spoken. If he so desired, he could turn that understanding to shape the Paths.

Was this what it meant to be a webweaver, like Leita? Like Riana?

And what becomes of Maya if you mean to set yourself among the gods?

The derisive thought sent him scrambling back to his hunt. He flung himself through the tangle, calling for the Mayavana he knew. The first time he found her was in the cave in the Sandien Mountains, where they had once weathered the killing winds together. Snowflakes drifted down the natural stone chimney and evaporated over the fire. She was sipping something steaming from a cup. He knew it was her. He said her name.

She glanced in his direction, and a look of horror iced her features. The cup fell from her fingers and shattered on the stone.

For a moment he could do nothing but stand motionless, stunned. "Maya, come to me. Quickly! I'm here to help you back."

Anger shadowed her fear as she rose. She flung up her wrist, exposing the copper and silver god charms there. "Do not think me foolish! I have walked in the lands of your people. I know better than to speak your name. I know how you seduce in dreams."

Jhared took another step toward her and reached out with one hand, fighting to keep his voice level. "Maya, it's me, Jhared. You *have* spoken my name. You have seduced me in dreams and in waking. Please take my hand."

She settled back a step, doubt hazing her gaze. "Prove to me you are Jhared Denaban. Tell me the first time we met on the Paths."

He despaired at the frightened rage in her voice. He thought of the time he had perceived the Bearer as a raven on the Paths and wondered what it was Maya saw when she looked at him. No time to wonder. He considered the first time they had met. Did she recall the same moment he did? For her it had happened years ago. "You were running on the beach. Under the moon. I saw your mother catch you. You were trying to fly. She was trying to keep you safe. Please, Mayavana. Take my hand now so I can bring you back."

Doubt remained in her eyes as she leaned toward him, but she did it. He grasped her wrist, and with an effortful turn of his thoughts, threw them back into the tangle.

Over and over he relived that scene. She did not accuse him on every Path, but too many times she showed fear or anger before recognition. Over and over he fought the tangle as it sent out coiled serpents to drag away bits of his self. Exhaustion enwrapped him as he retrieved piece after piece of Maya's splintered spirit and held them together. When he felt his grip slipping, he drew deeper from the cache of energy that had so often sustained him beyond what a man should be able to endure. Maya's name was the litany that kept his thoughts coherent. The knowledge that flowed through him allowed him to travel where he should not and to find what he had lost. He pushed himself through unknown doors until he could not imagine taking one more step in that airless half-world, and then he pushed himself farther.

Travel had become purely an act of will by the time he finally felt something different about the woman holding his hand, a sense of completion. He dared to look back and realized that clinging to him was one Maya—*all* of his Maya. The pieces had come together: she was complete and he was holding her. Gratefully, he prepared to make the journey home to their rightful place.

The doors of his own Path exploded open. One moment the tattered ribbons of the tangle twisted about him; the next, the damp ground pressed against his shoulders and the stars spun above him. Maya moaned. He crept closer, until he could whisper at her ear.

"Open your eyes. Focus on the now. Listen, Maya. You must cling to this moment."

Her eyelids fluttered. He could feel her struggling, but she was too near the threshold. She still lay within the tangle. If he did not move now, nothing else would matter to either of them. He pushed himself to his feet, took her arm, and gradually, gently dragged her free. When her body had cleared the tangle, he bent and scooped her into his arms. Her wings hung lax to the ground so that he had to take care not to trip over them.

He made it around the fallen tree before a faint tremor ran through her limbs, warning him, then a deeper tremor. Jhared dropped to his knees, clutching her close. Her body had been empty of her spirit for too long. The cold could take her now. As the tremors claimed her entirely, he held her, whispering reassurances that came from his own ravaged spirit. Her body writhed and her wings beat in uncoordinated spasms. He inhaled deep and slow, willing warmth and calm into her.

He couldn't have said how much time passed before her trembling eased. He held her tightly, no longer able to whisper, but still rocking her. When he felt her muscles gather and she began to shift, he set her down, afraid of the expression he might see if she awoke in his embrace.

An anxious whinny warbled into his awareness. Some distance through the trees, Seravina paced and called. Jhared left Maya wrapped in his cloak and approached the mare quietly. It took convincing to bring her back. Poor Brenka was long past any aid he could offer.

By the time he returned, Maya was sitting with her knees drawn up and her head resting on her folded arms. She stirred, but didn't lift her head.

"Maya, we need to put more distance between us and that tangle," he said softly. "Can you stand?"

"I can even walk, I think. But I'm not getting back on the horse."

"Brenka is dead, but we must move on. If we're not far enough away, I fear the Paths might shift and drag us in again."

"How can you be sure how far is far enough?"

"I can't be sure. But we're at least going to keep moving until the vultures stop trying to pluck pieces of me off this Path."

She didn't answer at first. Then her hand rose to her throat where a line of blood marred her skin. She stared at the blood on her fingertips. "It's this way for you every time, isn't it?"

"I'm sorry," he said wearily. "I didn't want to use the knife. I didn't know how else to reach you."

"I meant the cold. The sense that life is being torn away from you."

Sera snorted and stepped sideways. Jhared laid a hand on the mare's shoulder. "Yes. That's the way it's always been."

Maya closed her eyes and shivered, a soul-deep gesture. "You don't even understand how wrong that is."

"Keep your eyes open!" he ordered. "You could slip!"

She obeyed without protest. Her gaze was dull with shock, her voice heavy and far away. "I saw what happens. Every door you pass explodes open. And they stay open, even when you try to return across the Gate. While you struggle to find your own place, all those unsealed Paths are drawing parts of your spirit back toward them. Tearing away pieces of yourself. Stealing your life. Every time, Jhared."

He looked at her in horror. "But this time the doors I opened tore your spirit instead of mine."

You don't even understand how wrong that is.

He did understand. It was what he had tried so hard to explain to her. But no energy remained to go through it again. He crouched beside her. "Come. We'll ride together."

It was a miserable journey. His strength was bled out, and Maya was silent and sick behind him. Only the Avelun's rigid grasp around his chest kept him vigilant. He wouldn't allow himself to sink while she was helpless. In the darkness, the green world of Sona was dead and grey. The remnants of the tangle continued to pluck at his mind. Jhared turned away from them as best he could and pushed Sera onward. The mare's steady jog tapped the dirt in a soporific rhythm. Eventually Maya's grip loosened. Her weight sagged against Jhared's back and her head sank onto his shoulder.

"You mustn't sleep," he said, wriggling his shoulder to rouse her. "Not yet."

She groaned and nestled closer, her forehead tucked into his shoulder blade.

"Talk to me," he told her.

He felt the tired resistance in her. He flexed his shoulder again. "Perhaps this calls for more drastic measures."

He gathered his breath and rolled out the first lines of a marching song, trying to stir them both with its merciless beat, but such bawdy cheer only pained the senses after the immensity of what they had survived. The words flattened and died. Maya shivered against him. He was quiet for a time as the mare's hooves thudded on the soft ground. Then he started again. It was a song Maya had sung for him in the Sandien Mountains when he had needed an anchor to hold him to his Path. A Sonan lullaby. He grasped most of its meaning now. It was sweet and sad, a memory of a fertile land much loved. Of the tender sound of flowing waters smothered by the invaders' drums. He connected himself to the moment by focusing on the foreign scale. For a short time, his thoughts remained centered, and something gentle and generous began to form, a counter to the ruptured night. Then, somewhere in the third verse, an echo of desperation rang through him. He had come so close to failing. Maya had come so close to death. The words of the song dissolved. He floundered and surrendered to silence.

The silence held for a lonely span. Then faintly, no stronger than a tendril of new grass, Maya's sweet, untrained voice budded in the darkness. Jhared listened, aware of what she was giving him. Carefully this time, he drew a breath, as though any discordant sound might tear her fragile melody. When the refrain returned, he joined her, his low, steady voice interlacing with her delicate one. They sang together, with only the mare and the stars as witnesses.

Before the song ended, Seravina halted and lowered her head with a whicker. Jhared roused himself to take in their surroundings. The forest rose thick on all sides, but they were close enough to the river that he could smell its clean scent. He stretched his senses further and realized that the vultures had gone. Nothing of the torn and tangled space in the Paths pulled at him. He helped Maya to dismount and find a dry place under the trees. He dragged off Sera's tack and their remaining packs, and tethered the mare beside them. Gathering firewood in the dark took time, but tonight it was necessary. When the flames had grown strong enough to throw light on Maya's pale features, Jhared unpacked the food they hadn't touched earlier. Neither of them ate any of it. Maya soon pushed it away and curled up on her bedroll. Her wings, pulled close around her shoulders, didn't conceal her shivering. Jhared covered her with his blanket and lay down beside her. With one arm, he drew her close, until her wings pressed against his chest. She didn't resist. He wasn't certain she was conscious.

He rested his cheek against the silk of her feathers and kept a silent vigil to be certain the Path around them remained safely in its place.

19.
SAIMBOR

Maya was still asleep when Jhared opened his eyes. He lay silent in the darkness, dealing with ugly thoughts on the killing winds, the tangle of Paths, and the nature of True Chaos. Gently, he disengaged from the Avelun, feeling a sudden chill where her body no longer rested against his. He tucked the blankets around her, took his cloak, and turned toward the distant sounds of community that were rising in the predawn gloom.

As he made his way back to the road, he saw they had stopped closer to Nebov than he had realized during the night. Not so far ahead, the wide river reflected the last of the stars. Once he turned a bend, a silhouette of the village rose against the sky, with the docks beyond it. Penned animals bayed and bleated for their morning feed; men and women exchanged greetings; and from somewhere further down the river, a horn blared thrice in quick succession. Jhared walked toward the activity, curious despite the lightheadedness that lingered, as if his body hadn't completely settled back onto his proper Path.

He joined the growing bustle with caution. Even in the dusky light, it was obvious he didn't fit in among the short, wiry Sonans. As he strode toward the docks, head and shoulders above nearly everyone he passed, he felt the stares: some wary, some speculative, and none of them particularly welcoming. He kept his pace brisk and his expression neutral. Across from the docks, women sold ladles of steaming, sweet-scented beverages from fat-bellied kettles. One woman laid out woven baskets for sale. Another sold leaf-wrapped packets of smoked fish. Men pulling carts or carrying crates lashed to their backs were loading and unloading the half-dozen barges that bobbed and squeaked in their berths. A ferry began to pole across the river, its cargo bleating their protests. A grizzled man with a kitten peeking out of his pocket sang out about the quality of his fish.

Jhared ran his gaze over the barges, knowing it unlikely that he would catch Zinderdali's Vjeran in his downriver run, but hoping for it as he hadn't before. He didn't think Maya would be recovered enough for them to continue on their own, and he had no wish to delay at the edge of a town where an Avelun would receive a reception even less welcoming than his. At the first barge—a shield-shaped, clumsy-looking vessel—men trod up and down the gangplank, their shoulders straining under sacks of grain, their bright hair plastered to their brows. A grim-faced overseer on the deck of the barge wielded his short whip liberally among them, cursing in a dialect that was not quite Sonan.

Loud, frightened squawking behind Jhared jerked his attention around to a crate that was nodding past on the shoulders of a dockhand. Between the wooden slats flashed colorful feathers, scaled feet, and panicked avian eyes. Jhared gritted his teeth. How quickly he had forgotten the shock of such cruelties. It only surprised him when, instead of upending the crate of birds into the water to drown them, the dockhand carried it up the gangplank and laid it gently onto the deck.

The dockhand straightened, scowling as he caught Jhared watching him. Jhared continued on. When the sound of a single word lifted above the morning clatter, it caught him out, like hearing his name spoken across a noisy room. *Velenin*, the Sonans' name for Avelos. He shifted his gaze in the direction from which the word had been spoken and spied two Sonan men near the busy gangplank of the third barge. He slowed, straining to catch and interpret their conversation.

". . .that one, *se'yo*. I wonder what he's selling. We should . . . and take a peek, eh?" The speaker was short, as were all the Sonans, but with the same muscled arms and strong shoulders as the dockhands rolling barrels up the plank beside him. He glanced at the tablet in his hands and marked it as another barrel trundled past.

The second man, neatly built, with sun-toughened skin, and curly, nut-colored hair, chewed thoughtfully on something pushed into his cheek. His eyes flicked from Jhared back to the men who were loading the barrels. "Any man from Avelos who makes it this far south, Ravatin, has nothing left to sell."

"Maybe. But this one's got a look some would pay for."

The slender one named as *se'yo* stepped in front of the next barrel rumbling toward the gangplank. He stopped it with a booted foot and shook his head at the boy delivering it. There was a pause before the boy shrugged and, stepping around the barrel, began to roll it back the way he had come. The *se'yo* spat into the water. "Should we make him an offer? A diversion on the way to the city would be pleasant, eh? From the looks of it, he might be desperate enough to accept."

The one named Ravatin swore at his captain. His features and stance told of a man who worked often in the elements and didn't mind wading into a brawl. Both of the rivermen appeared utterly comfortable where they stood before their barge. As Jhared lifted his gaze to warn them off, he saw the craft behind them. It was trim, shaped like a willow leaf, with a single mast and clean-scraped flanks. On board, men and women moved efficiently to accept and stow the cargo. Then Jhared spied the pennant waving off the bow—a field of blue with two fish in gold twisted about one another; salmon, he realized—and he knew Cael was laughing at him.

Instead of moving away, he stepped closer. "*Se'yo* Vjeran, I hope the current runs with you this morning," he called, using the Sonan greeting Maya had taught him.

The man so addressed leaned back and spat another gob into the water. "See, Rav?" he said in perfect Velos. "Avelos has gained an interest in swamp rats. We may yet have a chance. Tell us, Avelos, are you selling or buying?"

"I seek passage to Saimbor for myself and a companion."

"Now, that's a shame. The *Mila Jul* isn't a passenger ship. Try elsewhere."

Jhared observed the barrels and boxes being stowed aboard the barge. "You don't like prying eyes."

"No. And I don't like wagging tongues. Especially those sharpened across the northern border."

"My companion and I take no interest in the work of an honest captain. All we seek is transport."

"I said, try elsewhere."

"And what would you say to a friend of Zinderdali Imiro?"

The *se'yo*'s expression didn't flicker. Ravatin, however, had stopped counting barrels and was openly staring.

"I'd say he seemed an unlikely friend in an unlikely place," the captain answered.

"It happens that Zinderdali said the same of you." Jhared reached into the pouch at his belt and pulled out Branlen's talisman. Lumati's carved face winked at him in the early light. "Perhaps this might reassure you."

The *se'yo* took it with clean, elegant fingers. His features remained unrevealing, but Ravatin beside him gave a little gasp. "Yes, Zinderdali speaks to Lumati," the captain said. "I don't."

He tossed the pebble back to Jhared. "There are risks to carrying Avelonian men to Saimbor. What would you offer to make the risk worthwhile?"

"Something rare and precious, *se'yo*."

"Ah, Zinderdali sent you with stones, then. I should have known. Damned Sahisten is shameless. Well, let's see them."

Jhared intended to say something about the gifts Zinderdali had sent with Maya, but he held his tongue, observing the captain instead. He wished it were possible to open himself to the blue flames and peer into this man's Path in order to discover his true nature. All he had of Vjeran was Zinderdali's trust and his own instincts. They felt inadequate weighed against Maya's safety. He needed something more. Then he realized he did have something more, although it came with a different risk. "Nothing so common as stones, *se'yo*."

"What then?"

"Feathers," he replied, hoping that Maya would forgive him.

"Now I am disappointed. Feathers are easily had in Sona. Not like in Avelos, where they're . . ." The *se'yo* hesitated. For the first time, interest sparked in his gaze. "What type of feathers?"

"What assurance do I have that my companion and I will have safe passage to Saimbor?"

"Everyone who comes aboard the *Mila Jul* reaches his destination intact. Ravatin will vouch for it. True, there was the one time with a drunken dockhand and a large snake, but that was no fault of mine, was it? What type of feathers?"

Jhared took a step closer to the captain, lowering his voice. "The summer plumage of an Avelun."

"Plumage of an . . ." The *se'yo* offered a small, impersonal smile. "I will give you points for creativity and charm, Avelos, but not for cleverness. You think I will be fooled into accepting the dyed feathers of a goose for that of some mythical creature?"

"I don't believe anyone fools you in trade, *se'yo*."

A considering expression played over the man's lean face. "Who's your companion?"

"Do you agree to provide us passage?"

"Bring the feathers. If I decide they are what you say, you'll have safe passage to Saimbor and back again."

"Excellent. I'll return promptly."

"Do not count your passage so easily won, Avelos. I don't believe in legends or listen to rumors."

Jhared smiled. "I'll return with my companion and the feathers. When do you depart?"

"Before the morning's spent." The captain glanced at his first mate, who was still looking astounded. "If Ravatin can trouble himself to finish loading our cargo."

"We'll return before then," Jhared promised.

He turned away and headed up the pier. Something in the riverman's cool, sardonic manner made him want either to knock the man into the water or sit down to drink a jug of *slu* and discuss the state of the world with him. The mention of Avelune hadn't ignited anger or fear or hatred in the *se'yo*; something different drove him. That was enough. It would have to be. As Jhared strode toward the bank, his boots echoing against the dock, he looked back and caught the captain's eye. "There will be no snakes, *se'yo*, but perhaps you should be aware: there is a horse."

As it happened, the horse ended up the least of a number of challenges. Presented with the gangplank, the bobbing vessel, and the noise and smell of the docks, Seravina had flicked her ears, arched her neck, and strode aboard the *Mila Jul* with the haughty confidence of a priestess. Mayavana had displayed a similar confidence upon meeting Vjeran, with the flash of a smile and warm greetings from

Zinderdali. But she had leaned heavily upon Jhared as they crossed the deck, and her hands had trembled before she concealed them beneath her cloak.

Vjeran led them past his bustling crew into the relative quiet of a deckhouse set amidships. A small galley filled with the odor of fried onions and damp wood held a table and benches, a tiny hearth, and against one wall, a rank of drawers. Through a doorway beyond, Jhared glimpsed bunks. Vjeran took them the opposite way, across a narrow breezeway to his own stateroom. There Jhared offered five of Maya's ombré primary feathers, each as long as his forearm, in exchange for passage to the capital. The *se'yo* had studied them, his fingers running over the shafts and smooth vanes with something near to tenderness. When he had lifted his head and studied Maya, she had reluctantly slid one wing out from under her cloak into the filtered light.

"Well, look at that," he murmured, eyeing Maya with a singular appreciation that set Jhared on edge. "A legend come to life. You must be the smuggler."

"I see Zin has shared his stories," Maya replied coolly.

"Oh no, beauty. At least, not your story. But a man who works among traders sometimes hears farfetched rumors, doesn't he? I remember a unique one about a fantastic creature who knows her way through the mountains of Avelos. A woman who soars over Forest Guard patrols by the light of the stars."

Maya withdrew her wing from observation and pulled her cloak close about her. "You should not believe rumors, Captain."

Vjeran leaned his wiry frame against a small desk bolted to the wall. "Oh, I don't. No thinking man would now, would he? Ravatin will hang a curtain here to give you some privacy. I'll do what I can to keep the others away, but I must warn you: not all my crew can be considered thinking men."

"If they do or say anything untoward," Jhared replied, "I will make them think twice."

Vjeran turned a frankly measuring gaze upon him. "Don't mistake me, Avelos, on my boat there will be no trouble. Occasionally, though, there may be a bit of foolishness. Have you any skill with that bow?"

"Some." Jhared remained unmoving at Maya's side.

"Good. You can take a turn at the night watch. Now and again the raiders get bold enough to try their luck on the river. It would be a nice turn to surprise them."

"The feathers have already paid our passage," Jhared said mildly. "My services as a guard are an additional cost."

The *se'yo* switched the leaf he was chewing from one side of his mouth to the other. "Good for you, Avelos. I don't trust a man who places no value on his own work. What'll it be?"

After some further negotiation in which fodder for Seravina and provision for Jhared and Maya was added to their travel, Vjeran whisked Maya's feathers into the folds of a soft, clean cloth and departed.

Maya sagged toward the deck, her arms wrapping around her middle as though to hold herself together. Jhared caught her by the elbow and eased her onto the stool beside the table.

"I despise this," she hissed. "My limbs feel backward and my innards upside down. My thoughts . . . my thoughts come through a fog. Like they belong to someone else."

"I know," Jhared said, wanting to draw her close, but respecting the warning in her eyes. "The confusion will fade. You will come together again. After a time." The barge lurched. Beyond the open door came the splash of oars and men's voices rising. "Come out with me. It will help you to stay focused on this Path."

She bowed her head. "I can't. Not now. I can't be the fantastic creature of legend, Jhared."

Her misery pushed at his heart. "No, of course not. Never mind. I'll help you to settle. You should eat something and then you can—"

He stopped as her expression turned forbidding. "Ah. Forgive me."

She sat very straight and didn't look at him. "Go out and learn something of the ship. It would be wise to cultivate Vjeran. I'm not certain our link to Zinderdali is enough to keep him from considering other ways we could profit him."

That had been three days ago. He had done as she asked. There was nothing else of use he could do for her.

If not for his concern for Maya, Jhared would have found the trip an easy one, a pleasure even. He had never traveled by boat and discovered that he enjoyed it: the wind whipping against his body as they raced with the current, the sail curving like a gull's wing as it filled with the morning breeze, the landscape ever changing on the shore. Water travel was a cousin to flight. It awoke his senses in a way that had long been proscribed and he indulged in it.

Despite the captain's warning, the crew tried nothing foolish. There were six of them—four men and two women—in addition to the *se'yo* and first mate. They were a rough and rugged lot and treated Jhared with distant curiosity at first, staring at him on the deck and during the predawn meal over bowls of thick porridge and mugs of strong tea. As he revealed his interest in the barge and his willingness to bend his back to necessary tasks, however, they warmed in a way that surprised him. Most of the crew spoke no Velos, which gave him the chance to test his Sonan, and to pick up a few words of Amurian and Laebekken as well. He enjoyed their gruff banter, not so different from what he had known among the Forest Guard. One grey and leathery woman named Thime went so far as to share some of the elements of river navigation with him. It was a welcome change from dodging the taunts aimed at Trianor's Folly.

While they all seemed ready to engage him, they grew careful when speaking about Mayavana. They seemed to hold the Avelun in a wary awe that bordered on reverence. Jhared deflected their questions as smoothly as possible and ignored their inquisitive glances; nevertheless, little gifts began to appear at the door to the captain's stateroom, where Jhared and Maya had been given sleeping space: a pretty white shell veined with green; a small sack of hard candy neatly tied with twine; a grey stone flecked with sapphire. The little collection of offerings began to line up next to Maya's pallet. She accepted them with grace, then retired again, as though pushed deeper into seclusion by the attention.

Each evening before twilight, the *Mila Jul* anchored off shore; the shifting sandbars making night travel too perilous, even for the shallow-drafted vessel. The first night, with Nebov well behind them, nothing so organized as a village existed on either side of the river, but only a collection of dwellings scattered among the trees where the fisherfolk had raised them. After the evening meal taken in the small galley, Vjeran sent a boat ashore with two sailors and one of the barrels from the cargo. *Slu*, Thime had told Jhared. The men returned with four small wooden chests, packets of smoked fish, and a bulging leather pouch that Ravatin had promptly stowed.

As Vjeran had negotiated, Jhared was given a night watch, which he took gladly. He spent the hours under the sky, scanning the star-speckled water that flowed endlessly from upriver, past the barge, and away toward the future. As the water flowed on, carrying Jhared farther south, he realized it was a place where lives might change as drastically as the landscape. Perhaps the river might mark a transition for him, carrying him away from the life of an exiled soldier toward another possibility he couldn't yet imagine. When he stepped off the barge, he would enter a city where no one need learn who and what he had been. Might he carve a space for himself there? Was this time on the river his opportunity to shed one identity and find another?

The trim barge was peaceful at the high moon watch, its sail furled and its crew asleep. Ravatin stood duty as well, more to watch Jhared than to watch with him, Jhared knew. When late that first night Jhared spied a small boat swiftly slipping toward them from upriver, a boat with too many men showing the glint of steel, he had discouraged them with two well-placed arrows. The would-be bandits hastily stood down as they passed the barge. Ravatin's laughter rose low and deep in the darkness. "Raiders?" Jhared had asked in Sonan.

"Naw, local opportunists," the mate replied derisively. "Hoped to catch us unawares. Cowards when it comes to it. No doubt their *se'yo* wet himself when you pinned his sleeve to the bench."

After that night, Ravatin's presence on the watch became more like the company of a comrade. The Sonan riverman had sailed with Vjeran for nearly a decade and talked readily about their travels and trade. Ravatin's stories showed him to be a good-natured man whose sailor's swagger embellished an unassuming spirit. His easy friendliness reminded Jhared of Anzo more than a little. Jhared realized just how far from Avelos he had traveled, however, the night that Ravatin dropped a hand casually onto his shoulder and slid him a smile of invitation at the end of their watch.

"Celebrate life with me under the stars, soldier?"

Startled, Jhared searched the other man's face for mockery or threat. It was common enough for Forest Guard soldiers to take lovers among their own, but no one whole touched a Shorn man. He couldn't deny that the combined novelty of the riverman's willing friendship and unconcealed desire held curious appeal. His thoughts turned again to transitions, to the need for an identity for himself separate from the one Avelos had crafted. Was it possible to be anyone other than an exiled soldier and oath breaker? What would happen if he reached for images of himself outside of all expectations—an image like the one Ravatin offered? He tried to visualize that person, but instead saw Mayavana and the vast sea of things she meant to him. She despised Avelos. How long before her antipathy for the country became antipathy for him? That was a transition he dreaded, but he discovered himself unwilling to run toward it. He declined Ravatin's offer with words of unfeigned thanks.

The riverman slapped Jhared on the back, grinning. "So there is a claim on your heart. I wondered. Still, it never hurts to reach for a bit of joy wherever a man can find it, eh?"

Night and day, Jhared's thoughts never strayed far from Maya. She remained cloistered most of the time, although he had at least cajoled her into continuing his daily lessons in Sonan. Since the tangle, her quick fire had been doused. During the brief hours when she wasn't sleeping, she moved about the cabin listlessly, as though some vital part of her had been lost. Jhared began to fear that he had failed to retrieve every part of her spirit from the Paths, or that the splintering of her self had caused an injury that hadn't healed. He wondered whether he should reach out to the Paths to search for her.

By the fifth night, the *Mila Jul* had sailed past even the scattered fishing hamlets, anchoring in a place where the river coursed through dense, wild forest. The calls, grumbles, and hoots from the woods were reminiscent of home. No, not home, Jhared revised, only the place in Avelos he had once lived. That night, the only creatures near the river were the waterfowl, the beasts that came to drink, and the predators. A family of glossy-headed ducks glided past the barge, their Paths passing Jhared's gently, present but without intruding or pulling him across the Gate. It was a peculiar but not unpleasant sensation, feeling the Gate shiver with the approaching Paths and himself still independent and intact. He smiled at the cousins and wished them well.

At the end of his watch, he went to the deckhouse, still smiling. He stepped into the breezeway between the galley and the *se'yo*'s stateroom. Inside the room, he slipped past Vjeran's desk and pallet, into the small space partitioned off for him and Maya. Moonlight cascaded through the open window across the Avelun. She lay curled on her side, her wings drawn tightly around her like a cocoon. Her face shone pale against her black hair.

More than anything, Jhared wanted to take her in his arms and reassure himself that she was safe and whole, but she would not welcome his concern. Before he could give in to his desire and do something infinitely foolish, he turned back to the doorway, narrowly avoiding a collision with Vjeran.

They stared at one another. Moonlight gilded the *se'yo's* curly hair and slender frame. His impassive features remained in shadow.

"I don't suppose that jug in your hand means you've tapped one of your barrels of *slu*," Jhared said.

"Almost," the *se'yo* replied in Velos. "Come. You've earned a cup."

Vjeran padded toward the afterdeck in bare feet, running a sharp eye over his barge and sleeping crew. Jhared followed. Close to where Seravina drowsed in a makeshift loosebox, the *se'yo* folded himself onto a low stack of crates. He nodded Jhared to another stack and began to pour the drinks with graceful hands.

"You've taken to the water as quick as ducklings, Avelos. I'm surprised. You struck me as a man who likes stable ground beneath his feet."

"Once perhaps. I've grown accustomed to it otherwise."

Vjeran handed Jhared a cup and, taking one for himself, leaned back against his crate. "Adaptable. Now there's a good word. My language doesn't have any one word that means quite the same thing. You like sailing, then?"

Jhared flashed a grin; he couldn't help it. "Your boat running with the wind is as near to flight as a man like me will ever come."

"I suppose I'm vain enough to be pleased by such poetry," said the *se'yo*. "I only regret the Avelun doesn't feel the same. I must have frightened her earlier. I made her shy of showing herself. And *that* is a terrible shame."

Jhared's grin vanished. "Don't make the mistake of believing her easily frightened. Mayavana has faced far greater dangers than overenthusiastic rivermen. And she's not some wild creature to be enticed out of hiding."

"You're quick to stand up for her. As you should be. Don't hear me wrong, Avelos. She is likely the only one of her kind living. She needs strong friends. Still, I will consider it one of the missed opportunities of my lifetime if I never have the chance to see her mantle her wings and take to the sky."

Jhared raised his cup. It wasn't *slu* but something akin to cider, thick and cold with the sweet-tart taste of ripe plums. "I suspect, *se'yo*, that anyone who has met her has felt the same."

"Aha. You are saying, I think, that I must be but another unrequited admirer." The captain's neutral expression grew rueful. "I understand. I am *not* accustomed to it otherwise."

Jhared didn't smile at the smoothly charming *se'yo*. Vjeran had some goal in inviting him to drink. He hoped it would not involve Mayavana; Jhared wanted to like the man. "What news have you of matters between Avelos and Sahiste?"

The captain's neat brow rose. "I have news?"

"Of course you do. War will impact trading. And that pouch we picked up outside of Nebov had something in it other than plums."

"Well, done." Vjeran's tone took on a note of appreciation. "We do receive communications from time to time."

"From those who find the *Mila Jul* a more appealing option than the *Simata'yo*'s couriers?"

"Perhaps." Vjeran's smile was foxlike. "As it happens, I can speak to your question. At least as of three weeks past, Sahiste and Avelos had not yet come to blows. High Chieftain Rumar has sent gifts to King Javahari in hopes that he may buy the king's good will."

"Gifts?"

"A woman from your goddess's temple. She has been named as an envoy escorted by Rumar's closest advisor. My correspondent suspects both have been sent as a symbolic sacrifice."

Jhared stopped breathing. "Do you mean the Lady of Avelos?"

"Indeed. With an elder of some renown. Javahari will likely try them for past crimes against Sahiste. He will call it justice. It might allow him to save face with his court and step back from open war. If he desires it."

"Such an act would stop nothing," Jhared said a little hoarsely, trying not to think about Lady Nemiah and Elder Trianor on their way to Sahiste. "Avelos would never allow Sahiste to go unpunished for such a thing."

"Perhaps not. Unless the high chieftain means to use Javahari as an excuse to be rid of some inconvenient connections. I have never heard anything that suggests Adan Rumar is a fool."

Jhared thumped his cup down. Plum cider sloshed over the side. "He is not."

The *se'yo*'s cup halted on the way to his lips. "Oh. Oh, I am sorry. I thought you had disentangled yourself from the country. I would not have been so flippant otherwise."

"I have no entanglements with Avelos," Jhared replied. "And I believe flippant is your natural state."

"Already determined my character so thoroughly, have you?" Vjeran's brow lifted in something that might have been mockery or self-mockery. "Well, regardless, it seems that Sahisten skystones and linen will continue to reach the west for a little while yet." He took a long drink. "Tell me," he said when he rose from his cup, "I can guess why you fled your frigid, mountain-marred land. And I've no need to ask why you follow the Avelun. But on my life, I cannot guess what makes you both hurry toward Saimbor."

Jhared was grateful for the change of subject. He scrubbed a hand over his face. "What first drove *you* to Saimbor?"

"I heard the food was better."

"From what I hear, the food anywhere is better than it is in Laebek."

Vjeran glanced up. "Ah, good for you again, Avelos. I have worked hard to stamp the sound of Laebek from my voice. Having Laebeki blood does not win a man a reputation for honest dealing."

"It wasn't your accent. I've spent time on the borders. I've seen the Laebeki raiders."

"And?" The *se'yo* twitched his head to one side.

"And it happens I have just enough Sonan to know it has a perfectly adequate translation for 'adaptable.'"

The man's laughter was quick and deep. "Gods, you must have had Zinderdali eating his heart out. He appreciates the clever ones."

Jhared set down his cup; the *se'yo* refilled it. "What made you *disentangle* yourself from Laebek?"

"To my misfortune, I have my mother's Sonan frame. I couldn't lift a Laebeki sword and I'm not clever enough to compete with Laebeki merchants." The man offered an idle grin. "My point is Saimbor is no easy city. For anyone."

Jhared shrugged. "I survived a childhood in Velantar. I understand the dangers."

"That's different. Velantar's hatred is old and established. Codified and ritualized. It's possible to avoid if one remains vigilant. Saimbor's hatred is fresh and restive. She's full of resentful men desperate to prove they are no longer powerless. That can lead to unexpected savagery."

"Do you mean to warn us off?"

"Now, that would be wasted time, wouldn't it? This is no smuggler's run for you. Zinderdali would have discouraged you else."

"What then?"

"Tell me your purpose. I might be a help."

"For a price?"

Vjeran sighed. "There always must be a price, eh? After all, I'm a Laebeki trader and you are from Avelos. Profit must be made. Someone must be owed. What if I just have a notion to give a gift?"

"Why?"

"You aren't much for trust, are you, Avelos?" Vjeran pushed one hand through his curly hair. "All right. Maybe because I also have an appreciation for the clever and the beautiful ones. Maybe because as a man with a smallish life, I would like to play a part in something that touches near to sacred."

"And maybe because Zinderdali would hunt you down if you could help Mayavana and didn't?"

"Oh, that was certain at the start."

It was said with such profound candor that Jhared laughed. "It seems we are in similar positions as far as that's concerned."

"I am glad she has strong friends," Vjeran said again.

It grew quiet. In the loosebox beside Jhared, Seravina snorted in her sleep. He sat back, trying to think about what lay ahead of him, but he kept returning to the thought of Lady Nemiah hazarding the journey to Sahiste. He knew why the high priestess would see it as her duty to go: she would be trying to carry Lady Amalia's story into a place they might be willing to hear it, trying to make her own reparation for the blood spilled on Riana's altar. Setting him free had been a part of that. Then there was "Rumar's closest advisor." Elder Trianor—Jhared was sure of it. Rumar would need to distance himself from the minister whose Shorn son was accused of treason. Likely, Vjeran was correct: the Sahistens would seek to punish Avelos by punishing Nemiah and Tierzen. Jhared knew what that would mean, and he knew their fates should no longer matter to him.

Many weeks had passed since he had troubled to form a prayer. He did so now. "Avelos?"

With an exhaled breath, Jhared turned his attention back to where it belonged, back to where it could make a difference. He was in a place of transition, a time when he might change not merely the direction he traveled but who he was on the Paths.

"Very well, *se'yo*. I would be grateful for anything you can tell me about how to find the *Simata'yo*'s new archive."

As they approached the city, the river traffic increased—mostly medium-sized, shallow-drafted barges like the *Mila Jul*—carrying goods to the capital, but some smaller vessels as well. Sailors called to one another from across the water, exchanging news and bawdy comments as they steered out of the main current and into the canals that split from the river on either side, cutting waterways through the outskirts of the city. The smaller vessels took the shallowest ways, bringing their fresh fish and fruits, their reed baskets, woven mats, and spices directly to the waterside markets scattered across the city. The *Mila Jul*, Vjeran said, would dock at the primary port of Saimbor just before the river met the sea.

Once they touched the outskirts of the city, the ragged shoreline quickly grew tamed, with sprawling old homes in place of the trees, and gated gardens in place of reeds. At times the houses stretched to the very edge of the river, their docks leading to once manicured lanes and elegant entryways. Although the scars of the occupation marred their splendor, and many of the homes had been abandoned, Jhared saw that Sona had not always lacked for talented artisans and wealthy patrons. Even in the broken houses, life continued. Shutters were thrown open to the sunny day, and laughing children leaned out from the casements, waving to the boats or tossing small coins, competing with one another to land them on the passing decks despite bellowed threats from the sailors. From some windows hung cunning brass and wooden cages in various shapes and sizes.

Jhared drew a breath as he realized what the cages contained. "Maya, in that window. Look!"

She had come out that afternoon, wan beneath her hood and cloak, but her hands were steady when they touched the rail. Her gaze followed to where Jhared pointed at a pair of red birds whistling in a small, square cage.

"The birds of Saimbor," she said quietly.

The next window held a larger cage with a grey-crested bird. Its long, elegant tail poked through the cage bars. One house beyond that, a bird with feathers as bright and varied as a rainbow swung on a hanging perch.

"Ah yes, the birds of Saimbor," Vjeran agreed. "A rare and lovely sight."

"The Sonans keep birds as *pets*?" Jhared didn't bother to hide his uneasiness.

"As art, Avelos. As inspiration. As something to make a man believe he can touch perfection."

Jhared shifted to sever Vjeran's line of sight to Maya. The Laebeki man winked and smiled at him. "Well, I'm no poet. Only a man who appreciates the beauty before him. Come, Avelos. We'll be steering in soon. You'll find little of beauty on Saimbor's docks."

The smell reached them first: dead fish and rotting vegetation melded with the reek of livestock and human occupation. When the *Mila Jul* rounded a bend, propelled by the current and directed by her rowers, the docks came into view, crowded with vessels: barges from the river and sea vessels come upriver to the deep harbor where it was safer from storms and Amurian pirates. A tower of wood and stone loomed over one of the ships, a crane more complex than any Jhared had seen in Avelos. Mule-drawn wagons waited to be loaded before they rumbled toward the blue-grey sprawl of the city beyond. At first glance, it was an imposing sight. From a distance, the activity around the moored vessels and across the pier seemed the mark of a thriving city as Jhared had never imagined it.

As they drew closer, he saw the men responsible for that activity: not the sailors or the traders, but the laborers who were hauling cargo and shoveling dung. The lined faces and bowed shoulders of those men spoke of a burden beyond weariness. Jhared recognized the look of men whose lives offered nothing more than a constant scrabbling for survival. Some among them were not men at all, but boys hardly older than Branlen or Trevazio. They worked under the hard eyes of the dock masters, individuals in vests of green and gold who each bore a staff in one hand and a whip in the other. The laborers who were trudging off duty headed not into the city, but toward a row of grim-looking drinking houses just above the docks. Women were beginning to emerge from the darkened doorways, and the men flocked around them like hungry gulls.

It was impossible not to observe that most of the laborers and the harlots stood a head taller than the Sonan dock masters and sailors. Instead of the dun and earth coloring of the others, these were fair or sandy-haired.

"They're Amurians," Jhared murmured.

"Part Amurian," Vjeran said behind him. "Part Sonan. Reminders of the occupation that Sona prefers not to acknowledge."

"So instead they've been pushed to the edge, where they have no voice, and a new story can be told about them."

"Their grandfathers and great-grandfathers murdered a generation of Sonans," Vjeran said mildly.

"Their ancestors," Jhared answered. "Not them."

He watched a half-dozen women, all with long, bright hair, dancing for a crowd of men while two young boys beat on small drums. Bells jingled merrily around the dancers' bare ankles. The women's sinuous movements invited attention, but their overbright smiles were fixed. As they danced through the crowd, one man after another grabbed at them, kissing and fondling. Adeptly, the women slipped or twisted out of each man's grasp, until one of the assailants rattled the coins in his fist. Each woman offered no resistance when such a one dragged her from the circle to the hoots of the crowd and the beat of the drum. One by one, couples disappeared into the alley or through the darkened doorways of the drinking houses.

Farther down the docks, as a crew of sailors disembarked, a knot of women with their children ran to greet them. Bouncing and wriggling nervously, the children held out little bouquets of wilting flowers to the men, while the women welcomed them with warm embraces. It might have been a reunion of families. Then one of the mothers nudged her little girl toward a lanky man who, grinning, bent and kissed the girl hard on the mouth. She writhed against him and he clutched at her and petted her copper hair.

Jhared turned away, sickened. He hadn't expected so much in Saimbor to be the same as Velantar.

Vjeran stopped him. "Stay one more night on board, Avelos. I wouldn't sleep easy if I sent you into the city at nightfall."

Jhared glanced at Maya, pale and cloaked, and nodded at the *se'yo*. "Appreciated. We'll wait for daybreak."

Dawn had hardly cracked the shell of darkness when Jhared rose, eager to be away from the stench and misery. During the night, a customs agent had come aboard to assess their cargo. Now, the crew of the *Mila Jul* hustled to unload it. Barrels of *slu* rumbled across the deck toward the gangplank and an empty mule wagon waited on the wharf. Maya stood at the bow, subdued and darkly dressed. If one didn't know what she was and didn't stare too closely, it was possible to think she carried a pack beneath her cloak. Jhared thought it safe enough for a short time. No one was likely to guess at the improbable truth.

As they prepared to disembark, Maya roused herself enough to offer Vjeran a kiss on his cheek and words of gratitude expressed in Sonan. The self-possessed *se'yo* returned a proper bow that would have served him well before the High Chieftain. He surprised Jhared with a gift: a jug of plum cider.

"Good luck to you, Avelos. The new moon will see us back in Saimbor. I still owe you a trip upriver, should you need it."

Then they were down the gangplank, the *Mila Jul* behind them and the city ahead.

Seravina pranced nervously at the end of her lead, hooves ringing against the stones, ears pricked at the strange scents and sounds. Jhared was determined to find an honest place to stable her before spending the day searching for the archive. Vjeran had given him recommendations and a sense of the city's layout. He had also given them a name. Jhared followed the riverman's directions toward one of the more affluent markets, Maya close at his side. Although she seemed steady and made a show of peering about, the flatness in her eyes gave no hint that she was within reach of her dream.

When Sera had been put up safely, Jhared stepped back into the dirty street where Maya huddled with her back to a wall. He set a hand on her arm. "You aren't well, Maya. There must be something I can do. I will go back to the Paths and search for what the tangle has kept of your spirit."

"It's not the tangle. Not as you mean it." Her gaze scraped over the people passing in the streets. "We needn't speak of it now."

"We must speak now. You've hardly even looked at me for days. I'm afraid my ignorance has led to your injury. If not the tangle, then what's happened?"

She gathered herself. He saw the effort it took and felt a chill.

"Jhared, you've always considered your traveling to be a sign of something wrong with you. At first, I even thought it. But what you did to save me from the tangle was astonishing. You tracked me on Path after Path. You opened every door that stood before you. I could never have opened those doors."

"Of course you could have. Just not on that terrible night. Maya, you were injured as surely as if you had taken an arrow. The tangle fractured your spirit."

"It had nothing to do with my injury. Except for that night, I've never even traveled beyond my own lifetime." She drew a long breath and slowly let it go. "Jhared, what if you are exactly what you should be? What if I'm the one who's damaged?"

He drew back from her. "That's impossible. I'm Shorn. What I am is unnatural. Broken."

"Is that what you know? Or what you were taught to believe?"

"Maya, it's the truth. Other Pathwalkers prove it."

"What other Pathwalkers? Me? Alende? Your Lady Nemiah? The Bearer of Cael's Blade? What do you know from us?"

Jhared pushed aside his reflexive protests and considered: Maya traveled very little, and never without effort. Leita had always moved within an aura of power, but in truth, he had only seen her travel twice, and both times she had hovered just at the edge of the Gate. Alende traveled widely and without intention. Jhared had always feared himself to be like the unbound man, but Alende showed no aptitude for tracking and didn't seem capable of finding his own way. If periodically he did track his way, what did that prove? They were both Shorn Pathwalkers, creatures not meant to exist. If pressed to compare, Jhared saw it was Lady Nemiah's travel that most mirrored his own: the priestess fell often and without conscious intention, but she traveled to distant moments and was a natural tracker. She had found Lady Amalia again and again along the same Parallel.

Jhared looked into the Avelun's anguished gaze. "Mayavana, you are one of the most capable people I know. Do not mourn that the Gate does not steal you away. It's not a gift."

"It's not traveling I mourn. Not precisely. I've begun to wonder if traveling is somehow connected with flight. What if I cannot fly because I do not travel?"

"The only way we'll answer that question is by finding the archive," Jhared said firmly. "Let's seek the building under construction and see if we might learn where the documents are currently housed. We might learn where to find this General Hrvan as well. Vjeran says his name has been spread as the archive's founder."

"I thought I would start near the estates." Maya gestured vaguely away from the city's center. "The money of the city lives there. And likely some of the *Simata'yo*'s advisors. Perhaps they've temporarily housed the documents among private libraries."

"If you prefer it, of course. That's where we'll start."

"No. I mean you go on to the market. You're eager to explore. Find the new building. Enjoy your first look at a foreign city."

"Ah." He glanced aside, trying to keep his disappointment to himself. Protesting that it wasn't safe for her to wander alone would not be taken well, and he didn't want to provoke her. "Shall we meet at midday then? To share what we've learned?"

"Yes. Midday. I'll meet you on the southern edge of the great market near the main canal." She smiled faintly. "Farewell."

He watched her walk away until the crowds and the buildings hid her from sight.

As he turned in the direction of the city's center, he spied a petite woman with a long braid the color of loam and a vest the color of buttercups. She was sitting at one of the tables outside a drinking house and, from over the rim of her cup, she was watching him watch Maya. Their eyes met for an instant. Hers were the color of sunlight on honey, but the shrewdness in them was far from sweet. With no shift in her expression to acknowledge that she had seen him, her gaze drifted away.

He gladly left the stranger behind and tried to set his mind on exploring the city. Most of the traffic—men and women on foot, some with laden donkeys or dogs, and some with a long-legged variety of goat—flowed toward the center. He flowed with it, his eyes on the old, ruined buildings and the new ones being constructed, on the Sonan people and the muddy canals. According to Vjeran, the great market twisted up and down the widest of the north-south canals, with stalls lining the smaller cross-lanes most of its length. The heart of the city beat in a healthier rhythm than the docks. Here Jhared spied individuals important to the development of any land: merchants and craftsmen, clerks and laborers, mothers with their children, lovers walking hand-in-hand. The Sonan women wore colorful vests and wove bright scarves into their plaited hair. In place of a belt, men wrapped pleated sashes of varying colors and fabrics around their waists. As Jhared reached the market, he discovered vendors who offered variety enough to prove that trade had been much influenced by the Amurian occupation, and customers flashing money enough to prove that the occupation was slowly fading into the past.

He marveled at the difference between the lonely marshes of central Sona and this crowded, coastal city. He had never seen such diversity—in the items for sale or the people selling them. There were yarns and fine fabrics and the tailors to shape them, bowls made of wood and bowls made of clay, rope of various weights, pearls—as Zinderdali had promised—buttons and needles and other fine tools of ivory, spears for fishing and spears for hunting, leather items from boots to tack— leather of the quality that suggested Amurian craftsmanship—and assorted daggers of good steel that suggested the same. Peering with some interest at the booth of a smith, Jhared spied a familiar design: a dagger with a guard shaped as a leaping fish and a grip worked in a pattern of interlocking palm fronds. Noting his interest, the broad-shouldered smith named a price. Jhared declined politely in Sonan, pleased to note that the man looked only disappointed but not puzzled by the words he spoke. As he returned to the noise and smells and activity of the street, Jhared considered how much his life had changed since he had been cut by a similar knife in Riana's high temple. He walked through the bright, dusty, vibrant city and thought of Alende, wondering whether the waylayer was also in Sona, sheltering with his people as winter approached.

He walked for a long while, as he had so often walked through Velantar. As in Velantar, the market drew entertainers of all types: musicians and firedancers, acrobats and animal trainers. One woman displayed a pedestal upon which mice with fur dyed green and yellow and pink raced through a miniature obstacle course with hoops and hurdles and little tubs of water. Bystanders crowded around the pedestal laying bets. Musicians and players stood at the edges of the canals and on the steps of the buildings. Some managed to capture small spaces in front of the drinking houses. Jhared paused at the window of one drinking house and bought a cup of *slu*, mostly for the excuse to stay and listen to the singers. The place was crowded, but he found an unobtrusive space to lean against a stone wall, drinking and enjoying the songs of the two weathered men, who on another day might have been sailors. When a large silver and white gull landed at his feet, Jhared froze and darted a look toward the crowd. No one pointed at him. No one threw stones or tried to beat the bird with their mugs. He emptied his own mug and decided it was time to move on. The gull hopped aside, nonplussed.

Entirely unlike Velantar, here the birds were everywhere, squawking, chirping, and screeching. Pigeons bobbed along the streets, unmolested, plucking at crumbs between the stones. Gulls, like the handsome creature who had greeted Jhared, wheeled overhead, landing on top of the booths or sometimes, brazenly, atop a tavern table, causing customers to gently shoo them off. At the market, there were ducks and geese in pens; small, exquisite finches flitting about in cages; and large birds bejeweled in feathers the color of emeralds, swinging on perches. It was a wonder. Although Jhared had no use for the cages and tethers, he made a space in his heart for the Sonans who threw crumbs to the wild birds.

Eventually, he found the building under construction, as Vjeran had promised, where the archive would one day be housed. It was deep in the city's center and east of the canals, in what once might have been a pretty square. Cracked and missing flagstones were all that remained of the lanes that bordered a small, overgrown park. Around the park, stone buildings, all in various stages of demolition or renovation, jutted like broken teeth. Dust hung in the air and hazed the men and teams of oxen working among the cranes or with the wagons to cart in and drag away stone. Across piles of rubble, Jhared spied a blue-white portico and the shell of a structure behind it. Although he had known what to expect from Vjeran, he couldn't help but feel disheartened. Years would pass before the building could become the grand center of learning about which Mursa Vin had boasted.

Frustrated, Jhared gave his Sonan another trial, asking a group of passing laborers if they knew where the archives were held during the construction of the library. The question earned him hard, appraising glares. One man aped Jhared's accent to the laughter of the others. Another man muttered something derogatory about prying foreigners. The first then declared that the archive was for learned Sonans, not tree-tall, ignorant strangers; he added an inventive description of what he would do to Jhared before sending him to the bottom of a canal if he didn't get on his way. All of them tightened their grips on their shovels and picks. Jhared gritted his teeth, considering his most likely route of escape. For an outsider, some things didn't change no matter what city he was in. Only the whistle of a headman standing on the portico caused the crew to give him up and lumber off.

Jhared left the park and started back in the direction of the canals, moving more quickly now. He began searching for Maya among the crowds, his vigilance revived by the unfulfilled promise of violence.

By the time he reached the south end of the market, the morning had scooted away. People filled the food vendors' lanes in search of a meal. The avalanche rumbling in Jhared's stomach reminded him of his own hunger. Over smoking braziers, vendors turned skewers heavy with roasting meat. Men and women ate savory combinations of sauce-covered grains or grilled fish, while children licked fruit pastes wrapped around sticks of hard-baked dough.

He followed the rich scents to a row of food vendors near the edge of the market. In the middle of the row, an old woman bent over a wide, shallow pan that hung above a small fire. Within the pan, chunks of meat sizzled in a thick, plum-colored sauce. The steam drifting from it offered the most appetizing scent Jhared had ever smelled. As his shadow fell over the booth, the woman nodded and grinned at him, beckoning him closer. His stomach roared. When he hesitated, she repeated the same words, an invitation, as she offered him a generous piece of the meat on a steel prong. Jhared declined in Sonan, but she pushed the prong toward him and spoke more emphatically. At her tone, a few of the passersby glanced over. Someone laughed. Equally reluctant to offend as to leave such a succulent dish untasted, Jhared accepted the offering from the prong.

A fierce cry pierced the air. As Jhared turned, a woman leaped between him and the food vendor. She was small and wiry. Her long braid of earth-brown hair whipped over her shoulder as she spun and slapped his hand. The meat flew from his fingers into the dirt. Instantly, one of the roaming dogs pounced and swallowed it. At the same time, the old food vendor hopped forward with an indignant cry. She swung the heavy prong at Jhared's assailant, catching her across the face and knocking her backward.

"Hold! Let her be!" Jhared demanded. The petite assailant didn't even reach his shoulder and appeared unarmed. He recognized her. She was the one watching when he had parted from Maya. Now she was barking at the food vendor in Sonan too fast for Jhared to understand. The tone could not be mistaken, however. It was accusatory and furious. With one hand, she slapped Jhared on the back. The old vendor shook her head vehemently as she brandished her weapon. The small woman slapped Jhared again, then pointed into the crowd that was beginning to gather. Jhared spied Mayavana hurrying toward the fray.

Before the Avelun even reached them, she was shouting in Sonan at the other two women. Then all three were yelling at once: Maya confronted Jhared's assailant, while the assailant continued barking at the vendor. The old vendor, still gripping the prong, seemed mainly to be defending herself and her wares. Jhared was thoroughly ignored.

As he debated whether to insert himself between the combatants, Maya jerked backward, away from the other women. Her expression twisted with shock and revulsion. Abruptly, she shook free of her cloak. Her wings unfurled with a loud *fooshhh*. Nodding hard, the slender stranger slapped Jhared on the back a third time.

The food vendor paled. Her prong hit the ground and her hands came up to her chest in an urgently repentant gesture. She repeated a phrase Jhared knew: *"Vushiya!"* "Forgive!"

"Come," the stranger said in Velos, grabbing Jhared by the arm and turning her back on the old woman.

"Wait," Jhared said, frowning over her. "Are you all right?"

A livid welt had risen just below the woman's cheekbone where the steel had left its mark. She reached up to touch it, then cast a scornful glance at the vendor. "Fine. Very fine. She understands now."

"Understands what?" he demanded. "What happened?"

"Not here. Too much of a crowd here." The woman gestured with her free hand. "You both must come away. Out of the crowd."

Jhared gazed over the woman's head at the way shopkeepers and passersby were staring. A hiss of whispers filled the street. Maya hastily folded her wings and cloaked them, but the stares didn't change. Something in the mood of the crowd made Jhared eager to be away. It wasn't hatred or fear, but something more subtle, more insidious that he couldn't label.

"Out of the crowd," he agreed.

He and Maya followed the Sonan woman in silence along the canal, out of the market and up a smaller street, quieter and cleaner than the one they left behind.

"What made you do it?" he asked Maya as they walked. "In front of so many people. Why would you ever . . . ?" He gestured at her cloak.

A muscle tensed in the Avelun's jaw. "The meat the old woman offered you. It was duck."

Jhared thought of the gentle creatures he had touched on the river. Cousins. Then he thought of the savory meat that had made his mouth water. A wave of nausea rushed through him. "Oh."

"Oh," the Sonan woman echoed sardonically. "You should not be here if you do not know such things."

"How did you guess what I am?" Jhared asked.

The woman stopped and looked up at him. "I work with birds all my life. I recognize a sky seeker when I see him."

"But how?" Maya pressed, her cheeks still bright with anger.

"Flight is not in the wings," the woman answered. "It is in the spirit. See it in the grace of movement. In the yearning."

Jhared opened his mouth, but he had no response.

"What are you doing here?" the woman asked, scowling at him. "It is dangerous for strangers. More dangerous for you."

She spoke bluntly, with no courtesies. Despite her size, she carried herself with an air of unwavering confidence. Jhared thought he might like her, but he didn't yet know how much he trusted her. "Why were you watching us before? When we entered the market. Why did you follow me?"

"So he sees better than he listens," she said tartly. "I follow with curiosity. She is not easy to hide, this one." The woman looked up at Maya with a sharp, guarded gaze, then back at Jhared. "Your kind we do not see here. I ask again. Why?"

"We're looking for General Hrvan," Jhared answered. "We thought he might be found in Saimbor."

The woman set her hands on her narrow hips. "Hmm."

Her expression shifted almost imperceptibly. He wouldn't have seen it if he hadn't been studying her face, a sun-warmed oval with a scattering of freckles the same golden shade as her eyes.

"You know where we can find him, don't you?"

She flipped her long braid over her shoulder. "My name is Falucha. I own a shop not far. Come with me. I will feed you. Food to be trusted. You are still hungry, after all."

After his close call with the duck, Jhared wasn't certain he could eat, but he did want to know what the woman would tell him. He exchanged a look with Maya, who gave a reluctant nod.

"I'm Jhared Denaban," he told the woman. "This is Mayavana. We will come with you."

"Good. After food, if you are set on it, I will tell you where to find the general. Perhaps, though, you will grow wiser before then."

20.
BIRD WALKERS

Falucha's shop was a fawn-colored stone building in a lane that might once have been elegant but had fallen far out of reach of that term. Beyond the blackened tree stumps that lined the broken road, a row of houses huddled, roofs sagging over split shutters and boarded windows. Still, the children playing among the wild gardens looked relatively clean and recently fed. Two women sat on the crooked porch of one house, shelling nuts. They stared openly when Jhared and Maya passed.

"This must have been a beautiful neighborhood once," Jhared observed quietly.

Falucha snorted. "Beautiful. And wealthy. Amurian soldiers came and killed many important families. Stole what they could. Burned the rest."

"Yet you are rebuilding," Maya said. "It is good to see."

"Of course we rebuild. Our *Simata'yo* would have Sona stand straight. No more bowing before the other nations. But this is no topic for the streets. Come in."

She pulled open the door and a breeze whisked past Jhared, enveloping him in a host of scents: fresh-cut wood, damp earth, dried fish, and birds—the feathery, pungent smell of birds.

"Go on," Maya urged from behind him before he realized he had halted.

He took several steps inside. Large windows spilled bright light over the interior. At first glance, it seemed little different from any shop in Velantar. Two sets of tall shelves cut the room into aisles. A row of covered barrels lined a side wall, and a long counter stretched half the distance across the back wall. Above all, hanging from chains in the rafters, were ranks and ranks of odd boxes—cages, Jhared realized—plain cages made from cane; cages of carved wood; small, shiny cages of brass; and large, long cages that took three chains to suspend them. With a jolt, Jhared observed that several of the cages were occupied. The captives set up a squawking and calling as Falucha entered.

"Gods of skies," Maya muttered.

In the center of the shop, a boy of thirteen or fourteen winters was sweeping the floor. He stopped when they entered. As his gaze landed on Maya, he gasped and tripped backward over his broom.

Falucha snapped at him in Sonan. He straightened, his sandy hair falling across his brow, but his eyes darted anxiously from the Avelun to Jhared and back. His next words sounded like a question.

"*Nat, nat,*" Falucha said. "Close your mouth. You look like a hungry nestling. Have you made the deliveries yet?"

The boy shook his head mutely.

"Then go! *Se'yo* Vasst will be waiting for his fish for Pertha! Be sure to tell him the fresh *scelf* will arrive tomorrow."

As the boy jumped to obey, Falucha led Jhared and Maya farther into the shop.

"Was that your son?" Maya asked, watching the boy depart.

"Not my own. My sister's child." The reply vibrated like a plucked cord, anger there or perhaps sadness. Falucha gestured around the room. "Look about. I will warm food."

"What is this place?" Jhared asked.

"A place needed for the birds. For the Bird Walkers." Falucha nodded toward a wire cage occupied by a large green and blue bird. "Say hello to Juf. I warrant you have never seen one like him in your land. If he is in the mood, he will answer you." Then she disappeared behind the counter through a door at the back of the shop.

Jhared frowned at Maya, who strolled toward the cage Falucha had indicated. "Bird Walkers. You mentioned them before. What do you know of them?"

"Not very much," she replied.

"They're the reason Zinderdali feared you coming south, aren't they?"

"I told you they wouldn't hate me here," she said with a sigh.

"You didn't tell me they would love you."

She grimaced and turned her back on him.

Reluctantly, Jhared accepted Falucha's invitation. Although he heard Maya murmuring in Sonan to the green and blue parrot, he couldn't bring himself to look closely at any of the birds. Instead, he peered under the lids of the barrels, finding various types of seeds in some, dried fish in another, and in yet another, rich earth crawling with small bugs. The shelves held trays and bowls of different sizes, an assortment of perches, small toys carved of wood or made with seeds, and polished copper mirrors no larger than his palm. One aisle held leather straps of various lengths and neatly sewn bits of colorful silk: tethers and hoods.

He shuddered. What he had said to Maya had been incorrect. All the exotic supplies and ornate cages did not speak of the Sonans' love of birds but of their obsession with them. That was what he had sensed in the market when Maya uncloaked—the desire to own and control. Yet he hadn't seen any such desire in Falucha. She had been nothing but matter-of-fact with him, and her attitude toward Maya held no heat at all, only intense caution. He wished he knew what that meant; they could use an ally in this strange city. He glanced at Maya. The ebony tip of one wing peaked out from under her cloak as she moved toward the cage of a golden lark.

"He's been injured," she said softly. "A broken foot. That other one, Juf, has been sick. I don't like this place. I don't like her." Maya nodded her head toward the door where Falucha had gone.

"This doesn't fit," Jhared said. "The cages, the tethers. I don't think those are really who she is."

"Jhared, you haven't looked *inside* the cages," Maya whispered.

She was right. Finally, he forced himself to look at the birds. As he moved from one cage to another, his own broken body responded in sympathy. The green and blue parrot had patches of raw, unfeathered skin on its breast and back; the lark's left foot was twisted from an old break; a white and black waterbird in a bronze cage was missing an eye.

Jhared came to a halt at a wooden cage with slatted bars that could be opened or closed like shutters, shedding more or less light inside. Through the narrow opening, he saw a silver-faced owl, no bigger than his fist, perched near the top of the cage. One black-striped wing hung awkwardly at its side, bent like a broken twig. Jhared stared at her. She stared back with unblinking amber eyes.

He couldn't glance away, even when he heard Falucha's returning step.

"That's Bavja," she told him.

"What happened to her?" he asked.

"An eagle. Maybe fox," the woman replied. "No way to know. Children found her outside the city. Brought her here."

He watched the little owl flap ineffectively with one wing, then sink back onto the perch. "She'll never fly again," he murmured.

Falucha smiled, a well-intentioned expression, he thought. "She manages fine enough."

"Perhaps she manages. But she doesn't live."

The bird flapped again, overbalanced, and toppled from her perch. With a squawk, she landed at the bottom of the cage. Jhared sucked a breath through his teeth as the severed muscles in his back contracted.

Falucha narrowed her eyes at him.

He met her gaze. "It would have been kinder to let such a damaged creature die."

"Kinder only for those too cowardly to look at her imperfections." The woman swung open the cage door and reached in with one hand. With care, she set the little owl back upon its branch. "These ones I nurture are the ones that survive. They have survived predators, illnesses, storms."

"So you collect aberrations," he replied. "Freaks and curiosities."

"No need for such a bitter tone," Falucha answered. "Nothing is shameful about surviving. Every creature is born with *yeeva*, a destiny to do something beautiful and good in the world. Sometimes darkness interrupts that destiny, pushes us toward pain. Whatever darkness we face in life, it need not steal our ability to do something worthwhile, even something wonderful."

Jhared's back contracted again. He tried to straighten against it.

"It hurts you to look at her," Falucha said, watching him once more. "At all the injured ones."

"Of course it does," he replied.

The Sonan shook her head. "Not sadness only. Physical pain. Look how you stand, hunched and stiff. All grace gone." She pointed at one of the covered barrels. "Sit there."

"What?"

"Sit. I can help."

Something in her demeanor caused him to do as she commanded. When she stepped behind him and set her hands on his back, however, he nearly jumped from the seat again.

"Hold still!" She cuffed him on the side of the head. "Scars I have touched before. Your kind are not the only ones who bear them."

She pushed him back down. He forced himself to be motionless as her hands began exploring the mass of damaged flesh along the length of his spine. "Ah, here. Mm. Yes, and here." She murmured to herself while her fingers dug into the knot of twitching muscles. She seemed to know just where to find the most painful points. She pinched and folded the severed muscles until cold sweat beaded across Jhared's forehead.

"Breathe!" she yelled suddenly, swatting him again. "Hurts more if you don't."

Her shout made him startle, and he laughed a little. He had been holding his breath. He settled himself and tried to focus. Inhaling deeply, he reached for the calm at his center. Under her deft fingers, something began to loosen. One cord of muscle unclenched.

"Good. A start. Stay put."

She continued working up his spine to his shoulders. Her thumbs wedged under the edges of his shoulder blades. "A hawk they will think when they look at you," she said. "Sharp eyes, strong arms, a warrior's bearing: a hawk. But they will be wrong. Your *yeeva* is hidden." She carved his shoulder with the boney edge of her hand. "The hawk is only the armor. Inside is what? A starling? A warbler? No, not a songbird. You do not enjoy this attention, I think. There is music in you, but no songbird showiness."

Falucha paused her kneading. "In the market, you might have batted me aside. But you say hold. Ask if I am hurt." She reached over his shoulder and took his right hand, turning it palm up to reveal the calluses of long sword practice. "I see you know how to harm, but maybe your own scars teach you something of the value of healing too. You feel the pain of my birds, take it as your own. Ferocity and compassion, both. Perhaps a swan."

"What are you doing trying to read him?" Jhared couldn't see Maya's face from where she was studying the cages, but he could hear her annoyance.

The woman released Jhared's hand and again set to work on his shoulders. "If you do not know what this is—"

"We shouldn't be here," Maya said dryly. "I know. We only want to speak with the general."

"Then you must know where you belong in the order of things or the general will not tolerate you. Ignorance will quickly drop you into trouble. Trouble will land you in a cage."

Maya came out from the row of shelves, her expression wary. "You're talking about the Bird Walkers. Is the general one of them?"

"To say he is one of them is to say the sea is one of the puddles on the beach. What so presses you to meet him?"

"We want access to the archive," Jhared said.

"Indeed." The woman's hand tensed on his shoulder. "What do you think to find?"

"I am searching for knowledge of my ancestors, the early Avelune," Maya answered.

"Our ancestors," Jhared said.

The gaze Falucha turned on Maya had nothing of possessiveness in it, but neither did it hold any warmth. "Save time and do not take the risk," she replied. "Foreigners are not given access."

Jhared twisted around to look at her. "I thought the archive was to be something for all the border nations to envy."

"Envy, yes," the woman said grimly. "You envy most what you see but cannot touch."

"Perhaps the general can be bribed," he mused.

"With what would you bribe him?"

Mayavana crossed her arms over her chest. "If the man is what you say, he will want to speak with me."

"You do not want that type of attention, feathered girl. That much I believe even you can guess." Falucha patted Jhared's shoulder and stepped away from him. "Come sit with me. Share a meal. Then decide."

Jhared followed the woman into a small room behind the shop. Lit only by a shallow hearth and what light trailed in from the front windows, it was sparsely furnished with a table, a narrow bed, and a set of drawers. A solitary bowl from a previous meal sat near the hearth. The grim room contrasted starkly with the bright shop and showed no sign that Falucha shared it with any others. Jhared wondered whether this space and the captive birds encompassed all of her life. He felt an unexpected sadness at the thought.

The meal she set before them was simple and delicious: a nut-flavored reddish grain and hot fish stew, with fish that was fresh and sweet, nothing like the rancid cissanu. Jhared added the jug of plum cider from Vjeran to the table, for which Falucha seemed grateful. He found he had no trouble eating after all, and was glad at first to leave conversation to the women. Falucha, however, was frosty and quiet with Maya, and the Avelun showed no interest in engaging the Sonan. He signed inwardly; it would win them nothing if the Sonan decided to throw them back into the street. Finally, he set down his spoon and interrupted the growing silence.

"Falucha, I don't understand. You are not one of these Bird Walkers. How is it you keep a shop for them?"

The Sonan woman stopped toying with her food and looked up sharply. "You think you already know so much of me?"

"Forgive me, but I saw how people stared at Mayavana in the market. I wager none of them see anything worthy in scarred creatures, as you do."

Falucha gave him a hesitant nod. "The shop belonged to the mother of my mother. In her day and for long before, my family owned the building. It was a grand place, our home, with all the color and sounds of the birds. When my mother died, my sister had her own family, no time for a shop. And my brother . . ." Falucha hunched in her chair. "I was the one left to take it. I have served the Bird Walkers since I was old enough to make deliveries. Their patronage is my living."

"But you have reason to dislike them," Jhared pressed.

"Do you know how we say Bird Walker in Sonan? *Voj'hrena*. It means to stroll very slowly. To be lazy, you would say. The families of the *Voj'hrena* grew rich during the occupation. Some by cooperating with Amuria, some by misusing their country-men. Now Amuria is gone, and they own very much power. It is not for me to like or not like them."

"Is it the *Voj'hrena* who fund the archive?" Jhared asked.

"The general and a group of his allies, yes. They are close to the *Simata'yo*. They fund many projects. The archive. Much of the rebuilding. Other things."

"And do you know where the books and other treasures are being housed while the new archive is built?"

"At *Kaleb Uto*."

Jhared frowned over the translation. "Haven of Gulls?"

"Haven, yes. It is the general's estate." The woman scowled as her hand rose to her left earlobe, where a small, faceted stone winked with the colors of sunset. "You ask many questions that are dangerous. Perhaps in Avelos that is a fine thing. Our *Simata'yo* does not like questions about his friends or his decisions."

"I apologize," Jhared replied. "You've been kind. I don't mean to trespass."

"Perhaps it is safe enough to ask where the Bird Walkers gather?" Maya said.

Falucha flipped a cool glance toward the Avelun. "The park at the west edge of the city. High above the water. Very lovely. A good place for birds."

"Will we find the general there?"

The Sonan nodded. "Today for a little while longer. He visits many afternoons, when he is in the city."

Jhared looked at Maya. "I'll go speak with him. You should stay out of sight."

Maya's expression turned instantly forbidding, but Falucha was already shaking her head. "Not wise. Not safe. Now that others know what you are, Jhared Denaban, many will want something from you."

"I have nothing." He laughed and showed his empty palms. "What could they possibly want?"

Falucha looked at him directly. "Your seed."

"What?" Maya coughed. "Do you mean they would try to breed Avelune children?"

"Oh yes," Falucha said. "Envy there for certain. What they see but cannot touch."

Jhared grimaced, imagining how Avelos would respond to such a thing. Then he shook his head, trying not to imagine it. "Maya remains the one in danger. They're not likely to take what I'm unwilling to give. Nor can they see what I am."

"You think not? I saw you clear enough. And Saimbor is not so big a city. News flies. The Bird Walkers will know what you are by the time you reach them. Listen to me: do not travel without the Avelun. She is your best protection and you are hers. You must be servant to her. If she is seen as important and strong enough to command a hawk, they may leave her be. You must do all she tells you. Do not speak unless she gives you permission. The general is old enough to remember the occupation. He will not let a foreign soldier move freely in Saimbor. Only if you are safely bound to her, he may not make you a slave or have you killed."

"You seem to know the general quite well," Maya said pointedly.

"I know his birds," the Sonan woman answered, touching a finger to the stone at her earlobe once more. "A man can be read through his birds."

Maya met Jhared's gaze across the table with an expression of longing he understood. "What would you risk for the chance to reach the skies?" she whispered.

Everything.

It was her birthright, and he had committed to helping her. The success of his own cause, to learn to control the killing winds, could mean the difference between safety and destruction for the Shorn.

"We will go together, as you say," he told Falucha.

The Sonan woman gave a resigned nod. "Very well. You will find the general under a pavilion with his own people. Do not approach him directly. Wait until he requests that you join him. By accepting his request, you give him some obligation to you. A good thing. Do not allow yourself to be obligated to him."

"I understand," Jhared answered.

"Not yet," she said, "but I fear you will."

"Thank you," Maya said, rising from the table. "For the advice and the food. We've too long taken you from your duties. It's time we let you be."

"Maya?" Jhared sensed her impatience, but he didn't like to rush away. She didn't respond, however. The tips of her wings brushed the door as she hurried from the little room.

"I'm sorry," he said to Falucha, rising to follow. "We've been searching for a long while."

"No. Do not apologize for her. You are not the same as the Avelun. You have not that sense of entitlement." Falucha set a hand on his arm. "Come back when you have met the general, Jhared Denaban. Let me know how you fare. Yes?"

"I will try. I will."

"Good. Listen to what I have said. Be careful of him. And be wary of his birds."

The depth of concern in her eyes took Jhared aback. He regretted that he had not asked her more about what she knew of scars and surviving, but Maya had disappeared into the shop and he could hear the door opening to the street. "Thank you. I'm sorry," he said again, both inadequate sentiments.

When he reached her, Maya was moving restlessly along the edge of the street. If he hadn't hurried out, he suspected she wouldn't have bothered to wait for him.

"We could use a friend in this city, Mayavana. That was foolish."

"I couldn't stand being in that place one more moment." She rustled her feathers against her back. "That woman hates me."

"What? You have it wrong. Look what she's done to help us."

"To help you, perhaps. Me she would just as soon see plucked and tossed into the ocean. Do you not think it odd she asked nothing of where I come from or how I've survived?"

Jhared glanced back at the shop, afraid Falucha might overhear them. "You're not seeing her straight. You intimidated her. You cannot imagine how it is to come face to face with an Avelun."

"No. What I saw in her had nothing to do with awe." Maya caught his glance at the shop and scoffed. "Never mind. I wouldn't expect you to have noticed."

He felt her words like a slap and didn't understand how he had earned them. "Maya, stand down. I won't fight with you. We must plan our approach to the general."

"My plan is to find him. And to convince him to open the archive to us."

"Fine. But we needn't rush in without understanding what we'll encounter. Let's find a place where you can stay out of the way of the crowds. I'll scout out the park and the Bird Walkers. After, if it seems safe, we can return together."

She shrugged her cloak more closely around her. "I am going now. Are you willing to play the bodyguard? Or shall I go alone?"

"Maya, throwing yourself into danger like this won't help you to fly any more than throwing yourself off a cliff!"

It was an unfair jibe, and too provocative. She shot him a withering glance, and without another word, straightened her shoulders and stepped into the street. Jhared followed, feeling the shape of his scars where Falucha had touched them and thinking about the flightless owl in its cage.

They followed the street through a number of neighborhoods: some in ruins, with few signs of life but for hungry dogs slinking in the alleyways; others with evidence of revival, like Falucha's neighborhood, that were busy with foot traffic. Most of the people they passed went about armed with at least a staff if not a knife or sword. Jhared walked close to Maya, uncomfortably aware of the avid stares arrowed in her direction.

The residential street ended abruptly at the foot of a steep hill, where the stone pavers turned to hard-packed dirt. As Falucha had directed, they followed the dirt road up the hill in a series of switchbacks. The steep rise obscured the ocean, at first, but close to the top, the road curved around the slope, and the water appeared before them. Jhared halted. Before Saimbor, he had never seen an ocean. The mountain heights had always been the heart of desire for him. When he had left Vjeran's boat at the docks, the sight of human misery had blunted any beauty the water might offer. Now Jhared stood above the city, gazing upon a rippled mirror of silver-blue that stretched without bounds to the edge of the world. Water and sky merged at that edge. The breeze that swept over him carried the scent of salt and freedom. He swayed, filled with longing.

"Goddess, Maya. Does it not call you to test your wings above it?"

"I have," she replied crisply, casting a perfunctory glance at the water. "I was nine winters. I broke my wrist, strained an ankle, and knocked myself silly. If Mother hadn't seen me fall, I would have drowned. Come on. We've another cliff to leap from now. We're almost there."

Jhared drew himself away from temptation. In a few precarious steps, the road opened onto a flat tableland and a thoroughly different scene. Slender trees grew in rows, their black trunks and green-needled branches bowing away from the water. Neat gravel trails wound like grey ribbons through the grove, leading to particolored pavilions and tables decorated with flowers. Elegant men and woman sat at the tables, some conversing, some bent over game boards. Others strolled along the trails, while servants hovered with steaming pots of drinks and trays of food. The well-born were adorned in fluttering silks and feathers. *Feathers.* Jhared had to look again to be certain of it: the women wore bright feathers woven into their hair; men and women both displayed feathery ruffs at their wrists and throats. Jhared felt increasingly unsettled and out of place. Above the feathered folk and all about the park hung a range of cages that might have been purchased in Falucha's shop: small cages of gleaming bronze, large cages of pale wood. They dangled from the trees, while their occupants called and preened.

Less conspicuous than the opulent strollers were the guards dressed in blue livery standing attentive and still at the edges of the trails. To Jhared's surprise, these men bore the height and coloring of the Amurian half-breeds.

"This isn't wise, Maya. We would do better to seek a private meeting."

"I don't think so," she replied. "The general will want the others to see him speaking with us."

"Perhaps. But he's a soldier, not a diplomat. He won't yield before so many witnesses."

"Too late to retreat!" she hissed, tossing him her cloak. "Step back and remember your place."

They had been spotted. A man in green silks pointed and a sea of eyes turned in their direction. A young woman dropped the piece of cake in her hand. It tumbled across the grass. Those at the game boards stood, and those on the farthest trails hurried closer. All of them bore expressions of awe and avarice.

Maya cupped her wings behind her like a swan. Her winter plumage gleamed white and ebony as she started toward the pavilions.

The Bird Walkers stared, their eyes alight, whispering behind feathered fans. The crowd had closed in a way that set Jhared's limbs humming with energy. As Mayavana strode among them, a regal symbol of what they desired, some Bird Walkers backed up hastily to make way. Others, most of the younger members of the crowd, offered a graceful gesture that began at the heart and touched lips, eyes, and brows. A sign of respect, Jhared thought. Still others boldly stretched out their hands to touch Maya's wings. Jhared scanned them all, searching for the man who might be the general. Those who stood gawking revealed nothing martial in their manners. The soft hands of the men were framed with feathers and weighted with silver. Women wore long gowns or wide, loose trousers. Clothing was cut to catch the eye.

As he studied the groups of Bird Walkers, Jhared realized that what at first had seemed a great mingling was actually an assortment of cliques distinguished by the type of birds hanging around the tables—songbirds, owls, raptors, and water fowl. The type of bird seemed to reflect the Bird Walker who collected it—the silver-studded gentlemen and their gregarious warblers; the scholars with their books and their quiet doves; the fine ladies and their colorful tanagers.

Maya bore the stares and whispering with apparent equanimity, drifting through the gardens like a priestess among her supplicants. Jhared knew the others saw only her remote grace, not the subtle signs of her anxiety: the fine tremble of her primary feathers and the unwonted tautness in her gait. Subjected all his life to the scrutiny of his Teachers and the judgment of the crowd, it hadn't occurred to Jhared how difficult it might be for Maya to place herself before so many eyes.

Just when he thought she had revealed herself for nothing, Jhared spied a fighting man striding out of the largest of the pavilions. Straight-shouldered and strongly built, the man could not be mistaken for anything other than a soldier. His dun-colored clothes were cut for utility, not display. He was clean-shaven with thick silver hair, and his movements expressed the effortless confidence of someone accustomed to command. Jhared watched as the man beckoned a guard, then, thinking of Falucha's warning, he looked to the others' birds. They made an eclectic collection: a small falcon mantling on its perch, a pair of ravens chortling together, a handful of tiny finches in a gleaming cage, and three bright parrots.

As Jhared watched, the guard—one of the tall and fair among the Sonans—hurried to comply with the soldier's orders. They spoke together, glancing in Maya's direction. Then the soldier nodded, and the young guard headed toward them.

"Here it comes," Jhared warned.

The guard gave Jhared a glance and halted a respectable distance from them. He bowed his head and one shoulder, as if not certain what honor to offer Mayavana. "Riza, if I may intrude?"

Maya tilted her head imperiously. "If you have a worthy reason for it."

The guard straightened. "Yes, Riza. General Hrvan, Leader of the Armies of Sona, Great *Se'yo* of the Southern Quarter, Prime Advisor to the *Simata'yo* has noted your most exceptional presence and would enjoy the grace of your company at his pavilion."

The invitation was extravagantly worded, but Jhared heard the command in it.

"I would be delighted to accept General Hrvan's kind invitation," Maya replied charmingly. The guard led them to the grand pavilion where it overlooked the ocean. He gestured for Maya and Jhared to enter. As Maya stepped into the shade of the tent, she rustled her wings uneasily. The general's eyes lit at the sight.

"I have heard of you, Riza," he said in a pleasant baritone. "I had hoped to have the opportunity to greet you, but never guessed it would be so soon. I am deeply honored you have accepted my invitation."

It was something other than honor Jhared saw. He tried to catch Maya's eye but she kept her back to him. He heard the smile in her voice.

"It is my privilege, General Hrvan. All of Sona knows the name of the man who has helped the *Simata'yo* to rebuild Saimbor."

Pleased surprise flickered in the general's face. "Sit, then. You will share my food and wine."

The others at the pavilion's tables moved speedily to make room for Maya, though none of them wandered far. The intensity of their interest was palpable. Only when the general flicked a finger at one of his guards, who with three other men began herding the onlookers out of the tent, did the audience turn away. Jhared stood behind Maya, watching as a dozen people sent their consuming gazes over her before drifting away to gossip.

"They cannot resist the sight of you, Riza," the general said, watching the others' disappointment with obvious satisfaction. "But we shall not be disturbed here. Now. Tell me something of the story that brings you to Saimbor."

General Hrvan spoke with courtesy. His Velos was excellent, though oddly old-fashioned, and colored with a strong Sonan lilt. He was gentle with his birds and polite to his staff, but that was not all of the man. The general had survived to adulthood in a time of war and occupation, had risen high in Sonan leadership, and was overseeing the looting of historical treasures from the surrounding nations. Such a man understood subtlety and how to manipulate others. Jhared feared that Maya's candor would not serve her well.

They spoke for some time. The general's first questions seemed benign—he showed much interest in knowing from where Maya had come and the lands through which she had traveled. She spoke honestly of her life in the northern parts of Sona and the tolerance the people had shown her there. Incapable of guile, she didn't try to hide her role as a smuggler or her work in Avelos. Gradually, the general's questions grew subtler and the topics more laden. He took particular interest in Maya's attitudes toward Avelos, the elders, and the border nations. Then the general asked if she had met others of her kind in her travels. An expression of unadulterated pleasure crossed his face when he learned that Maya was the only Avelun known living.

"You are truly a queen among us, then," he told her.

Jhared couldn't see her face, but he saw her shoulders rise and her wings settle and knew what would come next.

"General, you have no doubt guessed that my travels to Saimbor are not without purpose. You have been so hospitable, perhaps you would grant me leave to ask a favor."

The man chuckled, one callused hand tightening around the slender stem of his wine glass. "Ah, Riza, you truly are a stranger to my land. You must offer me a gift before you ask a favor. We do not shun debts here as they do in Avelos. Give me a gift and I will owe you."

Jhared shifted his stance. The situation could change rapidly. He wished Maya would look at him.

"I fear you leave me without hope, General. I have no gift worthy of the Great *Se'yo* of the Southern Quarter, Prime Advisor to the *Simata'yo*."

General Hrvan freed the delicate glass from his heavy fingers and made a soothing gesture with one hand. "Come now, I could not cause such a queen despair. Tell me of your fighting man. I recognize a Forest Guard when I see one. Avelos is jealous of her soldiers. She would not easily let one of them go."

Maya hesitated. "Perhaps not, but men who do not condone the actions of the elders sometimes find a way to break their bonds."

"Ah. A deserter. As I thought." Disapproval sharpened the general's words, but his eyes held something different. "Some are saying he is also of the winged line. One of the Ravaged. I want to know if this is true."

Maya nodded. "It is."

The general smiled indulgently. "You misunderstand me, Riza. I would like to *see* the truth of it. Though I have heard much of these people, I have never seen one. I have some trouble believing they exist."

"You do not believe Avelos is so cruel?" Maya said, heat touching her words.

"Oh no. I have witnessed the cruelties of which all men are capable. It is the folly I do not comprehend. I would no more tear the wings from a fighting man than geld my best stallion. Let me see if what is said is fact."

Maya fanned the air with one wing, but her tone remained impassive. "Do as the general requests," she commanded Jhared.

Jhared ground his jaws together. Maya knew the depth of the shame to which she was exposing him. He told himself she had little choice if they wished to gain the general's favor. As he turned and slowly lifted his shirt, the men and women still in the pavilion stopped their conversation to stare. The air hissed with their murmurs of pity and disgust. Jhared sent his gaze past the tent flaps, past the Bird Walkers to the open ocean.

"What tremendous pain that must cause," the general mused. "There is strength in the man who survives such a thing. Strength and perhaps a great capacity for hatred."

The last was said as if assessing a colt's capacity for speed. Jhared remained motionless. The cool air prickled the skin along his back.

"A waste to spill such noble blood, but then Avelos has wasted many of her treasures. She is ignorant and undeserving of what she has. Do you not agree?"

As Jhared lowered his shirt and turned, he realized the general was addressing him. "You are proposing, sir, to make better use of what she has wasted?"

"Perhaps I am." The general glanced at Maya. "In other ways, he remains whole, your man?"

"He is a wholly skilled tracker and guard," Maya replied.

The general smiled faintly. "Very well. Give me the gift of his services for a season."

"General Hrvan, I cannot give up my guard. Are your own fighting men not satisfactory?"

"I do not want him for fighting, Riza. I want him as stud for my household."

Although Falucha had warned him, Jhared went hot with a sharp mix of anger, humiliation, and something other he didn't care to examine.

"I keep him for his skill as a guard," Maya said coldly, "not for breeding."

The general laughed, but there was danger in it. "Do you say that a young warrior would shun the chance to bed a collection of lovely women? To mix his blood with an honored house?"

"Yes, I do," Maya replied. "If I tell him to."

The general sobered, took a sip of his wine and set it aside, his gaze thoughtful. "Lovely Riza, do you know why we collect birds in Sona? Most will say it is for their beauty or their songs or their ferocity in the hunt. Those are half-truths. The Amurians understand something of what we do. But Amurians, clumsy and obtuse, only try to grasp at the skies with the curve of their sails. They put wings on a boat and believe it is the same as the wings of a living creature. We collect birds, Riza, because to hold a winged creature is to hold a portion of the power of the sky."

The general's bronze gaze glinted with the same need that Jhared had sensed from the crowd in the market, a need evidenced in the ornaments and tethers in Falucha's shop. He moved in front of Maya, his body light with Shorn energy.

"Be careful what creatures you try to cage," he growled at the general, composed and ready. "Some power is not meant to be held by a man."

Hrvan's expression grew keen as he rose. Jhared slid into a fighting stance. He would need to strike decisively to have any chance of surviving. Behind him, Maya was moving, but he didn't look. She would understand she must run. He only prayed she didn't hesitate. He didn't see her fist until she slammed it against the side of his head.

"Never!" she snarled. "Never speak in my stead!"

Jhared stared, open-mouthed. Without warning, she struck him again, a backhanded slap across the face.

"Lower your gaze! Do not shame me further."

Laughter, low and guttural, came from the general, who was standing but had not drawn his blade. Three of the guards closest to him had their hands on their swords. "Oh, that is quite marvelous. Quite marvelous indeed."

Maya spun to face him. "I do not tolerate disrespect."

"Nor should you." The general smiled. "You do truly rule him. Forgive me. I am a skeptical man. I had to wonder."

"And what have you concluded?" Maya replied hotly.

"That you are a magnificent woman. And your guard, your guard intrigues me greatly."

"He should not. He is troublesome."

"Not at all. One needs fire to survive. A docile man is of no use. If more of my people had owned such fire in my great-grandfather's time, the Amurians would not have crossed our borders without suffering or stayed so long in our lands."

Maya hesitated. "Then you see a gift fit for the prime advisor to the *Simata'yo*?"

The general nodded. "Of course, I would never suggest depriving you of your protection, Riza. Let him but linger with us, and perhaps you would consider doing the same."

Maya looked considering. "I might be convinced to consider what you ask. In the interest of fostering friendship."

The general licked his lips, his smile deepening. "In the interest of friendship, I would be willing to entertain your favor."

Jhared remained still, fury singing through his veins. He knew Maya did not intend to barter him for books, but she dangerously misjudged the general if she thought she could dangle the man's desire before him, then snatch it away.

"We should speak of this further," the general said, "but it is unseemly for me to keep you longer in such poor comfort. You must grace my home, *Kaleb Uto,* with your visit."

"I would be pleased to do so."

"Good. We will go directly. Only sip your wine while my people prepare."

The general clapped his hands and servants sprang into motion around the tables. Crates appeared, filled with straw, to hold the delicate platters and cups. Silk hoods came out and were slipped over each cage. The birds on tethers were placed into a long cane cage bound to one of two pretty painted carts drawn by black mules. In the midst of the bustle, Jhared spied the general speaking with the same guardsman who had first approached Maya. The yellow-haired man bowed, then disappeared from the park at a run.

When all had been packed and loaded, the general handed Maya up into the smaller of the two carts. Jhared made to follow her, but the general stayed him.

"I fear there is no room," the man said apologetically. "With your mistress's permission." He gestured at Maya.

Though Jhared put all his distrust into his gaze, Maya turned her head in the slightest denial. "Walk beside us," she ordered. "I'm sure to be quite safe beside the General of Sona. He has offered us his hospitality, after all."

Jhared gave a stiff nod and stepped backward as the general's guardsmen fell into file on both sides of the cart. The other Bird Walkers looked on enviously as the little caravan made its way out of the park and slowly down the hill.

21.

DREAMS AND NIGHTMARES

The sure-footed mules pulled the carts down the twisting road, then away from Saimbor for several miles along a rocky ridge above the beach. Jhared tried at first to listen to Maya's conversation with the general, but they were speaking too quietly to be heard over the creak of the wheels and the endless roar of the surf.

He turned his attention instead to the landscape, which differed wildly from any other he had known. Long, coarse sea grass, flowering plants, and thorned bushes full of berries grew in clumps from the sandy soil. Small grey gulls posed on rocks and darted over the water, while flocks of large black-and-white birds gathered on the shore, their wings spread to dry in the sun. The antics of the cousins caused the world to sway.

As the cart came over another stony hill, General Hrvan circled his arm and pointed in an unmistakable gesture of possession and pride. Jhared saw Maya smile in appreciation. Below, walls of uncut stone encompassed grounds on three sides; the fourth side opened to the cliff and the pounding ocean. Outbuildings faced a regal main house built of the same sea stone as the wall. On the north side of the buildings, Jhared spied pasturelands with grazing livestock. South, uneven rows of fruit trees waved their glossy leaves in the breeze. Just beyond the orchards, the trees gave way to dark pine forest.

As they came within the walls onto the general's estate, nausea twisted Jhared's innards and blue sparkled at the edges of his awareness. He dug his nails into his palms and glanced behind him, watching with a sense of foreboding as the massive wood and iron gate swung shut. The cart drivers trotted their mules down a rutted road that curved into a sandy yard. The entire caravan halted in front of the house.

Outside of Velantar in the Parnas Valley, imposing estates with their high, arched passages, colored glass windows, and finely carved stones rivaled the grandeur of the mountains surrounding them. The general's manor made no attempt to rival the rough, beautiful seascape but to mirror it: three rows of windows—small and narrow on the first level, tall and wide on the third—created an impression of lightness and space despite the massive stones the color of sand and sea that formed the building. Changes in the design and the color of the stone suggested that the upper levels had been added much later. Jhared suspected the original building had been little more than a fortified hall, but the later architects had skillfully integrated the original with the new. Like the ocean, it appeared severe and beautiful. Jhared found the effect oddly familiar.

Above the roofline of the house, two towers rose sleek and austere, one on the sea side and one landward. Between the towers, Jhared could see what seemed to be a rooftop garden. Potted trees and blossoming plants tossed in the breeze. The rooftop would be an excellent position from which to survey the surrounding lands, and the view of the water from that height would be spectacular. A dark-haired man in a red cloak stood near the worked iron railing; his gaze lay on the arrivals, not the ocean.

Blue flames crackled across Jhared's vision. A wave of Paths slammed against his awareness. With one hand, he caught himself on the cart. Another ugly wave struck him, threatening to rip him from his own place. He arrowed his gaze about the courtyard, but could not find the tangle.

"What's wrong, you? You drunk?"

The scornful voice came from one of the guards, a pale-haired man with a scar across his chin, who had spoken in broken Velos. Jhared drew himself straight and planted his feet against the shifting terrain.

"Not drunk," he gasped.

"What then? Ill? Hungry? Does she not feed you?" The guard laughed and said something quickly in Sonan. Jhared didn't need any translation to tell it was a slur. The guard's comrades hushed him hastily, casting apprehensive glances not toward the general but toward the rooftop. The man in the red cloak was no longer visible. Jhared left the muttering guards and strode as steadily as he could toward Maya. The tangle must be close. It buzzed against his awareness, a painful wrongness.

His hand fell more heavily onto Maya's shoulder than he meant it to. Beneath his fingers, he felt her startle, but when she whipped around, she shot him a gaze so frigid and foreign he backed up a step.

"You forget yourself," she growled. "Shall I reconsider your contract after all?"

The general paused from where he was giving orders to his men, his head lifting like a hound catching a scent.

"I would expect you to do so, Riza, the moment I fail to observe a threat to your safety," Jhared replied, then hesitated, unwilling to admit vulnerability in the midst of armed strangers. Instead, he gestured vaguely toward a pile of coiled ropes near the house. "There are many tangles here to be avoided."

If Maya understood what he was telling her, she gave no sign. "The yard is perfectly ordered," she said tersely. "And my vision is still clear enough. Take your place, and do not affront our host."

The general returned, a smug smile tipping his lips upward, and ushered them with some ceremony through the main entrance into a great garden courtyard. In contrast to the wild landscape outside the walls, the courtyard garden was orderly and tame. Finely trimmed bushes defined geometric spaces where small trees shivered in the breeze. Around the courtyard, columns of blue-veined marble formed porticos that lined the four wings of the house. In each corner, a staircase spiraled to the upper level, where galleries led to numerous doorways into more private spaces. The general guided them down a wide gravel path, across the courtyard, and into the wing of the house facing the ocean. The shutters of every unglazed window had been thrown open, revealing a dizzying view of the water. Whitewashed walls and stone floors echoed with the sounds of men and women hurrying through the halls. Dressed in the general's blue livery, they all moved efficiently, receiving crates and cages from the returning party and scurrying away with them. The crates disappeared down the southeastern hall—where Jhared guessed the kitchens must lie—but the birdcages went in every direction: some were placed on pedestals in the courtyard; some disappeared into rooms; many were carried up the stairs.

Out of the scurry, two women marched toward the general. The woman leading the march might have been Falucha's aunt, although a fragile, papery version of Falucha. By contrast, the woman who trailed behind her was tall and solid, with hair a fascinating riot of copper and gold hanging in a thick curtain of small braids. Jhared couldn't see her eyes because she kept them downcast. Her stride, twice the length of the older woman's, was paced to keep her a demure step behind.

The older woman stomped before the general and addressed him in a tone an irate mother might use. From her angry Sonan, Jhared gathered she was none too happy to see guests in the house on such short notice. She seemed to be accusing the general of playing a prank. Then she looked more closely at Maya and sucked a quick, startled breath. Rather than the awe and desire Jhared was beginning to expect, her expression turned cautious.

The general made a bluff response, grinning as he clapped his large hand over the woman's shoulder. She didn't seem placated, but both she and the younger woman made the flowing hand gesture of respect, showing their open palms to Maya as the general introduced them: Livja was the small, intense one; Vyla was stately and reserved. As far as Jhared could gather, they ranked highly in the hierarchy of the house staff or perhaps were some distant relatives to the general.

With Maya's permission, he was given into the care of the one called Vyla. He tried to protest the separation, but another wave pushed over him, flooding him with tides of blue. He watched a hawk take flight and vanish through the ceiling. As he pondered that strangeness, a file of broad-shouldered soldiers marched through the atrium, passing a silver-haired man near the window who rocked a babe.

"You will come with me now?"

The woman was standing patiently, her hands clasped at her waist. No soldiers filled the entrance. Maya and the general had disappeared. Jhared wondered how many times the woman had repeated her question. He scrubbed a hand over his eyes. "Where?"

"To prepare for supper. The Riza has been invited to dine with General Hrvan. It is right that you should be present."

Her Velos was clipped and correct, as good as the general's and better than Falucha's. Amidst the tugging of the Paths, Jhared wondered where she had learned it. "Yes. Maya . . . my lady will expect me."

She looked at him oddly, and he realized in dismay that he had answered in Sonan. One small advantage gone. He urgently needed to collect himself. "The Riza has taught me a little," he continued in Sonan, stammering without effort.

The woman shrugged. "Of course," she replied in Velos. "Come. It will take you some time to prepare."

As she led him down one long hall, the reserved manner she had shown before the general transformed into something more vigorous. To any servants who paused to watch them pass, she sent an imperious glare, and she pulled up short to snap at a young boy who had stopped midstride to gape at Jhared. Although her Sonan was very fast, Jhared thought he caught most of her reprimand: *You have seen wings. We have birds all over this house. What is so interesting about no wings? Return to work!*

Jhared had some sympathy for the boy, who sketched a quick salute to the woman and scurried off. "Do you have many guests to the estate?" he asked.

"None like you," she said briskly.

"I'm surprised to hear it. Your Velos is excellent. I thought perhaps you entertained others from Avelos."

Her step faltered just a little. "No, none from Avelos," she said. "But some who have cause to know the language."

"Ah. Of course." The constant shifting of the Paths was clouding his thoughts. Mursa Vin traveled extensively in Avelos and spoke better than fair Velos. The woman might have learned from exposure to such border guards. Perhaps the general hired a Sonan traveler to teach his staff. Or perhaps the woman was partnered to a soldier or a smuggler. All the possibilities washed over him in another wave of tumbling Paths.

The hall was bright and airy. Closed doors alternated with open windows that carried in the sweet-salt smell of the ocean and nearby forest. At many of the windows, birds twittered in their cages. Near the end of the hall, Vyla opened a door and gestured him in. After the well-lit rooms, it took several moments for his eyes to adjust. It was a cozy space, with cushioned chairs and couches and a thickly piled rug. The only light came from lamps with chimneys of thin, colored stone that shed a rosy glow. Beyond the little chamber, a set of double doors opened upon a bathing room, warm and humid and scented with cedar. Two tubs of smooth wood stood before a fireplace large enough for a man to stand inside it. The grey flagstones of the floor had been subtly canted to let water roll into a narrow channel that ran along the wall and out a small drain. Beneath a shuttered window, a bench held a bowl filled with balls of soap and two porous-looking, roughly shaped spheres that appeared meant for scrubbing.

Vyla marched into the bathing chamber, dipped her hand into the water of one tub, and made a face of irritation. With an efficient motion, she scooped a bucket of steaming water from the kettle over the fire and poured it into the tub. As she flicked water droplets from her hands, two young women hurried into the room, their arms laden with towels and linens. They murmured apologies to Vyla as they hung the towels on a bar over the hearth. One of the two women hung a cream-colored robe and set a pair of slippers near the fire. She smiled at Jhared, her expression inquisitive, a dimple showing in the curve of her cheek. The other woman, tawny haired and slender, pinned her gaze to the floor.

"Yeva and Ri will attend you," Vyla said, turning to go. "You may . . . take your time. Have them send for me when you are finished."

"Attend me?" Jhared said uneasily. One of the girls, the smiling one, giggled.

Vyla appeared unamused. "Indeed. You are an honored guest. We are a civilized house."

Jhared glanced at the two women, not much older than girls. The dark-haired one who met his gaze had a vivid gleam in her eyes, but the other refused to look at him, and in fact seemed to be shrinking into herself, as if she hoped to vanish. Jhared realized belatedly just what it meant to be *attended*. The general apparently didn't intend to wait before he tried to gain what he wanted.

"I am only a once-soldier of Avelos," he said. "I deserve no honor and have no need of assistance, lovely and gracious though it may be."

"Are you rejecting the general's offer of hospitality?" Vyla asked, her features shaped with disapproval.

"Not at all," he replied, aware that a misstep could ruin his and Maya's chance to explore the archive. "I am grateful for the beauty with which I've been surrounded. I only mean . . . in Avelos, a Shorn man does not show his scars to honorable women."

Vyla's expression flickered. Sonans placed great weight on outward displays of respect, or so Maya had told him. "Very well," she said after a moment. She proceeded to instruct him on where to leave his clothes and how to make use of the soap and linens, as though she believed he had not seen a bath before.

When the women had gone, Jhared stripped off his clothes and slid into the hot water with a sigh of relief. Now was his chance to put some distance between himself and the Gate, but he could not quiet his mind enough to find his center. The thought of Maya laughing and talking with the general turned his stomach. He pictured the two young women sent to *attend* him: one, at least, had been terrified. As he had suspected, the general was but another powerful elder accustomed to shaping the Paths of those around him.

As Elder Trianor had shaped him.

Jhared grabbed the soap and scrubbed at his skin until it was red and stinging. He splashed out of the tub, flung the robe around himself, and stuck his feet into the slippers. When he threw open the door to the antechamber, Vyla was there. She startled at his abrupt appearance. That she had been waiting irritated him more.

"My clothes?" he asked, looking at the empty pegs where he had hung his travel-stained gear. "My things?"

"A room has been made ready for you."

After the bath girls, he wasn't certain he wanted to know just what that meant, but he decided that regaining his clothes would be the wisest first step. The thin robe clung to his damp shoulders as he followed Vyla back into the courtyard, up one of the four spiral staircases, and along the west gallery into a chamber that would have garrisoned a half-dozen soldiers. Sun poured in from a window overlooking the water and illuminated a desk of dark wood. On one side of the room, chairs and pillows formed a comfortable sitting area. On the other side, brightly woven blankets covered a mattress raised a hand's span from the floor with rectangular stones. Beside the bed, a table held a domed silver cage. As he entered, the grey bird inside smacked its orange beak and fluttered on its perch. A wave broke against him; he touched the wall for support.

"These aren't servants' quarters."

"No. They're for you," Vyla replied. "You must see that the general has great respect for your Riza to treat her guard so."

His boots had been cleaned and polished and set beneath a stand where his bag and cloak hung. His Forest Guard uniform appeared the only thing missing. Instead, spread on the bed was a suit of clothes in a familiar shade of blue.

"That is the general's livery," Jhared said, gesturing at the fine breeches and jacket.

"Yes. Very lovely, is it not? The color will suit you."

"I cannot wear it."

She frowned. "It is my understanding you are to join us for a season. That you will . . . labor under the general's colors."

So it had started. It might very well grow dangerous before the end. "That is incorrect. Nothing has been settled."

"I see." She sounded bemused. "Well, you cannot stand for dinner in the clothes of an Avelonian soldier. It would be an affront to the general."

"Not a greater affront than it will be to my lady if I appear in another's colors," he said.

Vyla was quiet, but her foot tapped rapidly on the stone. "Very well. I will find you something else. Wait here."

It took time, but she returned clutching a shirt of ivory and breeches of sable. They were cut from a tightly woven fabric, softer than linen but sturdier than silk. The simple style flaunted no absurd frills or loose panels of cloth meant to flutter. The only fussy part of the costume was a length of gleaming black fabric, wide in the middle and tapered at the ends, that wrapped tightly around the waist. Jhared had seen the style on men in the market and on some of the serving boys in the house who wore the same sash in a coarser fabric.

When Jhared emerged from the room, Vyla flicked a considering gaze over him. "Good."

What he could hear in her tone was "better." He tried not to fiddle with the cuffs or pluck at the collar. He hadn't worn such elegant garments since he had been a child in Elder Trianor's home. They felt very foreign.

"You must not believe the general has insulted your Riza," the woman said hastily. "The livery was my own fault. You are a soldier. They said you were a deserter. I didn't expect you to have . . ."

"A sense of loyalty?" he finished.

She flushed.

"Vyla, in my life I have had little say about which direction my Path turns. Now that I may give my loyalty without coercion, I give it to May . . . my lady. I will not march to the general's order."

"No? Then you may be the first," she said. The taut curve of her lip was not a smile.

"Vyla!"

At the whip-snap of her name, the woman's posture altered abruptly: she dropped her gaze, hunched her shoulders, and bowed her head, making herself smaller as the older, dun-colored woman, Livja, marched up to her. A boy carrying a tray of food trotted after.

"Vyla, is it proper for you to be conversing with a guest while he stands in the hall without the least comfort?"

"Not at all, Mer Livja." Her tone was low with remorse.

"When I paused in the kitchens just now, I discovered you had ordered nothing for the Riza's man to eat. Is this how you display our general's regard?"

"I am sorry, Mer Livja. I was—"

"Don't apologize to me, stupid *hofja*! Apologize to our guest!"

"No apology needed," Jhared said quickly. "I'm at fault. I was admiring General Hrvan's home. Has it been his family's seat for many years?"

As Livja swiveled her hard gaze toward him, he recognized what she was: a powerful lieutenant upbraiding a soldier she despised. "For generations," she answered. "How kind of you to ask. Now, let me amend the neglect you have suffered. I have brought some simple refreshments. You will want to eat, I am certain." With a gesture, she directed the boy with the laden tray. He entered the room and set it on the desk, carefully arranging the utensils and a little vase of flowers around the platters.

Jhared accepted the refreshments; then, trying out his status as an "honored guest," he dismissed Livja with what he hoped was gracious thanks.

"She is right," Vyla said, her voice once more stiff and cold. "I have kept you without comfort. Forgive me. I will leave you to take your respite."

Jhared's innards remained unsettled by the tilting world, but he knew it would only grow worse if he didn't put something into his stomach. There was a plate of flat, square cakes, a mug of something fruity smelling, and a bowl heaped with a grain similar to that which Falucha had fed him topped with chopped vegetables and pieces of grilled meat. He hesitated over the meat, glancing at the grey bird in its cage.

"What type of—"

"Boar," Vyla said. "You will find no birds slain for meat or feathers here."

"Thank you." He smiled in gratitude. "Perhaps you would stay. I have questions, and I suspect that Livja won't be the one to answer them."

Vyla glanced at him sharply, but she closed the door and came to stand, alert and aloof, beside the desk. "What is it you would know?"

"My lady will ask for a favor from the general."

"I have heard. It has raised the curiosity of the household."

Jhared tried a bite of food. The dish was flavored with spices he didn't recognize. Ignoring the roiling of his innards, he swallowed and took a drink from the mug: some type of lightly fermented fruit juice. He waited, but Vyla remained quiet, with no evidence of her own curiosity. "She intends to ask for access to the great archive."

More than surprise licked over the woman's face; Jhared saw relief. "You expected something other," he observed.

"The general is a powerful man with access to an army," she replied. "Your Riza is Avelun. She has a cause for vengeance, does she not? One might guess what she would ask."

"I see." He did see now. The general played in the large arenas of state. Maya's request, yet unspoken, was already being weighed in the context of the well-being of Sona. The very existence of an Avelun had implications the general would no doubt share with the *Simata'yo*. Raised by Elder Trianor, Jhared understood such things, but he had never taken Sona seriously enough to consider that they would matter here. It was, he supposed, the reason Falucha had been trying to warn him.

"How might the general respond?" he asked more soberly.

Vyla folded her hands before her. "That will depend on what your Riza says she seeks."

"Our heritage. The story of the Avelune. It is a small and personal request. Nothing to alarm the leader of the Sonan forces."

"He is not easily alarmed. Nor, however, is he quickly moved by the plea of a pretty woman. Although the Avelun touches something dear to him."

To hold a winged creature is to hold a portion of the power of the sky.

Jhared shifted, acutely aware of the vulnerable position into which he and Maya had willingly run. "Have other outsiders been allowed to see the archive?"

"In Sona, an 'outsider' is defined by more than simply the location of one's birth," the woman replied, an edge sharpening her tone. "Your Riza will be shown great favor. It is all I may say of such things."

There was hope in that, at least. What the general wanted from Maya or from him was another matter. He took a last bite of the flat cake and pushed the tray away, no steadier for the food.

Vyla's presence was a cool stream, rippled by an aggressive undercurrent. It intrigued him. Her gaze held flames, while her hands remained folded decorously at her waist. Her hair, a gleaming meld of copper, silver, and gold, serpentined in multiple beaded plaits that swayed enticingly as she moved. He didn't realize he was staring until she glanced down, pink blossoms on her cheeks.

"Vyla, why does Livja dislike you?"

Only a blink of blue-grey eyes betrayed her surprise this time. "Livja is an excellent Mer Riza. She simply means to maintain the ideals of hospitality where I have failed."

"Not so," he countered. "If her goal were only to correct some deficiency, she would have reprimanded you in Sonan. As you did to the little boy in the hall. She spoke in Velos so she could humiliate you in front of me. Why? What does *hofja* mean?"

The woman recoiled from his questions. "It is late. The bell will ring for dinner soon. You must not make your Riza wait."

She took him to the courtyard and abandoned him with a hasty excuse. Jhared regretted having offended her. He might very well need a friend in this house. Alone, he stood at attention, listening to the sounds of the birds fluttering and whistling in their cages up and down the galleries. Waves of Paths bumped his consciousness, threatening to tumble him from his own present. Something different was happening in this place: the waves buffeted him like a tangle—a massive gathering of Paths. Yet he did not sense the misshapen and knotted Paths he had sensed in the tangles. He did not sense the pain of the web where the pattern had been snarled. He did not sense the web at all.

"Jhared, are you all right?"

He tore himself free of his thoughts and looked up to the west gallery. For that moment, the shifting Paths did not torment him. Maya wore a gown of shimmering silver-green silk nearly the same shade as her eyes. The bodice of the gown hugged her form and curved over her breasts, leaving her shoulders and arms entirely bare. Cleverly gathered fabric emphasized her supple waist and dropped into a narrow, elegant bell at her feet. As she glided down the stairs and into the courtyard, he saw that the dress plunged to the small of her back, exposing the ripples of muscle there and allowing her wings to fold against her shoulders. Her black hair had been brushed until it shone, and was caught at the nape of her neck with a silver clip in the shape of a diving crane.

"Jhared?" She glanced around the courtyard before touching his arm. They were alone.

"I'm sorry, Maya. It's just that you look so . . ." He cleared his throat and made an effort to collect himself.

"I know. It's not who I am," she muttered ruefully. "You needn't point that out. I thought it best to play at being Riza for now."

"Be careful," he begged. "This game is bigger than we considered. The general is trying to win you not just for himself but for Sona. If charm doesn't work, he will not hesitate to act."

"Don't." She set a finger to his lips. "Hrvan is not all you think. You noted the men and women among his household who have the look of Amurians? Like the woman who led you off? When others would let them starve, Hrvan has taken them in, given them a place and protection."

"Why?" Jhared asked, noting unhappily that Maya had already dropped the general's title.

"Out of compassion?" Maya frowned. "Perhaps your shopkeeper has some veil that prevents her from seeing the truth of the man."

"The man who would breed children like puppies in hopes of caging an Avelun?"

Maya stiffened. "I won't be foolish. I see the possible dangers. But you—"

"Riza, the general awaits."

Jhared took a swift step away from Maya, who turned smoothly, regaining her bearing as a lady by the time she addressed Vyla. Jhared followed the two women through the hall, trying to appear complaisant, though anger and worry warred in his chest.

In contrast to the west-facing wing of the manor, with its wide windows and airy, arched ceiling, the dining room lay in the older part of the house and was built for defense instead of beauty. Narrow window slits allowed shafts of the evening air to shiver the lamplight across a table of scarred wood and to stir the woven hangings that did not completely conceal old damage to the walls. The ravens Jhared had seen at the park muttered to one another from their perch in a corner. With a pang, Jhared thought of Leita. He would have valued her counsel now. The constant swinging of the room made him wish he hadn't eaten, but he spread his feet and stood against the wall, as Maya and the general sipped wine and ate and spoke in animated tones. General Hrvan shifted the conversation into Sonan early in the first course. Jhared struggled to keep up, but as courses came and went and the shadows of other Paths lapped around him, he found himself floating with images that couldn't belong to his own story: parties of Sonans gathered around the table; a younger general speaking to a roomful of soldiers; a petite young woman with a long, thick braid cleaning cages and caring for birds that were no longer in the room.

Jhared swallowed and pulled himself straight. General Hrvan was setting aside his glass and rising with a gesture to Maya. The lamps had been turned up as the daylight faded. "Riza, it is time," he said in Velos, catching Jhared's eye briefly. "I have promised to let you meet my birds, and they are waiting. Vyla will take you to the rooftop. I believe you will want some time alone." He put a hand over his heart. "After, you and I will speak again. About favors. About the future."

On the portico, Vyla stood with her eyes lowered and no sign of the spirit she had revealed to Jhared. "If you will come this way, Riza."

She led them across the courtyard, up the spiral staircase in the northwest corner, to a small landing above the galleries, before a closed door. When she reached for the latch, Jhared stopped her.

"What is it we'll find here?" he demanded.

"Cousins," she said softly.

Be careful of the general. Of his birds.

"Does the general mean us ill?"

Vyla shook her head, eyes wide with dismay. "On the contrary! General Hrvan only wishes to please the Riza."

Her protest seemed genuine, but Jhared stepped around Vyla and Maya and threw open the door himself. Only in the last instant did it occur to him that Vyla had no way to know Maya referred to birds as cousins.

A warm breeze rushed against him, carrying the roar and hiss of the ocean. Within the balcony rail that framed a portion of the rooftop grew a lush glade of flowering trees in great copper pots. Benches and couches were strategically placed among them to offer the best views of the water and the bank of lofty clouds drifting toward the shore. Long-tailed birds preened on branches among the flowers. Jhared admired the elegant space as it tilted in his vision. Several moments passed before he perceived the four Avelune among the greenery, and another handful of breaths fled before he convinced himself they stood on his Path.

Avelune, majestic and compelling. His people. His history. Avelune, intact and surviving among the Sonans. Where no elder of Avelos would ever consider looking for them.

He stumbled a little as Maya nudged him aside. Recovering, he tried to calm the roiling around him. Near the trees stood two well-built young men, perhaps brothers. One was markedly taller and broader than the other, but both displayed wings the deep, bright color of heart's blood. Closer to the door, a soft-featured woman with summer-sky eyes and pale yellow wings stroked a parrot. Beside her, an ethereal-looking man leaned on a staff, his features delicately carved, his shoulders bowed by massive wings barred in black and bronze.

All four of them were glorious. More compelling than a lifetime of dreams.

The bronze-winged man stepped forward. Wisps of dark hair floated around his serene features. He took Maya's hand. "I am Drijan, sister. We rejoice at this reunion."

His Velos was old fashioned, like the general's, and heavily accented. Maya's fingers trembled as the man lifted them and touched them briefly to his heart.

"You're real," she murmured. "It's only that I've been searching so long. And suddenly here you are. I never thought. . . ."

The woman with yellow wings laughed, a pretty, musical trill. "Never thought to seek us in the rank swamps of Sona?"

Maya looked chagrined. "I had given up hope of finding you anywhere."

"Katian, don't speak so coarsely before our guest," a low voice drawled. "She won't understand the irony. She doesn't know we owe our lives to the swamps." The larger of the red-winged men approached the group. He was striking, dressed all in grey. His black hair and crimson wings gleamed. Jhared thought of Silvien's tale of the red-winged hero Tormelay.

Yellow-wing smiled. "I see you hope to play the Storyteller here, Kest. But not today. Not for a guest of such import."

Storyteller. The yellow-wing's emphasis on the word left no doubt it was a title. Jhared's mother had been a Storyteller, desperately keeping the broken remnants of Avelune history. What knowledge, what history these people must hold.

His thoughts were jarred as he saw the yellow-winged woman sneer at Maya, an ugly, resentful expression. By the time he caught his breath, however, her smile had returned.

"Unfair, Katian," the red-wing replied. "I would never usurp the place that belongs to our most wise and experienced Storyteller, honored nephew of Nemaye." He bowed gracefully to Drijan, who shifted his weight and looked uncomfortable. Jhared realized that the barred bronze-wing was younger than he first appeared.

"Oh, enough. By the light and dark, Kest, do stop showing off and let her in." Abandoning the parrot, the woman swooped upon Maya and drew her further onto the balcony. "Come, come, dear. Let us see you."

Yellow-wing gave Maya a little push, encouraging her to turn in a circle. "Go on, love, spread your wings for us. Let us see what you were meant to be."

Maya flushed with excitement and awe. "I'm sorry. I don't understand."

The handsome red-wing grinned. "Katian wants to see the shape of your wings to know whether you are meant for speed or distance, soaring or hovering. Don't be shy. Surely you've nothing to hide. You've lovely coloring."

Maya looked briefly reluctant, then hope lit her features. Flight. They were talking about how she would fly. Jhared drew a breath as she suddenly mantled and spread her wings to their full span. Her winter plumage, snow and ebony, was clean and elegant amidst the clash of colors around her.

The red-wing made a sound of appreciation. "Ah, look at those primaries," he whistled. "Wide and long like a raptor, she is. She'll hold the thermals and no mistake." He licked his lips. His own wings rose over his shoulders, revealing the long, tapered shape of a falcon, a predator fast and agile enough to kill in the air.

"I didn't know," Maya said, as the red-wing reached out and ran a finger along one of her ebony feathers. "I didn't know that we could . . ."

"Come in such different shapes?" yellow-wing finished. "Why should we not? Do not women vary in every other dimension? Do not men measure themselves by the length of their—"

"Leave her be!" The barked command caused the others to pause. It came from the smaller red-wing, who had lingered near the railing, staring out at the ocean. Although he had the same glorious scarlet and black coloring of the one called Kest, by comparison he was unprepossessing. When he turned, Jhared observed a bruise beneath his jaw and several broken feathers in his left wing.

At the interruption, Drijan cleared his throat with a sound of relief. "Good, Moravel. Do join us. Katian, my dear, please let us greet Mayavana properly." The others left off their admiring of Maya's wings and she furled them. Drijan gestured to the yellow-wing, who bobbed her head in a sudden show of modesty.

"Forgive my enthusiasm," the woman said with exquisite charm. "We've never had a visitor of our own kind. I'm afraid we're already treating you like family. It is quite rude, I confess."

Maya returned the smile. "And I confess to being overwhelmed. I've so much I must ask. So much I must learn."

"Good, good," Drijan said cheerfully, leaning on his staff. "It is a time for celebration. So many years we've been waiting. This is Katian, of course. The scarlet brothers are Kest and Moravel. Moravel, bring the wine. Shall we sit?"

Maya followed Drijan to a bench. As the brothers joined them, Jhared would have sworn that they glared at one another and touched knives at their belts. When he squeezed his eyes shut and looked again, however, they were not wearing knives. Not on this Path. Then he heard the voice, a woman's low, urgent hiss in his head.

Careful, I said! Don't ignore him. We need him. Until we can be certain of her.

Drijan turned to Jhared, who saw contempt for an instant before nothing but pleasure lit the Avelun man's green-gold eyes. "Little brother, we owe you great thanks for helping Mayavana to reach us. Be certain you are also welcome."

Some part of Jhared remembered to nod. Fragments of Paths darted past him like fish in a pool, and he couldn't close his hand around the one that belonged to him. Maya didn't appear to see his confusion. She was smiling and breathless, her gaze consuming the winged figures around her. With a word of thanks, she accepted a glass of wine from Moravel, who bowed silently in return.

"How did you escape the Shearing?" she asked. "How have you each come here? Are there others?"

Yellow-wing laughed, her chin lifted, exposing the graceful column of her throat. Her sea-colored dress was cut in a revealing fashion similar to Maya's "Drijan, will you honor us—soon—with your story? Before our sister bursts with her questions."

With a roguish grin, Kest took the space next to Maya on the bench. Sober Moravel moved a chair closer for Drijan.

"Mayavana, we are not what you imagine," the young Storyteller began. "None of us has ever glimpsed Avelos. More than one hundred fifty years have passed since our people walked in the land of our ancestors. We are the descendants of the survivors of the Exile War."

Descendants of the survivors. *Survivors.* Jhared had asked of them once, when he was a boy. Madam Trianor had mocked him and declared the Exiles all dead, then punished him for his lack of focus.

"How is it possible?" Maya murmured.

"While General Maren chased our ancestors toward death between the archers of Avelos and the spears of Sahiste, a few escaped the army and flew west. Those few vanished into the marshes of Sona."

"Where most died of disease and heartbreak," Kest growled.

"Peace, Kest," Katian said, touching the man's arm lightly.

"A handful of survivors crept south," Drijan continued. "They hid in the mud and scraped a life out of the swamps."

"A colony of Avelune all these years in Sona." Maya shook her head. "And I was here. So close."

"What happened during the invasion of Sona? Are there Avelune in Amuria, as well?" Jhared asked.

The others stared at him as though he had asked how to lace his boot. Drijan tilted his head in acknowledgment. "The Amurian occupation drove our people deeper into hiding and no place remained to flee. But Sonans persecuted for their loyalty were also escaping into the marshes. When our great-grandparents encountered a band of ragged Sonan soldiers, they discovered their common goal was to survive the Amurians. They helped one another through the years of violence. As we continue to help one another."

Maya's gaze was wide and wondering. "General Hrvan?"

"Yes. His great-great-grandfather and twice-great-uncle led the soldiers who first encountered our people. Of those who follow him still—the guards, his household staff—most are heirs to that alliance."

"How is it that all of Sona doesn't know of you?" she asked. "Why hasn't word reached Avelos?"

"We are but a small community beholden to the general for our lands and defenses," Katian replied. "He and those who follow him maintain their silence, not merely for our good but for the good of the country. What do you think would happen to poor Sona if Avelos or Sahiste should discover us?"

Maya was frowning. "You believe it would lead to another invasion."

"Not an invasion," Jhared interjected. "Avelos wouldn't need an invasion to bully Sona into surrendering the last of the Avelune." He was listening hard for the hissed voice. The waves bumping against him made it increasingly difficult to divide his attention. He felt he was missing something. Something important.

"Where we would be slain, along with any who gave us succor," Katian added.

Maya nodded.

"Some of us share the manor with the general's people," Drijan said. "The rest live well enough on the estate."

"Well enough? Hardly!" Kest declared, coming to his feet. "We should be in our own mountain keeps soaring from the highest cliffs! Instead, we live on another man's sufferance, hunkering in the damp with nothing left of our own."

"And your unmodulated anger has done so much to amend that," Moravel said mildly.

"Anger stirs men to action," Kest replied. "I will not ask forgiveness for refusing to age and die here, as our parents and grandparents did."

"And once you have stirred men to action—telling them they have the right to quench their hatred with violence—how then do you expect to shape a place where our children can grow whole and safe? Where our people can once more study the spheres?"

"You prattle of safety like a scared old man, brother. Go tend to your precious plants and leave the future to those who are unafraid to break free of our benign captivity. Nemaye has seen the Paths where we triumph!"

The Paths. Jhared knew the thing he was missing had something to do with the Paths. History existed here. His living history. "Your Travelers must be skilled. And your maps! They must reach all the way back to the Exile."

"Maps?" Kest barked. "We left those artifacts behind when we fled. We travel where we want, when we want. We need no maps!"

Jhared frowned, heated by a mix of doubt and anger. "Maps of the Paths can reveal patterns across Time and Place. They can show points of influence that might change the direction of the world."

Kest's laugh was deep and patronizing. "You sound like my brother, still chained to the past. We will have no one tracking us as Tumal tracked our ancestors."

"Kest, love, now who is being coarse?" Katian said quickly. "Let us not bore our guests with our family squabbles."

"Mayavana does not look bored," the big red-wing replied, turning to Maya. "Unless I very much miss my guess, you are one who understands the need to claim your own Path. You would never have found us else. My brother, on the other hand, would have you discuss and ruminate and consider until the opportunity for change has passed."

"I would only have you take care not to lose that which cannot be recovered," Moravel answered. "And perhaps to consider that you have never actually seen a mountain."

Kest's eyes remained on Maya. "What would you risk to win your heart's longing, Mayavana?"

Slowly, Maya leaned forward and ran her hand over the leading edge of Kest's wing, her eyes dark with desire. Jhared coughed and bit the inside of his cheek until he tasted blood and his vision cleared. Maya was not touching Kest, but only looking at him with an expression of understanding. Jhared gritted his teeth.

"For years, I have been traveling through Avelos," she said, "risking everything to learn what I could of my heritage."

"I thought as much! You are a brave and determined woman." Kest shot his brother a meaningful glance. Moravel shook his head and looked away.

"Foolish is likely a better word than brave," Maya replied with a laugh. "But determined, I'll accept. I've so yearned to find you. You are the cord that ties directly to our ancestors, all of you. Will you teach me what you know?"

"Of course. And we hope you will teach us." Kest sat back, looking supremely self-assured. He smiled at Maya, a deep, inviting expression.

Jhared could no longer bear it. "Mayavana would have you teach her how to fly."

Maya froze. Her cheeks turned beet and her mouth opened in silent mortification. Clearly, she had not intended to disclose her flaw before the group. Perhaps she might have whispered it to Kest or to his quiet brother later, a plea for them to show her how to reach the skies.

Silence strained the room. Maya's expression was shifting from embarrassment to anger.

"What do I do now?" The new voice rose a little desperately. Jhared couldn't mistake Drijan's tone.

"Idiot! I told you to attend to him!" The woman's reply crackled with frustration.

"I could tell her now what we need from her. Why should we wait?"

"No! It's too soon. He'll guess what we are if we reveal too much. End this. There will be time later. We must have her alone."

A wave swept over Jhared, dousing him with other Paths, other stories. He clutched the back of the bench with one hand and stared straight ahead, forcing his features to remain neutral, while his joy and his jealousy crumbled into cold fear.

"Forgive me for speaking above my place," he murmured. "I am Shorn and as clumsy in my speech as in my actions. I have strained your hospitality. Maya, perhaps we should leave. Tomorrow. Tomorrow, we will return."

Maya glared at him. "What are you talking about? I can't leave."

Drijan's gaze moved over Jhared suspiciously.

"Curse your ineptness," the woman spat. *"What does he guess? Calm him. Calm him!"*

"It is no burden to welcome our own back to the flock," the Storyteller said hastily. "We already have rooms made up for you both. We have years to discuss."

Jhared shook his head. "Forgive us. I fear we have obligations to others."

"*You* claim obligations to others, Jhared. Not I. And here you've never been closer to filling them. Why would you seek to leave?"

"Don't let him leave, but be restrained."

"Restrained?" Drijan's tone was all disgust. *"He is Tainted. Ravaged. The stink of Avelos is upon him."*

"And she is a whore who loves Sahistens. But if you harm him in front of her, we may lose her. For now, Ilaye says we need them both. For now.

Jhared didn't understand. Why did he sense such profound hatred in the voices? Did the words belong on this Path or on one of the infinite Paths weaving around him? "Maya," he gasped, "please come away."

When had Drijan come to his feet? When had the others spread around him?

"I could leave him to Kest."

"You can't. The general has some use for him. Another pretty face for his guard, no doubt. We'll have the woman and her skills. Hrvan will keep this gelded hofja *for display. Now, fix this!"*

Maya's expression broke open. "Jhared, what is it?"

"We must leave. Right now."

"Easy, little brother. Be easy." Drijan took a step closer, gripping his staff with a level of urgency that belied his tranquil words. "You have traveled too long among foes and are ill with it. You have no enemies here. Sit. Drink with us."

Jhared took Maya under the elbow and propelled her toward the door. "Come along. We can return. If all is well here, of course we will return."

Katian stepped into his way. Her wings had risen above her shoulders. Her voice was gentle, but her smile was full of lies. "Jhared Denaban, it is clear how deeply you care for Mayavana. Now that she is here among her own people, perhaps you fear we mean to take her from you. You needn't fear us. We are your cousins too."

Jhared was aware of his fingers digging into Maya's arm. Her breaths rose loud and outraged beside him. She didn't pull away; that much trust existed between them. Yet she had yearned all her life for her own kind. For flight. He didn't have much time before she balked.

"If we have no reason to fear, then let us leave," he demanded.

"Wait! Stop harassing him. Katian, leave off." It was Moravel. He crossed the distance between them, waving the others away. Unexpected sympathy softened his expression.

"You're a Traveler, aren't you?" the red-wing said quietly.

Jhared hesitated. Maya leaned close to his ear. "You're too open," she murmured. "Please stop this, Jhared. We are safe here." To Moravel she nodded. "He is."

The young red-wing canted his head. "Have the Paths befuddled you, my friend?"

They had. Jhared knew he was losing track of his own present. But he had heard the voices speaking of him. He had heard the woman speaking ill of Maya. Hadn't he? "Why are you so desperate to keep us here?" he asked. "Why do you seek to separate Maya and me?"

"You misunderstand. I fear perhaps you have seen some strange Path before us. But that does not make it so at this moment in this place."

The man's voice was gentle and his words logical. Jhared longed to stop fighting the waves that battered him. He wanted to bask in the warmth and beauty of the Avelune. His people. He wanted Maya to look on him with the same admiration she had given to Kest. He shook his head. Complexities existed he could not sort out right now, but he clung to what he knew. "Let us leave. That's all I ask."

"The truth is I am afraid to let you leave," Moravel continued in his rational tone. "I'm afraid that if you leave us in this state, your confusion and distorted thoughts will keep you from returning. You have been hurt, Jhared Denaban. Stay. Let us heal you."

Ah goddess. More than anything Jhared wanted what Moravel offered, but he could not be healed. He was Shorn. The skies would never be his. A sweep of blue shrouded his vision, and he saw Kest drawing the blade from his belt. Did he draw it on this Path? Jhared shook his head, staggering a little. He must get Maya to safety. He had promised Zinderdali to keep her safe. Still gripping her arm, he hurried her around Moravel toward the door. Drijan stood there, his staff turned end out. The wood bumped Jhared's chest, pushing him backward, keeping him from escape.

"Jhared, please come back. You're wandering."

Maya's plea held the last cogent words he knew before the balcony exploded into chaos.

Drijan jabbed again, and the staff thudded with bruising force against Jhared's breastbone. The Storyteller's face was a mask of revulsion. Or was that mask the truth the man was trying to conceal? When the staff came at Jhared a third time, he twisted his body to the side. With one arm he knocked the stick toward Drijan's chest and lunged. Someone screamed an urgent command. Someone moved to obey. In a heartbeat, Jhared had checked Drijan's attempt to swing back at him and spun behind the Avelun. Black and bronze wings flapped aggressively, but Jhared already stood too close for them to be dangerous. As feathers slapped at him, he slammed the side of his hand against Drijan's neck, grabbed the man by the shoulders and forced him to his knees. The staff came readily into his hands. He pulled it tight against the Avelun's throat, felt the man struggle, slump, and shoved him away.

He had moved fast, but not fast enough. The others had closed on him. Someone kicked him from behind, throwing him forward. The staff clattered to the ground as he landed on his knees. Kest rushed at him, arms extended as though to pin him. With effort, Jhared managed one shuffled, kneeling step, planted his foot, and drove himself toward the big red-wing's abdomen. Kest *woofed* out a lungful of air as Jhared's shoulder rammed into him. Quickly, with his hands on Kest's legs, Jhared heaved upward, hurling the man over his shoulder. A cry of pain escaped Kest as he landed on his back, one wing spread flat, the other folded beneath him.

No time for regret. In that moment, Jhared was completely exposed. Moravel didn't hesitate to come to his brother's aid: wings furled tightly, he spun and kicked Jhared squarely in the chest. Jhared's heart skipped and lurched. He fell backward and his head slammed against the marble floor. Red clouds hazed his vision. Beyond the rails, he saw the blue-grey water and the sky.

"Maya, run. Run!" He had lost sight of her, didn't know if she had made it down the stairs.

Dizzily, he rolled into a crouch, one knee on the ground, one foot beneath him. Moravel aimed another kick. Jhared ducked clumsily and dove for the man's grounded ankle. With both hands he jerked Moravel's leg out from under him and sent the Avelun onto his back

If he were quicker, if the blows and the Paths hadn't fogged his perception, he might have had a chance to flee. But he was still on the ground when Kest and Katian came for him.

"Restrained! I said restrained!" the woman's voice shouted.

Then a wave of shining blue knocked Jhared away from the clash and he found himself in an entirely different kind of struggle.

22.

HUNTED

At night, in deep woods, with a fog so thick it masked the stars, Nemiah lay on her blankets unseeing and tried to imagine what she would feel if she knew the darkness would never lift.

They had crossed out of Clan Delsio lands, trod through the wet wooded hills and muddy pastures of Clan Everen, and were camped somewhere near the border of Clan Makri. Nemiah wasn't certain she could have pointed out her location if shown a map. Lieutenant Sevar had led them off the roads along a route that they hoped would confound their hunters.

In a short time, Nemiah had learned much of what it meant to travel rough and at speed with seasoned soldiers. Certain bruised parts of her body made that clear when she lay down each night after a long day in the saddle and an evening sharing in the tasks of setting camp. Her Arionade had tried to stop her from taking on the physical tasks at first—caring for her mare and Leita's gelding, setting up their necessities for the night, and contributing to the preparation or cleanup of the evening meal. Rom knew her well enough and respected her abilities enough to do no more than scowl when she sent him off to other duties. Rien, however, Ansa's man, insisted on pressing his solicitousness. Nemiah told him, somewhat crisply, that Riana's Chosen had a duty to restore order wherever she could, not to watch others do it for her. One of the Forest Guardsmen gave a bark of surprised laughter at that; Anzo Nevia, she thought. She was small and not particularly strong—she couldn't be of use chopping firewood or hauling the kettle filled with water—but she had grown up on a farm, the daughter of a healer and a weaver. Some practical things she could still do to care for herself and others.

Her Arionade were learning from their travels as well. Nemiah only hoped they learned fast enough to avoid coming to blows with the soldiers. So far, habitual discipline kept the tension between her men and Sevar's from igniting, but the close quarters tested that discipline daily. The Forest Guardsmen knew the land, were accomplished trackers, and understood the sources of danger in the wilds. Of course it made sense for Lieutenant Sevar to direct the company. But she saw Rom gritting his teeth as he accepted the lieutenant's leadership, and saw the rebellious expressions of the younger, more impulsive Arionade.

The Bearer's presence only fed the conflict, like dry leaves to the flame. Leita was the horrible reminder of what happened when the Arionade yielded their positions as guardians. Nemiah knew that some of Rom's anger and that of his men arose from their own feelings of responsibility for what Leita had suffered. They yearned to make reparation for their perceived failure, and tried to do so by flanking her as they rode, hovering close to address whatever need she might express, and offering to serve as her guide the moment she dismounted. Each time that Leita rejected one of their offers, lashed out at their hovering, or reached instead for the arm of Lieutenant Sevar, the strain between Arionade and Forest Guard grew more dangerous. It didn't help matters that Nemiah had started their journey by stabbing one of the patrolmen in the face. It didn't help that Lieutenant Sevar possessed his own reasons for despising her: Ziabela was his sister; Jhared Denaban had been his scout. Nemiah worried that before they reached the Sahisten border war might break out, but not between Sahiste and Avelos.

They couldn't afford to indulge such disorder. Each day, the lieutenant sent his outriders to comb the wilds as the company continued south. For the past three evenings, they had reported that someone appeared to be following them. A man on his own, the shy, burly soldier named Esran said. They hadn't managed to spy him yet, only his trail, but from it the outriders reported he was underfed and ill. He was someone deeply familiar with the wilds and with no interest in being seen. Esran was the most devout of the soldiers; the only one who participated, bashfully, in the devotions when Nemiah conducted them morning and night. Tonight he had glanced at the Bearer when he reported finding the tracks for a third time. The news appeared to disturb her. Nemiah had spoken to Leita after, offering words of reassurance, reminding her that one malnourished man could offer no threat to them amid the Arionade and the Forest Guard. Nemiah had not commented on the fact that a man on foot who kept pace with a mounted company for three days must have some pressing cause.

Lieutenant Sevar had ordered the outriders to find the man. Then fog sank onto the landscape, shuttering the world. Not even the Forest Guard could find a person in such unrelenting darkness. It had touched Nemiah to see how the soldiers took particular care to cheer the Bearer. Anzo had jested with her. Esran had asked her for a story. Even Grion had subdued his typical, fatalistic ranting. Despite the rising tensions, Nemiah could not regret the camaraderie Leita enjoyed with the soldiers. Watching her with the four Forest Guards and their lieutenant—the way she talked and even laughed with them; the easy way they engaged her—Nemiah realized how isolated Leita had been in the high temple. The aura of darkness and disorder that had always kept other women at a distance from the Bearer of Cael's Blade had somehow become the explanation for her tragedy. Few women had been willing even to approach her, as if the horror she had experienced in the north was contagious. Nemiah felt ashamed she had not recognized that subtle shunning earlier. In contrast, these men treated Leita without fear or guilt or pity. They had shared her nightmare. They understood what she had suffered in a way no others could. And they respected her courage. No matter what the soldiers thought of Nemiah, she felt deep gratitude toward them for helping Leita to remember who she was.

Now, thinking on blindness and shunning and sacrifice, Nemiah lay awake somewhere near the border between the lands of Clans Makri and Amerre. Her eyes were open and sightless in the predawn darkness. Rom and Sevar had taken the last watch together: a step toward collaboration, perhaps. Or perhaps just an unwillingness in either one to cede control. She was aware of them sitting on opposite sides of the camp. The others slept on around her, known only by the various sounds of their breathing. No fire tonight—not enough dry wood for it. No tents: that bit of privacy had been surrendered for the sake of speed. Beside her, Leita shifted on her bedroll.

"Can you not sleep?" Nemiah asked softly.

"I don't want to," the Bearer answered.

"Nightmares?" Nemiah said, even more softly.

"No. Well, not just now. The fog is heavy, isn't it? No stars."

"None. It's impenetrable."

"This won't make sense to you, but I take some comfort in that. My own darkness doesn't feel so wrong."

Nemiah kept quiet for a time. "I think I can almost understand. I've been lying here . . . trying to."

"I know."

Leita's tone remained clean of fury or despair. Some balance seemed to be returning to her. She shifted again on her blankets. "What is it *you* fear, my friend?"

Nemiah drew a breath. It had been a long time since Leita called her friend. "Am I so easily read?"

"You are holding your breath and letting it out in counts of six. You do so when you're worried."

She supposed she did; she hadn't supposed anyone noticed. "It was just . . . I wonder, when the web has unraveled, when the land and sky and even the stars are undone, will the fog be all that remains, do you think?"

The rustling beside Nemiah stopped. "No. Not even the fog."

"Have you seen it?" Nemiah hadn't dared to ask before; she hadn't wanted to know. As Bearer, Leita was proscribed by temple law from crossing the Gate and traveling the Paths for her own purposes. But Nemiah had come to understand that many of the old laws had been meant to restrain Riana's servants rather than to protect them, leaving her without the defenses she had always trusted. Learning to walk outside of those boundaries still terrified her, but was necessary. She forced herself to say it explicitly: "Leita, have you witnessed the moments when the Paths unravel?"

The Bearer's voice changed, some of the fragileness returning. "Only an echo of those moments, Nemiah. A foreshadowing. Nothing exists on that Path. No, that's inaccurate. The unraveled Path *is* nothingness. If ever a Pathwalker touches it, I suspect she will cease to exist."

"Death?"

"Annihilation. Elimination from the infinite web." The Bearer shuddered.

With terrible certainty, Nemiah realized that Leita's experiences of the unraveling had burdened her with a torment even worse than blinding: an inescapable vision of the end of all Paths. From that perspective, if Nemiah were willing to broaden her understanding of order just a little further, it was possible to see how her friend had been driven to accept a heresy that offered an alternative to the nothingness. Nemiah hadn't decided if she could broaden her understanding that far.

"Nemiah."

"I'm here."

"I asked you at Sevar's farm if you had seen my role in the unraveling. When you answered, did you . . . Please tell me you wouldn't have . . . No, never mind."

"Leita, please tell me."

"I said leave it!" There was a pause; then abruptly Leita sat up. Blankets whooshed softly as if they'd been thrown aside.

"What is it?"

"Quiet!" Leita ordered. "Listen! Someone's out there."

Nemiah strained to hear what the Bearer did. She heard only the soft chirrups and squeaks and rustling foliage that she would have named typical of the nighttime. She regretted that her question had sparked Leita's terrors. "My friend, I hear only the forest."

Leita didn't answer. Then Nemiah did hear someone: a man rising at the edge of camp and stepping in near silence toward her and the Bearer. The lieutenant crouched at Leita's side.

"Something disturbed you, Lady?"

"I heard rustling. Like someone in the brush. Someone moving stiffly after being still for a long time. I suppose it couldn't have been, though. You would have heard it. Or Captain Rom."

Sevar's voice dropped lower. "Trust what you sense, Leita. I've told you. We make more mistakes when we talk ourselves out of what our perceptions tell us than when we attend to them. My scouts know this."

"Do they? I've heard you say something very different. At least to one scout."

The Bearer's tone held a fine whip of irony. The lieutenant's boots creaked as he shifted his weight.

"Since the farm, you might have some better sense of why I spoke so to that one scout." His voice remained mild. In the dark, it was impossible to read whether there was anger in him. "I've only ever told you truths as I know them, Leita. I'll check the perimeter."

"It may have been nothing. A fox."

"Then I will come back and tell you it was nothing."

"Of course. Thank you, Matio."

Sevar walked off. He spoke a word to his second, Commander Lenaro, then again, nearly silent, left the camp. He led a company of men trained to move without being observed, and was himself one of General Nadel's chief scouts. The way the ground trembled under Nemiah in that moment had nothing to do with the lieutenant's tread. Something in his words or Leita's, or perhaps something in what Nemiah had not said as she lay awake listening, had twisted the Path in a new direction. At least, that's what she thought until the first, dizzying thud was followed by another and another and a third.

Footsteps. From the other side of the Gate. A Pathwalker traveling.

Leita grasped Nemiah's arm. "Do you feel it?"

Heavier footsteps ran toward Nemiah, not silent, and solidly on this side of the Gate. The Arionade were house guards, bodyguards, trained to be seen and to intimidate. They would never match the Forest Guard for stealth. Rom dropped to his knees at her side. He knew her better than any other, was attuned to her. He didn't need to be a Pathwalker to know that she had touched the blue flames. Through the fog, Nemiah glimpsed steel in his hand.

"No, Rom, wait!"

"Lady, you mustn't wander! You may be trapped again."

"It's not me. Someone else is traveling. Someone close." The last time she had sensed another's steps on the Paths, they had been powerful and focused. She had thought them to be Leita's steps, but they had belonged to one who had long been denied any access to the Gate. They had been the steps of a Shorn man. She had sent that man away to save his life.

Nemiah disengaged from the Bearer and pushed to her feet. "Leita, do you think it's him?"

"I'm not sure. It might be. "

A man had been following the company for three days. Someone weary and sick. Someone who had a reason to keep pace with them. Who perhaps had a reason to fear approaching them.

"I'll find out."

"Nemiah, I said I'm not sure."

The Bearer's voice held apprehension. Nemiah thought she understood it. She pulled on her boots and grabbed her cloak. "We can keep him safe, Leita. I have authority here. I don't believe the elder will try to gainsay it."

"But Lieutenant Sevar is constrained by Forest Guard Law."

The implication was clear: the Forest Guard executed deserters. And Jhared Denaban had fled with charges of deceit marking his name.

The footsteps of the Pathwalker lurched, revealing exhaustion with each resounding, unstable step. "We must worry over that later. Whoever this is may need help to return. I will not abandon a spirit to endless wandering. Rom, with me."

"Take Anzo, too."

"Leita, a lost Pathwalker is nothing to fear."

"Please."

It was the pleading that changed Nemiah's mind. Even though there was no time to delay. Even though admitting the need for a soldier would cut at Rom. The Bearer begged for nothing, not in all the years Nemiah had known her, and she was begging now.

Around the camp, the others were rising. The grizzled patrolman from Clan Everen was already buckling his sword belt. "What do you need of me, Lady Bearer?"

"The Lady of Avelos is seeking strangers in the forest, Anzo. When I . . . we have reason to be wary of predators right now."

The soldier glanced at Rom, but didn't make a comment before turning to his commander for the order.

"What's this?" Lenaro snapped. "Why can't it wait until the lieutenant returns with word?"

"There is no waiting," Nemiah replied. "If the Pathwalker returns to his or her proper place, I will no longer have any trail to follow. Rom and I are going now, with or without a patrolman."

"Lenaro, she speaks only the truth," the Bearer added.

The commander uttered a quiet curse. "Go, Nevia. But you men take care not to mistake the lieutenant for some threat in the fog and run him through."

Nemiah grimaced. The commander's words were clearly meant for Rom. She could imagine her Arionad's scowl, but he kept his peace.

"Come," she said hastily. The Pathwalker's footsteps continued to drum against the back of her head and the center of her chest. She needed to turn inward, to orient herself before those steps faded away. "Captain, Patrolman, follow me. Follow only! Do not speak."

She hurried from the camp, letting the footsteps guide her—pull her—while the two men trailed behind. In this, *she* was the tracker. The fog and the darkness could not prevent her from reading the signs of the Pathwalker's passing. The signs were internal, changing pressures deep within her, an acute sense of a spirit who was out of place on the web. The traveler formed a small, sharp wrongness as he—Nemiah thought it truly was *he*—staggered about the infinite moments of the world without care, or perhaps without the capacity to stop. Moving as quickly as she dared in the damp darkness, her hands outstretched, she scraped against barely visible trees and tripped over unseen rocks. Even the experienced patrolman behind her cursed—then silenced himself—when the three of them slid down an unexpected slope into a shallow creek.

Nemiah splashed across the water and stood panting on the opposite bank. She stood so close to the Pathwalker now she could sense some of what drove him. Although illness and exhaustion greyed the traveler's spirit, determination ran at his core, a need that burned flesh and immolated reason. She sensed hatred, but not the sort that fueled action, only a faded remnant of something that might once have raged. Instead, fear gave the traveler strength, deep and abiding fear. Countering that coldness, Nemiah was surprised to sense in him a wide river of love twisted inseparably with sorrow.

"Hurry," she breathed, as much to herself as to Rom and the soldier at her side. "We cannot lose this one. We've lost too many."

She oriented herself once more to the thudding of the Path. Not far. Not very far at all. But the footsteps had slowed and grown fainter. She set off again at a jog, arms outstretched to prevent her from bashing into trees. The forest grew thicker here. She pushed through the brush, impatient, her thoughts already with the Pathwalker. The possibility existed she would need to cross the Gate to retrieve him. Someone so deeply entangled in the web might not be dragged back by the pain of the knife. Something rustled in the bushes ahead of her. She imagined the Pathwalker—she didn't yet dare to think of him by name—flailing in the grip of his journey. She was so close. One of the men behind her hissed a breath, cried out a warning. Too late.

Nemiah's feet struck nothing and she flew.

On one of the rare, quiet nights when Ziabela had relaxed her guard enough to reveal something of herself, she had spoken of her nightmares, of how she had so often taken the desired, destructive step from a glorious height in order to know, for the briefest instant, the embrace of the sky. The fall itself held no terror for her, Zia said, it was the understanding that she was capable of taking such a deadly step that made her ill. Nemiah had nodded as if she understood: she had not. In her dreams, it was the fall that undid her.

She flew through the darkness, a single, urgent cry torn from her lips. For an instant, she knew a sense of wonder as the wind caressed her face. Then the earth reclaimed her. Brush scratched and grabbed at her. Her left side slammed against the ground, and pain as she had never before known it exploded through her.

"Nemiah!"

The world shuddered. She didn't move, didn't dare, only tried to draw one careful breath to see if she could. More pain in that. Fragmented images flashed before her: a small bird smashing against a window and falling broken to the ground; a ripe plum dropping from the tree and bursting open in the dirt; a fine cup shattering upon the stones and spattering the ground with wine.

"Lady, can you hear me?"

She could hear, couldn't talk. Not enough breath yet. She heard the soft bubbling murmur of water. The sound came from directly beneath her, but she remained dry. Her body lay at an angle, shoulders higher than her feet. Not on the ground. Where? Thoughts came slowly and in pieces. The fingers of her right hand twitched over an uneven surface: striations. Wood. Bark. A tree. Had she fallen onto a downed tree? Caught and held by the branches? Some kind of irony there. A little way up the trunk she heard crackling and wondered what type of creatures her landing had disturbed.

"Only Cael causes others' torments."

It was a woman's voice, very soft. Nemiah's head rang with a sound like the temple's bell. Behind her came the noises of two men sliding and skidding down the side of the gully.

"Only Cael! Only Cael determines our destruction."

Nemiah shifted her gaze without moving her head. Through the silver fog, she saw the line of the tree trunk angling up toward the other side of the ravine. A dark figure perched on the trunk. Above the figure's narrow shoulders, Cael's raven head with its human skull gripped in its jaws glared down at her.

"Riana, shield me!"

A reflexive prayer. Nemiah had told Leita she understood some of Cael's beauty. Was that still sacrilege? Would she pay for it when she left the Paths of the Living? Would she leave those Paths in this predawn fog?

"The goddess offers us no shield!" snapped Cael. "I am his shield. And he has lost enough. Too much. Leave him be!" The eyes behind the skull shone savage and unyielding, but Nemiah heard something vulnerable in the demon's tone.

"Nemiah, are you there?" Rom's voice was low with restrained emotion.

The figure of Cael scampered up the trunk and vanished. Nemiah rested her forehead against the rough bark. "I'm . . . all right. Just dazed."

Her Arionad crouched at her side. The soldier, Anzo Nevia, stood behind. Nemiah could see their outlines now. Early light was beginning to touch the mist with grey.

"We'll get you out. Can you move?" Rom set a hand on her shoulder.

"Of course I can move. I must just—"

Deep within her, at the center of her self, a thud echoed one last time and fell silent.

"No! No, don't!"

Rom pushed closer. "Lady, what is it?"

"Gone. He's gone!"

"The Pathwalker?"

"Oh, Goddess, I think he crossed the Gate." She couldn't really know. If the Pathwalker had died, she supposed the abrupt end to his footsteps would have been the same. "We have to go after him. He can't be far." She drew both hands beneath her and pushed against the trunk. Pain, sharp and dazzling, stabbed through her chest. With a cry, she collapsed back onto the tree trunk.

"Nemiah, you fell hard," Rom said, gently touching the left side of her face. His fingers came away with blood on them. "You mustn't go anywhere but back to camp."

"Not yet. We must find him. Cael is watching him. From the tree."

"The tree? Nemiah?"

"She took quite a blow to the head." The gruff voice behind her belonged to the soldier.

She had taken a blow. Her head throbbed, and bells rang in her ears. But Cael had been there, hadn't he? Speaking in a woman's soft voice?

"Rom, you and Nevia go. Find him."

Rom's body tensed with his protest, but before he could voice it, the old soldier spun away from them. "Someone's coming."

Nemiah tried to turn her head to see, but was hit with a wave of dizziness and another stab of pain through her chest.

Rom stood. "Maybe the Pathwalker's found us."

"I don't think so," Nevia replied.

Dead leaves crackled as the two men shifted their balance. Nemiah lay on the log, maddened by her helplessness. Would the Pathwalker approach them of his own will? Leita had been afraid, had begged her to take a soldier. Nemiah didn't understand why.

A stiff quiet fell among them. The creek muttered and cackled. Whatever Nevia had heard to warn him of an approach, Nemiah didn't hear it.

"Ho, Nevia!"

The call came from far above them. The old soldier let out an audible breath. "Ho, Esran! Strength to the Fourth!"

"What're you doing down there? Fishing?"

"Could use a hand. Not your smart mouth. We're occupied. Need a tracker to go on after our quarry."

"Can't do it, old man. Time for you to be back in camp. Lieutenant's order."

"What? What're you on about?"

"By the Lady, stop screeching for all Avelos to hear. I'm coming down."

Skidding, snapping sounds spoke of a man speedily descending to the ravine bottom. A variety of curses embellished the descent before Nemiah heard Esran stumble to a halt near the water.

"Goddess protect you," he panted. "Lady, are you all right?"

"Well enough," she lied. "What's happened?"

Esran looked unhappily from Nemiah to the other men. "We need to move out. Now. Far too exposed down here."

"Esran, say what's happened?" Nevia demanded.

"Lieutenant found signs of observers. Just as the Lady Bearer said. Someone skilled. Thinks they might be Abrigado's people. Might be they know where we are now. He sent me to bring you back. And to give you an extra sword arm. In case."

Nevia spat into the dirt. "We're supposed to be taking care against Sahistens and highwaymen, not worrying about attacks from our own leaders."

Rom remained steady as the shore against the sea. "Lady Nemiah won't be able to climb. We'll have to rig a litter."

"No litter, Rom. No time. I'll do it."

The old soldier was examining the ridge again. Nemiah realized he had altered his position to stand in front of her, shoulder to shoulder with her Arionad. "Lady, I suspect you've broken some ribs. Walking up isn't going to be pleasant."

In answer, Nemiah carefully and slowly sat up. She kept her breathing shallow and ignored the way the world rocked around her. *That* she was accustomed to. "Then we'd best begin. So we can see an end to it."

Nevia swore, then stopped himself. "Forgive me, Lady. It's just that the temple breeds its women of iron and fire."

"I wish that were true. Then I wouldn't be sitting here bleeding into the dirt. Let's go."

She allowed herself Rom's arm for aid. No need to be foolish and fall again. Nevia put himself one pace ahead of them and Esran took the rear. As they climbed, both soldiers continuously scanned the landscape.

The ravine wall didn't run sheer all the way along the creek bed. By Riana's weaving or Cael's chance, Nemiah had fallen at one of the points where it did. Nevia took them back to the place where he and Rom had scrambled down. Although one might argue that it wasn't sheer, it was still terrifyingly steep and rocky. The rising sun touched the edge of the ridge now, but didn't yet dip into the ravine to light their way. Nemiah took slow, small steps, trying to avoid the need to suck a deep breath. Stones slid out from under her boots. Rom supported her with his arm around her waist.

"I wonder, Lady, what it is exactly that makes you run through a forest in fog at the naked edge of morning."

The comment came from Nevia. A Forest Guard patrolman. She needn't answer him, but considering how to frame a response forced her to think on something other than how hard it was to breathe and how far she had yet to climb. She suspected that he meant it to. "Someone was . . . journeying. Touching Riana's ways. Does that mean anything . . . to you?"

"I know little of Riana's mysteries, Lady. Mostly I've not thought on them beyond the prayers any soldier mutters at the start and end of his watch. But I saw some things while traveling with the Bearer of Cael's Blade. And after."

"When she tried to save you?"

Nevia remained silent a moment. "In the moment she did whatever it was she did to the northerners, I saw a hundred different ways my life could end. The *consequences* of things. Paths of my own, I suppose."

"Me too. I saw them too," Esran said, devotion subduing his tone.

"A gift," Nemiah whispered.

If she had owned the breath for it, she would have asked them both questions about what they had seen. The men were no Pathwalkers, but they had been nearby when Leita called the Paths to converge upon Commander Ciam. Leita had been fighting for her life and the lives of others; she would have thrown every bit of her significant strength into the battle. Had her immense power done something that allowed others to glimpse their own potential Paths? Nemiah didn't know if such a thing were possible. So many things she didn't know: Ziabela had asked once why she didn't just explore the Paths before her in order to spy out the consequences of her actions before they were woven. Amalia had been capable of traveling so closely on her Arionad's Path they could communicate at will from a distance. A deep pang of loss echoed in Nemiah's heart. They had lost an entire way of life—a way of existing in Riana's web. Now just the slender hope of one wandering Pathwalker had become like a promise of light through the fog.

"Do you know who it is, this someone touching Riana's ways?"

She returned to the moment. It was a pointed question from an observant man. Nevia had glanced back and was staring at her.

"I think so."

"Ah." A musing expression sketched the soldier's grizzled features. He scratched at the stubble across his chin. "I see. Just a little farther to go, Lady. You're almost there."

"Almost" seemed miles. Despite the careful pace, Nemiah was panting shallowly long before they reached the top. As they finally clambered over the edge of the ridge, she dropped to her hands and knees and was immediately, convulsively ill.

Rom's arms came around her. She sank backward against him, clammy and limp. Unexpectedly, the little veteran was also bending close, helping her to take a sip of water from his flask, and brushing the lose strands of hair off her damp brow.

"Soldier . . . you don't even *like* me."

The man shook his head. "Lady, I spoke thoughtlessly that day. I can't pretend to be ignorant of the things you saved the boy from. And I've never wished you harm. Is it too late to ask forgiveness for an ill-spoken old man?"

In that strange moment, Nemiah felt as if she could truly see the old veteran, beyond his gruff manner and scarred features. He had served as a warrior all of his life, a scout at the uncertain and violent borders of Avelos, yet his ferocity was balanced by intelligence and his intelligence was balanced by acceptance of what life offered. A new thought came to her: one did not need to name the goddess to be worthy of her.

"The weaving needs such men. Even the ill-spoken ones."

His lips quirked. "A rough patch I make in the tapestry, Lady. But thank you. I think now it's time for you to let your fine Arionad carry you, eh?"

No more protests remained in her. She nodded.

She had not known that pain could be a wall, tall and impenetrable. It entrapped her, kept her from reaching any farther than the faces and the voices beside her. She recalled Rom carrying her along the stony terrain. She knew his rumbling voice and his reassuring scent.

She knew when she could no longer keep the walls from closing in.

"Obey the Bearer, Rom. And send Nevia after the Pathwalker. We need him."

Her mind hurtled across all the years when she had held the bloody knife: How many babes had she cut in the Shearing? How many youths had she maimed and left to die after a failed Becoming?

A sacrifice would be required.

Foolish, Nemiah chided herself. This was no sacrifice: she had accomplished nothing and done nothing but fallen into a ditch.

23.
RISING FLAMES

The bed was warm and very soft. Nemiah felt like a splintered stick of wood swaddled in it. Glowing embers in a brazier on the floor painted the room with faint orange light. A feather of smoke carried the sweet-acrid scent of burning herbs.

There shouldn't have been a room or a bed.

A hand moved from her shoulder. She hadn't realized it had been there until it was gone.

"Water, my lady?"

She nodded, heard the sound of earthenware clinking, water pouring. The hand returned, helping her with the cup. A whimper escaped her as she tried to sit up. She realized that the swaddled feeling came from the bandages wrapped tightly around her chest.

"You must move slowly," Rom said. "Nevia was right. Three ribs broken."

The water felt good, although her jaw and face ached drinking it. She held the cup between both hands. In the quiet, Nemiah recalled the moment of flight from the ravine's edge. It had been the incarnation of a nightmare, and yet in the space of that fall, she had known a flash of longing for something that couldn't be hers. She thought of Cael on the tree above her, angry and vulnerable. The demon had spoken of loss. It occurred to her how very closely desire and loss were entwined; neither one could exist without the other. Then, for no reason she could articulate, she thought of Amalia and of Ziabela.

"The Shorn are the embodiment of loss and desire both, Rom. Did you know that?"

Her Arionad met her gaze; his eyes were black hollows in the dim light, his tone uncertain. "Lady?"

"We made it so. When we cut them apart and forced them each to live in a body they weren't meant to have. They lost their greatest desire then: the glory of the sky. Can you see it?"

"I can see it, my lady. But nothing about it will change tonight. Close your eyes now."

341

"Oh, Rom, there are so many parts of the weaving we can no longer see. We need to understand what's been lost before we can turn this Path. When I fell, I felt as if I almost could."

She trailed off breathlessly, seeing the concern in Rom's expression. With a shallow sigh, she leaned back onto the pillow. From somewhere beyond the room rose a roar of laughter. Men's voices, loud with drink.

"Ravia? The garrison?"

"No, my lady. An inn. The Blue Filly. We only made it as far as Nerre."

Nemiah tried to remember her maps. Stretching her thoughts that far hurt her head. The town of Nerre lay within Clan Amerre's territories, a crossroads town a day's ride from the tower at Ravia. Clan Amerre's lands. Abrigado's territory.

"You gave up the wilds for a healer?"

"In part, my lady." Rom hesitated. After a moment, Nemiah saw why.

"Oh. Of course. If Abrigado has already found us, then isolation is no longer a good idea."

Rom nodded grimly. "Busy roads, busy towns offer a kind of protection. In this, I agreed with the lieutenant."

An effortful admission there, but Nemiah heard a level of disapproval in it. *In this . . .* She wasn't sure what that meant. She closed her eyes as another roar of laughter stabbed the quiet.

"The innkeeper's sister left dreamsease for you," Rom said. "She's a fair hand as a healer I'm relieved to say."

"No dreamsease." Walls she could manage, but in this state, Nemiah dared not risk drugs that could thrust her spirit across the Gate. "Where's Leita?"

"She's well. Your injuries upset her, but she's fine now. Rest, Nemiah. Guria says you should be allowed to sleep for at least three days. To let the mind and spirit reunite. It's still many hours until morning."

Nemiah made a face. She didn't intend to delay them for three days, but she wasn't going to have that argument with Rom right now. "What of the Pathwalker? Has Nevia gone after him?"

"All Sevar's men are out. He sent two to Ravia with word for the general."

Was her Arionad evading her? Nemiah couldn't be certain; meanings seemed hard to pin down. "Good. Nadel will send support. More men."

"That's the expectation." Rom brushed strands of hair off her brow. "Nemiah, Captain Kajhar left word for us. His decoy company was attacked north of Nerre." Rom saw her start. "It's all right. None of our people were injured."

She exhaled a prayer of thanks on a careful breath. A woman had gone in her place, purposefully drawing danger to herself. "And the attackers?"

Rom shook his head. "They weren't identified. But it means the decoy is exposed. Kajhar couldn't have known we would stop in Nerre. He was concerned enough to leave word, in case."

"Very well." She closed her eyes again. Then forced herself to open them. Too soon to fade. "We need the Pathwalker, Rom."

"Spare your breath, my lady. Please."

"I'm not going to die from tripping over a tree," she replied irritably.

An anguished chuckle rose from her captain. "Indeed not, but it may very well kill me."

"Riana keep you always, my Arionad." She inhaled. The herbs from the brazier were sweet, something to lighten dreams, she supposed. "I will sleep, I think. If you promise to do so as well."

"Of course, my lady."

Rom would never damage the web with a lie, but she doubted he would do more than drowse in the chair by her bed.

As she drifted back into darkness, she realized something important. "We must claim him, Rom. When they bring in the Pathwalker. Claim him for Riana. Don't let the elder get to him." *Deserter*, Elder Trianor had called the boy. Trianor and Sevar together could destroy him. "Tell the Bearer. She will stand for Jhared Denaban, if I cannot."

"Riana weave you long in the web, my lady," her Arionad said gently. It wasn't agreement. Nemiah breathed in the sweet smoke from the brazier. She would have to deal with that another time.

Somewhere nearby a bird whistled a quiet morning tune. Sunlight splashed over Nemiah's face. She'd slept too long. The morning was well underway; the others would be restless to go on. The Sahistens were waiting. She opened her eyes and looked around the small, bright room. It took her several heartbeats to recall where she was. The shutters of two windows stretched wide upon a sunny day and welcomed the fresh air. Across the room, a woman whistled to herself as she poked through Nemiah's things.

"Is there something you need?"

The woman squeaked and spun to face the bed. "That's a good way to send someone right off this path, Lady."

"What are you doing?"

The woman didn't falter. Her hair was white and clipped short; her thin lips curved downward over a blunt chin, giving her wrinkled face a distinctly testudine appearance. "The Lady Bearer asked me to see to laundering your travel clothes. I noticed a few things that could do with some mending as well." She held up a pale green tunic and flapped the torn sleeve in Nemiah's direction.

"Where are—?"

"The others are in the common room eating. It took your Lady Bearer and his own men before your captain would move from your side. Solid as stone, that one. And dedicated, eh? But he needed to eat. Could use some sleep, too, if you ask me. Though you didn't."

"How long have I—?"

"Been sleeping the better part of three days."

"While I slept, I had such vivid—"

"Dreams. Of course you did. You've had my herbs on the brazier every night, haven't you?"

Nemiah blinked. This brisk old woman was her healer? She wondered whether she should try calling for Rom. But when the woman marched to the bed and poured a cup of water from the pitcher, Nemiah took it.

"I'm Guria. Mistress Fim's sister." The woman reached out familiarly and tilted Nemiah's bruised cheek to the light. "Curse them, Lady. Just curse them all. What have they done with you?"

Nemiah found her chin thoroughly captured in the woman's knobby fingers. "That's no one's fault but my own."

"It's not your fault you're tramping through the wilderness toward violence at the border. What's wrong with the elders, eh? Don't they realize what they have in you? They think it's so smart to risk our Lady? To tear the web apart?"

Nemiah glanced up in surprise. "You're devoted."

The old healer released her. "A childhood spent in my village temple taught me some things about order."

"Then you were an acolyte?"

"Hardly." The woman chuckled. "Riana took me in when my parents died. Before my sister had a place for me here. But that was too long ago to interest anyone." Guria turned to Nemiah's bags and pulled out a pale peach robe. "It's time to remind your spirit how to cooperate with your body, Lady. Before it considers other paths. You will rise now."

"I see you learned the healing arts in the temple."

"Well, not in this inn for sure. Now, you promise me you'll go slowly and I'll help you dress."

Presumptuous and demanding the woman might be, but she had the type of innate authority that didn't brook refusal. To Nemiah's annoyance, she found herself complying.

Guria helped Nemiah to shed her shift and dress in the loose robe that didn't bind her chest or require any acrobatics to don. Then she brushed out the tangles from Nemiah's hair. Her crabbed hands were unexpectedly clever as she plaited the long bright strands into one sleek braid.

"Thank you, Guria. I feel more myself now."

"There's no debt you owe me. Your road is hard enough." The healer straightened her shoulders, as if preparing to say more, but instead she folded her arms over her sunken breasts. "You will try walking later. Just a short turn. And only if it doesn't cause too much pain."

"A short turn? Guria, I must be on my way to the border. We've already delayed too long."

"Not long enough, I'll say. You mustn't go to Sahiste. Do you understand that, Lady?"

"I understand that your devotion is a balm, Madam Healer." Nemiah reached out to touch the woman's arm. A stab of pain in her side ripped her breath away.

The old woman let out a growl. "See now? I have dreamsease for that."

Nemiah shook her head wordlessly.

"Oh, you think so, do you? I know others as stubborn as you. My sister and her daughter's son, for examples. But they aren't the Lady of Avelos, so I let them go ahead and do stupid things as they will." Guria settled Nemiah back against the pillows. "I'll bring more herbs for the brazier. You'll use those."

"Very well." Nemiah closed her eyes and focused on breathing. There was something else she must do. She wasn't certain why she felt the urge to avoid it. It had something to do with Leita's tone when the Pathwalker had marched across the web. There had been fear in the Bearer's voice. It was a reminder of all that Leita had been through, a reminder that she should be safely back in Velantar. Nemiah knew Guria was right about at least one thing: the only two trained Pathwalkers in Avelos should not both be doing stupid things.

"Good morning, Lady."

Nemiah's eyes snapped open. As though her thoughts had summoned the Bearer, Leita stood at the door, one hand on the frame. Rom loomed behind her, tall and gaunt. His black eyes brightened when they landed on Nemiah.

The healer gauged the newcomers with a wicked glower. "A bit of company is acceptable. So long as they don't stir any excitement." With one gnarled hand, she offered Nemiah a graceful spiral. "I'll be back, Lady. Send for me if you need anything before."

"I thank you, Guria."

"No debt, Lady. I've already said it." The woman smacked Rom with a warning glare. "No excitement. Or I'll see you sleep elsewhere."

Nemiah expected her Arionad to answer with a scowl, but he offered the healer the slight curve of his lip that signaled approval. The healer nodded brusquely and disappeared into the hall.

Leita remained at the doorway, her head tilted. Then she smiled, not her old expression that hinted at her power, but a small smile that seemed genuine.

"I'm glad you're awake at last. You're feeling better."

It wasn't a question. Nemiah leaned back, watching the Bearer move slowly, but with confidence, across the room. Not once did she reach for Rom. "I am. What is it you discern?"

"Your breathing is still shallow, but it's regular now. You have less pain."

"I do. I'm sore, but clear of thought. Please sit down."

The Bearer stiffened a little and her smile vanished. There was nothing for it; if Leita could assess Nemiah's breathing from across the room then she would have no trouble catching a change in her tone.

"What's happened?" Nemiah said.

The Bearer bumped against the chair next to the bed and sat. Rom stood beside Nemiah. "People are beginning to run from the border in the face of rumors about a Sahisten military force. Only a few so far. But Nerre's starting to see some of them."

Nemiah frowned. "If Sahiste had truly crossed the border there'd be more than a few."

"That's what we thought. General Nadel's courier arrived last night and confirmed it. There is no military action. Only a small company of Sahistens who applied to enter Ravia."

"For what purpose?"

"To escort us across the Barren. They mean to wait for us."

"Ah. They aren't risking an incident at the border."

"Indeed. They have their own factions who oppose peace," Leita replied. "They're being careful."

Just a day's ride away the Sahistens were waiting. Very soon Nemiah would know whether they meant to negotiate in good faith or only sought a target for their generations of anger. In Velantar, for so many reasons, offering herself for this task had seemed the only sensible course. It was impossible not to wonder now if she had merely fallen victim once more to Abrigado's maneuvering.

"Leita, we are risking too much by both going into Sahiste. Avelos cannot afford to lose her only trained Pathwalkers."

The Bearer's brow lifted above the silk that concealed her hollowed eye sockets. "Does that mean you have decided to stay behind?"

Irony was Leita's key evasive strategy, but Nemiah had learned some things over the past months: how to ignore her taunting, how to change direction and flow around her resistance.

"Where is the other Pathwalker, Leita? The one I tracked."

The Bearer shifted in the chair. "Fled, I'm afraid."

"Fled? Beyond the reach of Forest Guard scouts?"

Leita fluttered a hand nervously. Rom hadn't moved, but Nemiah sensed his tension.

"You will tell her now," he said, softly but with steel in his words.

"It is not your place to command the Bearer, Lord Arionad!"

"Not a command," Rom agreed. "An opportunity. To speak before I do."

Nemiah sagged against the pillows. "Oh Leita, what have you done?"

"What must be done: I told Sevar he should not send anyone after the Pathwalker."

Nemiah darted her gaze from Rom to the Bearer. He had known. He had known when she had awoken in the night and he hadn't told her.

"Captain?"

Her Arionad looked miserable. "You ordered me to obey the Bearer while you were gone, my lady."

She had. Of course she had. She had never imagined this.

"Leita, why? We need to find what we've lost. You tried for so long to make me understand that, and now I do."

"Because it's unwise for us to find him."

"Do you think a Shorn Pathwalker is safer on his own? Wandering with no guide?"

The Bearer sat straighter. "I will not speak on it."

"And if the Lady of Avelos demands that you speak?"

The Bearer lifted her chin. "Then it will be one more way in which I have defied you."

"No," Nemiah answered. "Not today. You will not condemn a man to the possibility of a horrible death and not explain!"

Leita flinched, as though she had touched a kettle that she hadn't expected to be hot. "Nemiah, please. They stole much of my courage when they stole my eyes."

"Leita, you own more courage than—"

"Stop. It makes you feel better to say so. It is not the truth."

Nemiah drew another careful breath. "Leita, you rode out of Velantar in darkness. To confront Sahiste. For the faint hope of conquering the killing winds. Don't disparage that truth. Why do you fear finding the Pathwalker? Why do you think I can't keep him safe?"

Leita wrapped her arms around her chest. The knuckles of her fists were white. "The footsteps you sensed on the Path did not belong to Jhared Denaban."

Stunned, Nemiah didn't remove her gaze from Leita. Fear was in the Bearer's voice, as it had been in the fog in the early morning hours when they had both sensed the Pathwalker tumbling about the web. But Nemiah heard something else this time. "You don't fear *for* the Pathwalker, do you? You fear him."

"I did try to tell you," Leita said.

"That another Pathwalker survives untrained in the wilds? I think not."

Rom had taken a step backward, leaving Leita alone before Nemiah. They had never been comfortable with one another, the Bearer and the Arionad. Rom had no tolerance for the Bearer's defiance and Leita fussed at what she saw as the captain's rigidity. Such petty feuds had no place here, however. Nemiah needed Leita to speak openly. What she must do now to force that to happen would not be easier for Leita with a man looming over her.

"Captain, please leave us."

Rom looked startled, but when he gazed at Nemiah, he nodded and started for the door. "I'll be close, my lady."

When her Arionad had gone, Nemiah turned back to the Bearer. "Who is he, Leita? By your oath to Riana, you will tell me now."

The Bearer pressed the heel of her palm against her brow. She didn't speak. Nemiah waited in silence.

"Do you recall the waylayer who attacked us in the temple's outer courtyard before I left for the north?" Leita asked finally.

Nemiah couldn't forget. The waylayer had thrown a knife in a sacred place, had tried to kill the Lady's servants. Death had passed very close to the Bearer that night. "The unbound Shorn man? You're sure of it?"

"I am." Leita's tone held a challenge inconsistent with the way she huddled against the back of the chair. Nemiah didn't understand the challenge, but she did think she understood the fear.

"You're saying that he wants to hurt not just any of Riana's servants but you specifically. It was what he wanted weeks ago in Velantar?"

"Yes."

"Why you?"

The Bearer sat stiffly. Her head remained lifted, but her features grew increasingly pale.

"Leita?"

"His name is Alende and he remembers the woman who cut him after his failed Becoming. The woman who left him to die."

Nemiah took a shallow breath and let it out. It wasn't so much of a surprise, really. Not when young Shorn men and women had been maimed and abandoned by the temple for more than a century. Something more astonishing existed here than the fact that one man had survived a failed Becoming with anger in his heart. "If retribution is his goal, Leita, why wouldn't you let Sevar bring him in? You would have been safe then. And we might have had a chance to restore some order to his life."

"Nothing will restore him. Retribution is the only thing he recalls when the Paths have muddled everything else in his memory!"

Something seemed wrong about that, about the defensive way Leita sat, and the tension that pulled her low voice skyward.

"You know so much of him?" Nemiah asked. "I didn't feel any such thing."

"What? You touched his Path?" Leita's hands clenched into fists in her lap. Something terrible seemed near to consuming her, though Nemiah couldn't tell if it was fear or fury.

"I only brushed his boundaries," she answered. "I didn't feel hatred overwhelming the man. What I felt most strongly was dread."

"No doubt," Leita snapped. "If he was considering how to attack a company of soldiers."

"Do you truly believe he will act against you?"

"He already has!" The Bearer twitched her head sideways. "I don't understand why you defend him."

"He is a Pathwalker. We might teach him. He might have something to teach us."

"Teach us?" Leita was incredulous.

"About the killing winds, perhaps. Or the unraveling. That is why you wanted Jhared Denaban, isn't it? To send him to Times and Perspectives that you couldn't reach? Leita, you crossed every boundary a Bearer is ever given, all to gain control of a Shorn Pathwalker. Don't act now as if you can't understand what I'm saying."

"Then you care nothing for my fear?"

"If you hadn't followed me, you'd have no reason to fear."

"No reason?" Leita uttered an unsettling laugh. "I have seen the unraveling of Riana's web. Fear has been my shadow for years. Do you not understand that? The only difference now is I no longer have the strength to bear it."

Pain and frustration and Nemiah's own anxieties shredded her patience. "Then why don't you let me help you? Tell me what you are holding back! Why do you think a Shorn Pathwalker is so dangerous that a company of Arionade and Forest Guard cannot protect you?"

Leita shot to her feet, sending the chair flying backward. She stumbled, then caught her balance against the bed. Tears leaked from the corners of her empty eye sockets. "Stop, Nemiah! Stop! Is it your goal to break me again?"

Nemiah gasped at the unexpected blow. "Leita—"

"Perhaps you think this is the way to keep me from traveling to Sahiste. It is not. I'll not be cowed by what was done to me. I'll not be cowed by the journeys of a madman. Nothing he sees is the truth! Nothing!" Leita whipped around and started for the door. Near the center of the room she tripped, caught herself, then halted abruptly, her hands outstretched, her head twisting back and forth.

Nemiah swallowed. "The door is seven paces ahead and two steps to the right."

The Bearer said nothing, only shuffled gingerly across the floor until her hands caught the doorframe.

"Leita, please don't go." Nemiah trailed off. There were words she should say, limits she should enforce upon the Bearer, but watching her friend struggle just to leave the room with her dignity intact, she couldn't say anything.

Leita fumbled until she found the door latch, yanked open the door, and marched out.

Nemiah lay stunned for a strand of heartbeats, then slid herself off the bed. Bending to pull on her boots sent black bees swarming across her field of view. After that, however, walking was not as bad. Her room lay at the end of short, dark hall, lit only by the sunlight bleeding out from her open door and a lamp perched on a side table. Nemiah followed the hall, turning right with it past several closed doors, until she pushed through a gauzy curtain into the common room.

It was a busy place on a sunny afternoon, with most of the tables filled. Clanfolk were taking a midday meal, drinking ale or wine, and sharing the news of the day: apprentices, merchants, a few clanguard. Heads lifted from their cups or bowls as Nemiah entered the room. Curiosity showed in some faces, indifference in others, antipathy in more than a few. Nerre might be a crossroads town, but it belonged to Clan Amerre. Tumal's Legacy governed here.

Nemiah felt exposed and vulnerable. The intricate embroidered spirals on her robe identified her as a priestess for anyone who hadn't yet heard the rumor that the Lady of Avelos was staying at the inn. Glaring at her from a stool near the hearth was a pale-haired young man with eyes as blue as a jaybird and a bruise over his brow. An image of Amalia flashed into Nemiah's thoughts: Amalia surrounded by the people who had gathered to see her die. They had bound her with barbed chains around her neck and wings. The black bees returned to Nemiah's vision.

"Lady, maybe it's best you take a seat, eh?"

Nemiah started, then turned, grateful to find Anzo Nevia at her side. "Yes. Yes, I think so."

The old patrolman led her to a table in the corner of the room and let her slide in first, putting his stocky figure between her and the staring faces. "We're not the favorites here," he murmured as he flagged down a serving girl for a jug of wine.

She nodded. "I thought it was just me they despised. The temple."

"Oh, no. The closer we get to Ravia, the more they hate the Forest Guard."

Nevia poured a cup of wine and handed it to her. She wrapped her fingers around the cool stoneware. "Because of the Shorn soldiers? The Legacy's efforts against them?"

"Only in part." The old soldier shrugged. "Mostly it's because the clans resent how much they rely on us."

The patrolman was astute. The clans railed against Rumar for reducing their autonomy, but in truth, borderlands like those of Clan Amerre needed the better organized, better equipped Forest Guard to protect them.

"You mean the more they fear Sahiste, the more they despise you."

Nevia sipped his own wine and made a face. "Exactly that."

Nemiah nearly dropped her cup onto the table, causing wine to splash over the edge. "The Bearer! She came out shortly before I did. Did you see where she went?"

"Out. With the lieutenant. For a walk, it looked like."

"Oh no." Nemiah turned to scramble out of the booth. The patrolman didn't move. "Soldier, I must go after her. She was . . . not calm when she left me."

He shook his head. "No need. Your captain was not far behind them. Your Arionad might just as well have left it to the lieutenant. I could have told him so, but I wasn't going to start a parade going after them all."

"Lieutenant Sevar is no Arionad," she protested.

"That he's not, but he's a sensible man, and there's more than one way to show devotion."

Nemiah threw a sharp look at the old soldier, uncertain if he meant what she heard.

"And he's seen the Bearer *not calm* before this," Nevia added, offering a little smile and saluting Nemiah with his cup.

She sighed shallowly. *Oh Leita, what are you doing? Have you crossed yet another border?*

"You're not well, Lady. Should I help you back to your room?"

She blinked up at him. Anzo Nevia was solid as an oak door, but short for a man; he didn't tower over her as most did. "I must wait for the Bearer to return, but you needn't feel obligated to stay. Avjay or Rien or one of the other Arionade are here. Captain Rom wouldn't have left otherwise."

The veteran shrugged. "I don't mind staying. The wine isn't very good, but the company outshines anything an unmannered soldier might hope for."

Nemiah smiled in response to his gentle flirting. Most of the women in her Higher Circle would have recoiled at the thought of sitting elbow to elbow with this scarred fighter, a man who lived amid chaos and walked in the shadow of Cael, but Nemiah had not been a pampered daughter of Elders' Circle, given to the temple in return for favors. She had grown up a healer's youngest child on a small farm. And this soldier was more a man of order than most of the council elders she knew.

To her surprise, the old soldier blushed and looked away from her smile.

"I'm sorry, Patrolman. I've offended you."

"Oh no, Lady. That's not it at all. It's your openness, I suppose. The intensity of it. You are a very different person from the Lady Bearer."

Nemiah laughed carefully. "You're not the first to notice."

"But you're strong. As she is."

A droplet of dark wine had spilled and was slowly rolling toward the edge of the table. Nemiah wiped it away with one finger. "I don't know that I could ever match the strength Leita has shown."

"In Sahiste, Lady, you may find out." He said it matter-of-factly, but Nemiah shuddered.

"Patrolman, you've lived on the borders. Hunted Sahistens. Fought them."

"That's right," he replied. "For more than a few years."

"Will you tell me what you know of them?"

He looked at her, tugging at his chin as if at some time he'd worn a beard. "Are you certain, Lady? I'm no scholar or statesman. I've no refined analysis for you."

"What the scholars know they learned mostly from rumor and soldiers' stories. And no statesman has been inside Sahisten borders for more than a century. You're an observant man. Tell me what you've seen in the Sahistens."

"Well, they're clever. Fierce fighters. Dogged. I've known a phalanx of spearmen to cut apart a company twice its size." He trailed off, shaking his head. "You don't want to know these things."

Nemiah took a large swallow of wine and set it down. "Why do they fight? Is it all about retribution? I don't mean the king's reasons for fighting. I mean the reasons of the individual soldiers. Do they hate us as much as . . ."

"As much as we hate them?"

"I suppose that's part of what I'm asking. Yes."

Nevia frowned and leaned back in his seat. "When a man commits to living with the constant threat of death, it's less about who he hates and more about what he desires: for himself or his family. Glory. Land. A road out of servitude. In that, I suspect Sahistens are no different than we are."

"What was it for you, soldier?"

He looked surprised, an expression she didn't think he wore very often. "Escape," he said. "From an unwise marriage and a life trudging behind the back-end of an ox."

Nemiah smiled again. "Not a good fit for you?"

"No. Not the farm or the wife."

"Soldiering seems to have suited you."

"Well enough," he replied. "Whichever way things go in life, you learn to make the best of it or you spend your years unhappy."

"What is it the Sahisten people will find a good fit, do you think? Will it be the sight of an elder and a priestess executed before the palace gates?"

The old soldier sobered and looked down at his wine. Across the room, a serving girl dropped a cup. It bounced over the wooden floor, splashing ale. Someone laughed. Nevia raised his gaze. "Has the Lady Bearer spoken of what happened? In the north?"

Nemiah shifted uncomfortably. "Some of it."

"Then perhaps she told you something of the games the Northerners played with us. How eight or ten of them would bring us all out to watch as they tormented her. They kept us heavily chained, but they always left the lieutenant unbound. Gave him a sense he might have the ability to stop them. Gave him the obligation to try, even though it was impossible. Oh, he always took several of them down before they could control him again, but they would control him in the end. One afternoon, he made it all the way to the Bearer. They made him pay for that, of course."

Anger and horror surged in Nemiah like bile. "I don't understand. The Bearer was a valuable hostage. Sevar as well. Why would the Northerners injure their bargaining tools?"

"Because the Northern prefects are full of rage for what they see as Velantar's abuses. They believe the Northern clans are the most heavily taxed—the silver from their mines, the young men from their families—and the least favored. They've heard their grievances rebuffed and mocked. They've been seething since Rumar took the high chieftain's staff from his father. After all this time, the lieutenant and the Bearer were targets they could reach."

"A Forest Guard officer, the son of an elder, with a priestess from the high temple." Nemiah saw the horrific logic of it. "They were two perfect symbols of Velantar."

Nevia nodded and swallowed the rest of his wine. "The evil men do isn't caused by the side of the border they live on, Lady Nemiah. My years as a scout give me no reason to think Sahistens are any different from us. No doubt some of them want to see you dead. Would happily see us all dead and the serpent flag flying over Avelos. Not all of them feel that way. You and Elder Trianor will have to reach the ones who don't—"

The soldier's attention shifted abruptly. Nemiah followed his gaze toward the entrance, and her heart sped. Rom marched into the common room from the main entryway. He stomped toward the hall that led to her room and halted at the curtain. His back was to her, but his stance was coiled, angry.

Nevia frowned. "Uh, oh."

Nemiah started to rise, but the patrolman caught her arm. "Wait," he muttered.

It happened quickly. Instead of heading toward her room, Rom spun away from the hall. He marched up to a serving girl, grasped one of the cups on her tray, and tossed back the liquor. Then he grabbed another cup and swallowed its contents as well. Only as he dropped several coins onto the girl's tray did his eyes scour the room. When they landed on Nemiah, he froze. His sealed and steely expression plummeted into chagrin. Dust stained the right side of his coat. A bright red bruise blossomed over the left side of his cheek and jaw.

"He's been attacked," Nemiah whispered, fear washing through her. "Where's the Bearer?"

Rom moved toward her like a man being dragged.

Nevia stood. "Your return is well timed, Captain. The Lady was just saying she could use a rest. Would you help me escort her back to her room?" The soldier's pleasant tone never faltered, but he shook his head once, stiffly, at Rom.

The Arionad hesitated, glanced at Nemiah. She wasn't certain what Nevia had sensed, but she trusted him. She sagged in her seat. It wasn't necessary to feign weariness.

"Thank you, Patrolman. I'm afraid I've overestimated the extent of my recovery." She held out her hand. Rom reached to support her.

"Of course, my lady."

Nevia moved from the bench to let her out, casting his gaze across the room as he did so. As Nemiah came to her feet, she discovered that she genuinely needed Rom's support. The wine had been a mistake.

The gazes of a dozen strangers followed the three of them as they disappeared past the curtain. Elder Trianor caught them in the passageway as he stepped from his room.

"What's happened?"

"You'd better come along and find out," Nevia answered.

The elder fell in beside them. Nemiah was grateful to reach her room and hear the door shut and latch.

"Why?" she demanded of the old patrolman.

"Too many unfriendly ears," he replied. "In particular, that tall boy with eyes the color of a jaybird and a bump over his brow. He never stopped staring at you. Whatever this is, he didn't need to hear it."

Nemiah nodded and threw her gaze at Rom. "Was it Legacy who did this? Where's Leita? Why isn't she with you?"

Her Arionad paced across the room, only turning to face her when he came up against the opposite wall. "It wasn't the Legacy," he said, annunciating carefully around his swollen jaw. "The Bearer is safe. She isn't with me because she sent me away."

"If it wasn't the Legacy, then who . . . ?" Nemiah hesitated, not wanting to say what she guessed. The tensions between the two men had been arrowing toward disaster since the Forest Guard had joined them. When she glanced at Nevia beside her, he looked as if he'd rather be back in the common room with another cup of wine.

"Lieutenant did it," the old soldier said.

Nemiah took a step toward her Arionad, her heart banging against her chest. "Rom? Sevar *attacked* you?"

"Yes. He—"

"No, it's too much! An act of violence against Riana! I'll send to General Nadel for another escort."

"Nemiah, wait. Sevar did right. What I would have done."

She halted halfway across the room. "Explain!"

"When the Bearer left with the lieutenant, she was visibly upset. She needed a guard, and I didn't want to cause her more distress. I followed them."

"You mean you didn't want her to refuse your escort, so you snuck after her." It was perhaps unfairly harsh, but Nemiah had no more tolerance for evasions.

Rom didn't flinch. "I didn't want to disrupt the weaving merely by doing my duty, my lady.

"The Bearer and Sevar wandered, talking. They ended up in the market. Not an easy place to be today. It's noisy and crowded. Pickpockets taking advantage of the chaos. Even from a distance, it was obvious the Bearer was nervous, and the lieutenant put himself . . . too close. I wanted to reassure her that I was near. I managed to come up behind her, but the crowd was pressing. I reached out and set my hand on her shoulder." Rom shook his head, remorse in his black gaze. "It frightened her. Badly. She screamed."

"Causing the lieutenant to swing around with a fast right fist," Nevia said.

"Very fast," Rom observed, touching his swollen cheek with the back of his hand.

Nevia's expression lost all levity. "You're lucky he didn't pull his knife."

"Oh, he did. As it happens, I can also be fast."

"Goddess, Rom!"

After talking with Nevia about his time in the hands of the Northerners, Nemiah could guess where Sevar's thoughts had gone in that instant when the Bearer had screamed. Could guess that he would defend her at all costs, but the cost had nearly been the life of another devoted man. A man whose absence she couldn't even fathom. Nemiah pressed a hand to her mouth, aware how close they had come to a terrible, tragic Path.

"When the Bearer realized what had happened, she ordered me back to you, my lady."

"Where did they go?" Nevia asked.

"When I left them, they were on the road heading toward the west gate. Toward the forest."

"Why would the lieutenant take her there?" the elder asked.

The forest. A place beyond the walls. Leita had always found order in the wild spaces. Nemiah had begun to understand more deeply just why. In the wilds—among the trees, within the currents of the rivers, in the heart of a storm—order entwined with chaos. Just the type of place the Bearer would go to pray.

"I rather suspect *she* was taking *him,*" Nemiah replied.

Rom's gaze was dark. He would have had a similar thought. The others remained quiet; the elder looked thoughtful, the old soldier unfazed.

Ah, Leita. Riana return order to your way.

Behind Nemiah, a quick knock sounded and the door opened. Guria marched in, a tray in her hands that held a bowl of water, clean rags, and a cheesecloth bag filled and tied. The scent of oat-mash followed her into the room.

"Lady, that's quite enough time out of bed. And here you all are keeping this good captain telling stories, when he needs something on that jaw. He's going to have trouble talking at all tomorrow."

"How did you know the captain was injured, Madam Healer?" The chill in Elder Trianor's voice pulled Nemiah's gaze to him.

"You mean how did anyone in a room full of people notice a tall, armed man in white with a blackening bruise across his face?"

"Yes, that's exactly what I mean," the elder persisted. "Specifically, who told you?"

The healer snuffed as she herded Rom into the chair by the bed and set down her tray. "My niece's boy. Patience of a squirrel. But a good enough set of eyes."

"A young man of Clan Amerre with nothing to do but drink on a market day?"

The healer smacked Elder Trianor with her testudine expression. "Oh, ho! Are you volunteering to make a diligent man of my self-indulgent nephew?"

"No." The elder's features remained frozen. "You don't care to entrust a young man's moral guidance to me, Madam."

Nemiah winced at the bitterness in Tierzen's words. "My thanks to your observant nephew," she said quickly, "And to you, Guria. If you come back later, we can speak the devotion together."

Guria gave her a sidelong look. "I understand, my lady. You intend to continue being foolish."

"Indeed," Nemiah said, mildly enough, but with a hint that the healer was pressing a boundary.

The old woman looked a little penitent. "I hold close to her order, my lady. I'll be back later with herbs for the fire. You should sleep tonight."

"It's appreciated, Guria."

When the old woman left the room, Nemiah leaned back against the door and felt her body's stabbing opposition.

"It would be wise if we leave sooner rather than later," Elder Trianor said.

"Does this have something to do with your concern about who's been observing us?" Nemiah asked.

"I needed to know. I recognized two of the men who came into the inn this morning. One of them was a Teacher in Clan Amerre for a time. The other is a cousin of the prefect."

"Legacy men," Rom said.

"More than that. Both are supporters of Abrigado."

"They heard we were here," Nevia said. "The healer's right: it's not as though we're hard to spot."

Rom nodded. "And Abrigado would have had people watching the road."

Nemiah hadn't taken her eyes from the elder. She knew him for a deliberate, reflective man, but what she saw now was cynical and grim. "You spoke with them, Tierzen?"

"I wanted to assess their purpose. They were pleased to wish me well on my way to Sahiste."

"We needn't fear Abrigado on his own lands, surely," Nemiah said. "Suspicion would fall on him if we were attacked."

"Unless he no longer cares. Perhaps he's counting on the people to see any attack on us as just. The prefect's cousin was rather explicit about the kind of justice he expected the Sahistens to mete out. To me. And to you, Lady."

The others went silent. A high-pitched keening rang in Nemiah's ears. Amalia had been bound with barbed chains and pushed off the wall by her own people.

It staggered Nemiah to realize her countrymen hated her enough to want her dead. The crushing weight of that hatred could smother her courage, smother her ability even to stand upright and look another person in the eye. She couldn't help but think of Amalia. Then she thought of Ziabela and Jhared Denaban and the little boy imprisoned in Velantar and realized something it had taken her far too long see: the Shorn faced such hatred each day of their lives.

She wiped the sweat from her palms and drew a measured breath. "When will the general's reinforcements arrive?"

"Late tonight or early tomorrow," Nevia answered.

The idea of mounting a horse or bouncing along the rutted roads in a cart made Nemiah want to weep, but she wrapped her arms around her broken ribs and stood straighter. It was pain, nothing more, nothing at all compared to what Ziabela had suffered. She hoped for what might come about in Sahiste, for the story she might finally tell. Then she hoped she wasn't a fool for imagining the response might be different just because she crossed a border.

"Good," she answered finally. "We'll leave with them as soon as they're ready to depart."

They all looked at her with varying expressions of doubt or concern, but no one spoke against her. The elder rubbed a hand across his eyes and nodded. Since the start of the journey, he had been the only one who had shown any genuine excitement about meeting the Sahistens. Nothing of excitement showed in him now.

"Here's a presumption," Nevia offered. "I'd say it's best for all to stay close to the inn until we leave."

Elder Trianor looked at the soldier. "To avoid potential accidents in a crowded market?"

"Or something of the sort. Does the lieutenant know about your visitors?"

"Not yet. I'll speak with him when he returns."

"Right. Then I'd best find where Esran and the others have gotten to. A bit more of a presence wouldn't hurt, eh?"

Nevia offered Nemiah a nod before leaving them. The elder departed as well, and Rom went away to address his men before they heard some twisted rumor of what had happened to him.

Left on her own, Nemiah tried to make use of the waiting time. From her bags, she drew out the documents Rumar had given her: a map of Sahiste, copies of letters from Prince Ashani, a report on important Sahisten trade routes. She frowned at the meager stock of information, then pulled it closer. She had read the documents more than once already, but perhaps something new would come to her. Sahiste's primary imports and exports revealed something about the needs and desires of the people. The heir's letters offered clues as to the goals of the man.

Sunlight climbed through the window and tiptoed across the floor as she worked. Leita didn't return. Nemiah restrained the urge to send the Arionade after her again. With Sevar beside her, there was no need to worry about the Bearer's physical safety, and whatever other damage might occur would be of Leita's own choosing.

Perhaps predictably, Nemiah's thoughts slipped from Leita and Sevar in the forest to memories of a recent night with an unexpected man and an unexpected blessing. Nemiah had also walked outside the walls that night, breaking through boundaries long held as inviolable. She didn't know yet what that would mean for Avelos or for herself. Although those old boundaries had constrained her, for so many years they had also kept her safe. Crossing them had led her here and was taking her into Sahiste.

There was a knock at the door. Nemiah looked up from the desk to find that only a sliver of pale light remained near the bed. At her answer, Rom entered.

"I thought to find you resting, Lady."

"I've already wasted too much time resting. Have General Nadel's men arrived?"

"Not yet." Her Arionad came to her and offered his spiral. "Nemiah, you were patient with me when I was helpless. Be patient with yourself now. Once we are on the road again, there will be no time for rest."

He drew back the blanket on the bed and waited, his habitual scowl made fiercer by the mottled bruises across his cheek and jaw. With a sigh, Nemiah relented. Once she had carefully stretched out on the mattress and closed her eyes, she couldn't deny it felt good to lie still. Rom sat beside her on the floor.

"I will need to find him, Rom. Despite the Bearer's fear. Despite Abrigado. We need the Pathwalker."

Her Arionad stroked her hair with callused fingers. "If I could be to you what Ambri was to Lady Amalia, you would not need to chase after a Shorn man."

She opened her eyes. "No, Rom. Do not regret what you are to me. Not ever. What Ambri did—"

He stopped her with a finger to her lips. "I do not regret, Nemiah. Not in the way you mean. But I should have been able to cross the Gate with you. To keep you safe on every Path."

"If you had been born a Pathwalker, you would not have survived to become my Arionad."

He gazed down at her, his expression contemplative. "Will we change that?"

"I mean to, Rom. It is past time."

"Then you will."

They remained quiet as the light continued to fade. Finally, Rom stirred from her bedside. "I must see to the evening watch."

She blinked at him in the dusk. "Will you return?"

"Always while I live, Nemiah. You have heard my oath."

"It is dear to me, Captain Rom."

He kissed her brow, a kind of tenderness he hadn't shown since before she had offered a blessing to the high chieftain.

Sometime later, she was distantly aware of the sound of the door creaking open. Rom returning. She waited to hear his step, his voice. Did not. A scent like incense filled the room. Guria. It had to be the healer at the brazier.

"Thank you," Nemiah whispered.

"No debt, my lady," murmured a disembodied voice.

Twilight silvered the inner courtyard of the high temple. Nemiah sat on a blanket under the dead Ularian tree, while Zia played an ancient melody on her flute. Listening to the music as it flitted on the evening air, peace seemed a possibility. The Path would turn; the old stories would be retold. Nemiah didn't recognize the melody Zia played. She wondered whose story it preserved. Did Zia know? Did anyone know? Lord Tumal had destroyed the written records of the Avelune, but some songs survived. If Avelos were to recapture her lost history, musicians would become especially important in the years ahead.

"You can't stay to listen to the music, Nemiah. The Ularian tree is on fire."

Nemiah glanced up. Rom loomed over her. "The tree is long dead, my Arionad. Riana's Chosen spirit is gone. Sit with me here and learn from the music."

Rom caught her arm as if to pull her to her feet. "Nemiah, it is not yet time to tell the old stories, not even through music. The fire will only spread. You must rise now. Hurry, my heart."

"Rom?"

"I have loved you, my lady. Now you must go. Take the music with you. Quickly!"

"Quickly! It's spreading! Fire in the inn!"

Rom shook her. Nemiah coughed. She opened her eyes to a hazy half-darkness. Something wasn't right; she needed to find Ziabela. Ziabela could explain the song. "Leave me be. The stories must be told!"

The pressure on her arm increased abruptly, a rough jerk that shot pain through her chest. "Wake up, my lady! We need to get out!" The man was yelling now. Not Rom. Somewhere far away the air roared. Nemiah let herself be dragged half-upright. The blankets tangled around her legs. She had been sitting on a blanket in the temple courtyard. The air in her lungs burned. The Ularian tree was burning. All the Shorn would burn. She could not allow the Path to end this way.

She tried to kick herself free of the blankets. "Which way?"

"The window," gasped the man.

As he said it, a rush of cool air struck Nemiah's face. A figure outside the casement was flinging back the shutters, another man, shorter, stocky.

"Nevia?"

The figure climbed into the room, leaned one shoulder into Nemiah's middle, and slung her over his shoulder. The fierce pressure against her ribs caused her to gasp, which started her coughing harder.

"Out," growled the first man. "Hurry! The door is going to give."

As her rescuers leaped out of the window, it was all Nemiah could do to claim a few shallow breaths. The rough cloth of a shirt scratched her cheek. Smoke and the tang of a stranger's sweat filled her nose.

The dead Ularian tree in the courtyard. Ziabela had been playing the ancient songs.

Orange light threw shadows that writhed over the ground and across the legs running in and out of Nemiah's field of vision. Cries for water rang into the night. Somewhere horses squealed. A child cried.

"What have you done?" It was the first man's question. A tall, lanky stranger, yet somehow familiar. His voice raged like the flames. "She slept! They all did. There was no need of fire."

"That wasn't going to get us far outside the inn, was it?" snapped the one who carried Nemiah. "No! Don't stare over your shoulder, fool. You'll draw attention. If we're doing this, then help me with the girl!"

"We're doing it. It's necessary." A hand fell heavily on Nemiah's back. "Past the stables. Then we're clear."

"You did choose the right one this time?" A derisive tone from Nemiah's bearer.

"Shut up, Mer. I couldn't have known they'd do that. Just go."

The pair didn't slow. Cold streamed over Nemiah, stripping away some of the wool that clogged her thoughts. Her head throbbed in time to the stranger's heavy stride.

"Put me down. You can put me down now."

"You're awake," the tall one observed. "Be still, my lady. You're free. No need to fear."

"I must find Leita. And Rom." Her throat stung. She choked on the taste of smoke.

"Don't try to talk. Explanations will come when you're well away from here. When you're safe."

Safe? The word didn't match anything Nemiah felt. "Where are my Arionade? The Forest Guard?"

"All in the yard by now, I'm sure. No doubt looking for you."

The fire from her nightmares crackled cheerfully behind her. People were still screaming. She'd been speaking with Rom about Pathwalkers, about helplessness. She didn't remember the Bearer returning to the room. Didn't remember where

Rom had gone. He had spoken to her of music. "I'll come back to add herbs to the brazier," Guria had said. Herbs. Dreamsease? Or something even more potent? Nemiah had been deeply unconscious. Abruptly she understood that this wasn't a rescue.

Bundled out of the building in only her shift, Nemiah didn't have even her belt knife for a weapon. She clutched the man's shirt collar, wondering if she owned the strength to throttle him. "You're Abrigado's men."

Sharp laughter caused the man's shoulder to bounce beneath her. "Told you she'd be disappointed. It's not too late to take her to them. The Legacy'd pay us well."

"Shut your mouth, Mer!" The hand on Nemiah's back patted her soothingly. "No, my lady. The Legacy doesn't move me. I'm just a man doing what he must for Riana. For Avelos."

"What you must?"

"I know the truth, Lady. I know our blasphemous high chieftain forced you to accept the role of emissary to the treacherous Sahistens. He means you to be a sacrifice. To die in that goddessless land. They told me."

"Who told you?"

"Someone who will make sure you stay out of Sahiste."

"No! I must speak with the Sahistens. Amalia's story must be told!"

"Hush now, my lady. You're befuddled by the smoke."

Nemiah kicked against her assailant's abdomen. He grunted once, then simply gripped her tighter, one hand wrapped around her waist. Was it possible they weren't Legacy? If so, who could this *someone* be? Where was the Bearer? *Oh Leita, forgive me.* Nemiah said a prayer, then had to focus on drawing breath as the man's shoulder dug into her injured side.

The noise and running receded. The narrow lanes grew empty and still. Everyone had rushed to the inn; such a fire could threaten the entire town. They reached the gate. No guards. The men went through. Farmyards gave way quickly to trees. "This way," said the tall one, leading them off the road. Gradually, a forest closed around them, blocking the pale light of the stars. The forest where Leita had gone with Sevar this afternoon. Had Riana been with them then? Was she here now? The men didn't falter in the dark. They must have been following a trail. After only a short time, they stopped, and without warning, her captor hoisted Nemiah into the air. Cold whisked around her body. Then she was in a controlled fall and landing on wood.

"Steady there, my lady. In you go," said the tall one.

A horse nickered. It was a cart.

Nemiah struggled to her knees. "Stop this! By Riana's order, you must take me back!"

"Shut up, woman, and get *down*!"

She didn't see the hand that flew at her, but the slap knocked her flat onto the cart bottom. Through the ringing in her head, she heard another smack, of fist against flesh, then a hissed command.

"Don't *ever* lay a hand to her again or I'll string you up in these trees! Understand?"

"Idiot! If someone sees her, we'll both be swinging."

"I swear it, Mer. By the Lady's Order. Keep your hands off."

The stocky man gave an ugly grunt. "My mistake, Kelprin. I didn't realize she was meant only for you."

"Get off the ground," the tall one said, disgust clear in his voice. "Let's move."

Quieter cursing followed, and the cart squeaked as the one called Mer stepped up to the driver's bench. Nemiah lay on her side, her cheek burning and her ribs a throbbing anguish. She wondered if she could throw herself out of the cart and run. Then the tall one, Kelprin, climbed into the back with her. He dug into a bag in the corner of the cart and lifted something out.

"I'm sorry, my lady. You may curse me now. I know you don't understand. I only hope when your mind has cleared and they have you safe away, you will."

The rope hung loose in his grip. With a rush of panic, Nemiah rolled away from him, hit the far edge of the cart, and heaved herself upright. She was halfway over the side when he grabbed her from behind. She threw her head backward, felt her skull meet his face. He sucked a breath, but didn't lose his hold on her. With one hand he caught her wrists; with the other, he flung several coils of rope around them, and pulled the rope tight. Once her hands were bound, he tied her ankles as well. Then he pulled a blanket around her shoulders and patted her gently before settling into the corner beside her.

"Try to sleep," he said, infuriatingly calm. "We have some ways to go."

A whip cracked the air and the horse leaped forward against the traces. Nemiah slid backward as the cart lurched into motion. She tried to sit up. The cart hit a rut, tossing her flat again. She didn't rise. Fury and dread churned inside her. Where were the others now? Had they been drugged as well, leaving them unconscious as the flames spread? Nemiah squeezed her eyes closed. No. It wouldn't do to think like that. Rom would have been on watch or one of his men. They would have roused the others. But why hadn't they reached her room? Was it possible they'd been attacked? When the survivors emerged, would they come after her or assume she had perished in the flames?

Disorder threatened to undo her. She reached for prayers as the world suddenly fragmented. A voice cried out in protest, her own, as new Paths exploded into being and her own Path vanished. Only chaos existed around her. Her heart pounded out grief, a loss too large to comprehend. Awareness was slipping away.

Somewhere in that fog, Ziabela still played her flute. Rom sat beside Nemiah, listening. The Ularian tree creaked and swayed as fire danced in its dead branches.

24.

Lost and Wandering

Jhared tread water in a stormy sea, battling to keep his head above the waves. They crashed over him, one after another, in no rhythm, waves shaped from fragments of the Paths: pasts, presents, and futures. Wars were held in those waves, times of plague and drought. He saw his ancestors, experienced their glory, shared their loss and pain. He saw Katian, Kest, and the others across myriad moments, but no moment was complete; no Path had a beginning or an end. The waves crushed him and slapped him under with the sensations and experiences of a thousand thousand people in a thousand thousand instants, until he was certain he would drown. Only some core of defiance kept him treading.

Despite the skills he believed he had gained practicing with Maya, nothing he tried returned him to stable land: not reciting his litany of names, not building an image of locked walls, not tracking his own trail back to his Path. The longer the sea tossed him, the more he felt the wrongness of the place. It was a violation even more insidious than the tangle, for the tangle had remained connected to the immense pattern of the infinite web. From the tangle, Jhared had managed to travel back to a place of order. Within this flood, he perceived no pattern. The images, thoughts, and sensations that created the sea seemed to be cut apart from the weaving entirely. With no pattern and no weaving, he could not conceive how to track his way back to his own present. He swam and struggled, but knew himself to be sinking.

As the fragments from other Paths washed away the memories of his own, he clung to a sense of himself by singing. The old songs from his mother came to him first, then songs he had learned from Zia. When he had exhausted those, he drew out the melodies he had heard among the unbound. He was urgently humming "Alende's Flight," grasping at memories of the unbound Shorn man who had called him brother, when something changed. The waves spat him back upon the shore.

Jhared opened his eyes to a space that did not threaten to drown him. The chamber was large and airy. A grey bird with an orange beak whistled and chattered from its silver cage beside the bed. The place felt familiar, though not truly his. He sat upright, hissing at the pain in his head and chest. The waves fell further into the distance, clearing his vision of the present. It was the pain that had dragged him free. His own memories trickled back to him as he investigated his injuries: his ribs had been bound, a bandage wrapped the knuckles of his right hand, and at the back of his head, a row of tiny stitches closed a gash. He remembered General Hrvan, the Avelune, and his battle with them. Had the Avelune been the ones to care for him? Slivers of light slid through the closed shutters into the dusky room. Daylight. But how many days had slipped by while he fought the waves? On this Path, he could hear the sound of the true surf breaking rhythmically against the shore. He rolled to his feet, stumbled to the door, and grasped for the latch. Locked. Not a surprise perhaps, but no less disconcerting for that. He pounded on the door. The effort brought grey motes swarming into his vision. He leaned against the wall for support. His head throbbed in time with his heartbeat.

On the other side of the door, voices rose, then the latch clicked and the door opened slowly. Two of the general's guards entered, with Vyla behind them. Jhared lifted his gaze. The men spoke to one another in Sonan. Vyla snapped at one of them to run and tell the general the soldier was awake.

Her voice struck Jhared like cold rain. "You should not be moving about. The marble was not kind to you."

"Ah, right. It was the marble that was unkind." He pushed himself away from the wall.

At her order, the second guard hastened to help him. He waved the man away, moving carefully toward a seat on the bed. "Where is Maya? What have they done with her?"

"Your Riza is Avelun. She has nothing to fear. You needn't waste your energy worrying for *her*."

Jhared heard her implication. "I don't understand. If the general has the Avelun, why am I an interesting captive?"

"You are no captive," she snapped. "The general has placed a watch at your door for your own safety. Avelune are not quick to forgive, and you have given them a reason to seek reprisal."

Jhared gripped the edge of the bed in an attempt to steady the room. "Do they seek reprisal on all who wish to leave their company or only on Shorn soldiers they despise?"

The guard said something in Sonan that Jhared didn't catch. Vyla made a harsh, sudden sound that wasn't quite a laugh.

"What did he say?"

"Something very foolish," she replied. "I am surprised you didn't understand it. I thought one fool would recognize another."

Stomping across the room to the desk, she poured a cup of water from a ewer and offered it to Jhared. He caught her scent, warm and earthy, as she bent close. The grey bird squawked and hopped from side to side on its perch.

"You were an honored guest of the general. He wished nothing but for you to be welcomed. In return, you have brought violence into his house and threatened his closest allies."

"*That* was foolish," Jhared admitted, distracted by a wave that lapped against his consciousness.

"Then why?" she demanded.

Avelune tumbled from the sky into the fiery forest below. Jhared coughed as smoke filled his lungs. He braced himself, hands on knees, as though it might keep him above the waves. "The Paths here are broken. Do you know that?"

She straightened abruptly. "What do you mean?"

Through the smoke and flames, he saw that her gaze had sharpened. "I cannot find any pattern among them. I cannot find the weaving."

Vyla's response fell from a long distance. "Some are saying that your scars and your upbringing have weakened your mind. That your jealousy of the Avelune has driven you mad. Are you going to prove them right, Jhared Denaban?"

For another moment, he was pinned beneath the glare of a fierce-featured woman who wanted him to understand something important. The next moment, broken wings and burning trees filled his senses.

Awareness never left him; it was only that the moments of which he was aware continuously shifted. When he recognized his own place, he did what he could to bind himself there. The door to his chamber remained secured and watched. When Jhared asked to speak with General Hrvan, the guards responded with patient nods and reassurances in broken Velos that the general had been to see him several times. However, they always demonstrated a willingness to send one of the servant boys running with another message. If Jhared had ever remained present long enough to hear a response, he had no memory of it.

In the moments when he existed where he belonged, he spent time peering through the book of map notes, which had been left among his things. He talked with the grey bird, a cheerful creature called Blik, who chattered at him in Sonan and asked repeatedly for seeds. With his anger and yearning, he tied little threads between himself and his present, as though they could hold him steady. When the waves effortlessly snapped the threads and sent him floundering, he resorted to pain. The Avelune had left him no weapons. He tried the fine, hard edge of the desk at first, until the back of his left hand was swollen and striped with bruises to match the right, and he realized that breaking bones would not serve him. Instead, he scrabbled at the unfinished wood inside a drawer until he could rip free a long, sharp splinter. When he jabbed the splinter beneath his fingernails, the sharp, clean pain pushed back the waves and left him standing on his own Path for a time.

The changes that occurred in his room during the periods of his absence told him how very much he was drifting. Bowls of food appeared and disappeared on the desk by the window. Sometimes he smelled it and knew he should eat, though the strong spices turned his stomach. The necessary pot in the corner of the room was regularly emptied and the grey bird fed. One afternoon, he returned to his own Path to discover the stitches in his scalp had been removed. The thought of lying helpless while strangers who loathed him explored his unconscious body simultaneously shamed and enraged him. He wondered if Maya had been there. He searched his memories. He could have said that Maya was often with him—her presence full of concern—but he had no notion whether what he remembered came from one of the thousands of broken Paths among the waves or whether it was a Path he had actually walked.

The guards did not speak of Maya. Jhared feared what the Avelune had done to her after he had fallen, but a nagging part of him feared they hadn't needed to do anything at all. They were her own people, a community she had never expected to find. She longed for them and for flight more than anything else in life. She didn't know they hated her with nearly as much passion as they despised him. Or did they hate her? He paused, uncertain. The conversation he had overheard between Drijan and the unseen woman might have occurred on his Path or on any other fragment within the roiling sea. He had attacked the Avelune, after all. In response, they had set a guard on the door, but they had also given him a comfortable chamber, food, and gentle care. If the malice he perceived had come from another Path, then he might have been the agent of his own captivity.

And yet, and yet . . . The woman's voice had warned the others to treat him carefully. They sought to maintain Maya's good will. His thoughts churned. All his life Avelos had stamped into him the belief that his kind were treacherous and cruel. He knew better now, but did those years of immersion in the evils of the Avelune mean he could not see them any other way? The waves buffeted him, making each possibility equally vivid. Just recognizing his own place grew difficult. Sometimes he couldn't imagine how the locked room and the grey bird could possibly have anything to do with him, a soldier of Avelos. Other times he had trouble remembering anything of his life beyond that room. He needed a way to lift himself above the waves before he drowned. He needed to find Maya.

Shards of orange evening light cut through the shutters and sliced across the rug in the center of the room. With a fingernail, Jhared gouged another crescent into the corner of the desk. Ten gouges so far, though he had no way to know how many evenings he had missed. Although his injuries had mostly healed, he felt listless and vague. He had been submerged by so many bits of lives and so many other people's emotions that he couldn't always recall which emotion he should be feeling for himself. He was tired. He had lived more lifetimes than he could count. Sometimes the thought of pursuing his own meaningless Path seemed pointless.

Murmured voices rose in the hall, moving closer, along with the scent of food. Jhared stirred from his dull wondering. Food didn't interest him: it was merely something to note. The voices didn't concern him, either. Most Paths had nothing at all to do with him. Only long-trained habit made him listen and try to translate the Sonan.

"Yah, he is Ravaged but he knows of Avelos, doesn't he? Important things, maybe. Too bad this wasting sickness. A bad end for a soldier. The general is disappointed."

A higher, younger voice: *"In the kitchen, Selvka takes bets on who Riza Mayavana will go to—"*

"Hush. Not in the halls, stupid child."

"I bet on Riv Kest." Unrepentant enthusiasm trilled in the boy's tone.

"Say that where Riza Katian can hear and you will eat glass with your porridge."

The mention of Maya arrowed past Jhared's apathy. The voices reached the door. He thrust the waves back with a vicious thump of his fist against his still-healing ribs, then lurched to his feet. In three great strides, he crossed the room and dropped onto the bed just as the bolt scraped and the door opened. Through slitted eyelids, he saw a guard and the kitchen boy enter. The guard cast a casual glance in his direction then followed the boy, who began to clear the untouched food and replace it with fresh. The guard continued chatting in Sonan with the boy, more kitchen gossip, it seemed. They spoke freely, not even bothering to whisper. Jhared realized with dismay just how accustomed they were to his unresponsiveness. There was the sound of chewing as the guard took a bite of something on the tray, followed by the boy's mild protest.

Silently, Jhared rolled off the bed and slipped through the doorway. He was already hurrying down the gallery when the guard called out.

"Up? You're up? Wait! Where are you going?"

Jhared mustered a smile, but he didn't stop. "For a short walk, *se'yo*. I mean to speak with Riza Mayavana."

"We will send. The Riza will come."

"Don't trouble yourself. I'll find her." With a flick of his fingers in the Sonan salute, he continued on.

A confused pause registered behind him, then steps pursuing. Not running, but moving quickly. As he had hoped, the guard appeared reluctant to start a tussle in the hall. Jhared peered through open doors, slipping soundlessly toward the stairs and down into the courtyard.

"Come back, you!" the guard hissed. "My hide for this."

Others were beginning to appear on the gallery and in the courtyard, staring at Jhared and whispering behind their hands. Someone bumped him. Jhared turned, prepared for a struggle, only to spy a sandy-haired boy made awkward with the weight of yoked buckets dangling from his shoulders. The buckets swung wildly as the youth backed away, mumbling apologies in Sonan. Jhared saw seed scatter across the floor and caught the scent of fish. Something familiar nudged him—the seed, the buckets, the boy. He shook his head. Of course it was familiar: the sea had shown him hundreds of sandy-haired boys. On this Path, the youth stared at him, his eyes going wide, then he lumbered off in the other direction, head down and shoulders hunched.

Jhared increased his pace into the courtyard and along the portico. The double-doored entrance that led from the house into the yard loomed before him. Escape. He hesitated, but only for an instant. Maya must hear what he knew of the Avelune. He wouldn't leave without her.

A heavy door banged open at the end of the portico. Late sunlight streamed through the windows, silhouetting the stocky frame of the general and the three men who hovered behind him. Drijan's bronze wings glinted. Jhared didn't recognize the other two men.

"What will you do about General Lovron?" a well-built, white-haired man asked. "We need the border guards with us."

General Hrvan glanced over his shoulder at the speaker. "Lovron will do what his *Simata'yo* orders him to do."

"Lovron has more influence with the *Simata'yo* than you credit him."

General Hrvan only gave a dismissive snort and turned back toward the portico. As his gaze landed on Jhared, his features lifted with pleasure.

"At last, he is awake!"

"I must speak with Riza Mayavana," Jhared growled. "Where is she?"

Pleasure slid from the general's face. "Your devotion to your Riza is commendable, soldier. You had best reconsider your tone."

Years of Forest Guard training stopped Jhared short. The general's words were that of a superior officer to a subordinate, and there were rules to such interactions. With a deep breath, he unclenched his fists.

"Forgive me, General Hrvan. As you say, my duty is to my Riza. When I have been bound against my will and kept from her side, I can only fear for her well-being."

Jhared's guard came running up, his face a rictus of dismay as he saluted the general. He began speaking in pressured Sonan, but Hrvan ordered him silent.

"Bound against your will?" Drijan spat, taking a stiff step forward. "You attacked us! We offered you an honored place and you leaped upon us like a savage animal."

The third man with the general scowled at the interruption. He was a peacock of middling height and narrow build. His hair and beard were elegantly arranged and oiled. The silk coat that covered his soft frame fluttered as he moved, pretty to look at and entirely impractical. In contrast, his white-haired, weathered companion, the one who had asked about the border guards, was dressed in sturdy garments that had seen hard use. Jhared recognized a seasoned soldier.

"It is never wise to put two cocks in the same cage," the general said to Jhared, subduing Drijan with a warning gaze. "Knowing Kest as I do, I should not have let you meet him unprepared. I imagine you were baited. Your Riza is not in the house at the moment, soldier, but I invite you to talk with us while we await her return. This gentleman," he pointed to the peacock, "is Secretary Stoja, internal advisor to our august *Simata'yo*. And this is Captain Odemir. As it happens, we were just worrying over your fate."

"Sir, my fate is of little enough concern to me. It is hard to fathom that it's of concern to the leaders of Sona."

The one named Odemir gave a bluff laugh and spoke in startlingly superb Velos. "Hrvan, you needn't be diplomatic with this one. It's just as well you tell him that some of us think him a spy."

The secretary frowned and asked something in a petulant voice. He spoke in Sonan, not comprehending or perhaps refusing to speak Velos.

General Hrvan continued to consider Jhared. "A spy would hardly be likely to draw attention to himself with an impulsive attack on his hosts, Captain. What he is, I suspect, is young and distracted by desires he hasn't yet satisfied or adequately curbed."

Jhared ground his jaws together, wishing he needn't *curb* his desire to hit the man. That his and Maya's presence had been made known to the *Simata'yo* was unlikely to mean anything to their benefit. Not if labels such as spy were being bandied about. Maya represented a different type of threat. They would see her as a spark to light Avelonian rage. Vyla had thought she would ask for an army.

"I am no spy," Jhared said evenly. "I will answer any questions put to me. However, I would first know where my Riza has gone."

"Out with Moravel!" Drijan huffed, giving Jhared a look of contempt. "Testing her wings."

Testing her wings. Flying. Jhared had long imagined he would be there when Maya touched the sky, but she was with her own kind now.

"Mayavana is one of us," Drijan echoed, as though reading Jhared's thoughts. "Leave her be. You can do nothing but confuse her."

"I am sworn to her protection. We are bound!"

"Her pity for you is what has bound her! And a desperate need to cling to anything reminiscent of her heritage. Now that she is home, you no longer serve any purpose."

"Enough, Drijan," the general interrupted. "This soldier is a consequence of what you disdain, not its cause."

The general considered Jhared again, steepling his fingers over his belt. "I am not without sympathy for your situation, Jhared Denaban. I understand Mayavana will be joining her own people and will no longer need your services. As one of the Ravaged trained by the Forest Guard, you would be an asset to the *Simata'yo*. I would offer you a position of regard."

The general looked too smug for any claim of sympathy to be meaningful. Jhared didn't know what this man and his *Simata'yo* were seeking. Why did Hrvan court a Shorn man when he sheltered Avelune? Why did Drijan claim to want Maya among them when his manner toward her dripped with scorn? Jhared shook his head to clear it. He thought he had left such intrigues behind.

"Drijan! Why have you let that gelded hofja *join you? He'll learn too much!"*

Jhared gasped. The voice at the edge of his Path belonged to the same woman who had spoken with Drijan on the rooftop.

"Not now!" Drijan begged.

"Don't tell me 'not now,' boy. Not after the debacle in the garden."

"Does my offer startle you so?"

Jhared forced some part of his awareness back to the general, even as his sense of the woman sharpened: a face composed of boney planes; short, blunt wings the color of steel; a spirit filled with vitriol. He gripped the doorframe so hard it cut into his fingers.

"I can consider no offer until I hear from my Riza that I have been released from her service," he managed.

"Hrvan, you waste your time," Captain Odemir muttered. "The necessary hatred has been beaten out of him."

"Oh, I think not, Captain. Look at him there, wishing to strike someone, even now. The hatred is in him. It need only be given better direction."

"Refuse to speak with the general further in the presence of this Ravaged. Do it now!"

"I cannot. General Hrvan won't let me push so far. He wants the soldier."

"Drijan, you are the Storyteller of the Avelune. Surely you can tell one story to which he will listen." A groan of disgust from the woman. *"Gods cursed me the day we lost Rathael."*

The woman's derision had an edge to it that Jhared recognized. He didn't understand why at first, and then he did.

"She's your Teacher!"

Drijan started, whipping his gaze toward Jhared. The others stared.

"Curse your incompetence. You left your Path open!"

"I did not!"

Jhared tried to guard himself as the woman's presence arrowed toward him. He knew this kind of invasion, had experienced it for the first time when he was but a child, on the day his mother went to the pyre.

"Who do you think you are, little soldier, little scout? Do you think one tainted by the hands of Avelos owns the skill to sneak up on me?"

"I did not seek you," Jhared replied, holding tight to his thoughts. *"You are walking through my Path. Who are you and why have you breached the doors to my moments?"*

"If you are threatened, little soldier, why don't you close those doors? Or perhaps you need my help. Shall I rip away your memories of me when I leave?"

"It is a poor Teacher who can only move others with threats. Almost I could pity Drijan."

Cold, ironic laughter crackled in his head. *"Teacher? Me?"*

He would swear he had never heard that laughter before, yet it too reminded him of another's laughter, another's contempt. He might have been a boy again, wrapping his arms around his head until his Teachers stopped flogging him and left him alone with his shame.

She must have caught his thought, for without warning, she tore through his memories, upending a cascade of images of his own life: from the brief, sweet time before he knew what it meant to be Shorn, to his first years with Elder Trianor's family, to the time beyond his mother's death.

"You served a purpose once, little scout, but that time is coming to an end!"

Instinct told him to run, to get clear of Drijan, of the general, of the house. He spun around and flung himself down the portico. Red-gold light from the open shutters formed a square before the manor entrance. He could make it.

"Oh, I don't think so," the woman growled.

Abruptly, his limbs stopped obeying him. His feet stumbled on the smooth flagstones. Fear, deep and primal, shot through him as his control of his own body was stolen away. His knees struck the ground and he tipped forward. Inside of him, eyes of lead bored through all the fortifications he urgently tried to build. Helpless, he lay exposed to that gaze and all its loathing.

"For the love of all the gods," the general swore, "what did your people do to him, Drijan? You knew I wanted him undamaged."

"He was damaged long before he came to us," the Avelun replied. "How Mayavana ever tolerated such a creature I cannot imagine."

Jhared was clutching his thoughts of Maya when he left the Path entirely.

The stable on the south side of *Kaleb Uto* offered an aisle of neat loose boxes that opened onto a paddock close to the orchards, home for the carriage mules, the general's neat-footed stallion, and several compact geldings with carved crescent faces. As the sun slid toward the ocean, the beasts grazed placidly. Only the stallion raised his head, snorting and blowing at the angry squeals that echoed from within the barn.

Maya stood motionless, one pace back from the stall door, watching Seravina lash out against her new surroundings and anyone who came too close. A stable hand had already skittered away, nursing a bruised shin and a bleeding arm.

A man's footsteps crunched on the gravel just outside the door to the yard. A voice asked a question of the stable hand. Maya didn't hear the girl's answer over the mare's calls, but she heard the same footsteps enter the barn.

"Hello, Riza. Katian told me your horse had arrived. I hoped I might find you here."

Maya didn't turn, but only gave a cool nod by way of greeting. The man's expression, one of tentative pleasure, grew more reserved. "Forgive me for intruding. Perhaps you were expecting someone else?"

"Your brother has no claim on me," Maya said, watching the mare. A pause, then she added, "And neither do you."

Moravel accepted her words without comment. For a man accustomed to standing second all his life, it was at least a chance. Seravina turned a baleful eye on him and returned to kicking the wall. The sound of splintering wood rang in the barn. Moravel took a step back. "A rare large beast, she is. And demon spirited. You truly *ride* her?"

"No. Not me. She has no regard for me."

"Nor for any of us, I think." The red-wing cleared his throat. "How does your guard fare?"

Maya shook her head. "The same."

"I am sorry to hear it."

The words sounded genuine, a surprise that. He waited without pressing her. Perhaps he understood the need for grief to have its own space. Perhaps he only feared that she would send him away if he spoke again.

"I am useless," she said eventually. "I cannot move beyond the Gate to reach him. I've always had little skill. Now I have nothing. Jhared is the true Traveler."

Quiet fell between them, leaving only the rustle of straw and the arrhythmic thud of Seravina's hooves against the wood.

"Would you like for me to try?" the red-wing asked.

It was enough to startle her from her remote posture. She turned and met Moravel's gaze. "You would offer that kindness? After he attacked you?"

"He had cause."

Maya's wings stopped their fanning. Her eyes narrowed. "What do you mean?"

"I mean that he . . ." Moravel glanced down at his boots and drew a breath. A handsome man when judged on his own merits; clever, it seemed, and with a capacity for generosity. But the hesitance in the younger red-wing said he had been judged beside his brother for too long. It led him to doubt his own decisions. "I mean that the Paths had confused him. He imagined there was cause, seeing danger where none existed."

"Oh. I feared that was so." Maya's wings drooped. "Ilaye has come with me every morning. She says she senses no sign of him, and she is the strongest among you."

Moravel was still. "She told you that?"

"Is it not true?"

"No, no. It is the precise truth. Ilaye has never been shy about her talent."

"She's been quite attentive," Maya added, two short furrows deepening between her brows. "I believe this is the first time she's let me out of her sight since he fell."

A silence. The red-wing rustled his feathers as if troubled, but again he hesitated. "I am sorry for what you've lost," he said finally.

Maya nodded and turned away.

This time Moravel reached out a hand and touched her shoulder. "Would you allow me to share something with you?" he asked. "Something that might at least draw your mind away from grief for a time?"

"I can't imagine what that might be."

"Can't you? Together, Mayavana, you and I might touch the clouds."

Her breath caught. Her gaze flew to his. "You've come to teach me to fly? Now?"

"Tell me, do you know the purpose of the Becoming? Before High Chieftain Tumal turned the holy rite into a tool to break our people?"

"It was the rite of first flight."

"That is only the surface of what it was meant to be. Do you know what the Becoming truly tested?"

She shook her head. Seravina squealed.

"Our ability to feed and control desire."

Maya drew back, but not enough to dislodge his hand from her shoulder. "I don't understand."

"I think you do."

Moravel slid his hand from her shoulder to the leading edge of her right wing. She stiffened slightly, but he didn't release her. Instead, gradually, he drew his fingers along her gleaming white covert feathers, first along one wing and then the other, until both strained above her shoulders.

"To propel ourselves into the mountain heights, to soar over the crags, to give our bodies to the winds. That is the heart of yearning for our kind. Flight is the perfect manifestation of desire: it is both the striving and the fulfillment. I think you understand the connection."

"I do," she said, a little breathlessly.

Hesitantly, Moravel ran the back of his hand down the length of her wings. Her feathers flexed and straightened under the light pressure. She sucked an audible breath and tried to step away. He shifted to face her.

"Please don't run. What I am saying is not new to you. You have seen what happens when desire is thwarted. We are creatures of the wind, Mayavana, meant to caress the skies. Meant to move the thermals to our need. You have seen the destruction that results when we are chained to the ground."

Meant to move the thermals to our need.

She had been so young that she had barely climbed to her feet the first time she had dreamed of herself soaring, dreamed herself commanding the breeze that supported her body and filled her wings. To hear the reality of that dream made her shiver. Jhared saw it too, realized he should have seen it long ago. How perfect it was, the connection between his body and the glorious sky: the way he yearned for the clouds; the way they responded to his yearning. He was born to command the sky. How beautiful and how terrible. Every part of him cried out at the futility of that power.

Mayavana's expression twitched, as though hearing someone call her name, but Moravel's hand was on her feathers and she had just understood a terrible truth: "Gods of seas and skies, Moravel. You're talking about the killing winds."

"Another crime against Avelos that they can be named so. They were never meant to kill. Nothing in the archive speaks of such a horror. Abuse and desperation breed violence. It is ever so."

"Oh no. Oh, Moravel." Anguish thickened Maya's voice. "Are you are saying—"

"The winds that now kill come from the strength that once gave us flight. Yes, Mayavana."

She let out an inarticulate groan.

He drew her closer. "I know. You must not blame yourself for what you destroyed. It was only justice. You could never have known you held the key."

"What? No. You misunderstand!" She straightened out of his arms, the absurdity clouding her sage gaze. "Moravel, if the killing winds are meant to fuel flight, I cannot—"

"Wait. Please. Before you protest. Mayavana, you are needed here."

She trembled. "Please don't say it."

"I must. My people have lost the knowledge to let us transform desire into flight. We can no longer open ourselves to call the winds. With your help, however, we will."

"You mean you do not fly," she said brokenly.

"We do not command the winds in any form," he said, so softly she had to lean closer to hear him. "We do not fly. But that will no longer be so. We have waited so long for one of you to find us."

"One of us?"

"Of course you have guessed that others like you must exist. How else could it be that the winds have appeared all over Avelos? For so long, our guides have been looking for you among the Paths."

"But they could not find us. Moravel, you have it wrong."

"Don't, Mayavana. Now that you are here, I can show you how to loose your desires, if you will show me how to transform them." He closed his eyes, his hands still on her shoulders. His scarlet wings mantled. "Please. We cannot continue to live chained. You must show us, Mayavana. Show me. Together we will brush the sky."

As she turned to face him, a stream of sunlight struck her brilliant white primaries, turning them to gold. Seravina kicked the stall door and squealed.

Moravel slid his hand into Maya's. His voice turned rough with need. "Come to the beach with me. Come to the open skies."

Hurt and anger and relentless loneliness flooded through Jhared. He struggled to escape the scene, railing against what must surely happen in the next moment.

Born from the strength of his own emotion or merely by the chance that is always a part of chaos, a wave rose up and closed over his head before he could watch Mayavana accept Moravel's embrace.

Jhared sucked a smothering breath and flung a knot of blankets off his face. He rolled onto his back, staring at the ceiling and breathing hard. It was his chamber, his prison. From which Path, he could not yet be sure. Light from the single lamp licked at the darkness. The cool damp air and silence in the halls said it was somewhere near the heart of the night. It might be the place where he belonged or merely some close version of it. He no longer cared. He lay still, listening to the ocean crashing against the rocks, trying not to imagine Maya in Moravel's arms. Failing.

Testing her wings, Drijan had said. Maya had won the knowledge she had sought for so long: the killing winds and winds of flight arose from the same source. Desire and flight, two parts of the same experience. Across the room came a soft shift of air. Someone nearby. Jhared leaped upright, and just as swiftly sank back down. The woman sitting beside the desk was not the one he longed to see.

"You sing in your sleep," Vyla said quietly.

Jhared blinked. "So you've come in the dark to ask for a concert?"

"It was a Sonan lullaby," she murmured. "I didn't know a soldier could touch something so delicate without crushing it. It was . . . lovely."

He closed his eyes, thinking of the last time he had sung that song, with Maya leaning sleepily against him.

"You have been gone two days, but the kitchen tells me it has been much longer since you truly ate. I brought you something you might find palatable."

"Food is not what I need," he said flatly.

"Food is at least one of the things you need. You are growing weak. You know it, or I suspect you would have escaped us two days ago."

About the last, she was wrong. It would not have mattered how fit he was; the woman who had entered his Path had stolen his ability to act for himself. She had invaded his moment so deeply, in essence, for a handful of moments, she had become him. He wrenched himself upright, sickened by the memory. "Why are you here?"

"You have questions you wish answered," Vyla said. "If I stay and answer them, will you eat?" She clasped her small hands in her lap, as precise and decorous as he had yet seen her.

He glanced at the bowl on the desk, heaped with carrots and chunks of meat. In spite of his claim, his stomach rumbled. "Any question?"

"Any question that does not compromise my service to General Hrvan."

"Do the Avelune fly?"

She pointed to the bowl. "Try the meat."

He rose from the bed, ignoring the snow that filled his vision, and spooned a bite into his mouth. It held no foreign spice, but might have been something Neta cooked. The warmth made its way to his stomach. "Well?"

Vyla broke off a chunk of bread and offered it to him. "They do not."

He took the bread. "Why not? What happened?"

"I don't know. The last Avelun to fly died long before I was born."

"Does that mean there is something deformed about them? Are they ill?"

Exasperation pinched her expression. "Do you understand they do not talk to me? That I am of no more significance than a goat or a pack mule in their eyes?"

"You don't deny you know the answer, though. The general allows you access to the archive, doesn't he? Is the answer there? Among the histories?"

Her expression crackled with frost. "Why does it matter? Flight has no part in your life."

"It bears on what the Avelune want of my Riza."

"Is she your Riza, Jhared Denaban?"

A muscle in his back twitched. "I believe the arrangement was for you to answer my questions."

She smiled, a small, cool curl of her lip. "Yes. I have seen the writings from Avelos in the archive. Some letters and treatises came with the Exiled and are ancient. They speak of flight as a captain might record the movements of his army or a pilgrim might log her journey. None detail *how* to fly. Why would they? No treatise exists on how to walk or run."

That made him pause. She was right. The great historians did not record the details of daily life. No need and no glory existed in such a work. He put down a rush of disappointment. "Do the records imply that the Avelune must call the winds to lift their wings?"

She twisted her head so that her fine braids slid over her shoulder. "You overheard someone speaking. Drijan or Katian?"

The waves threatened around him again. He slapped the back of his hand against the pointed corner of the table near the bed. The bird squawked. "No."

Vyla sat forward, as though she meant to ask another question, then paused. "The Avelune believe Riza Mayavana will give them the knowledge they lack. That is the reason they woo her."

The words destroyed any hope he had of discarding what he had witnessed between Maya and Moravel. He kept a tight rein on his response. There were other things he needed to learn—about Drijan's Teacher, about the *Simata'yo*—but the image of Moravel gathering Maya into his arms wouldn't leave him.

"You should know that Riza Mayavana has come to you daily," Vyla murmured, as if she realized she had cut him and wished to make amends. He wondered why she bothered.

"With an Avelun named Ilaye?"

"Then you do remember."

"In a sense. I thought I was locked away from the Avelune for my own safety. That they would seek retribution."

He thought Vyla colored, but the single tongue of light in the room made it difficult to be certain. "Ilaye seems to have grown attached to your Riza. They are often together. It is good if she is seen to take your part. She is powerful among her people. One of their guides. Nemaye's daughter."

Ilaye. Nemaye. Names reserved for the Aye, Riana's Chosen. The Avelune guides were not just leaders; the names proclaimed them related to the immortal. Vyla's expression, however, did not suggest awe.

"You don't like her."

"It is not my place to like her. Only to respect her."

Similar words to those Falucha had expressed about the Bird Walkers. Jhared thought of the guarded way Falucha had dealt with Maya. She had tended the estate's birds since she was a girl, had made regular deliveries here. *Be wary of the general's birds.* Belatedly he understood that she had been trying to warn him of the Avelune. The Avelune, who wanted Maya to teach them how to call the winds. The irony could make a man laugh.

As Vyla reached for another piece of bread, the light shone through the fabric of her gown. It had been woven of such fine stuff that it floated over her frame, outlining the shape of her breasts, the curve of her waist. She was tall for an unfeathered woman, but not as tall as Maya, and where Maya was lean and lithe from years spent surviving in the wilds, Vyla was soft and full as a ripe berry.

Jhared swallowed, his long muddled senses abruptly clearing. He marveled at the range of forms beauty could take. With some effort, he stilled his untoward reaction, claimed the remainder of the bread, and strode to the other side of the room, where he leaned against a window casement.

"Tell me more about the archive."

"What do you care to know?" Her voice turned mocking. "Shall I tell you of the heroics of Alende Isan and the wisdom of Riana's Chosen? Of Tavia's beauty or the courage of Fariven? Of the wars between the first clans? Scrolls exist on all of these subjects."

"And on the travels of the Avelune? Those sacred journeys the guides take along Paths not yet seen or those long gone?"

Vyla appeared unfazed by the question. "I've seen some such records."

Hope existed in that. Jhared pressed his back against the casement until the sharp stone cut the fog away once more. "Do you know why I keep slipping away?"

She hesitated longer this time.

"Do not say the Avelune do not speak of such things with you. You've already talked once of the rumors." He paused, a new thought coming to him. "Will they hurt you if they know you have shared these things with me?"

"They would not trouble themselves. You do not matter to them any more than I do."

He did laugh then, wondering what they would do when they realized the Ravaged soldier, whose wings had been sacrificed on Riana's altar, was the one who could draw the winds. "Tell me the rumors."

"All the household knows the manor is special," she said with a shrug. "They say it is an unavoidable consequence of the Avelune's travels. They call it a crossroads."

"It is not special," Jhared growled. "It is broken. A sea of ragged moments roiling with no pattern. I would call it evil if it were not entirely void of intent. It is pure disorder."

Vyla raised one dubious brow. "They say you are weak-minded and will go mad."

"I am not mad," he replied. "The wrongness here is not me. Not this time. It is—" He stopped and looked at her more closely, her diaphanous gown, her sideways glances. "I see. They say I'll go mad, but General Hrvan intends to use me for at least one purpose before I do. He sent you to me."

"Yes. The general asked me to come."

Jhared folded his arms across his chest. "Then I fear you have interrupted your night to no purpose. I will sing you another ballad, if you like. Otherwise, you should leave."

As she stood, her gown shifted over her hips with a soft rustle. "Why do you believe that I did not also elect to be here?"

It did not surprise him that she would want her presence to be seen as a thing she chose. Women were surely no different from men in their need to perceive some control over their own fates. He understood that need, understood that it offered an opportunity. "What I believe matters very little. This place is drowning me. I'll be lost soon. Unless you help me."

She straightened. "If I do, will you give me what I seek?"

"Vyla, why does the general need me when he harbors a community of Avelune?"

Beware the general's birds.

"Do not be fooled, Jhared. His 'community of Avelune,' as you say, is very jealous of its bloodlines. They would sooner throw themselves from a cliff than breed with one of the unfeathered. Some years ago, when I was too young to fully understand what it meant, one of their kind dared to dally with a Sonan girl. I saw something of the grief that came of it. They shunned the man as soiled. He will never now be accepted by one of his own. Though their women rarely quicken, they would allow the line to die out before tainting themselves."

Jhared shook his head. "That's not all to it. There's more than Avelune arrogance in this. The general wants an Avelun he can control, doesn't he? A symbol of status he does not have to hide. Vyla, does he intend to challenge the *Simata'yo*?"

She startled. "My general is devoted to our honorable leader!"

"Yet the child is only one piece. He has plans to do with Maya, with me. What am I missing?"

She didn't answer, but went very still.

"Very well," Jhared sighed. "We won't play that game. Answer another question instead. Why could *you* wish such a thing?"

Her expression changed. Something fierce drove her across the room, causing her gown to flutter in a short train behind her. "What I wish is to have charge of my own life," she said, glaring up at him. "I am the bastard of a bastard with the blood of a raping Amurian soldier in my veins. If not for the general, I would be on the docks selling whatever parts of myself others might buy. Even with his protection, my life is not my own. If I bear an Avelun, I will be lifted free of shame."

Jhared's heart turned over in his chest. He knew the pain of being tainted. He knew the longing to escape from shame. But she was asking for a life. A life to be surrendered to a man who thought of others only in terms of how he might use them. Another reason prevented Jhared from stepping forward as well, a reason he felt but could not pull cleanly from among the years of Paths he had witnessed.

Her blue-grey gaze, defensive and demanding, held his. "Does it disgust you? That I bear Amurian blood? Is that why you won't touch me?"

"No. Vyla, no. I see your strength and beauty."

"Don't!" She flung out a hand like an icy wall between them. "What I am asking of you does not require lies. This is not a seduction."

Despite her bold words, she was trembling. Jhared's anger surged toward the general, who had sent the woman to him; toward the heartless Avelune, who held themselves above him; and toward Mayavana, who had turned to Moravel's embrace and abandoned him.

"You must go, Vyla."

"I cannot. This is a chance I will not have again."

"I will not be a part of Hrvan's plotting."

She smiled sadly. "It speaks to your strength of will that you think it possible to avoid such a fate. It is not."

"Of course it is. You are alone with me, and I am a soldier. Do you think the decision to do what I've been trained to do would be so difficult?"

Her smile this time was tight and bitter. "Threats will not win you an escape. The general has plenty of pretty bastards to take my place. He will not grieve if I should die."

Cerulean flashed across Jhared's vision. He slammed his hand against the casement and came back to himself clutching the wall. Vyla's hand was caressing his cheek, her fingers gentle and cool. He caught her earthy scent, like the forest after a rain.

"Do this thing for me and I will find a way to help you," she murmured. "You could be free of this place."

"What if the child is not Avelun?" he said, hating himself for what it meant that he could ask. "There is no certainty."

"Then another bastard will be born in Sona. The general would keep it, as he kept me."

Jhared's heart raced. He closed his eyes.

"There is no wrong in this," she whispered.

"Yes. There is."

But he set one hand on her shoulder and lifted the other to stroke her sun-touched hair. She stood stiff and unblenching under his scrutiny. Of their own accord, his fingers dropped to explore the shape of her. His hands shook. He had only ever touched one woman so intimately; he tried not to think of that woman now. There were reasons not to do this . . . or there once had been, on some other Path. Vyla pressed closer. As the little acorn-caps of her nipples hardened against Jhared's palms, his breath caught. Need pounded through him. With gritted teeth, he held himself in check. He could do what she asked of him—his body ached for it—but the price would be high. Too high? The seas tossed about him. A relentless sadness closed around his heart. From the fragment of a distant Path, a child wailed.

He pulled back with a groan. "I cannot. I cannot sacrifice another life for my own."

"Do not see it so." Her cool hands settled lightly on his chest. "With this gift, you would redeem me."

If he hesitated, her moth-light touch would drive him beyond rational thought. Gently, he removed her hands and took a step backward. "Neither of us will escape our shame by creating a new life to bear the burden."

Vyla wrenched her gaze upward to meet his, and Jhared froze. While floating within the sea of Paths, he had lived the emotions of thousands of others over thousands of moments. Looking at Vyla now, he discovered those experiences had given him unanticipated understanding. He saw her longing to rise above her shame, to live a life of her own choosing; he saw her pride in the skills she had honed, her anger at those who called her tainted, and the insidious doubt that they were right. Then he caught a different kind of longing, one he had not guessed: a soul-deep need to love, without caution, without limit, and without hiding her heart. A child was not merely a tool to alter her position, but a gift she would treasure and adore. He, who had never dared to consider the possibility of offspring, might give her that treasure, and in exchange, she might return to him his sanity.

"Vyla . . ." His voice broke.

Empathy shone in her expression. "I do not ask you to lay your heart before me, Jhared Denaban. It is safe. I cannot touch what is meant for another."

She leaned the length of her body against his and drew his head down to her kiss. The world swung, and every reason to restrain himself, the possibility of harm or horror, became too distant to ever have been real.

Nothing mocking or triumphant hid in her eyes when she led him to the bed, when she slipped free of her gown and reached for his belt. He was awkward at the start, too aware of the strangeness of his role, of his inexperience and rising desire. But Avelos had taught him to bridle his body's demands, and Maya had shown him how to give and take pleasure from that. A lifetime of curbing his desire now heightened it: an irony he was certain would mortify his Teachers. He slid his hands over the taut silk of Vyla's belly, the unstrung bows of her muscled thighs, her smooth, flawless back. He savored the ache of his own need, restraining himself, and her as well. When she reached for him with increasing desperation, he caught her hands and drew them away. He had not lied earlier: he found beauty in her determination, in her blue-grey eyes, and her long, strong limbs. He immersed himself in the scent and feel of her. It was a kind of escape, he knew, but he allowed himself that. Time enough to mourn later. Attuned to her subtle signals, he caught the quick gathering of tension in her body but thought it something different before her nails raked across his cheek.

He jerked upright. "Have I hurt you? Forgive me!"

"I should have known you meant to deny me!" she hissed. "That you would only torment and humiliate me. Have you judged my body unworthy to receive the seed of the Avelune?"

"Vyla!" Her self-hatred chilled him. He knew it too well. Jhared leaned forward, his heart drumming, his body exposed. With one deft motion, he caught her wrist and dragged her close, until he could press her hand to his back. Her face trembled inches from his; her spine bowed to keep from falling against him. He saw and felt her shock as her fingers splayed across his scars.

"I am *not* Avelun."

She swallowed, her expression anguished. "But you refuse me."

"What do you—? Oh." He released her and sat back, cursing. "You expected ravishment, didn't you? You expected I would be a brute and be done with it."

Her gaze held his accusingly. "I know what the general's men say of the Forest Guard. How you are bred with a need for violence. I have heard what Riza Ilaye says about the ways Avelonian women are used. Moments ago, did you not threaten my life?"

Jhared cursed again. "And believing me capable of such things, still you offered yourself to me?" He scrubbed a hand across his face. "Vyla, you asked for something sacred. Though we do not share our hearts, this moment need not be ugly or empty. Would you not have a measure of grace for yourself? For the future?"

"Grace is not something I have been permitted," she said coldly.

"You are worthy of it." Jhared shook his head. "Riza, I am honored and terrified by what you have allowed me, but if you have changed your mind, I beg you to go."

She remained motionless. Her gaze softened, though he did not mistake it for surrender. "I have not changed my mind."

He nodded, his throat having tightened around any more articulate response. He forced himself to wait for her. Only when she once more drew close did he lightly kiss her face, then her throat. Gradually, he moved his lips lower and then lower again, until she relaxed against him with a sweet, unsculpted sigh.

"I am sorry," she breathed. "You are nothing they have named you."

He answered in a manner that he hoped made his forgiveness clear.

When he finally drew her to him and they fit themselves together as roots to earth, he thought they had created, if not love or grace, at least a moment in which shame was beaten back. In the culmination of their striving, she became his anchor, clasping him to his Path. He gave what she asked of him, but not more. She was not the one for whom he was willing to lose himself, and danger existed in releasing all control. He remembered that at the last. He did not allow his mind to soar toward the past or what might become of the future, but he did let go of his fear. The blue flames did not rise to greet him and the winds did not lift from the skies.

After, Vyla surprised him by lingering. She lay on her side with one hand pressed against his heart, her head tucked under his chin. And then she surprised him again.

"Are you here only for your Riza, Jhared Denaban, or did you come to Saimbor for reasons of your own?"

She might have been probing for information for the general, but the question felt as if it arose from someplace more vulnerable. Jhared stroked one of her braids, thinking of his hopes at the start of his journey, thinking of the killing winds. "I wished to study in the archive. To learn something of my people, and of the world outside of Avelos."

"I would have thought by now you'd learned enough about your people."

He went still, his hand entwined in her hair.

She bowed her head against his chest. "I am sorry. That was cruel."

He put his arm around her and said nothing.

"Riza Mayavana does care for you," she murmured into the quiet. "You need not doubt it."

"And yet?" he whispered.

"Yet she is Avelun. She will not remain with you."

"Do you mean that as an invitation?" he asked.

One silky shoulder lifted. "You have heard the general's offer."

"I have. Vyla, whatever I might make of my future, it won't include serving as a mercenary. I don't belong under the command of a Sonan general."

She propped herself on one elbow, her eyes crinkled with bemusement. "Jhared, you don't belong anywhere. You are like me. *Hofja.* The best for which we dare hope is a position of respect. We will never belong or be loved."

"*Hofja,*" he echoed grimly, recalling the venom with which he had twice heard the word spoken.

"You asked me once what it means, but I think perhaps you know already. It is not a pretty name. It is 'split-souled' or 'half-souled.' For those of us born on the border of two worlds without fitting into either."

He exhaled heavily. "Yes. I know what that means."

"Consider what you have been offered. The general is a fair man. You would be treated according to your talents." Gently, she disengaged from him. "I must go now. Before the watch changes."

A sudden impulse caused him to stop her as she rose. "Vyla, we will go our own directions. I know you don't seek my interference. But will you tell me?" With a reverent hand, he touched her belly.

Her lips formed a soft, startled circle. "Yes. I . . . yes."

She bent and pressed her lips against his brow. "Whatever road you choose, Jhared Denaban, you should sing more often. And not only in the dark."

When she had slipped out, he did not sleep, unwilling to waste the precious moments of clear thought for however long they might last. Instead, he considered the pieces of knowledge Vyla had confirmed for him. It kept him from contemplating the consequences of what he had just done and the words she had spoken at the end. The Avelune of Sona longed for flight as deeply as Mayavana, but the general who sheltered them wanted something different. Hrvan had lifted himself out of two generations of Amurian exploitation. When the pride of Sona had been destroyed and nothing remained in the country worth the trouble of maintaining an occupying force, the Amurian army had withdrawn without sanction. It was Hrvan with his *Simata'yo* who had set about to rebuild Saimbor from the ashes. He had constructed a library from the stolen treasures of the surrounding nations. He was rebuilding the canals and seeking avenues for trade. What General Hrvan sought was something more than status.

The man who holds a winged creature holds a portion of the power of the sky.

A man did not grasp at power for its own sake. Always some need lay beneath ambition. The Avelune yearned for flight. They expected Maya to provide them with it. What could the general desire for his small, angry country but retribution and ascendency?

The general was not likely acting alone; Vyla had not been dissembling when she spoke of Hrvan's loyalty. This must be a strategy of the *Simata'yo* and the Avelune as well. With the power of the winds, the Avelune could touch the skies again and Amuria could be forced to endure the suffering she had once inflicted upon Sona.

Jhared realized he had caught at one truth in the weaving. As he reached for the next part of the pattern, where it hovered just out of sight, a fleeting sense of blunt, steel-colored wings caused his heart to jump. Before he could try to guard himself, a wave of shattered Paths smashed down upon his awareness.

25.

BROTHERS AND SISTERS

He did not see Vyla again. Years passed on some Paths. On his own Path, he could not be certain. Two weeks? A moon? He wondered if he had misjudged Vyla or whether she had found no way to help him after all. His disappointment floated like jetsam among waves that grew more savage. They kept him diving after thoughts that eeled away before he could organize them. At some point, he grew aware of Avelune speaking to him, but he had seen thousands of Avelune over centuries and knew no reason to respond to these. One of them laughed. There were three: a fair woman with wings the color of daisies, a big man with wings of heart's blood, and a shorter, older woman with a toast-colored birthmark on her cheek and wings of speckled brown.

A mild sting caught his attention, a distant sensation like a riding whip smacked across a gloved palm. A second sting followed. Then a pair of lovely green eyes glared at him and more words drowned among the waves.

He shook his head. "If you mean those questions for me, my darling, I'm afraid I've lost the thread of this story. You have no relevance here." The words came from his throat in a voice he knew but could not claim. He felt a third sting.

"Katian, stop. You will gain nothing from him that way. Kest, sit him down." They were the older woman's commands, clear and untouched by the waves.

The floor tilted. Jhared realized he was sitting when he looked down and saw a spider fleeing its web to skitter across his fingers onto the arm of a chair. He watched the little weaver with interest. Leita had been a weaver once.

"Look at me, boy. I'm going to—"

The fishing boats set out with the tide in a fog-blurred dawn. The bright-eyed girl waved goodbye to her father and uncle, her bare toes curling against the wet sand. The soldiers were waiting when she returned to the house. She knew one of them. He had spoken to her at the well, looked at her. She knew herself to be strong and smart, had been named so with pride by her brothers, but there were four men and they were armed.

No one else heard the girl scream as the copper-haired babe came into the world. Another girl-child who could know nothing but sadness. Bring nothing but sadness. A mother's grieving hands picked up the infant, certain what must be done. At the bottom of the cliffs, the ocean pounded against the rocks. She might find freedom there. For the babe. For herself. She steeled herself to welcome it. Would have done so without hesitation. The strong arms that prevented her from jumping were not cruel ones this time.

Another Path, another mother mourning. Her babe had left the weaving before he ever drew a breath. Damp strands of hair the color of earth, like his mother's, clung to his cold brow. Beneath closed lids, his eyes might have been green, like his father's. He might have been a Traveler, if the poison hadn't wrenched him too soon from the womb—

"Be still."

Jhared's thoughts struck something solid, a rock thrust up from the thrashing waves. Thankfully, he grasped it. The rock lifted him above the broken moments. He found himself sitting on the chair near the desk. A wren of a woman stood before him, one hand pressed against his brow, her eyes half closed and her speckled wings drooping. She was the rock.

"I see you," he breathed. "You are in this moment."

"Yes. We are both here. For now." Her words sank, weighty and immovable, into his understanding.

"Thank you." He turned his gaze slowly. Kest stood on one side of his chair. Behind the Wren, Katian stood with her yellow wings pressed against her back and her arms folded over her chest. It seemed he should know what they wanted. They had sought something from Mayavana, so what were they doing here with him? There had been a girl on the shore, tears and blood on her face. The soldiers had not been gentle. Did they intend to kill him after all? Unlikely. Why retrieve him from the Paths only to see him dead? A child had been murdered. A child had survived.

The Wren made a face and glanced at the others. "How long has he been this way?"

"Since the garden," answered Katian.

"Has Ilaye seen him?"

"With Mayavana."

"And as she ever sees him," Kest added.

"Not something she should brag about," the Wren replied, her tone loud with disapproval.

Jhared started to rise, and Katian took a swift step backward. Jhared had a partial recollection of his elbow sinking into soft flesh and pale yellow feathers in his hands. He twisted his body to snake out of Kest's grip. A mistake. The sharp movement caused the Wren to lose her contact with him. Waves roared up, pasts, presents, and futures washing him away.

"What's wrong with him?" someone asked from a distance.

A hand grabbed his shirt. The rock rose beneath him again, steadying him. He sagged with relief.

"He's wide open," the Wren declared. "Not a door closed between him and the flames. He needs to be away from the house."

Kest looked dubious. "Ilaye will say no."

"Then ask Ilaye how demented she wants him," the Wren said. "Confused and distracted? Lost and wandering? Or drooling and doddering?"

"Perhaps we could take him out for a walk later today. Or maybe tomorrow." Katian frowned down at Jhared as if he were an incontinent hound.

"I'm talking about now. Right now," the Wren replied. "And not just a walk. He needs sleep and food and someplace where he can stay put long enough to make use of them. There's strength here. Ilaye will want to consider that before she destroys it. Completely untutored, but strength all the same. He'd already be gone, otherwise."

"There's no strength in the Tainted." Katian's tone was scornful.

The Wren shrugged. "It's none of my concern. If you don't intend to listen to me, I'll gladly return to the garden."

Katian hesitated, her expression twisting. Jhared suddenly recognized what was happening. She had acted as the authority to which the Wren must concede, but she was not. Now, forced to acknowledge her lack of power, Katian looked aggrieved and sullen. He knew this woman, had seen her repeatedly in the fragments of Paths, not always with the same face, but always with the same ugly spirit: resentful of those above her, contemptuous of those below, and always reaching for something she did not have. The Wren was another matter entirely, one he couldn't see as clearly.

"Madam Healer, I am grateful for your care. I am Jhared Denaban, once soldier of Avelos. I have come among you with no intention other than to learn more of the history of our people."

"She knows who you are," Katian muttered.

The Wren looked at him with a bitter half-smile on her lips. "You hope that in giving me your name and calling to mind our ancestral ties, Jhared Denaban, I might not turn my back on your suffering. You don't realize that I am no longer a healer. And you have come among a people who inflict pain on others in an attempt to master their own history of suffering."

"Zelka, guard your tongue!" Kest snapped. "You've spent too much time with Rathael."

The Wren didn't answer. Jhared straightened under her regard. "All I ask is that you allow me to stand steady on my own Path so I might face this undeserved captivity with my self intact."

"Undeserved?" Kest snorted.

"I am certain you know exactly why I tried to leave," Jhared replied, addressing the Wren, not Kest. "No one has yet explained to me why force has been used to see that we stay."

The Wren looked some combination of annoyed and remorseful. "This is absurd. I'm taking him out. Kest, set him loose."

After a brief hesitation, the big red-wing gave way to the woman, who shoved Jhared's cloak into his hands and put an arm around his back before shepherding him up and through the door.

"Ilaye will be furious!" Katian hissed.

"Ilaye has other problems to resolve," replied the Wren.

The woman hustled him along the gallery and down the stairs at a pace that said she wasn't entirely confident of making it out. Jhared cast his gaze through open doors and among the staring servants.

"She's not here," the Wren muttered.

"Where then?"

"The archive."

Jhared said nothing. He might have guessed. When he accepted Vyla, General Hrvan had received the gift he sought. In return, Maya was allowed access to the archive. According to Vyla she would not find what she needed. He decided he couldn't care.

Once they escaped the house, the Wren turned toward the orchard without slackening her pace. Her hand remained a firm guide against Jhared's back. Ignoring the gazes of laborers coming in for the evening, they left the house behind, passed the stables, the smith, and a row of sheds. Beneath Jhared's boots, the terrain changed from stone to rutted mud, to coarse grass. The season had matured since he and Maya had arrived. In the orchard, the trees' glossy leaves were still bright, but their red and yellow fruits were picked or fallen. Fruit crushed under his boots, releasing a sweet perfume that mixed with the mineral scent of rain. Not far from shore, a storm dropped a blue-black curtain from the sky to the water, masking the setting sun. Lightning danced and skipped across the clouds.

Abruptly, Jhared halted, causing the woman to trip against him.

"What's wrong?" she asked.

"Order. It's such a relief for moments to be ordered again." He turned in a slow circle, absorbing every bit of his surroundings. "Everything I sense belongs to the same Path."

"Better, eh?" The Wren observed him, her speckled wings briefly fluttering. "They call me Hzelka. Before you give any thought to knocking me down and running for the walls, you should know that I can push you back into the chaos as easily as I pulled you free."

"I appreciate the warning." It didn't subdue him. He was striding through his own moment as he hadn't in weeks. He could sense the flow of his Path: one twisting ribbon of blue in the web with the beginning somewhere behind him and before him an eventual end.

"Why are you grinning?" The Wren's frown stretched the birthmark on her cheek.

"I am a part of the pattern again," he said. "The sea has receded. No, I imagine it's more accurate to say we've left it behind."

"The sea, you say. How interesting."

Jhared threw her an irritated expression.

"Don't give me that look. I'm not dismissing your experience. Those fragments of Paths are an artifact of too much travel in one small place. They're preternatural. We only understand them through the filter of our own perceptions. Katian perceives them as a labyrinth of tunnels. Drijan sees falling leaves. Kest, a very literal boy with no hint of the poet in him, sees them as city roads." The Wren smiled. "I've always perceived them as a room full of mirrors, reflecting things better not studied too closely."

Jhared stared at her. "You're saying that all of you perceive this sea—these broken Paths. The flaw truly is not something in me?"

"Yes and no," she said more soberly. "We sense them. You become them."

He could not pretend he didn't know what she meant. None of the others appeared to spend days at a time unconscious. "Why?" he asked simply.

"I suspect it is because you have been torn, Jhared Denaban. You have no barrier to protect you. Think of it so: if you put a handful of beach sand into a sack, it is now untouched by the tides. It is a new thing, a different thing that may be dry when the beach is wet or wet when the beach is dry. If, however, that sack is ripped open—"

"The grains fall and scatter to become a part of the shore."

She nodded. "As your self becomes a part of the endless Paths."

You have been torn. An inner scar to match the ones in his flesh. Maya had suggested that very thing to him once. "Would such an injury explain why the Paths throw themselves open to me?"

"Do they? That *is* interesting. I suppose with no barrier to define you, you belong to no pattern . . . and any pattern. Any Path might accept you as a part of it."

Jhared rubbed a hand over his heart, recalling a death he had caused, a hawk falling from the sky, and the agony afterward ripping him apart. "The Becoming did this to me."

The Wren made a face.

"You think not? Then you don't know what Avelos has made of the Becoming."

"I think you have been torn many times," she said, then seemed to regret it. She turned away from the orchard toward the forest. "It will be best if you do not return to the manor. I've a place I think will be safer. Come with me."

Thunder rumbled deep in Jhared's bones. The curtain of the storm was pushing toward land, grey chains of rain streaming before it. He offered the woman a fey smile. "Forgive me for being untrusting. Tell me now what you want. It may be I would rather run for the walls and risk the chaos."

She snorted. "A man who pulls himself through weeks of battering by broken Paths isn't eager for his own destruction. What I've offered is what it seems. As for what I want, I have not yet decided. But that is another's concern."

Vyla's aid, then. At last. He closed his eyes. Only now that his thoughts were ordered did he fully grasp what it meant that he had earned her help.

The Wren touched his arm. "Dizzy?"

He shook his head. It was not a thing that could be undone. "Do you mean to set me free?"

"Ha! Not while I place value on my own skin. Let us be clear, Forest Guard. I do not intend to suffer the joint fury of Nemaye and General Hrvan. I mean to see you safe." The Wren glanced at the house. "Which grows more difficult the longer we dawdle."

Jhared spied a guard in livery at the steps of the manor, another by the stable, and two in the distance near the wall. "We are being watched."

"They aren't the ones who concern me. They report only to Hrvan. Come on."

She pushed him toward the forest once more. He allowed it. Whatever happened now, he was no longer helpless to face it. His thoughts remained his own. Ahead, the pine grove offered familiar terrain, while the storm swiftly closed over them, cloaking the sky in midnight.

"Perhaps we should run," he said, grinning again in spite of everything.

"You've been weeks on a sickbed. You couldn't keep up with a three-legged kitten."

"Then you've no need to fear I'll leave you behind."

She didn't say anything, but gathered her skirts in her gnarled fists and broke into a rolling gallop toward the outstretched arms of the pines. Jhared glanced once at the stone wall, where the road led back to Saimbor, where ships would be anchored—perhaps the *Mila Jul*. Then he set off after her. He matched his jog to hers, glorying in the sensation of his muscles stretching, slowly recalling rhythm and pace. When he entered the forest, the resinous scent welcomed him. Tall, straight trees grew a distance from one another and the thick bed of grey needles kept the forest floor free of undergrowth, leaving the way clear. The only impediments to speed were the winds rushing inland from the storm and the limits of his own body.

She led him along the ridge, keeping the water on their right. By the time the rain had begun falling in large, slow cups, Jhared's breathing had become somewhat effortful. By the time the cups had turned to swift pellets, his lungs ached. She had been right: captivity and poor nourishment had taken more of a toll than he cared to admit. Half blinded by the rain, he stumbled as the Wren stopped abruptly before a narrow gate in a crumbling wall. Another of the general's men warded the gate, but he stared only at the wet forest as Hzelka fought with her wind-whipped skirts to tug a key from her pocket, unlocked the gate, and hastily gestured Jhared through.

On the far side of the wall, the forest continued. The Wren pulled Jhared away from the shore now, inland and uphill as the storm belted them with sudden gusts that drove the rain sideways. Lightning speared the trees, lining the boughs in blue-white brilliance to the deafening snarls of the thunder. Jhared no longer attempted to run.

"Why here?" he shouted, waving one arm at the forest.

"The forest is ours," Hzelka replied, and pointed toward a mass of darkness through the trees: a shed or a small cottage. A second similar shape squatted beside it and another one on the other side. A small village, it seemed. "Kept free of prying eyes by the general and his men. Most of us live here."

"How many?"

"Fewer than thirty remain." Even over the wind, he heard her sadness before she brushed the rain and the emotions from her features. "You and I go farther. A place less visited."

He refrained from asking how much farther. Instead, he lowered his head and bulled his way against the storm. He only noticed the clearing for the way the wind increased its offensive against him. Then he spied the ancient sentinel and stopped.

The tree stood alone in the clearing, its bold trunk shooting eighty feet through the rain toward the warring clouds. At alternating intervals, branches formed shelves wide enough for an agile man to stand upon. The ends of those shelves bobbed and bowed to the wind. Water ran from the deep green needles and slicked the bark to a slippery black.

A spear of lightning stabbed an instant of daylight through the forest. On a lower branch stood an Avelun, a painfully elongated figure, all fluid limbs and tapered wings. If not for the astonishing blue and green of his feathers, the man's black hair and dark clothes would have melded with the storm, but Jhared had the sense he would have found the Avelun no matter the dark and the storm. Something about the man's manner compelled him: the reckless grace with which he climbed; the way he grabbed the branch above him, and swung, forward and back, until with a flash of strength, he hauled his long body onto the branch. When the gap between branches proved too great to reach, the Avelun simply leaped, wings outstretched, not bothering to catch at the tree again until he started to fall. From the ground, the performance appeared an effortless act by a creature who belonged among the clouds.

"Who is it?" Jhared shouted.

"No one you need meet." Hzelka clutched his arm more tightly. "I'm soaked. Shelter is close. Come."

Jhared didn't move. He knew what it was to clamber into such heights: the deliciously precarious footing, the open space all about one's body, the gates of desire thrown open. They all begged a man to test himself against the chains that bound him to the ground. Watching the stranger climb, Jhared found it hard to believe the Avelun could not fly.

"Who?" he insisted.

The Wren made a sound that registered exasperation. "Ilaye's brother Rathael. Misfortune in the guise of a man. Come."

"I can't leave him." Somehow the words made sense. In the Avelun's urgent, careless manner Jhared recognized Alende, and a part of himself he didn't like to acknowledge. The man's gaze remained fastened on the sky, even as his feet slid over the uneven branches, even as he leaped against the bonds that tethered him. Calm descended over Jhared. He saw the tragedy about to occur. It was no wild projection of his own fears. At his core, he understood the beautiful blue-winged stranger—understood the anguish of his defeated desire—and knew what would happen.

Tearing free of Hzelka and his sodden cloak, he arrowed toward the tree. She grabbed for him and missed. Over the storm, he heard her cursing with a creativity he had rarely found outside the Forest Guard.

The lower branches welcomed him. As soon as he leaped for a higher branch to pull himself up, however, he was in trouble. The slippery bark resisted his grip. For several heartbeats his fingers slid and the bark tore his flesh. Ignoring the pain, he wrenched his fists tightly, dangling in midair as the wind and rain flayed him. His grip began to slip again. With an immense thrust of effort, he heaved his body partway onto the branch. A brief pause, a gasp for breath. Then with a second surge of effort, he drew both legs up and scrambled onto his feet. Above, the Avelun bounced on a branch and scrambled higher still, sending water and needles coursing over Jhared. He clenched his jaw, steadied his breathing, and prepared to leap again.

Nothing about his climb was elegant or effortless. Determination released a hot buzz of energy into his blood, feeding his muscles and allowing him to move gradually up and then up again. Cold rain sluiced his body. His fingers bled and then went numb. Every moment, he anticipated an outcry and the sight of the Avelun hurtling toward the ground. He sent futile thoughts into the storm that the stranger would hold fast. Then he could do nothing but continue to climb.

He felt more than saw when he finally caught up to the man. They stood on opposite branches, the tree trunk between them. Jhared leaned against the trunk, gulping great breaths. The Avelun had paced to the end of his branch, his face lifted to the storm, oblivious or indifferent to the danger. This close, even through the rain, his wings glowed with uncountable shades of blue and green, like an alpine lake, like sun-touched opals.

Jhared straightened and swung himself around the trunk to the other's branch. It trembled as it took his weight, but surprise was not his intention. He wanted the man to know he was there. He needed to break the hypnotic pull of the heights.

The Avelun didn't turn.

"Come," Jhared called. "Do not throw away your life for seconds of release."

"Should I not?" the Avelun replied. "Those seconds might be the worthiest of my life."

Jhared took another step away from the trunk, controlling his breathing. "They needn't be. Not when your people are so close to winning the sky."

The rain had begun to slow, though the wind still buffeted the tree in sporadic gusts, setting the branch to swaying. The Avelun swayed with it.

"And if I cannot live with the manner in which they have won it?" he asked, his voice rumbling low and heavy, like the thunder beginning to subside across the forest.

Jhared heard Hzelka's words like an echo: *You've come among a people who inflict pain . . ..* Unwelcome memory showed him Maya taking Moravel's hand, but he maintained a studied calm. "Will you climb down with me and speak of what burdens you, Rathael?"

At his name, the Avelun spun and strode up the branch with cat-light balance. For the first time, his face tilted in Jhared's direction, a sharply angled face, with the mark of Avelonian aristocracy in the broad, high cheekbones and slender nose. A neat, dark beard partially masked the level jaw. This man had been bred from the Avelune of the Exile, those who had known Lady Amalia, those who had survived the horror of Maren's Burn. Perhaps that was why his large, jade eyes reflected something familiar and painful, something that whipped Jhared's heart to a gallop.

The Avelun halted a half-step out of reach, his features lifting from the slack of apathy into taut concentration. He closed his eyes.

"You should never have followed me, my aberration. You should have fled when first you saw me."

The low voice penetrated Jhared's thoughts, rumbling like an animal growl. A known voice, incongruous with the reality of the winged man on the branch. A known voice, sometimes loved, long feared. A known voice . . .

"No." Jhared staggered, his foot slipped. He threw his weight backward to catch his balance and his shoulders connected hard with the trunk. He straightened, steadied. The Avelun's eyes remained closed, his body stiff.

"Yes, boy. Yes. An enlightened Teacher from another Path, you once named me. Boar, you called me more often, for the strength you sensed. Did you not imagine this broken man, with no remnant of honor or loyalty, standing sodden and snot-nosed before you?"

The sea no longer held him. Jhared's thoughts tumbled with terrible clarity. Boar. His Teacher. One who had crept over his Path for more than half his life. Never in his wildest imaginings had he considered the excoriating voices in his head might belong to Avelune. An Avelun, who should have had exquisite empathy for a Shorn child's pain, but instead had battered him again and again for every transgression, ripping through his memories, slamming him with agony, leaving him gasping and helpless, stripped of all pride and pleading his repentance.

Jhared stood at the edge of the branch, quiet, unmoving, while inside, he clung precariously to composure. *"I believed that you meant to teach me."*

"But we did! We taught you to doubt your heart and to fear your own strength."

"Yes. You did. By retelling the lies of Avelos."

A flicker of dark amusement from the Avelun. *"Shrill enjoyed the irony."*

"Where is Shrill? Who is she?" Jhared knew. He didn't want to know.

"Who is the question, isn't it? I've started to refer to her as Shrill myself. She hasn't found it as entertaining as I do."

Jhared strained to hold himself apart, to be just an impassive observer of this play. *"Ilaye. Your sister."*

"Good. It seems our meddling hasn't completely destroyed your reason."

Ilaye. Shrill. The Teacher who had once told Jhared to surrender and die on a field outside of Velantar, who had twisted his perceptions until he had come an instant away from violating the woman he loved, who had told Maya that her soldier was lost beyond the Gate.

"Does it mean nothing to you that you have warped the lives of all those who called you Teacher? We are the Shorn. Your cousins!"

"Lives? We? My dear aberration, you were always the only one."

"The only　？" Another blow outside of all imagining. Jhared tried to absorb it. He had lived in a world where all the Shorn accepted the internal voices of authority as a part of the Teaching. He had lived with the belief that no matter how isolated he was from his own kind, they shared a common experience.

"Do you not remember, boy, the first time we came to you?"

The nostalgia in the man's tone turned Jhared's stomach. *"I was a grieving child. You taught me to be ashamed of the tears I spilled for my mother. You told me it would save my life."* Jhared choked. *"I thanked you for it!"*

"Something about you drew us. Perhaps your vulnerability. Perhaps your innocent, untested strength. I don't recall. Once we found you, of course, Ilaye had no trouble tearing through the doors onto the Path of a lonely Shorn child."

"Why?" Jhared heard the anguish in his tone and knew his hold was slipping. *"To witness the torment you had escaped? To spy for General Hrvan?"*

"It would help you to make sense of it if I told you we had such a motive from the start, wouldn't it? Sadly, I've nothing left in me but the truth. That first time, the day was beastly hot. Ilaye and I were stuck inside, so as not to be seen by the general's visitors. We were bored. We turned to exploring beyond the Gate. We found you."

We were bored.

Jhared launched himself at the Avelun.

Embedded so deeply within him, Boar knew his intention. It gave the man the heartbeat necessary to duck his blow, but Jhared anticipated the evasion and rotated in the air, striking the Avelun full in the chest and sending him backward. They crashed onto the branch with an impact that jarred Jhared's teeth. Beneath him, the man's wings splayed and his head smacked against wood. Jhared twined his legs around the Avelun's waist and the branch. Years of contained fury gave his blows power.

"I was Avelun! I was whole! How could you make yourself the partner of the elders? How could you batter me with their weapons?"

Somewhere far distant from his thoughts, his fists rose and fell. Little resistance came between one blow and the next. He felt flesh yield and bone meet bone. Despite his long captivity, he was a soldier. The body did not soon forget its training. The man beneath him had assisted in that training.

Pain-soaked memories tore loose from where he had contained them. Shrill and Boar had been his Teachers. They had lived within him. They had known the torment they caused.

. . . a people who inflict pain to master their own history of suffering.

In the dusky light, steel glinted at the Avelun's waist. An opportunity. Jhared twisted to reach it. The man's dwindling attempts to block him meant nothing. Jhared batted them away and closed his palm around the grip of the dagger. With an easy tug, it slid free. Relief surged through him with unexpected intensity. The years of lies had worn him thin. Finally, the blade would silence the boy's voice, would end the remorse. Jhared hefted the knife. Some part of him noted the perfect balance. From beyond his own boundaries came the whoosh of wings beating futilely against the darkness, the frightened cry of a woman, the patter of raindrops weeping onto the forest. One thrust would end the struggle. Jhared had been shaped for violence. Some part of him, small and silent now, still regretted that. Steel flashed in his competent hands.

"Stop! Boy, stop this! Do not prove yourself the vicious thing we sought to make you!"

The command crashed against Jhared and flung him away from his bloody target. He staggered to the end of the bough, reeling with shame and confusion. The man rolled toward the tree trunk and began pulling himself to his feet. A cry of helpless fury welled in Jhared as his fingers opened and the knife dropped into the darkness.

He didn't know if the Avelun meant for him to die then, but the cracking branch made intention irrelevant. With a swift series of pops, Jhared's ledge tipped downward. The ground waited far below. He heard a wild sound and realized it was his own laughter. Finally, he would have his opportunity to fly, and Maya wasn't there to see it.

As the end of the branch gave way, he leaped toward the trunk, landed on his stomach, and clutched at the slippery bark with both hands. The fractured branch bowed under his weight. His feet dangled in the air as his body continued to dip and slide. He glanced down, but the dark and the storm made the footholds below impossible to pick out. The wood popped. He slid again. His struggle with Boar had bled out the last of his strength. He clenched his fists around the branch, but his fingers were losing their grip. The wind streamed over his body. He slid again, too far this time.

His body jerked to a sudden, excruciating halt. Stunned, he tilted his head upward. The Avelun, sprawled flat out, had caught Jhared's left wrist in both hands. His lips were drawn back in a snarl of effort. Jhared had time to register anguish in the other's gaze before the remainder of the branch snapped. Surprise stretched the Avelun's face and his blue-green wings flailed to their full length. Then they both fell.

Branches smacked Jhared's legs, knocked him about the head, cracked against his shoulders, and clawed at his face. For a moment, he caught himself, one arm draped fast over a slender bough, until the Avelun tumbled into him, bounced him free, and they both continued downward. But for the pained gasps and the thumps of flesh against wood, it happened in silence. Jhared thought how ridiculous they must look, two flightless birds barreling through the tree, snapping branches and possibly bones. He hoped Hzelka enjoyed the sight of the absurd. He didn't know how far he'd fallen or what had happened to the Avelun when a peel of thunder cracked just behind his head and blue-white lightning exploded in his face.

A stream of curses entered his muzzy awareness, along with a murderous ache that started at the back of his head and radiated through the rest of his body. Above him, the pine tree creaked and muttered. The ground beneath him must have been wet; he was soaked through. He wondered vaguely if he had broken anything, but didn't yet try to move. The cursing was Hzelka's, aimed, it seemed, at Boar.

"…and irresponsible. Ilaye and Nemaye will be on their way out here. This is not what I took on. I do not intend to pay for your cruelty."

"You should be careful when you speak of cruelty, Zelka." Soft, calm, detached: only the breathlessness of the voice bespoke physical pain. Jhared almost didn't recognize the voice as Boar's.

"Don't use my weakness to excuse yours," the Wren snapped. "You have plenty to answer for on your own."

"I know," the man replied emotionlessly. "You needn't fret over Ilaye and Nemaye. They won't come."

"Of course they'll come. They'll—no. What have you done?"

"Closed the doors to this Path. Mine. Yours. His. They will not know we are here."

"Foolish, boy! You spread yourself too far! That effort could end you!"

"You should perhaps decide, Zelka, whether you *want* me to pay for my errors or are afraid that I will pay."

Jhared pushed himself upright through a gauntlet of mallets. "What he means is that he doesn't care." The Wren startled at his voice; Boar did not. "He drew me to the tree because he knew I would try to stop him from jumping. He knew what would happen when he revealed himself as my Teacher. He never meant to fall. He meant for me to kill him."

Darkness hazed Hzelka's expression, but her indrawn breath was audible. "You refused?"

"I . . . think so." Jhared couldn't say for certain whether he had left Boar alive because at the last moment his Teacher had commanded it or because he had owned the strength to name the murder wrong. He couldn't say why the man had stopped him, if he had. The one thing Jhared had sensed with certainty was the other's desire for his twisted life to end.

The Avelun called Boar, called Rathael, said nothing.

"A nasty snarl you've both created. A snarl that's none of my concern. Yet here I am in the middle of it. As always." The Wren opened her wings and clapped them shut. "Both of you, up. Now. We're going."

She reached out a hand to Jhared. He clenched his jaw and rose to his feet on his own. She watched him a dubious moment, then shrugged and gestured for him to follow.

"You don't want me," said the Boar.

"No. I don't." Hzelka snorted. "But if you're going to continue to seal those Paths, I want an eye on you. And when you've let them go, I'm going to need help figuring out what to do with the boy. This jest is your mother and sister's doing and none of my affair."

Keeping up with the Wren proved a painful endeavor, but not enough to defend Jhared from his furious thoughts. He was glad when the terrain grew unpredictable, a hillside slicked by gravel and large stones that required all his attention to maneuver. Hzelka hustled them up the hill to a thick hedge of thorn bushes that had laid siege to a great stone wall. Jhared wrestled through the hedge behind Hzelka, the buckthorn tearing at the Avelune's feathers and his clothing, until they came to a broken gate. The wall was much older than the one that divided the forest and bordered the general's estate. The large, even stones under Jhared's palm had been carved with intricate patterns once, but wind and water had worn them smooth.

Inside the gate lay the ruins of a compound, small for a fortress, not badly situated, with the strength of the wall and the vantage of the hilltop overlooking the ocean. The remains of buildings and exposed foundations suggested kitchens, stables, a forge, quarters for the garrison, and perhaps for the commander and his family. It was a familiar layout, with patterns in the crumbling architecture that he almost knew. Jhared's eye traveled over the inner yard to the single remaining tower: a round tower with high, yawning windows and a domed roof. He left the others and crossed the yard, thinking suddenly of Alende and a night in the shelter of ruins. Peering through one of the windows, he was astonished to discover the same image he remembered.

"A sky tower," he murmured. "In Sona."

"Why not?" Hzelka had come up behind him. "Our ancestors were drawn to the ocean as well as to the mountains. And they owned no dread of others' customs. Long before the Exile, they had schools in many places."

"Schools?"

"The sky towers were not just places to observe the spheres and their spirals. They were centers of learning. Don't you see?" She flung her hand at the broken stones. "It would have been the library there. Dormitories over there, on the other side. Surrounding the courtyard were the masters' and mistresses' studios and workshops. What? Did you think it a place of war, soldier?"

His gaze dipped away from hers. "Your people don't know of it?"

"Of course they know. They despise it."

Jhared lifted his eyes to the inside of the tower with its ring of unreachable balconies and the taunting gallery far above near the open oculus of the dome. "I see."

"I'm sure you do. Come along."

She led them from the tower along the remains of a portico, its roof collapsed, its columns tumbled like gambling bones. Past the portico, they turned through an arched passage into a courtyard. It was a sad, sober place. The tall fountain at the center had been silenced. Mud and dead leaves clogged its basin. All around the fountain lay the bodies of felled Avelune: toppled statues with missing limbs and broken wings. The most intact structure was a narrow building at the northwest corner of the courtyard. Its two sturdy doors looked much newer than the rest and opened silently when the Wren released their locks.

Jhared hesitated at the dark entrance, while the Wren scuttled inside. Her shadowed figure bent to a banked hearth. In a moment, the scent of char curled in the air, then a red-gold flame revealed a neat, busy chamber with a little round table, mismatched chairs, and overflowing shelves, all made snug with rugs piled on the floor and draped on the walls. A faint animal scent came from a small cage near the hearth, where something furry slept in a tight curl.

"We won't spare the oil tonight," Hzelka muttered as she flitted about the room lighting hanging lamps and candles. "Come in, both of you. Before the sound of your teeth chattering wakes the forest."

Jhared stumbled into the house toward the hearth, aware of Boar limping at his side. He moved to put distance between them, although he realized it didn't matter: distance had never mattered. Despite the borders between them, the Avelun had always been able to penetrate his Path and steal his thoughts.

He hunkered before the small fire, absorbing what heat it offered. Hzelka's thick fingers splayed on his forearm and she gestured for him to take a seat near one of the hanging lamps. She held a box filled with rags and jars and the gleam of assorted instruments.

"I thought you weren't a healer," Jhared said.

"Oh, she was once an excellent healer." Across the room, Boar lowered himself carefully onto a rug, his wings lax. Blood and rain dripped from his face. "She was particularly adept at dealing with poisons, weren't you, Zelka?"

For the first time, the Wren's bluff, concealing attitude became something breakable. "I was never skilled enough to purge the poison that drips from your tongue, Rathael."

"Some poisons should never be purged. They should twist your innards for a lifetime, a reminder of your crimes." Boar's gaze shone, bitter and arch. "Perhaps we should number our victims together."

The woman's speckled brown wings snapped the air so hard a jar tumbled from her box. "Damn you, Rathael! Do not seek to play my conscience. This boy is not my responsibility."

"Then why did you bring him out of the house?"

She stooped and nipped up the jar. "The general asked a favor. He wants the soldier intact. Nothing more. It wasn't a thing I could refuse."

"Why didn't Hrvan deal with Nemaye?"

"He will have to now, won't he? There wasn't time before. Nemaye would have led him along a merry negotiation, and the boy couldn't wait. Vyla said he—"

Boar straightened, wincing. "Vyla? Hrvan's house girl brought the message to you?"

"Of course. If Hrvan had come to me himself, Nemaye would have heard of it."

Boar's overbright gaze speared the Wren and then Jhared, who drew his feelings close and tried not to think on the touch and the scent of the woman who had come to him in the darkness. He returned Boar's stare with his own stiff anger. "You needn't speak around me. I'm not a horse up for auction. You've known for weeks I was coming. You encouraged it."

"Did I?" The low voice remained tightly modulated.

"'Go find the archive,' you said, 'bring your sweet Avelun.' It was your way to gain control of the winds. Shrill tried and failed to force the knowledge out of Maya through me. You took a subtler approach to make certain Maya would walk directly into your influence."

"Ilaye has never understood the value of the subtle approach." Boar folded his arms on his knees and peered up from the caverns of his eyes. "But then you fooled her after all: Mayavana does not have the ability to call the winds, does she?"

A chill feathered down Jhared's back. He remained silent.

"I had begun to wonder at the possibility long ago," Boar continued. "I only became certain after Ilaye told me what happened at Parnas Pass. I am not so blind to the potential of the Shorn as she is."

"Why have you not told her?"

Boar's expression remained mild. "Why do you believe I have not?"

"In nine years, you did not hide everything of yourselves from me. If you had told her, she would have rushed to take them from me."

"Take them?" Hzelka interrupted with a snort of disgust. "If Ilaye believed you owned the secret of the killing winds, she would tear through your Paths until she uncovered your every experience of them. She would wring the knowledge from you, not caring if she left you after with the wits of a toothless babe."

Jhared leaped up, knocking over a chair. No cache of energy flowed buzzing through his veins. That cache had sustained him for weeks as he floundered about the broken Paths; it had carried him into the tree to rescue the Avelun, then fed his violence against the man. Now he was empty, a husk.

"That is one reason I have not told her," Boar observed.

"You would not have her deprive you of your own amusement?"

Behind Jhared, the Wren picked up the chair. Her hand fell upon his injured shoulder, heavily enough to make him grimace.

Boar smiled, his teeth white between his torn lips. "Do you know, it is so strange to look upon you with my own eyes. I have only ever known you through your perception of yourself: scarred and disfigured, with the features and the morals of the damned. Indeed, a sight to terrify. Instead, I find you well-built, with an innocence of manner that likely attracts a certain type of woman. And a predatory spark that no doubt attracts a very different type."

"I suppose you are attempting to be subtle again," Jhared said. "You would like me to think you might also be different from the cruel voice that played my Teacher. You ignore that what you showed me for nine years was the mask of your deliberate deception, and therefore you are really no different at all."

The Avelun's laugh was humorless. "Oh, I am different. Be assured. You have never yet seen the depravity of which I am capable. Zelka, you win. I leave the boy to you." Boar rose with a whistled breath and a rustle of broken feathers.

"You can't go, Rathael. You must stay close—"

"Just to the tower. It's easier to track the Paths when I'm under the stars. And this one won't rest while I'm here."

Her next words twisted out of Jhared's understanding, familiar but not quite comprehensible, like a language from a fever or a dream. As Rathael responded, Jhared strained to pick apart the sounds. He recognized the pattern: it was an elegant mix of ancient Velos, a Velos, he suspected, that was older than anything he had ever read or heard spoken, sprinkled with Sonan and what he thought to be Amurian. It was a language descended from his ancestors: it bore witness to the trials of their exile. Boar seemed to be assuring the Wren that he would keep their Paths secure. In response, she said something that was a warning and a complaint and one thing softer Jhared couldn't translate.

He didn't see the Wren's expression when the other Avelun limped away. A gust of wind bullied the flames as the door opened and closed, then the room grew warm and quiet again.

"So you're the one who draws forth the winds of flight. A Shorn man. It serves us right. It serves us all right."

Jhared watched her, unmoving. "What do you intend to do with that knowledge?"

"Hah. You needn't worry. I couldn't use the Paths to force you, as Ilaye would, even if I cared to." Hzelka set a pot of water over the hearth, then fluttered her wings and gave him a judging eye.

"Don't you want the winds for yourself, Hzelka?"

The Wren flashed a keen glance at him. "Don't bother. I didn't bring you out to conspire against my own. I've done what the general wanted. That's it. Share your knowledge. Don't share it. These old feathers will never be good for anything other than stirring dust. Now, will you let me clean those injuries or are you going to take your chances with the wound rot?"

"Leave me be, Hzelka. If you've a need to act the healer, see to your kinsman. His cracked ribs will cause him trouble if they shift. And I suspect there's a fracture in his left wing."

Her dun brows stretched upward. "You have a healer's eye."

"No. A soldier's."

"Useful in another way, I suppose." She busied herself about the room, pulling jars and plates from shelves, setting a second pot over the fire. In a short time, food appeared on the table: several types of sausage, some dried fish, and a bowl of cooked grain topped with honey and warm fruit. When the table was laden, she vanished into a back room and returned wrapped in a dry cloak that enveloped her wings and her plum-shaped body.

"You must eat something," she said. "Then sleep. There's a bed in the back. I need not be a healer to know how the broken Paths ravage the body and spirit. You are safe from them here."

"And from Ilaye and the others? From the invasion of my own Path?"

Plucking a piece of fruit from the bowl, she fluttered over to the cage near the hearth. A bushy-tailed rodent smaller than a squirrel and larger than a mouse neatly uncurled, hastened to the cage bars, and stole away the offering. The Avelun lifted the grey creature in one hand and cuddled it against her weathered cheek. "So long as Rathael has the strength to guard you, you are safe."

"Why? Why would he do so now, after hounding me for so many years?"

"I couldn't truly say. I suppose if a man is not corrupt at his core, he can sometimes look behind him and regret his actions."

"Not without cause. Not after so long. What has changed, Hzelka?"

She lowered the furry rodent back into its cage. "Why must there be any single cause? We cannot experience life and remain unchanged. And as you say, Rathael has traveled your Path for years."

"For years his deception made me an Avelune plaything."

We were bored. . . .

"It works both ways, Forest Guard. He could not share your perspective without also experiencing some of the consequences of what he did to you. Some men just take longer to figure out the role they are playing in their own suffering."

She gathered up her rags and the little box. One small jar she plunked onto the table. "I must go to him. Use this, and do what I say about the rest, or in a very short time you won't be capable of figuring out anything."

Hzelka hustled her round figure to the door. At the threshold, she turned. "Do not try to escape tonight, Forest Guard. If you think me an odd old woman with a streak of kindness, you are wrong. General Hrvan wants you for his collection. My people rely upon our connections with him. What I have done is merely to protect those connections, nothing more. If you try to run, I will hurt you."

"Interesting," Jhared replied mildly.

The Wren huffed. "What?"

"That is the third time you've found it necessary to tell me you have no kindness in you."

Hzelka's mouth opened, but she said nothing. Instead, she yanked open the door and walked into the storm.

26.

STRAINED BONDS

Once Hzelka had gone, Jhared didn't waste energy on senseless defiance. He washed with the heated water, smeared his cuts with the ointment, and ate the food she had left for him. After, he forced himself to move, stretching his bruised and neglected body. Hzelka's shelves beckoned to him with their burden of books, but he was disappointed to find most of them written in Amurian. He browsed vaguely through a few. At another time they would have intrigued him, but his thoughts traveled to Boar and Shrill and to the reason he and Maya had been drawn here.

As he slid a book back into place, he caught a disapproving glare above him. When he looked up, he found himself held by a vicious silver gaze. It was the gaze of a goddess, terrible, lovely, and ancient. Fine-grained wood, stained with age, showed beneath faded and flaking paint of blue, green, and gold. Her right hand, lifting gracefully from the folds of her robe, disappeared into twists of blue flame. Chains bound her right arm to a man facing the opposite direction at her back. A sense of the infinite reverberated through Jhared. Riana he recognized from the complex Path maps painted across her robes. They were the only way he knew her. The violence in her expression matched no image Jhared had ever known. Likewise, he did not doubt that the man with a raven on his shoulder was Cael, although the sculptor had portrayed him as a laughing young man with a plume of water spouting from his left hand, the hand chained to Riana's right. Jhared stepped back until he felt the wall behind him, unable to look away from the sculpture. What he looked upon was something he had never before seen and would not have believed remained in existence: a portrayal of Riana and Cael created before the Exile. It could only be that: a piece created before the Avelune became the symbol of evil, before the image of the demon was wiped out of the temple's reach. Cael's carved wings rose to their full, magnificent span, while Riana was unfeathered. In her right hand, Riana held the flames that guarded the Gate to the infinite Paths and all their doors. Cael held . . .

Jhared laughed aloud. "It's not a plume of water."

He understood what the artist had meant to depict. A handful of weeks ago he would never have allowed himself to see it, but Lady Nemiah had told him High

403

Priestess Amalia's story, and the Bearer of Cael's Blade had spoken of a certain heresy. He wondered if Hzelka realized that an explanation of the winds' power sat upon her shelves: a key to what Maya and all of them sought.

A smile twitched his lips. *"What use has the Demon of Disorder for closed doors?"* Shira had once asked him. The answer had been clear: none at all. Cael would open the ways wherever he desired. Riana held the blue flames that secured the doors to all the Paths, and Cael held the winds that blew them open. Jhared leaned his head back against the wall. Balance existed here, order that included both Cael and Riana, order strong enough to encompass and modulate chaos. Jhared found an unexpected peace in that thought. He sat on the soft rug, considering the statue until sleep pulled him into a dreamless darkness.

He awoke with the sense that someone had spoken his name, though it might have been only the thunder. Rain spattered the shuttered windows in concerted volleys, rising from time to time into the crack of hail. Somewhere in the courtyard, a loose door or shutter slammed repeatedly. Inside, the room was warm and still. Rose-gold light flitted about the ceiling and across the walls as the fire popped and chuckled. Boar had folded his elongated figure close to the fire. His weighty gaze rested on Jhared.

Jhared returned the gaze. Although the blood had been washed from the Avelun's face, bruises marred his aristocratic features. His opalescent wings hung from his sloped shoulders and trailed against the floor. The sardonic curve of the man's lips and his mocking green eyes seemed a poorly fitted mask over something more troubling.

Boar looked away first, glanced at the sculpture, and gave a dark grin. "You found Cael and his Holy Captive. How do you enjoy the rendering? Chains suit Riana, do they not?"

Jhared peered at the sculpture, at the goddess's grim face and Cael's laughing one. "She's not his captive."

"The words of a Shorn man taught by Avelos."

"And taught by you." Despite the complaints of his battered body, Jhared felt more alert than he had since entering the general's estate. "I know you mean to bait me, but you actually don't see it, do you?"

Boar gave an uneven shrug. "I see you remain stuck where we put you. Little about such artifacts interests me."

Jhared thought to explain what he had recognized; then changed his mind. He had given enough explanations to his Teachers. He watched the light twist over the flames in Riana's palm and the gust of wind in Cael's. "Where's Hzelka?"

"Resting. I kept her awake most of the night. She didn't trust me on my own."

"Of course not. She feared you would find another tree. Your life means something to her."

The Avelun chuckled. "Guilt and concern can look much the same, I'm afraid. She only wanted to know if I lost my grip on our Paths. Apparently, she told you that you would be safe here. Foolish woman."

Boar rested his chin on his fists and stared into the fire, his wings rising and falling with each careful breath. It grew quiet. Jhared closed his eyes, then opened them, awkward with the unwanted sense of intimacy.

"How did you do it?" he finally asked.

The Avelun didn't lift his head. "How? An innate callousness. A characteristic lack of concern for others. The gods provide you with wings or scruples. You may not claim both."

Jhared groaned. "That's what Tumal believed. It's why he created Shorn Law. For a short time before arriving in Saimbor, I had cause to think he was wrong. But that's not what I meant."

"Oh?"

"How did you and Shrill come to me over the years? How do you find a person repeatedly on your own Parallel, with only the Place and Time ever changing?"

"Ah. You want to reach your Mayavana."

"It would be one way."

"For another person, perhaps. Not for you."

"Tell me how. I'll decide for myself what's for me."

Boar shrugged with an elegant lift of his shoulders. "Very well. Batter yourself against the flame like a doomed moth. Three things are needed: you must know something distinctive about the person you seek; you must be able to picture the context in which you want to find her; and you must understand which doors to open and which to leave shut. It's the last that matters most. If you do not open the right doors, you cannot share thoughts with the one whose Path you've occupied. If too many doors are opened, however, you never find the specific person you seek. You only end up chasing her Prisms on every Parallel across the infinite weaving."

Jhared thought of his struggle to find Maya among the tangled Paths. "Prisms. The various versions of a person that exist throughout the weaving?"

"What else? We are the ones through whom the weaving is divided. Our every decision splits a Path into its conceivable parts."

"In the garden and later in the hall, I heard Drijan speaking with someone across the Paths, although I did not seek to open or close any doors between us. Why?"

Boar's laughter was deep and bitter. "Because Drijan is young and bright and eagerly incompetent. Do you know the primary duty of the Storyteller? The Storyteller has become the one tasked to keep alive the memories of all the harms done to us. To tell and retell every story of our exile and suffering. To endlessly relive that pain. Thus, for the Storyteller to remain sane, he must be a person as incapable of reflection as Drijan. The consequence, however, is that the others must regularly advise him to prevent him from doing things that are spectacularly idiotic. They don't always save the moment. Witness Drijan's failure to befriend you in the garden."

"What happened in the garden didn't come from Drijan," Jhared said. "Or not directly. I saw the malice within him, within each of them. All thoroughly different faces from the ones they showed me. As if I saw them on different Paths." Jhared paused, watching the Avelun closely. "Though I didn't see your face. Why weren't you present that night?"

"Do I seem to you someone who finds entertainment in sipping bad wine and listening to romantic recollections of our past?"

"You seem to find entertainment in deception, as the others do. You and Ilaye weren't there because you feared I might recognize you. But you were close, weren't you? I thought that the malice I saw in the others came from some random part of the broken Paths, but it couldn't have. What I saw had nothing to do with disorder. It was organized and meaningful. As though it were offered deliberately. Someone gave me those perceptions."

"That seems unlikely." Boar leaned carefully against the hearthstone. "Why would anyone do such a thing?"

"Either to warn me or to provoke me into acting as impulsively as I did. I suspect your intention was the latter, although I have trouble understanding why you now waste your strength concealing me from Ilaye. Unless you hope to take the secret of the winds and keep it for yourself. In that case, though, why the tree? I could have killed you."

The man sucked a partial breath as if to sigh, winced, and exhaled gingerly. "The tree was a mistake. I needed a way to draw you. It turns out there is danger in acting out one's fantasy."

"Which was the fantasy? That I would save you from yourself? Or that I would kill you in retribution for your evils?"

Boar lifted a heavy-lidded gaze. "Why do you think those two things are different?"

"And the garden?" Jhared asked. "The unmasked faces of Drijan and the others?"

"I didn't expect you to attack them. A very short time ago you would never have dared to release your anger."

Jhared took some comfort in knowing that the Avelun who had been his Teacher could not always predict his actions. "Then you wish me to believe you did these things for my benefit?"

"What you believe is of little significance. There are many reasons for what I did."

Boar's tone held no passion or rancor. It held no emotion at all. Jhared studied the man's face, struggling past his own anger to understand something of what was not offered. Rathael's gaze owned the kind of mad intensity that Alende's often did, but Alende drew a fey joy from his life and took pride in his guardianship of the Kin. The Avelun's intensity rose from a bleakness that stole all pleasure from his Path and turned every season to grey. Grief and loss composed that bleakness, filling Jhared's spirit until he ached with it. This was a man who knew what it meant to fail those he loved; who understood the damage inflicted upon himself and others by years of lies; who knew the futility of life after losing all that was dear to him. Rathael possessed strength and skills that no others living could claim. He should have been a leader, a guide, but instead he floated like debris along the current of his life, his strength sapped, his intelligence wasted, his heart broken—

Jhared sprang to his feet, cursing. "Stay off my Path!"

The other man raised a puzzled green gaze. "I'm not on it."

"You are. You're warping my perceptions. As you did in the garden. As Shrill did. I feel it." The unwanted empathy lingered in him like a bruise.

"I cannot secure your Path from others and travel it at the same time," Rathael said. "Whatever you feel, it comes from no one but you."

Jhared turned his back, closed his eyes, and sought deep within himself for signs of Shrill or Boar. Nothing. He plunged his hand over a flickering lamp. Pain, sharp and hot, but no new clarity came upon him.

"It must have been a repugnant perception, indeed," the man observed.

"It was." Jhared curled his fingers around the red spot on his palm and turned. "You desire the secret of the winds."

"How could I not? Flight is the only thing of worth this Path might still offer."

"Very well. There are things I want from you. If you give them to me, I will tell you everything I know or guess about the winds."

The Avelun's features remained impassive. "What do you want?"

"First, if what it takes to touch another's Path is to close the right doors, you will teach me just how to do so. Nothing remains closed when I'm near. I'm done with that kind of helplessness. Next, you will find a way for me to speak with Maya. Without Ilaye and the others spying us out—on either side of the Gate."

"Choose something other. Those things I cannot."

Jhared smiled thinly. "You *will* not."

"No. Ilaye and I breached your child's defenses over years. By the time you reached your Becoming, we had stripped you so completely, we could enter and leave your Path almost without your notice. Nothing can be done to compensate for that damage."

"A lie! Until I came within reach of the chaos in this place, I was gaining strength. Gaining control."

Rathael looked aside. "Whatever success you perceived, it was luck or coincidence. Jhared, what we did to you was not like breaking through a wall, not something that can be rebuilt. It was like amputating a limb. You will never fully control your own Path."

An ugly stillness shrouded the room. Only distantly did Jhared register that it was the first time in half a lifetime his Teacher had used his name.

Rathael's features knotted. He rolled his shoulders, as though shifting a heavy load. "There is a thing I can tell you that might offer another kind of protection. If you would have it."

"What is it?"

"I know why you were able to throw Ilaye out of your awareness during the battle in Parnas Pass."

Jhared didn't bother to conceal the intensity of his response; the Avelun knew it already. "Tell me."

"If I do, in exchange I ask you for one thing."

"One *more* thing, you mean."

Rathael bowed his head in acknowledgment. "You must speak no word of the winds—not to any Avelun or anyone associated with the general."

"Except for yourself."

"Not to *any* Avelun," Rathael repeated. "Not to me. And not to Mayavana. I will tell you now how best to protect yourself from Ilaye. Tomorrow, I will find a way to distract both Ilaye and Nemaye while you escape. You will leave and not turn your thoughts to this place again."

"But you want the winds. I've felt how much you want them. Why—"

"I am no longer your Teacher. I have no need to indulge your questions!" The Avelun's voice regained some of its power. "Do you agree or not?"

There was a silence, punctuated by the sweep of rain across the roof. "I will not leave without speaking to Mayavana," Jhared replied. "In the end she may stay, but she must tell me herself it is what she wishes."

Rathael's jaw tightened in a gesture of frustration that Jhared recognized. He wondered with disgust whether the Avelun had copied it from him or he from the Avelun. After a long, tense moment, the other man sank against the hearth. "Very well. You will see her. Then you will leave."

It was what Jhared had sought all along, but his goals should not have aligned with Rathael's. He didn't understand what the Avelun meant to gain from him. It made him wary. "Do you mean to coerce her to stay?"

"Do you believe we will need to?"

A log popped and the flames flared higher to consume it. "No."

Unexpectedly, it was the Avelun who flinched at the naked assessment. "Be that as it may, you will have your fair chance to win her. Now, put it aside. Quiet your mind and I will tell you a story." He offered Jhared a round, jade gaze. "I recall a time when you enjoyed stories."

Somewhere within Jhared, a memory stirred of cold nights when the absence of his mother was still an open wound and a rumbling voice deep within him offered him calm and a sense of purpose. He pushed the memory away.

The Avelun cleared his throat. "This story begins with two young Travelers, reckless and silly, who threw themselves through the gleaming blue flames and went in search of the Paths of their homeland, a place both despised and desired. They hungered for something they could not name and discovered a child as hungry as they were. He greeted them eagerly, and they gave him what he sought—a whip with which to flay himself. They fashioned themselves as his Teachers. The power of authority was irresistible, and the Travelers were born to wield it. By the time they realized the strange status of their young pupil and exactly how useful it could be to walk his Path, nothing could have torn them away—"

"Stop!"

The Avelun turned to him, one fine dark eyebrow arched high. Jhared shuddered with a terrible need to finish what had been started in the tree.

"You have already survived it," Rathael said matter-of-factly. "The truth has little power now. And if you were to kill me, it would not purge the sound of my voice from your thoughts."

Jhared gave a caustic laugh, knowing his Teacher was right. "Go on."

"Our visits to your Path swiftly grew to something greater than a game. Nemaye learned of it from Ilaye and encouraged us to continue. She wanted what we could learn of the Council and the Forest Guard."

"So you made me the perfect spy. Unknown even to myself."

"You were in an excellent position," the Avelun said, his eyes not meeting Jhared's. "So long as you complied with Shorn Law. So long as your elder and your commanders trusted you."

"Of course. When I began to lose their trust, I began to lose value. That's why Shrill decided I should die in the killing winds, isn't it? Ziabela and Elian had just demanded my aid for the unbound. Shrill knew that Tierzen would sense my guilt and withdraw from me. That I would lose my usefulness." Jhared's gaze fell hard on the bruised Avelun. "You fought with her on that. Why?"

Rathael shrugged. "We had invested too many years to lose you and what you might still offer. Ilaye strikes out impulsively when angered. She never bothers to consider what might be lost by doing so."

"As when she and I met during the battle at Parnas Pass."

"Yes. As then. Whenever we entered your Path as your Teachers, we approached the very core of you, but kept the doors to our own Paths tight. You heard us but did not see us, sensed something of our emotions but never knew our true thoughts. You could not touch us. But that day in Parnas Pass when you encountered Ilaye, neither of you were on your Path."

"We were in the Nowhere. On no Path," Jhared said.

"Precisely. Where no doors exist. In the Nowhere, you are on the same terrain. Whomever you face, you do so with only your own strength to protect you. When you struck at Ilaye, you caught her. You threw her far enough from her own Path that she nearly did not make it home."

Jhared grimaced. "I didn't intend that."

"Do not apologize. She would have killed you. When she realized that the high priestess had learned what you are, she believed Avelos would execute you and that her final chance to find the winds' secret was lost."

"Why didn't she come after me later? I expected it. I expected you both."

"She would have, but you hurt her quite badly. Enough to keep her from travel for several weeks. By the time she recovered from the physical injury, fear had undone her. Ilaye always imagined herself inviolate in her dealings with you. She always underestimated the strength a Shorn man might wield as a Traveler, and she believed you revered her. That you couldn't do her harm. You shook her understanding, of you and of herself."

"And you?" Jhared asked. "I didn't hear from you after that day. Not until you came to me with lies about giving up my Teaching."

"I did not lie. We did give up your Teaching." Rathael rubbed a hand over his eyes with the expression of a man exhausted past the capacity for sleep. "The day you came near to killing my sister, I learned the truth of her longing for the winds. I learned what Nemaye had promised General Hrvan. I learned once again how foolish I am."

Before Jhared could speak, a knock barely louder than the rain startled him silent. It came again, immediate and insistent. He stood with a wave of misgiving. "They've come."

"Not Ilaye. She wouldn't bother knocking." Rathael tilted his head, as though straining to hear something just beyond perception. "Fetch Hzelka."

The knocking continued, rising in urgency. As Jhared called at the doorway to the bedroom, Hzelka appeared, her grey-brown hair sticking from her head in twin tufts, giving her an owlish look. She belted her robe and shoved her feet into shoes. "I'm coming. I'm coming," she called with drowsy resentment.

A voice rang out in Sonan. "Let me in, Hzelka! I know who you hide."

Jhared spun toward the doors. Rathael jolted backward, as if stabbed. "No. No!" the Avelun hissed, staggering to his feet.

"No, for certain. Rathael conceal yourself." Hzelka overtook Jhared, nothing drowsy remaining in her manner. She pushed him after the other man. "Go to the bedroom. Both of you."

Jhared didn't move. "Hzelka, I needn't. I know her."

The Wren turned away. She drew one door open a sliver and put her ample body between it and the room.

"Falucha! By Cael's stars, what are you doing? There's nothing for you here."

"I have not come for myself."

Jhared stepped behind Hzelka and yanked the door out of her grasp. Wind whipped into the room, causing the fire to spit. He gazed down at the slender, sodden bundle that was Falucha.

Her tawny eyes took him in with a quick, competent appraisal. "You are in one piece still? Body and spirit?"

"I should have paid more heed to your warning, my friend."

Falucha wiped rain from her eyes. Strands of wet hair curled around her oval face. "I should have spoken more clearly."

Hzelka flung her gaze from the Sonan woman to Jhared and back. "*He's* the reason you've come?"

"Why else?" Falucha turned on the Avelun woman with sudden vehemence. "Do you think hatred dies so easily? It does not. Nor the pain of loss."

The Wren flinched, but her voice was resolute. "You cannot be here. Not now."

"Let her in," Jhared said, pushing around the barrier of Hzelka's speckled wings. "She's come a long way. She's cold and wet."

Against Hzelka's protests, he drew the Sonan woman inside and led her to the fire, where he helped her to peel off her rain-weighted cloak. Water dripped from her long braid and caused her garments to cling to her spare form.

"I never expected to see you. How did you guess that something had gone wrong?"

She rubbed her hands together before the flames. "My nephew. When he came with the delivery, he saw you. He recognized—" Wings rustled behind them. Falucha straightened and turned.

She halted as if she'd hit a wall. Jhared followed the line of her gaze to where Rathael stood in the doorway, his wings furled tightly against his shoulders, his gaze wide and disbelieving. Jhared saw Falucha absorb his presence like a blow, just as Rathael had done a moment before, when he heard her voice. Her fingers touched the sunset-colored stone in her left ear. Her expression closed. She pulled her hand away and turned her back on the Avelun.

"Let the soldier come away with me, Hzelka. I am owed a life. Two."

The Wren looked pained. "Falucha, we cannot simply set him free. Nemaye has walked his Path now, and Ilaye can always find him. He wouldn't get far before they stopped him."

"Then tell Rathael to keep the doors of this Path closed. I recall he is skilled at that."

"He is. And he has." Hzelka's tone remained patient, although her features contorted with a muddle of emotion. "It will not last much longer. He cannot sustain that kind of exertion indefinitely. You have cause to know it."

"I do. I know also how self-preserving you both are. I do not see him collapsed with trying to help this man. No. You owe me two lives, Hzelka. Do not think I will allow you to destroy another one."

Hzelka's mouth opened, as if she would protest, but she said nothing.

"Does forgiveness ever grow where pain and hatred cannot die?"

Slowly, Falucha looked at Rathael, her face pale and her gaze hard. "You have no right to speak to me."

"I know, Falucha."

"He would be eight winters."

"I know." The two words, repeated, were hardly a breath.

"He had your eyes. He might have been a Traveler, like you."

"I think on that. I think on him every day. I see the Paths . . ." The handsome Avelun shivered and closed his eyes.

"Which Paths, Ratha? The one where you did not brag of your conquest to Ilaye? The one where Hzelka found the courage to defy your mother? Did you think they would be proud you had dallied with the unfeathered? Did you truly believe they would let my child live?"

"I did not believe Ilaye would betray us. She is my sister. I was too young to see her clearly. Please, Falucha." Despair darkened the man's green gaze.

"Keep your explanations. Or better, tell them to my brother. He still carries the scars Kest gave him for trying to redeem me. I am here only to rescue another person from your viper nest. Nemaye and the general have what they want. They have the woman. Free this soldier."

Such a moment of heartbreak should never have been witnessed by a stranger. Jhared had no peace to offer and no right to intrude, but knew he must speak before more harm was done to the brave, bright spirit who had, astonishingly, come for him. He laid a hand on her shoulder.

"Falucha, I cannot go. Not yet."

She turned, her amber eyes questing. "Because of the woman?"

"Yes."

"You are different from her, Jhared. From them all. I saw it. You know loyalty. Do not stay and—"

Jhared lost her words as the world jerked beneath him. He stumbled, jostled by something or someone shoving against his boundaries.

At the same moment, Rathael let out a low moan and lurched forward. He caught himself on a bookshelf. The shelf rocked, tumbling books to the floor.

"Zelka, where is your viremur?" he gasped.

Hzelka's gaze went wide. "Not now, Rathael. Not worn as you are."

"Give it," the Avelun man said, collecting himself and aiming for the door. "Or you will pay the price for the company you're keeping. Ilaye's started searching."

Fear paled Hzelka's round face. "Right. Well, we knew it wouldn't last." She turned, but Jhared reached her collection of jars first. He rustled through the medicinals until he found a familiar plug of russet leaves and tossed it to Rathael.

Rathael caught it and grasped it close. "I'll distract them while I can. When they do come, tell them it's been days since you've seen me. Zelka, make sure she's well away from here before then. I charge you with that. Make sure of it."

Rathael turned to Falucha, his eyes beseeching. A muscle moved in the Sonan woman's throat and her fingers dug into the flesh of her arms, but her amber stare remained empty and cold.

Rathael lifted his head in a barely perceptible nod. He left without saying another word. The door closed noiselessly behind him.

"What will he do?" Falucha's question came out small and reluctant.

"Drug himself so the others can't reach him," Jhared said. He had done the same thing with *slu* to shield himself from Shrill. He frowned at Hzelka. "Such a barefaced move will only make them suspicious."

"It won't," the Wren muttered. "Familiar patterns provide the best camouflage."

"Ah, I see."

Hzelka smacked her dun wings together. "He'll keep them occupied for a time, but he'll lose his grip on our Paths in the meanwhile. Damn him! I'm going to have to march over to see Hrvan. If he still wants you in one piece, he'll need to rein in Nemaye."

"Nemaye wants me in one piece," Jhared said. "She just doesn't know it yet. Use that if you must, Hzelka."

Rathael didn't want him to speak of the winds, but he owed no loyalty to Rathael and cared nothing for his feuds with his family. To three women, however, he did owe something: One of them had left him. One of them had put herself in danger for him. And one of them had risked everything in giving herself to him. That risk he hadn't understood until now.

"We'll see," Hzelka replied, but she was staring at Falucha. "You will take yourself back to the city before the others realize you have seen him."

"No. I stay until Jhared Denaban walks free from this place. The general already knows he needs me in one piece. My people have cared for his family's birds since before the occupation."

"Falucha—" Jhared started simultaneously with Hzelka, but the Sonan woman pushed out a hand, refusing them both.

"You know my reasons. Do not act as if no wings and no scars mean no intelligence. I can help. Nemaye and Ilaye have never touched me on the Paths."

"It will be the end of him if something happens to you," Hzelka said. "You do know that."

Falucha's chin came up and her features turned brittle. "He can choose his own end, as he wishes."

"Flight is not in the wings," she had said to Jhared in the market. *"It is in the spirit. In the grace of movement. In the yearning."*

She had known that truth not because of her birds, but because of her love. She had loved Rathael and paid a ghastly price for it. Jhared could not find it in him now to belittle her courage.

"Hzelka, Falucha and I will stay. You go to the general."

The Wren hesitated, then sputtered acquiescence. "Listen closely: Katian or Kest will have told Ilaye where you are. It was never meant to be a secret. It's Rathael's interference they won't tolerate."

"I know what to do," Jhared said evenly. "Go, Hzelka. Only the general's authority matters now."

She didn't take long to prepare herself, though she muttered over it the entire time. Jhared warmed cider by the hearth and poured for Falucha, who sat in silence sipping her drink.

When Hzelka said her goodbyes and the door had closed behind her, Falucha looked up, her expression shrewd despite the pain there. "Does the Avelun carry your secrets, Jhared Denaban? Is that why you don't leave her?"

27.
RETRIBUTION

"Does the Avelun carry your secrets, Jhared Denaban?"
Jhared was standing behind Falucha's chair, so she couldn't see his reaction to her question. "Yes," he answered simply.

"I could say I do not understand. It would be a lie. They are beautiful and clever and far too perceptive. It is impossible not to be moved by them. Even if it is a move toward hatred."

"Falucha, I need to return to the house. To speak with Maya."

She turned to face him. "If you do, the broken Paths will take you again."

"They won't. At least I don't believe so. Rathael has secured the doors to my Path so that no one can reach in. That must also mean I cannot tumble out. But I must go before he loses his grip. I won't ask you to return home, but will you at least stay here and safe while I'm gone?"

"Why should you think I long for safety? I said I could help and I will. It is not your place to protect everyone."

He touched her arm. "No, not everyone, Falucha."

She smiled. Her freckled face had regained some color. "Thank you for that. You are a good man. But I choose my own risks. Let us go."

The walk back to the manor was less of an ordeal than the escape from it had been the previous afternoon. The storm had blown itself out and the breeze drifted soft and salty through the trees. Jhared's thoughts had already flown to the house and what he might encounter there. To avoid catching up with Hzelka, Falucha directed them along an abandoned game trail that skirted closer to the water. When they came upon the wall that marked the edge of Hrvan's pastureland, Jhared hoisted Falucha to his shoulders and she scrambled over. Then he sprang, caught the lip, and pulled himself up. Once on the other side, they hiked down the sandy ridge to the beach, where they could approach the manor from the waterfront. If they could avoid being spotted by anyone in the rooftop garden, Jhared knew he could find his way to Maya's chamber. If she were not there, he knew how to leave her a message. The other message he must leave would be somewhat more challenging.

They spoke little as the house came into view, its beige and green stone melding with the landscape. Packed sand crunched under their feet. At Jhared's left, beyond a stretch of cream-colored shore, the ocean rolled up the beach and slid away. At his right, the ridge curved up to the tableland just above his head. He strode close to Falucha and kept them both near the ridge's base, counting on the land to block them from the line of sight of anyone in the yard or the orchard. Alert as he was, the roar and hiss of the ocean still nearly masked the subtle change in the pattern. He halted.

Falucha glanced up. "What?"

He grabbed her and pulled her toward the shadow of the ridge just as another determined smack against his boundaries threw him off balance. Pitching sideways, he tumbled them both beneath the undercut tableland as men's voices barked over their heads.

Jhared gritted his teeth and braced himself against an anticipated invasion of his Path. Beside him, Falucha flattened her body against the land. They remained motionless as sand trickled onto their heads from the men pacing at the edge above them.

There were three men. The language they spoke differed somewhat from the Sonan Maya had taught Jhared, but he didn't need any translation to recognize the sound of orders being given. He drew quiet breaths; his awareness split between the stirring Paths inside of him and the threat above them. After a time, the tone of the conversation changed, as though with their duty acknowledged, the men relaxed. Jhared caught the scent of pipe smoke and heard someone laugh. Finally, with a last thump that sent a runnel of sand down his back, the men marched away.

Falucha gripped his hand. "You are whole? She has not broken through yet?"

"Not yet." Jhared stepped out of the shadow and peered over the ridge. The three men were heading toward the stables. Not the *hofja* personal guard in Hrvan's blue livery, these men were wiry Sonans in the dun garments of soldiers. More soldiers milled about the yard. At a glance, Jhared spied nearly twenty. From the extent of the mud churned up in front of the manor, there were more. "Who are they?"

"From the garrison in the east," Falucha replied. "Near Laebek. They are on their way north. Jhared, they say General Hrvan is gone."

"Gone where?"

"North. He left last night with Captain Odemir and a small escort. The garrison is to join him. They are uncertain why, but they are pleased. They trust Hrvan and say he is doing great things for Sona."

Jhared scrubbed a hand over his face. General Hrvan was the one man who could bridle Nemaye and the others. But he had gone off to do great things. Why not? He was rebuilding Saimbor, bringing hope for renewal to the people of Sona. Good things for his people. Great things? He was stealing the knowledge of the centuries from all the surrounding nations and hoarding it for his *Simata'yo*. He was trying to breed his own Avelune children. A vague memory bobbed toward the surface. Jhared reached for it, but it eeled away. A question came to him instead.

"Falucha, what does an ambitious man want for his battered country?"

The Sonan woman looked up sharply. "Power. Position."

"Of course, but what does he mean to do with them? This is a man who saw the heart of Sona beaten into the mud. Who watched his people bowed by hunger and humiliation."

From another place in his mind, Jhared recalled what Rathael had told him just before Falucha arrived. *The day you came near to killing my sister, I learned the truth of her longing for the winds. I learned what Nemaye had promised General Hrvan.*

"What does an ambitious man want for his battered country?" Understanding sparked in Falucha's gaze. "Retribution."

Jhared's heart thudded against his ribs. "Did the soldiers say anything about a woman traveling north with the general? Would they know of the Avelune?"

"Nothing of a woman. Odemir knows the Avelune. Likely a few commanders do also. What is it?"

Pieces came together, one after another, like individual footprints laid down until they formed a trail. Jhared recognized where they were heading: General Hrvan meant to use the killing winds against Amuria.

He opened his mouth, glanced at Falucha, and shut it. They were her people who had suffered in the occupation.

She met his gaze. "You wonder if I would cheer for death in Amuria."

"I have no right to ask for your help, Falucha. It may be that I must act against the general."

"Ask," she replied. "General Hrvan is a symbol of Sona to some. Not to me. You think he plans to devastate? I tell you that if offered such power, he will use it."

"Do they speak widely in Sona of the winds that kill?" Jhared said.

She nodded slowly, her amber gaze growing round.

"The Avelune know the winds' source. It is the same source that allows them flight. I believe they have promised it to Hrvan."

"But they do not yet possess it," she murmured. "What they see but cannot touch! Oh, I understand. I understand. They promised him the destruction of Amuria, and he promised to help them find what they so crave: the skies!"

"That must be right," Jhared said. "It is the reason Hrvan created the archive and began a search in every land."

"Has the archive finally given them what they wanted?" Falucha trailed off, her expression sober. "Oh. Not the archive. They found a different source."

"A different source," Jhared agreed. "That's why the general needs Maya in the north. At least he believes she's the one he needs. Come."

He marched them swiftly along the last stretch of sand and back up to the tableland. When they reached the southwest corner of the manor, they paused. Falucha leaned panting against the stone. Jhared put his back to the wall and peered along the building's ocean side. There were no trees or outbuildings to conceal an approaching man, just seagrasses and wildflowers and a long expanse of wall interrupted by windows, with shutters latched tight or open to the breeze.

Falucha moved beside him. "Go. I will watch here."

He looked down at her, hesitated, then nodded. "Give a piper's whistle if someone should approach. Then get yourself away."

"The soldiers are no threat to me. You just be quick."

He touched her shoulder in farewell. Then he was gliding away, moving with long-practiced stealth along the back wall of the manor.

From his previous misadventures in the house, he knew the approximate location of Maya's room. It meant a climb to the second level. Years of blasting from sand and wind had carved the stones of the wall into random holds. Jhared took a breath and started scaling.

Despite the damp weather, the shutters to Maya's chamber were thrown wide. Jhared adjusted his hold on a slippery stone and smiled a little. Accustomed to living in the open, Maya would hardly be likely to close herself in.

Soundlessly, he climbed onto the casement, crouched, and scanned the room. In size and furnishing it was similar to the one in which he had been caged, although in this room flowering plants offered color and a sweet, green scent. No bird twittered by the low bed. On the floor lay Maya's packs, with her clothes and gear drooping out of them. Maya stood before an open wardrobe, her back to the window.

But for one great wing slowly fanning the air, she was motionless, staring at the wardrobe's contents as if she didn't see them. Jhared lowered himself into the room and took a silent step toward her. From their first meeting, she had often known where he stood before she saw him. This time, she didn't turn.

He halted in the middle of the room, uncertain. *It is pity that has bound her to you. Pity and a desperate need for anything reminiscent of her heritage.* Drijan's words had been spat out of malice, but it did not make them wrong. Maya cared for him; Jhared did not doubt that, but she had never tried to hide how much she despised everything that made him who he was. One did not expect to shape a future from that.

"You are going north with the general," he said softly. "You haven't told them the truth."

She whipped around so fast her wings unfurled to give her balance. Light and shadow filled the room as her primaries splayed like reaching fingers. Her eyes caught his, and for an instant, fear sparked in their sage depths. It drove through him like a spear. He backed away, but she lunged after him. He had a heartbeat to wonder whether she had time to draw her knife. Then her arms slipped under his cloak and around his shoulders and she fit herself against him, warm and close.

"Thank the gods of skies and seas, Jhared. You're back. How? *How?*"

She smelled of sunlight and salt and flowers. Jhared couldn't speak at first, but only stood absorbing the stunning reality of her. "We don't have time for how," he finally managed. "I dare not stay in the house too long. Maya, General Hrvan still believes you can call the killing winds. The others don't know it's me. You didn't tell them?"

"Oh Jhared, I did tell them. How could I not when they asked for my help?"

"Then they know? Ilaye knows?"

Maya unclasped her hands and disengaged from him. "They helped me to see that I . . . that we were wrong."

"What do you mean wrong?"

"Jhared, come sit. You look battered. Where have you been?"

He didn't join her. He had expected her to demand an accounting for his attack on the Avelune or to openly reject him and send him away. He hadn't counted on this confusing approach and withdrawal. "With the Avelune healer, Hzelka. Have you met her?"

"No." Maya frowned at the floor. "But I've heard her name."

"I doubt it was said with any great fondness. Maya, what are you trying to say about the killing winds?"

"The others have taught me so much, Jhared. I understand many things that I didn't before. Just think on it: consider the strength that was stolen from you at the Shearing. I have touched your scars. I have seen the pain of them come near to crippling you. No one who is Shorn could possibly possess the power of the skies. It was me all along. It must have been."

The room swayed gently. Jhared knew a building dread. "Maya, you've felt the doors open within me. You've seen what it takes for me to stop them. Is this Moravel talking? Did he find a way to convince you?"

She flushed, but did not lower her gaze. "Ilaye."

"Ilaye. Ah." He drew a steadying breath. "Let me tell you about Ilaye. In the guise of a Teacher, she intruded on my Path for nine years, punishing me at her whim as only someone who knows my worst nightmares could. In Vris, she tried to force me to violate you because she thought it would win her the winds. Outside Velantar and again in Parnas Pass, she tried to kill me because she believed I was of no more use. She has done far worse to others. She is a malevolent spirit. Nothing, nothing that comes out of her mouth is—"

He stopped short. Maya's agonized expression told him he had made a mistake. It was too much too soon. She so longed for a community of her own people. Of course she could not bear to believe evil of one of its leaders. She leaned her head in her hands and pressed her palms against her brow. In that pained gesture, he saw her deny his words. When she lifted her head, something subtle had changed in the way she looked at him.

"Jhared, do you realize you have been gone more than two moons? All that time, Ilaye stayed close to me. She helped me to endure the knowledge that you might be lost. She gave me reasons to look toward the future."

"She gave you reasons to believe I was gone when all I needed was to be away from their chaos. Maya, she and Nemaye plan to use the killing winds to destroy Amuria. They promised it to General Hrvan. That is why you are being sent north."

"I know why they're sending me north, Jhared. I cannot very well practice calling the killing winds in the midst of Saimbor. Hrvan has gone ahead to prepare a place for me. This is just the beginning. There are debts to be paid." A small smile played at the edge of her lips. "Retribution is not always a terrible thing."

Her expression chilled him. It held nothing of the insightful and considering woman he knew. And her words held something more. He felt sick. "It isn't only Amuria they mean to attack, is it?"

"It wasn't only Amuria who watched while Sona suffered. It wasn't Amuria who lit the arrows and threw the spears and drove the Avelune broken from the skies."

Jhared closed his eyes, working to still the images of burning wings and falling bodies. "No, it wasn't. So Sona and the Avelune are the warmongers that Zinderdali warned us about. They pushed Sahiste and Avelos to the precipice. Not the unbound."

The treacherous Avelune.

"Encouragement was hardly needed to spark conflict between Sahiste and Avelos," Maya said derisively. "With the growing resources of the *Simata'yo,* Hrvan had little trouble hiring men in both countries willing to press the cause. When the winds are howling from the Barren to the Sandien Mountains, Sahiste and Avelos will continue to blame one another. And swampy little Sona, which has never been a threat to anyone, will rise in the vacuum they leave. You should be pleased, Jhared. Avelos will be razed and all its evils wiped away. Isn't that what you wished? To see all the Paths of Avelos unravel?"

"In my weakest moments," he admitted. "And only as a bullied child wishes agony to his tormentor. It is not my purpose. It has never been. Maya, how can you be a part of this?"

Her eyes flashed with anger. "You can ask me that? When my uncle gave his life and my mother sacrificed her future to save me from the knives? When I have spent years hiding what I am, living alone at the fringes of any community, always running to survive?"

Elder Trianor. Branlen. Lady Nemiah. Leita. Thousands of others from Amuria to Sahiste. If Ilaye came to acknowledge the destructive power he possessed, they would all be lost. Jhared's only hope was the Avelune's continued disregard.

"I know why you love them," Maya went on. "I do see that now. You had no choice. You had to embrace the warped logic behind everything they did to you or be driven mad by the cruelty of it. If you have the courage to look under the brittle shell of that love, you will find your anger. You will understand the importance of what we are doing."

"Mayavana, I have seen you on a thousand Paths. I knew you beyond the Gate before we ever met in this present. This is not you. Come away with me. Do not poison yourself so."

Her laughter clawed the air. "How could I possibly flee with a Shorn man? My own people are here, whole and strong." She closed on him. Her capable fingers grasped his arm. "All those times you denied your desire to punish those who cut you, you never asked me what I wished. I will tell you something, soldier. No one is ever who you hope they will be. Do not believe you have seen the truth of me."

Her hand tightened, then withdrew. She turned to the wardrobe and yanked a shirt from its hook. "You should go. I must finish packing. I depart in the morning with Ilaye and the garrison."

Jhared watched her in silence, the exquisite curve of her wings, the beloved angles of her face. A chasm opened wide in his chest. "Goodbye, Mayavana."

As he crossed to the door, her glare made him halt. "Where do you think you're going?" she snapped.

"I've a message to deliver. From Hzelka for General Hrvan's house girl."

"The girl with the braids? Vyla? She's gone with the general's people."

Surprise startled Jhared out of his caution. "What? Why would Hrvan take a housekeeper to the garrison?"

"Not the general. Apparently, Captain Odemir has claimed her for a mistress. All the house staff are whispering over it. What does the healer want with her?"

"Vyla . . . asked for an ointment for one of the general's birds. Madam Hzelka sent to say she does not have what the girl was seeking."

Claimed as a mistress by an advisor to the general. It meant protection for Vyla and, goddess forgive him, for any child she might bear. No doubt Hrvan had arranged it. He must have known the danger in sending her to Jhared, even if Vyla had not. Jhared wondered if she had been allowed any part in the decision before she had been handed over to another man. If the babe were born Avelun, would she be allowed to keep it? Her child. His child. A Path lit before him that he would never have the chance to walk. Something he recognized as regret hollowed out his middle. He didn't realize how long he had been standing at the door until Maya barked at him again.

"Go out the way you came. Do you think I want the others to see you leaving my room?"

"As you wish." Turning on his heel, he spied Maya's staff and bow canted against the far side of the wardrobe. His own bow and quiver leaned companionably beside them. Without a word, he caught up his gear, strode back to the window, and swung himself over the casement. He didn't look back as he scaled the stone, dropped to the ground, and slipped away.

At the corner of the house, he seized Falucha by the arm and dragged her along with him, ignoring her round-eyed alarm as he stormed away from the manor, along the ridge, and back to the beach. The damp wind lashed his face as he ran across the sand. The beach stretched for miles. He could run for days, until he could no longer see Maya's face or hear her cold tone.

"Jhared, slow! Slow down!" Falucha grabbed at his sleeve, her breath whistling with effort. "I am no courser."

After another moment, he forced himself back to a walk. "I'm sorry."

"I am the one sorry," she panted. "I feared this."

"No. Not this. Maya's in trouble."

Falucha offered him a look that held as much doubt as sympathy. "She did not strike me as one to walk where she does not wish it. Tell me."

"She knows what Hrvan and the other Avelune are planning. She's a part of it. She was contemptuous and cruel, and she sent me away."

"Well, then?"

"It was a show. I'm sure of it. One of the others was traveling her Path. Or trying to." Jhared looked out at the ocean, wishing he were as certain as he sounded.

"Do not believe you have seen the truth of me."

"How could I flee with a Shorn man?"

How. "She was trying to ask for help without alerting them."

Falucha sighed and sat down on a boulder. The breeze danced with strands of her loam-colored hair. "You must know it is not possible to lie to the one walking on your Path. Unless you bury it very deep, the Traveler knows your thoughts as you know them. There is no such thing as a 'show.' What the girl says, she must believe. At least some."

"I know. It is the *some* to which I must hold." The breeze gusted, cupping his cloak like a sail.

"What is this now?" With one hand, Falucha grabbed the edge of his cloak and flipped the inside up. Neat and quick, she tugged an object out of the dark wool.

It was a feather, oblong, about the length of his hand. It took some effort to free it; the quill had been thrust deep into a fold. When Falucha held it up, it shone a rich, bloody red.

Jhared recognized the shape of the feather as well as the man to whom it belonged. "She must have put it there."

Falucha twirled the feather between her forefinger and thumb. "It comes from the younger red-wing. Moravel. See the darker red at the edge of the vanes? That means a young one still."

"Do you know him?" Jhared asked.

"A bit. He was at the edge of manhood when I still made the deliveries. Curious about the outside, so he talked to me sometimes. Bullied by his brother for being quieter, gentler. Different from the others. A little . . . a little like Rathael in that. But less brilliant, more steady. Why did she give his feather to you?"

It was a heart feather, like the one Maya had given him from her own wing on that first day of their meeting in the Sandien Mountains, when they had each sworn to abide by the custom of peace at a shared fire. It was a symbol of trust. Jhared turned away from it. "If I am to escape with Maya, we must have a way to block Ilaye and Nemaye from her Path. Is there any chance Rathael could shield us another day?"

"Already he has lasted past anything I have known of him. You will be open again soon. Very soon."

"And Hzelka? Could she do it?"

"Only Ilaye and Rathael can lock all doors to a Path at once. Not even Nemaye can."

Jhared sank down wordlessly beside her.

"You do not want to go to Moravel because you think he has claimed your feathered girl, but if that is true, then your guess is wrong and she does not want to leave with you after all. So you lose nothing by speaking to him that you have not already lost."

The loss meant nothing; he told himself that. He was Shorn and didn't mean to be foolish about his place on the Path. "I must only see her safe."

"Then come." Falucha slid off the rock and turned, offering him her hand. "I will take you to his home. We cannot linger. Unless you think what you saw in her was only your own wish and not the truth. Then you should run from here. Now."

He took her hand and stood. "Let's go."

Falucha led him into the forest very close to the trail where Hzelka had taken him the night before, near the clearing and Rathael's tree. The day had turned muggy. Forest flies droned in patches of sunlight. The cottages that had been only vague mounds in the darkness in the daylight formed a sprawling hamlet that merged with the trees. Each well-tended home was built of fragrant pine and decked with garlands of dark needles. From a distance, a stranger might overlook them, though it would be difficult to overlook the dozen or so Avelune going about the ordinary tasks of living: sweeping a porch, working in a garden, tending to a rabbit hutch. The tall, lithe figures clothed in practical garments bore wings of grey and blue, black and rose, brown and white, all neatly furled over their muscled backs. It was a scene Jhared could never have imagined. Still, something was missing. Despite the activity, the hamlet seemed unnaturally quiet.

"Where are the children?" he murmured.

"The last child born living to an Avelun woman was Drijan," Falucha said crisply. "Nineteen summers ago."

"I had no idea it was so long. They truly are dying. Yet they won't—" Jhared bit off the words, cursing inwardly.

The Sonan woman walked more quickly.

"Forgive me, Falucha."

She made a face. "Do not stop. The mood of these birds I do not like."

He studied their observers surreptitiously. The stares of revulsion he provoked were so familiar he hadn't even marked them. "They know what I am."

"Worse, I think. They believe you are a pet of Nemaye. Not all the exiles like the way their guides lead them."

Falucha chose a trail that twisted away from the heart of the forest toward the water. Soon it opened upon a tiny clearing and an odd little house cleverly built around the base of a tree. The house was more window than wall, with all its wide shutters open to the humid afternoon. Above the shingled roofline, steps spiraled thirty feet around the straight, wide trunk of a sentinel pine to a circular balcony. No railing fenced the balcony, but flowering vines around the tree dripped large, horn-shaped blossoms all about it. Plants of curious shapes and unexpected colors trickled out of clay pots that hung from hooks on the balcony's edge.

Moravel was in front of the house, kneeling in the dirt of a flowerbed. Dappled light pied his face as he bent close to a sad-looking trio of stalks with wilting blue flowers. It appeared he was talking to them. Jhared slowed, but Falucha marched on. As the Avelun's dark head lifted, the smile he gave her illuminated his features with unexpected sweetness.

"Hello, Moravel."

"Little Falucha! What are you doing here? I never hoped—" Abruptly the red-wing's pleasure fractured. He surged to his feet in one powerful motion, his storm-green gaze on Jhared.

Jhared took another step and halted. Moravel was slight but tall, taller than he was. Beside the hulking figure of Kest on that first night, Jhared hadn't noticed. As he stood before the Avelun, Jhared knew himself measured and evaluated; he saw conclusions drawn, even as he did the same.

"Have I been found sufficiently lacking?" the red-wing said mildly. "After all, you have already met Kest."

"Perhaps you should pose the question to Mayavana," Jhared said. "I care nothing for your rivalry with your brother. I am here only because of this." He drew out the heart feather.

Moravel looked at it, his features darkening. "How did that come to you?"

"Maya gave it to me."

"And I gave it to her for what she gave to me. Did you come to hear the details?"

Jhared lifted a shoulder. "About all you are lacking?"

"About the intricate balance two can achieve when both are winged."

"How strange," Jhared said, pushing a bland look across his face. "I did not realize balance was the ultimate goal. I thought it was to soar to the highest peak together and go plummeting off of it. Perhaps we have hit upon the reason Avelune women no longer quicken."

Moravel's wings mantled in a sudden blur of red. Jhared altered his stance, prepared for an attack.

"Stop!" Falucha ordered. "Both of you. Moravel, your brother's act does not become you. Jhared, no time remains for dueling."

For all Falucha's small size, Jhared had recognized from the first that she possessed the kind of authority to which animals and men responded. At her reprimand, the red-wing drew back a step. Jhared uncoiled slowly, although he did not relax his vigilance.

"Fine," Falucha muttered. "Now, Moravel, you will please invite us in before things are said others should not hear."

The Avelun man's gaze went to the ground, to the dying blue flowers. He nodded silently.

"Widow's tears," Jhared observed. "They grow rampant in the meadows of Avelos."

"The general had them brought here," the red-wing said. "He knew I had a notion to create an Avelonian garden. They don't like the sandy soil." Moravel looked up, his features turned still and emotionless. "Falucha is right. If we plan to continue insulting one another, we'd best do it inside."

He took them into the house, an airy space simply furnished, with the great tree trunk at its center. Jhared hardly felt as though he had come inside. Windows framed the forest in each direction and made the most of the breeze. The steps that encircled the tree trunk began in the house, leading to a trap door in the roof that could be opened to allow access to the balcony.

Moravel gestured to a table surrounded by stools and decorated with a vase of fragrant yellow flowers. Jhared didn't know their name, but they were another variety from the meadows of home. He remained standing, until Falucha glared him into a seat.

"I am glad you stayed in your mother's house," Falucha said, smiling at the pretty room.

The red-wing plunked onto the table a bowl full of small round fruit with translucent pink skin. "It wasn't a choice I was offered. Kest decided he preferred the manor, so the house came to me."

"Do not act as if you wanted it another way, Moravel. You never liked the manor. Even as a boy you craved the wilds."

The red-wing dropped onto a stool and looked at the Sonan woman. To Jhared's surprise, a partial smile turned the corners of his mouth. "It is good to see you, Falucha."

"I am not certain if it is good to see you," the woman replied tartly. "I thought by now you would be out of your cage. Not doing Nemaye's bidding."

"Lucha, there is no out. I was a child when I dreamed otherwise. If I were to leave the general's protection, I would end as a part of some Bird Walker's exhibit. If by luck I made it free of Sona, the Amurians would slay me out of hand. Avelos and Sahiste would be pleased to kill me as well, but they would take their time about it."

"Maya has managed to make a life," Jhared said.

"You call what Mayavana has a life?" Moravel replied. "She does not. She is tired of endless wandering and worn to an edge from living with danger as her shadow."

The revelation struck Jhared like an arrow. He had believed Maya thrived on her wandering. "You know she would have done almost anything to make her life here," he said. "We both would have. You and the others were the unhoped-for incarnation of a dream."

"I *do* know that!" Moravel snapped. "You think it doesn't kill me we have nothing but venom to offer? You think I enjoy playing the games Nemaye has set for us? Mayavana is a gift our people desperately need. If not for Nemaye's hatred and my brother's warmongering . . ." The Avelun slammed his fist onto the table and bowed his head. Tension drew every line in his body. Jhared understood the man's struggle, but he had no time for it.

"If Maya gave you anything, it was her trust. Was she right in doing so or was that another part of the game?"

Moravel looked up. Jhared thought the Avelun might actually attempt to strike him this time, but instead the man sank back onto his stool. "I know what it means that she offered you the feather. What do you want of me?"

"I think Nemaye or Ilaye is traveling with her. Is that true?"

"I wouldn't have thought they would risk offending her so soon, but it's possible."

"Then I need help dealing with them. I cannot take Maya away unless we are both shielded."

"Take her?" The Avelun's feathers shifted. "Have you spoken with her about leaving?"

Jhared flattened his palm against the table. "Not directly."

"Yet you are so certain she will go?"

"After all you just admitted, Moravel, do you believe she would be willing to stay?"

A pained smile scored the Avelun's face. "It is a difficult thing to disown one's family, no matter how venomous they are. And we are the only family Maya will ever know."

Jhared stared at the beautiful winged man and knew a cold rush of doubt. Had he misread Maya after all? How could he presume she would welcome back her shadow of a life? The Avelune were her people. He was nothing but Shorn. Even Vyla had said it. He was *hofja*: he did not fit in any world. Perhaps Maya saw a chance for her to fit in here.

Then Jhared thought of her arms around him and the smile with which she had once greeted him and he shut out all other possibilities. "She means to flee. She needs my help."

Moravel leaned back with a sigh. "Very well. You returned to the house. How did you manage that without falling? Or, no. You had help, didn't you?" Moravel glanced at Falucha and back to Jhared, his expression uneasy. "I see. Rathael has guarded your Path. But his strength is not endless and his will is unpredictable."

"That's right," Jhared said.

"I don't possess half Rathael's skill and I am no part of Nemaye's trusted circle. What do you expect me to do?"

"I want you to poison them."

The red-wing laughed, a deep, round sound that caused his wings to bounce slightly above his shoulders. "Poison Nemaye? You don't wish my help. You wish my death."

"I do not wish it," Jhared said, "but neither would it pain me."

Moravel laughed again. "Maya said you were an honest soldier."

"If I cannot block Nemaye and the others from our Paths, then they must be made incapable of traveling. You must send them into oblivion long enough for us to be safely away."

"And once you are away? What then to keep Ilaye from crippling you?"

Jhared took one of the fruits from the bowl, smoothed his thumb thoughtfully over the pink skin. "I have some thoughts on that. It isn't your concern."

"You ask a lot," Moravel said. "All of it against my own interests."

Falucha touched the red-wing's arm. "It is not in you to hold her, Mor. You are not Kest."

"That is something I am reminded often enough. Shall I stand my ground this time, refuse you, and finally prove myself to him?"

"You will never prove yourself to Kest," Jhared said. "You reflect a side of the mirror he cannot bear to look upon. He will always demand something from you that you cannot give."

Moravel scoffed. "What do you know of my brother?"

"More than I wish to. I have seen you on uncountable Paths. If you do this thing, you will prove you can be true to yourself. A goal that so far seems to have eluded you."

Moravel didn't respond. A sea breeze breathed across the room and played with the petals of the flowers in the vase.

"There is a reason you gave the girl your feather," Falucha murmured. "Would you undo all it means?"

"No. I am not so far gone as that." The red-wing sighed. "Not yet. I will do what you ask. For Mayavana. And for you, Falucha."

"How will you reach them all?" Jhared asked.

"Oh, I have the lure to reach them. You needn't worry."

Jhared didn't like the bitter expression the red-wing offered, but he couldn't fault Moravel's commitment. Once the man agreed to help, he proved himself to be thoughtful and clever. Together, they worked out where and when Jhared would meet Maya and how she would make it to him without Hrvan's personal guard on her heels. It must be carefully timed to avoid the garrison patrol as well. Moravel plucked his heart feather out of Jhared's hand, promising to pass it back to Maya to alert her to their collaboration. It was Moravel who took the note Falucha scribbled out that would send her nephew to the docks to check the next expected landing of the *Mila Jul*.

"Hzelka will have what draught you need," Falucha said when the rest had been settled.

Moravel gave her a rueful look. "You think I don't possess the herbs necessary to send a man into oblivion when he needs it?"

Jhared saw Falucha shaking her head. Then the scene blurred into a sheen of blue. The first blow knocked him clear off the stool. The second threw him to his knees. He slammed up barriers against the Gate, as though that might do any good to keep intruders out if Rathael had lost his hold. Distantly, he was aware of Falucha grasping his shoulder. He repeated his litany of names, as the blows reverberated against him like a hammer against an anvil. When the hammer finally stopped and he was left panting on the ground, his boundaries continued to tremble. He wouldn't be alone on his Path much longer.

"They're looking for you!" Moravel was on his feet, his face dark with horror. "And you came here. To my home! If Ilaye or Nemaye breaks through your Path and sees you with me, you can burn all the plans we've made. And any other future you might have hoped for."

"I had no choice," Jhared panted. "You wouldn't have committed to it if I hadn't brought you the feather." He pulled himself upright. "You needed proof Maya still has some connection to me. You seek a reason to keep her here."

"I did. I do! But I don't crave my own painful end." The Avelun drew his wings close, breathing hard.

The attempt against Jhared's Path had left behind an unholy ache. He rubbed the heels of his palms against his brow. "They don't know. Not yet."

Moravel rustled his wings again, working visibly to regain his composure. "It was not a role I sought, you know. When Nemaye asked it of me, I tried to convince her to wait. We have not thoroughly cataloged the archive. I am sure we could find a way to call the winds without using Maya, but the others are done with waiting. Kest would have taken her, willing or not. I thought I might offer her some protection. What else could I do?"

"Are you apologizing for helping your people or for not helping them?" Jhared said bitterly.

"I am offering you an explanation I thought you might understand."

"Why would you ever believe *I* am the one who needs an explanation? Maya is the one you have exploited, and she is her own person." Jhared turned away from the red-wing. Had the Paths turned just a little differently, he might have found a home here; the unbound Kin might have come eagerly to help renew the community; this man might have been a friend. So many possibilities had slipped away because High Chieftain Tumal had not overcome his fear and the Avelune could not surrender their hatred. Jhared stared out the window at the garden.

"The widow's tears. In Avelos, they grow over battlefields. They are a symbol of loss and memory."

Moravel joined him at the window, head bowed. "My people are trapped by memories. So trapped we can find no new solutions to our problems. We can create nothing new—not even children. We only reenact the horrors done to us."

Jhared nodded and turned to the door, ready to be away from Moravel, from them all. Falucha hurried behind him. He had already stepped into the sunshine when Moravel called from the window.

"Tell me, Jhared Denaban. Please. Is there anything of beauty left in Avelos?"

Jhared caught himself in mid-stride, taken off guard by the question and by the cascade of images that followed it. "The mountains," he answered. "The mountains of Avelos were meant for those who soar."

He went on, leaving the red-wing alone, understanding with sudden clarity that not all the scars from the Exile War had been carved into the flesh of the Shorn.

28.
FLIGHT

On the trail back to Hzelka's, Jhared walked beside Falucha in silence. He sensed she needed the distance as much as he did. Only as they approached the ancient compound did he venture to speak. "Will he do it? Poison his own people?"

"Yes," Falucha said simply.

Neither of them spoke again as they wrestled through the hedge and passed through the broken gate. By the time they reached Hzelka's little haven, the ache in Jhared's head had become an arrow of fire embedded in his skull. He drew slow, even breaths and kept his thoughts neutral. No one came trampling over his Path, but the arrow burned where it had lodged. He knocked at Hzelka's door with a studied calm. If Ilaye or Nemaye could sense anything of his response, he refused to reveal the damage they were causing with this new attack.

The door flew open and slammed against the inner wall. "Where have you been?" the Wren cried, pouncing on him and dragging him inside. "How was I to know whether Nemaye had carted you off or you had just decided to flee? I am trying my best to keep you in one piece, and you run around flaunting danger."

"We know the general's gone," Jhared said, pushing free of Hzelka's grasp. "I've seen Mayavana. I'm leaving tonight. You'll have nothing more to worry over."

"You what?" Hzelka pressed a hand against her lips.

"I'm leaving. And Maya as well."

The Wren peered up at him unhappily. "Jhared, what are you saying? Rathael lost his hold on our Paths not an hour ago. You are open. Whatever you have planned, Nemaye will already know it."

Jhared pinched his brow between his fingers, but the arrow continued to prod his brain. "Well, that might explain something. Why my head has turned into a cracked eggshell."

"Jhared?" Falucha's warm amber gaze came into focus before him.

"The problem is . . . it's rather a challenge to think."

"Oh dear. Ilaye has already been kicking her way through his Path." Hzelka's tone was grim. "Sit him down."

"Wait. Wait!" Jhared threw off the hands that reached for him. "I'm not addled." He sucked a breath.

"Damn, boy, what have they done with you?"

"Stop talking. I need to look more closely. It's not what you think. Hzelka, can you bring me back?"

"Bring you back? You enter the Gate right now and Ilaye will smear you across the Nowhere like a glop of bird shit. Sit down, damn you. I'll take a look myself."

She pushed him to the hearth. Unresisting, he dropped onto the stone. With one hand, Hzelka cupped his cheek, her gaze growing vague as her focus turned toward the Gate and she sought his Path. He tried to imagine what it would be like to reach for a new Perspective, a known Perspective, as it ran along the same Parallel and Place as his own. What would it be to open the right doors and take one sideways step into another person's life? How else might he use the Paths if he had such control? His Teachers had used their control to shape him. What influence might he have? Hzelka's wings relaxed and sagged to the ground. Beyond the pain, Jhared sensed something stirring inside him. He closed his eyes and tried not to fight it.

Gradually, he grew aware of having drifted to the deepest point within himself. He sensed two spirits shifting among his thoughts, as his Teachers so often had shifted there. One presence, still and silent, gripped his Path like a drowning man clinging to a log. The other moved into the pulsing heat of his pain and cried out, a sound of shocked agony. Swiftly, Jhared drew back, but another outcry split his thoughts. Hzelka. Jhared's awareness of the outer world popped back as she stumbled, her wings flailing, her hands pressed against her skull as if to keep it from breaking apart. She landed in a heap in front of the hearth.

"It's Rathael," she panted. "He's put himself on your Path. He must have slipped in when he lost his hold on the rest of us."

Jhared nodded and instantly regretted it. "He's using the pain deliberately, isn't he? To fog me from the others."

"I think so. I couldn't reach him. He means not to be reached."

"Hzelka, it's not something he's doing to me. The pain. It's his pain."

Hzelka groaned, still pressing a hand against her temple. "That's what I felt as well. He has opened himself to allow his perceptions onto your Path."

"He's injured then."

The Wren clambered to her feet, awkwardly folding and refolding her wings. "He has traveled too long. I warned him. I'm going to look for him."

Jhared gathered himself and stood. "A search will be faster with two."

"It won't be faster when you collapse from his exhaustion. No, don't argue. You must stay in case he manages to return on his own." She sent a sharp gaze to Falucha. "If he does return, he will need care, not conflict. Now is the time for you to go home."

"I will stay."

Jhared heard the new tone in the Sonan woman's voice. Her decision this time did not have to do with freeing him. This time something fragile was exposed beneath the determination. Hzelka must have heard it too. Her blunt features softened.

"Falucha, I will not be responsible for more injuries. Yours or his."

"For this, you are not responsible," Falucha answered.

"Very well. You can be a help here in the meantime. Keep this one occupied." The Wren tilted her chin toward Jhared. "Don't go out again. No sense in drawing more attention." She bent over her medicinals, selecting jars and clean cloths and nestling them into a satchel. Jhared saw her drop in another plug of viremur.

"Whatever happens, I am leaving before moon's rising," he said.

"Stop," she ordered. "Tell me nothing further. I've a good hold on my own ways, but Ilaye is strong and sly. Don't take anymore foolish risks."

With no other farewell, Hzelka slung the satchel across her shoulder and left them.

"Jhared, do you hear? You must rise. It is near time."

Although the voice was gentle, a streak of iron existed in it. Maya would speak to him so, but this wasn't Maya. He shifted slightly, reluctant to leave the tranquil place where he floated. Something cool and soft rested over his brow.

"Yes, you are awake, Jhared Denaban. There is no peace this side of sleep."

He opened his eyes. Daylight had fled the room. After Hzelka had left, Falucha had convinced him to be still, and he had dropped into a sleep so deep that he suspected it had more to do with Rathael's need than his own. Falucha sat on the floor beside him, all her cream and amber and loam coloring leached to grey and black.

"Good," she murmured, reaching over and removing a damp folded rag from his forehead.

He pushed himself up, searching the room, disturbed by the quiet. "Hzelka hasn't returned."

"Not yet. How do you feel?"

"Better. Perhaps not fighting fit, but able to think."

She nodded without looking at him. As if of its own accord, her hand fluttered up to her ear and brushed across the sunset-colored stone there.

Jhared caught her fingers in his. "He is alive. He's still on my Path and still in pain, but it is less intense, or maybe more distant. Hzelka may be with him."

"Good," she said again. "I was afraid . . . afraid you would be too unwell to go to your feathered girl."

"Falucha, I could try to open the final doors between us. To put myself on his Path and reach his thoughts. If it would ease you."

"Do not!" She withdrew her fingers and stood. "Hzelka's care is more than he deserves. I am foolish for giving him this much consideration. Come. I have collected things you will want on your journey."

The bag she showed him had been thoughtfully packed: food, a flask, one of Hzelka's small pots, a select few of her herbs, a knife.

"Hzelka keeps no kind of fodder for your horse," she said.

"Maya will take it from the stable when she retrieves Seravina. I pray that decision wasn't a mistake. Sera and Maya are not on the best of terms." Jhared lifted his head to the quiet crunch of gravel outside. Falucha stopped what she was doing, her eyes on him.

"Hzelka?" she asked.

"Only if she's brought a party with her. There are at least five." Jhared started for the door, his innards churning. The leaders of the Avelune should be falling toward oblivion by now. Unless Moravel had gone back on his word. Unless Nemaye had discovered the truth. Unless Mayavana had never meant to flee with him.

The footsteps accelerated. A sharp blow cracked against the doors just as Jhared reached for them. An axe at the lock. There was no bar.

"Hide!" he ordered Falucha.

She hesitated. "I have nothing more to fear from them."

"Falucha, if this goes badly, I will need you to tell Hzelka what happened."

Her eyes widened. She paused only long enough to grab the packed bag from the table before disappearing into the back room.

The door shuddered under another blow. Dull and tinny notes dented the air as pieces of wood and metal fragmented. Jhared backed away. His bow leaned against the wall, useless in the small room. He had no place to escape. This was to be a different type of battle.

A salt breeze huffed through the doors as they shot open. Two Avelune marched into the room and threw back their hoods: Kest and a tall spear of a woman whom Jhared had never seen but was certain he knew. Four well-armed guards followed.

As the intruders formed a half-circle around him, Jhared leaned back against the table and folded his arms loosely across his chest.

"Greetings to you, Riv Kest, Riza Ilaye. Please forgive the complexity of the doors. I imagine it is the long isolation from our homeland and civilization that has caused you to lose your ability to knock."

The Avelun woman's flinty smile and large, mineral gaze revealed amusement, irritation, and loathing, all swiftly shifting, like sand blown across the shore. A severe twist constrained her dark hair at the crown of her head, leaving exposed the knife-edge of her jaw and the tendons of her slender neck. Her wings were tapered, like her brother's, but in the dusky room showed grey as glass. She was beautiful, as a finely crafted blade is beautiful or a freshly fletched arrow.

"We finally meet on the same Path, my aberration, and all you have for me is a poor show of wit? Will you not greet your Teacher properly, as you have been taught?"

It was the same wintry voice that for nine years had chimed in his head, meting out punishment and scorn. Jhared fought an intense, unreasoned need to drop to his knees before her.

"You taught me to greet an Avelun with a sword," he said quietly, though his heart was galloping.

"Ah, yes. I was a dutiful Teacher for Avelos, was I not? As with so many other lessons, however, you failed to learn it. A piece of luck for my people, as it happens. Where are Mayavana and Moravel?"

"Out testing her wings, I should imagine. Where else?" The bitterness came without effort.

"Where else, indeed?" replied Shrill. "You spoke with her today."

"Yes."

"You attempted to turn her against me."

"I attempted to tell her the truth."

Shrill's swift-changing expressions turned again as she stepped forward and swung a hand to slap him. Neatly, he slid aside, leaving her to stumble with the force of her failed blow. As she straightened, her lip lifted in a snarl. "*Your* truth. Wrested from your crippled understanding of what I do. What part did you play in poisoning my mother and the others?"

Jhared blinked at her, unmoved. Faintly from the back room, he heard the sound of wood creaking. "A needless question, Riza. You know me. You know I would never use the coward's way to take a life."

Shrill's gaze narrowed. "I did not say they were slain. If I thought you had killed them, you would be dead already." She snapped her fingers at the guards. "Prvas. Zelemir. Search the house."

Two of the guards moved to do her bidding. Jhared stepped into their way, his hands lifted in warning. "You wear General Hrvan's colors. You've seen how he values Riza Mayavana. Why do you allow this woman to use you against the general's own interests?"

One of the men, the younger of the two, hesitated. The other tried to barrel Jhared aside, grunting in frustration as Jhared stood firm and then ducked his swung fist. Shrill flung a command and the remaining two guards joined the others. Jhared's mistake was glancing in their direction. In that distracted instant, the first two knocked him off balance, allowing the third to land a blow. Jhared staggered and caught himself, but the others were on him now. The days he had lost among the Paths had weakened him. Three of the men bore him to the ground. He heard the fourth find Falucha, heard the sound of her protest and a fist striking flesh. He fought futilely as Falucha was half-dragged, half-carried back into the front room.

"She was trying to go out the window," the guard reported in Sonan.

"More vermin in Hzelka's nest." Shrill drew back in disgust. "Here's the mouse who thought she could catch the owl. The little bird collector who thought she could collect my brother. How have you become a part of this?"

Falucha lifted her head. Just below her right eye, a bruise darkened her cheek. Jhared's heart turned over. The first time he met her she had also taken a blow for him.

"General Hrvan sent for me," she replied coldly. "He said he had a broken bird in need of care. This one." She nodded her chin toward where three guards tried to keep Jhared subdued.

The man who had dragged her into the room shifted his weight uncomfortably. Kest hissed in displeasure. "There is a balance here, Ilaye. We need the general."

"And he needs us."

"Not if he learns that the soldier can call the winds!"

"An absurdity. I don't believe it and neither does the general. Jhared Denaban has been mine since he was a child. I will do with him what I like. Get him to his feet."

Kest gave a command and the guards jerked Jhared upright. Although the big red-wing's hand remained on his blade, uncertainty clouded his expression. Doubt would slow him. Jhared blessed Falucha for her daring lie.

"Take care," he pressed Kest. "Ilaye does not reason clearly when she is angered. You may not wish to suffer the consequences. Unless, of course, you believe Riza Nemaye will be quick to forgive you for damaging your people's standing with General Hrvan."

The young guard who had hesitated before halted now, his eyes wide. Kest glared death at Jhared. "Riza Ilaye is the Guide of the Avelune. She has seen the Paths before us. She would not risk our futures for her own purpose."

"How excellent you have no cause to doubt her."

"Tie him!" Shrill shouted. "Tie him now!"

Jhared tilted his head, as if no more than bemused by her fury. "You never used to need others to protect you when you came to me, Ilaye."

Kest gestured hastily to the guards to obey. Jhared tensed as they moved on him again. He could fight now; he could cause them significant damage. But unarmed against four fighting men and the vicious Kest, he wouldn't win free. He could do nothing for Falucha or himself if they beat him down. With ruthless effort, he subdued his instinct to resist, letting them bind his hands. They threw the rope's end over a heavy wooden beam in the ceiling. He gritted his teeth and bore it. Kest drew the rope taut across the beam until Jhared's arms strained above him and his feet barely found purchase on the floor. The guards secured the end of the rope to a cooking rod bolted into the hearthstone.

Ilaye frowned at the guards' vacillating expressions as they stepped away from their captive. "Prvas, take the others back to the manor," she ordered. "Riv Kest and I have no further need of them."

"What of the woman?" the guard asked, nodding at Falucha.

"You heard her: she must stay to help care for this broken bird."

Prvas paused, but was unwilling or unable to conjure a protest against Shrill. With a dutiful salute, he led the other three guards out of the house. Their footsteps crunched the gravel outside as they marched away.

"So the general sent this little mouse to care for you, my aberration. Is that what she told you?"

Ilaye stripped Jhared with a withering gaze. He met that gaze and offered back his own, unwavering. "I wonder that you must ask, Riza. You are the Guide of the Avelune. I wonder that you haven't gone beyond the Gate to answer such a question yourself. Why haven't you sought Maya's Path, or Moravel's?"

Something less ordered tweaked her features before she gave him her brutal smile. "You assume the answers are my goal. As it happens, I have already sent a search detail after Moravel and our missing sister. I have Hzelka caring for those who were foolish enough to drink Moravel's wine. And you and I have matters still to resolve."

Falucha made a sound of dismay. Shrill began to turn toward her. Swiftly, Jhared lunged against his bonds. "Do you mean the matter at Parnas Pass? As I recall, we had a lovely dance. Did you intend to repeat it?"

Shrill whipped back to him, her eyes filled with antipathy. "I intend to hurt you. Do you understand? Mayavana has no more use for you. I need no longer restrain myself from doing to you what I should have done months ago."

Behind Jhared, the big red-wing shifted his weight. "Ilaye, are you certain—"

"Silence, Kest! If you are too faint-hearted for such things, you may leave with the others. I thought you were a warrior."

Jhared had known Shrill this angry, had known the pain she could inflict upon others to manage her own hurts. He shook his head slowly. "Whatever you do to me, it will not satisfy you, Ilaye. You hate me because I remind you of everything you despise about yourself: That you have no country. That you've lost the lore of our ancestors. That despite your wings, you are as chained as I am."

This time, her blow caught him across the face. Her ring scored a stinging line down his cheek. "Your death will be enough to satisfy me for now. We will have a country very soon and I will soar over it."

"No, Ilaye. You won't."

Her anger threatened to flare. With it, Jhared recognized some possibilities. The time had come to gamble. He showed her the extent of his pity. "I know what it is you want, Ilaye, and I know what it is that escapes you."

The knife flashed into her hand so quickly it could only have come from her sleeve. Jhared tried to twist aside, but Kest's bulk behind him kept him in place. The blade entered his body just under his collarbone near his right shoulder.

He exhaled hard. Falucha pressed a hand over her mouth, her expression full of fear. For a span of heartbeats, Jhared held her gaze, willing her to understand what he meant to do, begging her to stay quiet.

Blood oozed warm and sticky down his chest. He licked his lips and controlled the speed of his breathing. Painful, not mortal. On the bookshelf behind his Teacher stood the ancient statue of Riana and Cael: the Guardian of the Paths and the Keeper of the Winds chained together. The Sonan Avelune had preserved the artifact but had forgotten its meaning. He smiled. "You do understand, Ilaye, that if you kill me, you will never know flight?"

Shrill studied the blade in her hand. "You are grasping for the only thing you think can give your life value. But I know better. For years, you have been cut and cowed by Avelos, by my brother, and by me. You have no such strength."

"Other than the strength I found in Parnas Pass?"

The knife flashed again. This time, it scored his ribs. Jhared closed his eyes and turned inward. This part of his gamble was the one on which he most depended and the one over which he had no control. His last sense of Rathael had been little more than a distant, throbbing ache. Now he couldn't sense the man at all. He opened his own doors wide, praying Rathael was still capable of touching his Path.

"You traveled that day with your Lady of Avelos," Shrill was saying. "She lent you her strength."

"Are you certain it was hers?"

"Of course I'm certain! Do you think I cannot find the Lady of Avelos on the Paths? How do you think I knew where to send Hrvan's men to kill her?"

At the boundary of Jhared's self, someone stirred weakly. Jhared sent out a silent entreaty. "You haven't," he said in an iron tone. "The Lady has nothing you want."

"Alive she has nothing. Dead on the road impaled by Sahisten spears? The war will come then. Avelos and Sahiste will shred one another. And we will reclaim our own lands." Shrill's voice had a ring of victory in it. "You have no skill on the Paths other than what we lent you, my aberration. And what physical strength you possess is now bleeding out of you. You are useless. Mayavana called the winds: she was the flame; you were nothing more than the fuel. When I retrieve her, she will light that flame once again."

Lady Nemiah was on her way to Sahiste with Elder Trianor, if Vjeran was right. Both of them would be seeking a kind of reparation. Lady Nemiah carried the truth of Amalia's story. Tierzen had always been fascinated by Sahiste, had dreamed of open borders and a sharing of knowledge. Jhared shoved away those thoughts. His final gamble must succeed.

"You do not believe what you claim, Ilaye. I see your doubt, even now. But you could find out the truth if you walked my Path. I would open myself to you."

Falucha cried out. "Jhared, she will kill you!"

"The mouse is right. Is that the way you wish to die?"

Shrill paced around him, her boots tapping the flagstone in an angry rhythm, her narrow wings opening and closing. Never still. Never at ease. Jhared knew that about her. As he watched her, recognizing her anger and her dread, something else came clear. "It wasn't you who tried to reach me today. It was Nemaye."

"What? Why would my mother seek your Path?"

"Perhaps it is because she does not share your belief about the weakness of the Shorn. Or perhaps it is because you are too afraid."

Ilaye wheeled on him, indignation blazing over her sharply carved features. "Look at you! Scarred. Impotent. From infancy, a slave to the unfeathered. Now a helpless, mindless animal on the Paths. I saw you lying unconscious in the general's bed, drooling and twitching among sweat-stained sheets. It was so easy to push you into the swamp of broken Paths. I could do it again, right now. I could drown you like a malformed pup. You are nothing like I am! Nothing of our ancestors' talent remains in you!"

"Look at you," Jhared responded quietly, "frantic and undone. You never expected me to defy you in Parnas Pass. You never imagined I owned the will to attack you. Even now, a part of you expects I will beg you for forgiveness for my transgressions. But I am no longer the small child who held you in awe. I can see you are no different from the ones who cut me, and I have left them behind."

Murder gleamed in her eyes as she came at him.

He was ready. He threw himself backward, dropping his weight into Kest's arms and onto the ropes that held him. The rope gave just enough. Instinctively, Kest's grip tightened, bearing him and making it impossible for the Avelun to free his hands. The knife Ilaye wielded already shone with Jhared's blood.

He intended his kick to catch her in the head, giving him a clear instant to strike Kest. He needed to daze her if he was to have a chance at the red-wing. Ilaye took another step and another. One more would bring her within range.

Motion flashed behind her. Jhared glimpsed Falucha, her lips pressed in effort, her fingers clenched around the neck of a jug. He cried out to warn her off. Too late. Sound exploded in the small room: the sound of pottery shattering against flesh and feathers, of a woman's startled outcry and pained retching. Ilaye, bent nearly double from the blow, staggered sideways, too far for Jhared to reach. Shards of pottery slid from her shoulders and off her wings, ringing against the stone as they struck. Broken feathers and puffs of down floated around her.

Kest struggled to disengage from Jhared. With a noise between a growl and a gasp, Ilaye flung all her mortal rage toward Falucha. The knife remained in her hand.

"No. No!" Jhared hurled himself against the ropes. The cooking rod screeched. The rope stretched, but refused to release him. Ilaye turned on the small Sonan woman, her intention unmistakable.

Pushing away fear, Jhared closed his eyes and dove inward. The blue flames burned there, as they ever did. He shuddered at the border, overwhelmed with memories from the sea of Paths and his long battle to keep from drowning. He braced himself. He had no other means of protecting Falucha. With determination as his shield, he strode through the Gate. The flames crackled over his memories, burning them briefly. Then he was out and hovering over the blue and red ribbons that wound out the possibilities of every life. He repeated the litany of himself, countering the pull of the web and holding steady. One sideways step was all he needed. This was not like flinging himself across Times and Places and uncountable Perspectives to reach Lady Amalia. Ilaye's Path ran beside his. All he needed was one sideways step.

You will never fully control your own Path.

Rathael's voice. Jhared shut it out and sent his thoughts toward the Avelun woman named Ilaye. Named Shrill. The woman who had been closer to him than a mother or a lover. The woman who needed to kill to escape the truth of her own impotence.

He saw her pattern gleaming in the web, entwined with his own. He took the step it required.

A current of rage crashed against him; followed by disbelief and a shrieking pain in his left wing. The little Sonan bitch had dared to attack him! No doubt she harbored some notion of caging the Guide of the Avelune. An abhorrence, she was. Without even the reverence of the Bird Walkers. She acted as if it were her right to trap and cage birds. To the ill and the injured she denied even the right to a clean death: stringing out their futile lives, teaching them to perform like dogs. He stalked toward her and had to bite back a scream as the broken bones in his wing ground against one another. The bitch had known just where to slam that heavy jug. An abhorrence. She trapped and doomed injured birds to a life at the bottom of some dark cage. Just as she had trapped and doomed the foolish, trusting Rathael. Almost she had tainted a line that traced all the way back to Alende Isan and Lady Sabela. Almost. She should have died with her misbred offspring. She would die now.

As he closed on her, the woman backed into the bookshelf, wielding the jagged neck of the broken jug. He could see fear under the defiance in her eyes. It would be a relief to kill her. She deserved it. As the Shorn boy deserved it. This, at least, would be a clean death. More than the woman allowed her birds. Fury carried him the final distance and gave strength to his arm as he hoisted the blade.

The Sonan woman flung up her makeshift weapon defensively. Her amber eyes met his, no longer fearful, but full of the knowledge of her death. A clean death. Better than she deserved. She did not turn away as the knife rose. She had never lacked courage, after all. This small, Sonan woman. The one who had seen something of grace in him. Falucha.

"Hold, Ilaye! You will not harm her! You will not!*"*

Jhared scrambled to rise above Ilaye's Perspective. The force of her fury shoved him down again. The knife clutched tightly in their fist wavered over Falucha's heart. Once more, Jhared rose up, holding urgently to his purpose. He had dropped onto

Ilaye's Path with all his own doors thrown wide. A mistake. The knife came slashing downward, veered from its target, found purchase, dropped.

"Vile creature! Violator! Get off my Path!"

Nothing of deliberation or restraint existed in Ilaye as she turned on him. They tumbled, locked together, across one another's Paths: slamming against his memories of border patrols; rolling over her knowledge of Sona's coastal towns; barreling through his opinions on Velantar's bowyers; devastating her understanding of the Saimbor canal system. He kept up with her at the outset, striving to keep his awareness intact. But she owned all the advantage: she had spent nine years riding his Path and knew the architecture of his thoughts and memories. Gradually, she forced the battle into more critical parts of his self: the day he murdered a hawk and swore his life to Avelos; the first time he saw Mayavana beyond the Gate; the night Zinderdali shared his secrets about the Hands of Lumati; the moment Jhared knew he held the power of the killing winds.

Shrill squealed. *"No! It isn't possible. It's Mayavana! Mayavana holds the key!"*

With a sickening thud, she leaped fully into his moment and took it for her own. At her command, Jhared's heart lurched out of rhythm. His lungs refused to draw air. Agony torqued through him as she ripped through his thoughts, through the places where he defined himself, through every experience that had shaped his understanding of the world. His Path and the weaving beyond began to darken. He struggled, but he knew the struggle existed only in some small corner that remained his own. His body no longer belonged to him. Images began to float across his vision, recalling the past, and the futures that would never be. As his energy dwindled, he whispered the names of those who had mattered.

The ripple started somewhere very far away. A gathering of effort. Slow and unsteady at first, but building, like a storm gathering power. The roar, when it came, reverberated through the core of Jhared's bones.

"Mayavana holds nothing, you ignorant bitch! She's just like the rest of us. None of us own the discipline to call the winds. It is all the Shorn. Only the Shorn!"

Rathael smashed against Shrill's presence, fracturing her grip on Jhared's Path. A whisper brushed Jhared's consciousness: *"Go!"* Then Rathael peeled away, catapulting off both Paths into the Nowhere, pursued by the raging Shrill. For long moments, Jhared could do no more than gasp grateful breaths and try to sweep together the fragments of his self. When finally he could lift his awareness, he limped toward the Gate.

Kest was waiting. His adamant presence hunkered directly before the blue flames. His fatal grin stretched wide. *"Show me how to call the winds or suffer the Gate's scorching fire."*

Jhared didn't pause, knowing hesitation would finish him. Once before in the Nowhere, anger and desperation had lent him the skill he needed. He hurled his emotion around the big Avelun, and sensed the man's burst of shock as it caught him. With all his will, Jhared whipped Kest about until the man's thoughts rattled and his smugness turned to fear. When the red-wing hung limp in his grasp, like a snake in the talons of a raven, Jhared flung him away from the blue flames deep into the black emptiness.

Somewhere in that emptiness, Rathael battled Shrill. For a moment, Jhared might have gone hurtling after them, but agony throbbed through his thoughts, the agony his Teachers had cultivated over nine years. The time had come to pull his Path in his own direction.

When he sang his litany of names, the doors to his own place opened. He discovered himself sprawled across the floor. His arms, stretched above him, were still bound, but the rope lay slack. The force of his falling body had finally torn the cooking rod free of the hearthstone. It dangled over the beam near the ceiling.

Kest lay unconscious beside him. Fine tremors ran through the red-wing's large frame as the cold of the Nowhere began to take its toll. Ilaye had fallen facedown, her body half under the overturned table: one wing stretched to its full span; the other askew against her shoulder. Jhared turned away and found Falucha.

Ah goddess. Falucha.

She had collapsed against the bookshelf, books tumbled around her. Her hands, pressed against her middle, were slippery with blood. Jhared scrambled toward her. Ilaye's knife lay at her feet. Sitting on the floor, he clutched the grip between his knees and sawed at the rope around his wrists until it fell away.

He touched Falucha's cheek. Her eyes fluttered open, their amber darkened with pain.

"It is over?" she asked faintly.

He glanced at Ilaye's still form. "Almost."

"I did not . . . intend this. Do not let them think I sought this."

He brushed loose strands of hair from her face. Her skin was cold and sweat-slicked. "I understand. You needed to strike a blow."

"I did," she whispered, falling wearily into her native Sonan. "For my child."

Gently, he moved her hands away from the jagged wound in her left side. It was deep and low. The blade had slipped down her ribs, missed her heart and lungs, but found something vital at her core. He had done this. His fist had gripped the knife as well as Ilaye's, and he had not been skilled enough to stop it. He grabbed Hzelka's shawl from the back of a chair and pressed it against the gash.

Falucha flailed one hand feebly against his. "Leave it. Nothing can be done. Better not to linger."

Jhared met her round gaze, crying out inwardly against this turn in the Path. In the brief time he had known her, Falucha had been a friend.

She must have seen the uncertainty in his expression for she nodded her confirmation and closed her fingers over his.

Something beat, faint but rhythmic, deep within Jhared, an urgent stroke of wings still riding his Path. A weak voice hissed from far away. *"What . . . ? What's happened? Falucha?"*

Jhared drew a calming breath, but sorrow still rang in his thoughts. *"I have her. She will not be alone."*

Instant understanding and horror arrowed into him. *"No! Ah, no!"*

The force of the cry knocked Jhared backward against the table. He caught himself and flung his thoughts toward the madness that was Rathael. *"Where are you? Can you come to us?"*

In a rush, he caught the scent of sand and seaweed and heard waves breaking unevenly against rocks. Somewhere off shore, a horn blew, long and mournful.

"Too far. Never make it." Jhared sensed a quick series of gasps, like a man trying to catch his breath. *"Let me speak with her. Please!"*

"Has he come?"

Falucha's fading voice pulled Jhared back. He drew her close, sheltering her torn body with his own, as though he could preserve her from this final pain. "You need not speak with him. I will send him away, if you wish it."

She winced. A host of emotions crowded her features. "I will not go as Ilaye did. With hatred for a guide. Let him through."

Once again, Jhared turned inward and pushed open the doors of his own Path. *"Have a care,"* he warned his Teacher. *"Do not cause her another moment of pain."*

Rathael staggered into Jhared's Perspective like a drunkard falling down stairs. Suddenly, Jhared's arms holding Falucha became his Teacher's also. Suddenly, a desperate, remorse-filled love flushed through him, and the grief-stricken voice that spoke in Sonan was not quite his own.

"My heart. Ah, my heart. She will never harm you again."

"I believe that is safe to say," Falucha murmured, her dry manner rising above her agony. "Did you come to ask me, Ratha? Are you going to plead one last time?"

"No." The Avelun faltered and nearly slipped from Jhared's Path. With a wrench of effort, Jhared caught the man and steadied him.

"No," Rathael repeated. "I do not deserve your forgiveness. I came only to promise that on the next Path, I will not fail you."

"The next?" Falucha stiffened, with anger more than pain, Jhared thought. "Do not follow me."

"No one can prevent that now, my heart."

"Do not! I will . . . refuse you on the Hidden Paths." Falucha's breath hissed quick and shallow.

With Jhared's hand, Rathael touched the sunset-colored stone at Falucha's ear. His presence in Jhared was a pale thing. "We went into the forest once . . . to watch the hawk teach her fledglings to fly."

"Yes," Falucha said hoarsely.

"I will wait for you there. On every Path. I will wait until you return to me. I will—"

The blue flames flared high, severing Rathael's low voice. His presence winked out, like the sun dropping into the sea. Jhared grabbed for him, but nothing remained to grab.

Falucha cried his name, half rising out of Jhared's arms with the force of her anguish.

"I am sorry," Jhared murmured. "He's gone."

"His life . . . should not be wasted," she gasped. "The world should not lose his strength and beauty. Please. Do not let him follow me."

Only now did tears spring into her eyes: the tears she had not shed for herself spilled for the man she had loved; the man who had betrayed her. The man who had spent years tormenting a Shorn child.

With Falucha in his arms and the remnants of Rathael's love and remorse pounding through him, Jhared found only one answer possible: "I promise it. Whatever can be done, I will not let him abandon this Path."

He held her as Falucha fought her last, desperate battle. Softly, he sang the Sonan lullaby Maya had sung for him. He kept singing, even when Falucha could no longer hear the song.

Nothing existed to mark the passage of time when sounds from outside the house penetrated his melody. The noise grew, entered the house, and became the sounds of alarm and dismay. Jhared stroked Falucha's cheek. He had once seen Riana's guide come to lead a fallen man's spirit to the Hidden Paths of the Dead. He wondered if the doors of those Hidden Paths would open themselves as readily for him as the Paths of this world seemed to do. He wondered if he would find Falucha there.

"She's dead." Hzelka's voice slammed against Jhared like the jug had slammed against Ilaye's wings. "I knew it could happen. I told them there was strength in you."

A heavy hand landed on his shoulder. He looked up into Hzelka's homely face. Moravel stood behind her, staring at the carnage with a sick expression. "Little Lucha," the red-wing said brokenly.

Anger bulled across Jhared's grief. He shook off Hzelka's hand. "Where have you been? Where's Rathael? You went to find him hours ago."

Hzelka took a startled step backward. Wetness gleamed at the corners of her eyes. "I don't know. I searched the woods. I didn't find him. Ilaye caught me heading north. She had guards with her. I had to go back to the house to care for Nemaye and the others. I tried to return to you. I—"

"Quiet!" Jhared ordered. "You needn't bother with excuses. Falucha can no longer hear them."

The Avelun woman bowed her head.

Moravel caught site of Kest. He dropped to his brother's side. "What happened?"

"Ilaye meant to kill me. Falucha intervened. I failed to protect her."

"And Kest?"

"Is struggling his way back from the Nowhere. I suspect it will be a long trip."

Moravel took off his cloak and tucked it around his brother's trembling body. "I don't understand."

"I do." Hzelka watched Jhared with wary regret. Slowly, she lowered her round figure beside him. "I told them there was strength in you," she repeated faintly.

Jhared did not respond. His gaze lingered on Moravel. "Why did you not send warning that Ilaye had evaded you? You said you would gather them all."

"I did gather them." Moravel's expression turned bitter. "Ilaye and Kest appeared to drink with the others. They dropped as the others did. It was a sham. Ilaye must have doubted me from the start. She has been too close to Mayavana. She must have guessed the truth."

"What truth?" Jhared snapped.

"I told her that Mayavana carries my child. Nemaye called them together herself to celebrate."

Hzelka turned away from the red-wing and reached out a hand to stroke Falucha's brow. "Rathael must not learn of this."

"He already came to say goodbye," Jhared answered.

"But how did he . . . ? Oh." Astonishment passed over the Wren's features once more. "You realize that you must flee now. Whatever you pledged to Falucha, you must leave it and run. You have killed Nemaye's daughter, the Guide of the Avelune. The general's men will come after you."

"Falucha asked only one thing, Hzelka. I will see it done. If he will let me."

The Wren sighed. "It will do no good to find Rathael unless you mean to take him with you. He will not survive here now she is gone."

"Then I will take him."

"If that's what you promised, Jhared, you must do it. You must go."

Jhared looked down at the shell of the woman in his arms, his vision blurring with unexpressed sorrow. "I cannot."

Understanding softened the Wren's features. "I will tend to her myself. She will not be alone. I will light the candles that Riana's guides might find her. Then I will send to her family. No others will touch her."

"It is the least of what she deserves," Jhared said.

"I know."

With Falucha cradled against his chest, Jhared rose. He laid her body upon the table. Moravel's shadow fell over him as he straightened her braid and folded her arms.

"Mayavana is waiting for you," the red-wing said.

"Is she?" Jhared hadn't even thought to ask. A short time ago it had seemed the only thing of importance. "What word of the *Mila Jul*?"

"Left Saimbor this afternoon. Heading upriver."

Half a day's head start, but rowing against the current. Not unreachable. He had to find what was left of Rathael. He had to get them all to Vjeran. It was the only way they might stay ahead of the general's men. That must be his goal now. "Rathael is somewhere along the beach. An outcropping of rocky shoreline. I heard a horn. Does that give you some clue as to where he might be?"

"Yes." Hzelka's wings opened and closed; her head bent over Falucha. "It's on the other side of the estate. I didn't believe he could wander so far. If I would have considered it sooner—" She cut herself off, but a single track of silver traced her wrinkled cheek. "The others don't bother with it. It's nothing more than a barren spine of rock close to the city."

"The Spearhead?" Moravel looked surprised. "It's just a bit short of where you'll find Mayavana. Past the rocks there's a stretch of abandoned warehouses. She'll be there. It was the best hide I could think of. I feared Ilaye might send searchers."

"She did." At last Jhared turned away from Falucha and began to gather his things. "What of you both? What will Nemaye do to you?"

"She'll have no time for us. With Ilaye gone, Nemaye will have to take her place again at the general's side. They have plans for Amuria."

"Plans, Hzelka? They intend to use the killing winds to obliterate Amuria. And then Avelos and Sahiste." As Jhared walked away to retrieve his travel sack, he heard the stunned gasp from Moravel and the silence from Hzelka.

"You and Mayavana are leaving. Their plans will come to nothing," the Wren finally said.

"Do you think so?" Jhared retorted. "Kest knows the truth of the killing winds now. I suspect Nemaye is ready to believe what he tells her."

And the Sonan border guard, Mursa Vin and his men, had befriended the unbound. Even if they didn't have him, they knew Alende's people. They could reach Shira.

"Well, what will happen will happen," Hzelka said, hunching into herself. "Just get yourself gone. I'll try to win you some time. That's all I can do. I owe nothing to Avelos or any of them."

The rill of acid rage that ran through Jhared seemed only partially his own. "You choose strange times to play at indifference, Hzelka. I wonder how things might have gone for Falucha and Rathael, if you had refused to be involved when Nemaye came to you eight years ago. If you had refused to give her the poison to kill their unborn child."

In the brittle wake of his words, Jhared rested his hand over Falucha's brow, then picked up the sack she had packed for him and turned to leave.

"I'll come with you," Moravel said into the silence. "You will need another set of hands to help with Rathael and perhaps to defend you from the others."

Jhared glanced back at the slender red-wing. Moravel stood over his unconscious brother, his conflict clear in the contradiction between his tentative posture and his determined gaze.

"Help by staying here and reminding your people that Paths exist other than vengeance," Jhared replied. He paused, considering for an instant. Then, moving to Hzelka's bookshelves, he grasped the ancient sculpture of Cael and Riana. Neither of the others said a word as he placed it into his pack.

The door closed behind him without a sound. He strode across the courtyard, past the broken statues and the shattered fountain, past the long-abandoned dormitories and the sky tower. In the star-speckled darkness, he reached the crumbling wall of the compound and pushed through it, glad to leave behind the ruins of Avelune civilization.

29.

UPRIVER

Jhared moved along the dark trail, vigilant for signs of the general's men. As the coast slithered its way from the forest, past the estate, toward the city, it grew challenging to remain close to the beach without becoming a clear target on the wide, flat stretches of pebbled sand. A sea-tainted wind rushed him with its scent of decay. When a horn blew off shore, the familiar sound warned Jhared he must be approaching Rathael's hide. Even in the near-dark, he could tell when he had reached the Spearhead by the change in the sounds of the breaking waves. Instead of the regular roll and crash that described the tide striking the open shore, an erratic thud, roar, and splash told of uneven rocks and a barrier that stretched beyond the sand. Jhared stood at the foot of the Spearhead, watching the plumes of water as they caught the faint moonlight and fell in a pale blue foam across the narrow span. He didn't underestimate the strength of those plumes. It would be easy enough for one of them to smash a man against the stone. Only by the most unlikely twist would Rathael have avoided being swept out to sea, yet Jhared couldn't help feeling that he would know it if the man who had been his Teacher had already drowned.

He called Rathael's name. His voice lifted over the sea for an instant before the wind tore it away. There was no response.

With a sound somewhere between a sigh and a growl, Jhared deposited his pack and his bow in a spot where they would stay dry and started down the precarious plank of rocks. The first wave did not surprise him: he braced himself against a sea-slimed bolder until the wave broke over him and slid away. The second wave caught him sooner than expected. It struck him behind the knees, buckling his left leg. He grasped the sharp rocks, forbidding the water from pushing him free. When the wave retreated, his clothes were sodden and salt ran stinging into his wounds. As quickly as possible, he rose and strode forward before the next wave could reach him.

He found Rathael near the tip of the spear, where the land flared and flattened into a rough triangle. The Avelun's body was sprawled face down, half over the rocks and half in the water, his wings splayed like a dead gull's. Jhared climbed down to him, a dark, angry part of him hoping the man was dead after all. Only when he knelt in the waves and laid his hands on the Avelun could he feel the shallow rise and fall of his rib cage.

He called the man's name again and shook him by the shoulder. A low, pained moan rose in protest. As Jhared rolled Rathael onto his back, his eyes opened slowly, gleaming like glass in the sliver of moonlight.

"Don't. Please, just let me follow her." The man's slow, heavy words could barely be heard above the sound of the sea.

"I promised her I wouldn't allow that."

"I could find her on the Hidden Paths. I am sure of it."

"Perhaps," Jhared agreed. "But not today."

A faint, familiar wryness passed across Rathael's features. "For the others, mask your retaliation as compassion. There is nothing you can mask from me."

"Don't waste your energy on cleverness," Jhared said, shoving his arm behind the Avelun and prying him upright. "We have a ways to walk."

"You presume a lot if you think I have energy left to save."

Cold spray misted them as Jhared compelled Rathael to his feet and half-carried him across the slippery rocks back toward the beach.

"Where?" Rathael panted.

"Somewhere not here," Jhared replied, tugging his Teacher's arm more securely across his shoulders. Rathael gave one short, shallow chuckle and fell silent.

They stumbled up the Spearhead and began the trek along the beach. The scattered lights and dense, blocky shapes of sleeping Saimbor gradually grew closer. When the breeze shifted, it brought the stench of city offal. A dog barked as they limped past a cluster of houses. Jhared began to fear that they had passed the place where Moravel had sent Maya. He scanned the dark, turning clumsily with Rathael to rake his gaze across the way they had just come. Finally, across from the rotting carcass of what must have once been a pier, Jhared spied a set of buildings in various stages of collapse.

"Wait here," he said, lowering the Avelun to the rough stones.

Jhared made himself a shadow, gliding among the fallen beams and scorched walls of the old warehouses. There were three. The first looked the most intact, with much of the walls and roof in place. Before he reached the doorway, however, the sweet, grim scent of death filled his nostrils. He halted, sucking air through his teeth. The stench was potent: something large had died in there. He didn't go further to discover what. The second building had burned more thoroughly, but tumbled stone and rotting wood created an intricate maze of hiding places. He entered, stepping with care over debris. Around a corner, he heard someone speaking. Maya. He froze, until he heard her soft curses and an answering equine snort. His heart jigged in his throat. Although Maya's tone was quiet, he could imagine in it the derision she had turned on him that afternoon. He despised the images of her that came unbidden: laughing with the general, confiding in Ilaye, embracing Moravel. He would have given years of his life to travel back to the moment when Falucha had warned them away from the general, when they might have left the city without encountering the Avelune.

Hooves scraped on stone. Abruptly, Seravina whinnied a greeting. Maya's voice bit the air: "Who is it? Show yourself."

Jhared stepped into view. The Avelun stood as sharp and alert as the mare beside her. A heavy cloak and hood enwrapped her wings and shadowed her face. With one hand, she gripped her staff, with the other, Seravina's lead. The mare danced and sidled, her sculpted head lifted high.

"Jhared. Gods of seas and skies."

In that utterance, all of Maya's uncertainty lay exposed. She hadn't believed he would come for her. Her doubt stung.

"Perhaps you were expecting someone else?" he said quietly.

The words echoed Moravel's on a Path Jhared shouldn't have seen. Maya flinched.

With a bright whicker, Seravina pranced the short distance to reach him, dragging Maya with her. Jhared stroked the mare's silver neck.

"Moravel feared that Ilaye had escaped the drug," Maya said, answering and not answering his question.

"Ilaye is dead."

Under the folds of her hood, the Avelun's features registered shock. "You?"

"No. Her brother. Which is why he's coming with us.

"Rathael? The traitor?"

Jhared doubted he could explain how Nemaye and the others defined "traitor" without losing his grip on his anger. "Rathael, my Teacher. Come. They will be searching for us. Despite your best efforts, Nemaye knows the truth about the killing winds."

Maya nodded, her mute expression revealing that his irony had reached her. Jhared took Seravina's reins and led the way back to the beach.

Rathael hadn't moved. Jhared crouched beside him. "Wake now, Rathael. Wake. We must hurry."

Maya placed an assessing hand on the man's brow. "Did Ilaye do this?"

"In a sense. He spent himself over the past two days holding my Path closed to keep her away from me."

"Two days! That's why you were able to return to the house?"

"Yes."

Maya muttered a curse.

"Impressive, I know," Rathael drawled, opening his eyes. Profound exhaustion was evident in his every word. His overbright gaze slid from Maya to Jhared. "You won't let me go where I wish, so tell me where we are going instead."

"North," Jhared answered. "There's a barge heading upriver that will carry us. She has a half-day lead. We must reach her before she sets out again."

"A good trick that. A pity none of us can fly, eh?"

"You are going to ride."

Rathael's brow lifted. Jhared gave the man no chance to protest, but heaved him upright once more.

"Hold Sera," he said to Maya. He hoisted Rathael onto the mare, gritting his teeth as his torn muscles strained. Rathael roused enough to scramble onto the horse and hunker in the saddle. Sera bent her neck to peer sidelong at her strange rider, but to Jhared's relief made no other mischief.

"Are you capable of staying on or should I tie you?" he asked Rathael.

The Avelun adjusted his wings so that they drooped over the mare's flanks. "I've always preferred the excitement of falling to the indignity of bondage, thank you."

Jhared pulled the man's damp cloak over his opalescent feathers as best he could. "Very well. Let's go."

To reach the river required them to follow the coastline through the city. A fractured moon lit the way, snagging light on closed shops and abandoned houses. Near the docks, Jhared sensed eyes watching them. He straightened his bow over his shoulder and hoped that the three of them looked to be more trouble than profit.

Beyond the docks, they turned north and slightly east, finally catching up to the river and starting to move away from Saimbor. Even as they slowly gained distance from the general's estate, Jhared's back prickled. Traveling the river road left them in the open and vulnerable, but they had to remain within sight of the water or risk missing the *Mila Jul*. As they passed small settlements, Jhared scanned the moored boats, seeking the familiar lines of the *Jul* and her pennant of blue and gold. It was miles yet before they might expect her to have docked, unless some twist in the Path had caused Vjeran and his crew to put up early, closer, but Jhared remained watchful and hoped.

His damaged body, recalling its long habit of night patrols, continued to answer his demands. The crackle of blue at the edges of his vision he simply ignored. At his side, Maya moved with swift, easy grace. Neither of them spoke, other than to give a direction or request a pause. The things they must eventually say would endanger defenses they both needed just now. Beyond his tight focus, Jhared sensed an ocean of grief and remorse that he wasn't certain belonged entirely to him. Atop Seravina, Rathael remained silent, his head drooping over his chest until Jhared thought he had fallen asleep.

"Not asleep. Just . . . thinking."

Jhared startled and stumbled over a rut in the road. "Stop!"

"Thinking? Would that I could."

"You know what I meant. Get off my Path."

"Not certain I can. All my doors are open. I wonder if this is what it's like for you. I feel thin like . . . oil slicked across water."

Jhared clenched his jaw. "You're not trying."

"How do you know?"

"I can feel things from you I usually don't."

"Oh?" Rathael peered at him curiously. *"Did you know that our ancestors had se-cret words they gave only to loved ones? Only those who could speak the trust words were allowed to enter their Path and sense their emotions. A pretty idea, isn't it?"*

"Beautiful," Jhared muttered. *"Perhaps we might resurrect it."*

"A bit late for such romantic notions, I think."

"Jhared, what are you doing?"

The knife-edge of concern in Maya's voice yanked him out of his own head. He had slipped inward without realizing it.

"It's not me. It's Rathael. He's . . ." Jhared shrugged, then reached up and shook his Teacher's shoulder. "Stop drifting! I'll not lose you to the Gate. Not tonight."

"Of course," Rathael said, his tone unapologetic.

"Aloud!" Jhared commanded. "From your own Path."

"I understand." A strain of anger touched Rathael's weary despair.

"Good. Tell us more about the trust words. How did you discover them?"

Rathael's silence stretched until Jhared feared the man had lost consciousness. "That's an old dull story," he finally said.

"Tell it. It will keep you in your own perspective."

"I despise that perspective."

Jhared barely stifled his exasperation. "Very well, keep it to yourself, but stay off my Path. I need my senses to be my own."

They moved on through the night, passing through wilderness and sleepy ham-lets, turning with the river, and praying that the *Mila Jul* might be anchored around the next bend. Near morning, as the false dawn pushed its grey blade into the sky, Rathael awoke. He straightened on Seravina and darted a look about him, a stricken expression on his face.

"What is it?" Jhared asked.

Maya gasped abruptly. "Look, both of you! Look there. The dark space on the water before that cluster of sheds. What do you see?"

They were approaching the skirts of a settlement that Jhared recalled. On the downriver trip, the *Jul* had stopped there to take on small casks of spices, and Vjeran had given him a taste of a dark red powder that smelled of earth and made his tongue burn. He recalled a serviceable jetty and a scattering of homes and farmyards. Now, with the sun struggling to rise on their right flank, they had just passed a crossroads. The village lay ahead. Jhared followed Maya's pointing finger toward where the early light had begun to pick out the lines of several moored boats. He looked, closed his eyes, and dared to look again. It was a barge. But dozens of barges traveled this waterway. "Can you see her flag?"

"Not yet," Maya panted.

In that moment, the nightmare Jhared had been dreading since they fled *Kaleb Uto* caught them.

Six mounted men roared out from behind a barn and launched themselves up the road. As Jhared shouted for Maya and Rathael to flee, he knew it was already too late. The men wore Hrvan's livery. They had been waiting. On their quick Sonan coursers, they had cut northeast from Saimbor and reached the river road ahead of them. It wasn't truly a surprise: Moravel and Hzelka had both known which route they would take.

"Go, Maya, go! Up with Rathael!"

"Jhared, don't be stupid. I'll fight—"

"Maya, if they catch Rathael, they will kill him. Get him away. I'm right behind you!"

Seravina screamed at the challengers as Jhared flung Maya up behind the saddle. No time for a farewell. No time to untangle all that had knotted. As Sera raced away, Jhared snatched his bow from his shoulder and set an arrow to the string. Pain greyed his vision when he pulled against the great bow's tension, but he sucked a deep breath and widened his stance. His first arrow soared, as perfect as a hawk's flight. One of the men cried out and tumbled from the saddle. Jhared tracked another Sonan thundering toward him. The second arrow took the guard in the shoulder, throwing him backward off his mount. Jhared wondered if the Avelune would kill him also, in retribution for Ilaye, or just imprison him until he lost himself on the sea of broken Paths. Maya would be dragged back to serve the general's need. His third arrow went wide.

Maya was shouting at him to run. He did run, even though they had nowhere to go. A flat, tamed landscape surrounded them, the forest still miles north. They were strangers in this land, and their assailants wore the badge of one of the most powerful men in Sona. Yet Jhared refused to hold out his arms to accept their chains. One of the remaining riders pounded toward him; the other three went after Seravina. As he pushed himself onward, as fast as he could move without flight, Jhared recalled a maneuver he had managed in the practice yard at Ravia—a challenge one of his patrolmates had issued. He had never tried it in battle.

The guard was closing on him. Jhared didn't look back, not daring to lose momentum. Behind him, the galloping horse huffed and snorted. Hoofbeats drummed the road at his back, so close that Jhared smelled the sweat of the beast. Just before horse and rider barreled over him, Jhared spun aside and grabbed at the animal's withers. For one long stride they cantered together; then Jhared leaped, swinging his body through the air and up onto the horse's back behind the saddle. The animal stumbled with the sudden weight, flinging its rider against the pommel. Jhared hammered his elbow into the man's ribs. Already unstable, the guard slid sideways. Another blow from Jhared and he hit the ground. Jhared seized the reins.

Seravina led their flight, but the three remaining guards were harrying her toward the village, where it would be easy to trap her on the narrow streets. Maya had her staff in hand. As one of the guards came within range, she smashed it across his face. The man roared and dropped back. People in the early morning streets scattered out of the way of the plunging horses.

Jhared scanned ahead, searching desperately for safer ground, but Maya pulled his gaze back to the riverside with her cry: "It's her! It's the *Jul*!"

A familiar pennant waved over the jetty: entwined salmon on a blue field. Hope surged in Jhared. "Ho, the barge! Ho, the *Mila Jul*!"

At the bottom of the gangplank, Vjeran and Ravatin were speaking with a villager. Ravatin had a cask under one arm. The *se'yo* turned and stared, wide eyed. "Ho, Avelos! You've trouble on your tail."

Jhared drew his mount to a staggering halt. Seravina wheeled onto the dock and pulled up, jigging beside him. Vjeran glanced from Jhared to Maya to Rathael and back. The river captain had no reason to allow them aboard, and sheltering them was likely to earn him the enmity of more than one of the leaders of Sona.

"*Se'yo*, if you aid us now, I will be in your debt until the weaving is completed. Please. For Maya, and for the sake of influencing something near to sacred."

Jhared held his breath, watching as a series of emotions crashed over Vjeran's narrow face. Finally, the man seemed to settle on one. "Come aboard, Avelos. You and your company. Quickly!"

Seravina thudded up the gangplank. Jhared followed on the Sonan beast. On the dock, two of the crew were already casting off the mooring lines. Two others hauled up the gangplank. Ravatin had exchanged the cask in his hands for a sword. He glared down as two of the general's men raced up to the edge of the dock, shouting up impotently as their lathered horses fretted over the wooden planks. Vjeran gave them one cold glance before turning to bellow orders to the crew.

Jhared took Sera and the Sonan mount in hand to keep them out of the way as the *Mila Jul* pushed off. The grizzled navigator scooted Maya and Rathael out of sight toward the deckhouse. Jhared watched the rest of the crew move with brisk efficiency to ease the *Jul* into the river. When they were well underway, Vjeran found him putting up the horses in the barge's makeshift loose box.

"Unexpected, Avelos. After our last conversation, I thought you might find a place in Saimbor and stay. Instead, you appear to have upset a beehive."

A breeze shoved across the water. Jhared felt the growing chill in it as he secured the horses. "A wasp nest, I'm afraid."

The *se'yo* glanced up at the clouds, then back at Jhared. "A storm in that breeze," he noted. "What happened?"

"General Hrvan tried to cage Mayavana."

"And the other Avelun?"

"Has also escaped captivity. I don't know that Hrvan will let them go."

"Well, I suppose we'll deal with that if we need to," the captain said mildly.

As the horizon dipped and twitched in Jhared's vision, he steadied himself against the barge's railing. "*Se'yo*, I am deeply grateful to you for taking us on. You had no cause to do it."

"I've already shared my weaknesses with you, Avelos."

Jhared grimaced. "You have dangerous tastes."

"It has been said." Vjeran grinned. "But for now, friend, you are safe from those dangers and from the general. Go see to your feathered ones. We'll speak of other things later."

Inside the deckhouse, yellow light soaked through the cloth that separated the captain's space from the small sleeping area provided to them on their first trip. Jhared announced himself quietly and stepped around the curtain. Rathael lay asleep or unconscious on the narrow pallet, the leading edge of his blue-green wings peeking above a blanket. Maya sat beside him on the deck, her eyes closed. Her head came up instantly as Jhared entered.

Jhared's breath caught at the way the light illuminated her green gaze and touched the flush on her cheeks. Her wings, furled against her shoulders, drew a double-arched shadow across the wall. Her manner bespoke strength and skill, and a subtle reserve not everyone would recognize. She remained the most compelling being he had ever met.

Pity is what has bound her to you.

"Thank you, Jhared," she murmured. "I haven't yet had the chance to say it. Thank you for coming after me."

"You didn't think I would?"

"I . . ." Her gaze skirted away from his, then rose, a little defiantly. "There are so many things I didn't know . . . you didn't tell me. I wasn't certain what to expect. You didn't tell me Ilaye meant to kill you."

"In fact, I did tell you. While you were explaining what a great friend she had become."

Maya winced and said nothing.

Jhared stood motionless, watching her and wondering things he wished he never had reason to wonder. He cleared his throat. "Thank you for settling Rathael. How is he?"

"Sleeping," she said. "On his own Path, for now. I fear he has no great care to remain there."

"He doesn't," Jhared agreed.

Maya looked away again. Her wings rustled. "Jhared, I don't know what to say to address all that has happened."

He smiled humorlessly. "Then it's good I have not asked it of you."

She is Avelun. She does not belong with you.

"Please, Jhared. It's only that I'm trying to—"

"Forgive me," he interjected. "I didn't intend to speak of such things. I only wanted to see that you and Rathael were safe and settled. I will let you be." He turned to go.

"Wait. I'm sorry . . . about Falucha."

He tensed. Slowly, he shifted to meet Maya's gaze.

"Rathael told me," she said.

"He shared it deliberately? Or did you steal it from his rambling?"

Her flush deepened, suggesting it was the latter. "He loved her," she said in wonder. "Even though she was unfeathered."

"Indeed. Baffling that he could suffer himself to touch her."

Maya drew an audible breath. "That's not what I meant."

"Maya, Rathael abandoned Falucha, allowing Ilaye and Nemaye to murder their child. It's not love that causes him to seek escape now. It's guilt."

Jhared pushed aside the curtain, anger rising off of him like steam. He strode out of the deckhouse and across the deck, avoiding others as much as was possible on the small vessel. His composure held until he reached the boat's side. Then the world turned upside down. His sweat-slicked palms failed to find any grip, and he slid to the deck.

The wood beneath his hands was smooth. The flanks of the barge sheltered him from the rising wind. The burning pain in his chest made him think of a hawk plummeting out of the sky and the arrow-sharp words that still cut deep.

You are hofja. *Half-spirited. You belong nowhere.*

Blue flames roared up to consume him. Only as he passed through the Gate did he make an effort to direct his fall, recalling at the last moment the names of the two women he needed to reach. Two needed a warning, but the web drew him toward the one whose names he knew best, the woman whose own shame had allowed her to recognize his.

His awareness settled upon a forest, on the sweet and spicy scents of pine trees near water and the call of a hawk circling above the canopy. It was an Avelonian forest—not the wet, moss-draped woods of Sona. On the sun-dappled trail before him lay the tracks of someone tall and light moving swiftly. They ended under the trees where he stood. He looked up. The owner of the tracks perched on a branch overhead, kicking her booted feet like a child on a swing. Under one arm, she clutched the avian mask of Cael, with its human skull staring from within the raven's black beak.

"Shira. I didn't think I would find your Path so readily. Do you know me?"

The woman looked down, pursing her lips. "Beloved of Alende?"

"Once you called me that. I am no longer anyone's beloved."

"Do not presume," she said coyly. "Only Cael knows all your names."

"And you, I think. I must speak with you. Will you come down?"

She darted a glance over her shoulder. "You should not be here. You will not be welcome."

"I bear a warning, Shira. For you and the Kin. You must hear it."

"Wait," she ordered. She pulled the mask over her head, like a soldier donning armor, then turned on the branch and dropped neatly to the ground.

"Why are you here, Jhared Denaban? The Kin have named you traitor."

He held his hands out to her, palms up. "In the eyes of the Kin, it is the only name that fits. I never wished you harm. I do not now. I have been with the Sonans."

"With the Sonans? Why? What warning could you possibly bring—" Cael's corvid beak twitched upward. Her entire body stiffened. "They know. I see the truth in your fear and in the blood spilled across your chest. The Sonans know what violence Cael has created in you. And in me."

"They know," Jhared agreed. "You must stay clear of them. They want the killing winds for themselves. Can you convince Alende to remain in Avelos? He must not move the Kin to Sona."

Jhared could see nothing of her expression, but sadness filled her tone. "Alende has left the Kin."

Grey and leaden dread poured through him. Alende had loved his Kin—Kilzaro, Rani, Shira, Silvien. They were his purpose. "What happened? Was it Lusian?"

The masked head twisted back and forth. "Alende's journeys have pushed him to act. He has gone to seek the cause of the weaving's unraveling."

"What cause?" Jhared feared he knew the answer.

"The one like me who bears the burden of Cael's love. She who carries his Blade."

"Leita," Jhared hissed. "Shira, you must not let him harm her. Like you, she has suffered Cael's torments."

"Alende no longer listens to me," she said helplessly. "Cael can do nothing but shadow him."

"Then I will come to you. Where are you?" He glanced again at the forest, at the birds, and at a river he knew. "You're in the south. Near Clan Amerre's lands. If Alende is after Leita, why isn't he heading for Velantar?"

"Cael follows the chaos," she replied softly.

Perhaps it was because of the shame they shared or perhaps it was Jhared's ability to see the patterns of a thing that allowed him to understand her. "Follows the chaos," he echoed. "Leita's traveling with Lady Nemiah, isn't she? They're on the way to Sahiste. And General Hrvan is after you and the Lady both. Shira, please. You must convince Alende to wait for me."

"He would not welcome you, Jhared Denaban."

"Welcome doesn't matter. Our stories are entwined."

"Only one story matters to him now. He travels toward it. Toward the ending. Cael can hardly keep up with him. But he will be drawn to you. You should leave now."

"I cannot," he answered. "Alende will not do me harm."

"Do not presume!" she cried again. "He is not who he was meant to be. Torment and violence alter all of us!"

Her voice scaled upward, toward panic. Jhared took several steps backward to open the distance between them. As he did, a rhythmic beat resonated through him, like drumbeats, like footsteps. "Someone's coming."

"Him. It's him. I knew he would be drawn here. In the past days, he has no more volition on the Paths than a moth before the fire. You must go. Now!"

"Let him come. I will speak with him myself."

"I said *GO!*"

She flung her will at Jhared with a strength he had never imagined in her. Although he threw his thoughts over the forest to anchor himself, her blow struck him full across the chest and sent him flying backward, body and spirit. He tumbled off the Path, past the blue and red strands of the web. Only his quick rehearsal of his own litany of names sent him through the Gate rather than into the black of the Nowhere.

He landed on the barge, his body cramped in the same position where he had fallen. Cold water splashed over him. His sodden clothing stuck to his skin. It took time to orient to his own moment enough to realize it was raining. No matter. Hurriedly, he gathered himself, and all the names he knew for Alende, and prepared to cross the flames once more. Falucha had been sacrificed to Ilaye's hatred. He would not allow Leita to be sacrificed to Alende's fear.

"Hold, Shorn child! I forbid you from touching the web once more!"

Jhared froze, chained reflexively by the voice that had whipped him into obedience for more than half his life. Footsteps he recognized hastened across the deck. A cloaked figure crouched at his shoulder.

"Jhared? Are you here?"

"Where else? I've been ordered to keep my Shorn taint off Riana's Paths."

Awkwardness registered in Maya's posture as it never would have before she met the Avelune. "Rathael?" she murmured.

"Yes. He thought to play the Teacher again." Jhared levered himself upright, surprised by how much effort it took. The wind gusted, slapping him with a sheet of rain. It didn't cool his anger.

"I don't think that's it," Maya said, her tone unwontedly careful. "Nemaye will have the others searching for us. Rathael warned me not to travel. Now come out of this mess."

Jhared followed her. When they reached the deckhouse, she pushed the door open just enough that they might sidle inside without bringing too much of the rain with them. As her arm crossed the threshold, however, the wind caught the door and swirled madly into the chamber, rolling scrolls off Vjeran's desk. Jhared leaped forward to grab the whipping door, but Maya's arm hindered him and he missed.

Something familiar in the moment made him pause: the way the small intrusion of her arm allowed the storm to slip through the doorway, carrying chaos with it. He thought of Rathael fluttering on and off his Path all day and of the blue flames hounding him. He thought of his Teachers watching him across the years: an arm in the door of his Path that kept it from shutting. An insight there, something of value.

"Jhared, come in! It's wet!"

He forced himself back into motion. Maya was already on the other side of the room. He turned and latched the door, then carefully crossed to the curtained chamber. The wind had blown out the lantern.

"I felt the Gate shift," Maya said. "Where did you go?"

Jhared bent over Rathael, touched his brow lightly. The Avelun appeared deeply asleep, although somewhere in his dreams he had slipped onto Jhared's Path, at least for a moment. Shivering, Jhared sank down beside him. "I went to Shira."

"To warn the unbound."

"Yes."

"Were you successful?"

The answer to that question was more complex than he felt like explaining. He settled for a shrug.

"Jhared? What is it?"

He did have a thought, but it seemed to have washed away with the rain. Weariness was claiming him. Had he closed his eyes for a moment? Maya stood beside him. As her hand closed on his right shoulder, an odd sound tore from his throat. Maya snatched away her hand. Jhared cursed his lack of control.

The following moments took place within a dusky haze; perhaps he dropped to sleep for a time. When next he opened his eyes, the Avelun stood with two sailors frowning down at him. One of the men crouched and began to remove Jhared's cloak. Jhared had a sudden, incongruous memory of a generous invitation offered by a riverman under the stars. Something wry could be said about that man now sliding callused hands over Jhared's torso. He might have noted it aloud, for there was laughter and a clever response. From Vjeran, Jhared thought. Then they lifted his cloak away and the laughter stopped.

Jhared smelled his own blood. His shirt crackled with it. When they pulled open his collar, the fragile scab below his shoulder tore also. Then came a rough cloth and hot water and the necessary burn of *slu* in his wounds. He would have preferred to drink the *slu*. He said as much. Then he slid gratefully into darkness.

Cool air whisked across his skin. He was lying on the bunk that was Vjeran's, and water was falling on him again, wetting his bare chest. The droplets this time were warm and gentle.

He opened his eyes. Vjeran and Ravatin had gone. Lamplight limned Maya's profile as she set clean, dry bandaging to the ragged gash where Ilaye's knife had cut him. The tears gliding silently down her cheeks caught the light and transformed to gold before falling.

"I wanted them to be my family," she said. "I had dreamed of them for so long without any real hope they might exist. I just . . . I needed them to be what I imagined."

"I know." Jhared turned his palm upward to catch one teardrop as it fell. "I wanted to believe in them too."

She bowed her head. "They were—"

"Everything Avelos claims them to be. What I was taught to fear. What I feared I was doomed to become."

Her head lifted. "And what have I become?"

"That is not a fair question to ask me, Maya."

She sighed, then stopped herself and nodded. "But there are questions you would like to ask me."

He looked at her as she waited unflinching: her wings of light and shadow, her sage gaze, her strong hands. He thought of Moravel. And of Vyla.

"I have no right to ask. You sought what you most needed. I have no claim to question that. In the end, both of us chose different paths than we were offered. It is the only thing that matters."

A lie, that last, but a lie they both needed.

She let out a breath, as though she had been holding it, and nodded once more. "You mean to go back to Avelos, don't you? To warn them about Sona."

He watched her unwind a strip of cloth and sat up to aid her as she began to bind his shoulder. "I do."

"They will kill you."

"I'm not going to Velantar to hand myself to the council," he said quietly. "There are people at the Sahisten border I might convince to listen. I must find Lady Nemiah before Hrvan does."

And Shira. Shira was in the south too. If he didn't find her, Hrvan's men would kill Nemiah and then claim the killing winds. In two moves, they could start a war and give Sona the weapon to win it.

"You go because you love them?" Maya asked.

I know why you love them. You had no choice.

He shivered at the recollection of her scorn and at the knowledge that she must be, at least partially, correct. "I no longer claim to be free of them," he said, searching for the right words. "But it's more than my own need. One evil act cannot balance another. You told me that, Maya. I know you see the right in this, whatever your time in Sona has done to you."

She bit her lip and did not meet his gaze as she wrapped the cloth over his shoulder and under his arm. "Do you wish me to come with you?"

He wished he had never witnessed her among her own kind. "Go home," he said. "I wish you to be out of danger. I only ask you to take Rathael. I can't have him with me."

She smoothed the bandage once more under his arm and over. "The house by the lake is no longer safe, Jhared. Nemaye knows of it. They will search for me there."

He closed his eyes. "Would Zinderdali make a place for you?"

"I . . . yes, I think so."

"Then come with me as far as the border. I will help you to reach him."

Her hands paused on his chest. "Is that all?"

He opened his eyes. "It is all I can promise just now."

She finished the binding, then tied off the bandage and sat back. Her gaze on his was dark and sad.

He knew her as she knew him; a kind of miracle existed in that: he knew just how the light would return to her eyes if he stretched out his hand to hers and uttered a word of forgiveness. He knew just as well what to say to injure her, perhaps beyond healing.

They held their tableau. The vibrating tension between them reminded him of another moment, when their paths first crossed in the Sandien Mountains. Then *she* had owned the blade. Given the choice, she had chosen mercy.

He inhaled slowly. As his lungs expanded, he felt the ache of Ilaye's hatred where she had torn him and the strength of Mayavana's binding holding him together. What he most needed now, he realized, was to look into Maya's eyes and touch her wings and remember all that was honest and kind and trusting in her. He needed to blot away the images of Ilaye and Katian and Kest—at least for tonight.

His hand rose to touch her hair. Tentatively, he stroked the silky black strands. With a hitched breath, she accepted his touch. After a little while, she slipped down and laid her head in his lap.

"You've won the secret you most longed for," he whispered. "Do not regret that."

She looked up at him. "What I sought was the grace of the skies. Instead, I found terror and death."

"But you know the connection now, Maya. You will figure out the rest. You will figure out how to fly."

"You told me once you would be there when I do."

Jhared's hand stilled in her hair. He gazed at her, at the hopefulness in her eyes. "I know."

The wall of the deckhouse pressed against his back. Jhared let it hold him, his hand moving softly across Maya's brow. They remained that way as the storm hooted and cried about the barge. At some point, Jhared slid flat onto the bunk and Maya stretched out beside him. In the quiet, he breathed deeply of her familiar scent, slowing his heart and gentling his sorrow.

He thought on the road that lay ahead of them and everything they had left behind. He had discovered a boundary between himself and those who might have been his people. Although it was one more way in which he would never belong, he felt secure in this new understanding of himself: he would never share their hatred.

As he slipped toward dreams, he wrapped his arm around Maya's shoulders. Maya unfurled one snow and ebony wing and covered them both.

DEAR READER

I hope you enjoyed *Avelune*, book three of The Sky Seekers. More than ever, authors depend on readers like you to get the word out about their books. It would mean so much to me if you would take five minutes to leave your review on Amazon or Goodreads to let others know what you thought about the book.

To stay updated about the release of *Cael's Legacy*, book four of The Sky Seekers, get a sneak peek at a chapter, and find an author interview about the series, please go to www.StoneRavenPress.com. You will find more about my work at www.LarissaNNDavila.com.

WARMLY,

LARISSA N. N. DAVILA

Book Club Discussion Questions for Avelune

1. Alende tells Jhared that he no longer belongs to Avelos but to the Unbound Shorn. Why does Jhared disagree?

2. How do Leita's capture and torture affect her determination to seek the source of the killing winds?

3. The time Nemiah spends at Madam Sevar's estate yields important revelations. How do they change Nemiah's perspectives on the Paths, the Shorn, and her mission?

4. Do the revelations about Lieutenant Sevar's connection to Ziabela shed light on his antipathy for Jhared?

5. How does Jhared's downriver journey on the *Mila Jul* help him to imagine new possibilities for himself?

6. What do Falucha and the Bird Walkers show us about Sonan culture?

7. Rathael manipulated and abused Jhared for years, so why does Jhared insist that the other man escape with him?

8. To what extent do you think the tensions between Avelos, Sahiste, and Sona are cultural, economic, or political? How do the tensions reflect international relations in our world?

9. How does the discovery of the Avelune alter Mayavana's understanding of herself and her relationship with Jhared?

10. At the end of the novel, Jhared realizes he is still connected to those who cut and bound him. Is this acknowledgment a sign of his abuse or his resilience?

Photo by Gail Spiro

About the Author

Daughter of first-generation Latine and Polish parents, Larissa N. N. Davila is a child psychologist and professor. She lives in Michigan, where in addition to writing fiction, she directs a mental health clinic for children and conducts research to improve psychological treatments for underserved families. Her work has been highlighted in outlets such as NBC's *Today* and National Public Radio. When not writing, Davila can be found riding horses through Michigan forests. Find out more at www.LarissaNNDavila.com.